"Compelling and complex. . . . [ ]
writes a winning heroine in Nahri."
—WASHINGTON POST

"It's hard to describe just how gorgeous and
intricate this fantasy novel is."
—SYFY WIRE

"A superbly written, lush fantasy story that deserves
to be at the top of your to-read list."
—HYPABLE

"Not only does it open up an imaginative space we
had all but lost, it raises important issues of inclusion
and diversity with engaging flair."
—WALL STREET JOURNAL

"A gorgeous epic as rich in its language as it is in characterization. . . .
Simply one of the best debuts I've read."
—KEVIN HEARNE

"Beguiles all the way."
—VULTURE

"An opulent masterpiece."
—ROSHANI CHOKSHI

"Leaves you wishing for more."
—MICHAEL J. SULLIVAN

"Each page reveals a new wonder."
—FRAN WILDE

"EVEN A FEW PAGES WILL ENMESH YOU IN ITS MAGIC." —ROBIN HOBB

THE CITY
OF BRASS

THE

CITY

OF

BRASS

S. A. CHAKRABORTY

HARPER Voyager
An Imprint of HarperCollins*Publishers*

THE CITY OF BRASS. Copyright © 2017 by Shannon Chakraborty. Excerpt from THE KINGDOM OF COPPER © 2018 by Shannon Chakraborty. All rights reserved. Printed in the United States of America. No part of this book may be used or reproduced in any manner whatsoever without written permission except in the case of brief quotations embodied in critical articles and reviews. For information, address HarperCollins Publishers, 195 Broadway, New York, NY 10007.

HarperCollins books may be purchased for educational, business, or sales promotional use. For information, please email the Special Markets Department at SPsales@harpercollins.com.

P.S.™ is a trademark of HarperCollins Publishers.

Harper Voyager and design are trademarks of HarperCollins Publishers LLC.

A hardcover edition of this book was published in 2017 by Harper Voyager, an imprint of HarperCollins Publishers.

FIRST HARPER VOYAGER PAPERBACK EDITION PUBLISHED 2018.

Designed by Paula Russell Szafranski
Map by Virginia Norey
Frontispiece art by Aza1976/Shutterstock, Inc.
Half title and chapter opener art by yuliasupova/Shutterstock, Inc.

The Library of Congress has catalogued a previous edition as follows:

Names: Chakraborty, S. A., author.
Title: The city of brass / S. A. Chakraborty.
Description: First edition. | New York, NY: Harper Voyager, 2017.
Identifiers: LCCN 2017020068 | ISBN 9780062678102 (hardcover) | ISBN 9780062678126 (eBook)
Subjects: LCSH: Imaginary places—Fiction. | Jinn—Fiction. | BISAC: FICTION / Fantasy / Historical. | FICTION / Fantasy / Epic. | FICTION / Action & Adventure. | GSAFD: Adventure fiction. | Fantasy fiction.
Classification: LCC PS3603.H33555 C58 2017 | DDC 813/.6—dc23
LC record available at https://lccn.loc.gov/2017020068

ISBN 978-0-06-267811-9 (pbk.)

20 21 22   LSC   20 19 18 17 16 15 14 13 12

FOR ALIA, THE LIGHT OF MY LIFE

The Six Tribes
of the Djinn

THE GEZIRI

Surrounded by water and caught behind the thick band of humanity in the Fertile Crescent, the djinn of Am Gezira awoke from Suleiman's curse to a far different world than their fire-blooded cousins. Retreating to the depths of the Empty Quarter, to the dying cities of the Nabateans and to the forbidding mountains of southern Arabia, the Geziri eventually learned to share the hardships of the land with their human neighbors, becoming fierce protectors of the shafit in the process. From this country of wandering poets and zulfiqar-wielding warriors came Zaydi al Qahtani, the rebel-turned-king who would seize Daevabad and Suleiman's seal from the Nahid family in a war that remade the magical world.

THE AYAANLE

Nestled between the rushing headwaters of the Nile River and the salty coast of Bet il Tiamat lies Ta Ntry, the fabled homeland of the mighty Ayaanle tribe. Rich in gold and salt—and far enough from Daevabad that its deadly politics are more game than risk, the Ayaanle are a people to envy. But behind their gleaming coral mansions and sophisticated salons lurks a history they've begun to forget . . . one that binds them in blood to their Geziri neighbors.

THE DAEVAS

Stretching from the Sea of Pearls across the plains of Persia and the mountains of gold-rich Bactria is mighty Daevastana—and just past its Gozan River lies Daevabad, the hidden city of brass. The ancient seat of the Nahid Council—the famed family of healers who once ruled the magical world—Daevastana is a coveted land, its civilization drawn from the ancient cities of Ur and Susa and the nomadic horsemen of the Saka. A proud people, the Daevas claimed the original name of the djinn race as their own . . . a slight that the other tribes never forget.

THE SAHRAYN

Sprawling from the shores of the Maghreb across the vast depths of the Sahara Desert is Qart Sahar—a land of fables and adventure even to the djinn. An enterprising people not particularly enamored of being ruled by foreigners, the Sahrayn know the mysteries of their country better than any—the still lush rivers that flow in caves deep below the sand dunes and the ancient citadels of human civilizations lost to time and touched by forgotten magic. Skilled sailors, the Sahrayn travel upon ships of conjured smoke and sewn cord over sand and sea alike.

THE AGNIVANSHI

Stretching from the brick bones of old Harappa through the rich plains of the Deccan and misty marshes of the Sundarbans lies Agnivansha. Blessedly lush in every resource that could be dreamed—and separated from their far more volatile neighbors by wide rivers and soaring mountains—Agnivansha is a peaceful land famed for its artisans and jewels . . . and its savvy in staying out of Daevabad's tumultuous politics.

THE TUKHARISTANIS

East of Daevabad, twisting through the peaks of Karakorum Mountains and the vast sands of the Gobi is Tukharistan. Trade is its lifeblood, and in the ruins of forgotten Silk Road king-doms, the Tukharistanis make their homes. They travel unseen in caravans of smoke and silk along corridors marked by humans millennia ago, carrying with them things of myth: golden apples that cure any disease, jade keys that open worlds unseen, and perfumes that smell of paradise.

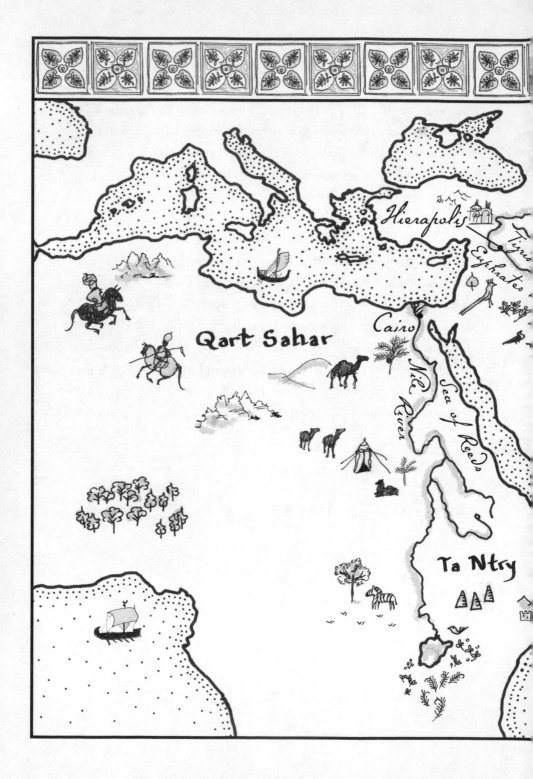

Hierapolis

Tigris

Euphrates

Qart Sahar

Cairo

Nile River

Sea of Reeds

Ta Ntry

THE CITY
OF BRASS

NAHRI

He was an easy mark.

Nahri smiled behind her veil, watching the two men bicker as they approached her stall. The younger one glanced anxiously down the alley while the older man—her client—sweated in the cool dawn air. Save for the men, the alley was empty; fajr had already been called and anyone devout enough for public prayer—not that there were many in her neighborhood—was already ensconced in the small mosque at the end of the street.

She fought a yawn. Nahri was not one for dawn prayer, but her client had chosen the early hour and paid handsomely for discretion. She studied the men as they approached, noting their light features and the cut of their expensive coats. Turks, she suspected. The eldest might even be a basha, one of the few who hadn't fled Cairo when the Franks invaded. She crossed her arms over her black abaya, growing intrigued. She didn't have many Turkish clients; they were too snobbish. Indeed, when the Franks and Turks weren't fighting over Egypt, the only thing they seemed to agree on was that the Egyptians couldn't govern it themselves. God forbid. It's not as though the Egyptians were the inheritors of a great civilization whose mighty monuments still littered the land. Oh, no. They were peasants, superstitious fools who ate too many beans.

Well, this superstitious fool is about to swindle you for all you're worth, so insult away. Nahri smiled as the men approached.

She greeted them warmly and ushered them into her tiny stall, serving the elder a bitter tea made from crushed fenugreek seeds and coarsely chopped mint. He drank it quickly, but Nahri took her time reading the leaves, murmuring and singing in her native tongue, a language the men most certainly wouldn't know, a language not even she had a name for. The longer she took, the more desperate he would be. The more gullible.

Her stall was hot, the air trapped by the dark scarves she hung on the walls to protect her clients' privacy and thick with the odors of burnt cedar, sweat, and the cheap yellow wax she passed off as frankincense. Her client nervously kneaded the hem of his coat, perspiration pouring down his ruddy face and dampening the embroidered collar.

The younger man scowled. "This is foolish, brother," he whispered in Turkish. "The doctor said there's nothing wrong with you."

Nahri hid a triumphant smile. So they were Turks. They wouldn't expect her to understand them—they probably assumed an Egyptian street healer barely spoke proper Arabic—but Nahri knew Turkish as well as she knew her native tongue. And Arabic and Hebrew, scholarly Persian, high-class Venetian, and coastal Swahili. In her twenty or so years of life, she had yet to come upon a language she didn't immediately understand.

But the Turks didn't need to know that, so she ignored them, pretending to study the dregs in the basha's cup. Finally she sighed, her veil fluttering against her lips in a way that drew the gazes of both men, and dropped the cup on the floor.

It broke as it was meant to, and the basha gasped. "By the Almighty! It's bad, isn't it?"

Nahri glanced up at the man, languidly blinking long-lashed black eyes. He'd gone pale, and she paused to listen for the pulse of his heart. It was fast and uneven due to fright, but she could sense it pumping healthy blood throughout his body. His breath was clean of sickness, and there was an unmistakable brightness in his dark eyes. Despite the graying hairs in his beard—ill hidden by henna—and the plumpness in his belly, he suffered from nothing other than an excess of wealth.

She'd be glad to help him with that.

"I am so sorry, sir." Nahri pushed back the small cloth sack, her quick fingers estimating the number of dirhams it held. "Please take back your money."

The basha's eyes popped. "What?" he cried. "Why?"

She dropped her gaze. "There are some things that are beyond me," she said quietly.

"Oh, God . . . do you hear her, Arslan?" The basha turned to his brother, tears in his eyes. "You said I was crazy!" he accused, choking back a sob. "And now I'm going to die!" He buried his head in his hands and wept; Nahri counted the gold rings on his fingers. "I was so looking forward to marrying . . ."

Arslan shot her an irritated look before turning back to the basha. "Pull yourself together, Cemal," he hissed in Turkish.

The basha wiped his eyes and looked up at her. "No, there must be something you can do. I've heard rumors— People say you made a crippled boy walk by just *looking* at him. Surely you can help me."

Nahri leaned back, hiding her pleasure. She had no idea what cripple he was referring to, but God be praised, it would certainly help her reputation.

She touched her heart. "Oh, sir, it grieves me so to deliver such news. And to think of your dear bride being deprived of such a prize . . ."

His shoulders shook as he sobbed. She waited for him to grow a bit more hysterical, taking the opportunity to appraise the thick gold bands circling his wrists and neck. A fine garnet, beautifully cut, was pinned to his turban.

Finally she spoke again. "There might be something, but . . . no." She shook her head. "It wouldn't work."

"What?" he cried, clutching the narrow table. "Please, I'll do anything!"

"It will be very difficult."

Arslan sighed. "And expensive, I bet."

Oh, now you speak Arabic? Nahri gave him a sweet smile, knowing her veil was gauzy enough to reveal her features. "All of my prices are fair, I assure you."

"Be silent, brother," the basha snapped, glowering at the other man. He looked at Nahri, his face set. "Tell me."

"It's not a certainty," she warned.

"I must try."

"You are a brave man," she said, letting her voice tremble. "Indeed, I believe your affliction has come about from the evil eye. Someone is envious of you, sir. And who wouldn't be? A man of your wealth and beauty could attract only envy. Perhaps even someone close . . ." Her glance at Arslan was brief but enough to make his cheeks redden. "You must clear your home of any darkness the envy has brought in."

"How?" the basha asked, his voice hushed and eager.

"First, you must promise to follow my instructions exactly."

"Of course!"

She leaned forward, intent. "Obtain a mixture of one part ambergris to two parts cedar oil, a good amount. Get them from Yaqub, at the apothecary down the alley. He has the best stuff."

"Yaqub?"

"Aywa. Ask for some powdered lime rind and walnut oil as well."

Arslan watched his brother with open disbelief, but hope brightened in the basha's eyes. "And then?"

"This is where it might get difficult, but, sir . . ." Nahri touched his hand, and he shuddered. "You must follow my instructions exactly."

"Yes. By the Most Merciful, I swear."

"Your house needs to be cleansed, and that can only be done if it is abandoned. Your entire family must leave, animals, servants, all. There must not be a living soul in the house for seven days."

"Seven days!" he cried, then lowered his voice at the disapproval in her eyes. "Where are we to go?"

"The oasis at Faiyum." Arslan laughed, but Nahri continued. "Go to the second smallest spring at sunset with your youngest son," she said, her voice severe. "Gather some water in a basket made of local reeds, say the throne verse over it three times, and then use it for your ablutions. Mark your doors with the ambergris and oil before you leave and by the time you return, the envy will be gone."

"Faiyum?" Arslan interrupted. "My God, girl, even you must know there's a war on. Do you imagine Napoleon eager to let any of us leave Cairo for some useless desert trek?"

"Be *quiet*!" The basha banged on the table before turning back to Nahri. "But such a thing will be difficult."

Nahri spread her hands. "God provides."

"Yes, of course. So it is to be Faiyum," he decided, looking determined. "And then my heart will be cured?"

She paused; it was the heart he was worried about? "God willing, sir. Have your new wife put the powdered lime and oil into your evening tea for the next month." It wouldn't do anything for his nonexistent heart problem, but perhaps his bride would better enjoy his breath. Nahri let go of his hand.

The basha blinked as if released from a spell. "Oh, thank you, dear one, thank you." He pushed back the small sack of coins and then slipped a heavy gold ring from his pinkie and handed that over as well. "God bless you."

"May your marriage be fruitful."

He rose heavily to his feet. "I must ask, child, where are your people from? You've a Cairene accent, but there's something about your eyes . . ." He trailed off.

Nahri pressed her lips together; she hated when people asked after her heritage. Though she wasn't what many would call beautiful—years of living on the streets had left her much thinner and far dirtier than men typically preferred—her bright eyes and sharp face usually spurred a second glance. And it was that second glance, the one that revealed a line of midnight hair and uncommonly black eyes—*unnaturally* black eyes, she'd heard it said—that provoked questions.

"I'm as Egyptian as the Nile," she assured him.

"Of course." He touched his brow. "In peace." He ducked under the doorway to leave.

Arslan stayed behind; Nahri could feel his eyes on her as she gathered her payment. "You do realize you just committed a crime, yes?" he asked, his voice sharp.

"I'm sorry?"

He stepped closer. "A crime, you fool. Witchcraft is a crime under Ottoman law."

Nahri couldn't help herself; Arslan was only the latest in a long line of puffed-up Turkish officials she'd had to deal with growing up in Cairo under Ottoman rule. "Well, then I suppose I'm lucky the Franks are in charge now."

It was a mistake. His face instantly reddened. He raised his hand, and Nahri flinched, her fingers reflexively tightening over the basha's ring. One sharp edge cut into her palm.

But he didn't hit her. Instead, he spat at her feet. "By God as my witness, you thieving witch . . . when we clear the French out of Egypt, filth like you will be the next to go." He shot her another hate-filled glare and then left.

She took a shaky breath as she watched the arguing brothers disappear into the early morning gloom toward Yaqub's apothecary. But it wasn't the threat that unsettled her: It was the rattle she'd heard when he shouted, the smell of iron-rich blood in the air. A diseased lung, consumption, maybe even a cancerous mass. There was no outward sign of it yet, but soon.

Arslan had been right to suspect her: there was nothing wrong with his brother. But he wouldn't live to see his people reconquer her country.

She unclenched her fist. The gash in her palm was already healing, a line of new brown skin knitting together beneath the blood. She stared at it for a long moment and then sighed before ducking back inside her stall.

She pulled off her knotted headdress and crumpled it into a ball. *You fool. You know better than to lose your temper with men like that.* Nahri didn't need any more enemies, especially not ones now likely to post guards around the basha's house while he was in Faiyum. What he'd paid today was a pittance compared to what she could steal from his empty villa. She wouldn't have stolen much—she'd been doing her tricks long enough to avoid the temptations of excess. But some jewelry that could have been blamed on a forgetful wife, a quick-fingered servant? Baubles that would have meant nothing to the basha and a month's rent to Nahri? Those she would take.

Muttering another curse, she rolled back her sleeping mat and dislodged a few bricks from the floor. She dropped the basha's coins and ring in the shallow hole, frowning at her meager savings.

It's not enough. It's never going to be enough. She replaced the bricks, calculating how much she still needed to pay for this month's rent and bribes, the inflated costs of her increasingly unsavory profession. The number always grew, pushing away her dreams of Istanbul and tutors, of a respectable trade and actual healing instead of this "magical" nonsense.

But there was nothing to be done about it now, and Nahri wasn't about to take time from earning money to bemoan her fate. She stood, winding a rumpled headscarf around her messy curls and gathering up the amulets she'd made for the Barzani women and the poultice for the butcher. She'd need to come back later to prepare for the zar, but for now, she had someone far more important to see.

YAQUB'S APOTHECARY WAS LOCATED AT THE END of the alley, crammed between a moldering fruit stand and a bread bakery. No one knew what had led the elderly Jewish pharmacist to open an apothecary in such a grim slum. Most of the people living in her alley were desperate: prostitutes, addicts, and garbage-pickers. Yaqub had moved in quietly several years ago, settling his family into the upper floors of the cleanest building. The neighbors wagged their tongues, spreading rumors of gambling debts and drunkenness, or darker charges that his son had killed a Muslim, that Yaqub himself took blood and humors from the alley's half-dead addicts. Nahri thought it all nonsense, but she didn't dare ask. She didn't question his background, and he didn't ask why a former pickpocket could diagnose illnesses better than the sultan's personal physician. Their strange partnership rested on avoiding those two subjects.

She entered the apothecary, quickly sidestepping the battered bell meant to announce customers. Crowded with supplies and impossibly chaotic, Yaqub's shop was her favorite place in the world. Mismatched wooden shelves crammed with dusty glass vials, tiny reed baskets, and crumbling ceramic jars covered the walls. Lengths of dried herbs, animal parts, and objects she couldn't identify hung from the ceiling while clay amphorae competed for the small amount of floor space. Yaqub knew his inventory like the lines of his palms, and listening to his stories of ancient Magi or the hot spice lands of the Hind transported her to worlds she could hardly imagine.

The pharmacist was bent over his workbench, mixing something that gave off a sharp, unpleasant scent. She smiled at the sight of the old man with his even older instruments. His mortar alone looked like something from the reign of Salah ad-Din. "Sabah el-hayr," she greeted him.

Yaqub made a startled noise and glanced up, knocking his forehead into a hanging garlic braid. Swatting it away, he grumbled, "Sabah el-noor. Can't you make some noise when you enter? Scared me half to death."

Nahri grinned. "I like to surprise you."

He snorted. "Sneak up on me, you mean. You get more like the devil each day."

"That's a very unkind thing to say to someone who brought you a small fortune this morning." She pushed up on her hands to perch on his workbench.

"Fortune? Is that what you call two bickering Ottoman officials banging down my door at dawn? My wife nearly had a heart attack."

"So buy her some jewelry with the money."

Yaqub shook his head. "And ambergris! You're lucky I even had some in stock! What, could you not convince him to paint his door in molten gold?"

She shrugged, picking up one of the jars near his elbow and taking a delicate sniff. "They looked like they could afford it."

"The younger one had quite an earful to say about you."

"You can't please everyone." She picked up another jar, watching as he added some candlenut kernels to his mortar.

He put the pestle down with a sigh, holding his hand out for the jar, which she reluctantly handed back. "What are you making?"

"This?" He returned to grinding the kernels. "A poultice for the cobbler's wife. She's been dizzy."

Nahri watched another moment. "That won't help."

"Oh, really? Tell me again, Doctor, who did you train under?"

Nahri smiled; Yaqub hated when she did this. She turned back to the shelves, hunting for the familiar pot. The shop was a mess, a chaos of unlabeled jars and supplies that seemed to get up and move on their own. "She's pregnant," she called over her shoulder. She picked up a vial of peppermint oil, swatting away a spider that crawled over the top.

"Pregnant? Her husband said nothing."

Nahri pushed the vial in his direction and added a gnarled root of ginger. "It's early. They probably don't know yet."

He gave her a sharp look. "And you do?"

"By the Compassionate, don't you? She vomits loudly enough to wake Shaitan, may he be cursed. She and her husband have six children. You think they'd know the signs by now." She smiled, trying to reassure him. "Make her a tea from these."

"I haven't heard her."

"Ya, grandfather, you don't hear me come in either. Maybe the fault lies with your ears."

Yaqub pushed away the mortar with a disgruntled noise and turned to the back corner where he kept his earnings. "I wish you'd stop playing Musa bin Maimon and find yourself a husband. You're not too old, you know." He pulled out his trunk; the hinges groaned as he opened the battered top.

Nahri laughed. "If you could find someone willing to marry

the likes of me, you'd put every matchmaker in Cairo out of business." She pawed through the random assortment of books, receipts, and vials on the table, searching for the small enamel case where Yaqub kept sesame candies for his grandchildren, finally finding it beneath a dusty ledger. "Besides," she continued, plucking out two of the candies, "I like our partnership."

He handed her a small sack. Nahri could tell from its weight that it was more than her usual cut. She started to protest, but he cut her off. "Stay away from men like that, Nahri. It's dangerous."

"Why? The Franks are in charge now." She chewed her candy, suddenly curious. "Is it true Frankish women go about naked in the street?"

The pharmacist shook his head, used to her impropriety. "French, child, not Frankish. And God prevent you from hearing such wickedness."

"Abu Talha says their leader has the feet of a goat."

"Abu Talha should stick to mending shoes . . . But don't change the subject," he said, exasperated. "I'm trying to warn you."

"Warn me? Why? I've never even talked to a Frank." That wasn't for lack of effort. She'd tried selling amulets to the few French soldiers she'd encountered, and they'd backed away like she was some sort of snake, making condescending remarks about her clothing in their strange language.

He locked eyes with her. "You're young," he said quietly. "You have no experience with what happens to people like us during a war. People who are different. You should keep your head down. Or better yet, leave. What happened to your grand plans of Istanbul?"

After counting her savings this morning, the mere mention of the city soured her. "I thought you said I was being foolish," she reminded him. "That no physician would take on a female apprentice."

"You could be a midwife," he offered. "You've delivered babies before. You could go east, away from this war. Beirut, perhaps."

"You sound eager to be rid of me."

He touched her hand, his brown eyes filled with concern. "I'm eager to see you *safe*. You've no family, no husband to stand up for you, to protect you, to—"

She bristled. "I can take care of myself."

"—to *advise* you against doing dangerous things," he finished, giving her a look. "Things like leading zars."

Ah. Nahri winced. "I hoped you wouldn't hear about those."

"Then you're a fool," he said bluntly. "You shouldn't be getting caught up in that southern magic." He gestured behind her. "Get me a tin."

She fetched one from the shelf, tossing it to him with a bit more force than was necessary. "There's no 'magic' to it at all," she dismissed. "It's harmless."

"Harmless!" Yaqub scoffed as he shoveled tea into the tin. "I've heard rumors about those zars . . . blood sacrifices, trying to exorcise djinn . . ."

"It's not really meant to *exorcise* them," Nahri corrected lightly. "More like an effort to make peace."

He stared at her in utter exasperation. "You shouldn't be trying to do anything with djinn!" He shook his head, closing the tin and rubbing warm wax over the seams. "You're playing with things you don't understand, Nahri. They're not your traditions. You're going to get your soul snapped up by a demon if you're not more careful."

Nahri was oddly touched by his concern—to think that just a few years ago he'd dismissed her as a black-hearted fraudster. "Grandfather," she started, trying to sound more respectful. "You needn't worry. There's no magic, I swear." Seeing the doubt on his face, she decided to be more frank. "It's nonsense, all of it. There's no magic, no djinn, no spirits waiting to eat us up. I've been doing my tricks long enough to learn none of it's real."

He paused. "The things I've seen you do—"

"Maybe I'm just a better trickster than the rest," she cut in, hoping to assuage the fear she saw in his face. She didn't need to scare off her only friend simply because she had a few strange skills.

He shook his head. "There are still djinn. And demons. Even scholars say so."

"Well, the scholars are wrong. No spirit has come after me yet."

"That's very arrogant, Nahri. Blasphemous, even," he added, looking taken aback. "Only a fool would speak in such a way."

She lifted her chin defiantly. "They don't exist."

He sighed. "No one can say I didn't try." He pushed the tin over. "Give that to the cobbler on your way out, will you?"

Nahri pushed off the table. "Are you doing inventory tomorrow?" Arrogant she might be, but she rarely passed on an opportunity to learn more about the apothecary. Yaqub's knowledge had greatly advanced her own instincts for healing.

"Yes, but come early. We have a lot to get through."

She nodded. "God willing."

"Now go buy some kebab," he said, nodding at the purse. "You're all bones. The djinn will want more to eat should they come for you."

BY THE TIME NAHRI REACHED THE NEIGHBORHOOD where the zar was taking place, the sun had blinked behind the crowded landscape of stone minarets and mud-brick flats. It vanished into the distant desert, and a low-voiced muezzin began the call to maghrib prayer. She paused, briefly disoriented by the loss of light. The neighborhood was in southern Cairo, squeezed between the remains of ancient Fustat and the Mokattam hills, and it wasn't an area she knew well.

The chicken she was carrying took advantage of Nahri's distraction to kick her in the ribs, and Nahri swore, tucking it tighter under her arm as she pushed past a thin man balancing a board of bread on his head and narrowly avoided a collision with a gaggle of giggling children. She picked her way through a growing pile of shoes outside an already packed mosque. The neighborhood was crowded; the French invasion had done little to stop the waves of people coming to Cairo from the countryside. The new migrants arrived with little more than the clothing on their backs and the traditions of their ancestors, traditions often denounced as perversions by some of the city's more irritated imams.

The zars were certainly denounced as such. Like belief in magic, belief in possession was widespread in Cairo, blamed for everything from a young bride's miscarriage to an old woman's lifelong dementia. Zar ceremonies were held to placate the spirit and heal the afflicted woman. And while Nahri didn't believe in possession, the basketful of coins and the free meal earned by the kodia, the woman who led the ceremony, were too tempting to pass up. And so, after spying on a number of them, she started hosting her own—albeit extremely abbreviated—version.

Tonight would be the third one she held. She'd met with an aunt from the afflicted girl's family last week and arranged to hold the ceremony in an abandoned courtyard near their home. By the time she arrived, her musicians, Shams and Rana, were already waiting.

Nahri greeted them warmly. The courtyard had been swept clean, and a narrow table, covered with a white cloth, set in the center. Two copper platters sat at either end of the table, laden with almonds, oranges, and dates. A fair-size group had gathered, the female members of the afflicted girl's family as well as about a dozen curious neighbors. Though all looked poor, no one would dare come to a zar empty-handed. It would be a good take.

Nahri beckoned to a pair of small girls. Still young enough to find the whole thing terribly exciting, they raced over, their little faces eager. Nahri knelt and folded the chicken she'd been carrying into the arms of the elder.

"Hold him tight for me, okay?" Nahri asked. The girl nodded, looking self-important.

She handed her basket to the younger girl. She was precious, with big dark eyes and curly hair pulled into messy braids. No one would be able to resist her. Nahri winked. "You make sure everyone puts something in the basket." She tugged one of her braids and then waved the girls away before turning her attention to the reason she was here.

The afflicted girl's name was Baseema. She looked about twelve and had been outfitted in a long white dress. Nahri watched as an older woman attempted to tie a white scarf around her hair. Baseema fought back, her eyes wild, her hands flapping. Nahri could see that her fingertips were red and raw from where she'd bitten her nails. Fear and anxiety radiated off her skin, and kohl streaked her cheeks from where she'd tried to rub it from her eyes.

"Please, beloved," the older woman begged. Her mother; the resemblance was obvious. "We're just trying to help you."

Nahri kneeled beside them and took Baseema's hand. The girl stilled, only her eyes darting back and forth. Nahri pulled her gently to her feet. The group fell silent as she laid a hand upon Baseema's brow.

Nahri could no more explain the way she healed and sensed illness than she could explain how her eyes and ears worked. Her abilities had so long been a part of her that she had simply stopped questioning their existence. It had taken her years as a child—and a number of painful lessons—to even realize how different she was from the people around her, like being the only sighted person in a world of the blind. And her abilities were so natural, so organic, that it was impossible to think of them as anything out of the ordinary.

Baseema felt unbalanced, her mind alive and sparking beneath Nahri's fingertips but misdirected. *Broken.* She hated how quickly the cruel word leaped to mind, but Nahri knew there was little she could do for the girl other than temporarily soothing her.

And put on a good show in the process—she wouldn't get paid otherwise. Nahri pushed back the scarf from the girl's face, sensing she felt trapped. Baseema held one end in a clenched fist, giving it a shake as her eyes locked on Nahri's face.

Nahri smiled. "You can keep that if you like, dear one. We're going to have fun together, I promise." She raised her voice and turned to the audience. "You were right to bring me. There is a spirit in her. A strong one. But we can calm it, yes? Bring about a happy marriage between the two?" She winked and motioned to her musicians.

Shams started on her darbuka, banging out a fierce beat on the old skin drum. Rana took up her pipe and handed Nahri a tambourine—the one instrument she could use without making a fool of herself.

Nahri tapped it against her leg. "I will sing to the spirits I know," she explained over the music, though there were very few southern women who didn't know how a zar worked. Baseema's aunt took up an incense burner, waving plumes of aromatic smoke over the crowd. "When her spirit hears its song, it will make her excitable, and we can proceed."

Rana started on her pipe, and Nahri beat the tambourine, her shoulders shaking, her fringed scarf swaying with every movement. Transfixed, Baseema followed her.

"Oh, spirits, we beseech thee! We implore and honor thee!"

Nahri sang, keeping her voice low so it didn't crack. While legitimate kodia were trained singers, Nahri was anything but. "Ya, amir el Hind! Oh, great prince, join us!" She started with the song of the Indian prince and moved on to that of the Sea Sultan and then the Great Qarina, the music changing for each one. She'd been careful to memorize their lyrics if not their meanings; she was not particularly worried about the origins of such things.

Baseema grew more animated as they went on, her limbs loosening, the tense lines in her face gone. She swayed with less effort, tossing her hair with a small, self-contained smile. Nahri touched her every time they passed, feeling for the dim areas of her mind and pulling them closer to calm the restless girl.

It was a good group, energetic and involved. Several women stood, clapping their hands and joining the dance. People typically did; zars were as much an excuse to socialize as to deal with troublesome djinn. Baseema's mother watched her daughter's face, looking hopeful. The little girls clutched their prizes, jumping up and down in excitement as the chicken squawked in protest.

Her musicians also looked to be enjoying themselves. Shams suddenly struck out a faster beat on the darbuka, and Rana followed her lead, playing a mournful, almost unsettling tune on the pipe.

Nahri drummed her fingers on the tambourine, growing inspired by the group's mood. She grinned; maybe it was time to give them something a little different.

She closed her eyes and hummed. Nahri had no name for her native tongue, the language she must have shared with her long-dead or forgotten parents. The only clue to her origins, she had listened for it since she was a child, eavesdropping on foreign merchants and haunting the polyglot crowd of scholars outside El Azhar University. Thinking it similar to Hebrew, she'd once spoken it to Yaqub, but he'd adamantly disagreed, adding, unnecessarily, that his people had enough problems without her being one of them.

But she knew it sounded unusual and eerie. Perfect for the zar. Nahri was surprised she hadn't thought of using it before.

Though she could have sung her market list and no one would have been any the wiser, she stuck to the zar songs, translating the Arabic into her native language.

"Sah, afshin e-daeva . . . ," she started. "Oh, warrior of the djinn, we beseech thee! Join us, calm the fires in this girl's mind." She closed her eyes. "Oh, warrior, come to me! Vak!"

A bead of sweat snaked past her temple. The courtyard grew uncomfortably warm, the press of the large group and crackling fire too much. She kept her eyes closed and swayed, letting the movement of her headdress fan her face. "Great guardian, come and protect us. Watch over Baseema as if—"

A low gasp startled Nahri, and she opened her eyes. Baseema had stopped dancing; her limbs were frozen, her glassy gaze fixed on Nahri. Clearly unnerved, Shams missed a beat on the darbuka.

Afraid of losing the crowd, Nahri struck her tambourine against one hip, silently praying Shams would copy her. She smiled at Baseema and picked up the incense brazier, hoping the musky fragrance would relax the girl. Maybe it was time to wrap things up. "Oh, warrior," she sang more softly, returning to Arabic. "Is it you who sleeps in the mind of our gentle Baseema?"

Baseema twitched; sweat poured down her face. Closer now, Nahri could see that the blank expression in the girl's eyes had been replaced by something that looked a lot more like fear. A bit unsettled, she reached for the girl's hand.

Baseema blinked, and her eyes narrowed, focusing on Nahri with an almost feral curiosity.

WHO ARE YOU?

Nahri blanched and dropped her hand. Baseema's lips hadn't

moved, yet she heard the question as though it had been shouted in her ear.

Then the moment was gone. Baseema shook her head, the blank look reappearing as she began to dance again. Startled, Nahri took a few steps back. A cold sweat erupted across her skin.

Rana was at her shoulder. "Ya, Nahri?"

"Did you hear that?" she whispered.

Rana raised her brows. "Hear what?"

Don't be a fool. Nahri shook her head, feeling ridiculous. "Nothing." Raising her voice, she faced the crowd. "All praise is due to the Almighty," she declared, trying not to stammer. "Oh, warrior, we thank you." She beckoned for the girl holding the chicken. "Please accept our offering and make peace with dear Baseema." Her hands shaking, Nahri held the chicken over a battered stone bowl and whispered a prayer before cutting its throat. Blood spurted into the bowl, spattering her feet.

Baseema's aunt took the chicken away to be cooked, but Nahri's job was far from over. "Tamarind juice for our guest," she requested. "The djinn like their sours." She forced a smile and tried to relax.

Shams brought over a small glass of the dark juice. "Are you well, kodia?"

"God be praised," Nahri said. "Just tired. Can you and Rana distribute the food?"

"Of course."

Baseema was still swaying, her eyes half closed, a dreamy smile on her face. Nahri took her hands and gently pulled her to the ground, aware that much of the group was watching. "Drink, child," she said, offering the cup. "It will please your djinn."

The girl clutched the glass, spilling nearly half the juice down her face. She gestured at her mother, making a low noise in the back of her throat.

"Yes, habibti." Nahri stroked her hair, willing her to be calm. The child was still unbalanced, but her mind didn't feel as frantic. God only knew how long it would last. She beckoned Baseema's mother over and joined their hands.

There were tears in the older woman's eyes. "Is she cured? Will the djinn leave her in peace?"

Nahri hesitated. "I have made them both content, but the djinn is a strong one and has likely been with her since birth. For such a tender thing . . ." She squeezed Baseema's hand. "It was probably easier for her to submit to his wishes."

"What does that mean?" the other woman asked, her voice breaking.

"Your daughter's state is the will of God. The djinn will keep her safe, provide her with a rich inner life," she lied, hoping it would give the woman some comfort. "Keep them both content. Let her stay with you and your husband, give her things to do with her hands."

"Will . . . will she ever speak?"

Nahri looked away. "God willing."

The older woman swallowed, obviously picking up on Nahri's discomfort. "And the djinn?"

She tried to think of something easy. "Have her drink tamarind juice every morning—it will please him. And take her to the river to bathe on the first jumu'ah, the first Friday, of every month."

Baseema's mother took a deep breath. "God knows best," she said softly, seemingly more to herself than to Nahri. But there were no more tears. Instead, as Nahri watched, the older woman took her daughter's hand, looking more at peace already. Baseema smiled.

Yaqub's words stole into Nahri's heart at the tender sight. *You've no family, no husband to stand up for you, to protect you . . .*

Nahri stood up. "You'll excuse me."

As kodia, she had no choice but to stay until the meal was served, nodding politely at the women's gossip and trying to avoid an elderly cousin whom she sensed had a mass spreading in both breasts. Nahri had never tried to heal anything like that and didn't think it was a good night to experiment—though that didn't make the woman's smiling face easier to stomach.

The ceremony finally drew to a close. Her basket was flush, filled with a random assortment of the various coins used in Cairo: battered copper fils, a scattering of silver paras, and a single ancient dinar from Baseema's family. Other women had put in small pieces of cheap jewelry, all exchanged for the blessings she was supposed to bring them. Nahri gave Shams and Rana each two paras and let them take most of the jewelry.

She was securing her outer wrap and ducking the repeated kisses of Baseema's family when she felt a slight prickling at the back of her neck. She'd spent too many years stalking marks and being followed herself not to recognize the feeling. She glanced up.

From the opposite side of the courtyard, Baseema stared back. She was completely still, her limbs in perfect control. Nahri met her gaze, surprised by the girl's calm.

There was something curious and calculating in Baseema's dark eyes. But then, just as Nahri really took notice, it was gone. The younger girl pressed her hands together and began to sway, dancing as Nahri had shown her.

2

NAHRI

Something happened to that girl.

Nahri picked through the pastry crumbs of her long-devoured feteer. Her mind spinning after the zar, she'd stopped in a local coffeehouse rather than head home and, hours later, she was still there. She swirled her glass; the red dregs of her hibiscus tea raced across the bottom.

Nothing happened, you idiot. You didn't hear any voices. She yawned, propping her elbows up on the table and closing her eyes. Between her predawn appointment with the basha and her long walk across the city, she was exhausted.

A small cough caught her attention. She opened her eyes to find a man with a limp beard and a hopeful expression idling by her table.

Nahri drew her dagger before he could speak and slammed the hilt against the wooden surface. The man vanished, and a hush fell across the coffeehouse. Someone's dominos clattered to the floor.

The owner glared, and she sighed, knowing that she was about to be thrown out. He'd initially refused her service, claiming no honorable woman would dare venture out unaccompanied at night, let alone visit a coffeehouse full of strange men. After repeatedly demanding to know if her menfolk knew where she was, the sight of the coins from the zar had finally shut him up, but she suspected that brief welcome was about to end.

She stood up, dropped some money on the table, and left. The street was dark and unusually deserted; the French curfew had scared even the most nocturnal of Egyptians into staying inside.

Nahri kept her head down as she walked, but it wasn't long before she realized she was lost. Though the moon was bright, this part of the city was unfamiliar to her, and she circled the same alley twice, looking for the main road without success.

Tired and annoyed, she stopped outside the entrance to a quiet mosque, contemplating the idea of sheltering there for the night. The sight of a distant mausoleum towering over the mosque's dome caught her eye. She stilled. El Arafa: the City of the Dead.

A sprawling, beloved mass of burial fields and tombs, El Arafa reflected Cairo's obsession with all things funerary. The cemetery ran along the city's eastern edge, a spine of crumbling bones and rotting tissue where everyone from Cairo's founders to its addicts were buried. And until plague had dealt with Cairo's housing shortage a few years ago, it had even served as shelter for migrants with nowhere else to go.

It was an idea that made her shudder. Nahri didn't share the comfort most Egyptians felt around the dead, let alone the desire to move in with a pile of decaying bones. She found corpses offensive; their smell, their silence, it was all wrong. From some of the more well-traveled traders, she heard stories of people who burned their dead, foreigners who thought they were being clever in hiding from God's judgment—geniuses, Nahri thought. Going up in a crackling fire sounded delightful compared to being buried under the smothering sands of El Arafa.

But she also knew that the cemetery was her best hope of getting home. She could follow its border north until she reached more familiar neighborhoods, and it was a good place to hide if she came across any French soldiers looking to enforce the curfew; foreigners usually shared her apprehension toward the City of the Dead.

Once inside the cemetery, Nahri stuck to the outermost lane. It was even more deserted than the street; the only hints of life were the smell of a long-extinguished cooking fire and the shrieks of fighting cats. The spiky crenellations and smooth domes of the tombs cast wild shadows against the sandy ground. The ancient buildings looked neglected; Egypt's Ottoman rulers had preferred to be buried in their Turkish homeland and therefore hadn't seen the upkeep of the cemetery as important—one of many insults they'd visited upon her countrymen.

The temperature seemed to have dropped rather suddenly, and Nahri shivered. Her worn leather sandals, threadbare things long overdue for replacement, padded on the soft ground. There was no other sound save the jingling coins in her basket. Already unnerved, Nahri avoided looking at the tombs, instead contemplating the far more pleasant topic of breaking into the basha's house while he was in Faiyum. Nahri would be damned if she was going to let some consumptive little brother keep her from a lucrative take.

She hadn't been walking long when there was a hush of breath behind her, followed by a flit of movement she caught out of the corner of her eye.

It could be someone else taking a shortcut, she told herself, her heart racing. Cairo was relatively safe, but Nahri knew there were few good outcomes to a young woman being followed at night.

She kept her pace but moved her hand toward her dagger

before making an abrupt turn deeper into the cemetery. She hurried down the lane, startling a sleepy cur, and then ducked behind the entrance to one of the old Fatimid tombs.

The footsteps followed. They stopped. Nahri took a deep breath and raised her blade, getting ready to bluster and threaten whoever was there. She stepped out.

She froze. "*Baseema?*"

The young girl stood in the middle of the alley about a dozen paces away, her head uncovered, her abaya stained and torn. She smiled at Nahri. Her teeth gleamed in the moonlight as a breeze blew back her hair.

"Speak again," Baseema demanded in a voice strained and hoarse from disuse.

Nahri gasped. Had she actually helped the girl? And if so, why in God's name was she wandering around a cemetery in the middle of the night?

She dropped her arm and hurried toward her. "What are you doing out here all alone, child? Your mother will be worried."

She stopped. Though it was dark, sudden clouds veiling the moon, she could see strange splotches staining Baseema's hands. Nahri drew in a sharp breath, catching the scent of something smoky and charred and *wrong*.

"Is that . . . blood? By the Most High, Baseema, what happened?"

Clearly oblivious to Nahri's worry, Baseema clapped her hands together in delight. "Could it really be you?" She circled Nahri slowly. "About the right age . . . ," she mused. "And I'd swear that I see that witch in your features, but you otherwise look so *human*." Her gaze fell on the knife in Nahri's hand. "Though I suppose there's only one real way to tell."

The words had no sooner left her mouth than she snatched the dagger away, her movements impossibly fast. Nahri stumbled back with a surprised cry, and Baseema laughed. "Don't worry, little healer. I'm no fool; I've no intention of testing your blood myself." She wagged the dagger in one hand. "Though I think I'll take *this* before you get any ideas."

Nahri was speechless. She took Baseema in with new eyes. Gone was the flapping, tormented child. Her bizarre declarations aside, she stood with a new confidence, the wind whipping through her hair.

Baseema narrowed her eyes, perhaps picking up on Nahri's confusion. "Surely you know what I am. The marid must have warned you about us."

"The *what*?" Nahri held up a hand, trying to protect her eyes from a sandy gust of wind. The weather had worsened. Behind Baseema, dark gray and orange clouds swirled across the sky, obliterating the stars. The wind howled again, like the worst of the khamaseen, but it was not yet the season for Cairo's spring sandstorms.

Baseema glanced at the sky. Alarm bloomed in her small face. She whirled on Nahri. "That human magic you did . . . who did you call for?"

Magic? Nahri raised her hands. "I didn't do any magic!"

Baseema moved in the blink of an eye. She shoved Nahri against the nearest tomb wall, pressing an elbow hard against her throat. "Who did you sing for?"

"I . . ." Nahri gasped, shocked by the strength in the girl's thin arms. "A . . . warrior, I think. But it was nothing. Just an old zar song."

Baseema stepped back as a hot breeze tore down the alley, smelling of fire. "That's not possible," she whispered. "He's dead. They're all dead."

"Who's dead?" Nahri had to shout over the wind. "Wait, Baseema!" she cried as the young girl fled down the opposite alley. "Where are you going?"

She didn't have long to wonder. A crack snapped the air,

louder than a cannon. All was silent, too silent, and then Nahri was thrown off her feet, blasted against one of the tombs.

She hit the stone hard as a bright flash of light blinded her. She crumpled to the ground, too dazed to protect her face from the rain of scorching sand.

The world went quiet, returning with the steady beat of her heart, the blood rushing to her head. Black dots blossomed across her eyes. She flexed her fingers and twitched her toes, relieved they were still attached. The thud of her heart was slowly replaced by ringing in her ears. She tentatively touched the throbbing bulge on the back of her skull, stifling a cry at the sharp pain.

She tried to twist free of the sand that half-buried her, still blinded by the flash. No, not from the flash, she realized. The white bright light was still in the alley, just condensing, growing smaller to reveal fire-scorched tombs as it collapsed in on itself. As it collapsed in on *something*.

Baseema was nowhere to be seen. Frantically, Nahri began to work her legs loose. She had just managed to uncover them when she heard the voice, clear as a bell and angry as a tiger, in the language she'd been listening for all her life.

"Suleiman's eye!" it roared. "I will *kill* whoever called me here!"

THERE'S NO MAGIC, NO DJINN, NO SPIRITS WAITING TO eat us up. Nahri's own decisive words to Yaqub came back to her, mocking her as she peeked over the headstone she'd dashed behind when she first heard his voice. The air still smelled of ash, but the light filling the alley dimmed, almost like it had been sucked in by the figure at its center. It looked like a man, swathed in a dark robe that swirled around his feet like smoke.

He stepped forward as the remaining light vanished into his body and immediately lost his balance, grabbing for a desiccated tree trunk. As he steadied himself, the bark burst into flames beneath his hand. Instead of pulling back, he leaned against the burning tree with a sigh, the flames licking harmlessly at his robe.

Too stunned to form a coherent thought, let alone flee, Nahri rolled back against the headstone as the man called out again.

"Khayzur . . . if this is your idea of a jest, I swear on my ancestors to pluck you apart feather by feather!"

His bizarre threat rang in her mind, the words meaningless, but the language so familiar it felt tangible.

Why is some lunatic fire creature speaking my language?

Unable to fight her curiosity, she turned back, peering past the headstone.

The creature dug through the sand, muttering to himself and swearing. As Nahri watched, he pulled free a curved scimitar and secured it to his waist. It was quickly joined by two daggers, an enormous mace, an ax, a long quiver of arrows, and a gleaming silver bow.

The bow in hand, he finally staggered up and glanced down the alley, obviously searching for whoever had—what had he said?— "called" him. Though he didn't look much taller than her, the vast array of weapons—enough to fight a whole troop of French soldiers—was terrifying and slightly ridiculous. Like what a little boy might don when playing at being some ancient warrior.

A warrior. Oh, by the Most High . . .

He was looking for her. Nahri was the one who had called him.

"Where are you?" he bellowed, striding forward with his bow raised. He was getting dangerously close to Nahri's headstone. "I will tear you into fours!" He spoke her language with a cultured accent, his poetic tone at odds with the terrifying threat.

Nahri had no desire to learn what being "torn into fours" meant. She slipped off her sandals. Once he was past her headstone, she quickly rose and silently fled down the opposite lane.

Unfortunately, she had forgotten about her basket. As she moved, the coins rang out in the silent night.

The man roared, "Stop!"

She sped up, her bare feet pounding the ground. She turned down one twisting lane and then another, hoping to confuse him.

Spotting a darkened doorway, she ducked inside. The cemetery was silent, free of the sounds of pursuing feet or angry threats. Could she have lost him?

She leaned against the cool stone, trying to catch her breath and wishing desperately for her dagger—not that her puny blade would offer much protection against the excessively armed man hunting her.

I can't stay here. But Nahri could see nothing but tombs in front of her and had no idea how to get back to the streets. She gritted her teeth, trying to muster up some courage.

Please, God . . . or whoever is listening, she prayed. *Just get me out of this, and I swear I'll ask Yaqub for a bridegroom tomorrow. And I'll never do another zar.* She took a hesitant step.

An arrow whistled through the air.

Nahri shrieked as it sliced across her temple. She staggered forward and reached for her head, her fingers immediately sticky with blood.

The cold voice spoke. "Stop where you are or the next one goes through your throat."

She froze, her hand still pressed against her wound. The blood was already clotting, but she didn't want to give the creature an excuse to put another hole in her.

"Turn around."

She swallowed back her fear and turned, keeping her hands still and her eyes on the ground. "Pl-please don't kill me," she stammered. "I didn't mean to—"

The man—or whatever he was—sucked in his breath, a noise

like an extinguished coal. "You . . . you're human," he whispered. "How do you know Divasti? How can you even *hear* me?"

"I . . ." Nahri paused, startled to finally learn the name of the language she'd known since childhood. *Divasti.*

"Look at me." He moved closer, the air between them growing warm with the smell of burnt citrus.

Her heart was beating so hard she could hear it in her ears. She took a deep breath, forcing herself to meet his gaze.

His face was covered like a desert traveler, but even if it had been visible, she doubted she would have seen anything but his eyes. Greener than emeralds, they were almost too bright to look into directly.

His eyes narrowed. He pushed back her headscarf, and Nahri flinched as he touched her right ear. His fingertips were so hot that even his brief press was enough to scald her skin.

"Shafit," he said softly, but unlike his other words, the term remained incomprehensible in her mind. "Move your hand, girl. Let me see your face."

He pushed her hand away before she could comply. By now, the blood had clotted. Exposed to the air, her wound itched; she knew the skin was stitching back together before his eyes.

He leaped back, nearly crashing into the opposite wall. "Suleiman's eye!" He looked her up and down again, sniffing the air like a dog. "How . . . how did you do that?" he demanded. His bright eyes flashed. "Is this some sort of trick? A trap?"

"No!" She held her hands up, praying she looked innocent. "No trick, no trap, I swear!"

"Your voice . . . you are the one who called me." He raised his sword and laid the curved blade against her neck, soft as a lover's hand. "How? Who are you working for?"

Nahri's stomach tied itself into a tight knot. She swallowed, resisting the urge to jerk back from the blade at her throat—no doubt such a motion would end poorly.

She thought fast. "You know . . . there was this other girl here. I bet she called you." She pointed down the opposite lane with one finger, trying to force some confidence into her voice. "She went that way."

"Liar!" he hissed, and the cold blade pressed closer. "Do you think I don't recognize your voice?"

Nahri panicked. She was normally good under pressure, but she had little practice outwitting enraged fire spirits. "I'm sorry! I-I just sang a song . . . I didn't mean to . . . ow!" she cried as he pressed the blade harder, nicking her neck.

He pulled it away and then brought it to his face, studying the smear of red blood on the blade's metal surface. He sniffed it, pressing it close against his face covering.

"Oh, God . . ." Nahri's stomach turned. Yaqub was right; she'd tangled with magic she didn't understand and now was going to pay for it. "Please . . . just make it quick." She tried to steady herself. "If you're going to eat me—"

"*Eat* you?" He made a disgusted sound. "The smell of your blood alone is enough to put me off eating for a month." He dropped the sword. "You smell dirt born. You're no illusion."

She blinked, but before she could question that bizarre proclamation, the ground gave a sudden and violent rumble.

He touched the tomb beside them and then gave the trembling headstones a distinctly nervous look. "Is this a burial ground?"

Nahri thought that fairly obvious. "The largest in Cairo."

"Then we don't have much time." He looked up and down the alley before turning back to her. "Answer me, and be quick and honest about it. Did you mean to call me here?"

"No."

"Do you have any other family here?"

How could that possibly be important? "No, it's just me."

"And have you done anything like this before?" he demanded, his voice urgent. "Anything out of the ordinary?"

Only my whole life. Nahri hesitated. But terrified as she was, the sound of her native language was intoxicating, and she didn't want the mysterious stranger to stop speaking.

And so the answer rushed out of her before she could think better of it. "I've never 'called anyone' before, but I heal. Like you saw." She touched the skin on her temple.

He stared at her face, his eyes growing so bright she had to look away. "Can you heal others?" He asked the question in a strangely soft and desperate tone, as if he both knew and feared the answer.

The ground buckled, and the headstone between them crumbled into dust. Nahri gasped and looked over the buildings surrounding them, suddenly aware of just how ancient and unsteady they appeared. "An earthquake . . ."

"We should be so fortunate." He deftly swept past the crumbled headstone and snatched her arm.

"Ya!" she protested; his hot touch burned through her thin sleeve. "Let me go!"

He gripped her tighter. "How do we get out of here?"

"I'm not going anywhere with you!" She tried to twist free and then froze.

Two thin, bowed figures stood at the end of one of the narrow cemetery paths. A third hung out a window, the smashed screen on the ground below. Nahri didn't need to listen for the absence of their heartbeats to know all three were dead. The tattered remains of burial shrouds hung from their desiccated frames, the scent of rot filling the air.

"God be merciful," she whispered, her mouth going dry. "What-what are—"

"Ghouls," the man answered. He let go of her arm and shoved his sword in her hands. "Take this."

Nahri could barely lift the damned thing. She held it awkwardly in both hands as the man pulled free his bow and notched an arrow.

"I see you've found my servants."

The voice came from behind them, young and girlish. Nahri whirled around. Baseema stood a few paces away.

The man had an arrow aimed at the young girl in the blink of an eye. "Ifrit," he hissed.

Baseema smiled politely. "Afshin," she greeted. "What a pleasant surprise. Last I heard, you were dead, having gone completely insane in the service of your human masters."

He flinched and drew the bow back farther. "Go to hell, demon."

Baseema laughed. "Aye, there's no need for that. We're on the same side now, haven't you heard?" She grinned and drew nearer. Nahri could see a malicious glint in her dark eyes. "Surely you'll do *anything* to help the newest Banu Nahida."

The newest what? But the term must have meant something to the man: his hands trembled on the bow.

"The Nahids are dead," he said in a shaky voice. "You fiends killed them all."

Baseema shrugged. "We tried. All in the past now, I suppose." She winked at Nahri. "Come." She beckoned her forth. "There's no reason to make this difficult."

The man—Afshin, Baseema had called him—stepped between them. "I will rip you from that poor child's body if you come any nearer."

Baseema gave a rude nod to the tombs. "Look around, you fool. Do you have any idea how many here owe debts to my kind? I have but to say a word and you will both be devoured."

Devoured? Nahri immediately stepped away from Afshin. "Wait! You know what? Maybe I should just—"

Something cold and sharp grabbed her ankle. She glanced

down. A bony hand, the rest of its arm still buried, held her tight. It yanked hard, and she tripped, falling just as an arrow whizzed over her head.

Nahri slashed at the skeletal hand with Afshin's sword, trying not to accidentally amputate her own foot. "Get off, get off!" she shrieked, the sensation of bones on her skin causing every hair on her body to stand on end. From the corner of her eye, she saw Baseema collapse.

Afshin rushed to her side, pulling her to her feet as she crushed the hand holding her ankle with the hilt of the sword. She twisted free and swung the sword. "You killed her!"

He jumped back to avoid the blade. "You were going to go over to her!" The ghouls moaned, and he snatched back the sword before grabbing Nahri's hand. "There's no time to argue. Come on!"

They raced down the nearest lane as the ground shook. One of the tombs burst open, and two corpses flung themselves at Nahri. Afshin's sword flashed, sending their heads tumbling.

He pulled her into a narrow alley. "We need to get out of here. The ghouls likely can't leave the burial ground."

"*Likely?* You mean there's a chance these things might get out and start feasting on everyone in Cairo?"

He looked thoughtful. "That would provide a distraction . . ." Perhaps noticing her horror, he quickly changed the subject. "Either way, we need to leave."

"I . . ." She glanced around, but they were deep in the cemetery. "I don't know how."

He sighed. "Then we'll need to make our own exit." He jerked his head at the surrounding mausoleums. "Do you think I can find a rug in any of these buildings?"

"A *rug*? How is a rug going to help us?"

The headstones near them shuddered. He made a hushing noise. "Be quiet," he whispered. "You'll wake up more."

She swallowed hard, ready to throw her lot in with this Af-shin if it was the best way to avoid becoming a meal for the dead. "What do you need me to do?"

"Find a rug, a tapestry, curtains—something fabric and big enough for us both."

"But why—"

He cut her off, motioning with one finger toward the ghastly sounds coming from the opposite alley. "No more questions."

She studied the tombs. A broom rested outside one, and its wooden window screens looked new. It was large, probably the kind that held a small room for visitors. "Let's try that one."

They crept down the alley. She tried the door, but it didn't budge.

"It's locked," she said. "Give me one of your daggers, I'll pick it."

He raised his palm. The door burst inward, wooden splinters spraying the ground. "Go, I'll guard the entrance."

Nahri glanced back. The noise had already drawn attention; a group of ghouls rushed in their direction. "Are they getting . . . *faster*?"

"The curse takes time to warm up."

She blanched. "You can't possibly kill them all."

He gave her a shove. "Then hurry!"

She scowled but hastily clambered over the ruined door. The tomb was even darker than the alley, the only illumination com-ing from the moonlight that pierced the carved screens and threw elaborate designs on the floor.

Nahri let her eyes adjust. Her heart raced. *It's just like casing a house. You've done this a hundred times.* She knelt to run her hands over the contents of an open crate on the ground. Inside was a dusty pot and several cups, stacked neatly inside each other, awaiting thirsty visitors. She moved forward. If the tomb was set up for guests, there would be a place to visit. And if God was kind and the family of this particular deceased respectable, they would have carpets there.

She moved farther inside, keeping one hand on the wall to orient herself as she tried to guess how the space was laid out. Nahri had never been inside a tomb before; no one she knew would want someone like her anywhere near their ancestors' bones.

The guttural cry of a ghoul pierced the air, rapidly followed by a heavy thump against the outer wall. Moving more quickly, she peered into the darkness, making out two separate rooms. The first had four heavy sarcophagi crammed inside, but the next looked like it contained a tiny sitting area. Something was rolled up in one dark corner. She hurried over and touched it: a carpet. Thank the Most High.

The rolled carpet was longer than she was, and heavy. Nahri dragged it through the tomb but had gotten only halfway when a soft noise drew her attention. She glanced up, catching a mouthful of sandy dust as it blew past her face. More sand swept past her feet, as if it was being sucked from the tomb.

It had grown eerily quiet. A little worried, Nahri dropped the carpet and peered through one of the window screens.

The smell of rot and decay nearly overwhelmed her, but she caught sight of Afshin, standing alone among a pile of bodies. His bow was gone; in one hand he held the mace, covered in viscera, and in the other the sword, dark fluid dripping from the gleaming steel. His shoulders were slumped, his head lowered in defeat. Down the lane, she could see more ghouls still coming. By God, did everyone buried here owe a debt to a demon?

He tossed his weapons to the ground. "What are you doing?" she cried as he slowly raised his empty hands as if in prayer. "There are more . . ." Her warning trailed off.

Every particle of sand, every mote of dust in sight, rushed to meet the motion of his hands, condensing and swirling into a twisting funnel in the center of the lane. He took a deep breath and flung his hands outward.

The funnel exploded toward the rushing ghouls, a snap breaking across the air. Nahri felt a wave of pressure rock the wall, sand blasting her from the open screen.

And they shall control the winds and be lords of the deserts. And any traveler who strays across their land shall be doomed . . .

The line came unbidden to her, something she'd heard during her years of pretending to be wise about the supernatural. There was only one creature that line ever referred to, only one being that struck terror in hardened warriors and savvy merchants from the Maghrib to the Hind. An ancient being said to live for deceiving and terrorizing mankind. A djinn.

Afshin was a djinn. An honest-to-goodness djinn.

It was a distracting realization, one that made her momentarily forget where she was. So when a bony hand yanked her back and teeth sank into her shoulder, she was understandably caught off guard.

Nahri shouted, more in surprise than pain as the bite wasn't deep. She struggled to get the ghoul off her back, but it wrapped its legs around her and knocked her to the ground, clinging to her body like a crab.

Managing to wrench an elbow free, she shoved it hard. The ghoul fell away but took a good piece of her shoulder with it. Nahri gasped; the burn of exposed flesh sent spots blossoming across her vision.

The ghoul snapped at her neck, and she scrambled away. Its body wasn't too old; swollen flesh and a tattered burial shroud still covered its limbs. But its eyes were a horrifying, pestilent wreck of writhing maggots.

Nahri sensed movement behind her too late. A second ghoul yanked her close, pinning her arms.

She screamed, "Afshin!"

The ghouls dragged her to the ground. The first ripped a gash in her abaya, raking sharp nails across her stomach. It sighed with contentment as it ran a rough tongue over her bloodied skin, and her entire body shuddered in response, revulsion coursing in her blood. She thrashed against them, finally succeeding in smashing her fist into the second ghoul's face as it leaned in toward her neck. "Get off me!" she screamed. She tried to hit it again, but it grabbed her fist, wrenching her arm away. Something popped in her elbow, but the pain barely registered.

Because at the same time, it tore into her throat.

Blood filled her mouth. Her eyes rolled back. The pain was receding, her sight dimming, so she didn't see the djinn approach, only heard an enraged roar, the swoosh of a blade, and two thuds. One of the ghouls collapsed onto her.

Sticky, warm blood pooled on the floor beneath her body. "No . . . no, don't," she murmured as she was picked up off the floor and carried out of the tomb. The night air chilled her skin.

She was on something soft and then suddenly weightless. There was the faint sensation of movement.

"Sorry, girl," a voice whispered, in a language that until today, Nahri had never heard another speak. "But you and I are not done."

3

NAHRI

Nahri knew something was wrong before she opened her eyes.

The sun was bright—too bright—against her still-closed lids, and her abaya clung wetly to her stomach. A gentle breeze played across her face. She groaned and rolled over, trying to take refuge in her blanket.

Instead, she got a faceful of sand. Sputtering, she sat up and wiped her eyes. She blinked.

She was definitely not in Cairo.

A shady grove of date palms and scrubby brush surrounded her; rocky cliffs blocked part of the bright blue sky. Through the trees, there was nothing but desert, gleaming golden sand in every direction.

And across from her was the djinn.

Crouched like a cat over the smoldering remains of a small fire—the sharp smell of burnt green wood filling the air—the djinn stared at her with a sort of wary curiosity in his bright green eyes. A fine dagger, its handle set with a swirling pattern of lapis and carnelians, was in one soot-covered hand. He trailed it across the sand as she watched, the blade glinting in the sunlight. His other weapons were piled behind him.

Nahri snatched up the first stick her hand landed on and held it out in what she hoped was at least a somewhat menacing manner. "Stay back," she warned.

He pursed his lips, clearly unimpressed. But the motion drew her attention to his mouth, and Nahri was startled by her first good look at his uncovered face. Though there was nary a wing nor a horn in sight, his light brown skin shone with an unnatural gleam, and his ears twisted into elongated points. Curly hair—as impossibly black as her own—fell to the top of his shoulders, framing a sharply handsome face with long-lashed eyes and heavy brows. A black tattoo marked his left temple, a single arrow crossed over a stylized wing. His skin was unlined, but there was something ageless about his jewel-bright gaze. He might have been thirty or a hundred and thirty.

He was beautiful—strikingly, *frighteningly* beautiful, with the type of allure Nahri imagined a tiger held right before it ripped out your throat. Her heart skipped a beat even as her stomach constricted in fear.

She closed her mouth, suddenly aware it had fallen open. "Wh-where have you taken me?" she stammered in—what had he called her language again? Divasti? Right, that was it. Divasti.

He didn't take his eyes off her, his arresting face unreadable. "East."

"*East*?" she repeated.

The djinn tilted his head, staring at her like she was an idiot. "The opposite direction of the sun."

A spark of irritation lit inside her. "I know what the word means . . ." The djinn frowned at her tone, and Nahri gave the dagger a nervous glance. "You . . . you're clearly occupied with that," she said in a more conciliatory tone, motioning to the weapon as she climbed to her feet. "So why don't I just leave you alone and—"

"Sit."

"Really, it's no—"

"*Sit.*"

Nahri dropped to the ground. But as the silence grew too long between them, she snapped, her nerves finally getting the better of her. "I sat. So what now? Are you going to kill me like you killed Baseema or are we just going to stare at each other until I die of thirst?"

He pursed his lips again, and Nahri tried not to stare, feeling a sudden stab of sympathy for some of her more lovestruck clients. But what he said next put such thoughts out of mind.

"What I did to that girl was a mercy. She was doomed the moment the ifrit possessed her: they burn through their hosts."

Nahri reeled. *Oh, God . . . Baseema, forgive me.* "I-I didn't mean to call it . . . to hurt her. I swear." She took a shaky breath. "When you killed her . . . did you kill the ifrit as well?"

"I tried. It may have escaped before she died."

She bit her lip, remembering Baseema's gentle smile and her mother's quiet strength. But she had to push away the guilt for now. "So . . . if that was an ifrit, then you're what? Some kind of djinn?"

He made a disgusted face. "I am no djinn, girl. I am Daeva." His mouth curled in contempt. "Daeva who call themselves djinn have no respect for our people. They are traitors, worthy only of annihilation."

The hatred in his voice sent a fresh rush of fear coursing through her body. "Oh," she choked out. She had little idea what the difference between the two was, but it seemed wise not to press the matter. "My mistake." She pressed her palms against her knees to hide their trembling. "Do . . . do you have a name?"

His bright eyes narrowed. "You should know better than to ask that."

"Why?"

"There is power in names. It's not something my people give out so freely."

"Baseema called you Afshin."

The daeva shook his head. "That's merely a title . . . and an old and rather useless one at that."

"So you won't tell me your actual name?"

"No."

He sounded even more hostile than he had last night. Nahri cleared her throat, trying to maintain her calm. "What do you want with me?"

He ignored the question. "You are thirsty?"

Thirsty was an understatement; Nahri's throat felt like sand had been poured down it, and considering the events of last night, there was a fair chance that was actually true. Her stomach rumbled as well, reminding her that she hadn't eaten anything in hours.

The daeva removed a waterskin from his robe, but when she reached for it, he held it back. "I am going to ask you some questions first. You will answer them. And *honestly*. You strike me as a liar."

You have no idea. "Fine." She kept her tone even.

"Tell me of yourself. Your name, your family. Where your people are from."

She raised an eyebrow. "Why do you get to know my name if I can't know yours?"

"Because I have the water."

She scowled but decided to tell him the truth—for now. "My name is Nahri. I have no family. I have no idea where my people are from."

"Nahri," he repeated, drawing the word out with a frown. "No family at all . . . you are certain?"

It was the second time he had asked about her family. "As far as I know."

"Then who taught you Divasti?"

"No one taught me. I think it's my native tongue. At least, I've always known it. Besides . . ." Nahri hesitated. She never spoke of these things, having learned the consequences as a child.

Oh, why not? Maybe he'll actually have some answers for me. "I've been able to learn any language since I was a child," she added. "Every dialect. I can understand, and respond to, any tongue spoken to me."

He sat back, inhaling sharply. "I can test that," he said. But not in Divasti, rather in a new language with oddly rounded, high-pitched syllables.

She absorbed the sounds, letting them wash over her. The response came to her as soon as she opened her lips. "Go ahead."

He leaned forward, his eyes bright with challenge. "You look like an urchin who's been dragged through a charnel house."

This language was even stranger, musical and low, more like murmuring than speech. She glared back. "I wish someone would drag you through a charnel house."

His eyes dimmed. "It is as you say then," he murmured in Divasti. "And you have no idea of your origins?"

She threw up her hands. "How many times must I say so?"

"Then what of your life now? How do you live? Are you married?" His expression darkened. "Do you have children?"

Nahri couldn't take her eyes off the waterskin. "Why do you care? Are *you* married?" she shot back, annoyed. He glared. "Fine. I'm not married. I live alone. I work in an apothecary . . . as an assistant of sorts."

"Last night you mentioned lock picking."

Damn, he was observant. "Sometimes I take . . . *alternative* . . . assignments to supplement my income."

The djinn—no, the daeva, she corrected herself—narrowed his eyes. "You're some kind of thief, then?"

"That's a very narrow-minded way of looking at it. I prefer to think of myself as a merchant of delicate tasks."

"That doesn't make you any less a criminal."

"Ah, and yet there's a fine difference between djinn and daeva?"

He glowered, the hem of his robe turning to smoke, and Nahri quickly changed the subject. "I do other things. Make amulets, provide some healing . . ."

He blinked, his eyes growing brighter, more intense. "So you *can* heal others?" His voice turned hollow. "How?"

"I don't know," she admitted. "I can usually sense sickness better than I can heal it. Something will smell wrong, or there'll be a shadow over the body part." She paused, trying to find the right words. "It's difficult to explain. I can deliver babies well enough because I can sense their position. And when I lay my hands on people . . . I sort of wish them well . . . think about the parts fixing themselves; sometimes it works. Sometimes it doesn't."

His face grew stormier as she spoke. He crossed his arms; the outline of well-muscled limbs pressed against the smoky fabric. "And those you can't heal . . . I assume you reimburse them?"

She started to laugh and then realized he was serious. "Sure."

"This is impossible," he declared. He rose to his feet, pacing away with a grace that belied his true nature. "The Nahids would never . . . not with a human."

Taking advantage of his distraction, Nahri snatched the waterskin off the ground and ripped out the plug. The water was delicious, crisp and sweet, like nothing she'd ever tasted.

The daeva turned back to her. "So you just live quietly with these powers?" he demanded. "Haven't you ever wondered why you have them? Suleiman's eye . . . you could be overthrowing governments, and instead you steal from peasants!"

His words enraged her. She dropped the skin. "I do not *steal* from peasants," she snapped. "And you know nothing of my world, so don't judge me. You try living on the streets when you're five and speak a language no one understands. When you get thrown out of every orphanage after predicting which child will die next of consumption and telling the mistress that she has a shadow growing in her head." She seethed, briefly overcome by her memories. "I do what I need to survive."

"And calling me?" he asked, no apology in his voice. "Did you do that to survive?"

"No, I did that as part of some foolish ceremony." She paused. Not so foolish after all; Yaqub had been right about the dangers of interfering with traditions that weren't her own. "I sang one of the songs in Divasti—I had no idea what would happen." Saying it aloud did little to alleviate the guilt she felt about Baseema, but she pressed on. "Aside from what I can do, I've never seen anything else strange. Nothing magical, certainly nothing like *you*. I didn't think such things existed."

"Well, that was idiotic." She glared at him, but he only shrugged. "Were your own abilities not evidence enough?"

She shook her head. "You don't understand." He couldn't. He hadn't lived her life, the constant rush of business she had to bring in to keep herself afloat, her bribes paid. There wasn't time for anything else. All that mattered were the coins in her hand, the only true power she had.

And speaking of which . . . Nahri looked around. "The basket I was carrying—where is it?" At his blank look, she panicked. "Don't tell me you left it behind!" She jumped to her feet to search but saw nothing besides the rug spread out in the shade of a large tree.

"We were fleeing for our lives," he said sarcastically. "Did you expect me to waste time accounting for your belongings?"

Her hands flew to her temples. She'd lost a small fortune in a night. And she had even more to lose stashed in her stall back home. Nahri's heart quickened; she needed to return to Cairo. Between whatever rumors would undoubtedly fly around after the zar and her absence, it wouldn't be long before her landlord sacked the place.

"I need to get back," she said. "Please. I didn't mean to call you. And I'm grateful you saved me from the ghouls," she added, figuring a little appreciation couldn't hurt. "But I just want to go home."

A dark look crossed his face. "Oh, you're going home, I suspect. But it won't be to Cairo."

"Excuse me?"

He was already walking away. "You can't go back to the human world." He sat heavily on the carpet under the shade of a tree and pulled off his boots. He seemed to have aged during their brief conversation, his face shadowed by exhaustion. "It's against our law, and the ifrit are likely already tracking you. You wouldn't last a day."

"That's not your problem!"

"It is." He lay down, crossing his arms behind his head. "As are you, unfortunately."

A chill went down Nahri's back. The pointed questions about her family, the barely concealed disappointment when he learned of her abilities. "What do you know about me? Do you know why I can do these things?"

He shrugged. "I have my suspicions."

"Which *are*?" she prodded when he fell silent. "Tell me."

"Will you stop pestering me if I do?"

No. She nodded. "Yes."

"I think you're a shafit."

He had called her that in the cemetery too. But the word remained unfamiliar. "What's a shafit?"

"It's what we call someone with mixed blood. It's what happens when my race gets a bit . . . *indulgent* around humans."

"Indulgent?" She gasped, the meaning of his words becoming clear. "You think I have daeva blood? That I'm like you?"

"Believe me when I say I find such a thing equally distressing." He clucked his tongue in disapproval. "I never would have thought a Nahid capable of such a transgression."

Nahri was growing more confused by the minute. "What's a Nahid? Baseema called me something like that too, didn't she?"

A muscle twitched in his jaw, and she caught a flicker of emotion in his eyes. It was brief, but it was there. He cleared his throat. "It's a family name," he finally answered. "The Nahids are a family of daeva healers."

Daeva *healers*? Nahri gaped, but before she could respond, he waved her off.

"No. I told you what I think, and you promised to leave me alone. I need to rest. I did a lot of magic last night and I want to be ready should the ifrit come sniffing for you again."

Nahri shuddered, her hand instinctively going to her throat. "What do you mean to do with me?"

He made an irritated sound and reached into his pocket. Nahri jumped, expecting a weapon, but instead he pulled free a pile of clothing that looked too big to have fit the space and tossed it in her direction without opening his eyes. "There is a pool near the cliff. I suggest you visit it. You smell even viler than the rest of your kind."

"You didn't answer my question."

"Because I don't know yet." She could hear the uncertainty in his voice. "I've called someone for help. We will wait."

Just what she needed—a second djinn to weigh in on her fate. She picked up the bundle of clothes. "Aren't you worried I'll escape?"

He let out a drowsy laugh. "Good luck getting out of the desert."

THE OASIS WAS SMALL, AND IT WASN'T LONG BEfore she came upon the pool he had mentioned, a shadowy pond fed by the steady trickle of springs from a rocky ledge and surrounded by scrubby brush. She saw no sign of horses or camels; she couldn't imagine how they'd gotten here.

With a shrug, Nahri pulled off her ruined abaya, stepped in, and submerged.

The press of the cool water was like the touch of a friend. She closed her eyes, trying to digest the madness of the past day. She'd been kidnapped by a djinn. A daeva. Whatever. A magical creature with too many weapons who didn't seem particularly enamored of her.

She drifted on her back, tracing shapes in the water and staring at the palm-fringed sky.

He thinks I have daeva blood. The idea that she was in any way related to the creature who'd summoned a sandstorm last night seemed laughable, but he had a point about ignoring the implications of her healing abilities. Nahri had spent her entire life trying to blend in with those around her just to survive. Those instincts were warring even now: her thrill at learning what she was and her urge to flee back to the life she'd worked so hard to establish for herself in Cairo.

But she knew her odds of surviving the desert alone were low, so she tried to relax, enjoying the pool until her fingertips wrinkled. She scoured her skin with a palm husk and massaged her hair in the water, relishing the sensation of being clean. It wasn't

often she got to bathe—back home, the women at the local hammam made it clear she was unwelcome, perhaps fearing she'd put
a hex on the bathwater.

There was little that could be done to save her abaya, but she
washed what remained, stretching it out on a sunny rock to dry before turning her attention to the clothing the daeva had given her.

It was obviously his; it smelled of burnt citrus and was cut
to accommodate a muscular man, not a chronically famished
woman. Nahri rubbed the ash-colored fabric between her fingers
and marveled at its quality. It was soft as silk, yet sturdy as felt. It
was also completely seamless; try as she might, she couldn't find a
single stitch. She could likely sell it for a good sum if she escaped.

It took effort to get the clothes to fit; the tunic hung comically
large around her waist and ended past her knees. She rolled the
sleeves up as best she could and then turned her attention to the
pants. After ripping a strip from her abaya to use as a belt and
rolling up the hems, they stayed on reasonably well, but she could
only imagine how ridiculous she looked.

With a sharp rock, she cut a longer section of her abaya for a
headscarf. Her hair had dried in a wild mess of black curls that she
attempted to braid before tying the makeshift scarf around her
head. She drank her fill from the waterskin—it seemed to refill on
its own—but the water did little to help the hunger gnawing at her
stomach.

The palm trees were thick with swollen gold dates, and overripe ones, covered in ants, littered the ground. She tried everything she could think of to get at the ones in the trees: shaking
the trunks, throwing rocks, even a particularly ill-fated attempt
at climbing, but nothing worked.

Did daevas eat? If so, he must have some food, probably hidden in that robe of his. Nahri made her way back to the small
grove. The sun had risen, hot and searing, and she hissed as she

crossed a patch of scorched sand. God only knew what had happened to her sandals.

The daeva was still asleep; his gray cap was tipped over his eyes, his chest slowly rising and falling in the fading light. Nahri crept closer, studying him in a way she'd been too wary to do before. His robe rippled in the breeze, undulating like smoke, and hazy heat drifted from his body as though he was a hot stone oven. Fascinated, she moved even closer. She wondered if daeva bodies were like those of humans: full of blood and humors, a beating heart and swelling lungs. Or perhaps they were smoke through and through, their appearance only an illusion.

Closing her eyes, she stretched her fingers toward him and tried to concentrate. It would have been better to touch him, but she didn't dare. He struck her as the type to wake in a foul mood.

After a few minutes, she stopped, growing disturbed. There was nothing. No beating heart, no surging blood and bile. She could sense no organs, nothing of the sparks and gurgles of the hundreds of natural processes that kept her and every other person she'd ever met alive. Even his breathing was wrong, the movement of his chest false. It was as though someone had created an image of a person, a man out of clay, but forgotten to give it a final spark of life. He was . . . unfinished.

Not an ill-formed piece of clay, though . . . Nahri's gaze lingered on his body, and then she stilled, catching sight of a green flash on the daeva's left hand.

"God be praised," she whispered. An enormous emerald ring—large enough for a sultan—rested on the daeva's middle finger. The base looked to be badly battered iron, but she could tell from a single glance that the jewel was priceless. Dusty but perfectly cut, with not a single blemish. Something like that had to be worth a fortune.

As Nahri contemplated the ring, a shadow passed overhead.

Idly, she glanced up. Then, with a yelp, she dove into the thick brush to hide.

NAHRI PEEKED THROUGH A SCREEN OF LEAVES AS the creature flew across the oasis, enormous against the spindly trees, and then landed next to the sleeping daeva. It was something only a deviant mind could dream up, an unholy cross between an old man, a green parrot, and a mosquito. All bird from the chest down, it bobbed like a chicken as it moved forward on a pair of thick, feathered legs ending in sharp talons. The rest of its skin—if it could be called skin—was covered in silvery gray scales that flashed as it moved, reflecting the light of the setting sun.

It paused to stretch a pair of feathered arms. Its wings were extraordinary, the brilliant, lime-colored feathers nearly as long as she was tall. Nahri started to rise, wondering whether to warn the daeva. The creature was focused on him and seemingly oblivious to her, a situation she preferred. Yet if it killed him, there'd be no one to get her out of the desert.

The birdman let out a chirp that made every hair on her body rise, and the sound roused the daeva, solving her problem. He blinked his emerald eyes slowly, shading his face to see who stood before him. "Khayzur . . ." He exhaled. "By the Creator, am I glad to see you."

The creature extended a delicate hand and pulled the daeva into a brotherly embrace. Nahri's eyes widened. Was this the person the daeva had been waiting for?

They settled themselves back on the rug. "I came as soon as I got your signal," the creature squawked. Whatever language they were speaking it wasn't Divasti; it was full of staccato bursts and low whoops like birdsong. "What's wrong, Dara?"

The daeva's expression soured. "It's better seen than explained." He glanced about the oasis, and his eyes locked on Nahri's hiding spot. "Come on out, girl."

Nahri bristled, annoyed to be found so easily and then ordered about like a dog. But she emerged anyway, shoving the leaves aside and coming forward to join them.

She stifled a gasp when the birdman turned to her—the gray tone of his skin reminded her far too much of the ghouls. It was at odds with his small, almost pretty pink mouth and the neat green brows that met in the middle of his forehead. His eyes were colorless, and he had just the barest wisps of a gray beard.

He gaped, looking equally surprised at the sight of her. "You . . . you've a companion," he said to the daeva. "Not that I'm displeased, but I must say, Dara . . . I did not take humans as your type."

"She's not my companion." The daeva scowled. "And she's not entirely human. She's shafit. She . . ." He cleared his throat, his voice suddenly strained. "She would appear to have some Nahid blood."

The creature whirled around. "Why do you think that?"

The daeva's mouth twisted in distaste. "She healed before my eyes. Twice. And she has their gift with languages."

"The Maker be praised." Khayzur lurched closer, and Nahri skittered back. His colorless eyes swept her face. "I thought the Nahids were wiped out years ago."

"As did I," the daeva said. He sounded unnerved. "And to heal the way she did . . . she can't merely be a distant descendant. But she looks entirely human—I plucked her from some human city even farther west than we are now." The daeva shook his head. "Something's wrong, Khayzur. She claims she knew nothing of our world until last night, but she somehow dragged me halfway across the—"

"*She* can speak for herself," Nahri said acidly. "And I didn't mean to drag you anywhere! I'd have been happier never to have met you."

He snorted. "You'd have been murdered by that ifrit if I hadn't shown up."

Khayzur abruptly raised his hands to silence them. "The ifrit know about her?" he asked sharply.

"More than I do," the daeva admitted. "One showed up just before I did and wasn't at all surprised to see her. That's why I called you." He waved his hand. "You peris always know more than the rest of us."

Khayzur's wings drooped. "Not on this matter—though I wish I did. You're right, the circumstances are strange." He pinched the bridge of his nose, the gesture oddly human. "I need a cup of tea." He abruptly returned to the rug, motioning for Nahri to follow. "Come, child."

He dropped into a half perch, and a large samovar, fragrant with peppercorns and mace, suddenly appeared in his hands. He snapped his fingers, and three glass cups appeared. He filled them and handed her the first.

She examined the cup in awe; the glass was so thin it seemed almost like the steaming tea floated in her hand. "What *are* you?"

He gave her a gentle smile that revealed sharply pointed teeth. "I am a peri. My name is Khayzur." He touched his brow. "An honor to meet you, my lady."

Well, whatever a peri was, they clearly had better manners than daevas. Nahri took a sip of her tea. It was thick and peppery, burning down her throat in an oddly pleasant way. In an instant, her whole body felt suffused with warmth—and more important, her hunger was sated.

"That's delicious!" She smiled, her skin tingling from the liquid.

"My own recipe," Khayzur said proudly. He gave a sidelong glance at the daeva and nodded to the third cup. "If you'd like to stop glowering and join us, that's yours, Dara."

Dara. It was the third time the peri had called him that. She flashed him a triumphant smile. "Yes, *Dara*," she said, all but purring his name. "Why don't you join us?"

He threw her a dark look. "I'd prefer something stronger." But he took the cup and dropped down beside her.

The peri sipped his tea. "Do you think the ifrit will come after her?"

Dara nodded. "It was hell-bent on taking her. I tried to kill it before it abandoned its host, but there's a good chance it escaped."

"Then it may have already told its fellows." Khayzur shuddered. "You've no time to puzzle out her origins, Dara. You need to get her to Daevabad as soon as possible."

Dara was already shaking his head. "I can't. I *won't*. Suleiman's eye, do you know what the djinn would say if I brought in a Nahid shafit?"

"That your Nahids were hypocrites," Khayzur replied. Dara's eyes flashed. "And what of it? Is saving her life not worth embarrassing her ancestors?"

Nahri certainly thought her life was a hell of a lot more important than the reputation of some dead daeva relatives, but Dara didn't look convinced. "You could take her," he urged the peri. "Leave her at the banks of the Gozan."

"And hope she finds her way past the veil? Hope the Qahtani family believes the word of some lost, human-looking girl should she somehow make it to the palace?" Khayzur looked appalled. "You are an Afshin, Dara. Her life is your responsibility."

"Which is why she'd be better off in Daevabad without me," Dara argued. "Those sand flies would likely murder her just to punish me for the war."

The *war*? "Wait," Nahri cut in, not liking the sound of this Daevabad at all. "What war?"

"One that ended fourteen centuries ago and over which he's

still holding a grudge," Khayzur answered. At that, Dara knocked over his teacup and stalked off. "A skill at which he's most adept," the peri added. The daeva threw him a jewel-eyed glare, but the peri pressed on. "You're only one man, Dara; you can't hold the ifrit off forever. They will kill her if they find her. Slowly and gleefully." Nahri shivered, a prickle of fear running over her skin. "And it will be entirely your fault."

Dara paced the edge of the rug. Nahri spoke up again, not particularly keen on a pair of bickering magical beings deciding her fate without any input from her.

"Why would this Daevabad be safer than Cairo?"

"Daevabad is your family's ancestral home," Khayzur replied. "No ifrit can pass its veil—none can, save your race."

She glanced at Dara. The daeva stared out at the setting sun, muttering angrily under his breath as smoke curled around his ears. "So it's full of people like him?"

The peri gave her a weak smile. "I'm sure you will find a greater . . . *breadth* of temperaments in the city itself."

How encouraging. "Why are the ifrit after me in the first place?"

Khayzur hesitated. "I'm afraid I'll have to leave that explanation to your Afshin. It's a lengthy one."

My Afshin? Nahri wanted to ask. But Khayzur had already turned his attention back to Dara. "Have you come to your senses yet? Or do you intend to let this nonsense over blood purity ruin another life?"

"No," the daeva grumbled, but she could hear the indecision in his voice. He clasped his hands behind his back, refusing to look at either of them.

"By the Maker . . . go *home*, Dara," Khayzur urged. "Have you not suffered enough for this ancient war? The rest of the Daeva tribe made peace long ago. Why can't you?"

Dara twisted his ring, his hands trembling. "Because they didn't witness it," he said softly. "But you are correct about the ifrit." He sighed and turned around, his face still troubled. "The girl is safest—from them anyway—in Daevabad."

"Good." Khayzur looked relieved. He snapped his fingers, and the tea supplies disappeared. "Then go. Travel as fast as you can. But discreetly." He pointed to the rug. "Do not overly rely on this. Whoever sold it to you did a terrible job on the charm. The ifrit might be able to track it."

Dara scowled again. "*I* did the charm."

The peri lifted his delicate brows. "Well . . . then perhaps keep those close," he suggested with a nod to the weapons piled under the tree. He rose to his feet, shaking out his wings. "I will not delay you further. But I'll see what I can learn of the girl— should it be useful, I'll try to find you." He bowed in Nahri's direction. "An honor to meet you, Nahri. Good luck to you both."

With a single flap of his wings, he rose in the air and vanished into the crimson sky.

Dara stepped into his boots and swung the silver bow over one shoulder before smoothing the carpet out. "Let's go," he said, tossing his other weapons onto the rug.

"Let's *talk*," she countered, crossing her legs. She wasn't moving from the carpet. "I'm not going anywhere until I get some answers."

"No." He dropped beside her on the rug, his voice firm. "I saved your life. I'm escorting you to the city of my enemies. That's enough. You can find someone in Daevabad to bother with your questions." He sighed. "I suspect this journey will already be long enough."

Enraged, Nahri opened her mouth to argue and then stopped, realizing the rug now held all their supplies, as well as she and Dara both.

No horses. No camels. Her heart skipped a beat. "We're not really going to—"

Dara snapped his fingers, and the carpet shot into the air.

4

ALI

It was a miserable morning in Daevabad.

Though the adhan, the call to dawn prayer, rang out across the wet air, there was no sign of the sun in the misty sky. Fog shrouded the great city of brass, obscuring its towering minarets of sand-blasted glass and hammered metal and veiling its golden domes. Rain seeped off the jade roofs of marble palaces and flooded its stone streets, condensing on the placid faces of its ancient Nahid founders memorialized on the murals covering its mighty walls.

A chilly breeze swept through the winding streets, past intricately tiled bathhouses and the thick doors protecting fire temples whose altars had burned for millennia, bringing the smell of damp earth and tree sap from the thickly forested mountains that surrounded the island. It was the type of morning that sent most djinn scurrying indoors like cats fleeing rain, back to beds of smoky silk brocade and warm mates, burning away the hours until the sun reemerged hot and proper to scald the city to life.

Prince Alizayd al Qahtani was not one of them. He pulled the tail of his turban across his face and shivered, hunching his shoulders against the cold rain as he walked. His breath came in a steamy hush, the sound amplified against the damp cloth. Rain dripped from his brow, evaporating as it crossed his smoky skin.

He went over the charges again in his mind. *You have to talk to him*, he told himself. *You have no choice. The rumors are getting out of hand.*

Ali stuck to the shadows as he neared the Grand Bazaar. Even at this early hour, the bazaar would be busy: sleepy merchants undoing the curses that had protected their wares throughout the night, apothecaries brewing potions to energize their first customers, children carrying messages made of burnt glass that shattered upon revealing their words—not to mention the bodies of barely conscious addicts wasted on smuggled human intoxicants. With little desire to be seen by any of them, Ali turned down a dark lane, a detour that took him so deep into the city that he could no longer glimpse the tall brass walls that enclosed it.

The neighborhood he entered was an old one, crowded with ancient buildings mimicking human architecture lost to time: columns carved with Nabatean graffiti, friezes of Etruscan satyrs, and intricate Mauryan stupas. Civilizations long dead, their memory captured by the curious djinn who'd passed through—or by nostalgic shafit trying to re-create their lost homes.

A large stone mosque with a striking spiral minaret and black and white archways stood at the end of the street. One of the few places in Daevabad where djinn purebloods and shafit still worshipped together, the mosque's popularity with traders and travelers from the Grand Bazaar made for an unusually transient community . . . and a good place to be invisible.

Ali ducked inside, eager to escape the rain. He'd no sooner slipped off his sandals than they were snatched away by a zealous ishtas, the small, scaled creatures obsessed with organization and footwear. For a bit of fruit and negotiation, Ali's shoes would be returned to him after prayer, scrubbed and fragrant with sandalwood. He continued, passing a pair of matching marble ablution fountains, one flowing with water for the shafit while its partner swirled with the warm black sand most purebloods preferred.

One of the oldest in Daevabad, the mosque consisted of four covered halls enclosing a courtyard open to the gray sky. Worn down by the feet and brows of centuries of worshippers, its red and gold carpet was thin but immaculate—whatever self-cleaning enchantments had been woven in with its threads still held. Large, hazy glass lanterns filled with enchanted flames hung from the ceiling, and nuggets of frankincense smoldered in corner braziers.

It was mostly empty this morning, the benefits of communal prayer perhaps not outweighing the vile weather for many of its usual congregants. Ali took a deep breath of the fragrant air as he scanned the scattered worshippers, but the man he was looking for had yet to arrive.

Maybe he's been arrested. Ali tried to dismiss the dark thought as he approached the gray marble mihrab, the niche in the wall indicating the direction of prayer. He raised his hands. Despite his nerves, as Ali began to pray, he felt a small measure of peace. He always did.

But it didn't last long. He was finishing his second rakat of prayer when a man knelt quietly beside him. Ali stilled.

"Peace be upon you, brother," the man whispered.

Ali avoided his gaze. "And upon you peace," he said softly.

"Were you able to get it?"

Ali hesitated. "It" was the fat purse concealed in his robe that contained a small fortune from his overflowing personal vault at the Treasury. "Yes. But we need to talk."

From the corner of his eye, Ali saw his companion frown, but before he could respond, the mosque's imam approached the mihrab.

He gave the rain-damp group of men a weary look. "Straighten your lines," he admonished. Ali stood as the dozen or so sleepy worshippers shuffled into place. He tried to concentrate while the imam led them in prayer, but it was difficult. Rumors and accusations swirled in his mind, charges he felt ill-prepared to lay on the man whose shoulder brushed his.

When prayer was over, Ali and his companion stayed seated, silently waiting as the rest of the worshippers filed out. The imam was last. He climbed to his feet, muttering under his breath. As he glanced at the two remaining men, he froze.

Ali dropped his gaze, letting his turban shadow his face, but the imam's attention was focused on his companion. "Sheikh Anas . . . ," he gasped. "P-peace be upon you."

"And upon you peace," Anas replied calmly. He touched his heart and gestured to Ali. "Would you mind giving the brother here and me a moment alone?"

"Of course," the imam rushed on. "Take all the time you need; I'll make sure no one disturbs you." He hurried out, pulling the inner door shut.

Ali waited another moment before speaking, but they were alone, the only sound the steady patter of rain in the courtyard. "Your reputation grows," he noted, a little unnerved by the imam's deference.

Anas shrugged and leaned back on his palms. "Or he's off to warn the Royal Guard."

Ali startled. His sheikh smiled. Though Anas Bhatt was in his fifties—an age at which pureblooded djinn were still considered young adults—Anas was shafit, and gray dusted his black beard, lines creasing his eyes. Though there must have been a drop or two of djinn blood in his veins—his ancestors couldn't have crossed into Daevabad without it—Anas could have passed for human and had no magical abilities. He was dressed in a white kurta and embroidered cap and had a thick Kashmiri shawl wrapped around his shoulders.

"It was a jest, my prince," he added when Ali didn't return his smile. "But what's wrong, brother? You look as though you've seen an ifrit."

I'd take an ifrit over my father. Ali scanned the dark mosque, half-expecting to see spies nestled in its shadows. "Sheikh, I'm starting to hear . . . certain *things* about the Tanzeem again."

Anas sighed. "What is the palace claiming we did now?"

"Tried to smuggle a cannon past the Royal Guard."

"A cannon?" Anas gave him a skeptical look. "What would I do with a cannon, brother? I'm shafit. I know the law. Possessing even an overly large kitchen knife would get me thrown in prison. And the Tanzeem are a charitable organization; we deal in books and food, not weapons. Besides, how would you purebloods know what a cannon looks like anyway?" He scoffed. "When's the last time someone in the Citadel visited the human world?"

He had a point there, but Ali pressed on. "There've been reports for months that the Tanzeem is trying to buy weapons. People say your rallies have grown violent, that some of your supporters are even calling for the Daevas to be killed."

"Who spreads such lies?" Anas demanded. "That Daeva infidel your father calls the grand wazir?"

"It's not just Kaveh," Ali argued. "We arrested a shafit man just last week for stabbing two purebloods in the Grand Bazaar."

"And I'm responsible?" Anas threw up his hands. "Am I to be called to account for the actions of every shafit man in Daevabad? You know how desperate our lives are here, Alizayd. Your people should be happy more of us haven't resorted to violence!"

Ali recoiled. "Are you condoning such a thing?"

"Of course not," Anas replied, sounding annoyed. "Don't be absurd. But when our girls are snatched off the street to be used as bed slaves, when our men are blinded for looking at a pureblood the wrong way . . . is it not to be expected that some will fight back any way they can?" He gave Ali an even stare. "It's your father's fault things have gotten this bad—if the shafit were afforded equal protection, we wouldn't be forced to take the law into our own hands."

It was a low, albeit justified, blow, but Anas's angry denial wasn't doing much to assuage Ali's concerns. "I was always clear with you, Sheikh. Money for books, food, medicine, anything like that . . . but if your people are taking up arms against my father's citizens, I can't be part of that. I won't."

Anas raised a dark eyebrow. "What are you saying?"

"I want to see how you're spending my money. Surely you've kept some type of records."

"*Records?*" His sheikh looked incredulous . . . and then offended. "Is my word not enough? I run a school, an orphanage, a medical clinic . . . I have widows to house and students to teach. A thousand responsibilities and now you want me to waste time on what exactly . . . an audit from my teenage patron who fancies himself an accountant?"

Ali's cheeks burned, but he wasn't backing down. "Yes." He pulled the purse from his robe. The coins and jewels inside jingled together when they hit the ground. "Otherwise this will be the last of it." He rose to his feet.

"Alizayd," Anas called. "Brother." His sheikh scrambled to his feet, putting himself between Ali and the door. "You're acting rashly."

No, I was acting rashly when I started funding a shafit street preacher without checking into his story, Ali wanted to say, but he held his tongue, avoiding the older man's eyes. "I'm sorry, Sheikh."

Anas's hand shot out. "Just wait. Please." There was an edge of panic in his normally calm voice. "What if I could show you?"

"Show me?"

Anas nodded. "Yes," he said, his voice growing firm, as if he had come to a decision. "Can you get away from the Citadel again tonight?"

"I-I suppose." Ali frowned. "But I don't see what that has to do with—"

The sheikh cut him off. "Then meet me at Daeva Gate tonight, after isha prayer." He glanced down Ali's body. "Dress as a nobleman from your mother's tribe, with all the finery you have to spare. You'll easily pass."

Ali flinched at the comment. "That doesn't—"

"You will learn tonight what my organization does with your money."

ALI FOLLOWED HIS SHEIKH'S INSTRUCTIONS EX-actly, slipping out after isha prayer with a bundle tucked under one arm. After taking a circuitous route through the Grand Bazaar, he ducked into a dark, windowless lane. He unrolled the bundle—one of the rich teal robes the Ayaanle, his mother's kinsmen, were fond of—and pulled it on over his uniform.

A turban of the same color went on next, wrapped loosely around his neck in Ayaanle fashion, and then a deeply ostentatious collar of gold worked with corals and pearls. Ali hated jewelry—truly a more useless waste of resources had never been devised—but he knew that no Ayaanle nobleman worth his salt would dare go out unadorned. Though his vault brimmed with treasure from his mother's wealthy homeland of Ta Ntry, the collar had already been on hand, some family heirloom his sister Zaynab had insisted he wear to an Ayaanle wedding he'd been forced to attend a few months ago.

Finally, he pulled a tiny glass vial from his pocket. A potion that looked like swirled cream churned inside, a cosmetic enchantment that would turn his eyes the bright gold of an Ayaanle man for a few hours. Ali hesitated; he didn't want to change the color of his eyes, not for a moment.

There weren't many people in Daevabad like Ali and his sister, pureblooded djinn nobles of mixed tribal heritage. Separated into six tribes by the human prophet-king Suleiman himself, most djinn preferred the company of their kinsmen; indeed, Suleiman had supposedly divided them with the express purpose of causing as much dissent as possible. The more time djinn spent fighting each other, the less they spent harassing humans.

But Ali's parents' marriage had been equally purposeful, a political match meant to strengthen the alliance between the Geziri and the Ayaanle tribes. It was a strange, often strained, alliance. The Ayaanle were a wealthy people who prized scholarship and trade, rarely leaving the fine coral palaces and sophisticated salons of Ta Ntry, their homeland on the East African coast. In contrast, Am Gezira, with its heart in the most desolate deserts of southern Arabia, must have seemed a wasteland, its forbidding sands filled with wandering poets and illiterate warriors.

And yet Am Gezira owned Ali's heart completely. He'd always preferred the Geziri, an allegiance his appearance thoroughly mocked. Ali resembled his mother's people so strikingly that it would have provoked gossip had his father not been king. He shared their lanky height and black skin, his stern mouth and sharp cheeks near replicas of his mother's. All he'd inherited from his father was his dark steel eyes. And tonight, he'd have to give even those up.

Ali opened the vial and tapped a few drops into each eye. He bit back a curse. God, it burned. He'd been warned that it would, but the pain took him aback.

He made his bleary-eyed way to the midan, the central plaza at Daevabad's heart. It was empty at this late hour; the neglected fountain in its center cast wild shadows on the ground. The midan was enclosed by a copper wall gone green with age, the wall in turn broken up by seven equally spaced gates. Each gate led to a different tribal district with the seventh opening into the Grand Bazaar and its overcrowded shafit neighborhoods.

The midan's gates were always a sight to behold. There was the

Sahrayn Gate, black-and-white-tiled pillars wrapped in grape-vines heavy with purple fruit. Beside it was that of the Ayaanle, two narrow, studded pyramids crowned with a scroll and a salt tablet. The Geziri Gate was next, nothing but a perfectly cut stone arch-way, his father's people preferring function over form as always. It looked even plainer beside the richly decorated Agnivanshi Gate with its rose-colored sandstone sculpted into dozens of dancing figures, their delicate hands holding flickering oil lamps so small that they resembled stars. Next to that was the Tukharistani Gate, a screen of polished jade reflecting the night sky, carved in an im-possibly intricate pattern.

And yet impressive as they all were, the final gate—the gate that would catch the first rays of sunlight each morning, the gate of Daevabad's original people—outshone them all.

The Daeva Gate.

The entrance to the Daevas' quarter—for the fire worshippers had arrogantly taken their race's original name as their own tribal one—sat directly across from the Grand Bazaar, its enormous pan-eled doors painted a pale blue that could have been plucked di-rectly from a fresh-washed sky, and embedded with white and gold sandstone disks set in a triangular pattern. The doors were held open by two massive brass shedu, the statues all that were left of the mythical winged lions the ancient Nahids were said to have ridden into battle against the ifrit.

He made his way toward the entrance, but he'd barely got-ten halfway there when two figures stepped out from beneath the gate's shadow. Ali stopped. One of the men quickly raised his hands and moved into the moonlight. Anas.

His sheikh smiled. "Peace be upon you, brother." He was dressed in a homespun tunic the color of dirty wash water, his head uncharacteristically bare.

"And upon you peace." Ali eyed the second man. He was shafit—that much was apparent from his rounded ears—but looked

Sahrayn, with the North African tribe's fiery red-black hair and copper eyes. He wore a striped galabiyya, its tasseled hood half drawn.

The man's eyes widened at the sight of Ali. "*This* is your new recruit?" He laughed. "Are we so desperate for fighters that we're taking crocodiles barely out of their shell?"

Outraged by the slur against his Ayaanle blood, Ali opened his mouth to protest, but Anas cut in. "Watch your tongue, Brother Hanno," he warned. "We are all djinn here."

Hanno didn't look bothered by the admonishment. "Does he have a name?"

"Not one that concerns you," Anas said firmly. "He's here merely to observe." He nodded at Hanno. "So go on. I know you like to show off."

The other man chuckled. "Fair enough." He clapped his hands, and a swirl of smoke shrouded his body. When it dissipated, his dirty galabiyya had been replaced by an iridescent shawl, a mustard-colored turban decorated with pheasant feathers, and a bright green dhoti, the waist cloth typically worn by Agnivanshi men. As Ali watched, his ears lengthened, and his skin brightened to a dark, luminous brown. Black braids crawled out from under his turban, stretching to sweep the hilt of the Hindustani talwar now sheathed at his waist. He blinked, his copper eyes turning the tin color of an Agnivanshi pureblood. A steel relic band clanged into place around his wrist.

Ali's mouth fell open. "You're a *shapeshifter*?" he gasped, hardly believing the sight before him. Shape-shifting was an incredibly rare ability, one which only a few families in each tribe possessed and even fewer managed to master. Talented shapeshifters were worth their weight in gold. "By the Most High . . . I didn't think the shafit even capable of such advanced magic."

Hanno snorted. "You purebloods always underestimate us."

"But . . ." Ali was still stunned. ". . . if you can look pure-blooded, why even live as shafit?"

The humor vanished from Hanno's new face. "Because I *am* shafit. That I can wield my magic better than a pureblood, that the sheikh here could spin intellectual circles around the scholars of the Royal Library—that is proof that we're not so different from the rest of you." He glared at Ali. "It's not a thing I mean to hide."

Ali felt like a fool. "I'm sorry. I didn't mean—"

"It's fine," Anas interrupted. He took Ali's arm. "Let's go."

Ali drew to a halt when he realized where the sheikh was leading him. "Wait . . . you don't mean to actually go *in* the Daeva Quarter, do you?" He assumed the gate had only been a meeting place.

"Afraid of a few fire worshippers?" Hanno teased. He tapped the hilt of his talwar. "Don't worry, boy. I won't let any Afshin ghost gobble you up."

"I'm not afraid of the Daevas," Ali snapped. He'd had just about enough of this man. "But I know the law. They don't allow foreigners in their quarter after sunset."

"Well, then I guess we'll just have to be discreet."

They passed under the snarling shedu statues and into the Daeva Quarter. Ali got a brief glance at the main boulevard—bustling at this time of night with shoppers browsing in the market and men playing chess over endless cups of tea—before Anas pulled him toward the back of the nearest building.

A dark alley stretched before them, lined with neatly stacked crates of garbage awaiting disposal. It snaked away, vanishing into the gloomy distance.

"Stay low and stay quiet," Anas warned. It quickly became clear that the Tanzeem men had done this before; they navigated the maze of alleys with ease, darting into the shadows every time a back door banged open.

When they finally emerged, it was in a neighborhood that bore little resemblance to the gleaming central boulevard. The ancient buildings looked hewn directly from Daevabad's rocky hills, ramshackle wooden huts squashed in every available space. A squat brick complex stood at the end of the street, firelight winking from behind its tattered curtains.

As they drew closer, Ali could hear drunken laughter and the strains of some sort of stringed instrument pouring out from the open door. The air was hazy; smoke drifted about the men lounging on stained cushions, swirling past steam pipes and dark goblets of wine. The patrons were all Daeva, many with black caste tattoos and family sigils emblazoned on their golden-brown arms.

A burly man in a stained vest with a scar splitting one cheek guarded the entrance. He climbed to his feet as they approached, blocking the door with an enormous ax.

"You lost?" he growled.

"We're here to see Turan," Hanno said.

The guard's black eyes shifted to Anas. He sneered. "You and your crocodile friend can come in, but the dirt-blood stays out here."

Hanno stepped up to him, his hand on his talwar. "For what I'm paying your boss, my servant stays with me." He jerked his head at the ax. "Mind?"

The other man didn't look happy, but he stepped away and Hanno entered the tavern, Anas and Ali following.

Besides a few hostile glances—mostly aimed at Anas—the patrons ignored them. It looked like the type of place people came to be forgotten, but Ali struggled not to stare. He'd never been to a tavern—he'd never even spent much time around the fire worshippers. Few Daevas were permitted to serve in the Royal Guard, and of those who did, Ali suspected none were interested in befriending the youngest Qahtani.

He dodged out of the way as a drunk man fell from his ottoman with a smoky snort. The sound of feminine laughter caught
his attention, and Ali glanced over to find a trio of Daeva women
conversing in rapid-fire Divasti over a mirrored table covered
in brass game pieces, half-empty goblets, and glittering coins.
Though their conversation was gibberish—Ali had never bothered to learn Divasti—each woman was more stunning than the
last, their black eyes sparkling as they laughed. They wore embroidered blouses that were cut low and tight across their breasts,
their slender golden waists wrapped in jeweled chains.

Ali abruptly lost the battle he'd been waging against staring.
He'd never seen an adult Daeva woman uncovered, let alone one
displaying the charms of these three. The most conservative of
the tribes, Daeva women veiled themselves when leaving their
homes, with many—especially from highborn families—refusing
to speak to foreign men at all.

Not these three. Noticing Ali, one of the women straightened
up, boldly meeting his eyes with a wicked grin. "Aye, darling, do
you like what you see?" she asked in accented Djinnistani. She
licked her lips, causing his heart to skip several beats, and nodded to the jeweled collar around his neck. "You look like you
could afford me."

Anas stepped between them. "Lower your eyes, brother," he
chided gently.

Embarrassed, Ali dropped his gaze. Hanno snickered, but Ali
didn't look up until they were led into a small back room. It was
better adorned than the tavern; intricately woven rugs depicting
fruit trees and dancers covered the floor while chandeliers of cut
glass hung from the ceiling.

Hanno pushed Ali onto one of the plush cushions lining the
wall. "Keep quiet," he warned as he took a seat beside him. "It
took me a long time to set this up." Anas stayed standing, his head
bowed in an uncharacteristically subservient manner.

A thick felt curtain in the center of the room swept away to reveal a Daeva man in a crimson coat standing at the entrance to a dark corridor.

Hanno beamed. "Greetings, sahib," he boomed in an Agnivanshi accent. "You must be Turan. May the fires burn brightly for you."

Turan didn't return the smile or the blessing. "You're late."

The shapeshifter lifted his dark brows in surprise. "Is the market for stolen children a punctual one?"

Ali startled, but before he could open his mouth, Anas caught his eye from across the room and gave a slight shake of his head. Ali stayed quiet.

Turan crossed his arms, looking irritated. "I can find another buyer if your conscience bothers you."

"And disappoint my wife?" Hanno shook his head. "Absolutely not. She's already set up the nursery."

Turan's eyes slid to Ali. "Who's your friend?"

"Two friends," Hanno corrected, tapping the sword at his waist. "Do you expect me to wander about the Daeva Quarter with the ridiculous amount of money you're demanding and not bring protection?"

Turan's cold gaze stayed fixed upon Ali's face. His heart raced; Ali could think of few places worse to be recognized as a Qahtani prince than a Daeva tavern filled with drunk men of various criminal persuasions.

Anas spoke for the first time. "He is delaying, master," he warned. "He probably already sold the boy."

"Shut your mouth, shafit," Turan snapped. "No one gave you permission to speak."

"Enough." Hanno cut in. "But come, man, do you have the boy or not? All this complaining about my tardiness and now you're wasting time leering at my companion."

Turan's eyes flashed, but he disappeared behind the felt curtain.

Hanno rolled his eyes. "And the Daevas wonder why nobody likes them."

There was an angry burst of Divasti from behind the curtain, and then a dirty little girl carrying a large copper tray was pushed into the room. She looked as human as Anas. Her skin was dull, and she was dressed in a linen shift wholly inadequate for the night's chill, her hair shaved so roughly there were scarred nicks on her bare scalp. Keeping her gaze down, she approached on bare feet, mutely offering the tray upon which sat two steaming cups of apricot liquor. She couldn't have been any older than ten.

Ali spotted the bruises on the girl's wrist at the same time as Hanno, but the shapeshifter straightened up first.

He hissed. "I'll kill that man."

The little girl scrambled back, and Anas hurried to her side. "It's okay, little one, he didn't mean to scare you . . . Hanno, *put your weapon away*," he warned as the shapeshifter drew his talwar. "Don't be a fool."

Hanno snarled but sheathed the blade as Turan reentered.

The Daeva man took one look at the scene before him and then glared at Anas. "Get away from my servant." The girl retreated to a dark corner, cowering behind her tray.

Ali's temper flashed. He'd heard Anas speak for years about the plight of the shafit, but to actually *witness* it, to hear how the Daevas spoke to Anas, to see the bruises on the terrified little girl . . . Maybe Ali had been wrong to question him earlier.

Turan approached. A baby—well-swaddled and fast asleep—was nestled in his arms. Hanno immediately reached for him.

Turan held back. "The money first."

Hanno nodded at Anas, and the sheikh stepped forward with the purse Ali had given him earlier. He spilled the contents on the rug, a mix of currencies including human dinars, Tukharistani jade tablets, salt nuggets, and a single small ruby.

"Count it yourself," Hanno said curtly. "But let me see the boy."

Turan passed him over, and Ali had to work to contain his surprise. He'd expected another shafit child, but the baby's ears were as peaked as his own, and his brown skin gleamed with the luminescence of a pureblood. Hanno briefly opened one closed lid, revealing tin-colored eyes. The baby let out a smoky whimper of protest.

"He'll pass," Turan assured him. "Trust me. I've been in this business long enough to know. No one will ever suspect that he's a shafit."

Shafit? Ali looked at the boy again, taken aback. But Turan was right: he didn't look like a mixed-blood in the slightest.

"Did you have any trouble getting him away from his parents?" Hanno asked.

"The father wasn't an issue. Agnivanshi pureblood who just wanted the money. The mother was a maid who ran off when he got her pregnant. Took a while to track her down."

"And she agreed to sell the child?"

Turan shrugged. "She's shafit. Does it matter?"

"It does if she's going to make problems for me later."

"She threatened to go to the Tanzeem." Turan scoffed. "But those dirt-blooded radicals are nothing to worry about, and the shafit breed like rabbits. She'll have another baby to distract her in a year."

Hanno smiled, but the expression didn't meet his eyes. "Maybe another business opportunity for you." He glanced at Ali. "And what do you think?" he asked, his voice intent. He turned the sleeping baby around to face him. "Could he pass as my own?"

Ali frowned, a little confused by the question. He glanced between the baby and Hanno, but of course Hanno didn't look like himself. He'd shapeshifted. He'd shapeshifted into a very particular Agnivanshi visage, and it suddenly became terribly clear why.

"Y-yes," he choked out, swallowing back the lump in his throat and trying to conceal the horror in his voice. It was the truth, after all. "Easily."

Hanno didn't seem as pleased. "Perhaps. But he's older than promised—certainly not worth the ridiculous price you're demanding," he complained to Turan. "Is my wife to have given birth to a toddler?"

"Then go." Turan raised his palms. "I'll have another buyer in a week, and you'll return to a wife waiting beside an empty crib. Spend another half century trying to conceive. It's all the same to me."

Hanno appeared to deliberate another moment. He glanced at the little girl still crouched in the shadows. "We're looking for a new servant. Include that one with the boy, and I will pay your price."

Turan scowled. "I'm not going to sell you a house slave for nothing."

"I'll buy her," Ali cut in. Hanno's eyes flashed, but Ali didn't care. He wanted to be done with this Daeva demon, to get these innocent souls away from this hellish place where their lives were weighed solely upon their appearance. He fumbled for the clasps on his golden collar, and it landed heavily in his lap. He thrust it at Turan, the pearls glistening in the soft light. "Is this enough?"

Turan didn't touch it. There was no greed, no anticipation in his black eyes. Instead, he glanced at the collar and then looked at Ali.

He cleared his throat. "What did you say your name was?"

Ali suspected he'd just made a terrible mistake.

But before he could stammer a response, the door leading to

the tavern swung open, and one of the wine bearers hurried in. He bent to whisper in Turan's ear. The slaver's frown deepened.

"Problem?" Hanno prompted.

"A man whose desire to drink outweighs his ability to pay." Turan rose to his feet, his mouth pressed in an irritated line. "If you will excuse me a moment . . ." He headed for the tavern, the wine bearer at his heels. They shut the door behind them.

Hanno whirled on Ali. "You *idiot*. Didn't I tell you to keep your mouth shut?" He gestured at the collar. "That thing could buy a dozen girls like her!"

"I-I'm sorry," Ali rushed. "I was just trying to help!"

"Forget that for now." Anas pointed to the baby. "Does he have the mark?"

Hanno shot Ali another aggrieved look but then gently coaxed one of the baby's arms out of his swaddling and turned his wrist to the light. A small blue birthmark—like a dashed pen stroke—marred the soft skin. "Yes. Same story as the mother's, as well. It's him." He pointed to the little girl still cowering in the corner. "But she's not staying here with that monster."

Anas eyed the shapeshifter. "I didn't say she was."

Ali was thunderstruck by what he'd just witnessed. "The boy . . . is this common?"

Anas sighed, his face somber. "Quite. The shafit have always been more fertile than purebloods, a blessing and a curse from our human ancestors." He gestured to the small fortune glittering on the rug. "It's a lucrative business—one that's gone on for centuries. There are probably thousands in Daevabad like this boy, raised as purebloods with no idea of their true heritage."

"But their shafit parents . . . can't they petition m—the king?"

"'*Petition the king*'?" Hanno repeated, his voice thick with scorn. "By the Most High, is this the first time you've left your family's mansion, boy? Shafit can't petition the king. They come to us—we're the only ones who can help."

Ali dropped his gaze. "I had no idea."

"Then perhaps you will think on this night should you decide to question me again about the Tanzeem," Anas cut in, his voice colder than Ali had ever heard it. "We do what's necessary to protect our people."

Hanno suddenly frowned. He stared at the money on the floor, shifting the sleeping baby still nestled in his arms. "Something's not right." He stood. "Turan shouldn't have left us here with the money and the boy." He reached for the door leading to the tavern and then jumped back with a yelp, the sizzle of burned flesh scenting the air. "The bastard cursed us in!"

Awakened by Hanno's shout, the baby started to cry. Ali shot to his feet. He joined them at the door, praying Hanno was wrong.

He let his fingertips hover just over the wooden surface, but Hanno was right: it simmered with magic. Fortunately, Ali was Citadel trained—and the Daevas were troublemakers enough that breaking through the enchantments they used to guard their homes and businesses was a skill taught to the youngest cadets. He closed his eyes, murmuring the first incantation that came to mind. The door swung open.

The tavern was empty.

It had been abandoned in a hurry. Goblets were still full, smoke curled around forgotten pipes, and scattered game pieces glittered on the table where the Daeva women had been playing. Even so, Turan had been careful to douse the lamps, throwing the tavern into darkness. The only illumination came from the moonlight piercing the tattered curtains.

Behind him, Hanno swore and Anas whispered a prayer of protection. Ali reached for his hidden zulfiqar, the forked copper scimitar he always carried, and then stopped. The famed Geziri weapon in the hands of a young Ayaanle-looking man would give him away at once. Instead, he crept through the tavern. Taking care to remain hidden, he peeked past the curtain.

The Royal Guard stood on the other side.

Ali sucked in his breath. A dozen soldiers—nearly all of whom he recognized—were quietly lining up in formation across the street from the tavern, their coppery zulfiqars and spears gleaming in the moonlight. More were coming; Ali could see shadowy movement from the direction of the midan.

He stepped back. Dread, thicker than anything he'd ever felt, ensnared him, like vines tightening around his chest. He returned to the others.

"We need to leave." He was surprised at the calm in his voice; it certainly didn't match the panic rising inside him. "There are soldiers outside."

Anas paled. "Can we make it to the safe house?" he asked Hanno.

The shapeshifter bounced the squalling baby. "We'll have to try . . . but it won't be easy with this one carrying on."

Ali thought fast, glancing around the room. He spotted the copper tray, abandoned by the shafit girl now clutching Anas's hand. He crossed the room, snatching up one of the cups of apricot liquor. "Would this work?"

Anas looked aghast. "Have you lost your mind?"

But Hanno nodded. "It might." He held the baby while Ali clumsily attempted to pour the liquor into his wailing mouth. He could feel the weight of the shapeshifter's gaze. "What you did to the door . . ." Hanno's voice brimmed with accusation. "You're Royal Guard, aren't you? One of those kids they lock up in the Citadel until their first quarter century?"

Ali hesitated. *I'm more than that.* "I'm here with you now, aren't I?"

"I suppose you are." Hanno swaddled the boy with practiced ease. The baby finally fell silent, and Hanno drew his talwar, the gleaming steel blade the length of Ali's arm. "We'll need to look for an exit out the back." He jerked his head at the red curtain. "You'll understand if I insist you go first."

Ali nodded, his mouth dry. What choice did he have? He pushed the curtain aside and stepped into the dark corridor.

A maze of storerooms greeted him. Barrels of wine were stacked to the ceiling, and towering crates of hairy onions and overripe fruit scented the air. Broken tables, half-constructed walls, and shrouded pieces of furniture were haphazardly scattered everywhere. Ali saw no exits, only spots to hide.

A perfect place to be ambushed. He blinked; his eyes had stopped burning. The potion must have worn off. Not that it mattered— Ali had grown up with the men outside; they would recognize him either way.

There was a small tug on his robe. The little girl raised a trembling hand and pointed to a black doorway at the end of the corridor. "That goes to the alley," she whispered, her dark eyes wide as saucers.

Ali smiled down at her. "Thank you," he whispered back.

They headed down the corridor toward the last storeroom. In the distance, he spotted a line of moonlight near the floor: a door. Unfortunately, that was all he saw. The storeroom was blacker than pitch and, judging from the distance to the door, enormous. Ali slipped inside, his heart pounding so loudly he could hear it in his ears.

It wasn't all he heard.

There was a hush of breath, and then something whooshed past his face, grazing his nose and smelling of iron. Ali whirled around as the little girl screamed, but he couldn't see anything in the black room, his eyes not yet adjusted to the darkness.

Anas cried out. "Let her go!"

To hell with discretion. Ali drew his zulfiqar. The hilt warmed in his hands. *Brighten*, he commanded.

It burst into flames.

Fire licked up the copper scimitar, scorching its forked tip and throwing wild light across the room. Ali spotted two Daevas:

Turan and the guard from the tavern, his massive ax in hand. Turan was trying to pull the screaming girl from Anas's arms, but he turned at the sight of the fiery zulfiqar. His black eyes filled with fear.

The guard wasn't as impressed. He lunged at Ali.

Ali brought the zulfiqar up in the nick of time, sparks flying from where the blade hit the ax. The ax head must have been iron, the metal one of the few substances that could weaken magic. Ali pushed hard, shoving the man off.

The Daeva came at him again. Ali ducked the next blow, the entire situation surreal. He'd spent half of his life sparring; the motion of his blade, his feet, it was all familiar. Too familiar; it seemed impossible to imagine that his opponent actually wanted to *kill* him, that a misstep wouldn't result in trash-talking over coffee, but a bloody death on a dirty floor in a dark room where Ali had no business being in the first place.

Ali dodged another blow. He'd yet to attack the other man himself. How could he? He'd had the best martial training available, but he'd never killed anyone—he'd never even intentionally harmed another. He was underage, years from seeing combat. And he was the king's son! He couldn't murder one of his father's citizens—a *Daeva*, of all people. He'd start a war.

The guard raised his weapon again. And then he went white. The ax stayed frozen in midair. "Suleiman's eye," he gasped. "You . . . you're Ali—"

A steel blade burst through his throat.

"—al Qahtani," Hanno finished. He twisted the blade, stealing the man's last words as he stole his life. He pushed the dead man off the talwar with one foot, letting him slide to the floor. "Alizayd *fucking al Qahtani*." He turned to Anas, his face bright with outrage. "Oh, Sheikh . . . how could you?"

Turan was still there. He glanced at Ali and then at the Tanzeem men. Horrified realization lit his face. He lunged for the door, fleeing into the corridor.

Ali didn't move, didn't speak. He was still staring at the dead Daeva guard.

"Hanno . . ." Anas's voice was shaky. "The prince . . . no one can know."

The shapeshifter let out an aggravated sigh. He handed the baby to Anas and picked up the ax. He followed Turan.

The realization came to Ali too late. "W-wait. You don't have to—"

There was a short scream in the corridor followed by a crunching sound. Then a second. A third. Ali swayed on his feet, nausea threatening to overwhelm him. *This isn't happening.*

"Alizayd." Anas was before him. "Brother, look at me." Ali tried to focus on the sheikh's face. "He sold children. He would have revealed you. He needed to die."

There was the distinct sound of the tavern door smashing open. "Anas Bhatt!" a familiar voice shouted. *Wajed . . . oh, God, no . . .* "We know you're here!"

Hanno rushed back into the room. He snatched up the baby and kicked open the door. "Come on!"

The thought of Wajed—Ali's beloved Qaid, the sly-eyed general who'd all but raised him—finding Ali standing over the bodies of two murdered purebloods snapped him to attention. He raced after Hanno, Anas at his heels.

They emerged in another trash-strewn alley. They ran until they reached its end, the towering copper wall that separated the Tukharistani and Daeva quarters. Their only escape was a narrow breach leading back to the street.

Hanno peeked out of the breach and then jerked back. "They've Daeva archers."

"*What?*" Ali joined him, ignoring the sharp elbow to his side.

At the distant end of the street was the tavern, lit up by the fiery zulfiqars of soldiers pouring through the entrance. A half-dozen Daeva archers waited on elephants, their silver bows gleaming in the starlight.

"We have a safe house in the Tukharistani Quarter," Hanno explained. "There's a spot we can get over the wall, but we need to cross the street first."

Ali's heart sank. "We'll never make it." The soldiers might have been focused on the tavern, but there was no way one of them wouldn't notice three men, a girl child, and a baby dashing across the street. The fire worshippers were devilishly good archers—the Daevas as devoted to their bows as the Geziris were to their zulfiqars—and it was a wide street.

He turned to Anas. "We'll have to find another way."

Anas nodded. He glanced at the baby in Hanno's arms and then at the little girl clutching his hand. "All right," he said softly. He knelt to face the girl, untangling her fingers from his own. "My dear, I need you to go with the brother here." He pointed at Ali. "He's going to take you someplace safe."

Ali stared at Anas, dumbstruck. "What? Wait . . . you don't mean . . ."

"I'm the one they're after." Anas stood. "I'm not going to risk the lives of children to save my own." He shrugged, but his voice was strained when he spoke again. "I knew this day would come . . . I-I'll try to distract them . . . to give you as much time as possible."

"Absolutely not," Hanno declared. "The Tanzeem need you. I'll go. I've got a better chance at taking out some of those purebloods anyway."

Anas shook his head. "You're better equipped than I to get the prince and the children to safety."

"*No.*" The word tore from Ali's throat, more prayer than plea.

He could not lose his sheikh, not like this. "I'll go. Surely I can negotiate some sort of—"

"You'll negotiate nothing," Anas cut in, his voice severe. "If you tell your father about tonight, you're dead, do you understand? The Daevas would riot if they learned of your involvement. Your father won't risk that." He placed a hand on Ali's shoulder. "And you're too valuable to lose."

"The hell he is," Hanno retorted. "You're going to get yourself killed just so some Qahtani brat can—"

Anas cut him off with a sharp motion of his hand. "Alizayd al Qahtani can do more for the shafit than a thousand groups like the Tanzeem. And he will," he added, giving Ali an intent look. "Earn this. I don't care if you have to dance on my grave. Save yourself, brother. Live to fight again." He pushed the little girl toward him. "Get them out of here, Hanno." Without another word, he turned back, heading for the tavern.

The shafit girl looked up at Ali, her brown eyes enormous with fear. He blinked back tears. Anas had sealed his fate; the least Ali could do was follow his last order. He picked up the girl, and she clung to his neck, her heart thudding against his chest.

Hanno shot him a look of pure venom. "You and I, al Qahtani, are going to have a long chat when this is over." He snatched the turban from Ali's head, quickly fashioning it into a sling for the baby.

Ali immediately felt more exposed. "Was there something wrong with yours?"

"You'll run faster if you're worried about being recognized." He nodded at Ali's zulfiqar. "Put that away."

Ali shoved the zulfiqar under his robe, shifting the girl to his back as they waited. There was a shout from the tavern, followed by a second, more exultant cry. *God protect you, Anas.*

The archers turned toward the tavern. One drew back his silver bow, aiming an arrow at the entrance.

"Go!" Hanno said and shot out, Ali at his heels. Ali didn't look at the soldiers, his world reduced to sprinting across the cracked paving stones as fast as his legs would take him.

One of the archers shouted a warning.

Ali was halfway across when the first arrow whizzed over his head. It burst into fiery fragments, and the little girl screamed. The second tore through his robe, grazing his calf. He kept running.

They were across. Ali threw himself behind a stone balustrade, but his refuge was short-lived. Hanno lunged for an intricate wooden trellis attached to the building. It was covered with sprawling roses in a rainbow of colors, stretching three stories to reach the distant roof.

"Climb!"

Climb? Ali's eyes went wide as he stared at the delicate trellis. The thing barely looked strong enough to hold its flowers, let alone the weight of two grown men.

An arrow doused in blazing pitch hit the ground near his feet. Ali jumped back, and the sound of trumpeting elephants filled the air.

The trellis it was.

The wooden frame shook violently as he climbed, the thorny vines shredding his hands. The little girl clung to his back, half-choking Ali as she buried her face in his neck, her cheeks wet with tears. Another arrow whizzed past their heads, and she shrieked—in pain this time.

Ali had no way to check on her. He kept climbing, trying to stay as flat as possible against the building. *Please, God, please*, he begged; he was far too terrified to come up with a more coherent prayer.

He was nearly at the roof, Hanno already clear, when the trellis began to peel away from the wall.

For one heart-stopping moment, Ali was falling backward. The wooden frame came apart in his hands. A scream bubbled up in his throat.

Hanno grabbed his wrist.

The shafit shapeshifter dragged him onto the roof, and Ali promptly collapsed. "The g-girl . . . ," he breathed. "An arrow . . ."

Hanno pulled her from his back and quickly examined the back of her head. "It's all right, little one," he assured her. "You'll be okay." He glanced at Ali. "She'll need a few stitches, but the wound doesn't look deep." He undid the sling. "Let's switch."

Ali took the baby, slipping into the sling.

There was a shout from below. "They're on the roof!"

Hanno yanked him to his feet. "Go!"

He dashed away, and Ali followed. They ran across the roof, leaping over the narrow space to the next building and then doing it again, racing past lines of drying laundry and potted fruit trees. Ali tried not to look at the ground as they jumped, his heart in his throat.

They reached the last roof, but Hanno didn't stop, instead speeding up as he neared the edge. And then—to Ali's horror—he launched himself over.

Ali gasped, drawing to a stop just before the edge. But the shapeshifter wasn't dashed on the ground below; instead, he'd landed atop the copper wall separating the tribal quarters. The wall was perhaps half a body length lower than the roof and a good ten paces away. It was an impossible jump, pure fortune that Hanno had made it.

He gave the shapeshifter an incredulous look. "Are you *insane*?"

Hanno grinned, baring his teeth. "Come on, al Qahtani. Surely if a shafit can do it, so can you."

Ali hissed in response. He paced the edge of the roof. Every sensible instinct he had screamed at him not to jump.

The sound of the pursuing soldiers grew louder. They'd be up on the roof any minute. Ali took a few steps back, trying to work up the courage to take a running leap.

This is madness. He shook his head. "I can't."

"You don't have a choice." The humor vanished from Hanno's voice. "Al Qahtani . . . *Alizayd*," he pressed when Ali didn't respond. "Listen to me. You heard what the sheikh said. You think you can turn back now? Beg your abba for mercy?" He shook his head. "I know Geziris. Your people don't fuck around with loyalty." Hanno met Ali's gaze, his eyes dark with warning. "What do you think your father will do when he learns his own blood betrayed him?"

I never meant to betray him. Ali took a deep breath.

And then he jumped.

5

NAHRI

"Don't fall asleep, little thief. We're landing soon."

Nahri's eyelids were as heavy as a sack of dirhams, but she wasn't asleep. There was no way she could be, with only a scrap of fabric preventing her from plummeting to her death. She rolled over on the carpet, a chilly wind caressing her face as they flew. The dawn sky blushed at the approach of the sun, the dark of night giving way to light pinks and blues as the stars winked out. She stared at the sky. Exactly one week ago, she'd been looking at another dawn in Cairo, waiting for the basha, unaware of how drastically her life was about to change.

The djinn—no, the daeva, she corrected herself; Dara had a tendency to fly into a rage when she called him a djinn—sat beside her, the smoky heat from his robe tickling her nose. His shoulders were slumped, and his emerald eyes were dim and focused on something in the distance.

My captor looks particularly tired this morning. Nahri didn't blame him;

it had been the most bizarre, challenging week of her life, and though Dara appeared to be softening toward her, she sensed they were both thoroughly exhausted. The haughty daeva warrior and scheming human thief were not the most natural of pairings; at times, Dara could be as chatty as a girlhood friend, asking a hundred questions about her life, from her favorite color to what types of cloth they sold in the Cairo bazaars. Then, with little warning, he'd turn sullen and hostile, perhaps disgusted to find himself enjoying a conversation with a mixed-blood.

On Nahri's part, she was largely forced to check her own curiosity; asking Dara anything about the magical world immediately put him in a bad mood. "You can bother the djinn in Daevabad with all your questions," he'd dismiss her, returning to polishing his weapons.

But he was wrong.

She couldn't do that. Because she was definitely *not* going to Daevabad.

One week with Dara was enough for her to know there was no way she was trapping herself in a city filled with more ill-tempered djinn. She would be better off on her own. Surely she could find a way to avoid the ifrit; they couldn't possibly search the entire human world, and there was no way in hell she'd ever perform a zar again.

And so, eager to escape, she'd kept an eye out for an opportunity—but there'd been nowhere to flee in the vast, unbroken monolith of desert they traveled, all moonlit sands by night and shady oases by day. Yet as she sat up now and caught a glimpse of the ground below, hope bloomed in her chest.

The sun had broken across the horizon to illuminate a changed landscape. Instead of desert, limestone hills melted into a wide, dark river that twisted southeast as far as the eye could see. White clusters of buildings and cooking fires hugged its banks.

The arid plains directly below were rocky, broken up by scrub and slender, conical trees.

She scanned the ground, growing alert. "Where are we?"

"Hierapolis."

"*Where?*" She and Dara might speak the same language, but they were centuries apart in geography. He knew everything by a different name, rivers, cities, even the stars in the sky. The words he used were entirely unknown, and the stories he told to describe such places even more bizarre.

"Hierapolis." The carpet swept toward the ground, Dara directing it with one hand. "It has been too long since I've been back. When I was young, Hierapolis was home to a very . . . *spiritual* people. Very devoted to their rituals. Though I suppose anyone would be devoted, considering they worshipped phalluses and fish and preferred orgies to prayer." He sighed, his eyes creasing in pleasure. "Humans can be so delightfully inventive."

"I thought you hated humans."

"Not at all. Humans in their world, and my people in ours. That is the best way of things," he said firmly. "It is when we cross that trouble arises."

Nahri rolled her eyes, knowing he believed her to be the result of such a crossing. "What river is that?"

"The Ufratu."

Ufratu . . . She rolled the word in her mind. "Ufratu . . . el-Furat . . . that's the Euphrates?" She was stunned. They were *much* farther east than she expected.

Dara took her dismay the wrong way. "Yes. Don't worry, it's too massive to cross here."

Nahri frowned. "What do you mean? We're flying over it anyway, aren't we?"

She would swear that he blushed, a hint of embarrassment in his bright eyes. "I . . . I don't like flying over that much water," he finally confessed. "Especially when I'm tired. We'll rest, then fly farther north to find a better spot. We can get horses on the other side. If Khayzur was right about the enchantment I used on the rug being easy to track, I don't want to fly much farther on it."

Nahri barely heard what he said about the rug, her mind racing as she appraised the dark river. *This is my chance*, she realized. Dara might refuse to talk about himself, but Nahri had studied him all the same, and his confession about flying over the river confirmed her suspicion.

The daeva was *terrified* of water.

He'd refused to put even a toe in the shady pools of the oases they visited and seemed convinced she was going to drown in the shallowest of ponds, declaring her enjoyment of water unnatural, a shafit perversion. He wouldn't dare cross the mighty Euphrates without the carpet; he probably wouldn't even go near its banks.

I just need to get to the river. Nahri would swim its whole damn length if that was the only way to freedom.

They landed on the rocky ground, and her knee slammed into a hard lump. She cursed, rubbing it as she climbed to her feet to look around. Her mouth dropped open. "*When* did you say you last visited?"

They hadn't landed on rocky ground; they'd landed on a flattened building. Broken and bare marble columns lined the avenues, most of which were missing sections of paving stones. The buildings were destroyed, though the height of a few remaining yellowed walls hinted at previous glory. There were grand arched entrances that led to nothing, and blackened weeds and brush growing between the stonework and snaking up the columns. Across from the rug, an enormous stone pillar the color of washed sky lay smashed on the ground. Carved into its side were the grimy contours of a veiled woman with a fish tail.

Nahri moved away from the rug and startled a dust-colored fox. It vanished behind a crumbling wall. She glanced back at

Dara. He looked equally stunned, his green eyes wide with shock. He caught her glance and forced a small smile.

"Well, it has been *some* time . . ."

"Some time?" She gestured to the abandoned remains surrounding them. Across the broken road was an enormous fountain filled with murky black water; foul scum stained the marble from where it had started to evaporate. It had to take centuries for a place to get like this. There were similar ruins in Egypt, and it was said that they belonged to an ancient race of sun worshippers who lived and died before the holy books were even written. She shivered. "How old *are* you?"

Dara gave her an annoyed look. "It's not your concern." He shook the carpet out with more force than necessary, rolled it up, and then threw it over one shoulder before stalking off into the largest of the ruined buildings. Voluptuous fish-women were carved around the entrance; perhaps it was one of the temples where people had "worshipped."

Nahri followed. She needed that rug. "Where are you going?" She stumbled over a broken column, envying the graceful way the daeva moved over the uneven ground, and then paused as she entered the temple, dazzled by the grand decay.

The temple's roof and eastern wall were gone, opening the ruin to the dawn sky. Marble pillars stretched far above her head, and crumbled stone walls outlined what must once have been an enormous maze of different rooms. Most of the interior was gloomy, shaded by the remaining walls and a few determined cypress trees that split through the floor.

To her left was a tall stone dais. Three statues were poised on top: another fish-woman, as well as a stately female riding a lion, and a man wearing a loincloth and holding a discus. All were stunning, their muscled figures and regal poise entrancing. The pleats in their stone garments looked so real that she was tempted to touch them.

But glancing around, she saw that Dara had vanished, his footsteps silent in the grand ruin. Nahri followed the trail he'd made in the thick layer of dust coating the floor.

"Oh . . ." A small sound of appreciation escaped her throat. The large temple was dwarfed by the enormous theater she entered. Hundreds, perhaps thousands, of stone seats were carved into the hill in a semicircle surrounding the large stage upon which she stood.

The daeva stood at the edge of the stage. The air was still and silent save for the early morning trill of songbirds. His midnight blue robe smoked and swirled about his feet, and he'd unwrapped his turban to let it fall to his shoulders, his head covered only by the flat charcoal cap. Its white embroidery shone pink in the rosy morning light.

He looks like he belongs here, she thought. *Like a ghost forgotten in time, searching for its long-dead companions.* Judging from the way he spoke of Daevabad, Nahri assumed him to be some sort of exile. He probably missed his people.

She shook her head; she didn't intend to let a flash of sympathy convince her to keep playing companion to a lonely daeva. "Dara?"

"I saw a play here once with my father," he reminisced. "I was young, probably my first tour of the human world . . ." He studied the stage. "They had actors waving brilliant blue silks to represent the ocean. I thought it magical."

"I'm sure it was lovely. Can I have the carpet?"

He glanced back. "What?"

"The carpet. You sleep on it every day." She let a note of complaint slip into her voice. "It's my turn."

"So share with me." He nodded at the temple. "We'll find a place in the shade."

She felt her cheeks grow slightly hot. "I'm not sleeping alongside you in some temple dedicated to fish orgies."

He rolled his eyes and dropped the rug. It landed hard on the ground, sending up a cloud of dust. "Do as you wish."

I intend to. Nahri waited until he had stalked back into the temple before dragging the carpet to the far end of the stage. She pushed it off and flinched at the heavy thump, half-expecting the daeva to run out and tell her to hush. But the theater stayed empty.

She knelt on the rug. Though the river was a long, hot walk away, she didn't want to leave until she was certain Dara was fast asleep. It didn't usually take long. The comment about flying over the river wasn't the first time he'd mentioned becoming exhausted by magic. Nahri supposed it was a type of labor like any other.

She reviewed her supplies. It wasn't much. Besides the clothes on her back and a sack she'd made from the remains of her abaya, she had the waterskin and a tin of manna—stale-tasting crackers Dara had given her that landed in her stomach like weights. The water and manna might keep her fed, but they wouldn't put a roof over her head.

It doesn't matter. I might not get another opportunity like this. Pushing away her doubts, she tied the bag closed and rewrapped her headscarf. Then she picked up some kindling and crept back into the temple.

She followed the smell of smoke until she found the daeva. As usual, Dara had lit a small fire, letting it burn beside him as he slept. Though she'd never asked why—it obviously wasn't for warmth during the hot desert days—the presence of the flames seemed to comfort him.

He was fast asleep under the shadow of a crumbling arch. For the first time since they'd met, he'd taken off his robe and was using it as a pillow. Underneath he wore a sleeveless tunic the color of unripe olives and loose, bone-colored pants. His dagger was tucked into a wide black belt tied tight around his waist, and his bow, quiver of arrows, and scimitar were between his body and the wall. His right hand rested on the weapons. Nahri's gaze lingered on the sight of his chest rising and falling in sleep. Something stirred low in her belly.

She ignored it and lit her kindling. His fire flared, and in the improved light, she noticed the black tattoos covering his arms, bizarre, geometrical shapes, as if a calligrapher had gone mad on his skin. The largest mark was a slender, ladderlike structure with what looked like hundreds of meticulously drawn, unsupported rungs snaking out from his left palm and twisting up his arm to disappear under his tunic.

And I thought the tattoo on his face was strange . . .

As she followed the lines, the light illuminated something else as well.

His ring.

Nahri stilled; the emerald winked in the firelight as if greeting her. Tempting her. His left hand rested lightly on his stomach. Nahri stared at the ring, transfixed. It had to be worth a fortune and yet didn't even look snug on his finger. *I could take it,* she realized. *I've taken jewelry off people while they were* awake.

The kindling grew warm in her hand, the fire burning uncomfortably close. No. It wasn't worth the risk. She gave the daeva one last glance as she left. She could not help but feel a pang of regret; she knew Dara represented the best chance to learn about her origins, about her family and her abilities. About, well . . . everything. But it wasn't worth her freedom.

Nahri returned to the theater. She dropped the kindling on the carpet. Years in a tomb and a week in the desert air had sucked out every drop of moisture from the old wool. It burst into flames like it had been doused in oil. She coughed, waving smoke away from her face. By the time Dara woke, it would be nothing but ash. He'd have to go after her on foot, and she'd have a half day's start.

"Just make it to the river," she whispered to herself. She picked

up her bag and started climbing the stairs that led out of the theater.

The bag was pathetically light, a physical reminder of how
dire her circumstances were. *I'm going to be nothing. People will laugh when
I say I can heal.* Yaqub's willingness to partner with her was rare, and
that was after she'd already established a reputation as a healer, a
reputation that had taken years of careful cultivation.

But she wouldn't have to worry if she had that ring. She could
sell it, rent a place so she wouldn't have to sleep on the street. Buy
medicines to use in her work, materials with which to make amulets. She slowed, not even halfway up the steps. *I'm a good thief. I've
stolen far more challenging things.* And Dara slept like the dead; he hadn't
even awakened when Khayzur nearly landed on him.

"I'm a fool," she whispered, but she was already turning
around, running lightly down the steps and past the blazing
carpet. She crept back into the temple, winding her way around
the collapsed columns and smashed statues.

Dara was still fast asleep. Nahri carefully put down her bag
and freed the waterskin. She sprinkled a few drops on his finger,
her heart racing as she watched for any reaction. Nothing. Moving cautiously, she gently pinched the ring between her thumb
and index finger. She pulled.

The ring pulsed and grew hot. A sudden pain blossomed
in her head. She panicked and tried to let go, but her fingers
wouldn't budge. It was as if someone had seized control of her
mind. The temple vanished, and her vision blurred, replaced by
a series of smoky shapes that quickly solidified into something
entirely new. A parched plain under a blinding white sun . . .

*I study the dead land with a practiced eye. This place had once been grassy and
green, rich with irrigated fields and orchards, but my master's army trampled all signs
of fertility, leaving nothing but mud and dust. The orchards are stripped and burned,
the river poisoned a week ago, in hopes that it would drive the city to surrender.*

Unseen by the humans around me, I rise in the air like smoke to better survey our forces. My master has a formidable army: thousands of men in chain and leather, dozens of elephants, and hundreds of horses. His archers are the best in the human world, honed by my careful instruction. But the walled city remains insurmountable.

I stare at the ancient blocks, wondering at how thick they are, how many other armies they have repulsed. No battering ram will bring them down. I sniff carefully; the stench of famine scents the wind.

I turn to my master. He is one of the largest humans I've ever encountered; the top of my head barely comes to his shoulders. Unable to deal with the heat of the plains, he is constantly pink and wet and utterly disagreeable. Even his ruddy beard is damp with sweat, and his ornately filigreed tunic stinks. I wrinkle my nose; such a garment is frivolous in a time of war.

I settle to the ground next to his horse and look up at him. "Another two to three days," I say, tripping over the sounds. Although I've belonged to him for a year, his language is still strange to me, full of harsh consonants and snarls. "They cannot hold out much longer."

He scowls and caresses the hilt of his sword. "That is too long. You said they'd be ready to surrender last week."

I pause, the impatience in his voice causing a small knot of dread to grow in my stomach. I do not want to sack this city. Not because I care about the thousands who will die—centuries of slavery have cultivated a deep hatred for humans in my soul—but because I do not wish to see the sack of any city. I do not want to see the violence, to imagine how my beloved Daevabad suffered a similar fate at the hands of the Qahtanis.

"It is taking longer because they are courageous, my lord. Such a thing should be admired." My master doesn't seem to hear me, so I continue, "You'll earn a more lasting peace by negotiating."

My master takes a deep breath. "Was I not clear?" he snaps, leaning down in his saddle to glare at me. His face is scarred from the pox. "I didn't buy you for advice, slave. I wish for you to give me victory. I wish for this city. I wish to see my cousin on his knees before me."

Admonished, I lower my head. His wishes settle heavily on my shoulders, wrapping around my limbs. Energy surges through my fingers.

There is no fighting it; I learned this long ago. "Yes, master." *I raise my hands and focus my attention on the wall.*

The ground begins to tremble. His horse shies away, and a few men cry out in alarm. In the distance, the wall groans, the ancient stones protesting my magic. Tiny figures race along the top, fleeing their posts.

I close my hands into fists, and the wall collapses as though made of sand. A roar runs through my master's army. Humans, their very blood dances at the prospect of brutalizing their own kind . . .

No! Nahri gasped, a tiny voice crying out in her mind. *This isn't me! This isn't real!* But the voice was drowned out by the screams of the next vision.

We are inside the city. I fly alongside my master's horse through bloody streets thick with corpses. His soldiers torch the shops and narrow homes, cutting through any inhabitants foolish enough to cross them. A burning man crashes to the ground beside me, thrown from a balcony, and a young girl shrieks as two soldiers pull her from an overturned cart.

Bonded by the wish, I can't leave my master's side. I wade through gore with a sword in each hand, killing any who approach. As we grow closer to the castle, the attackers are too numerous for my blades. I toss the weapons away, and the slave curse sweeps through me as I burn an entire group with a single glance. Their screams rise through the air, horrendous, animal–like groans.

Before I know it, we are in the castle and then in a bedchamber. The room is opulent and smells strongly of cedarwood, the scent bringing tears to my eyes. It was what my Daeva tribe burned to honor the Creator and His blessed Nahids . . . but I cannot honor anyone in my defiled condition. Instead, I tear through the guards. Their blood spatters the silk wall coverings.

A balding man cowers in one corner; I can smell his released bowels. A fierce–eyed woman throws herself in front of him, a knife in her hand. I break her neck as I toss her aside and then grab the sobbing man, forcing him to his knees before my master.

"Your cousin, my lord."

My master smiles, and the weight of the wish lifts from my shoulders. Exhausted by magic and nauseated by the smell of so much human blood, I fall to my own knees.

My ring blazes, illuminating the black slave record branded into my skin. I fix my gaze on my master, surrounded by the carnage he ordered, watching as he mocks his cousin's hysterics. Hate surges in my heart.

I will see you dead, human, *I swear.* I will see your life reduced to a mere mark on my arm . . .

The bedchamber dissolved before Nahri's eyes as her fingers were pried off the ring, her hand wrenched away so hard that she fell back against the stone floor. Her mind spun as she desperately tried to make sense of what had just happened.

The answer loomed over her, still clutching her wrist.

If anything, Dara looked more shocked to find himself awakened in such a manner. He glanced at his hand, his fingers still gripping her wrist. His ring blazed with light, mirroring the emerald brightness of his eyes. He let out a startled cry.

"*No!*" His eyes went wide with panic, and he dropped her wrist, backing away. His entire body was shaking. "What did you do?" he shrieked, holding his hand out like he expected the ring to explode.

Dara. The man in her vision had been *Dara.* And what she had seen . . . were those his *memories?* They seemed too real to have been his dreams.

Nahri forced herself to meet his gaze. "Dara . . ." She tried to keep her voice gentle. The daeva was pale with fright, his eyes wild. "Please, just calm down." He'd backed away without any of his weapons. She resisted the urge to look at them, fearing he would notice. "I didn't—"

The daeva seemed to read her mind, lunging for his weapons at the same time she did. He was faster, but Nahri was closer. She grabbed his sword and jumped back as he lunged at her with the dagger.

"Don't!" She raised the sword, her hands trembling as she gripped it tight. Dara drew back with a hiss that bared his teeth. Nahri panicked. There was no way she could outrun him, no way she could outfight him. The daeva looked like he'd gone mad; she half-expected him to start frothing at the mouth. The visions flashed through her mind again: bodies ripped apart, men burned to death. And Dara had done it all.

No. There had to be some explanation. And then she remembered. Master, he had called that man his master.

He's a slave. All the stories Nahri had heard about the djinn raced through her mind, and her mouth fell open in shock. *A wish-granting djinn slave.*

The realization didn't improve her situation. "Dara, please . . . I don't know what happened, but I didn't mean to hurt you. I swear!"

His left hand was pressed to his chest, the ring next to his heart—if daevas had hearts. He held the dagger out with his right, circling her like a cat. He closed his eyes for a moment and when he opened them, some of the wildness had dissipated. "No . . . I—" He swallowed, looking close to tears. "I'm still here." He took a shaky breath, relief flooding into his face. "I'm still free." He leaned heavily against one of the marble columns. "But that city . . . ," he choked out. "Those people . . ." He slid to the floor, dropping his head into his hands.

Nahri didn't lower the sword. She had no idea what to say, torn between guilt and fear. "I . . . I'm sorry," she finally said. "I just wanted the ring. I had no idea . . ."

"You wanted the ring?" He glanced up sharply, a hint of suspicion stealing back into his voice. "Why?"

Telling the truth seemed safer than his assuming some type of magical malice on her part. "I was trying to steal it," she confessed. "I am—I *was*," she corrected, realizing there was no way she was getting free now, "trying to escape."

"Escape?" He narrowed his eyes. "And you needed my ring for that?"

"Have you seen the size of it?" She let out a nervous laugh. "That emerald could get me back to Cairo with money to spare."

He gave her an incredulous look and then shook his head. "And the glory of the Nahids continues." He climbed to his feet, seemingly unaware of how quickly she backed away. "Why would you even want to escape? Your human life sounds dreadful."

"What?" she asked, offended enough to momentarily forget her fear. "Why would you say that?"

"*Why?*" He picked up his robe and whirled it around his shoulders. "Where do I even start? If simply being human isn't wretched enough, you had to lie and steal constantly to survive. You lived alone, with no family and no friends, in unceasing fear you'd be arrested and executed for sorcery." He blanched. "And you'd return to *that*? Over Daevabad?"

"It wasn't that bad," she insisted, taken aback by his answer. All those questions he'd asked about her life in Cairo—he really had been listening to her answers. "My abilities gave me a lot of independence. And I had a friend," she added, though she wasn't certain Yaqub would agree with that definition of their relationship. "Besides, you act as if I'm facing something better. Aren't you turning me over to some djinn king who murdered my family?"

"No," Dara said, adding somewhat more hesitantly, "it was not . . . *technically* him. Your ancestors were enemies, but Khayzur spoke correctly." He sighed. "It was a long time ago," he added lamely, as if that explained everything.

Nahri stared. "So being delivered to *my ancestral enemy* is supposed to make me feel better?"

Dara looked even more annoyed. "*No.* It's not like that." He made an impatient noise. "You're a healer, Nahri. The last of them. Daevabad needs you as much as you need it, maybe even more." He scowled. "And when the djinn learn I was the one who found you? The Scourge of Qui-zi forced to play nursemaid to a mixed-blood?" He shook his head. "The Qahtanis are going to love it. They'll probably set you up in your own wing of the palace."

My own wing of the what? "The Scourge of Qui-zi?" she asked instead.

"An endearment I've earned from them." His green gaze settled on the sword still clasped in her hands. "You don't need that. I'm not going to hurt you."

"No?" Nahri arched an eyebrow. "Because I just saw you hurt a whole lot of people."

"You saw that?" When she nodded, his face crumpled. "I wish you hadn't." He crossed the floor to retrieve her bag, dusting it off before handing it back. "What you saw . . . I didn't do those things by choice." His voice was low as he turned back and picked up his turban cloth.

Nahri hesitated. "In my country, we have stories of djinn . . . djinn who are trapped as slaves and forced to grant wishes to humans."

Dara flinched, his fingers fumbling as he rewound his turban. "I'm not a djinn."

"But are you a slave?"

He said nothing, and her temper flashed. "Forget it," she snapped. "I don't know why I bothered to ask. You never answer my questions. You let me panic over this Qahtani king for an entire week just because you couldn't bother to—"

"Not anymore." His reply was a whisper, a fragile thing that hung in the air—the first real truth he'd offered her. He turned around; old grief was etched in his face. "I'm not a slave anymore."

Before Nahri could respond, the ground trembled beneath her feet.

A nearby pillar cracked as a second rumble—far stronger— rocked the temple. Dara swore, snatched up his weapons, and grabbed her hand. "Come on!"

They raced through the temple and out onto the open stage,

narrowly avoiding a falling column. The ground shook harder, and Nahri gave the theater a nervous glance, looking for signs of the recently risen dead. "Maybe this one's an earthquake?"

"So soon after you used your powers on me?" He searched the stage. "Where's the carpet?"

She hesitated. "I may have burned it."

Dara whirled on her. "You *burned* it?"

"I didn't want you to follow me!"

"Where did you burn it?" he asked, not even waiting for an answer before sniffing the air and racing toward the edge of the stage.

By the time she caught him, he was crouching in the glowing embers, his hands pressed against the carpet's ashy remains. "Burned it . . . ," he muttered. "By the Creator, you really don't know anything about us."

Little worms of white-bright flame crawled out from under his fingers, reigniting the ash and twisting together into long ropes that grew and stretched under his feet. As she watched, they quickly multiplied, forming a fiery mat roughly the same size and shape as the carpet.

The fire flashed and died, revealing the tired colors of their old rug. "How did you *do* that?" she whispered.

Dara grimaced as he ran his hand over the surface. "It won't last long, but it should get us across the river."

The ground rumbled again, and a groan came from inside the temple, the sound all too familiar. Dara reached for her hand. She backed away.

His eyes flashed with alarm. "Are you mad?"

Probably. Nahri knew what she was about to do was risky, but she also knew the best time to negotiate was when your mark was desperate. "No. I'm not getting on that rug unless you give me some answers."

There was another loud, vaguely human shriek from inside

the temple. The ground shook harder, and a crack raced across the high ceiling.

"You want answers *now*? Why? So you'll be better informed when the ghouls devour you?" Dara snatched for her ankle, but she danced back. "Nahri, please! You can ask me whatever you want once we're gone, I swear!"

But she wasn't convinced. What was to stop him from changing his mind as soon as they were safe?

Then it came to her.

"Tell me your name, and I'll go with you," she offered. "Your real name." He had told her there was power in names. It wasn't much, but it was something.

"My name doesn't—" Nahri took a deliberate step toward the temple, and panic lit his face. "No, stop!"

"Then tell me your name!" Nahri shouted, her own fear getting the better of her. She was used to bluffing, but not with the threat of being eaten by the risen dead looming. "And be quick about it!"

"Darayavahoush!" The daeva pulled himself onto the stage. "Darayavahoush e-Afshin is my name. Now get *over* here!"

Nahri was certain she couldn't have repeated that correctly even if she'd been paid, but as the ghouls screamed again, and the smell of rot swept past her face, she decided it didn't matter.

He was ready for her, grabbing her elbow and pulling her down on the rug as he landed lightly beside her. Without another word, the carpet rose in the air, sweeping over the temple's roof as three ghouls stumbled out onto the stage.

DARA WAS THOROUGHLY RILED BY THE TIME THEY'D risen above the clouds. "Do you have *any* idea how dangerous that was?" He threw up his hands. "Not only did you try to destroy our only method of escaping the ifrit, you were ready to risk your life just to—"

"Oh, get over it," she said, dismissing him. "You're the one who drove me to such straits, Afshin Daryevu—"

"'Dara' will continue to do just fine," he interrupted. "You needn't mangle my proper name." A goblet appeared in his hand, filled with the familiar dark of date wine. He took a long sip. "You can call me a damn djinn again if you promise not to go running after ghouls."

"Such affection for the shafit thief?" She raised an eyebrow. "You weren't so fond of me a week ago."

He grumbled. "I can change my mind, can't I?" A blush stole into his cheeks. "Your company is not . . . *entirely* displeasing." He sounded deeply disappointed in himself.

Nahri rolled her eyes. "Well, it's time *your* company became a lot more informative. You promised to answer my questions."

He glanced around, gesturing to the clouds. "Right now?"

"Are you busy with something else?"

Dara exhaled. "*Fine.* Go on, then."

"What's a daeva?"

He sighed. "I already told you this: we're djinn. We just have the decency to call ourselves by our true name."

"That explains nothing."

He scowled. "We're souled beings like humans, but we were created from fire, not earth." A delicate tendril of orange flame snaked around his right hand and twisted through his fingers. "All the elements—earth, fire, water, air—have their own creatures."

Nahri thought of Khayzur. "The peris are creatures of air?"

"An astonishing deduction."

She shot him a dirty look. "He had a better attitude than you."

"Yes, he's extraordinarily gentle for a being who could rearrange the landscape below us and kill every life-form for miles with a single sweep of his wings."

Nahri felt the blood drain from her face. "Truly?" When

Dara nodded, she continued. "Are—are there a lot of creatures like that?"

He gave her a somewhat wicked smile. "Oh, yes. Dozens. Rukh birds, karkadann, shedu . . . things with sharp teeth and nasty temperaments. A zahhak nearly ripped me in two once."

She gaped at him. The flame playing around his finger stretched into an elongated lizard that belched a fiery plume. "Imagine a fire-breathing serpent with limbs. They're rare, thank the Creator, but don't give much warning when they attack."

"And humans don't notice any of this?" Nahri's eyes widened as the smoky beast left Dara's arm and flew around his head.

He shook his head. "No. Those created from dirt, like humans, usually can't see the rest of us. Besides, most magical beings prefer wild places, places already empty of your kind. If a human had the misfortune to come across one, they might sense something, see a blur on the horizon or a shadow out of the corner of their eye. But they'd likely be dead before they gave it a second thought."

"And if they came across a daeva?"

He opened his palm, and his fiery pet flew into it, dissolving into smoke. "Oh, we'd eat them." At the alarm in her face, he laughed and took another sip of wine. "A jest, little thief."

But Nahri wasn't in the mood for his jokes. "What about the ifrit?" she persisted. "What are they?"

The amusement vanished from his face. "Daevas. At least . . . they were once."

"Daevas?" she repeated in surprise. "Like you?"

"No." He looked offended. "Not like me. Not at all."

"Then like what?" She prodded his knee when he stayed silent. "You promised to—"

"I know, I know." He removed his cap to rub his brow, running his fingers through his black hair.

It was an entirely distracting motion. Nahri's eyes followed his hand, but she shut her wayward thoughts down, ignoring the flutter in her stomach.

"You do know that if you have Nahid blood, you're likely going to live a few centuries." Dara lay back on the carpet to recline on a propped wrist. "You should work on your patience."

"At this rate, it will take us a few centuries just to finish this conversation."

That brought a wry smile to his face. "You have their wit, I'll admit to that." He snapped his fingers, and another goblet appeared in his hand. "Drink with me."

Nahri gave the goblet a suspicious sniff. It smelled sweet, but she hesitated. She hadn't had a drop of wine in her life; such a forbidden luxury was well beyond her means, and she wasn't sure how she'd react to alcohol. Drunks had always been easy pickings for a thief.

"Rejecting hospitality is a grave offense among my people," Dara warned.

Mostly to appease him, Nahri took a small sip. The wine was cloyingly sweet, more like a syrup than a liquid. "Is it truly?"

"Not at all. But I'm tired of drinking alone."

She opened her mouth to protest, irritated that she'd been so easily tricked, but the wine was already working, rolling down her throat and spreading a warm drowsiness throughout her body. She swayed, grabbing for the rug.

Dara steadied her, his fingers hot on her wrist. "Careful."

Nahri blinked, her vision swimming for another moment. "By the Most High, your people must get nothing done if you drink things like this."

He shrugged. "A fair assessment of our race. But you wish to know of the ifrit."

"And why you think they want to kill me," she clarified. "Mostly that."

"We'll get to that bit of bad luck later," he said lightly. "First, you must understand that the earliest daevas were true creatures of fire, formed and formless all at once. And very, very powerful."

"More powerful than you are now?"

"Far more. We could possess and imitate any creature, any object we desired, and our lives spanned eras. We were greater than peris, maybe even greater than marid."

"Marid?"

"Water elementals," he replied. "No one's seen one in millennia—they'd be like gods to your kind. But the daevas were at peace with all creatures. We stayed in our deserts while the peri and marids kept to their realms of sky and water. But then, humans were created."

Dara twirled his goblet in his hand. "My kind can be irrational," he confessed. "Tempestuous. To see such weak creatures marching across our lands, building their filthy cities of dirt and blood over our sacred sands . . . it was maddening. They became a target . . . a plaything."

Goose bumps erupted across her skin. "And how exactly did the daevas *play*?"

A flash of embarrassment swept his bright eyes. "In all sorts of ways," he muttered, conjuring up a small pillar of white smoke that thickened as she watched. "Kidnapping newlyweds, stirring up sandstorms to confuse a caravan, encouraging . . ." He cleared his throat. "You know . . . worship."

Her mouth fell open. So the darker stories about djinn really did have their roots in truth. "No, I can't say that I do know. I've never murdered merchants for my own amusement!"

"Ah, yes, my thief. Forgive me for forgetting that you are a paragon of honesty and goodness."

Nahri scowled. "So what happened next?"

"Supposedly the peri ordered us to stop." Dara's smoky pillar undulated in the wind at his side. "Khayzur's people fly to the edge of Paradise; they hear things—at least they think they do.

They warned that humans were to be left alone. Each elemental race was to stick to its own affairs. Meddling with each other—especially with a lesser creature—was absolutely forbidden."

"And the daevas didn't listen?"

"Not in the slightest. And so we were cursed." He scowled. "Or 'blessed,' as the djinn see it now."

"How?"

"A man was called from among the humans to punish us." A hint of fear crossed Dara's face. "Suleiman," he whispered. "May he be merciful."

"Suleiman?" Nahri repeated in disbelief. "As in the *Prophet* Suleiman?" When Dara nodded, she gasped. Her only education might have consisted of running from the law, but even she knew who Suleiman was. "But he died thousands of years ago!"

"Three thousand," Dara corrected. "Give or take a few centuries."

A horrifying thought took root in her mind. "You . . . you're not three thousand years—"

"No," he cut in, his voice terse. "This was before my time."

Nahri exhaled. "Of course." She could barely wrap her mind around how long three thousand years was. "But Suleiman was human. What could he possibly do to a daeva?"

A dark expression flickered across Dara's face. "Anything he liked, apparently. Suleiman was given a seal ring—some say by the Creator himself—that granted him the ability to control us. A thing he went about doing with a vengeance after we . . . well, *supposedly* there was some sort of human war the daevas *might* have had a part in instigating—"

Nahri held up a hand. "Yes, yes, I'm sure it was a most unfair punishment. What did he do?"

Dara beckoned the smoky pillar forward. "Suleiman stripped us of our abilities with a single word and commanded that all daevas come before him to be judged." The smoke spread before them; one corner condensed to become a misty throne while the rest dissipated into hundreds of fiery figures the size of her thumb. They drifted past the carpet, their smoky heads bowed before the throne.

"Most obeyed; they were nothing without their powers. They went to his kingdom and toiled for a hundred years." The throne vanished, and the fiery creatures swirled into workers heating bricks and stacking enormous stones several times their size. A vast temple began to grow in the sky. "Those who made penance were forgiven, but there was a catch."

Nahri watched the temple rise, entranced. "What was it?"

The temple vanished, and the daevas were bowing again to the distant throne. "Suleiman didn't trust us," Dara replied. "He said our very nature as shapeshifters made us manipulative and deceitful. So we were forgiven but changed forever."

In an instant, the fire was extinguished from the bowing daevas' smoky skin. They shrank in size, and some grew hunched, their spines bent in old age.

"He trapped us in humanlike bodies," Dara explained. "Bodies with limited abilities that only lasted a few centuries. It meant that those daevas who originally tormented humanity would die and be replaced by their descendants, descendants Suleiman believed would be less destructive."

"God forbid," Nahri cut in. "Only living for a few centuries with magical abilities . . . what an awful fate."

He ignored her sarcasm. "It was. Too awful for some. Not all daevas were willing to subject themselves to Suleiman's judgment in the first place."

The familiar hate returned to his face. "The ifrit," she guessed.

He nodded. "The very same."

"The *very* same?" she repeated. "You mean they're still alive?"

"Unfortunately. Suleiman bound them to their original daeva bodies, but those bodies were meant to survive millennia." He gave her a dark look. "I'm sure you can imagine what three thousand years of seething resentment does to the mind."

"But Suleiman took their powers away, didn't he? How much of a threat can they be?"

Dara raised his brows. "Did the thing that possessed your friend and ordered the dead to eat us seem powerless?" He shook his head. "The ifrit have had millennia to test the boundaries of Suleiman's punishment and have risen to the task spectacularly. Many of my people believe they descended to hell itself, selling their souls to learn new magic." He twisted his ring again. "And they're obsessed with revenge. They believe humanity a parasite and consider my kind to be the worst of traitors for submitting to Suleiman."

Nahri shivered. "So where do I fit in all this? If I'm just some lowly, mixed-blood shafit, why are they bothering with me?"

"I suspect it's whose blood—however little—you have in you that provoked their interest."

"These Nahids? The family of healers you mentioned?"

He nodded. "Anahid was Suleiman's vizier and the only daeva he ever trusted. When the daevas' penance was complete, Suleiman not only gave Anahid healing abilities, he gave her his seal ring, and with it the ability to undo any magic—whether a harmless spell gone wrong or an ifrit curse. Those abilities passed to her descendants, and the Nahids became the sworn enemies of the ifrit. Even Nahid blood was poisonous to an ifrit, more fatal than any blade."

Nahri was suddenly very aware of how Dara was speaking of the Nahids. "*Was* poisonous?"

"The Nahid family is no more," Dara said. "The ifrit spent centuries hunting them down and killed the last, a pair of siblings, about twenty years ago."

Her heart skipped a beat. "So what you're saying—" she started, her voice hoarse, "is that you think I'm the last living descendant of a family that a group of crazed, revenge-obsessed former daevas have been trying to exterminate for the last three thousand years?"

"You wanted to know."

She was sorely tempted to push him off the carpet. "I didn't think . . ." She trailed off as she noticed ash drifting up around her. She looked down.

The carpet was dissolving.

Dara followed her gaze and let out a surprised cry. He backed away to a more solid patch in the blink of an eye and snapped his fingers. Its edges smoking, the rug sped up as it descended toward the glistening Euphrates.

Nahri tried to appraise the water as they skimmed through the air above it. The current was rough but not as turbulent as it had been in other spots; she could probably make it to shore.

She glanced up at Dara. His green eyes were so bright with alarm that it was difficult to look at his face. "Can you swim?"

"Can I *swim*?" he snapped, as if the very idea offended him. "Can you burn?"

But their luck held. They were already at the shallows when the carpet finally burst into burning crimson embers. Nahri tumbled into a knee-high patch of river while Dara leaped for the rocky shore. He sniffed disdainfully as she staggered toward the riverbank covered in muck.

Nahri adjusted the makeshift strap of her bag. And then she stopped. She didn't have Dara's ring, but she had her supplies. She was in the river, safely separated from the daeva by a band of water she knew he wouldn't cross.

Dara must have noticed her hesitation. "Still tempted to try your luck alone with the ifrit?"

"There's a lot you haven't told me," she pointed out. "About the djinn, about what happens when we get to Daevabad."

"I will. I promise." He gestured at the river, his ring sparkling in the light of the setting sun. "But I've no desire to spend the coming days being looked at like some villainous abductor. If you want to return to the human world, if you wish to risk the ifrit to return to bartering your talents for stolen coins, stay in the water."

Nahri glanced back at the Euphrates. Somewhere across the river, across deserts vaster than seas, was Cairo, the only home she'd ever known. A hard place but familiar and predictable—completely unlike the future Dara offered.

"Or follow me," he continued, his voice smooth. Too smooth. "Find out what you really are, what really exists in this world. Come to Daevabad where even a drop of Nahid blood will bring you honor and wealth beyond your imagining. Your own infirmary, the knowledge of a thousand previous healers at your fingertips. *Respect*."

Dara offered his hand.

Nahri knew she should be suspicious, but, God, his words struck her heart. For how many years had she dreamed of Istanbul? Of studying proper medicine with respected scholars? Learning to read books instead of pretending to read palms? How often had she counted her savings in disappointment and put aside her hopes for a greater future?

She took his hand.

He pulled her free of the mud, his fingers scalding her own. "I'll cut your throat in your sleep if you're lying," she warned, and Dara grinned, looking delighted at the threat. "Besides, how are we supposed to get to Daevabad? We've lost the rug."

The daeva nodded eastward. Set against the dark river and distant cliffs, Nahri could make out the bare brick lines of a large village.

"You're the thief," he challenged. "You're going to steal us some horses."

6

ALI

Wajed came for him at dawn.

"Prince Alizayd?"

Ali startled and looked up from his notes. The sight of the city's Qaid—the commander of the Royal Guard—would have made most djinn startle, even if they weren't expecting to be arrested for treason at any minute. He was a massively built warrior covered in two centuries' worth of scars and welts.

But Wajed only smiled as he entered the Citadel's library, the closest thing Ali had to his own quarters. "Already hard at work, I see," he said, motioning to the books and scrolls scattered on the rug.

Ali nodded. "I have a lesson to prepare."

Wajed snorted. "You and your lessons. Were you not so dangerous with that zulfiqar, one would think I'd raised an economist instead of a warrior." His smile faded. "But I fear your students—however few they are—will have to wait. Your father's had it with

Bhatt. They can't get any more information out of him, and the Daevas are clamoring for his blood."

Though Ali had been expecting this moment since he'd first heard Anas had been captured alive, his stomach twisted, and he struggled to keep his voice even. "Was he—?"

"Not yet. The grand wazir wants a spectacle, says it's the only thing that will satisfy his tribe." Wajed rolled his eyes; he and Kaveh had never gotten along. "So we'll both need to be there."

A spectacle. Ali's mouth went dry, but he rose to his feet. Anas had sacrificed himself so that Ali might escape; he deserved to have one friendly face at his execution. "Let me dress."

Wajed ducked out, and Ali quickly changed into his uniform, a tunic the color of obsidian, a white waist-wrap, and a gray tasseled turban. He secured his zulfiqar to his waist and tucked his khanjar—the hooked dagger worn by all Geziri men—into his belt. At least he'd look the part of a loyal soldier.

He joined Wajed at the stairs, and they descended the tower into the Citadel's heart. A large complex of sand-colored stone, the Citadel was home to the Royal Guard, housing the barracks, offices, and training ground of the djinn army. His ancestors had built it shortly after conquering Daevabad, its crenellated courtyard and stark stone tower an homage to Am Gezira, their distant homeland.

Even at this early hour, the Citadel was a hive of activity. Cadets drilled with zulfiqars in the courtyard and spearmen practiced on an elevated platform. A half-dozen young men crowded around a free-standing door, attempting to break past its locking enchantment. As Ali watched, one flew back from the door, the wood sizzling as his fellows burst into laughter. In the opposite corner, a Tukharistani warrior-scholar dressed in a long felt coat, fur hat, and heavy gloves presented an iron shield to a group of students gathered around him. He shouted an incantation, and a sheath of ice enveloped the shield. The scholar tapped it with the butt of a dagger, and the entire thing shattered.

"When's the last time you saw your family?" Wajed asked as they reached the waiting horses at the end of the courtyard.

"A few months ago . . . well, more than a few, I suppose. Not since Eid," Ali admitted. He swung into his saddle.

Wajed tsked as they passed through the gate. "You should make a greater effort, Ali. You're blessed to have them so close."

Ali made a face. "I'd visit more often if it didn't involve going to that Nahid-haunted palace they call home."

The palace came into view just then, as they rounded a bend in the road. Its golden domes gleamed bright against the rising sun, its white marble facade and walls shining pink in the rosy dawn light. The main building, an enormous ziggurat, sat heavy on the stark cliffs overlooking Daevabad's lake. Surrounded by gardens still in shadow, it looked as if the massive step pyramid was being swallowed by the spiky tops of blackened trees.

"It's not haunted," Wajed countered. "It simply . . . misses its founding family."

"The stairs vanished under me the last time I was there, uncle," Ali pointed out. "The water in the fountains turns to blood so often that people don't drink it."

"So it misses them a lot."

Ali shook his head but stayed quiet as they crossed the waking city. They ascended the hilly road leading to the palace and then entered the royal arena through the back. It was a place best suited for sunny days of competition, for boastful men juggling incendiaries and women racing scaled simurgh firebirds. For entertainment.

That's exactly what this is for these people. Ali gazed at the crowd with scorn. Though it was early, many of the stone seats were already taken, filled with an assortment of nobles vying for his father's attention, curious pureblood commoners, angry Daevas, and what looked to be the entire ulema—Ali suspected the clerics had been ordered to witness what happened when they failed to control the faithful.

He climbed up to the royal viewing platform, a tall stone terrace shaded by potted palm trees and striped linen curtains. Ali didn't see his father but spotted Muntadhir near the front. His older half brother didn't look any happier than Ali to be there. His curly black hair was mussed, and he seemed to be wearing the same clothes he'd probably gone out in last night, an embroidered Agnivanshi jacket heavy with pearls and a lapis-colored silk waist-wrap, both wrinkled.

Ali could smell the wine on Muntadhir's breath from three paces away and suspected his brother had probably just been dragged from a bed not his own. "Peace be upon you, Emir."

Muntadhir jumped. "By the Most High, akhi," he said, his hand over his heart. "Do you have to creep up on me like some sort of assassin?"

"You should work on your reflexes. Where's Abba?"

Muntadhir nodded rudely toward a thin man in Daeva clothing at the terrace edge. "That one insisted on a public reading of all the charges." He yawned. "Abba wasn't wasting his time on that—not when he has me to do it for him. He'll be here soon enough."

Ali glanced at the Daeva man: Kaveh e-Pramukh, his father's grand wazir. Focused on the ground below, Kaveh didn't appear to notice Ali's arrival. A satisfied smile played on his mouth.

Ali suspected he knew why. He took a deep breath and then stepped to the edge of the terrace.

Anas kneeled on the sand below.

His sheikh had been stripped to the waist, burned and whipped, his beard hacked off in disrespect. His head was bowed, his hands bound behind him. Though it had only been two weeks since his arrest, he'd clearly been starved, his ribs visible and his bloody limbs thin. And those were only the wounds Ali could see. There would be others, he knew. Potions that made you feel as if you were being stabbed by a thousand knives, illusionists who could make you hallucinate the deaths of your loved ones, singers who could reach a pitch high enough to drive you to your knees while your ears bled. Men didn't survive the dungeons of Daevabad. Not with their minds intact.

Oh, Sheikh, I'm so sorry . . . The sight before him—a single shafit man with no magical abilities surrounded by hundreds of vengeful purebloods—seemed a cruel joke.

"As for the crime of religious incitement . . ."

The sheikh swayed, and one of his guards jerked him upright. Ali went cold. The entire right side of Anas's face was smashed, his eye swollen shut, his nose broken. A line of saliva dripped from his mouth, escaping past shattered teeth and swollen lips.

Ali pressed his zulfiqar's scabbard. Anas met his stare. His eye flashed, the briefest of warnings before he dropped his gaze again.

Earn this. Ali remembered his sheikh's last command. He dropped his hand away from the weapon, aware of the eyes of the audience upon him. He stepped back to join Muntadhir.

The judge droned on. "The illegal possession of weapons . . ."

There was an impatient snort from the other side of the arena, his father's karkadann, caged and hidden by a fiery gate. The ground trembled as the beast stomped its feet. A horrid cross between a horse and an elephant, the karkadann was twice the size of both, its scaly gray skin stained and matted with gore. The dust in the arena was heavy with its smell, the musk of old blood. No one bathed a karkadann; none even got near save the pair of tiny sparrows caged next to the creature. As Ali listened, they began to sing. The karkadann settled down, placated for the moment.

"And as for the charge of—"

"By the Most High . . ." A voice boomed from behind Ali as the entire crowd shot to their feet. "Is this *still* going on?"

His father had arrived.

King Ghassan ibn Khader al Qahtani, ruler of the realm, Defender of the Faith. His name alone made his subjects tremble and glance over their shoulders for spies. He was an imposing man, massive really, a combination of thick muscles and hearty appetite. He was built like a barrel, and at the age of two hundred, his hair had just started to go gray, silver spotting his black beard. It only made him more intimidating.

Ghassan strode to the edge of the terrace. The judge looked ready to wet himself, and Ali couldn't blame him. His father sounded annoyed, and Ali knew the very thought of facing the king's legendary wrath had made more than one man's bowels give way.

Ghassan gave the bloodied sheikh a dismissive glance before turning to the grand wazir. "The Tanzeem have terrorized Daevabad long enough. We know their crimes. It's their patron I want, along with the men who helped him murder two of my citizens."

Kaveh shook his head. "He won't give them up, my king. We've tried everything."

"Banu Manizheh's old serums?"

Kaveh's pale face fell. "It killed the scholar who attempted it. The Nahids did not mean for their potions to be used by others."

Ghassan pursed his lips. "Then he's useless to me." He nodded to the guards standing over Anas. "Return to your posts."

There was a gasp from the direction of the ulema, a whispered prayer. *No.* Ali stepped forward, unthinking. There was punishment, and then there was *that*. He opened his mouth.

"Burn in hell, you wine-soaked ass."

It was Anas. There were several shocked murmurs from the crowd, but Anas pressed on, his fierce gaze locked on the king.

"Apostate," he spat through broken teeth. "You betrayed us, the very people your family was meant to protect. You think it matters how you kill me? A hundred more will rise in my place. You will suffer . . . in this world and the next." A savage edge entered his voice. "And God will rip away from you those you hold most dear."

His father's eyes flashed, but he kept calm. "Unbind his hands before you return to your posts," he told the guards. "Let's see him run."

Perhaps sensing its master's intentions, the karkadann roared, and the arena shook. Ali knew the rumbles would echo through Daevabad, a warning to any who would disobey the king.

Ghassan raised his right hand. A striking mark high on his left cheek—an eight-pointed ebony star—began to glow.

Every torch in the arena went out. The stark black banners signifying his family's rule stopped fluttering, and Wajed's zulfiqar lost its fiery gleam. Beside him, Muntadhir sucked in his breath, and a wave of dull weakness swept over Ali. Such was the power of Suleiman's seal. When used, all magic, every trick and illusion of the djinn—of the peri, of the marid, of God only knew how many magical races—failed.

Including the fiery gate that kept the karkadann enclosed.

The beast stepped forward, pawing at the ground with one of its three-toed yellow feet. Despite its massive bulk, it was its horn—the length of a man and harder than steel—that was most feared. It jutted straight from its bony forehead, covered in the dried blood of hundreds of previous victims.

Anas faced the beast. He squared his shoulders.

There ended up being little amusement for the king. Anas did not run, did not try to escape or beg for mercy. And it seemed the beast was in no mood to torture its prey. It rushed out with a bellow and impaled the sheikh at his waist before raising its head and tossing the doomed man to the dust.

It was done, it was quick. Ali let out a breath he didn't realize he was holding.

But then Anas stirred. The karkadann noticed. The beast approached more slowly this time, sniffing and snorting at the ground. It prodded Anas with its nose.

The karkadann had just lifted one foot over Anas's prone body when Muntadhir flinched and averted his gaze. Ali didn't look away, didn't budge even when Anas's short scream was abruptly ended by a sickening crunch. From some distance away, one of the soldiers retched.

His father stared at the mangled corpse that had been the leader of the Tanzeem and then shot a long, intent look at the ulema before turning to his sons. "Come," he said curtly.

The crowd dispersed while the karkadann pawed its bloodied prize. Ali didn't move. His eyes were locked on Anas's body, his sheikh's scream ringing in his ears.

"Yalla, Zaydi." Muntadhir, still looking sick, nudged his shoulder. "Let's go."

Earn this. Ali nodded. He had no tears to fight. He was too shocked to cry, too numb to do anything other than mutely follow his brother into the palace.

The king swept down the long hallway, his ebony robe kissing the ground. Two servants abruptly about-faced to hurry down an opposite corridor, and a low-ranking secretary threw himself on the floor in prostration.

"I want those fanatics gone," Ghassan demanded, his loud voice directed at no one in particular. "For good this time. I don't want another shafit fool declaring himself a sheikh and popping up to wreak havoc in the streets next month." He shoved open the door to his office, sending the servant meant to do so scrambling.

Ali followed Muntadhir inside, Kaveh and Wajed close at their heels. Tucked between the gardens and the royal court, the spacious room was a deliberate blend of Daeva and Geziri design. Artists from the surrounding province of Daevastana were responsible for the delicate tapestries of languorous figures and painted floral mosaics, while the simple geometric carpets and rough-hewn musical instruments were from the Qahtanis' far more austere homeland of Am Gezira.

"There will be displeasure in the streets, my king," Wajed warned. "Bhatt was a well-liked man, and the shafit provoke easily."

"Good. I hope they riot," Ghassan retorted. "It will make it easier to root out the troublemakers."

"Unless they kill more of my tribesmen first," Kaveh cut in, his voice shrill. "Where were your soldiers, Qaid, when two Daevas were hacked to death in their own quarter? How did the Tanzeem even pass the gate when it's supposed to be guarded?"

Wajed grimaced. "We're pressed thin, Grand Wazir. You know this."

"Then let us have our own guards!" Kaveh threw up his hands. "You've got djinn preachers declaring Daevas to be infidels, the shafit calling for us to be burned to death in the Grand Temple—by the Creator, at least give us a chance to protect ourselves!"

"Calm *down*, Kaveh," Ghassan cut in. He collapsed into a low chair behind his desk and knocked aside an unopened scroll. It went rolling away, but Ali doubted his father cared. Like many high-born djinn, the king was illiterate, believing reading was useless if you had scribes who could do it for you. "Let's see if the Daevas themselves can go a half century without rebelling. I know how easily your people get misty eyed about the past."

Kaveh shut his mouth, and Ghassan continued. "But I agree: it's time the mixed-bloods were reminded of their place." He pointed at Wajed. "I want you to start enforcing the ban on more than ten shafit gathering in a private residence. I know it's fallen into disuse."

Wajed looked reluctant. "It seemed cruel, my lord. The mixed-bloods are poor . . . they live as many to a room as possible."

"Then they shouldn't rebel. I want anyone with even the slightest of sympathies to Bhatt gone. Let it be known that if they have children, I'll sell them. If they have women, I'll give them over to my soldiers."

Horrified, Ali opened his mouth to protest, but Muntadhir beat him to it. "Abba, you can't really—"

Ghassan turned his fierce gaze on his eldest son. "Should I let these fanatics run free then? Wait until they've stirred the whole city into flames?" The king shook his head. "These are the same men who claim we could free up jobs and homes for the shafit by burning the Daevas to death in the Grand Temple."

Ali's head snapped up. He had dismissed the charge when Kaveh said it, but his father was not prone to exaggeration. Ali knew Anas, like most shafit, had a lot of grievances when it came to the Daevas—it was their faith that called for the shafit to be segregated, their Nahids who'd once routinely ordered the deaths of mixed-bloods with the same emotion one would rid a home of rats. But Anas wouldn't really have called for the annihilation of the Daevas . . . would he?

His father's next comment pulled Ali from his thoughts. "We need to cut off their funding. Take that away, and the Tanzeem are little more than puritanical beggars." He fixed his gray eyes on Kaveh. "Have you made any further progress in uncovering their sources?"

The grand wazir raised his hands. "Still no proof. All I have are suspicions."

Ghassan scoffed. "Weapons, Kaveh. A clinic on Maadi. Bread-lines. That's the work of the rich. High-caste, pureblooded wealth. How are you not able to find their patrons?"

Ali tensed, but it was clear from Kaveh's frustration that he held no further answers. "Their finances are sophisticated, my king; their collection system may have even been designed by someone in the Treasury. They rotate the different tribal currencies, trade supplies with some ridiculous paper money used among the humans . . ."

Ali felt the blood drain from his face as Kaveh listed just a few of the many loopholes in Daevabad's economy that Ali had complained about—with thorough explanations—to Anas throughout the years.

Wajed's face perked up. "Human money?" He jerked a thumb at Ali. "You're always harping about that currency nonsense. Have you taken a look at Kaveh's evidence?"

Ali's heart raced. Not for the first time, he thanked the Most High that the Nahids were dead. Even one of their half-trained children would be able to tell he was lying. "I . . . no. The grand wazir did not consult with me." He thought fast, knowing that Kaveh believed him a zealous idiot. He looked down at the Daeva man. "I suppose if you're having *trouble* . . ."

Kaveh bristled. "I've had the sharpest minds in the scholar's guild assisting me; I doubt the prince could offer more." He gave Ali a withering look. "I *am* hearing a number of Ayaanle names among their rumored patrons," he added coolly before turning back to the king. "Including one that might concern you. Ta Musta Ras."

Wajed blinked in surprise. "Ta Musta Ras? Isn't he one of the queen's cousins?"

Ali cringed at the mention of his mother, and his father scowled. "He is, and one I could easily see supporting a bunch of dirt-blooded terrorists. The Ayaanle have always been fond of treating Daevabad's politics as a chessboard set for their amusement . . . especially when they're safely ensconced in Ta Ntry." He fixed his gaze on Kaveh. "But no proof, you say?"

The grand wazir shook his head. "None, my king. But plenty of rumors."

"I can't arrest my wife's cousin over rumors. Especially not with Ayaanle gold and salt making up a third of my treasury."

"Queen Hatset is in Ta Ntry now," Wajed pointed out. "Do you think he would listen to her?"

"Oh, I don't doubt it," Ghassan said darkly. "He might already be."

Ali stared at his feet, his cheeks growing warm as they discussed his mother. He and Hatset weren't close. Ali had been taken from the harem when he was five and given to Wajed to be groomed as Muntadhir's future Qaid.

His father sighed. "You'll have to go there yourself, Wajed. I trust no one else to speak to her. Let her and her entire damned family know she doesn't return to Daevabad until the money stops. Should she wish to see her children again, the choice is hers."

Ali could feel Wajed's eyes upon him. "Yes, my king," Wajed said softly.

Kaveh looked alarmed. "Who will serve as Qaid while he's gone?"

"Alizayd. It's only for a few months and will be good practice for when I'm dead and this one"—Ghassan jerked his head in Muntadhir's direction—"is too occupied with dancing girls to rule the realm."

Ali's mouth dropped open, and Muntadhir burst into laughter.

"Well, that should cut down on theft." His brother made a chopping motion across his wrist. "Quite literally."

Kaveh went pale. "My king, Prince Alizayd is a *child*. He's not even close to his first quarter century. You cannot possibly entrust the city's security to a sixteen—"

"*Eighteen*," Muntadhir corrected with a wicked grin. "Come now, Grand Wazir, there's an enormous difference."

Kaveh clearly didn't share the emir's amusement. His voice

grew more pitched. "Eighteen-year-old boy. A boy who—might I remind you—once had a Daeva nobleman whipped in the street like a common shafit thief!"

"He *was* a thief," Ali defended. He remembered the incident, but was surprised Kaveh did; it was years ago, the first—and last—time Ali had been allowed to patrol the Daeva Quarter. "God's law applies equally to all."

The grand wazir took a breath. "Trust me, Prince Alizayd, it is to my deep disappointment that you are not in Paradise where we all follow God's law . . ." He didn't pause long enough for the double meaning of his words to land, but Ali picked it up well enough. "But under Daevabad's law, the shafit are not equal to purebloods." He looked imploringly to the king. "Did you not just have someone executed for saying much the same thing?"

"I did," Ghassan agreed. "A lesson you would do well to re-member, Alizayd. The Qaid enforces *my* law, not his own beliefs."

"Of course, Abba," Ali said quickly, knowing he'd been foolish to speak so plainly in front of them. "I will do as you command."

"See, Kaveh? Nothing to fear." Ghassan nodded in the di-rection of the door. "You may leave. Court will be held after the noon prayer. Let word get out about this morning; perhaps that will cut down on the number of petitioners harassing me."

The Daeva minister looked like he had more to say, but he merely nodded, throwing Ali a vicious look as he left.

Wajed slammed the door shut behind him. "That snake has a twisted tongue, Abu Muntadhir," he said to the king, switching to Geziriyya. "I'd like to make him wriggle like one." He caressed his zulfiqar. "Just once."

"Don't give your protégé any ideas." Ghassan unwound his turban, leaving the brilliant silk in a heap on the desk. "Kaveh is not wrong to be upset, and he doesn't even know the half of things." He nodded to a large crate sitting next to the balcony. Ali hadn't noticed it earlier. "Show them."

The Qaid sighed but crossed to the crate. "An imam who runs a mosque near the Grand Bazaar contacted the Royal Guard a few weeks ago and said he suspected Bhatt of recruiting one of his congregants." Wajed pulled free his khanjar and pried open the crate's wooden slats. "My soldiers followed that man to one of his hideouts." He beckoned for Ali and Muntadhir. "We found this there."

Ali took a step closer, already sick. In his heart, he knew what was in that crate.

The weapons Anas swore he didn't have were packed in tight. Crude iron cudgels and battered steel daggers, studded maces and a couple of crossbows. A half-dozen swords and a few of the long incendiary devices—rifles?—humans had invented, along with a box of ammunition. Ali's disbelieving eyes scanned the crate and then his heart skipped a beat.

Zulfiqar training blades.

The words were out of Ali's mouth before he could stop himself. "Someone in the Royal Guard stole these."

Wajed gave him a grim nod. "It had to be. A Geziri man; we only let our own near those blades." He crossed his arms over his massive chest. "They must have been stolen from the Citadel, but I suspect the rest were bought from smugglers." He met Ali's horrified gaze. "There were three other crates like this one."

Beside him, Muntadhir exhaled. "What in God's name were they planning to do with all this?"

"I'm not sure," Wajed admitted. "They could have armed a few dozen shafit men at most. No real match for the Royal Guard, but—"

"They could have murdered a score of people shopping in the Grand Bazaar," the king cut in. "They could have lain in wait outside the Daevas' temple on one of their feast days and massacred a hundred pilgrims before help arrived. They could have started a war."

Ali gripped the crate, though he had no memory of reaching for it. In his mind, he saw the warriors he'd grown up with— the cadets who'd fallen asleep on one another's shoulders after long days of training, the young men who teased and insulted one another as they headed out on their first patrols. The ones Ali would soon swear to lead and protect as Qaid. They were the ones who would have likely faced these weapons.

Anger, swift and fierce, coursed through him, but Ali had no one to blame but himself. *You should have known. When the first rumors of weapons reached you, you should have stopped.* But Ali hadn't stopped. Instead, he'd accompanied Anas to that tavern. He'd stood by while two men were killed.

He took a deep breath. From the corner of his eye, he saw Wajed give him a curious look. He straightened up.

"But why?" Muntadhir pressed. "What would the Tanzeem have to gain?"

"I don't know," Ghassan replied. "And I don't care. It took years to bring peace to Daevabad after the deaths of the last Na-hids. I don't intend to let some dirt-blood fanatics eager for mar-tyrdom tear us apart." He pointed at Wajed. "The Citadel will find the men responsible and execute them. If they are Geziri, do it quietly. I don't need the Daevas thinking our tribe supports the Tanzeem. And you will put in place the new restrictions on the shafit. Ban their gatherings. Throw them in prison if they so much as step on a pureblood's foot. For now, at least." He shook his head. "God willing, we'll get through the next few months without any surprises, and we'll be able to ease them again."

"Yes, my king."

Ghassan waved at the crate. "Get rid of that thing before Ka-veh sniffs it out. I've had enough of his ranting for one day." He rubbed his brow and sank back into his chair, his jeweled rings gleaming. He glanced up, fixing his sharp gaze on Muntadhir. "Also . . . should I need to execute another shafit traitor, my emir will watch without flinching else he'll find himself carrying out the next sentence."

Muntadhir crossed his arms, leaning against the desk in a familiar manner Ali never would have dared. "Ya, Abba, if I knew you were going to have his head crushed like an overripe melon, I would have skipped breakfast."

Ghassan's eyes flashed. "Your younger brother managed to control himself."

Muntadhir laughed. "Yes, but Ali is Citadel trained. He'd dance in front of the karkadann if you told him to."

Their father didn't seem to appreciate the jest, his face growing stormy. "Or perhaps spending all your time drinking with courtesans and poets has weakened your constitution." He glared. "You should be glad of your future Qaid's training—God knows you're likely to need it." He rose from his desk. "And on that note, I would speak to your brother alone."

What? Why? Ali was barely holding his emotions in check; he didn't want to be alone with his father.

Wajed squeezed his shoulder and briefly leaned in toward Ali's ear. "Breathe, boy," he whispered as Ghassan stood and strolled toward the balcony. "He doesn't bite." He flashed Ali a reassuring smile and followed Muntadhir out of the office.

There was a long moment of silence. His father studied the garden, his hands clasped behind him.

His back was still to Ali when he asked, "Do you believe that?"

Ali's voice came out in a squeak. "Believe what?"

"What you said before." His father turned around, his dark gray eyes intent. "About God's law applying equally— By the Most High, Alizayd, stop *shaking*. I need to be able to talk to my Qaid without him turning into a trembling mess."

Ali's embarrassment was tempered with relief—far better for Ghassan to blame his anxiety on nerves from being made Qaid. "I'm sorry."

"It's fine." Ghassan leveled his gaze on him again. "Answer the question."

Ali thought fast, but there was no way he could lie. His family knew he was devout—he had been since childhood—and their religion was clear on the issue of the shafit. "Yes," he replied. "I believe the shafit should be treated equally. That's why our ancestors came to Daevabad. That's why Zaydi al Qahtani went to war with the Nahids."

"A war that nearly destroyed our entire race. A war that ended in the sacking of Daevabad and earned us the enmity of the Daeva tribe until this day."

Ali startled at his father's words. "Do you not think it was worth it?"

Ghassan looked irritated. "Of course I think it was worth it. I'm simply capable of seeing both sides of an issue. It's a skill you should try to develop." Ali's cheeks grew hot, and his father continued. "Besides, there weren't this many shafit in Zaydi's time."

Ali frowned. "Are they that numerous now?"

"Nearly a third of the population. Yes," he said, noticing the surprise in Ali's face. "Their numbers have burgeoned immensely in recent decades—information you'd do best to keep to yourself." He gestured to the weapons. "There are now almost as many shafit in Daevabad as there are Daevas, and truthfully, my son, if they went to war in the streets, I'm not sure the Royal Guard could stop them. The Daevas would win in the end, of course, but it would be bloody, and it would destroy the city's peace for generations."

"But that's not going to happen, Abba," Ali argued. "The shafit aren't fools. They just want a better life for themselves. They want to be able to work and live in buildings that aren't coming down around them. To take care of their families without fearing their children will be snatched away by some pure—"

Ghassan interrupted. "When you come up with a way to provide jobs and housing for thousands of people, let me know. And if their lives were made easier here, they would only reproduce faster."

"Then let them *leave*. Let them try to make better lives in the human world."

"Let them cause chaos in the human world, you mean." His father shook his head. "Absolutely not. They may look human, but many still have magic. We'd be inviting another Suleiman to curse us." He sighed. "There's no easy answer, Alizayd. All we can do is strike a balance."

"But we're not striking a balance," Ali argued. "We're choosing the fire worshippers over the shafit our ancestors came here to protect."

Ghassan whirled on him. "The *fire worshippers*?"

Too late Ali remembered the Daevas hated that term for their tribe. "I didn't mean—"

"Then don't ever repeat such a thing in my presence." His father glared at him. "The Daevas are under my protection, same as our own tribe. I don't care what faith they practice." He threw up his hands. "Hell, maybe they're right to obsess over blood purity. In all my years, I've never encountered a Daeva shafit."

They probably smother them in their cradles. But Ali didn't say that. He'd been a fool to pick this fight today.

Ghassan ran a hand along the wet windowsill and then shook off the water droplets that had gathered upon his fingertips. "It's always wet here. Always cold. I haven't been back to Am Gezira in a century and yet every morning, I wake up missing its hot sands." He glanced back at Ali. "This is not our home. It never will be. It will always belong to the Daevas first."

It's my home. Ali was accustomed to Daevabad's damp chill and liked the diverse mix of peoples that filled its streets. He'd felt out of place during his rare trips to Am Gezira, always conscious of his half-Ayaanle appearance.

"It's their home," Ghassan continued. "And I am their king.

I will not allow the shafit—a problem the Daevas had no part in creating—to threaten them in their own home." He turned to face Ali. "If you are to be Qaid, you must respect this."

Ali lowered his gaze. He didn't respect it; he entirely disagreed. "Forgive my impertinence."

He suspected that wasn't the answer Ghassan wanted—his father's eyes stayed sharp another moment before he abruptly crossed the room toward the wooden shelves lining the opposite wall. "Come here."

Ali followed. Ghassan picked up a long, lacquered black case from one of the upper shelves. "I hear nothing but compliments from the Citadel about your progress, Alizayd. You've a keen mind for military science and you're one of the best zulfiqari in your generation. None would dispute that. But you're very young."

Ghassan blew the dust off the case and then opened it, pulling a silver arrow from a bed of fragile tissue. "Do you know what this is?"

Ali certainly did. "It's the last arrow shot by an Afshin."

"Bend it."

A little confused, Ali nonetheless took the arrow from his father. Though it was incredibly light, he couldn't bend it in the slightest. The silver still gleamed after all these years, only the scythe-ended tip dulled by blood. The same blood that ran in Ali's veins.

"The Afshins were good soldiers too," Ghassan said softly. "Probably the best warriors of our race. But now they're dead, their Nahid leaders are dead, and our people have ruled Daevabad for fourteen centuries. And do you know why?"

Because they were infidels, and God willed us to victory? Ali held his tongue; he suspected if he said that, the arrow would be getting a new coat of Qahtani blood.

Ghassan took the arrow back. "Because they were like this arrow. Like you. Unwilling to bend, unwilling to see that not everything fit into their perfectly ordered world." He put the weapon back in the case and snapped it shut. "There is more to being Qaid than being a good soldier. God willing, Wajed and I have another century of wine and ridiculous petitioners ahead of us, but one day Muntadhir will be king. And when he needs guidance, when he needs to discuss things only his blood can hear, he'll need you."

"Yes, Abba." Ali was willing to say anything at this point to leave, anything that would let him escape his father's measured gaze.

"There's one more thing." His father stepped away from the shelf. "You're moving back to the palace. Immediately."

Ali's mouth dropped open. "But the Citadel is my home."

"No . . . *my* home is your home," Ghassan said, looking irritated. "Your place is here. It's time you start attending court to see how the world works outside your books. And I'll be able to keep a better eye on you—I don't like the way you're talking about the Daevas."

Dread welled up in Ali, but his father didn't press the issue. "You can go now. I'll expect you at court when you're settled in."

Ali nodded and bowed; it was all he could do not to run for the door. "Peace be upon you."

He'd no sooner stumbled into the corridor than he ran into his grinning brother.

Muntadhir pulled him into a hug. "Congratulations, akhi. I'm sure you're going to make a terrifying Qaid."

"Thanks," Ali mumbled. He'd just witnessed the brutal death of his closest friend. That he was soon to be in charge of maintaining security for a city of bickering djinn was something he'd yet to dwell on.

Muntadhir didn't seem to pick up on his distress. "Did Abba tell you the other good news?" When Ali made a noncommittal sound, he continued. "You're moving back to the palace!"

"Oh." Ali frowned. "That."

His brother's face fell. "You don't sound very excited."

A fresh wave of guilt swept over Ali at the hurt in Muntadhir's voice. "It's not that, Dhiru. It's . . . it's been a long morning. Taking over for Wajed, the news about the weapons . . ." He exhaled. "Besides, I've never been very . . ." He searched for a way to avoid insulting his brother's entire social circle. ". . . *comfortable* around people here."

"Ah, you'll be fine." Muntadhir threw his arm around Ali's shoulder, half-dragging him down the corridor. "Stick by me, and I'll make sure you get embroiled in only the most delightful of scandals." He laughed when Ali gave him a startled look. "Come. Zaynab and I picked you out apartments near the waterfall." They turned the corner. "With the most boring furnishings and least comfortable amenities. You'll be right at ho—whoa."

The brothers drew to an immediate stop. They had to. A wall stood in their way, a jewel-colored mural splashed across the stone.

"Well . . ." Muntadhir's voice was shaky. "That's new."

Ali edged closer. "No . . . it's not," he said softly, recognizing the scene and remembering his long-ago history lessons. "It's one of the old Nahid murals. They used to cover the palace walls before the war."

"It wasn't here yesterday." Muntadhir touched the mural's bright sun. It flashed beneath his fingertips, and they both jumped.

Ali gave the mural an uneasy look. "And you wonder why I'm not excited about moving back to this Nahid-haunted place?"

Muntadhir made a face. "It's not usually this bad." He nodded to one of the figures on the cracked plaster facade. "Do you know who that's supposed to be?"

Ali studied the image. The figure looked human, a man with a flowing white beard and a silver halo above his crowned head. He stood before a crimson sun, one hand resting on the back of a roaring shedu, and the other holding a staff with an eight-pointed seal. The same seal that was on Ghassan's right temple.

"It's Suleiman," Ali realized. "Peace be upon him." He gazed at the rest of the painting. "I think it depicts the ascension of Anahid when she received her abilities and Suleiman's seal." His eyes fell on the bent figure at Suleiman's feet. Only her back was visible, the long taper of her ears giving away that she was a djinn. Or daeva, rather. Anahid, first of her line.

Blue paint flooded Suleiman's robes.

"Odd," Muntadhir remarked. "I wonder why it picked today of all days to start trying to repair fourteen centuries of damage."

A shiver went down Ali's spine. "I don't know."

7

NAHRI

"Raise your arm higher."

Nahri lifted her elbow, tightening her grip on the dagger. "Like this?"

Dara made a face. "No." He stepped up to her, the scent of his smoky skin tickling her nose, and adjusted her arm. "Loosen up; you need to be relaxed. You're throwing a knife, not beating someone with a stick."

His hand lingered a moment longer than necessary on her elbow, his breath warm against her neck. Nahri shivered; relaxing was a thing easier said than done when the handsome daeva was so close. He finally stepped away, and she fixed her eyes on the scrubby tree. She threw the dagger, and it sailed past the tree to land in a patch of bushes.

Dara burst into laughter as she swore. "I'm not sure we're going to be able to make much of a warrior out of you." He opened his palm, and the dagger flew back to him.

Nahri gave him an envious look. "Can't you teach me how to do that?"

He handed the knife back. "No. I've told you enough times . . ."

". . . magic is unpredictable," she finished. She threw the dagger again. She could have sworn it landed slightly closer to the tree, but that might have been her own wishful thinking. "So what if it is? Are you truly afraid of what I might do?"

"Yes," he said bluntly. "For all I know, you'll send fifty such knives flying back at us."

Ah, well, perhaps he had a point. She waved the knife away when he tried to hand it back. "No. I've had enough for today. Can't we just rest? We've been traveling as if—"

"As if a pack of ifrit are after us?" His raised his eyebrows.

"We'll travel faster if we're not exhausted," she replied, taking his arm and pulling him in the direction of their small camp. "Come on."

"We'd travel faster if we weren't carting around a caravan of stolen goods," Dara retorted, snapping off a twig from a dying tree and letting it burn to cinders in his hands. "How many clothes do you truly need? And you're not even eating the oranges . . . to say nothing of that entirely useless flute."

"That flute is ivory, Dara. It's worth a fortune. Besides . . ." Nahri held out her arms, briefly admiring the embroidered tunic and brown leather boots she'd snatched off a stall they passed in one of the river towns. "I'm just trying to keep our supplies well stocked."

They reached their camp, though "camp" might have been too kind a word for the little clearing where Nahri had stomped down the grass before dropping her bags. The horses were grazing in a distant field, eating any bit of greenery down to the roots. Dara knelt and rekindled their fire with a snap of his fingers. The flames jumped, illuminating the dark tattoo on his frowning face.

"Your ancestors would be horrified to see how easily you take to stealing."

"According to you, my ancestors would be horrified to learn of my very existence." She pulled out a well-wrapped heel of stale bread. "And it's the way the world works. By now, people have certainly broken into my home in Cairo and stolen my things."

He tossed a broken branch on the fire, sending up sparks. "How does that make it better?"

"Someone steals from me, I steal from others, and I'm sure the people I stole from will eventually take something that doesn't belong to them. It's a circle," she added wisely, as she gnawed on the chewy bread.

Dara stared at her for a good few heartbeats before speaking. "There is something very wrong with you."

"Probably comes from my daeva blood."

He scowled. "It's your turn to fetch the horses."

Nahri groaned; she had little desire to leave the fire. "And what are you going to do?"

But Dara was already retrieving a battered pot from one of their bags. She'd stolen it along the way, hoping to find something to cook that wasn't manna. And after listening to her complain about their food situation for days, Dara had taken it upon himself to try and figure out how to conjure up something different. But Nahri wasn't hopeful. All he'd managed thus far was a vaguely warm gray soup that tasted like the ghouls smelled.

Night had fallen by the time Nahri returned with the horses. The darkness in this land fell quick and was thick enough to feel, a heavy, impenetrable blackness that would have made her nervous if she didn't have their campfire to guide her. Even the thick canopy of stars above did little to alleviate it, their light captured by the white mountains surrounding them. They were covered in snow, Dara explained, a concept she could scarcely imagine. This country was completely foreign to her, and though it was novel and in some ways even beautiful, she found herself longing for Cairo's busy streets, for the crowded bazaars and squabbling merchants. She missed the golden desert that embraced her city and the wide, brown Nile that twisted through it.

Nahri tied the horses to a skinny tree. The temperature had dropped dramatically with the sun, and her cold fingers fumbled the knot. She wrapped one of the blankets around her shoulders and then took a seat as close to the fire as she dared.

Dara wasn't even wearing his robe. She stared jealously at his bare arms. *Must be nice to be made of fire.* Whatever daeva blood she had clearly wasn't enough to keep the chill away.

The pot steamed at his feet; he pushed it over with a triumphant smile. "Eat."

She took a suspicious sniff. It smelled good, like buttery lentils and onions. Nahri ripped off a strip of bread from her bag and dipped it into the pot. She took a guarded bite and then another. It tasted as good as it smelled, like cream and lentils and some type of leafy green. She quickly reached for more bread.

"Do you like it?" he asked, his voice rising in hope.

After all the manna, anything edible would have been appetizing, but this was legitimately delicious. "I love it!" She scooped more into her mouth, savoring the warm stew. "How did you finally do it, then?"

Dara looked tremendously pleased with himself. "I tried to concentrate on the dish I knew best. I think the focus helped—a lot of magic has to do with your intentions." He paused, and his smile faded. "It was something my mother used to make."

Nahri almost choked; Dara had revealed nothing about his past and even now she could see a guarded look slip across his face. Hoping he wouldn't change the subject, she quickly replied, "She must be a very good cook."

"She was." He drank back the rest of his wine, and the goblet immediately refilled.

"Was?" Nahri ventured.

Dara stared into the fire; his fingers twitched like he longed to touch it. "She's dead."

Nahri dropped her bread. "Oh. Dara, I'm sorry, I didn't realize—"

"It is fine," he interrupted, though the tone of his voice implied it was anything but. "It was a long time ago."

Nahri hesitated but couldn't contain her curiosity. "And the rest of your family?"

"Dead as well." He gave her a sharp look, his emerald eyes bright. "There's no one but me."

"I can relate," she said softly.

"Indeed. I suppose you can." A goblet suddenly materialized in her hand. "Drink with me, then," he commanded, raising his goblet in her direction. "You'll choke if you don't wash down that food. I don't think I've ever seen anyone eat so quickly."

He was changing the subject, and they both knew it. Nahri shrugged, taking a sip of the wine. "You'd do the same if you grew up like me. Sometimes I didn't know when I'd eat next."

"I could tell." He snorted. "You didn't look much thicker than the ghouls when I first found you. Curse the manna all you like, at least it filled you out some."

Nahri lifted an eyebrow. "'Filled me out some'?" she repeated.

Dara was immediately flustered. "I-I didn't mean in a bad way. Just that, you know . . ." He made a vague sweeping motion toward her body and then blushed, perhaps realizing such a gesture didn't help. "Never mind," he muttered, dropping his embarrassed gaze.

Oh, I know, believe me. For all Dara supposedly abhorred the shafit, Nahri had caught him staring at her more than once, and their dagger-throwing lesson hadn't been the first time his hand had lingered upon her a bit too long.

She kept her gaze on him, studying the broad line of his shoulders and watching as he played nervously with his goblet, still avoiding her eyes. His fingers trembled on the stem, and for a moment Nahri could not help but wonder if they would do the same upon her skin.

Because things are not tumultuous enough between us without adding that to the mix. Before her mind could go any further, Nahri changed the subject again to one she knew would thoroughly ruin the mood. "So tell me about these Qahtanis."

Dara startled. "What?"

"These djinn you keep insulting, the ones who supposedly fought my ancestors." She took a sip of her wine. "Tell me about them."

Dara made a face as if he'd eaten something sour. One objective achieved. "Must we really do this now? It's late—"

She shook a finger at him. "Don't make me go looking for another ghoul to threaten you into talking."

He didn't smile at the joke, instead looking more troubled. "It's not a pleasant tale, Nahri."

"All the more reason to get it over with."

He took a sip of wine, a long sip, as if he needed a dose of courage. "I told you before that Suleiman was a clever man. Before his curse, all daevas were the same. We looked similar, spoke a single language, practiced identical rites." Dara beckoned at their fire, and its tendrils of smoke rushed toward his hands like an eager lover. "When Suleiman freed us, he scattered us across the world he knew, changing our tongues and appearances to mirror the humans in our new lands."

Dara spread his hands. The smoke flattened and condensed to form a thick map in the sky before her, Suleiman's temple at the center. As she watched, blazing pinpricks of light spun out from the temple across the world, falling to the ground like meteorites and bouncing back as fully formed people.

"He divided us into six tribes." Dara pointed at a pale woman weighing jade coins at the eastern edge of the map, China perhaps. "The Tukharistanis." He gestured south at a bejeweled dancer twirling in the Indian subcontinent. "The Agnivanshi." A tiny rider burst out of the smoke, galloping across southern Arabia and brandishing a fiery sword. Dara pursed his lips and with a snap of his fingers lopped off its head. "The Geziri." To the south of Egypt, a golden-eyed scholar tossed a brilliant teal scarf over his shoulder as he scanned a scroll. Dara nodded at him. "The Ayaanle," he said and then pointed to a fire-haired man mending a boat on the Moroccan coast. "The Sahrayn."

"What about your people?"

"*Our* people," he corrected and gestured toward the flat plains of what looked like Persia to her, or perhaps Afghanistan. "Daevastana," he said warmly. "The land of the Daevas."

She frowned. "Your tribe took the original name of the entire daeva race as your own?"

Dara shrugged. "We were in charge."

He studied the map. The smoky figures silently shouted and gesticulated at each other. "It was said to be a violent, terrifying time. Most people embraced their new tribes, clinging together for survival and forming within the tribes caste groups determined by their new abilities. Some were shapeshifters, others could manipulate metals, some could conjure up rare goods, and so forth. None could do it all, and the tribes were too busy fighting each other to even consider revenge against Suleiman."

Nahri smiled, impressed. "Surely even you must admit that was rather a brilliant move on Suleiman's part."

"Perhaps," Dara replied. "But brilliant as he might have been, Suleiman failed to consider the consequences of giving my people solid, mortal bodies."

The tiny figures continued to multiply, building small villages and crisscrossing the vast world in spindly caravans. Occasionally a miniature flying carpet dashed across the smoky clouds.

"What consequences?" Nahri asked, confused.

He gave her a playful smile that didn't quite reach his eyes. "That we could mate with humans."

"And make shafit," she realized. "People like me."

Dara nodded. "Completely forbidden, mind you." He sighed. "You may have realized by now that we're not particularly good at following rules."

"I'm guessing those shafit multiplied pretty quickly?"

"Very." He gestured to the smoky map. "Like I say, magic is unpredictable." A tiny city in the Maghreb burst into flames. "Made even more so in the hands of mix-blooded, untrained practitioners." Enormous ships, in a variety of bizarre shapes crossed the Red Sea, and winged cats with human faces soared over the Hind. "Although most shafit don't have any abilities, the few that do have the capacity to inflict terrible damage on their human societies."

Damage like leading a pack of ghouls through Cairo and tricking bashas out of their wealth? Nahri had little argument there. "But why did the daevas—or djinn, or whatever you were calling yourselves at the time—even care?" she asked. "I thought your race didn't think much of humans anyway."

"They wouldn't have," Dara admitted. "But Suleiman made it quite clear that another would follow in his place to punish us again should we ignore his law. The Nahid Council struggled for years to contain the shafit problem, ordering that any humans suspected of having magical blood be brought to Daevabad to live out their lives."

Nahri went still. "The *Nahid* Council? But I thought the Qahtanis were the ones—"

"I'll get to that part," Dara cut in, his voice a little colder—and slightly more slurred—than usual. He took another long sip of wine. The goblet never seemed to empty, so Nahri could only imagine how much he'd consumed by now. Far more than her, and her head was starting to swim.

A city rose from the smoky map in Daevastana, in the center of a dark lake. Its walls gleamed like brass, beautiful against the dark sky. "Is that Daevabad?" she asked.

"Daevabad," Dara confirmed. His eyes dimmed as he stared at the tiny city, longing in his face. "Our grandest city. Where Anahid built her palace and from where her descendants ruled the realm until they were overthrown."

"Let me guess . . . by all the kidnapped shafit they kept locked up?"

Dara shook his head. "No. No shafit could have ever done such a thing; they're too weak."

"Then who did?"

Dara's face darkened. "Who didn't?" When she frowned in confusion, he continued. "The other tribes never paid much heed to Suleiman's decree. Oh, they *claimed* to agree that humans and daevas should be segregated, but they were the source of the shafit."

He nodded at the map. "The Geziri were the worst. They were fascinated by the humans in their land, praising their prophets and adopting their culture—with some inevitably getting too close. They're the poorest tribe, a pack of religious fanatics who believe what Suleiman did to us was a blessing not a curse. They often refused to surrender shafit kin, and when the Nahid Council grew more severe in their enforcement of the law, the Geziri didn't react well."

A black swarm rose in the Rub al Khali, the forbidding desert north of the Yemen. "They started calling themselves 'djinn,'" Dara said. "The word the humans in their land used for our race. And when their leader, a man named Zaydi al Qahtani, called for an invasion, the other tribes joined him." The black cloud grew enormous as it descended upon Daevabad and stained the lake.

"He overthrew the Nahid Council and stole Suleiman's seal." Dara's next words came out in a hiss. "His descendants rule Daevabad to this day."

Nahri watched as the city slowly turned black. "How long ago was all this?"

"About fourteen hundred years ago." Dara's mouth was a thin line. Within the smoky map, the tiny version of Daevabad, now black as coal, collapsed.

"Fourteen hundred years ago?" She studied the daeva, noticing the tense way he held his body and the scowl on his handsome face. Something stirred in her memory. "This . . . this is the war you were discussing with Khayzur, isn't it?" Her mouth fell open. "Didn't you say you *witnessed* it?"

He drank back the rest of his wine. "You don't miss much, do you?"

Nahri's head spun from the admission. "But how? You said the djinn only lived for a few centuries!"

"It doesn't matter." He dismissed her with a wave of his hand, but the movement wasn't as graceful as usual. "My history is just that: mine."

She was incredulous. "And you don't think this king is going to want an explanation when we show up in Daevabad?"

"I'm not going to Daevabad."

"*What?* But I thought . . . where are we going then?"

Dara looked away. "I'll take you as far as the city gates. You can make your way to the palace from there. You'll be received better alone, trust me."

Nahri drew back, shocked and far more hurt than she should have been. "You're just going to abandon me?"

"I'm not *abandoning* you." Dara exhaled and threw up his hands, gesturing rudely to the pile of weapons behind him. "Nahri, what kind of history do you think I have with these people? I can't go back."

Her temper flashed, and she rose to her feet. "You coward," she accused him. "You misled me back at the river and you know it. I never would have agreed to go to Daevabad with you if I'd known you were so afraid of the djinn that you were planning to—"

"I am *not* afraid of the djinn." Dara also rose to his feet, his eyes flaring. "I sold my soul for the Nahids! I'm not going to spend eternity languishing in a dungeon while I listen to the djinn mock them for being hypocrites."

"But they *were* hypocrites—look at me! I'm living proof!"

His face darkened. "I am all too aware of that."

That stung, she couldn't deny it. "Is that what this is about then? You're ashamed of me?"

"I . . ." Dara shook his head. Something like regret seemed to briefly flicker in his face before he turned away. "Nahri, you didn't grow up in my world. You can't understand."

"Thank God I didn't! I probably would have been killed before my first birthday!"

Dara said nothing, his silence more revealing than any denial. Her stomach twisted. She'd been imagining her ancestors as noble healers, but what Dara suggested painted a far darker picture. "Then I'm glad the djinn invaded," she said, her voice hoarse. "I hope they got vengeance for all the shafit my ancestors murdered!"

"Vengeance?" Dara's eyes flashed, smoke curling out from under his collar. "Zaydi al Qahtani slaughtered every last Daeva man, woman, and child when he took the city. My *family* was in that city. My sister wasn't even half your age!"

Nahri immediately backed down, seeing the grief in his face. "I'm sorry. I didn't . . ."

But he'd already turned away. He crossed toward their supplies, moving so fast the grass scorched beneath his feet. "I don't need to listen to this." He snatched his bag from the ground, slinging his bow and quiver over his shoulder before shooting her a hostile look. "You think your ancestors—*my* leaders—such monsters, the Qahtanis so righteous . . ." He jerked his head toward the encompassing darkness. "Why don't you try singing for a djinn to save you next?"

And then before Nahri could say anything, before she could really comprehend what was happening, he stalked off, vanishing into the night.

8

ALI

Where is he?

Ali paced outside his father's office. Muntadhir was supposed to meet him here before court, but it was getting late and there was still no sign of his perpetually tardy brother.

He gave the closed office door an anxious look. People had been passing through all morning, but Ali could not yet bring himself to go in. He felt terribly unprepared for his first day at court and had barely slept the night before, the spacious bed in his extravagant new quarters too soft and covered in an alarming number of beaded pillows. He'd finally settled for sleeping on the floor, only to be assailed by nightmares of being thrown to the karkadann.

Ali sighed. He took one last look down the corridor, but there was no sign of Muntadhir.

A flurry of activity greeted him when he entered the office, scribes and secretaries loaded with scrolls dashing past assorted ministers arguing in a dozen different languages. His father was at his desk, listening intently to Kaveh while one servant waved an incense burner of smoldering frankincense over his head and another adjusted the stiff collar of the white dishdasha he wore under his immaculate black robes.

No one seemed to notice Ali, and he was happy to keep it that way. Dodging a wine bearer, he pressed against the wall.

As if on some prearranged signal, the room began to disperse, the servants slinking away and the ministers and secretaries making their way toward the doors leading to the king's massive audience hall. Ali watched as Kaveh made a notation on the paper in his hand and nodded.

"I'll be sure to tell the High Priests that . . . ," he trailed off and then abruptly straightened up as he noticed Ali. His face turned stormy. "Is this some sort of joke?"

Ali had no idea what he'd already done wrong. "I . . . I was supposed to come here, right?"

Kaveh gestured rudely at his clothes. "You're *supposed* to be in ceremonial dress, Prince Alizayd. Robes of state. I had tailors sent to you last night."

Ali mentally cursed himself. Two anxious Daeva men *had* presented themselves to him last night, stammering something about measurements, but Ali had dismissed them, not thinking much of it at the time. He neither desired nor needed new clothes.

He glanced down. His sleeveless gray tunic had only a couple of gashes where he'd been slashed during practice, and his indigo waist-wrap was dark enough to hide its zulfiqar burns. It looked fine to him.

"These are clean," he argued. "I only wore them yesterday." He gestured to his turban; the crimson cloth indicated his new position as Qaid. "This is all that matters, no?"

"No!" Kaveh looked incredulous. "You're a Qahtani prince—

you can't go to court looking like someone just dragged you in from a sparring match!" He threw up his hands and turned to the king. Ghassan had said nothing, simply watching them fight with a strange twinkle in his eyes. "Do you see this?" he demanded. "Now we'll have to start late so your son can be properly—"

Ghassan laughed.

It was a full-throated, hearty laugh, one Ali hadn't heard from his father in years. "Aye, Kaveh, let him be." The king came from behind the desk and clapped Ali on the back. "He has Am Gezira in his blood," he said proudly. "Back home, we never bothered with all this ceremonial nonsense." He chuckled as he led Ali toward the door. "If he looks like he just finished thrashing someone with a zulfiqar, so be it."

His father's praise was not a thing doled out often, and Ali could not help but feel his spirits lift. He glanced around as a servant reached for the door leading to the audience chamber. "Abba, where's Muntadhir?"

"With the trade minister from Tukharistan. He's . . . *negotiating* a deal to reduce the debt we owe for the Royal Guard's new uniforms."

"Muntadhir's negotiating our debts?" Ali asked skeptically. His brother and numbers did not go well together. "I didn't think economics his strong suit."

"It's not that type of negotiation." When Ali's confused frown only deepened, Ghassan shook his head. "Come along, boy."

It had been years since Ali had last been in his father's throne room, and he paused to fully appreciate it as they entered. The chamber was enormous, taking up the entire first level of the palatial ziggurat, and held up by marble columns so tall they disappeared into the distant ceiling. Although it was covered in fading paint and broken mosaics, one could still make out the flowery vines and ancient Daevastani creatures that had once decorated its surface—as well as the pockmarks where his ancestors had pried out gems; the Geziri were not ones to waste resources on ornamentation.

The western side of the room opened onto manicured formal gardens. Enormous windows—nearly the height of the ceiling— broke up the remaining walls, shielded by intricately carved wooden screens that kept the cavernous space cool while letting in light and fresh air. Flower-filled fountains set against the wall did the same, the water enchanted to continuously flow over channels of cut ice. Bright mirrored braziers of burning cedar-wood hung from silver chains over a floor of green marble swirled with white veins. The floor rose as it reached the eastern wall and separated into five tiers, each level assigned to a different branch of the government.

Ali and his father walked out onto the top level, and as they approached the throne, Ali could not help but admire it. Twice his height and carved from sky blue marble, the throne originally belonged to the Nahids and looked it, a monument to the extravagance that had gotten them overthrown. It was designed to turn its occupant into a living shedu, the legendary winged lion that had been their family symbol. Rubies, carnelians, and pink and orange topaz were inlaid above the head to represent the rising sun, while the arms of the throne were similarly jeweled to imitate wings, the legs carved into heavy clawed paws.

The jewels sparkled in the sunlight—as did the thousands of eyes he suddenly realized were upon him. Ali promptly dropped his gaze. There was nothing that united the tribes more than gossiping about their leaders, and he suspected the sight of Ghassan's second son eying the throne on his first day in court would set every tongue wagging.

His father nodded to the jeweled cushion below the throne. "Your brother isn't here. You might as well take his seat."

More gossip. "I'll stand," Ali said quickly, edging away from Muntadhir's cushion.

The king shrugged. "Your choice." He settled into his throne, Ali and Kaveh flanking him. Ali forced himself to look at the crowd again. Though the throne room could fit ten thousand, Ali guessed about half that number were here now. Nobles from all the tribes—their regular presence required to prove loyalty—shared space with clerics in white turbans, while court scribes, lesser wazirs, and Treasury officials swarmed in a dizzying array of ceremonial dress.

But the majority of the crowd looked to be commoners. No shafit, of course, save servants, but plenty of mixed tribal heritage like Ali. All were dressed well—none would present themselves in court otherwise—but some were clearly from Daevabad's lower classes, their robes clean but patched, their ornaments little more than metal bangles.

An Ayaanle woman in mustard-colored robes with a scribe's black sash around her collar stood up.

"In the name of King Ghassan ibn Khader al Qahtani, Defender of the Faith, and on the ninety-fourth Rabi' al Thani of the twenty-seventh generation after Suleiman's Blessing, I call this session to order!" She lit a cylindrical glass oil lamp and placed it on the dais before her. Ali knew his father would hear petitions until the oil ran out, but as he watched court officials herd the crowd below into some semblance of order, he gaped at the sheer number. His father didn't mean to hear all these people, did he?

The first petitioners were brought forward and introduced: a silk merchant from Tukharistan and his aggrieved Agnivanshi customer. They prostrated themselves before his father and stood when Ghassan beckoned them to rise.

The Agnivanshi man spoke first. "Peace be upon you, my

king. I am humbled and honored to be in your presence." He jerked a thumb at the silk merchant, the pearls around his neck jangling. "I only beg your forgiveness for having dragged before you an unabashed liar and unrepentant thief!"

His father sighed as the silk merchant rolled his eyes. "Why don't you just explain the problem?"

"He agreed to sell me a half-dozen bales of silk for two barrels each of cinnamon and pepper—I even threw in three crates of mangos as a gesture of good faith." He whirled on the other merchant. "I delivered on my end, but by the time I returned home, half your silk had turned to smoke!"

The Tukharistani man shrugged. "I am merely an intermediary. I warned you that if you had problems with the product, you'd have to take it up with the supplier." He sniffed, unimpressed. "And your mangos of good faith were sour."

The Agnivanshi man bristled as if the merchant had insulted his mother. "*Liar!*"

Ghassan raised a hand. "Calm down." He turned his hawk-like gaze on the silk merchant. "Is what he says true?"

The merchant fidgeted. "It might be."

"Then pay him for the silk that disappeared. It's your responsibility to recover the loss from the suppliers. The Treasury will set the price. We'll leave the question of the mangos' acidity to God." He waved them away. "Next!"

The bickering merchants were replaced by a Sahrayn widow left destitute by her spendthrift husband. Ghassan immediately granted her a small pension, along with a spot for her young son in the Citadel. She was followed by a scholar requesting funds to research the incendiary properties of zahhak bladders (firmly denied), an appeal for help against a rukh savaging villages in western Daevastana, and several more accusations of fraud—one including knock-off Nahid potions with some rather embarrassing results.

Hours later, the complaints were a blur, a stream of demands—

some so utterly nonsensical Ali wanted to shake the petitioner. The sun had risen past the wooden window screens, the audience chamber growing warm, and Ali swayed on his feet, staring longingly at the cushion he'd refused.

None of it seemed to bother his father. Ghassan was as calmly impassive now as he'd been when they walked in—helped, perhaps, by the goblet a wine bearer had been keeping studiously full. Ali had never known his father to be a patient man and yet he showed no irritation toward his subjects, listening as intently to destitute widows as to wealthy nobles arguing over vast tracts of land. Truthfully . . . Ali was impressed.

But by God, did he want it to end.

When the light in the oil lamp finally snuffed out, it was all Ali could do not to drop to the floor in prostration. His father rose from his throne and was promptly swallowed by a crowd of scribes and ministers. Ali didn't mind; he was eager to escape for a cup of tea so strong it could hold a spoon upright. He headed for the exit.

"Qaid?"

Ali paid no mind to the voice until the man called again, and then he realized with some embarrassment that he was now Qaid. He turned to see a short Geziri man behind him. He wore the uniform of the Royal Guard, a black-hemmed turban indicating he was a military secretary. He had a well-trimmed beard and kind gray eyes. Ali didn't recognize him, but that wasn't surprising. There was an entire section of the Royal Guard dedicated to the palace, and if the man was a secretary, it might have been decades since he trained in the Citadel.

The man promptly touched his heart and brow in the Geziri salute. "Peace be upon you, Qaid. I'm sorry to bother you."

After hours of civilian complaints, a fellow Geziri warrior was a welcome sight. Ali smiled. "No bother at all. How can I help you?"

The secretary held out a thick roll of scrolls. "These are records of those suspected in manufacturing the faulty carpets that crashed in Babili."

Ali stared at him in utter incomprehension. "What?"

The secretary narrowed his eyes. "The Babili incident . . . the one whose survivors your father just granted compensation. He ordered us to arrest their manufacturers and seize the remaining stock of carpets before they're sold."

Ali dimly remembered something like that being mentioned. "Oh . . . of course." He reached for the scroll.

The other man held back. "Maybe I should give it to your secretary," he said delicately. "Forgive me, my prince, but you look a little . . . overwhelmed."

Ali cringed. He hadn't realized it was that obvious. "I don't have a secretary."

"Then who took notes for you during today's session?" Alarm rose in the other man's voice. "There were at least a dozen matters that pertained to the Royal Guard."

I was supposed to have someone take notes? Ali wracked his brain. Wajed had thoroughly explained Ali's new responsibilities before he left for Ta Ntry, but shocked by Anas's execution and the revelation about the weapons, Ali had struggled to pay attention.

"No one," he confessed. Ali glanced at the sea of scribes—surely one of them would have a transcript of today's session.

The other man cleared his throat. "If I may be so bold, Qaid . . . I typically take notes for myself regarding Citadel matters. I would gladly share them with you. And though I'm sure you would rather appoint a relative or member of the nobility as your secretary, if you need someone in the mean—"

"Yes," Ali cut in, relieved. "Please . . . ," he trailed off with some embarrassment. "I'm sorry. I don't think I asked your name."

The secretary touched his heart again. "Rashid ben Salkh,

my prince." His eyes sparkled. "I look forward to working with you."

ALI FELT BETTER AS HE HEADED BACK TO HIS QUAR-ters. His attire and failure to take notes aside, he didn't think he'd done terribly at court.

But, by God, those eyes . . . It was bad enough to stand and listen to inane petitions for hours; being examined by thousands of strangers while doing so was torture. He could hardly blame his father for drinking.

A palace guard bowed as Ali approached. "Peace be upon you, Prince Alizayd." He opened the door for Ali, then stepped aside.

His siblings might have tried to find Ali simple accommodations, but it was still a palace apartment, twice the size of the barracks he'd once shared with two dozen junior cadets. The bedroom was plain but large, containing the overly soft bed and the single chest of belongings he'd brought from the Citadel pushed against the wall. Attached to the bedroom was an office ringed in bookshelves already half filled—improved access to the Royal Library was the one benefit of palace living Ali intended to make use of.

He entered the room and slipped off his sandals. His apartment faced the wildest corner of the harem gardens, a verdant jungle complete with hooting monkeys and shrieking mynah birds. A covered marble pavilion lined with swings overlooked the cool waters of the rushing canal.

Ali unwound his turban. The late-afternoon light filtered in through the sheer linen curtains, and it was mercifully quiet. He crossed the carpet to his desk and rifled through the stacks of paperwork: crime reports, appropriation requests, invitations to a countless number of social events he had no intention of attending, oddly personal notes requesting favors, pardons . . . Ali quickly sorted it, discarding anything that sounded unnecessary or ridiculous and putting the more important papers in order.

The sparkle of the canal caught his eye, tempting him. Though his mother had taught him to swim as a child, it had been years since Ali had last done so, embarrassed to take part in a hobby so strongly associated with the Ayaanle—and one that was viewed with revulsion and horror by many in his father's tribe.

But there was no one around to see him now. He loosened his collar, reaching for the bottom of his shirt as he headed for the pavilion.

Ali stopped. He backed up to glance again through the open archway leading to the next room, but his eyes hadn't deceived him.

There were two women waiting in his bed.

They burst into laughter. "I think he's finally spotted us," said one of the women with a grin. She lay on her stomach, delicate ankles crossed overhead. Ali's eyes took in her layers of sheer skirts, soft curves, and dark hair before he quickly fixed his eyes on her face.

Not that it helped; she was beautiful. Shafit; that was clear from her rounded ears and dull brown skin. Her eyes were lined with kohl and bright with amusement. She rose from the bed, her ankle bells tinkling as she approached. She bit a painted lip, and Ali's heart started to race.

"We were wondering how long it would take you to look past all your papers," she teased. She was suddenly before him, her fingers trailing the inside of his wrist.

Ali swallowed. "I think there's been some sort of mistake."

She smiled again. "No mistake, my prince. We were sent to welcome you properly to the palace." She reached for the knot of his waist-wrap.

Ali stepped back so fast he nearly tripped. "Please . . . that's not necessary."

"Oh, Leena, do stop scaring the boy." The second woman

stood, moving into the sunlight. Ali went cold, the ardor he'd been struggling to check instantly gone.

It was one of the Daeva courtesans from Turan's tavern.

She walked forward with far more grace than the shafit girl, her liquid black eyes locked on his face. There didn't seem to be any recognition there, but the night came flooding back to Ali: the smoky tavern, the blade bursting through the guard's throat, Anas's hand on his shoulder.

The way his scream had abruptly ended in the arena.

The courtesan's gaze swept over him. "I like him," she said to the other woman. "He looks sweeter than they say." She gave him a gentle smile. Gone was the laughing woman enjoying a night out with friends; she was all business now.

"There's no need to be so nervous, my prince," she added softly. "Our master desires only your satisfaction."

Her words cut through the fog of fear and desire clouding Ali's mind, but before he could question her, there was another feminine laugh from the direction of the pavilion—this one all too familiar.

"Well . . . it certainly didn't take you much time to settle in."

Ali jerked away from the courtesan as his sister entered the room. The other women instantly fell to their knees.

Zaynab's gray-gold eyes sparkled with the malicious delight only a sibling's could hold. She was less than a decade older than Ali, and as teenagers they could have passed for twins though their mother's sharp cheeks and elongated features suited Zaynab far better. His sister was dressed in Ayaanle fashion today, a dark purple and gold gown with a matching head wrap embroidered in pearls. Gold ringed her wrists and neck, and jewels glittered in her ears; even in the privacy of the harem, Ghassan's only daughter looked the part of a princess.

"Forgive the interruption." She sauntered farther into the room. "We came to make sure court hadn't swallowed you alive, but clearly you need no help." She dropped onto his bed and kicked at the blanket that was neatly folded on the floor with a roll of her eyes. "Don't tell me you slept on the ground, Alizayd."

"I—"

The second part of "we" entered the room before Ali could finish his protest. Muntadhir looked more rakish than usual, his dishdasha unbuttoned at the collar and his curly hair uncovered. He grinned at the sight before him. "*Two?* Don't you think you ought to pace yourself, Zaydi?"

Ali was happy his siblings were enjoying themselves at his expense. "That's not what this is," he snapped. "I didn't tell them to come here!"

"No?" The amusement left Muntadhir's face, and he glanced at the courtesans kneeling on the floor. "Rise, please. There's no need for that."

"Peace be upon you, Emir," the Daeva courtesan murmured as she stood.

"And upon you peace." Muntadhir smiled, but the expression didn't meet his eyes. "I know I resisted the urge, so tell me . . . who requested that my little brother receive such a delightful welcome home?"

The two women exchanged a look, their playful attitude gone. The Daeva courtesan finally spoke again, her voice hesitant. "The grand wazir."

Instantly outraged, Ali opened his mouth, but Muntadhir raised his hand, cutting him off.

"Please thank Kaveh for the gesture, but I fear I'll have to interrupt." Muntadhir nodded at the door. "You can go."

Both women offered muted salaams and then hurried out.

Muntadhir glanced at their sister. "Zaynab, would you mind? I think Ali and I need to talk."

"He grew up in a Citadel full of men, Dhiru . . . I think he's had 'the talk.'" Zaynab laughed at her joke but rose from the bed, ignoring the annoyed look Ali shot in her direction. She touched his shoulder as she passed. "Do *try* and stay out of trouble, Ali. Wait at least a week before launching any holy wars. And don't be a stranger," she shot back over her shoulder as she headed toward the garden. "I expect you to come listen to me gossip at least once a week."

Ali ignored that, immediately turning for the doors leading to the palace. "You'll excuse me, akhi. Clearly, I need to have words with the grand wazir."

Muntadhir stepped in front of him. "And what are you going to tell him?"

"To keep his fire-worshipping whores to himself!"

Muntadhir raised a dark eyebrow. "And how do you think that will play?" he asked. "The teenage son of the king—already rumored to be some sort of religious fanatic—berating one of the most-respected Daeva men in the city, a man who's loyally served his father for decades? And over what—a gift most young men would be delighted to receive?"

"I'm not like that, and Kaveh knows—"

"Yes, he does," Muntadhir finished. "He knows very well, and I'm sure he's made certain to situate himself someplace where there will be a great number of witnesses to the scene you're ready to cause."

Ali was taken aback. "What are you saying?"

His brother gave him a dark look. "That he's trying to upset you, Ali. He wants you away from Abba, ideally away from Daevabad and back in Am Gezira, where you can't do anything to hurt his people."

Ali threw up his hands. "I haven't done anything to his people!"

"Not yet." Muntadhir crossed his arms over his chest. "But you religious types hardly make a secret of your feelings toward the Daevas. Kaveh is afraid of you; he probably thinks your presence here is a threat. That you'll turn the Royal Guard into some sort of morality police and have them beating up all men wearing ash marks." Muntadhir shrugged. "Honestly, I can't blame him; the Daevas tend to suffer when people like you come near power."

Ali leaned against his desk, taken aback by his brother's words. He was already trying to fill in for Wajed while hiding his involvement with the Tanzeem. He didn't feel capable of matching political wits with a paranoid Kaveh right now.

He rubbed his temples. "What do I do?"

Muntadhir took a seat in the window. "You could try sleeping with the next courtesan he sends you," he said with a grin. "Oh, Zaydi, don't give me that look. It would throw Kaveh for a loop." Muntadhir absentmindedly twirled a bit of flame around his fingers. "Until he turned around and denounced you as a hypocrite, of course."

"You're not leaving me with a lot of options."

"You could try not stomping around like the royal version of the Tanzeem," Muntadhir offered. "Actually, I don't know . . . attempt to befriend a Daeva? Jamshid's been wanting to learn how to use a zulfiqar. Why don't you give him lessons?"

Ali was incredulous. "You want me to teach *Kaveh's son* how to use a Geziri weapon?"

"He's not just Kaveh's son," Muntadhir argued, sounding a little irritated. "He's my best friend, and you're the one who asked me for advice."

Ali sighed. "Sorry. You're right. It's just been a long day." He shifted against the desk, promptly knocking over one of his carefully arranged stacks of paperwork. "A day with no sign of ending anytime soon."

"Maybe I should have left you with the women. They might have improved your attitude." Muntadhir rose from the window. "I just wanted to make sure you survived your first day at court, but you look like you have a lot of work. At least think on what I've said about the Daevas. You know I'm only trying to help."

"I know." Ali exhaled. "Were your negotiations successful?"

"My what?"

"Your negotiations with the Tukharistani minister," Ali reminded. "Abba said you were trying to reduce a debt."

Muntadhir's eyes brightened with amusement. He pressed his lips together as if fighting a grin. "Yes. She proved to be very . . . accommodating."

"That's good." Ali retrieved his papers, straightening the stacks on his desk. "Let me know if you'd like me to check the numbers you agreed on. I know mathematics isn't your—" He stopped, surprised by the kiss Muntadhir suddenly planted on his forehead. "What?"

Muntadhir only shook his head, exasperated affection in his face. "Oh, akhi . . . you're going to get eaten alive here."

9

NAHRI

Cold. That was her first thought upon waking. Nahri shivered violently and curled into a ball, pulling her blanket over her head and tucking her frozen hands under her chin. Could it be morning already? Her face felt damp, and the tip of her nose was completely numb.

What she saw when she opened her eyes was so strange, she immediately sat up.

Snow.

It had to be; it matched Dara's description perfectly. The ground was covered by a thin blanket of white with only a few dark patches of soil visible. The very air seemed more still than usual, frozen into silence by the snow's arrival.

Dara was still gone, as were the horses. Nahri wrapped her blanket around her shoulders and fed the dying fire the driest branch she could find, trying not to let her nerves get the better of her. Maybe he'd just taken the horses to graze.

Or maybe he really did leave. She forced down a few bites of cold stew and then started packing up her meager supplies. There was something about the silence and lonely beauty of the fresh snowfall that made the solitude more intense.

The stale bread and spicy stew left her mouth dry. Nahri searched their small campsite, but the waterskin was nowhere to be seen. Now she did start to panic. Would Dara really leave her with no water?

That bastard. That smug, self-righteous bastard. She tried to melt some snow in her hands but only got a mouthful of mud. She spat, growing annoyed, and then pulled on her boots. Dara be damned. She'd noticed a stream in the sparse woods behind their camp. If he wasn't back by the time she returned, well . . . she'd have to start making other plans.

She stomped toward the forest. *If I die out here, I hope I come back as a ghoul. I will haunt that arrogant, wine-soaked daeva until the Day of Judgment.*

As she walked deeper into the forest, the sounds of warbling birds faded. It was dark; the tall, ancient trees blocked what little light penetrated the cloudy morning sky. Unbending pine needles held up tiny cups of crisp snow in the air all around her.

A thin layer of ice covered the rushing stream. She broke it easily with a rock and knelt to drink. The water was so cold it made her teeth ache, but she forced a few mouthfuls down and splashed some on her face, her entire body trembling. She longed for Cairo, its heat and crowds the perfect remedy to this cold, lonely place.

A flash drew her attention back to the stream, and she glanced down to see a bright fish dash behind a submerged rock. It briefly reappeared to fight the swift current, its scales sparkling in the dim light.

Nahri pressed her palms against the muddy bank and leaned closer. The fish was a striking silver color with brilliant blue and green bands crossing its body. While it was only about the length of her hand, it looked plump, and she suddenly wondered how it would taste seared over her weak campfire.

The fish must have guessed her intent. Just as she was considering the best way to catch it, it vanished behind the rocks again, and a breeze blew straight through her thin headscarf. She shivered and stood; the fish wasn't worth staying here any longer.

She returned to the forest's edge and then stopped.

Dara was back.

She doubted he saw her. He stood between the horses with his back to the trees, and as Nahri watched, he pressed his brow against one's fuzzy cheek, giving its nose an affectionate scratch.

She wasn't moved by the gesture. Dara probably thought even animals were superior to shafit like her.

But there was visible relief in his face when she entered their campsite. "Where were you?" he demanded. "I was worried that something ate you."

Nahri pushed past him toward her horse. "Sorry to disappoint." She grabbed the edge of her saddle and shoved one foot into the stirrup.

"Let me help—"

"Don't touch me." Dara jerked away, and Nahri heaved herself awkwardly into the saddle.

"Listen . . . ," he started again, sounding admonished. "About last night. I was drunk. It's been a long time since I've had company." He chewed his lip. "I suppose I forgot my manners."

She whirled on him. "Your *manners*? You go into a wild rant about the djinn—you know, the ones who stopped the indiscriminate butchery of shafit like me, insult me when I show some relief at the news of their victory, and then announce you're planning to leave me at the gates of that damn city anyway? And you're blaming it all on wine and your lack of *manners*?" Nahri scoffed. "By the Most High, you're so arrogant you can't even apologize properly."

"Fine. *I'm sorry*," he said, exaggerating the words. "Is that what you wish to hear? You are the first shafit I've ever spent time with. I didn't realize . . ." He cleared his throat, playing nervously with the reins. "Nahri, you have to understand that when I was growing up, we were taught that the Creator himself would punish us if our race continued breaking Suleiman's laws. That another human would rise to strip away our powers and upend our lives if we didn't bring the other tribes into line. Our leaders said the shafit were soulless, anything out of their mouths a deception." He shook his head. "I never questioned it. No one did." He hesitated, his eyes bright with regret. "When I think of some of the things I've done . . ."

"I think I've heard enough." She jerked the reins out of his hands. "Let's just go. The sooner we get to Daevabad, the sooner we're done with each other."

She kicked her horse a bit harder than usual, and it gave an annoyed snort before rushing into a trot. Nahri clutched the reins and squeezed her legs, praying her rash move wouldn't land her on the ground. She was a terrible rider, while Dara seemed to have been born in the saddle.

She tried to relax, knowing from experience that the most comfortable way to ride was to let her body follow the animal's motions, leaving her hips loose to sway instead of bouncing all over the place. Behind her, she heard Dara's horse pounding the frozen ground.

He quickly caught up. "Oh, don't run off like that. I said I was sorry. Besides . . ." She heard his voice catch, and when he spoke again, she could barely hear him. "I will take you to Daevabad."

"Yes, I know. To the gates. We've been over this."

Dara shook his head. "No. I will take you *into* Daevabad. I will escort you to the king myself."

Nahri immediately pulled on her reins to slow her horse. "Is this a trick?"

"No. I swear on my parents' ashes. I will take you to the king."

Macabre oath aside, she found it hard to trust his rather abrupt change of heart. "Will I not embarrass the legacy of your precious Nahids?"

He dropped his gaze to study his reins, looking ashamed. "It matters not. In truth, I cannot predict how the djinn will react and . . ." A blush stole into his cheeks. "I could not bear it if something happened to you. I would never forgive myself."

She opened her mouth to mock his reluctant affection for the "dirt-blood thief" and then stopped, struck by the soft edge to his voice and the way he was anxiously twisting his ring. Dara looked as nervous as a prospective bridegroom. He was telling the truth.

Nahri stared at him, catching sight of the sword at his waist. His silver bow gleamed in the morning light. No matter the disturbing things that occasionally came out of his mouth, he was a good ally to have.

She'd be lying if she said her gaze didn't linger a moment longer than necessary. Her heart skipped a beat. *Ally*, she reminded herself. *Nothing more.*

"And how do *you* expect to be greeted in Daevabad?" she asked. Dara looked up, a wry smile on his face. "You mentioned being locked up in a dungeon," she reminded him.

"Then how fortunate I travel with Cairo's premier picker of locks." He gave her a wicked grin before spurring his horse. "Try to keep up. It seems I cannot afford to lose you now."

THEY TRAVELED THROUGHOUT THE MORNING, racing along the frost-encrusted plains, their horses' hooves loud against the frozen ground. The snow cleared, but the wind kicked up, sweeping rolling gray clouds over the southern horizon and whipping through Nahri's garments. With the snow gone, she could see the blue mountains surrounding them, capped by ice and belted by dark forests, the trees growing sparser as the rocky cliffs rose. At one point, they startled a group of wild goats grown fat on grass, with thick, matted coats and sharply curved horns.

She eyed them hungrily. "Do you think you could get one?" she asked Dara. "All you do with that bow of yours is polish it."

He glanced at the goats with a frown. "Get one? Why?" His confusion turned to revulsion. "You mean to *eat*?" He made a disgusted sound. "Absolutely not. We don't eat meat."

"What? Why not?" Meat had been a rare luxury on her limited income in Cairo. "It's delicious!"

"It's unclean." Dara shuddered. "Blood pollutes. No Daeva would consume such a thing. And especially not a Banu Nahida."

"A Banu Nahida?"

"The title we give to female Nahid leaders. A position of honor," he added, a little chiding in his voice. "Of responsibility."

"So you're telling me I should hide my kebabs?"

Dara sighed.

They kept riding, but Nahri's legs were aching by the afternoon. She twisted in her saddle to stretch her cramping muscles and pulled the blanket tighter, wishing for a cup of Khayzur's hot spiced tea. They'd been traveling for hours; certainly it was time for a break. She kicked her heels against the horse's side, trying to close the distance between her and Dara so she could suggest they stop.

Annoyed by his inexperienced rider, her horse snorted and skidded to the left before galloping forward and passing Dara.

He laughed. "Having some problems?"

Nahri cursed and yanked back on the reins, pulling her horse into a walk. "I think it hates—" She stopped speaking, her eyes drawn toward a dark crimson smudge in the sky. "Ya, Dara . . . have I gone mad or is there a bird the size of a camel flying toward us?"

The daeva whirled around, then pulled to a stop with a curse, snatching the reins from her hands. "Suleiman's eye. I don't think it's seen us yet, but . . ." He looked worried. "There's no place to hide."

"Hide?" she asked, lowering her voice when Dara hushed her. "Why? It's just a bird."

"No, it's a rukh. Bloodthirsty creatures; they'll eat anything they find."

"Anything? You mean like us?" She groaned when he nodded. "Why does everything in your world want to *eat* us?"

Dara carefully pulled his bow free as he watched the rukh circle the forest. "I think it's found our camp."

"Is that bad?"

"They have an excellent sense of smell. It will be able to track us." Dara inclined his head to the north, toward the thickly forested mountains. "We need to reach those trees. Rukh are too large to hunt in the forest."

Nahri glanced back at the bird, which had drifted closer to the ground, and then at the edge of the forest. It was impossibly far. "We'll never make it."

Dara pulled off his turban, cap, and robe and tossed them to her. Puzzled, Nahri watched as he secured his sword to his waist. "Don't be such a pessimist. I have an idea. Something I heard about in a story." He nocked one of his gleaming silver arrows. "Just stay low and hold on to your horse. Don't look back, and don't stop. No matter what you see." He pulled on her reins, jerked her horse in the right direction, and urged both animals into a trot.

She swallowed, her heart in her throat. "What about you?"

"Don't worry about me."

Before she could protest, Dara smacked her horse's rump hard. She could feel the heat of his hand from her saddle; the animal whinnied in protest and bolted toward the forest.

Nahri threw herself forward, one hand clutching the saddle

and the other wrapped in the horse's damp mane. It took every bit of self-control not to scream. Her body bounced wildly, and she tightened her legs, desperately hoping that she wouldn't be thrown off. She caught a brief glimpse of the racing ground before squeezing her eyes shut.

A long cry pierced the air, so high-pitched it seemed to tear right through her. Unable to cover her ears, Nahri could only pray. *Oh, Merciful One*, she begged, *please don't let this thing eat me.* She'd survived a body-possessing ifrit, ravenous ghouls, and a deranged daeva. This couldn't end with her being gobbled up by an overgrown pigeon.

Nahri peeked up from the horse's mane, but the forest didn't look much closer. Her horse's hooves beat against the ground, and she could hear it panting. And where was Dara?

The rukh screeched again, sounding furious. Worried about the daeva, she ignored his warning and glanced back.

"God preserve me." The whispered prayer came unbidden to her lips at the sight of the rukh. She suddenly knew why she'd never heard of them.

No one survived to tell the tale.

Camel size was a terrible understatement; larger than Yaqub's shop and with a wingspan that would have covered the length of her street in Cairo, the monstrous bird probably snacked on camels. It had ebony eyes the size of platters and glittering feathers the color of wet blood. Its long black beak ended in a sharply curved tip. It looked big enough to swallow her whole, and it was closing in. There was no way she'd make it to the forest.

Dara suddenly veered into view behind her. His boots jammed against the stirrups, he was damn near standing on the horse, turned around to face the rukh. He drew back his bow, unleashing an arrow that hit the beast just below its eye. The rukh jerked its head back and shrieked again. At least a dozen silver arrows pierced its body, but they didn't slow it in the slightest. Dara shot it twice more in the face, and the rukh dove for him, its massive talons outstretched.

"Dara!" she screamed as the daeva made a sharp eastward turn. The rukh followed, apparently preferring a reckless daeva to a fleeing human.

There was little chance he could hear her over the rukh's enraged shrieks, but she couldn't help but shout, "You're going the wrong way!" There was nothing east but flat plains—was he trying to get himself killed?

Dara shot the creature once more and then threw his bow and quiver away. He pulled himself into a squatting position on the horse's saddle and cradled his sword to his chest with one arm.

The rukh cried out in triumph as it closed in on the daeva. It opened its talons wide.

"No!" Nahri screamed as the rukh snatched up the horse and Dara, as easily as a hawk might seize a mouse. It rose in the air while the horse screamed and kicked, and then veered back south.

She yanked hard on the reins to pull her racing horse around. It reared, trying to throw her off, but she held on, and it turned. "Yalla, go! Go!" she shouted, reverting to Arabic in panic. She kicked hard, and it bolted after the rukh.

The bird soared away with Dara clutched in its talons. It cried out again and then tossed both Dara and his horse high in the air. It opened its mouth wide.

It was only seconds, but the moment between seeing Dara thrown in the air and seeing him vanish seemed to last an eternity, twisting something deep in her chest. The rukh caught the horse again with one foot, but the daeva was nowhere to be seen.

She searched the sky, expecting him to reappear, to flit into existence like the wine he conjured up. This was Dara, the magical being who traveled by sandstorms and saved her from a pack of ghouls. He had to have a plan; he couldn't just vanish down the gullet of some bloodthirsty bird.

But he didn't reappear.

Tears pricked her eyes, her mind knowing what her heart denied. Her horse slowed, balking at her kicks. It clearly had more sense than she did; the only thing they could offer the rukh was dessert.

She could see the crimson bird silhouetted against the mountains; it hadn't gotten very far but suddenly shot up in the sky, frantically flapping its wings. As she watched, it started to fall and then momentarily righted itself, letting out a screech that sounded more frightened than triumphant. Then it fell again, tumbling through the air and crashing to the frozen ground.

The force of the distant impact shuddered through her horse. Nahri wanted to scream. Nothing could survive a fall like that.

She didn't let her horse slow until they reached the shallow crater the rukh's body had smashed into the ground. She tried to steel herself but had to look away from Dara's dead horse. Her own animal startled and fussed. Nahri fought for control as she approached the rukh's massive body. It towered over them, one enormous wing crumpled under its dead weight. Its glittering feathers were twice her height.

She began to circle the bird, but the daeva was nowhere to be seen. Nahri choked back a sob. Had it really eaten him? That might have been faster than crashing to the ground, but—

A cold, sharp feeling cut through her and she reeled, overcome with emotion. She caught sight of the creature's bent head, black blood pouring from its mouth. The sight of it filled her with rage, displacing her grief and despair. She grabbed her dagger, overcome by the irrational need to tear at its eyes and rip out its throat.

Its neck twitched.

Nahri jumped, and her horse backed up. She tightened her grip on the reins, ready to flee, and then the neck twitched again . . . no, it *bulged*, like something was inside.

She'd already slipped off her horse when a dark blade finally emerged from inside the rukh's neck, laboriously cutting a long vertical gash before being dropped to the ground. The daeva followed, washed out in a wave of black blood. He collapsed to his knees.

"Dara!" Nahri ran and kneeled at his side, throwing her arms around him before her mind caught up with her actions. The rukh's hot blood soaked through her clothes.

"I . . ." He spat a gob of black blood onto the ground before shaking free of her grasp and climbing laboriously to his feet. He wiped the blood from his eyes, his hands trembling. "Fire," he rasped. "I need a fire."

Nahri looked around, but the ground was covered in wet snow, and there were no branches in sight. "What can I do?" she cried as the daeva gasped for air. He collapsed to the ground again. "Dara!"

She reached for him. "No," he protested. "Don't touch me . . ." He dug his fingers into the ground, sending up sparks that were quickly extinguished by the icy dirt. A terrible sucking sound came from his mouth.

She crept closer despite his warning, aching to do something as a deep shudder ran through his body. "Let me heal you."

He slapped her hand away. "No. The ifrit—"

"There are no damned ifrit here!"

Beads of ash rolled down his face. Before she could reach for him again, he suddenly cried out.

It was as if his very body momentarily turned to smoke. His eyes grew dim, and as they both watched, his hands briefly translucent. And though Nahri knew nothing about how daeva bodies worked, she could tell from the panic in his face that this was not normal.

"Creator, no," he whispered, staring in horror at his hands. "Not now . . ." He glanced up at Nahri, a mixture of fear and sadness in his expression. "Oh, little thief, I'm so sorry."

He had no sooner apologized than his entire body shimmered like steam, and he fell against the ground.

"Dara!" Nahri knelt at his side and checked him over, her instincts kicking in. She could see nothing but slick black blood, whether the daeva's or the rukh's, she had no idea. "Dara, talk to me!" she begged. "Tell me what to do!" She tried to pull open his robe, hoping to see some type of wound she could heal.

The hem crumbled into ash. Nahri gasped, trying not to panic as the daeva's skin took on the same hue. Was he going to turn to dust in her arms?

His skin briefly firmed up even as his body grew light. His eyes fluttered shut, and Nahri went cold. "No," she said, brushing the ash from his closed eyes. *Not like this, not after everything we've been through.* She wracked her memory, trying to think of anything useful he'd told her about how the Nahids healed.

He had said they could undo poisons and curses, she remembered that. But he hadn't told her how. Did they have their own medicines, their own spells? Or did they do it by touch alone?

Well, touch was all she had. She pulled his shirt open and pressed her trembling hands against his chest. His skin was so cold it numbed her fingers. *Intent*, he had mentioned more than once. Intent was critical in magic.

She closed her eyes, focusing entirely on Dara.

Nothing. There was no heartbeat, no breath. She frowned, trying to sense anything wrong, trying to imagine him healthy and alert. Her fingers grew frosty, and she pressed them harder against his chest, his body twitching in response.

Something wet tickled her wrists, growing faster and thicker, like steam off a boiling pot. Nahri didn't move, keeping the image of a healthy Dara, his smile sly as always, firmly in her mind. His skin warmed a bit. *Please, let it be working,* she begged. *Please, Dara. Don't leave me.*

A sharp ache crept up from the base of her skull. She ignored the pain. Warm blood dripped from her nose, and she fought a wave of dizziness. The steam was coming more quickly. She felt his skin grow firm beneath her fingertips.

And then the first memory flashed before her eyes. A green plain, lush and entirely unfamiliar, sliced in half by a brilliant blue river. A young girl with eyes as black as obsidian. She held out a badly constructed wooden bow.

"Look, Daru!"

"A masterpiece!" I exclaim, and she beams. My little sister, ever the warrior. The Creator help the man she marries . . .

Nahri shook her head, dispelling the memory. She needed to remain focused. Dara's skin was finally growing hot again, the muscles solidifying under her hands.

A dazzling court, the palace walls covered in precious metals and jewels. I breathe in the scent of sandalwood and bow. "Does this please you, my master?" I ask, my smile ingratiating as always. I snap my fingers, and a silver chalice appears in my hand. "The finest drink of the ancients as requested." I hand the beaming human fool the chalice and wait for him to die, the drink little more than concentrated hemlock. Perhaps my next master will be more careful in the wording of his wishes.

Nahri shook free of the horrifying image. She bent down to concentrate. She just needed a little more time . . .

But it was too late. The darkness behind her closed eyes swept away again, replaced by a ruined city surrounded by rocky hills. A sliver of moon splashed dim light on broken masonry.

I thrash against the ifrit, dragging my feet on the ground as they pull me toward the sinkhole, the remains of an ancient well. Its dark water glimmers, hinting at hidden depths.

"No!" I scream, for once not caring about my honor. "Please! Don't do this!"

The two ifrit laugh. "Come now, General Afshin!" The female offers a mock salute. "Don't you want to live forever?"

I try to struggle, but the curse has already weakened me. They bind my wrists with rope, not bothering with iron, and then wrap the rope around one of the heavy stones lining the well.

"No!" I beg, as they haul me over the edge. "Not now! You don't under—" The brick hits me in the stomach. Their black smiles are the last thing I see before the dark water closes over my face.

The brick plummets to the bottom of the well, dragging me along headfirst. I frantically twist my wrists, clawing and ripping at my skin. No, I can't die like this. Not with the curse still on me!

The stone thuds against the bottom, my body bouncing against the rope. My lungs burn, the press of dark water against my skin terrifying. I follow the rope, trying desperately to find the knot tying it to the stone. My own magic is lost to me, the ifrit's curse coursing through my blood, preparing to seize me as soon as I breathe my last.

I'm going to be a slave. The thought rings through my mind as I fumble for the knot. When I next open my eyes, it will be to look upon the human master to whose whims I'll be entirely beholden. Horror surges through me. No, Creator, no. Please.

The knot won't budge. My chest is collapsing, my head spinning. One breath, what I would do for just one breath . . .

There was a scream from another world, a faraway world on a snowy plain, shouting a strange name that meant nothing.

The water finally pries past my clenched jaws, pouring down my throat. A bright light blossoms before me, as lush and green as the valleys of my homeland. It beckons, warm and welcoming.

And then Nahri was gone.

"NAHRI, WAKE UP! NAHRI!"

Dara's terrified cries tugged at her mind, but Nahri ignored them, warm and comfortable in the thick blackness that surrounded her. She pushed away the hand shaking her shoulder, settling deeper into the hot coals and savoring the tickle of fire licking up her arms.

Fire?

Nahri had no sooner opened her eyes and seen a set of dancing flames than she shrieked and jumped up. She batted her arms and the fiery tendrils shimmied away, dropping to the ground like snakes and melting into the snow.

"It's okay! It's okay!"

Dara's voice barely registered as she frantically swept her body. But instead of scorched flesh and burned clothes, she found only normal skin. Her tunic barely felt warm to the touch. What in the name of all . . . She glanced up, giving the daeva a wild look. "Did you light me on *fire*?"

"You wouldn't wake!" he protested. "I thought it might help." His face was paler than usual, the crossed wing and arrow tattoo on his face standing out like charcoal. And his eyes were brighter, closer to how they'd looked in Cairo. But he was standing up, healthy and whole, and mercifully not translucent.

The rukh . . . she remembered, her head feeling like she'd had too much wine. She rubbed her temples, unsteady on her feet. *I healed him and then . . .*

She gagged, the memory of water pouring down her throat strong enough to make her sick. But it hadn't been her throat, hadn't been her memory. She swallowed, taking in the sight of the anxious daeva again.

"God be merciful," she whispered. "You're dead. I saw you die . . . I felt you *drown*."

The devastated shadow that overtook his face was confirmation enough. Nahri gasped and instinctively stepped back, bumping into the still warm body of the rukh.

No breath, no heartbeat. Nahri closed her eyes, everything coming together too fast. "I-I don't understand," she stammered. "Are you . . . are you some sort of ghost?" The word sounded ridiculous to her ears even as its implication broke her heart. Her eyes were suddenly wet. "Are you even *alive*?"

"Yes!" The words tumbled out in a rush. "I mean, I-I think so. It's . . . it's complicated."

Nahri threw up her hands. "Whether or not you're alive shouldn't be *complicated*!" She turned away, linking her fingers behind her head and feeling wearier than she had at any point during their exhausting journey. She paced down the length of the rukh's belly. "I don't understand why every . . ." And then she stopped, distracted by the sight of something lashed to one of the rukh's massive talons.

She was at the rukh's foot in an instant, tearing the bundle from its ties. The black scrap of fabric was filthy and torn but the cheap coins were recognizable. As was the heavy gold ring tied to one end. The basha's ring. She untied both, holding the ring up in the sunlight.

Dara hurried toward her. "Don't touch that. Suleiman's eye, Nahri, not even you could want those. They're probably from its last victim."

"They're mine," she said softly, quiet horror taking grip of her heart. She rubbed the ring, remembering how it had cut her palm so many weeks ago. "They're from my home back in Cairo."

"What?" Dara stepped closer and snatched the headdress from her hands. "You must be mistaken." He turned the filthy fabric over and pressed it to his face, taking a deep breath.

"I'm not mistaken!" She dropped the ring, suddenly wanting nothing to do with it. "How is that possible?"

Dara lowered the headdress; there was panic in his bright eyes. "It was hunting us."

"You mean it belonged to the ifrit? They broke into my home?" Nahri asked, her voice rising. Her skin crawled at the thought of those creatures in her tiny stall, rifling through the few precious things she owned. And what if that hadn't been enough? What if they'd gone after her neighbors? After Yaqub? Her chest tightened.

"It wasn't an ifrit. The ifrit can't control rukhs."

"Then what can?" Nahri didn't like the cold stillness that had overtaken him.

"Peris." He threw the headdress to the ground, the movement sudden and violent. "The only creatures who can control ruhks are peris."

"Khayzur." She took a shaky breath. "But why?" she stammered. "I thought he liked me."

He shook his head. "Not Khayzur."

She couldn't believe his naiveté. "What other peris even know about me?" she pointed out. "And he rushed off after finding out about my Nahid heritage—probably to go tell his friends." She started walking toward the rukh's other leg. "I bet my teacup is tied over . . ."

"No." Dara reached for her hand. Nahri flinched, and he immediately pulled back, a flash of hurt in his face. "I . . . Forgive me." He swallowed and turned toward the horse. "I'll try not to touch you again. But we need to leave. Now."

The sadness in his voice cut her deeply. "Dara, I'm sorry. I didn't mean—"

"There's no time." He gestured for her to climb into the saddle, and she did so reluctantly, taking the bloody sword when he handed it to her.

"I will need to ride with you," he explained, pulling himself up and settling in behind her. "At least until we find another horse."

He kicked the horse into a trot and despite his promise, she fell back against his chest, momentarily taken aback by the smoky heat and warm press of his body. *He's not dead*, she tried to assure herself. *He can't be.*

He pulled the horse to an abrupt stop where he'd thrown his

bow and quiver. He raised his hands, and they flew to him like loyal sparrow hawks.

Nahri ducked as he swung the weapons over her head, looping both over his left shoulder. "So what do we do now?" She thought back to Khayzur's easy banter and Dara's quip about how the peri could rearrange the landscape with a single sweep of his wings.

"The only thing we can," he said, his breath soft against her ear. He snatched up the reins again, holding her tight. There was nothing affectionate or remotely romantic about the gesture; it was desperation, like a man clinging to a ledge.

"We run."

10

ALI

Ali squinted and tapped the delicate stem of the scales on the desk in front of him, aware of the expectant eyes of the other three men in the room. "They look even to me."

Rashid bent down to join him, the silver scale platters reflected in the military secretary's gray eyes. "It could be hexed," he offered in Geziriyya. He jerked his head in the direction of Soroush, the Daeva Quarter's muhtasib. "He might have come up with some type of curse that would weigh the coins in his favor."

Ali hesitated, glancing at Soroush. The muhtasib, the market official in charge of exchanging Daeva currency with the myriad others used in Daevabad, was trembling, his black gaze locked on the floor. Ali could see ash staining his fingertips; he'd been nervously touching the charcoal mark on his brow since they entered. Most religious Daevas wore such a mark. It was a sign of their devotion to the Nahids' ancient fire cult.

The man looked terrified, but Ali couldn't blame him—he had just been visited by the Qaid and two armed members of the Royal Guard for a surprise inspection.

Ali turned back to Rashid. "We have no evidence," he whispered back in Geziriyya. "I can't arrest a man with no evidence."

Before Rashid could respond, the door to the office swung open. The fourth man in the room, Abu Nuwas—Ali's very gruff and very large personal guard—was between the door and the prince in a moment, his zulfiqar drawn.

But it was only Kaveh, not looking particularly impressed by the enormous Geziri warrior. He peered under one of Abu Nuwas's large raised arms, his face turning sour when he met Ali's eyes. "Qaid," he greeted him flatly. "Do you mind telling your dog to back down?"

"It's fine, Abu Nuwas," Ali said before his guard could do something rash. "Let him in."

Kaveh stepped over the threshold. As he glanced between the glittering scales and the frightened muhtasib, a hint of anger crept into his voice. "What are you doing in my quarter?"

"There've been several reports of fraud coming out of here," Ali explained. "I was just examining the scales—"

"Examining the scales? Are you a wazir now?" Kaveh raised a hand to cut off Ali before he could reply. "Never mind . . . I've wasted enough time this morning looking for you." He beckoned to the door. "Come in, Mir e-Parvez, and give your report to the Qaid."

There was some inaudible muttering from the doorway.

Kaveh rolled his eyes. "I don't *care* what you heard. He doesn't have crocodile teeth, and he isn't going to eat you." Ali flinched, and Kaveh continued. "Forgive him, he's had a terrible fright at the hands of the djinn."

We are all djinn. Ali bit back the retort as the anxious merchant came forward. Mir e-Parvez was thickset and older, beardless like most Daeva. He was dressed in a gray tunic and loose dark trousers, the typical garb of Daeva men.

The merchant pressed his palms together in greeting but kept his gaze on the floor. His hands were shaking. "Forgive me, my prince. When I learned you were serving as Qaid, I-I did not want to trouble you."

"It's the Qaid's job to be troubled," Kaveh cut in, ignoring Ali's glare. "Just tell him what happened."

The other man nodded. "I run a shop outside the quarter selling fancy human goods," he started. His Djinnistani was broken, colored by a thick Divasti accent.

Ali raised his eyebrows, already sensing where this was going. The only "fancy human goods" a Daeva merchant would sell outside their quarter were human-made intoxicants. Most djinn had little tolerance for human spirits, and they were banned by the Holy Book anyway, so it was illegal to sell them in the rest of the city. The Daevas had no such qualms and freely traded in the stuff, peddling it to foreign tribesmen at greatly inflated prices.

The man continued. "I've had some trouble in the past with djinn. My windows smashed, they protest and spit when I pass by. I say nothing. I don't want trouble." He shook his head. "But last night, these men break into my shop while my son is there and smash my bottles and set fire to everything. When my son tried to stop them, they hit him and cut his face. They accused him of being a 'fire worshipper' and said he's leading djinn to sin!"

Not exactly false charges. Ali refrained from saying so, knowing Kaveh would go running to his father at the slightest whisper of injustice against his tribe. "Did you report this to the guard in your quarter?"

"Yes, Your Majesty," the merchant said, bungling his title, his Djinnistani growing worse as he got upset. "But they do nothing. This happens all the time and always nothing. They laugh or 'make report,' but nothing changes."

"There are not enough guards in the Daeva neighborhoods," Kaveh interrupted. "And not enough . . . diversity among them. I've been telling Wajed this for years."

"So you requested more soldiers from Wajed—just not ones that look like him," Ali replied, though he knew Kaveh had a point. The soldiers patrolling the markets were often the youngest, many straight from the sands of Am Gezira. They probably feared protecting a man like Mir e-Parvez was as much a sin as drinking his wares.

But there was no easy solution; the bulk of the military was Geziri, and they were already stretched thin. "Tell me, whose district do I take these soldiers from, Kaveh?" Ali pressed on. "Should the Tukharistanis go without so the Daevas feel safer selling liquor?"

"The allocation of the guard is not my realm of responsibility, Prince Alizayd. Maybe if you took a break from terrorizing my muhtasib . . ."

Ali straightened up and came around the table, cutting off Kaveh's sarcastic remark. Mir e-Parvez actually stepped back, giving Ali's coppery zulfiqar a nervous look.

By the Most High, were the rumors surrounding him really that bad? Judging from the look on the merchant's face, one would think Ali spent every other Friday slaughtering Daevas.

He sighed. "Your son is okay, I trust?"

The merchant blinked in surprise. "He . . . yes, my prince," he stammered. "He will recover."

"God be praised. Then I will speak to my men and see what we can do about improving security in your quarter. Go over the damages to your shop and submit the bill to my aide Rashid. The Treasury will cover—"

"The king will have to approve—" Kaveh started to say.

Ali raised a hand. "It will come from my accounts if necessary," he said firmly, knowing that would end any doubt. The fact that his Ayaanle grandfather gave a lavish yearly endowment to his royal grandson was an open secret. Ali normally found it embarrassing—he didn't need the money and knew his grandfather only did it to annoy his father. But in this instance, it worked to his advantage.

The Daeva merchant's eyes popped, and he dropped to the ground and pressed his ash-covered forehead against the carpet. "Oh, thank you, Your Majesty. May the flames burn brightly for you."

Ali fought a smile, bemused at the traditional Daeva blessing being bestowed upon him of all people. He suspected the merchant was going to present him with a rather hefty bill, but he was nonetheless pleased, sensing he'd handled the situation correctly. Maybe he could manage the role of Qaid after all.

"I trust we are done?" he asked Kaveh as Rashid opened the door. Movement caught his eye up ahead: two small boys armed with makeshift bows were playing along one of the fountains in the plaza. Each had an arrow in hand, and they were bashing them together like swords.

Kaveh followed his gaze. "Would you like to join them, Prince Alizayd? You're near enough in age, no?"

He remembered Muntadhir's warning. *Don't let him get under your skin.* "I dare not. They look far too fierce," he said calmly. He grinned to himself, ducking out from under the balustrade and into the bright sunshine, as Kaveh's smirk turned to a scowl. The sky was a cheerful blue, with only a few lacy white clouds dancing in from the east. It was another beautiful day in a string of beautiful days, warm and bright—a pattern most unlike Daevabad and strange enough to start attracting attention.

And the weather wasn't all that was odd. Ali heard rumors

that the Nahids' original fire altar, extinguished after Manizheh and Rustam—the siblings who'd been the last of their family—were murdered, had somehow relit itself in a locked room. An abandoned, weed-choked grove in the garden where one of them had liked to paint was suddenly orderly and flourishing, and just last week one of the shedu statues that framed the palace walls had turned up on top of the ziggurat's roof, its brass gaze focused on the lake as if awaiting a boat.

Then there was that mural of Anahid. Against Muntadhir's wishes, Ali had it destroyed. Yet he walked past it every few days, nagged by the sense that there was something alive beneath the ruined facade.

He glanced at Kaveh, wondering what the grand wazir made of the whispers coming from his superstitious tribe. Kaveh was an ardent devotee of the fire cult, and the Pramukh family and the Nahids had been close. Many of the plants and herbs used in traditional Nahid healing were grown on the Pramukhs' vast estates. Kaveh himself had originally come to Daevabad as a trade envoy but had risen quickly in Ghassan's court, becoming a trusted advisor even as he aggressively pushed for Daeva rights.

Kaveh spoke again. "I apologize if my girls made you nervous the other week. It was meant as a gesture of kindness."

Ali bit back the first retort that came to mind. And the second. He was unused to this type of verbal sparring. "Such . . . gestures are not to my taste, Grand Wazir," he finally said. "I would appreciate it if you remember that for the future."

Kaveh said nothing, but Ali could feel his cold stare upon him as they continued to walk. By the Most High, what had he done to earn this man's enmity? Could he truly think Ali's beliefs represented that much of a threat to his people?

It was an otherwise pleasant stroll, the Daeva Quarter a far lovelier sight when he wasn't dashing through it pursued by archers. The cobbled stones were perfectly even and swept. Cypress trees shadowed the main avenue, broken up by flower-filled fountains and potted barberry bushes. The stone buildings were finely polished, their thatched wooden screens neat and fresh—one would never guess that this neighborhood was among the oldest in the city. Ahead, a few elderly men were playing chatrang and sipping from little glass vials, probably filled with some human intoxicant. Two veiled women glided from the direction of the Grand Temple.

It was an idyllic scene, at odds with the filthy conditions in the rest of the city. Ali frowned. He'd have to see what was going on with Daevabad's sanitation. He turned toward Rashid. "Make me an appointment with—"

Something whizzed past Ali's right ear leaving a sharp sting. He let out a startled cry, instinctively reaching for his zulfiqar as he whirled around.

Standing on the edge of the fountain was one of the little boys he'd seen playing, the toy bow still in his grasp. Ali immediately dropped his hand. The boy looked at Ali with innocent black eyes; Ali saw he had used charcoal to draw a crooked black arrow on his cheek.

An Afshin arrow. Ali scowled. It was just like the fire worshippers to let their children run around pretending to be war criminals. He touched his ear, and came away with a smear of blood on his fingers.

Abu Nuwas pulled free his zulfiqar and stepped forward with a snarl, but Ali held him back. "Don't. He's just a boy."

Seeing that he wasn't going to be punished, the boy gave them a wicked grin and jumped off the fountain to flee down a twisting alley.

Kaveh's eyes were bright with mirth. Across the plaza, a veiled woman held a hand across her hidden mouth, though Ali could hear her giggle. The old men playing chatrang had their eyes fixed on their game pieces, but their mouths twitched in amusement. Ali's cheeks grew warm with embarrassment.

Rashid stepped up to him. "You *should* have the boy arrested, Qaid," he said quietly in Geziriyya. "He's young. Give him to the Citadel to be raised properly as one of us. Your ancestors used to do so all the time."

Ali paused, nearly taken in by Rashid's reasonable tone. And then he stopped. *How is that any different from purebloods stealing shafit children?* And the fact that he could do it, that Ali could snap his fingers and have a boy kidnapped from the only home he'd ever know, wrested from his parents and his people . . . ?

Well, it suddenly explained why someone like Kaveh might look upon him with such hostility.

Ali shook his head, uneasy. "No. Let's just go back to the Citadel."

"OH, MY LOVE, MY LIGHT, HOW YOU HAVE STOLEN my happiness!"

Ali let out a grumpy sigh. It was a beautiful night. A thin moon hung over Daevabad's dark lake, and stars twinkled in the cloudless sky. The air was fragrant with frankincense and jasmine. Before him played the city's finest musicians, at hand was a platter of food from the king's favored chef, and the dark eyes of the singer would have driven a dozen human men to their knees.

Ali was miserable. He fidgeted in his seat, keeping his gaze on the floor and trying to ignore the jingle of ankle bells and the girl's smooth voice singing of things that made his blood rise. He tugged at the stiff collar of the new silver dishdasha Muntadhir had forced him to wear. Embroidered with a dozen rows of seed pearls, it was tight on his throat.

His behavior didn't go unnoticed. "Your little brother doesn't appear to be having a good time, my emir." An even silkier female voice interrupted the singer, and Ali glanced up to meet Khanzada's coy smile. "Are my girls not to your liking, Prince Alizayd?"

"Don't take it personally, my light," Muntadhir interrupted, kissing the hennaed hand of the courtesan curled at his side. "He got shot in the face this morning by a child."

Ali threw his brother an annoyed look. "Do you have to keep bringing it up?"

"It's very funny."

Ali scowled, and Muntadhir lightly smacked his shoulder. "Ya, akhi, can you at least try to look less murderous? I invited you here so we could celebrate your promotion, not so you could terrify my friends." He gestured at the dozen or so men arrayed around them, a handpicked group of the wealthiest and most influential nobles in the city.

"You didn't invite me." Ali sulked. "You ordered me."

Muntadhir rolled his eyes. "You're part of Abba's court now, Zaydi." He switched to Geziriyya and lowered his voice. "Socializing with these people is part of it . . . hell, it's supposed to be a perk."

"You know how I feel about these"—Ali waved his hand at a nobleman giggling like a little girl, and the man abruptly shut up—"*debaucheries*."

Muntadhir sighed. "You need to stop talking like that, akhi." He nodded at the platter. "Why don't you eat something? Maybe the weight of some food in your stomach will drag you off your high horse."

Ali grumbled but obeyed, leaning forward to take a small glass of sour tamarind sherbet. He knew Muntadhir was just trying to be kind, to ease his awkward, Citadel-raised little brother into court life, but Khanzada's salon made Ali terribly uncomfortable. A place like this was the epitome of the wickedness Anas had wanted to eradicate in Daevabad.

Ali stole a glance at the courtesan as she leaned in to whisper in Muntadhir's ear. Khanzada was said to be the most skilled dancer in the city, hailing from a family of acclaimed Agnivanshi illusionists. She was stunning, Ali would admit that. Even Muntadhir, his handsome older brother famous for leaving a string of broken hearts in his wake, had fallen for her.

I suppose her charms are enough to pay for all this. Khanzada's salon was located in one of the city's most desirable neighborhoods, a leafy enclave nestled in the heart of the Agnivanshi Quarter's entertainment district. Her home was large and beautiful, three floors of white marble and cedar-screened windows that surrounded an airy courtyard with fruit trees and an intricately tiled fountain.

Ali would have seen the entire place razed to the ground. He despised these pleasure houses. It wasn't enough that they were dens of every vice and sin imaginable, put on brazen public display, but he knew from Anas that most of these girls were shafit slaves stolen from their families and sold to the highest bidder.

"My lords."

Ali looked up. The girl who had been dancing stopped before them and bowed low to the ground, pressing her hands on the tiled floor. Though her hair had the same night-black sheen as Khanzada's and her skin shimmered like a pureblood, Ali could see round ears beneath her sheer veil. Shafit.

"Rise, my dear," Muntadhir said. "Such a pretty face does not belong on the floor."

The girl stood and pressed her palms together, blinking long-lashed hazel eyes at his brother. Muntadhir smiled, and Ali wondered if Khanzada would have some competition tonight. His brother beckoned her closer and hooked a finger into her bangles. She giggled, and he removed one of the strands of pearls that looped his neck, playing at placing it over her veil. He whispered something in her ear, and she laughed again. Ali sighed.

"Perhaps Prince Alizayd would like some of your attention, Rupa," Khanzada teased. "Do you like your men tall, dark, and hostile?"

Ali shot her a glare, but Muntadhir only laughed. "It might

help your attitude, akhi," he said as he nuzzled the girl's neck. "You're too young to have sworn off them completely."

Khanzada pressed closer to Muntadhir. She trailed her fingers down his waist-wrap. "And Geziri men make it so easy," she said, tracing the pattern embroidered on the hem. "Even their garments are practical." She grinned and removed her hand from his brother's lap to run it down Rupa's smooth face.

She looks like she's evaluating a piece of fruit at the market. Ali cracked his knuckles. He was a young man—he'd be lying if he said the pretty girl didn't stir him—but that only made him more uneasy.

Khanzada took his disdain the wrong way. "I have other girls if this one doesn't suit your interest. Boys, as well," she added with a wicked grin. "Perhaps such an adventurous taste runs in the—"

"Enough, Khanzada," Muntadhir cut in, a note of warning in his voice.

The courtesan laughed and slid into Muntadhir's lap. She pressed a wineglass to his lips. "Forgive me, my love."

The humor returned to Muntadhir's face, and Ali looked away, his temper rising. He didn't like to see this side of his brother; such profligacy would be a weakness when he was king. The shafit girl looked between them.

As if awaiting orders. Something in Ali snapped. He dropped his spoon, folding his arms across his chest. "How old are you, sister?"

"I . . ." Rupa looked again to Khanzada. "I am sorry, my lord, but I do not know."

"She's old enough," Khanzada interrupted.

"Is she?" Ali asked. "Well, I'm sure you would know . . . you'd be certain to get all the details of her pedigree when you bought her."

Muntadhir exhaled. "Simmer down, Zaydi."

But it was Khanzada who grew irate. "I do not *buy* anyone," she said, defending herself. "I have a list of girls wishing entrance to my school as long as my arm."

"I am certain you do," Ali said scornfully. "And how many of your customers must they sleep with to get off this list?"

Khanzada straightened up, fire in her tin-colored eyes. "Excuse me?"

Their argument was attracting curious glances; Ali switched to Geziriyya so only Muntadhir could understand him. "How can you even sit here, akhi? Have you ever given thought to where—"

Khanzada jumped to her feet. "If you want to accuse me of something, at least have the courage to say it in a language I can understand, you half-tribe brat!"

Muntadhir abruptly straightened up at her words. The nervous chatter of the other men died away, and the musicians stopped playing.

"*What* did you just call him?" Muntadhir demanded. Ali had never heard such ice in his voice.

Khanzada seemed to realize she had made a mistake. The anger vanished from her face, replaced by fear. "I-I only meant—"

"I don't care what you meant," Muntadhir snapped. "How dare you say such a thing to your prince? Apologize."

Ali reached for his brother's wrist. "It's fine, Dhiru. I shouldn't have—"

Muntadhir cut him off with a raised palm. "Apologize, Khanzada," he repeated. "Now."

She quickly pressed her palms together and lowered her eyes. "Forgive me, Prince Alizayd. I did not mean to insult you."

"Good." Muntadhir shot a look at the musicians so reminiscent of their father it made Ali's skin crawl. "What are you all staring at? Play on!"

Ali swallowed, too embarrassed to look at anyone in the room. "I should go."

"Yes, you probably should." But before Ali could rise, his brother grabbed him by the wrist. "And don't ever disagree with me in front of these men again," he warned in Geziriyya. "Especially when *you're* the one being an ass." He let go of Ali's arm.

"Fine," Ali muttered. Muntadhir still had a strand of pearls looped around Rupa's neck like some extravagant leash. The girl was smiling, but the expression didn't meet her eyes.

Ali pulled a heavy silver ring off his thumb as he stood up. He met the shafit girl's gaze and then dropped the ring on the table. "My apologies."

He took the dark steps that led to the street two at a time, struck by his brother's swift response. Muntadhir clearly hadn't agreed with Ali's behavior, but had still defended him, had humiliated his own lover to do so. He hadn't even hesitated.

We are Geziri. It's what we do. Ali was just clear of the house when a voice spoke up behind him.

"Not quite to your taste?"

Ali glanced back. Jamshid e-Pramukh lounged outside Khanzada's door, smoking a long pipe.

Ali hesitated. He didn't know Jamshid well. Though Kaveh's son served in the Royal Guard, he did so in a Daeva contingent whose training was segregated—and purposefully inferior. Muntadhir spoke highly of the Daeva captain—his bodyguard for over a decade and his closest friend—but Jamshid was always quiet in Ali's presence.

Probably because his father thinks I want to burn down the Grand Temple with all the Daevas inside it. Ali could only imagine the things said about him in the privacy of the Pramukh household.

"Something like that," Ali finally replied.

Jamshid laughed. "I told him to take you someplace quieter, but you know your brother when he sets his mind on a thing." His dark eyes sparkled, his voice warm with affection.

Ali made a face. "Fortunately, I think I've worn out my invitation."

"You're in good company then." Jamshid took another drag from the pipe. "Khanzada hates me."

"Really?" Ali couldn't imagine what the courtesan would have against the mild-mannered guard.

Jamshid nodded and held out the pipe, but Ali demurred. "I think I'll just head back to the palace."

"Of course." He motioned down the street. "Your secretary's waiting for you in the midan."

"Rashid?" Ali frowned. He didn't have any further business this evening that he could recall.

"He didn't get around to offering his name." A hint of annoyance flickered in Jamshid's eyes, gone in a moment. "Nor did he want to wait here."

Odd. "Thank you for letting me know." Ali started to turn away.

"Prince Alizayd?" When Ali turned back, Jamshid continued. "I'm sorry for what happened in our quarter today. We're not all like that."

The apology took him aback. "I know," Ali replied, unsure of what else to say.

"Good." Jamshid winked. "Don't let my father get to you. It's a thing at which he excels."

That brought a smile to Ali's face. "Thank you," he said sincerely. He touched his heart and brow. "Peace be upon you, Captain Pramukh."

"And upon you peace."

NAHRI

Nahri took a long swig of water from the skin, swirled it around in her mouth, and spat. She'd have given her last dirham to drink without feeling grit in her teeth. She sighed and leaned heavily against Dara's back, letting her legs hang loose on the horse.

"I hate this place," she mumbled into his shoulder. Nahri was used to sand—she dealt with the storms that coated Cairo in a hazy yellow dust every spring—but this was unbearable.

They'd left the last oasis days ago, stealing a new horse and making one last push across open, unprotected ground. Dara said there was no choice; everything between the oasis and Daevabad was desert.

It had been a brutal crossing. They barely spoke, both too weary to do more than hold on to the saddle and continue in companionable silence. Nahri was filthy; dirt and sand clung to her skin and matted her hair. It was in her clothes and her food, under her nail beds and in between her toes.

"It's not much farther," Dara assured her.

"You always say that," she muttered. She shook out a cramped arm and then wrapped it around his waist again. A few weeks ago she would have been too embarrassed to hold him so boldly, but now she no longer cared.

The landscape began to change, hills and scrubby, frail trees replacing the bare dirt. The wind picked up, blue clouds rolling in from the east to darken the sky.

When they finally stopped, Dara slid off the saddle and pulled away the filthy cloth that covered his face. "Praise be to the Creator."

She took his hand as he helped her down. No matter how many times she dismounted, it always took a few minutes for her knees to remember how to work. "Are we there?"

"We've reached the Gozan River," he replied, sounding relieved. "Daevabad's threshold is just across the water, and none but our kind can pass through it. Not ifrit, not ghouls, not even peris."

The land came to an abrupt end in a cliff that overlooked the river. In the gloomy light, the wide, muddy river was an unappealing brownish-gray, and the other side didn't look promising. All Nahri could see was more flat dirt. "I think you may have overstated Daevabad's charms."

"Do you really think we'd leave a vast magical city open to the eyes of any curious human onlooker? It's hidden."

"How are we going to cross?" Even from up here, she could see whitecaps cresting on the rushing water.

Dara peered over the edge of the limestone cliff. "I could try to enchant one of the blankets," he suggested, not sounding optimistic. "But let's wait until tomorrow." He nodded at the sky.

"It looks like it's about to storm, and I don't want to risk crossing in bad weather. I remember these cliffs being pocked with caves. We'll shelter in one for the night." He started to lead the horse down a twisting, narrow path.

Nahri followed. "Any chance I could make a trip to the riverbank?"

"Why?"

"I smell like something died in my clothes, and I have enough dirt caked on my skin to make a double of myself."

He nodded. "Just be careful. The way down is steep."

"I'll be fine."

Nahri trekked down the sharp hill, zigzagging past rocky boulders and stunted trees. Dara hadn't lied. She tripped twice and cut her palms on the sharp rocks, but the chance to bathe was worth it. She stayed close to the riverbank as she quickly scrubbed her skin, ready to jump back if the current grew too strong.

The sky grew darker by the minute; an unhealthy tinge of green lined the clouds. Nahri climbed out of the water, wrung out her hair, and shivered. The air was humid and smelled of lightning. Dara was right about the storm.

She was shoving her wet feet into her boots when she felt it. The touch of the wind, so firm it was like a hand upon her shoulder. She immediately straightened up and spun around, ready to hurl her boot at whatever it was.

There was no one. Nahri scanned the rocky shore, but it was empty and still save for the dead leaves blowing in the breeze. She sniffed and caught the oddly strong scent of peppercorns and mace. Maybe Dara was attempting to conjure up a new dish.

She followed the small trail of smoke drifting in the sky behind her until she found Dara sitting at the mouth of a dark cave. A pot of stew bubbled over the flames.

He glanced up and smiled. "Finally. I was starting to fear you drowned."

The wind whipped through her wet hair, and she trembled. "Never," she declared, cozying up to the fire. "I swim like a fish."

He shook his head. "All your swimming reminds me of the Ayaanle. I ought to check your neck for crocodile scales."

"Crocodile scales?" She snatched up his goblet in hopes the wine would warm her. "Truly?"

"Ay, it's just something we say about them." He pushed the pot in her direction. "Crocodiles are one of the preferred forms of the marid. Supposedly the ancient Ayaanle used to worship them. Their descendants don't like talking about it, but I've heard bizarre stories about their old rituals." He took the goblet back from her; the goblet refilled with wine the instant his fingers touched the stem.

Nahri shook her head. "What is it tonight?" she asked, looking at the stew with a knowing smile. The question had turned into a game. try as he might, Dara had never been able to conjure up anything other than his mother's lentil dish.

He grinned. "Pigeons stuffed with fried onions and saffron."

"How forbidden." She helped herself to the food. "The Ayaanle live near Egypt, yes?"

"Far to the south; your land is too fat with humans for the tastes of our people."

The rain began to fall. Thunder rumbled in the distance, and Dara made a face as he wiped water from his brow. "Tonight is not a night for stories," he declared. "Come." He picked up the pot, indifferent to the hot metal. "We should get out of the rain and get some sleep." He fixed his gaze on the hidden city beyond the river, and his expression turned unreadable. "We have a long day ahead of us."

NAHRI SLEPT FITFULLY, HER DREAMS BIZARRE AND full of thunder. It was still dark when she woke, their fire reduced to glowing embers. Rain battered the mouth of the cave, and she could hear the wind howling past the cliffs.

Dara was stretched out beside her on one of the blankets, but they'd grown familiar enough that she could tell from the cadence of his breathing that he was also awake. She rolled over to face him, realizing that he'd spread his robe over her as she slept. He lay flat on his back, his hands crossed over his stomach like a corpse.

"Trouble sleeping?" she asked.

He didn't move, his gaze fixed on the rocky ceiling. "Something like that."

A flash of lightning lit up the cave, followed shortly by a rumble of thunder. She studied his profile in the dim light. Her gaze trailed his long-lashed eyes down his neck and across his bare arms. Her stomach fluttered; she was suddenly aware of how little space separated them.

Not that it mattered—Dara's mind was clearly worlds away. "I wish it were not raining," he said, his voice uncharacteristically wistful. "I would have liked to look upon the stars in case . . ."

"In case?" she prompted when he trailed off.

He glanced at her, looking almost embarrassed. "In case it's my last night as a free man."

Nahri flinched. Too busy searching the sky for more rukh and trying to survive the last leg of their grueling journey, Nahri had barely given further thought to their reception in Daevabad. "Do you really think you're going to be arrested?"

"It's likely."

There was a hint of fear in his voice, but having learned how prone to exaggeration Dara could be—especially when it came to the djinn—Nahri tried to reassure him. "You're probably just ancient history to them, Dara. Not everyone is capable of holding a grudge for fourteen centuries." He scowled and looked away, and she laughed. "Oh, come now, I'm just teasing you." She pushed up on one elbow, and without thinking much of it, reached for his cheek to turn him back to face her.

Dara startled at her touch, his eyes bright with surprise. No, not at her touch, Nahri realized with some embarrassment, rather at the position she'd inadvertently put them in, her body half-draped over his chest.

She flushed. "I'm sorry. I didn't mean to—"

He touched her cheek.

Dara looked nearly as astonished as she did at the act, as if his fingers were lightly tracing her jaw of their own accord. There was so much longing in his face—as well as a good bit of indecision— that Nahri's heart began to race, heat pooling in her stomach. *Don't*, she told herself. *He's the literal enemy of the people you're about to ask for sanctuary, and you want to add this to the ties already binding you?* Only a fool would do such a thing.

She kissed him.

Dara made a halfhearted sound of protest against her mouth and then promptly tangled his hands in her hair. His lips were warm and urgent, and every part of her seemed to cheer as he kissed her back, her body filled with a hunger her mind was screaming warnings against.

He broke away. "We can't," he gasped, his warm breath tickling her ear, sending a thrill down her spine. "This—this is completely inappropriate . . ."

He was right, of course. Not about being inappropriate— Nahri had never much cared about that. But it was *stupid*. This was how lovesick idiots ruined their lives, and Nahri had delivered enough bastards and nursed enough broken wives through the last stages of syphilis to know. But she'd just spent a month with this arrogant, infuriating man, every night and day at his side, a month of his smoldering eyes and his scalding hands that lingered both a little too long and yet never long enough.

She rolled on top of him, and the look of stunned disbelief on his face was worth it alone. "Shut up, Dara." And then she kissed him again.

There was no sound of protest now. There was a gasp—half exasperation, half desire—then he pulled her down against him, and Nahri's thoughts stopped being coherent.

She was fumbling with the maddeningly complicated knot on his belt, his hands slipping under her tunic, when the cave shook with the loudest boom of thunder Nahri had yet heard.

She stilled. She didn't want to—Dara's mouth had just found a delightful spot at the base of her throat and the press of his hips against hers was doing things to her blood she'd never thought possible. But then a flash of lightning—brighter than the rest—lit up the cave. Another breeze swept in, extinguishing the small fire and sending Dara's bow and quiver clattering to the floor.

At the sound of his precious weapon hitting the ground, he looked up, and then froze, noticing the expression on her face. "What's wrong?"

"I . . . I don't know." The thunder continued to rumble, but beneath it was something else, almost like a whisper on the wind, an urging in a language she didn't understand. The breeze came again, rustling and tugging at her hair, smelling of those same spices. Peppercorn and cardamom. Clove and mace.

Tea. Khayzur's tea.

Nahri immediately drew back, filled with a foreboding she didn't understand. "I think . . . I think there's something out there."

He frowned. "I didn't hear anything." But he sat up anyway, untangling his limbs from hers to retrieve his bow and quiver.

She shivered, cold without the warm press of his body. Grabbing his robe, she slipped it over her head. "It wasn't a sound," she insisted, knowing she probably sounded crazy. "It was something else."

Another bolt of lightning cracked across the sky, its flash outlining the daeva against the dark. His brow furrowed. "No, they would not dare . . . ," he whispered, almost to himself. "Not this close to the border."

Still, he handed her his dagger and then notched one of his silver arrows. He crept toward the cave's entrance. "Stay back," he warned.

Nahri ignored him, shoving the dagger in her belt and joining him at the cave's mouth. Rain lashed their faces, but it wasn't as dark as it had been earlier; the light from the moon was reflected in the swollen clouds.

Dara raised his bow and gave her a pointed look as the fletched end of the arrow caught her stomach. "At least a *little* back."

He stepped out, and she stayed at his side, not liking the way he flinched when the rain hit his face. "Are you sure you should be going out in this weather—"

A bolt of lightning struck just ahead, and Nahri jumped, shielding her eyes. The rain stopped, the effect so immediate it was as if someone turned off a spigot.

The wind whipped through her damp hair. She blinked, trying to clear the spots from her vision. The darkness was lifting. The lightning had struck a tree right near them, setting the dead branches aflame.

"Come on. Let's go back inside," Nahri urged. But Dara didn't move, his gaze locked on the tree. "What is it?" she asked, trying to push past his arm.

He didn't answer—he didn't have to. Flames raced down the tree, the heat so intense it instantly dried her wet skin. Acrid smoke poured off the wood, seeping past the roots and pooling into hazy black tendrils that slithered and twirled, solidifying as they slowly rose from the ground.

Nahri backed up and reached for Dara's arm. "Is . . . is it

another daeva?" she asked, trying to sound hopeful as the smoky ropes twisted together, thicker, faster.

Dara's eyes were wide. "I fear not." He took her hand. "I think we should leave."

They had no sooner turned back toward the cave when more black smoke swept down from the cliffs above, surging past the rocky entrance like a waterfall.

Every hair on her body stood on end; the tips of her fingers buzzed with energy. "Ifrit," she whispered.

Dara stepped back so fast that he stumbled, his usual grace gone. "The river," he stammered. "Run."

"But our supplies—"

"There's no time." Keeping one hand clenched on her wrist, he dragged her down the rocky ridge. "Can you swim as well as you claim?"

Nahri hesitated, thinking back to the Gozan's fast current. The river was likely swollen from the storm, its already turbulent waters whipped into a frenzy. "I . . . maybe. Probably," she corrected, seeing alarm flash across his face. "But you can't!"

"It matters not."

Before she could argue, he pulled her along, racing and scrambling down the limestone hill. The steep decline was treacherous in the dark, and Nahri slipped more than once on the loose, sandy pebbles.

They were running along a narrow ledge when a low sound broke across the air, something between a lion's roar and the snap of an uncontrolled fire. Nahri glanced up, getting the briefest glimpse of something large and bright before it slammed into Dara.

The force knocked her back, her balance gone without the daeva's firm grip on her wrist. She grabbed for a tree branch, for a rock, for anything as she stumbled, but her fingers raked uselessly through the air. Her feet met nothing, and then she was over the ridge.

NAHRI TRIED TO PROTECT HER HEAD AS SHE HIT the ground hard and rolled down the incline, the jagged rocks gouging her arms. Her body bounced past another small ledge, and then she landed in a thick patch of mud. The back of her head smashed into a hidden tree root.

She lay still, stunned by the blinding pain, the wind knocked out of her. Every part of her hurt. She tried to take a small breath and cried out at the protest of an obviously broken rib.

Just breathe. Don't move. She needed to let her body heal. She knew it would; already the sting of her torn flesh was fading. She gingerly touched the back of her head, praying that her skull was still intact. Her fingers met bloodied hair but nothing else. Thank the Most High for that small piece of luck.

Something in her abdomen twisted back into place, and she sat up, wiping her eyes free of blood or mud or God only knew what. She squinted. The Gozan was ahead of her, the rushing water glistening as it crested into rapids.

Dara. She climbed to her feet and staggered forward, peering through the darkness at the ridge.

Another flash blinded her, and the air crackled, followed by a deafening boom that knocked her back. Nahri threw up her hands to protect her eyes, but the light was already gone, vanished in a haze of quickly evaporating blue smoke.

Then the ifrit was there, towering over her with arms as thick as tree boughs. Its flesh was pressed light, its skin shimmering between the ashy white of smoke and the crimson-tinged orange of fire. Its hands and feet were coal black, its hairless body covered with a scrawl of ebony markings even wilder than Dara's.

And it was beautiful. Strange and deadly, but beautiful. She froze as a pair of golden feline eyes settled on her. It smiled, its teeth blackened and sharp. A coal-colored hand reached for the iron scythe at its side.

Nahri jumped to her feet and dashed across the rocks to open water, landing in the shallows with a splash. But the ifrit was too fast, snatching her ankle as she tried to swim away. She clawed at the muddy river bottom, hooking her fingers on a submerged tree root.

The ifrit was stronger. He yanked again, and Nahri screamed as he dragged her back. He'd grown brighter, his skin pulsing with hot yellow light. A scar ran across his bald head like a smear of extinguished charcoal. The thief in her could not help but note the gleaming bronze chest plate he wore over a simple linen waist cloth. A string of raw quartz stones looped his neck.

He raised her hand as if in shared victory. "I have her!" he screamed in a language that sounded like wildfire. He grinned again and ran his tongue over his sharp teeth, a look of unmistakable hunger in his gold eyes. "The girl! I have—"

Recovering her senses, Nahri grabbed for the dagger Dara had given her in the cave. Nearly slicing off one of her fingers in the process, she plunged it deep into the ifrit's fiery chest. He cried out and dropped her wrist, sounding more surprised than hurt.

He lifted one painted eyebrow as he glanced down at the dagger, obviously unimpressed. Then he slapped her hard across the face.

The blow knocked Nahri off her feet. She reeled, black spots blinking before her eyes. The ifrit pulled the dagger free, barely glancing at it before he flung it past her.

She scrambled up, slipping and staggering as she tried to back away. She couldn't take her eyes off his scythe. The iron blade was stained black, the edge battered and dull. It would kill her, no doubt, and it would hurt. A lot. She wondered how many of her Nahid ancestors had met their end upon that scythe.

Dara. She needed the Afshin.

The ifrit followed at a leisurely pace. "So you're the one getting all the races riled up . . . ," he started. "The latest of Anahid's treacherous, blood-poisoning spawn."

The hate in his voice sent a new surge of fear through her body. She spotted the dagger on the ground and snatched it up. It might not hurt the ifrit, but it was all she had. She held it out, trying to keep as much distance as possible between them.

The ifrit grinned again. "Are you afraid, little healer?" he drawled. "Are you trembling?" He caressed his blade. "What I would do to see that traitor's blood run out of you . . ." But then he dropped his hand, looking regretful. "Alas, we made a deal to return you unharmed."

"*Unharmed?*" She thought back to Cairo, the memory of the ghoul's teeth ripping open her throat vivid in her mind. "Your ghouls tried to eat me!"

The ifrit spread his hands, looking apologetic. "My brother acted rashly, I admit." He cleared his throat as if he was having trouble speaking, and then tilted his head to regard her. "Astonishing really, I give the marid their due. At first glance, you're completely human, but look past that and . . ." He stepped closer to study her face. "There's the daeva."

"I'm not," she said quickly. "Whoever you're working for . . . whatever it is you want . . . I'm just a shafit. I can't do anything," she added, hoping the lie might buy her some time. "You don't need to waste your time on me."

"Just a *shafit*?" He laughed. "Is that what that lunatic slave thinks?"

The sound of a crashing tree drew her attention before she could respond. A line of fire danced across the ridge, consuming the scrub brush as if it was kindling.

The ifrit followed Nahri's glance. "Your Afshin's arrows might be sharper than his wits, little healer, but you are both outmatched."

"You said you meant us no harm."

"We mean *you* no harm," he corrected. "The wine-soaked slave was not part of our deal. But perhaps . . . if you come willingly . . ." He trailed off with a cough and took in a sharp breath.

As she watched, he wheezed and reached for a nearby tree to brace himself. He coughed again, clutching his chest where she had wounded him. He pulled the breastplate off, and Nahri gasped. The skin around the wound had turned black with what looked like infection. And it was spreading, tiny coal-colored tendrils snaking out like delicate veins.

"Wha-what did you do to me?" he cried out as the blackening veins gave way to a blue-tinged ash before their eyes. He coughed again, hacking up a dark viscous liquid that steamed when it hit the ground. He staggered closer and tried to grab her. "No . . . you didn't. Say you didn't!" His golden eyes were wide with panic.

Still clutching the dagger, Nahri edged back, fearing the ifrit might be trying to trick her. But as he clutched his throat and fell to his knees, sweating ash, she remembered something Dara had told her weeks ago over the Euphrates.

It was said the very blood of a Nahid was poisonous to the ifrit, more fatal than any blade. As if in a trance, her gaze slowly fell on the dagger. Mixed in with the ifrit's black blood was her own dark crimson from when she'd cut herself trying to stab him.

She looked back at the ifrit. He was lying on the rocks, blood leaking from his mouth. His eyes, beautiful and terrified, met hers. "No . . . ," he panted. "We had a deal . . ."

He hit me. He threatened to kill Dara. Acting on a rush of cold hate and instinct that likely would have frightened her if she had given it more thought, she kicked him hard in the stomach. He cried out, and she dropped to her knees, pressing her dagger against his throat.

"Who did you make a deal with?" she demanded. "What did they want with me?"

He shook his head and took a rattling breath. "Filthy Nahid scum . . . you're all the same," he spat. ". . . knew it was a mistake . . ."

"Who?" she demanded again. When he said nothing, she slashed her hand open and pressed her bloody palm against his wound.

The sound that came from the ifrit was unlike any she could imagine: a screech that tore at her soul. She wanted to turn away, to flee into the river and submerge herself, escaping all this.

Nahri thought again of Dara. Over a thousand years as a slave, stolen from his people and murdered, given over to the whims of countless cruel masters. She saw Baseema's gentle smile, the most innocent of innocents gone forever. She pushed harder.

With her other hand, she kept the dagger against his throat, though judging from his shrieks, it wasn't necessary. She waited until his cries turned to a whimper. "Tell me, and I'll heal you."

He squirmed under her blade, his eyes briefly dilating black. The wound bubbled, steaming like an overfilled cauldron, and a terrible liquid sound came from his throat.

"Nahri!" Dara's voice rose from somewhere in the dark, a distant distraction. "Nahri!"

The ifrit's fevered gaze fixed on her face. Something flickered in his eyes, something calculating and vile. He opened his mouth. "Your mother," he wheezed. "We made a deal with Manizheh."

"What?" she asked, so startled that she nearly dropped the knife. "My *what*?"

The ifrit started to seize, a rattling moan coming from somewhere low in his throat. His eyes dilated again, and his mouth fell open, a haze of steam rushing past his lips. Nahri grimaced. She doubted she'd get much more information from him.

His fingers scrabbled on her wrist. "Heal me . . . ," he begged. "You promised."

"I lied." With a sharp and vicious motion, she slashed her hand back and cut his throat. Dark vapor rose from his maimed neck and stifled his cry. But his eyes, fixed and hateful, stayed on her blade, watching as she raised it over his chest. *The throat...* Dara had once instructed, the weaknesses of the ifrit one of the few things he would tell her.

... the lungs. She brought the blade back down, plunging it into his chest. It didn't go in easily, and she fought the urge to vomit as she leaned her weight into the dagger. Viscous black blood gushed over her hands. The ifrit convulsed once, twice, and then fell still, his chest lowering like she'd emptied a sack of flour. Nahri watched another moment but knew he was dead, felt the lack of life and vigor immediately. She had killed him.

She stood; her legs trembled. *I killed a man.* She stared at the dead ifrit, transfixed by the sight of his blood seeping and smoking over the pebbly ground. *I killed him.*

"Nahri!" Dara skidded to a stop in front of her. He took one of her arms as his alarmed eyes raked over her bloodied clothing. He touched her cheek, his fingers grazed her wet hair. "By the Creator, I was so worried . . . Suleiman's eye!"

Spotting the ifrit, he leaped back, pulling her protectively behind him. "He . . . you . . . ," he stammered, sounding more shocked than she had ever heard him. "You killed an ifrit." He whirled on her, his green eyes flashing. "*You* killed an ifrit?" he repeated as he took a closer look.

Your mother . . . The ifrit's final claim taunted her. She couldn't forget that strange flicker in his eyes before he spoke. Was it a lie? Words meant to haunt the enemy who would kill him?

A hot breeze swept past her cheeks, and Nahri lifted her eyes. The cliffs were on fire; the wet trees snapped and cracked as they burned. The air smelled poisonous, hot and seeded with tiny burning embers that swept across the dead landscape and twinkled above the dark river.

She pressed one of her bloody hands against her temple as a wave of nausea swept over her. She turned away from the dead ifrit, the sight of its body triggering a strange sense of rightness that she didn't like. "I . . . he said something about . . ." She stopped speaking. More black smoke was coming down the cliff, twisting and slithering through the trees and growing into a thick roiling wave as it neared them.

"Get back!" Dara yanked her away, and the smoky tendrils flattened with a low hiss. Dara took the opportunity to shove her toward the water. "Go, you can still get to the river."

The river. She shook her head; even as she watched, an enormous tree branch shot past like it had been fired from a cannon, and the water roared as it crashed against the boulders littering its banks.

She couldn't even see the opposite shore—there was no way she could cross. And Dara would probably dissolve.

"No," she replied, her voice grim. "We'll never make it."

The smoke surged forward and began to separate, swirling and piling into three distinct shapes. The daeva snarled and drew his bow. "Nahri, get in the water."

Before she could reply, Dara gave her a hard push, knocking her into the cold current. It wasn't deep enough for her to submerge, but the river fought her as she climbed back to her feet.

Dara released one of his arrows, but it sailed uselessly through the nebulous forms. He cursed and shot again as one of the ifrit flashed with fiery light. A blackened hand grabbed the arrow. Still holding it, the ifrit burned back into its solid form, followed immediately by the other two.

The ifrit with the arrow was even larger than the one Nahri had killed. The skin around his eyes smoldered in a rough band, black and gold. The other two were smaller: another man and a woman wearing a diadem of braided metals.

The ifrit rolled Dara's arrow between his fingers. It began

to melt, the silver winking as it dripped into the dirt. The ifrit grinned, and then his hand smoked. The arrow was gone, replaced by an enormous iron mace. The spikes and ridges of its heavy head were dull with blood. He hoisted the horrific weapon up on one shoulder and stepped forward.

"Salaam alaykum, Banu Nahida." He gave her a sharp smile. "I have *so* looked forward to this meeting."

THE IFRIT'S ARABIC WAS FLAWLESS, WITH JUST enough of Cairo's flavor to make her flinch. He inclined his head in a slight bow. "You call yourself Nahri, yes?"

Dara drew back another arrow. "Don't answer that."

The ifrit lifted his hands. "There is no harm. I know it's not her real name." He turned his golden gaze back to Nahri. "I am Aeshma, child. Why don't you come from the water?"

She opened her mouth to reply, but then the female sauntered over to Dara.

"My Scourge, it has been far too long." She licked her painted lips. "Look at that slave mark, Aeshma. A beauty. Have you ever seen one as long?" She sighed, her eyes creasing in pleasure. "And oh, how he earned them."

Dara paled.

"Don't you remember, Darayavahoush?" When he said nothing, she gave him a sad smile. "A pity. I've never seen a slave so ruthless. Then again, you were always willing to do *anything* to stay in my good graces."

She leered at him, and Dara recoiled, looking sick. A surge of hatred swept through Nahri.

"Enough, Qandisha." Aeshma waved his companion off. "We are not here to make enemies."

Something brushed against Nahri's shins under the black water. She ignored it, focusing her attention on the ifrit. "What do you want?"

"First: for you to get out of the water. There is no safety in there for you, little healer."

"And there's safety with you? One of your people in Cairo promised the same and then set a pack of ghouls on us. At least there's nothing in here trying to eat me."

Aeshma raised his eyes. "A terribly ill choice of words, Banu Nahida. The denizens of air and water have already done you both more harm than you know."

She frowned, trying to untwist his words. "What do you . . ." She stopped speaking. A shudder went through the river, like something impossibly large heaving itself along the muddy bottom. She eyed the water around her. She could've sworn she saw a flash of scales in the distance, a wet glistening that vanished as quickly as it had come.

The ifrit must have noticed her reaction. "Come now," he urged. "You are not safe."

"He's lying." Dara's voice was barely more than a growl. The daeva was still, his hate-filled gaze fixed on the ifrit.

The skinny one suddenly straightened up, sniffing the burning air like a dog before rushing into the brush where the murdered ifrit lay.

"Sakhr!" The skinny ifrit cried, his luminous eyes wide in disbelief as he touched the throat Nahri had torn open. "No . . . no, no, *no!*" He threw his head back and let out a screech of despair that seemed to rend the very air before bending back over the dead ifrit and pressing his forehead to the corpse's.

His grief took her completely by surprise. Dara said the ifrit were demons. She wouldn't have thought they cared for each other at all, let alone so deeply.

The wailing ifrit silenced his cry as he caught sight of her, and hate filled his golden eyes. "You murderous witch!" he accused her, rising to his feet. "I should have killed you in Cairo!"

Cairo . . . Nahri backed up until the water surged around

her waist. *Baseema*. He was the one who'd possessed Baseema, who doomed the little girl and sent the ghouls after them. Her fingers twitched on her dagger.

He charged forward, but Aeshma grabbed him and threw him to the ground. "No! We made a deal."

The skinny ifrit jumped to his feet and immediately started after her again, snapping and hissing as he tried to wriggle free of Aeshma's grasp. The dirt beneath his feet sparked. "The devil take your deal! She blood-poisoned him—I'm going to rip out her lungs and grind her soul to dust!"

"*Enough!*" Aeshma threw him to the ground again and raised his mace. "The girl is under my protection." He glanced up and met Nahri's eyes. There was a much colder look to his face now. "But the slave is not. If Manizheh wanted her bloody Scourge, she should have told us." He lowered his weapon and gestured at Dara. "He's yours, Vizaresh."

"Wait!" Nahri cried as the skinny ifrit leaped on Dara. Dara smashed him across the face with his bow, but then Qandisha—bigger than both men—simply grabbed Dara by the throat and lifted him off his feet.

"Drown him again," Aeshma suggested. "Maybe this time it will take." The river danced and boiled around his feet as he started after Nahri.

Dara tried to kick Qandisha, his cry abruptly ending when she plunged him under the dark water. The ifrit laughed as Dara's fingers clawed at her wrists.

"Stop!" Nahri screamed. "Let him go!" She hopped back, hoping to lose Aeshma in the deeper water and swim back to Dara.

But as Aeshma closed in, the river swept back, almost like a wave drawing up. It pulled from the bank, pulled from her ankles, and in seconds, it was gone from her feet altogether, leaving her standing in a foot of muck.

Absent the sound of the rushing current, the world went quiet. There was not even a hint of wind, the air saturated with the scent of salt, smoke, and wet silt.

Taking advantage of Aeshma's distraction, Nahri darted toward Dara.

"Marid . . . ," the female ifrit whispered, her golden eyes wide with fright. She dropped Dara and grabbed the other ifrit by his skinny arm, yanking him away. "Run!"

The ifrit were fleeing by the time Nahri reached Dara. He was holding his throat, sucking for air. As she tried to pull him to his feet, his eyes locked on something past her shoulder, and the color left his face.

She glanced behind her. She immediately wished she hadn't.

The Gozan was gone.

A wide, muddy trench stood in the river's place, wet boulders and deep ridges marking its former path. The air was still smoky, but the storm clouds had vanished, revealing a swollen moon and a rich spread of stars that lit up the sky. Or at least would have lit up the sky had they not been steadily blinking out as something darker than night rose in front of them.

The river. Or what had been the river. It had drawn back and thickened, rapids and tiny waves still rippling across its surface, swirling and churning, defying gravity to rise. It wriggled and undulated in the air, slowly towering over them.

Her throat tightened in fear. It was a serpent. A serpent the size of a small mountain and made entirely of rushing black water.

The watery snake writhed, and Nahri got a glimpse of a head the size of a building, with whitecaps for teeth, as it opened its mouth to roar again at the stars. The sound broke across the air, some horrifying combination of a crocodile's bellow and the break of a tidal wave. Behind the serpent, she spied the sandy hills where Dara said Daevabad lay hidden.

He was frozen in terror now, and knowing how frightened he was of water, she didn't expect that to change. She tightened her grip on his wrist. "Get up." She pulled him forward. "Get up!" When he moved too slowly for her liking, she slapped him hard across the face and pointed toward the sandy dunes. "Daevabad, Dara! Let's go! You can kill all the djinn you want once we get there!"

Whether it was the slap or the promise of murder, the terror holding him seemed to break. He grabbed her outstretched hand, and they ran.

There was another roar, and a thick tongue of water lashed the spot where they'd been standing, like a giant swatting a fly. It crashed against the muddy bank, and water swept out to splash their feet as they fled.

The serpent twisted and slammed to the ground just ahead of them. Nahri slid to a halt, pulling Dara in another direction to sprint across the emptied riverbed. It was littered with damp waterweeds and drying boulders; Nahri stumbled more than once, but Dara kept her on her feet as they dodged the crushing blows of the river monster.

They had gotten a bit more than halfway across when the creature suddenly halted. Nahri didn't turn around to see why, but Dara did.

He gasped, his voice returning. "Run!" he screamed, as if they were not already doing so. "Run!"

Nahri ran, her heart pounding, her muscles protesting. She ran so fast she didn't even notice the ditch, a spot of what must have been deep water, before she was sailing over it. She hit the uneven bottom hard. Her ankle twisted as she landed, and she heard the snap before she felt the pain of the broken bone.

Then from the ground, she saw what had made Dara scream.

Having risen once again to howl at the sky, the creature was letting its lower half dissolve into a waterfall taller than the Pyramids. The water rushed toward them, the wave at least three times her height and spreading out in both directions. They were caught.

Dara was at her side again. He clutched her close. "I'm sorry," he whispered. His fingers snaked through her wet hair. She could feel his warm breath as he kissed her brow. She held him tight, tucking her head into his shoulder and taking a deep breath of his smoky scent.

She expected it to be her last.

And then something slammed down between them and the wave.

The ground shook, and a high-pitched screech that would have frozen the blood of the bravest man alive broke the air. It sounded like a whole flock of rukh descending upon their prey.

Nahri looked up from Dara's shoulder. Outlined against the rushing wave was an enormous sweep of wings, glittering with lime-colored sparks where the starlight touched them.

Khayzur.

The peri shrieked again. He spread his wings, raised his hands, and then took a breath; as he inhaled, the air around Nahri seemed to ebb—she could almost feel it being pulled from her lungs. Then he exhaled, sending a racing, funnel-shaped cloud toward the serpent.

The creature let out a watery bellow when the winds hit. A cloud of steam evaporated off its side, and it flinched, ducking away toward the ground. Khayzur flapped his wings and sent another giant gust. The serpent let out a defeated sound. It collapsed in the distance with a crash, flattening back out across the land, gone in an instant.

Nahri let out a breath. Her ankle was already healing, but Dara had to help her to her feet and give her a shove to get out of the ditch.

The river had lain down along different banks and was busily consuming the trees and ripping at the cliffs they had just escaped. There was no sign of the ifrit.

They had crossed the Gozan.

They had made it.

She stood up, giving her ankle a delicate twist before she let out a triumphant shout. She could have thrown her head back and howled at the stars herself, she was so thrilled to be alive. "By God, Khayzur has the *best* timing!" She grinned, glancing around for Dara.

But Dara wasn't behind her. Instead she spotted him rushing toward Khayzur. The peri landed on the ground and immediately collapsed, his wings falling around him as he crumpled.

By the time she reached them, Khayzur lay cradled in Dara's arms. His lime-colored wings were marked with white boils and gray scabs that grew larger before her eyes. He shuddered and several feathers fell to the ground.

". . . was following and tried to warn . . . ," he was saying to Dara. "You were so close . . ." The peri stopped to take a deep, rattling breath. He looked shrunken, and there was a purplish cast to his skin. When he looked up at her, his colorless eyes were resigned. Doomed.

"Help him," Dara begged. "Heal him!"

Nahri bent to take his hand, but Khayzur waved her off. "There's nothing you can do," he whispered. "I broke our law." He reached up and touched Dara's ring with one of his claws. "And not for the first time."

"Just let her try," Dara pleaded. "This can't be happening because you saved us!"

Khayzur gave him a bitter smile. "You still don't understand, Dara, about my people's role. Your race never did. Centuries after being crippled by Suleiman for interfering with humans . . . and you still don't understand."

Taking advantage of Khayzur's distracted rambling, Nahri

laid her palm over one of the boils. It hissed and grew icy at her touch and then doubled in size. The peri yelped, and she pulled away. "I'm sorry," she rushed. "I've never healed anything like you."

"And you can't now," he said gently. He coughed to clear his throat and lifted his head, his long ears pricked up like a cat's. "You need to go. My people are coming. The marid will be back, as well."

"I'm not leaving you," Dara said firmly. "Nahri can cross the threshold without me."

"It is not Nahri they want."

Dara's bright eyes widened, and he glanced around, as though he expected to see a new addition to their trio. "M-me?" he stammered. "I don't understand. I'm nothing to either your race or the marids!"

Khayzur shook his head as the shrill cry of a large bird pierced the air. "Go. Please . . . ," he croaked.

"*No.*" There was a tremor in Dara's voice. "Khayzur, I can't leave you. You saved my life, my soul."

"Then do the same for another." Khayzur rustled his wrecked wings and gestured at the sky. "What's coming is beyond you both. Save your Nahid, Afshin. It's your duty."

It was as if he'd cast a spell on the daeva. She watched Dara swallow and then nod, all trace of emotion vanishing from his face. He laid the peri carefully on the ground. "I am so sorry, old friend."

"What are you doing?" Nahri exclaimed. "Help him to his feet. We need to— Dara!" she shouted as the daeva picked her up and threw her over his shoulder. "Don't! We can't leave him here!" She kneed the daeva in the chest and tried to push off his back, but his grip was too tight. "Khayzur!" she screamed, catching a glimpse of the injured peri.

He gave her a long, sad look before turning his gaze back to the sky. Four dark shapes soared over the cliffs. The wind kicked up, seeding the air with sharp pebbles. She saw the peri wince and draw a withered wing across his face for protection.

"Khayzur!" She kicked at Dara again, but he only sped up, struggling to clamber over a sandy dune with her still on his shoulder. "Dara, please! Dara, don't—"

And then she could not see Khayzur any longer, and they were gone.

12

ALI

Ali's spirits felt lighter as he headed for the midan, cheered by Jamshid's kind words. He passed under the Agnivanshi Gate, its scattered oil lamps making it seem like traveling through a constellation. Ahead, the midan was still, the night songs of insects replacing the sound of the music and drunken revelers he left behind. A cool breeze blew bits of rubbish and silvery dead leaves across the ancient cobblestones.

A man stood at the fountain's edge. Rashid. Ali recognized him, though his secretary was out of uniform, dressed in a rather bland dark robe and slate-colored turban.

"Peace be upon you, Qaid," Rashid greeted him as Ali came forward.

"And upon you peace," Ali replied. "Forgive me. I didn't think we had any further business this evening."

"Oh, no!" Rashid assured. "Nothing official, anyway." He smiled, his teeth a bright flash in the dark. "I hope you'll forgive my impertinence. I didn't mean to pull you away from your evening amusements."

Ali made a face. "It's no bother, trust me."

Rashid smiled again. "Good." He gestured to the Tukharistani Gate. "I was on my way to see an old friend in the Tukharistani Quarter, and thought you might like to come along. You've mentioned wanting to see more of the city."

It was a kind, if slightly strange, offer. Ali was the king's son; he wasn't someone you casually invited for tea. "Are you sure? I wouldn't want to intrude."

"It's no intrusion at all. My friend runs a small orphanage. In truth, I thought it might be good for a Qahtani to be seen there. They've fallen on rough times recently." Rashid shrugged. "Your choice, of course. I know you've had a long day."

Ali had, but he was also intrigued. "I'd like that very much, actually." He returned Rashid's smile. "Lead the way."

BY THE TIME THEY REACHED THE HEART OF THE Tukharistani Quarter, clouds had drawn past the sky, veiling the moon and bringing a light mist of rain. The weather did nothing to dissuade the crowds of merrymakers and evening shoppers, however. Djinn children chased each other through the crowd, running after conjured-up pets of smoke while their parents gossiped under metal canopies hastily erected to block the rain. The sound of the raindrops striking their battered copper surfaces echoed throughout the quarter. Enclosed glass globes of enchanted fire hung from the storefronts, reflecting the puddles and dizzy array of colors on the bustling street.

Ali narrowly avoided two men haggling over a glittering golden apple. A Samarkandi apple, Ali recognized; a lot of djinn swore a single bite of its flesh was as effective as a Nahid's touch. Though Ali's Tukharistani wasn't great, he could hear pleading in the prospective buyer's voice, and he glanced back. Rust-colored metal growths covered the man's face, and his left arm ended in a stump.

Ali shuddered. *Iron poisoning.* It wasn't terribly uncommon, especially among djinn travelers who might drink from a stream without realizing it ran over banks rich in the deadly metal. Iron built up in the blood for years, before striking violently and without warning, causing limbs and skin to atrophy. Deadly and swift, it was nonetheless easily cured by a single visit to a Nahid.

Except there weren't any more Nahids. And that apple wouldn't help the doomed man, nor would the myriad other "cures" hawked to desperate djinn by unscrupulous con artists. There was no substitute for a Nahid healer, and that was a dark truth that most people—Ali included—tried not to think about. He averted his eyes.

Thunder rumbled, oddly distant. Perhaps a storm was brewing past the veil hiding the city. Ali kept his head down, hoping to avoid both the rain and the curious glances of passersby. Even out of uniform, his height and royal finery gave him away, provoking startled salaams and hurried bows in his direction.

When they reached a fork in the main road, Ali noticed a striking stone monument twice his height, built of worn sandstone, roughly shaped like an elongated bowl, almost like a boat placed on its stern. The top had started to crumble, but as they passed, he spotted new incense at its base. A small oil lamp burned inside, throwing flickering light on a long list of names in Tukharistani script.

The Qui-zi memorial. Ali's skin crawled as he recalled what happened to the ill-fated city. Which Afshin's handiwork had that atrocity been again? Artash? Or was it Darayavahoush? Ali frowned, trying to remember his history lessons. Darayavahoush, of course; Qui-zi was why people started calling him the Scourge. A nickname to which the Daeva devil had thoroughly committed, judging from the horrors he would later perpetrate during his rebellion.

Ali glanced again at the memorial. The flowers inside were fresh, and he wasn't surprised. His people had long memories, and what had happened at Qui-zi was not a thing easily forgotten.

Rashid finally stopped outside a modest two-story dwelling. It was not a particularly impressive sight; the roof tiles were cracked and covered in black mold, and dying plants in broken pots were scattered out front.

His secretary tapped lightly on the door. A young woman opened it. She gave Rashid a tired smiled that vanished as soon as she spotted Ali.

She dropped into a bow. "Prince Alizayd! I . . . peace be upon you," she stammered, her Djinnistani laced with the thick accent of Daevabad's working class.

"You can call him Qaid, actually," Rashid corrected. "At least for now." Amusement simmered in his voice. "May we come in, sister?"

"Of course." She held open the door. "I'll prepare some tea."

"Thank you. And please tell Sister Fatumai that we're here. I'll be in the back. There's something I want to show the Qaid."

There is? Curious, Ali wordlessly followed Rashid down a dark corridor. The orphanage looked clean—its floors were worn but well-scrubbed—but in terrible disrepair. Water dripped into pans from the broken roof, and mildew covered the books that were neatly stacked in a small classroom. The few toys he saw were sad things: animal bones carved into game pieces, patched dolls, and a ball made of rags.

As they turned the corner, he heard a terrible hacking cough. Ali glanced down the corridor. It was dim, but he spotted the shadowy form of an older woman supporting a skinny young boy upon a faded cushion. The boy started to cough again, the hacking sound interspaced by choked sobs.

The woman rubbed the boy's back as he fought for air. "It's okay, dear one," Ali heard her say softly, bringing a cloth to his mouth as he coughed again. She pressed a steaming cup to his lips. "Have some of this. You'll feel better."

Ali's eyes locked on the cloth she'd held to the boy's mouth. It glistened with blood.

"Qaid?"

Ali glanced up, realizing Rashid was halfway down the corridor. He quickly caught up. "Sorry," he mumbled. "I didn't mean to stare."

"It's all right. These are things I'm sure you're usually kept from seeing."

It was a strangely worded response, delivered with a hint of chiding that Ali had never heard from his mild-mannered secretary. But before he could dwell on it, they reached a large room fronting an uncovered courtyard. Tattered curtains, patched where possible, were all that separated it from the chilly rain falling in the yard.

Rashid pressed a finger to his lips and pulled back one of the curtains. The floor was crowded with sleeping children, dozens of boys and girls wrapped in blankets and bedrolls, packed close for both warmth and lack of space, Ali imagined. He took a step closer.

They were shafit children. And curled under a quilt, her hair already starting to grow out, was the girl from Turan's tavern.

Ali stepped back so quickly he stumbled. *We have a safe house in the Tukharistani Quarter* . . . Horrified realization swept over him.

Rashid's hand landed heavy on his shoulder. Ali jumped, half-expecting a blade.

"Easy, brother," Rashid said softly. "You wouldn't want to startle the children . . ." He clapped his other hand over Ali's as Ali reached for his zulfiqar. ". . . nor run from this place covered in another's blood. Not when you're so easily recognized."

"You bastard," Ali whispered, stunned by how easily he'd walked into a trap so obvious in hindsight. He wasn't usually one for swearing, but the words tumbled out. "You fucking trait—"

Rashid's fingers dug a little deeper. "That's enough." He pushed Ali down the hall, gesturing to the next room. "We just want to talk."

Ali hesitated. He could take Rashid in a fight, of that he was certain. But it would be bloody, and it would be loud. Their location was intentional. A single shout, and he'd awaken dozens of innocent witnesses. He had no good options, and so Ali steeled himself and walked through the door. His heart immediately sank.

"If it isn't the new Qaid," Hanno said, greeting him coolly. The shapeshifter's hand dropped to the long knife tucked in his belt, and his copper eyes flashed. "I hope that red turban of yours was worth Anas's life."

Ali tensed, but before he could reply, a fourth person—the older woman from the corridor—joined them at the door.

She waved Hanno off. "Now, brother, surely that's no way to treat our guest." Despite the circumstances, her voice was oddly cheerful. "Make some use of yourself, you old pirate, and pull me up a seat."

The shapeshifter grumbled, but did as he was told, laying a cushion upon a wooden crate. The woman made her way in, helped by a black wooden cane.

Rashid touched his brow. "Peace be upon you, Sister Fatumai."

"And upon you, Brother Rashid." She settled onto the cushion. She was shafit, that much Ali could tell from her dark brown eyes and rounded ears. Her hair was gray, half-covered by a white cotton shawl. She looked up at him. "My, you *are* tall. You must be Alizayd al Qahtani then." The slightest of amused smiles lit her pale face. "We meet at last."

Ali shifted uncomfortably on his feet. It was far easier to rage at the Tanzeem men than this grandmotherly figure. "Am I supposed to know you?"

"Not yet, no. Though I suppose these times call for flexibility."

She inclined her head. "My name is Hui Fatumai. I am . . ." Her smiled faded. "Rather, I was one of Sheikh Anas's associates. I run the orphanage here and many of the Tanzeem's charitable works. For which I should thank you. It was only through your generosity that we were able to do so much good."

Ali raised an eyebrow. "That's apparently not all you were doing with my 'generosity.' I saw the weapons."

"And what of it?" She nodded to the zulfiqar at his waist. "You wear a weapon to protect yourself. Why should my people not have the same right?"

"Because it's against the law. Shafit aren't allowed to carry weapons."

"They're also forbidden medical care," Rashid cut in, giving Ali a knowing look. "Tell me, brother, whose idea was the clinic on Maadi Street? Who paid for that clinic and stole medical books from the royal library to train its providers?"

Ali flushed. "That's different."

"Not in the eyes of the law," Rashid rebuked. "Both preserve the lives of shafit, and thus both are forbidden."

Ali had no response for that. Fatumai was still studying him. Something that might have been pity flickered in her brown eyes. "How young you are," she remarked quietly. "Far nearer in age to the children sleeping in the next room than to any of us, I imagine." She clucked her tongue. "I am almost sorry for you, Alizayd al Qahtani."

Ali didn't like the sound of that. "What do you want with me?" he asked. His nerves were starting to get the better of him, and his voice shook.

Fatumai smiled. "We want you to help save the shafit, of course. Ideally by resuming our funding as soon as possible."

He was incredulous. "You must be joking. Anas was supposed to buy food and books with the money I gave him, not rifles and daggers. You can't possibly think I'd give you a coin more."

"Full bellies mean nothing if we can't protect our children from slavers," Hanno snapped.

"And we already educate our people, Prince Alizayd," Fatumai added. "But to what end? Shafit are forbidden from skilled work; if our kind are lucky, they can find a job as a servant or bed slave. Do you have any idea how hopeless that makes life in Daevabad? There is no betterment save the promise of Paradise. We're not allowed to leave, we're not allowed to work, our women and children can be legally stolen by any pureblood claiming they're related—"

"Anas gave me the speech," Ali interrupted, his voice more cutting than he intended. But he had believed Anas's words before, and the knowledge that his sheikh had lied to him still stung. "I'm sorry, but I've done everything in my power to help your people." It was the truth. He'd given the Tanzeem a fortune and even now was quietly delaying the harsher measures his father wanted to put in place on the shafit. "I don't know what else you expect."

"Influence." Rashid spoke up. "The sheikh did not recruit you for money alone. The shafit need a champion at the palace, a voice to speak for their rights. And you need us, Alizayd. I know you're stalling those orders your father gave you. The new laws you're supposed to be enforcing? Hunting down the traitor from the Royal Guard who stole zulfiqar training blades?" A slight grin played on his mouth at that. "Let us help you, Brother Alizayd. Let us help each other."

Ali shook his head. "Absolutely not."

"This is a waste of time," Hanno declared. "The brat is Geziri—he'd probably let Daevabad burn to the ground before turning on his own." His eyes flashed, and his fingers again lingered on the hilt of his knife. "We should just kill him." Bitterness crept into his voice. "Let Ghassan know what it feels like to lose a child."

Ali drew back in alarm, but Fatumai was already waving him

off. "Give Ghassan a reason to slaughter every shafit in the city, you mean. No, I don't think we'll be doing that."

From out in the corridor, the little boy began to cough again. The sound—that hacking, blood-tinged cough, that sad little sob—cut deep, and Ali flinched.

Rashid noticed. "There's medicine for it, you know. And there are a few human-trained shafit physicians in Daevabad who could help him, but their skills don't come cheap. Without your aid, we can't afford to treat him." He raised his hands. "To treat any of them."

Ali dropped his gaze. *There's nothing to stop them from turning around and spending whatever I give them on weapons.* He'd trusted Anas far more than he trusted these strangers, and the sheikh had still deceived him. Ali could not risk betraying his family again.

A mouse darted past his feet, and a drop of rain landed on his cheek from a leak in the ceiling. In the next room, he could hear children snoring from their makeshift beds on the floor. He thought guiltily of the enormous bed back in the palace that he didn't even use. It would probably hold ten of those children.

"I can't," he said, his voice cracking. "I can't help you."

Rashid pounced. "You *must*. You're a Qahtani. The shafit are the reason your ancestors came to Daevabad, the reason your family now possesses Suleiman's seal. You know the Holy Book, Alizayd. You know how it requires you to stand up for justice. How can you claim to be a man of God when—"

"That's quite enough," Fatumai spoke up. "I know you're passionate, Rashid, but insisting a boy not even near his first quarter century betray his family lest he be damned isn't going to help anyone." She let out a weary sigh, tapping her fingers on her cane. "This is not a thing that needs to be decided tonight," she declared. "Think on what we've said here, Prince. On what you've seen and heard in this place."

Ali blinked in disbelief. He glanced nervously among them. "You're letting me go?"

"I'm letting you go."

Hanno gaped. "Are you mad? He's going to run right to his abba! He'll have us rounded up by dawn!"

"No, he won't," Fatumai met his gaze, her face calculating. "He knows the cost too well. His father would come for our families, our neighbors . . . a whole score of innocent shafit. And if he's the boy of whom Anas spoke so fondly, the one on whom he pinned so many hopes . . ." She gave Ali an intent look. "He won't risk that."

Her words sent a shiver down his spine. She spoke correctly: Ali did know the cost. If Ghassan learned about the money, if he then suspected others might know it was a Qahtani prince who'd funded the Tanzeem . . . Daevabad's streets would be flowing with shafit blood.

And not just shafit. Ali wouldn't be the first inconvenient prince to be assassinated. Oh, it would be done carefully, probably as quickly and painlessly as possible—his father wasn't cruel. An accident. Something that wouldn't make his mother's powerful family too suspicious. But it would happen. Ghassan took kingship seriously, and Daevabad's peace and security came before Ali's life.

Those weren't prices Ali was willing to pay.

His mouth was dry when he tried to speak. "I won't say anything," he promised. "But I'm done with the Tanzeem."

Fatumai didn't look even the slightest bit worried. "We'll see, Brother Alizayd." She shrugged. "Allahu alam."

She said the human holy words better than Ali's pureblood tongue would ever manage, and he couldn't help but tremble slightly at the confidence in her voice, at the phrase meant to demonstrate the folly of man's confidence.

God knows best.

13

NAHRI

It was as if they stepped through an invisible door in the air. One minute Nahri and Dara were scrambling over dark dunes, and the next, they emerged in an entirely new world, the dark river and dusty plains replaced by a small glen in a quiet mountain forest. It was dawn; the rosy sky glowed against silver tree trunks. The air was warm and moist, rich with the smell of sap and dead leaves.

Dara dropped Nahri gently to her feet, and she landed on a soft patch of moss. She took a deep breath of the cool, clean air before whirling on him.

"We need to go back," she demanded, shoving at his shoulders. There was no trace of the river, though through the trees, something blue glistened in the distance. A sea, perhaps; it looked vast. She waved her hands through the air, searching for the way through. "How do I do it? We need to get him before—"

"He's likely already dead," Dara interrupted. "From the stories

told about the peris . . ." She heard his throat catch. "Their punishments are swift."

He saved our lives. Nahri felt sick. She angrily wiped away the
tears rolling down her cheeks. "How could you leave him there?
It was him you should have carried, not me!"

"I . . ." Dara turned away with a choked sob and abruptly
dropped onto a large, moss-covered boulder. His head fell into
his hands. The weeds surrounding him started to blacken and a
hazy heat rose in waves above the rock. "I couldn't, Nahri. Only
those of our blood can cross the threshold."

"We could have tried to help. To fight—"

"How?" Dara glanced up. His eyes were dim with sorrow,
but his expression was resolute. "You saw what the marid did to
the river, how Khayzur fought back." He pressed his mouth in a
grim line. "Compared to the marid and peri, we are insects. And
Khayzur was right—I had to get you to safety."

Nahri leaned against a crooked tree, feeling ready to collapse
herself. "What do you think happened to the ifrit?" she finally
asked.

"If there's any justice in this world, they were dashed upon the
rocks and drowned." Dara spat. "That . . . *woman*," he said scornfully. "It was she who enslaved me. I remember her face from the
memory you triggered."

Nahri wrapped her arms around herself; she was still wet,
and the dawn air was cool. "The one I killed said they were working with my *mother*, Dara." Her voice choked on the word. "That
Manizheh they kept talking about." She reeled; Khayzur's death,
the mention of her mother, an entire damned *river* rising up to
smash them to pieces . . . it was all too much.

Dara was at her side in a moment. He took her by the shoulders, bending to meet her gaze. "They're lying, Nahri," he said
firmly. "They're demons. You can't trust anything they say. All

they do is deceive and manipulate. They do it to humans, they do it to daevas. They will say anything to trick you. To break you."

She managed a nod, and he briefly cupped her cheek with one hand. "Let's just get into the city," he said softly. "We should be able to find sanctuary at the Grand Temple. We'll figure out our next step there."

"All right." The press of his palm on her skin made her think back to what they'd been doing before the ifrit attack, and she flushed. She glanced away, looking around them for the city. But she saw nothing but silvery trees and flashes of the sun-dappled water in the distance. "Where *is* Daevabad?"

Dara pointed through the trees. The forest descended sharply before them. "There's a lake at the bottom of the mountain. Daevabad is on an island at its center. There should be a ferry down by the beach."

"The djinn use ferries?" It was so unexpected and so human, she almost broke into laughter.

He raised an eyebrow. "Can you think of a better way to cross a lake?"

Movement drew her eye. Nahri glanced up, catching sight of a gray hawk perched in the trees opposite her. It stared back, shifting on its feet as it settled into a more comfortable position.

She turned back to Dara. "I suppose not. Lead the way."

Nahri followed him through the trees as the sun climbed higher and filled the forest with a lovely, pale yellow light. Her bare feet crunched through the underbrush, and as she passed a thick bush with spindly dark green leaves, she let her hands drift out to briefly cradle a spray of salmon-colored buds. They warmed to her touch and began to blossom ever so slightly.

She glanced at Dara from the corner of her eye, watching as he gazed at the forest. Despite Khayzur's death, there was a new light in his eyes. *He's home,* Nahri realized. And it wasn't just his eyes that were shining; as he reached to clear away a low-hanging branch, she caught a glimpse of his ring, the emerald glowing bright. Nahri frowned, but as she moved closer to him, the glow vanished.

The forest finally began to flatten, the trees thinning out to give way to a pebbly shore. The lake was enormous, ringed by mountains of green hardwood forests on the southern side and sheer cliffs in the distant north. The blue-green water was completely still, an unbroken sheet of glass. She saw no island, nothing even hinting at a village, let alone a massive city.

But there was a large boat beached not far from where they stood, similar in shape to the feluccas that sailed the Nile. The sun flashed off the dizzying black and gold designs painted on the hull, and a triangular black sail flapped uselessly in the breeze, reaching for the lake. A man stood on the sharply curved bow with his arms crossed, chewing the end of a skinny pipe. His clothing reminded Nahri of the Yemeni traders she'd seen in Cairo, a patterned waist-wrap and simple tunic. His skin was as brown as hers, and his trimmed black beard the length of a fist. A tasseled gray turban was tied around his head.

There were two other men on the beach below the boat, both dressed in voluminous robes of dark teal and matching head wraps. As Nahri watched, one gestured angrily at the man on the boat, shouting something she couldn't hear and pointing behind him. From the trees on the other side of the forest, a few more men appeared, leading camels laden with bound white tablets.

"Are they daevas?" she asked in an eager hush, noting the way their robes shimmered and smoked and their black skin gleamed.

Dara didn't look as excited. "Probably not their preferred term."

She ignored his hostility. "Djinn then?" When he nodded, she returned to watching them. Even after the months she had spent with Dara, the sight before her still seemed unimaginable.

Djinn, nearly a dozen of them. The stuff of legends and campfire tales in the flesh, haggling like old women.

"The men in the robes are Ayaanle," Dara offered. "Probably salt traders, judging from their cargo. That other man is Geziri," Dara said, looking at the ferryman with narrowed eyes. "Probably one of the king's agents, although he certainly doesn't look very official," he added snobbishly. He glanced back at Nahri. "Pull your scarf—what remains of it anyway—across your face when we get closer."

"Why?"

"Because no Daeva would travel with a shafit companion," he said plainly. "At least not in my time. I don't want to draw attention." He plucked a bit of muck from his left sleeve and rubbed it carefully on his cheek to hide his tattoo. "Let me have my robe back. I need to cover the marks on my arms."

Nahri pulled it off and handed it over. "Do you think you'll be recognized?"

"Eventually. But apparently my choices are being arrested in Daevabad or returning to the Gozan to be murdered by marids and peris for some unknown offense." He wrapped the tail end of his turban close around his jaw. "I'll take my chance with the djinn."

She pulled her scarf across her face. The men were still fighting when they reached the boat. Their language was raucous, sounding like a mismatch of every language Nahri had ever heard in the bazaars.

"The king will hear of this, he will!" one of the Ayaanle traders declared. He angrily shook a piece of parchment at the boatman's feet. "We were given a fixed contract by the palace for transport!"

Nahri watched the men in awe. All the Ayaanle were at least two heads taller than she was, their brilliant teal robes flapping like birds. Their eyes were gold, but without the yellow harshness of the ifrit. She was utterly transfixed; she didn't even have to touch them to feel the life and energy sparking just beneath their skin. She could hear their breathing, could sense enormous lungs filling and puffing like bellows. The beat of their hearts was like wedding drums.

The Geziri boatman was far less impressive, though his slouch and stained tunic might have been to blame. He exhaled a long stream of black smoke and orange sparks, dangling the pipe from his long fingers.

"A pretty piece of paper," he drawled, gesturing at the traders' contract. "Perhaps it shall serve as a raft if you don't want to pay my price."

Nahri appreciated the man's logic, but Dara seemed less impressed. He stepped up, the others finally noticing them. "And what price is that?"

The boatman gave him a surprised look. "Daeva pilgrims don't pay, you fool." He grinned wickedly at the Ayaanle. "Crocodiles, however . . ."

The other djinn abruptly raised his hand, and sparks twisted around his fingers. "You dare insult us, you thin-blooded, wave-addled . . ."

Dara gently led Nahri to the other side of the boat. "They might be a while," he said as they headed up the narrow painted ramp.

"They sound like they're going to kill each other." She glanced back as one of the Ayaanle traders started to bang a long wooden staff against the boat's hull. The Geziri captain cackled.

"They'll agree on a fare eventually. Believe it or not, their tribes are actually allies. Though of course under *Daeva* rule, all passage was free."

She detected a hint of smugness in his voice and sighed. Something told her the squabbles between the various djinn tribes would make the war between the Turks and Franks look positively friendly.

But however nasty their argument, the captain and the merchants must have finally agreed on a price, because before she knew it, the camels were being led into the belly of the ship. The boat lurched and swayed with each step, the sewn wooden planks protesting. Nahri watched the merchants settle on the opposite end of the boat, gracefully crossing their long legs underneath their sweeping robes.

The captain jumped aboard and pulled the ramp up with a loud bang. Nahri felt her stomach flutter with nerves. She watched as he plucked a short rod from his waist-wrap. As he turned it over in his hands, it became longer and longer.

She frowned, peering over the boat's side. They were still beached on the shore. "Shouldn't we be in the water?"

Dara shook his head. "Oh, no. Passengers only embark from land. It's too risky otherwise."

"Risky?"

"Oh, the marid cursed this lake centuries ago. If you put so much as a toe in the water, it'll grab you, rip you to shreds, and send your remains to all the locations your mind has ever contemplated."

Nahri's mouth dropped open in horror. "*What?*" she gasped. "And we're going to cross it? In this rickety piece of—"

"There is no god but God!" the captain cried and slammed the rod—which was now a pole nearly as long as the boat—into the sandy shore.

The boat shoved off so fast it was briefly propelled in the air. It slammed into the lake with a great crash that sent a wave of water flying over its sides. Nahri shrieked and covered her head, but the captain quickly swept between her and the rising wave. He clucked his tongue at the water and threatened it with his pole like one would shoo away a dog. The water flattened out.

"Relax," Dara urged, looking embarrassed. "The lake knows to behave. We're perfectly safe here."

"It knows . . . Do me a favor," Nahri seethed, glaring at the daeva. "Next time we're about to do something like cross a marid-cursed lake that *shreds* people, stop and explain every step. By the Most High . . ."

No one else seemed bothered. The Ayaanle were chatting among themselves, sharing a basket of oranges. The captain balanced precariously on the edge of the hull and adjusted the sail. As Nahri watched, he tucked the pipe into his tunic and began to sing.

The words swept over her, sounding oddly familiar yet completely incomprehensible. It was such a strange sensation that it took her a moment to fully realize what was happening. "Dara?" She tugged on his sleeve, drawing his attention from the sparkling water. "Dara, I can't understand him." That had never happened to her before.

He glanced up at the djinn. "No, he's singing in Geziriyya. Their language can't be understood, can't even be learned by foreign tribesmen." His lips curled. "A fitting ability for such a duplicitous people."

"Don't start."

"I'm not. I didn't say it to his face."

Nahri sighed. "What was that they were speaking to each other then?" she asked, gesturing between the captain and the traders.

He rolled his eyes. "Djinnistani. An ugly and unrefined merchant tongue consisting of the most unpleasant sounds of all their languages."

Well, that was enough of Dara's opinions for now. Nahri turned away, lifting her face to the bright sun. It was warm on her skin, and she fought to keep her eyes open, the rhythmic motion of the boat lulling her toward sleep. She lazily watched a gray hawk circle and dip close, perhaps hoping for orange scraps, before it veered off toward the distant cliffs.

"I still don't see anything that looks like a city," she said idly.

"You will very shortly," he answered, peering at the green mountains. "There's one last illusion to pass."

As he spoke, something shrill rang in her ears. Before she could cry out, her entire body suddenly constricted, as if it had been compressed in a tight sheath. Her skin burned, and her lungs felt full of smoke. Her vision briefly blurred as the ringing grew louder . . .

And then it was gone. Nahri lay flat on her back on the deck, trying to catch her breath. Dara leaned over her, his face full of worry. "What happened? Are you all right?"

She pushed herself upright and rubbed her head, dislodging her shawl and wiping away the sweat that sheened her face. "I'm fine," she mumbled.

One of the Ayaanle merchants rose as well. Upon seeing her uncovered face, he averted his golden eyes. "Is your lady ill, brother? We have some food and water . . ."

"She's not your concern," Dara snapped.

The trader flinched like he'd been slapped and abruptly sat back down with his fellows.

Nahri was shocked by Dara's rudeness. "What's wrong with you? He was just trying to help." She let her voice rise, half-hoping the Ayaanle could hear her embarrassment. She pushed away Dara's hand as he tried to help her to her feet, and then nearly fell over again as an enormous walled city loomed before them, so large it blotted out most of the sky and entirely covered the rocky island upon which it sat.

The walls alone would have dwarfed the Pyramids, and the only buildings she could see in the distance were tall enough to peek over them: a dizzying variety of slender minarets, egg-shaped temples with sloping green roofs, and squat brick build-ings draped in intricate white stonework resembling lace. The wall itself shone brilliantly in the bright sun, the light glistening off the golden surface like . . .

"Brass," she whispered. The massive wall was entirely built of brass, polished to perfection.

She wordlessly walked to the edge of the boat. Dara followed. "Yes," he said. "The brass better holds the enchantments used to build the city."

Nahri's eyes roamed the wall. They were approaching a port of stone piers and docks that looked large enough to hold both the Frankish and Ottoman fleets. A large, perfectly cut stone roof sheltered much of the area, held up by enormous columns.

As the boat pushed closer, she noticed figures skillfully carved into the wall's brass surface, dozens of men and women dressed in an ancient style she couldn't identify, with flat caps covering their curly hair. Some were standing and pointing, holding un-furled scrolls and weighted scales. Others simply sat with open palms, their veiled faces serene.

"My God," she whispered. Her eyes widened as they grew closer; brass statues of the same figures towered over the boat.

A grin like Nahri had never before seen lit Dara's face as he gazed upon the city. His cheeks flushed with excitement, and when he glanced down at her, his eyes were so bright she could barely meet his gaze.

"Your ancestors, Banu Nahida," he said, gesturing to the statues. He pressed his hands together and bowed. "Welcome to Daevabad."

14

ALI

Ali slammed the stack of papers back on his desk, nearly knocking over his teacup. "These reports are lies, Abu Zebala. You are the city's sanitation inspector. Explain to me why the Daeva Quarter all but sparkles while a man in the Sahrayn district was crushed the other day by a collapsing pile of garbage."

The Geziri official standing before him offered an obsequious smile. "Cousin . . ."

"I am not your cousin." Not technically true, but sharing a great-great-grandfather with the king had gotten Abu Zebala his position. It wasn't going to let him squirm out of answering the question.

"*Prince*," Abu Zebala graciously corrected. "I am investigating the incident. It was a young boy—he should not have been playing in the trash. Truly, I blame his parents for not—"

"He was two hundred and eighty-one, you fool."

"Ah." Abu Zebala blinked. "Was he then?" He swallowed, and

Ali watched him calculate his next lie. "Either way . . . the idea of equally distributing sanitation services among the tribes is out-dated."

"I beg your pardon?"

Abu Zebala pressed his hands together. "The Daevas greatly value cleanliness. Their whole fire cult is about purity, no? But the Sahrayn?" The other djinn shook his head, looking disap-pointed. "Come now. Everyone knows those western barbarians would happily stew in their own filth. If cleanliness is important enough to the Daevas that they're willing to put a price on it . . . who am I to deny them?"

Ali narrowed his eyes as he untwisted Abu Zebala's words. "Did you just admit to being bribed?"

The other man didn't even have the decency to look ashamed. "I would not say bribed . . ."

"Enough." Ali shoved the records back at him. "Correct this. Each quarter gets the same standard of trash removal and street sweeping. If it's not done by the end of the week, I'll have you sacked and sent back to Am Gezira."

Abu Zebala started to protest, but Ali raised his hand so abruptly the other man flinched. "Get out. And if I hear you speak of such corruption a second time, I'll take your tongue to prevent a third."

Ali didn't really mean that; he was merely exhausted and an-noyed. But Abu Zebala's patronizing smile vanished and he paled. He nodded and quickly left, his sandals clattering as he fled down the steps.

That was poorly done. Ali sighed and stood, walking toward the window. But he didn't have the patience for a man like Abu Zebala. Not after last night.

A single ferry pushed over the calm water of the distant lake, bright sunlight reflecting on its black and gold hull. It was a beautiful day to sail. Whoever was on the ferry should count themselves lucky, he thought; the last time Ali crossed was in rain so heavy he'd feared the boat would sink.

He yawned, exhaustion creeping up on him again. He hadn't gone back to the palace last night, unable to bear the thought of seeing his luxurious apartment—or running into the family the Tanzeem wanted him to betray—after the disastrous encounter at the orphanage. But he hadn't gotten much sleep in his office; in truth, he hadn't gotten much sleep since the night he had followed Anas into the Daeva Quarter.

He returned to his desk, its flat surface suddenly tempting. Ali laid his head upon his arm and closed his eyes. *Maybe just a few minutes . . .*

A sudden knock jarred Ali from sleep, and he jumped, scattering his papers and knocking over the teacup. When the grand wazir barged in, Ali didn't bother to hide his irritation.

Kaveh closed the door as Ali swept wet tea leaves off his now-stained reports. "Hard at work, my prince?"

Ali glared at him. "What do you want, Kaveh?"

"I need to speak to your father. It is most urgent."

Ali waved his hand around the office. "You do know that you're in the Citadel? I understand it must be confusing at your age . . . all these buildings that look nothing alike, located on opposite sides of the city . . ."

Kaveh sat without invitation in the chair across from Ali. "He won't see me. His servants say he's busy."

Ali hid his surprise. Kaveh was a deeply annoying man, but his position was one which usually guaranteed access to the king, especially if the matter was urgent. "Perhaps you've fallen from favor," he suggested hopefully.

"I take it then that the rumors do not have you worried?" Kaveh asked, pointedly ignoring Ali's response. "The gossip in the bazaar about a Daeva girl who supposedly converted to your faith to elope with a djinn man? People say her family stole her back last night and are hiding her in our quarter."

Ah. Ali reconsidered Kaveh's concern. There wasn't much that sparked more tension in their world than conversions and intermarriage. And unfortunately the situation the wazir just laid out was fuel for a riot. Daevabad's law provided absolute protection to converts; under no circumstances were their Daeva families allowed to harass or detain them. Ali saw no problem with this: the djinn faith was the correct faith, after all. Yet the Daevas could be extremely possessive when it came to their kin, and it rarely ended well.

"Would it not be better for you to go back to your people and find the girl? Surely you have the resources. Return her to her husband before things get out of control."

"As much as I enjoy handing over Daeva girls to mobs of angry djinn," Kaveh started sarcastically, "the girl in question doesn't seem to exist. No one on either side knows her name or has any identifying information. Some say her husband is a Sahrayn trader, some say a Geziri metalworker, and others a shafit beggar." He scowled. "If she were real, I would know."

Ali narrowed his eyes. "So what is the problem then?"

"That it's a rumor. There's no girl to turn over. But that answer merely angers the djinn even more. I fear they're looking for any reason to sack our quarter."

"And who is 'they,' Grand Wazir? Who would be foolish enough to attack the Daeva Quarter?"

Kaveh raised his chin. "Perhaps the men who helped Anas Bhatt murder two of my tribesmen, the men I believe *you* were tasked with finding and arresting."

It took every bit of self-control Ali had not to flinch. He cleared his throat. "I doubt a few fugitives already on the run from the Royal Guard would be interested in attracting such attention."

Kaveh held his stare a moment longer. "Perhaps." He sighed. "Prince Alizayd, I'm simply telling you what I've heard. I know you and I have our differences, but I beg that you set them aside for a moment." He pursed his lips. "There's something about this that has me truly worried."

The honesty in Kaveh's voice struck him. "What would you have me do?"

"Put a curfew in place and double the guard at our tribal gate."

Ali's eyes went wide. "You know I cannot do that without the king's permission. It would cause panic in the streets."

"Well, you must do *something*," Kaveh insisted. "You're the Qaid. The city's safety is your responsibility."

Ali rose from his desk. Kaveh was probably being ridiculous. But on the very, *very* slim chance this rumor had a grain of truth, he did want to do what he could to avoid a riot. And that meant going to his father.

"Let's go," he said, beckoning Kaveh along. "I'm his son, he'll see me."

"THE KING CAN'T SEE YOU RIGHT NOW, MY PRINCE."

Ali's cheeks grew hot as the guard politely denied him. Kaveh coughed into his hand in a poor effort to hide his laugh. Ali stared at the wooden door, embarrassed and annoyed. His father wouldn't see the grand wazir and now was too busy for his Qaid?

"This is ridiculous." Ali barged past the guard and shoved the door open. He didn't care what sort of dalliance he was interrupting.

But the scene that met his eyes was not the flirtatious pack of concubines he expected, but rather a small group of men huddled around his father's desk: Muntadhir, Abu Nuwas, and even more strangely, a shafit-looking man he didn't recognize clad in a shabby brown robe and sweat-stained white turban.

The king glanced up, clearly surprised. "Alizayd . . . you're early."

Early for what? Ali blinked, trying to gather his composure. "I . . . ah, sorry, I didn't realize you were . . ." He trailed off. Conspiring? Judging from how quickly the men straightened up when he barged in and the vaguely guilty look on his brother's face, conspiring was definitely his first impression. The shafit man lowered his gaze, stepping behind Abu Nuwas like he didn't want to be seen.

Kaveh came in behind him. "Forgive us, Your Majesty, but there is an urgent matter—"

"Yes, I got your message, Grand Wazir," his father interrupted. "I'm handling it."

"Oh." Kaveh squirmed under the king's withering stare. "I just fear that if—"

"I said I'm handling it. You're dismissed."

Ali almost felt a moment of pity for the Daeva man as he quickly backed out of the room. Ignoring his younger son, Ghassan nodded at Abu Nuwas. "So we're understood?"

"Yes, sire," Abu Nuwas said, his voice grave.

The king turned his attention to the shafit man. "And if you get caught . . ."

The man simply bowed, and his father nodded. "Good, you may both go." He glanced at Ali, and his face hardened. "Come here," he commanded, switching to Geziriyya. "Sit."

He'd gone in as Qaid, but now Ali felt more like a boy bracing for a scolding. He took a seat on the plain chair opposite his father. He noticed for the first time that the king was in his ceremonial black robes and jewel-colored turban, which was odd. Court was being held later this afternoon, and his father didn't typically dress like that unless he expected public business. A steaming cup of green coffee sat by his bejeweled hand, and his pile of scrolls looked even messier than usual. Whatever he was working on, he'd clearly been at it for some time.

Muntadhir came around the desk and nodded at the cup. "Should I take that before you hurl it at his head?"

Ali bit back a wave of panic, fidgeting under his father's harsh stare. "What did I do?"

"Not much, it seems," Ghassan said. He drummed his fingers over the sprawl of papers. "I've been reviewing the reports from Abu Nuwas on your . . . *tenure* as Qaid."

Ali drew back. "There are reports?" He had figured Abu Nuwas was watching him, but there was enough paper on the desk to contain a detailed history of Daevabad. "I didn't realize you had him spying on me."

"Of course I had him spying on you," Ghassan scoffed. "Did you really think I'd blindly hand over complete control of the city's security to my underage son with a history of poor decision making?"

"I take it his reports are not glowing?"

Muntadhir winced, and his father's face darkened. "I hope you keep your sense of humor, Alizayd, when I send you to some wretched garrison in the wastes of the Sahara." He jabbed angrily at the papers. "You were supposed to hunt down the remaining Tanzeem and teach the shafit a lesson. Yet our jail is mostly empty, and I see no evidence of increased arrests or evictions. What happened to the new ordinances on the shafit? Should not half of them be out on the street?"

So Rashid had been correct last night in saying Ghassan would soon realize Ali wasn't putting the new laws in place. Ali fought for words. "Is it not a good thing for our jail to be empty? There has been no mass violence since Anas's execution, no increase in crime . . . I cannot arrest people for things they don't do."

"Then you should have drawn them out. I told you I wanted

them gone. You are Qaid. It's your responsibility to figure out how to accomplish my orders."

"By inventing charges?"

"Yes," Ghassan said vehemently. "If that is what's needed. Besides, Abu Nuwas says there have been several instances of purebloods having their foster children kidnapped in the past few weeks. Could you not have followed up on that?"

Foster children? Is that what they call them? Ali gave his father an incredulous look. "You realize the people who make those complaints are slavers, yes? They kidnap these children from their parents in order to sell them to the highest bidder!" Ali started to rise from his seat.

"Sit down," his father snapped. "And don't spout that shafit propaganda at me. People give up children all the time. And if these so-called slavers of yours have their paperwork in order, then as far as both you and I are concerned, they fall within the law."

"But, Abba—"

His father slammed his fist onto the desk so hard the scrolls jumped. An inkwell fell, smashing to the floor.

"Enough. I've already told Abu Nuwas that such transactions can now be done in the bazaar if it will make things safer." When Ali opened his mouth, his father held up his hand. "Don't," he warned. "If you say another word on the matter, I swear I'll have you stripped of your titles and sent back to Am Gezira for the rest of your first century." He shook his head. "I was willing to give you a chance to prove your loyalty, Alizayd, but—"

Muntadhir swept between them and spoke for the first time. "It is not yet at that point, Abba," he said cryptically. "Let us see what the day brings—that is what we decided, yes?" He ignored Ali's questioning look. "But perhaps when Wajed returns, Ali *should* go to Am Gezira. He is not even at his quarter century yet. Give him a garrison back home, and let him get seasoned for a few decades among our own people in a place where he can do less damage."

"That's not necessary." Ali's face grew hot, but his father was already nodding in agreement.

"It is something to consider, yes. But things will not continue like this until Wajed's return. After today, you'll have excuse enough to crack down on the shafit."

"What?" Ali sat up straight. "Why?"

A shrill bird cry from outside the window interrupted them, and then a gray hawk neatly swept through the stone frame, tumbling to the floor in the form of a Geziri soldier, his uniform perfectly pressed. He fell into a bow as smoky feathers melted back into his skin. A scout, Ali recognized, one of the shapeshifters that regularly patrolled both the city and the surrounding lands.

"Your Majesty," the scout started. "Forgive my intrusion, but I have news I thought urgent."

Ghassan frowned impatiently when the scout fell silent. "Which is . . . ?"

"There's a Daeva slave crossing the lake with an Afshin mark on his face."

His father's scowl deepened. "*And?* I have Daeva men going mad, painting themselves up in Afshin marks and running half-naked through the streets at least once a decade. That he's a slave only explains his lunacy."

The scout persisted. "He . . . he did not seem mad, my king. A bit *haggard* perhaps, but imposing. He looked like a warrior to me and wore a dagger at his waist."

Ghassan stared. "Do you know when the last Afshin died, soldier?" When the scout flushed, Ghassan continued. "*Fourteen hundred* years ago. Slaves don't last that long. The ifrit give them to the humans to cause chaos for a few centuries and when they're driven thoroughly insane, dump them back on Daevabad's doorstep to scare us." He raised his brows. "Rather effectively, in your case."

The scout dropped his gaze, stammering something unintelligible, but Ali noticed his brother suddenly frown.

"Abba," Muntadhir started. "You don't think . . ."

Ghassan threw him an exasperated glance. "Did you not hear what I just said? Don't be ridiculous." He turned back to the scout. "If it will console you both, follow him. Should he draw a bow and start scourging shafit in the street . . . well, then I suppose the day will be more interesting. Go."

The flustered scout bowed; feathers sprouted over his arms, and he flew out the window, looking eager to escape.

"An Afshin . . ." Ghassan shook his head. "Next Suleiman himself will be appearing on my throne to lecture the masses." He waved a dismissive hand at his sons. "You can go, as well, though you're both confined to the palace for the rest of the day."

"What?" Ali jumped to his feet. "I'm acting Qaid, there's a possible riot brewing in the streets, a crazed slave arriving, and you want to lock me in my room?"

The king lifted his dark brows. "You won't be Qaid for long if you keep questioning my orders." He inclined his head toward the door. "*Go.*"

Muntadhir grabbed Ali by the shoulders, literally turning him around and shoving him toward the exit. "Enough, Zaydi," he hissed under his breath.

They're up to something. Ali didn't like to think his father capable of intentionally stirring up such dangerous rumors, but even so, he didn't want the shafit lured into a riot. He started to break off down the corridor. As much as the idea turned his stomach, he knew he needed to find Rashid.

Muntadhir grabbed his wrist. "Oh, no, akhi. You don't leave my side today."

"I need to get some papers from the Citadel."

Muntadhir gave him a long look. Too long. Then he shrugged. "Well, then by all means, let's go."

"You don't need to come."

"I don't?" Muntadhir crossed his arms. "And that's where you would go? Just to the Citadel. Alone and back again without meeting anyone . . . *no*, Alizayd," he snapped, grabbing Ali's chin when he looked away, unable to meet his older brother's suspicious gaze. "You look at me when I talk to you."

A group of chattering courtiers rounded the bend of the corridor, and Muntadhir dropped his hand, stepping away from Ali as they passed.

The anger returned to his brother's face as soon as they were out of sight. "You fool. You're not even a good liar, do you know that?" Muntadhir paused and then let out an exasperated sigh. "Come with me."

He grabbed Ali's arm and pulled him in the opposite direction of the courtiers, through a servants' entrance near the kitchens. Too frightened to protest, Ali stayed silent until his brother stopped at an unassuming alcove. Muntadhir raised his hand, whispering an incantation under his breath.

The alcove's surface smoked. It vanished. A set of dusty stone steps greeted them, yawning into blackness.

Ali swallowed. "Are you going to assassinate me?" He was not entirely joking.

Muntadhir glared. "No, akhi. I'm going to save you."

MUNTADHIR LED HIM ON A DIZZYING PATH DOWN the stairs and through deserted corridors, lower and lower until Ali could hardly imagine they were still in the palace. There were no torches; the only light came from a handful of flames that Muntadhir charmed into existence. The firelight danced widely on the slick, damp walls, making Ali uncomfortably aware of how tight the corridor was. The air was thick and smelled of mildew and wet earth. "Are we under the lake?"

"Probably."

Ali shuddered. They were underground *and* underwater? He tried not to think about the press of stone and earth and water above his head, but his heart raced. Most pureblooded djinn were notoriously claustrophobic, and he was no different. Nor was his brother, judging from Muntadhir's ragged breathing.

"Where are we going?" he finally dared to ask.

"It's better seen than explained," Muntadhir said. "Don't worry, we're close."

A few moments later the corridor ended abruptly in a pair of thick wooden doors that barely came to Ali's chin. There were no knobs or door pulls, nothing to indicate how they opened.

Muntadhir's hand shot out when Ali reached for them. "Not like that," he warned. "Let me have your zulfiqar."

"You're not going to cut my throat and leave me in this godforsaken place, are you?"

"Don't tempt me," Muntadhir said flatly. He took the zulfiqar, bent down, and ran the blade lightly along his ankle. He pressed his palm against the bloody wound and handed the zulfiqar back to Ali. "Your turn. Take the blood from somewhere Abba won't see. He'd kill me if he found out I brought you down here."

Ali frowned but followed his brother's example with the blade. "Now what?"

"Put your hand here." Muntadhir gestured to a pair of grimy copper seals on the door, and they each pressed a bloody hand against a seal. The ancient doors opened with a whisper of dust into yawning blackness. His brother stepped through and raised his fistful of flames.

Ali ducked under the low doorway and followed. Muntadhir flung his hand out, scattering the flames to light the torches on the walls, illuminating a large cavern roughly hacked out of the city's bedrock. Ali covered his nose as he took another step on the soft, sandy ground. The cavern reeked, and as his eyes adjusted to the blackness, he stilled.

The floor was covered with coffins. Scores, he realized, as Muntadhir lit another torch. Some were neatly lined up in identical rows of matching stone sarcophagi, while others were simply jumbled piles of plain wooden boxes. The smell wasn't mildew. It was rot. The sharply astringent odor of the ashy decay of a djinn.

Ali gasped in horror. "What is this?" All djinn, regardless of their tribe, burned their dead. It was one of the few rituals they shared after Suleiman divided them.

Muntadhir scanned the room. "Our handiwork, apparently."

"*What?*"

His brother motioned him toward a large rack of scrolls concealed behind an enormous marble sarcophagus. All were sealed in lead containers marked with tar. Muntadhir cracked open one of the seals, pulled out the scroll, and handed it to Ali. "You're the scholar."

Ali carefully unrolled the fragile parchment. It was covered in an archaic form of Geziriyya, a simple line drawing of names leading to other names.

Daeva names.

A family tree. He glanced at the next page. This one had several entries, all following roughly the same format. He struggled to read one.

"Banu Narin e-Ninkarrik, aged one hundred and one. Drowning. Verified by Qays al Qahtani and her uncle Azad . . . Azad e-*Nahid* . . . Aleph noon nine nine," Ali read out the symbols at the end of the entry and raised his gaze to the pile of coffins before him. All had a four-digit pattern of numbers and letters painted in black tar on their sides.

"Merciful God," he whispered. "It's the Nahids."

"All of them," his brother confirmed, an edge to his voice. "All those who've died since the war anyway. No matter the cause." He nodded at one dark corner, so far back Ali could only make out shadowy shapes of boxes. "Some Afshins, as well, though their family was wiped out in the war itself, of course."

Ali gazed around. He spotted a pair of tiny coffins across the room and turned away, his stomach souring. Regardless of how he felt about the fire worshippers, this was ghastly. Only the worst criminals were buried in their world, dirt and water said to be so contaminating to djinn remains that they concealed one's soul from God's judgment entirely. Ali wasn't sure he believed that, but still, they were creatures of fire, and to fire they were supposed to return. Not to some dark, dank cave under a cursed lake.

"This is obscene," he said softly as he rolled up the scroll; he didn't need to read further. "Abba showed you this?"

His brother nodded and stared at the pair of small coffins. "When Manizheh died."

"I take it she's down here somewhere?"

Muntadhir shook his head. "No. You know how Abba felt about her. He had her burned in the Grand Temple. He said that when he became king he wanted to have all the remains blessed and burned, but he didn't think there was a way to do so discreetly."

Shame gnawed at Ali. "The Daevas would tear down the palace gates if they found out about this place."

"Probably."

"Then why do all this?"

Muntadhir shrugged. "You think it was Abba's decision? Look at how old some of these bodies are. This place was likely built by Zaydi himself . . . oh, don't give me that look, I know he's your hero, Ali, but don't be that naive. You must know the things people used to say about the Nahids, that they could change their faces, swap forms, resurrect each other from ash . . ."

"Rumors," Ali said dismissively. "Propaganda. Any scholar could—"

"It doesn't matter," Muntadhir said evenly. "Ali, *look* at this place." He pointed to the scrolls. "They kept records, they verified the bodies. We might have won the war, but at least some of our ancestors were so frightened of the Nahids, they literally kept their bodies to reassure themselves that they were truly dead."

Ali didn't respond. He wasn't sure how to. The whole room made his skin crawl; Suleiman's chosen, reduced to rotting in their burial shrouds. The cavern—no, the tomb—was silent save for the sound of spitting torches.

Muntadhir spoke again. "It gets worse." He jiggled free a small drawer in the side of the rack and plucked out a copper box about the size of his hand. "Another blood seal, though what you have on your hand should be enough to open it." He offered it to Ali. "Trust me, our ancestors never wanted anyone to find *this*. I'm not even sure why they kept it."

The box grew warm in Ali's bloody hand, and a tiny spring was released. Nestled inside was a dusty brass amulet.

A relic, he recognized. All djinn wore something similar, a bit of blood and hair, sometimes a baby tooth or flayed piece of skin—all bound up with holy verses in molten metal. It was the only means by which they could be returned to a body if they were enslaved by an ifrit. Ali wore one, as did Muntadhir, copper bolts through their right ears in the manner of all Geziri.

He frowned. "Whose relic is this?"

Muntadhir gave him a bleak smile. "Darayavahoush e-Afshin's."

Ali dropped the amulet as if it had bitten him. "The *Scourge of Qui-zi*?"

"May God strike him down."

"We shouldn't have this," Ali insisted. A shiver of fear ran down his spine. "That—that's not what the books say happened to him."

Muntadhir gave him a knowing look. "And what do the books say happened, Alizayd? That the Scourge mysteriously disappeared when his rebellion was at its height, as he prepared to retake Daevabad?" His brother knelt to retrieve the amulet. "Strange timing, that."

Ali shook his head. "It's not possible. No djinn would turn over another to the ifrit. Not even their worst enemy."

"Grow up, little brother," Muntadhir chided and replaced the box. "It was the worst war our people have ever seen. And Daraya-vahoush was a monster. Even I know that much of our history. If Zaydi al Qahtani cared for his people, he would have done any-thing to end it. Even this."

Ali reeled. A fate worse than death: That's what everyone said about enslavement. Eternal servitude, forced to grant the most savage and intimate desires of an endless slew of human masters. Of the slaves that were found and freed, very few survived with their sanity intact.

Zaydi al Qahtani couldn't have arranged such a thing, he tried to tell himself. His family's long reign could not be the product of such an awful betrayal of their race.

His heart skipped a beat. "Wait, you don't think the man the scout saw . . ."

"No," Muntadhir said, a little too quickly. "I mean, he can't be. His relic is right here. So he couldn't have been returned to a body."

Ali nodded. "No, of course not. You're right." He tried to put the nightmarish thought of the Scourge of Qui-zi, freed after centuries of slavery and seeking bloody vengeance for his slain Nahids, out of mind. "Then why did you bring me here, Dhiru?"

"To set your priorities straight. To remind you of our *real* enemy." Muntadhir gestured at the Nahid remains scattered around them. "You've never met a Nahid, Ali. You never watched

Manizheh snap her fingers and break the bones of a man across the room."

"It doesn't matter. They're dead anyway."

"But the Daevas are not," Muntadhir replied. "Those kids you were fretting about upstairs? What's the worst that will happen to them—they'll grow up thinking they're purebloods?" Muntadhir shook his head. "The Nahid Council would have had them burned alive. Hell, probably half the Daevas still think that's a good idea. Abba walks the line between them. We are neutral. It's the only thing that's kept peace in the city." He lowered his voice. "You . . . you are *not* neutral. People who think and talk the way you do are dangerous. And Abba does not suffer threats to his city lightly."

Ali leaned against the stone sarcophagus, and then remembering what it contained, quickly straightened back up. "What are you saying?"

His brother met his gaze. "Something's going to happen today, Alizayd. Something you're not going to like. And I want you to promise me you're not going to do anything stupid in response."

The deadly intent in Muntadhir's voice took him aback. "What's going to happen?"

Muntadhir shook his head. "I can't tell you."

"Then how can you expect me to—"

"All I'm asking is that you let Abba do what he needs to do to keep the city's peace." Muntadhir gave him a dark look. "I know you're up to something with the shafit, Zaydi. I don't know what exactly, nor do I want to. But it ends. *Today*."

Ali's mouth went dry. He fought for a response. "Dhiru, I—"

Muntadhir hushed him. "No, akhi. There is no fight to be had here. I'm your emir, your older brother, and I'm telling you: stay away from the shafit. Zaydi . . . *look at me*." He took Ali by the shoulders, forcing him to meet his eyes. They were filled with worry. "*Please*, akhi. There's only so much I can do to protect you otherwise."

Ali took a shaky breath. Here alone with the older brother he'd looked up to for years, the one he'd spent his life preparing to protect and serve as Qaid, Ali felt the terror and guilt of the past few weeks, the anxiety that weighed upon him like armor, finally loosen.

And then collapse. "I'm so sorry, Dhiru." His voice cracked, and he blinked, fighting back tears. "I never meant for any of this . . ."

Muntadhir pulled him into a hug. "It's all right. Look . . . just prove your loyalty now and I promise you that when I'm king, I will listen to you about the mixed-bloods. I have no desire to harm the shafit—I think Abba is often too hard on them. And I *know* you, Ali—you and your spinning mind, your obsession with facts and figures." He tapped Ali's temple. "I suspect there are *some* good ideas hiding behind your propensity for rash, terrible decisions."

Ali hesitated. *Earn this*. Anas's last order was never far in his mind, and if he closed his eyes, Ali could still see the crumbling orphanage, could hear the little boy's rattling cough.

But you can't save them on your own. And wouldn't the brother that he loved and trusted, the man who would actually have real power one day, be a better partner than the bickering remnants of the Tanzeem?

Ali nodded. And then he agreed, his voice echoing in the cavern.

"Yes, my emir."

15

NAHRI

Nahri glanced behind her, but the boat was already leaving, the captain singing as he returned to the open lake. She took a deep breath and followed Dara and the Ayaanle merchants as they made their way to the enormous doors, flanked by a pair of winged lion statues, set in the brass wall. The docks were otherwise deserted and in a state of disrepair. She picked her way carefully through the crumbling monuments, catching sight of a gray hawk watching them from high atop one of the statue's shoulders.

"This place looks like Hierapolis," she whispered. The decaying grandeur and deathly silence made it hard to believe there was a teeming city behind the high brass walls.

Dara cast a dismayed glance at a collapsed pier. "It was much grander in my day," he agreed. "The Geziri never had much taste in the finer aspects of life. I doubt they care about upkeep." He lowered his voice. "And I don't think the docks get much use.

I've not seen another daeva in years; I assumed most people became too afraid to travel after the Nahids were wiped out." He gave her a small smile. "Maybe now that will change."

She didn't return his smile. The idea that her presence might be reason enough to renew commerce was daunting.

The heavy iron doors opened as their group approached. A few men milled about the entrance, soldiers from the look of them. All wore white waist-wraps that went to their calves, black sleeveless tunics, and dark gray turbans. They shared the same bronze-brown skin and black beards as the boat captain. She watched as one nodded to the merchants and motioned them inside.

"Are they Geziris?" she asked, not taking her eyes off the long spears held by two of the men. Their scythed points had a coppery gleam.

"Yes. The Royal Guard." Dara took a deep breath, self-consciously touching the muddied mark on his temple. "Let's go."

The guards seemed preoccupied with the merchants, poking through their salt tablets and scouring their scrolls with pursed lips. One guard glanced up at them, his gunmetal gray gaze briefly flickering past her face. "Pilgrims?" he asked, sounding bored.

Dara kept his gaze low. "Yes. From Sarq—"

The guard waved him off. "Go," he said distractedly, nearly knocking Nahri over as he turned to help his fellows with the long-suffering salt traders.

Nahri blinked, surprised by how easily that had gone.

"Come on," Dara whispered, tugging her forward. "Before they change their minds."

They slipped through the open doors.

AS THE FULL FORCE OF THE CITY HIT HER, NAHRI realized the walls must have held sound in as well as magic because they were standing in the loudest, most chaotic place she'd ever seen, surrounded by waves of jostling people.

Nahri tried to peer over their heads to look down the crowded street. "What *is* this place?"

Dara glanced around. "The Grand Bazaar, I believe. We had ours in the same location."

Bazaar? She gave the frenzied scene a dubious glance. Cairo had bazaars. This looked more like a cross between a riot and the hajj. And it wasn't so much the number of people that astounded her, but the *variety*. Pureblooded djinn strode through the crowds, their odd and ephemeral grace marking their difference among the mob of more human-looking shafit. Their attire was wild—literally; in one case she saw a man pass by with an enormous python settled over his shoulders like a contented pet. People wore glowing robes the color of turmeric and dresses like wound-up sheets, held together by shells and razor-sharp teeth. There were headdresses of glittering stones and wigs of braided metals. Capes of bright feathers and at least one robe that looked like a skinned crocodile, its toothy mouth resting on its wearer's shoulder. A spindly man with an enormous smoking beard ducked by, and a girl holding a basket swept past Nahri, bumping her with one hip. The girl briefly glanced back, letting her gaze linger appreciatively on Dara. A spark of annoyance lit in Nahri, and one of the girl's long black braids let out a wriggle like a stretching snake. Nahri jumped.

Dara, meanwhile, just looked irritated. He eyed the bustling crowd with open displeasure, giving the muddy street an unimpressed sniff. "Come," he said, pulling her forward. "We'll attract attention if we just stand here gawking."

But it was impossible not to gawk as they pushed their way through the crowd. The stone street was wide, lined with dozens of market stalls and unevenly stacked buildings. A dizzying maze of covered alleys snaked off the main avenue, crowded with foul heaps of decaying garbage and stacked crates. The air was ripe with the smell of coal and cooking aromas. Djinn shouted and gossiped all around her; vendors hawked their wares while customers haggled.

Nahri couldn't identify half of what was being sold. Hairy purple melons quivered and trembled beside ordinary oranges and dark cherries, while midnight black nuggets the size of fists were piled between cashews and pistachios. Bolts of giant folded rose petals scented the air between those of patterned silk and sturdy muslin, and a jewelry merchant swung a pair of earrings toward her, painted glass eyes that seemed to wink. A stout woman in a bright purple chador poured a smoking white liquid into several different braziers, and a little boy with fiery hair tried to coax a golden bird twice his size from a rattan cage. Nahri nervously edged away; she'd had her fill of large birds.

"Where's the Grand Temple?" she asked, dodging a puddle of iridescent water.

Before Dara could answer, a man peeled off from the crowd and planted himself in front of them. He was dressed in stone-colored trousers and a close-fitting crimson tunic that reached his knees. A matching flat cap was perched upon his black hair.

"May the fires burn brightly for you both," he greeted them in Divasti. "Did I hear you say the Grand Temple? You are pilgrims, yes? Here to pay devotion to the glory of our dear, departed Nahids?"

His flowery words were so obviously recited that Nahri could only smile in recognition. A fellow hustler. She looked him over, noting his black eyes and sharp golden cheekbones. He was clean shaven save for a neat black mustache. A Daeva con artist.

"I can take you to the Grand Temple," he continued. "I have a cousin with a little tavern. Very fair prices for the rooms."

Dara shoved past the man. "I know the way."

"But there is still the matter of accommodation," the man persisted, hurrying to keep up with them. "Pilgrims from the countryside tend not to realize how dangerous Daevabad can be."

"Ah, and I bet you get a handsome cut from this cousin of yours with such fair prices," Nahri said knowingly.

The man's smile vanished. "Are you working with Gushnap?" He planted himself in front of them again and squared his shoulders. "I told him," he said, wagging a finger in her face. "This is my territory and . . . ah!" He shrieked as Dara seized him by his collar and yanked him away from Nahri.

"Let him go," she hissed.

But the Daeva man had already caught sight of the muddied mark on Dara's cheek. The color left his face, and he let out a muffled squeal as Dara lifted him off the ground.

"*Dara.*" Nahri felt a sudden prick behind her ears, the sensation of being watched. She abruptly straightened up and looked over her shoulder.

Her eyes met the curious gray gaze of a djinn across the street. He appeared to be Geziri and was dressed casually in a simple gray robe and turban, but there was a certain erectness to his posture that she didn't like. As she stared at him, he turned to a nearby stall as if browsing its wares.

It was then that Nahri saw the bazaar crowd was thinning. A few nervous faces disappeared down adjoining alleys, and a copper merchant across the way slammed his metal screen shut.

Nahri frowned. She'd lived through enough violence—the power struggles of various Ottomans, the French invasion—to recognize the quiet tension that overtook a city before it erupted. Windows were being latched and doors pulled closed. A woman shouted for a pair of dawdling children, and an elderly man limped down an alley.

Behind her, Dara was threatening to rip the con artist's lungs from his chest if he ever saw him again. She touched his shoulder. "We need to—"

Her warning was interrupted by a sudden clang. Down the avenue, a soldier used his scythe to strike a large set of brass cymbals strung from two opposing rooftops. "Curfew!" he cried.

Dara let go of the hustler, and the man fled. "*Curfew?*"

Nahri could feel the tension of the remaining crowd with every hurried heartbeat. *Something's going on here, something we know nothing about.* A quick glance showed her that the Geziri man she'd caught spying was gone.

She grabbed Dara's hand. "Let's go."

She caught snatches of whispers as they hurried through the emptying bazaar.

"That's what people are saying . . . kidnapped in the dead of night from their marriage bed . . ."

". . . gathering in the midan . . . the Most High only knows what they think they're going to accomplish . . ."

"The Daevas don't care," she heard. "The fire worshippers get whatever they want. They always do."

Dara tightened his grip on her hand, pulling her through the crush of people. They crossed through a tall ornamental gate to enter a large plaza enclosed by copper walls gone green with age. It was less crowded than the bazaar, but there were at least a few hundred djinn milling about the simple fountain of black and white marble blocks at the plaza's center.

The massive archway they had passed under was unadorned, but six other, smaller gates fronted the plaza, each decorated in a widely different style. Djinn, looking far better dressed and wealthier than the shafit in the bazaar, were vanishing through them. As she watched, a pair of flame-haired children chased each other through a gate of fluted columns with grapevines winding its length. A tall Ayaanle man pushed past her, headed for a gate marked by two narrow, studded pyramids.

Six gates for six tribes, she realized, as well as a gate for the bazaar. Dara pushed her toward the one directly across the plaza. The Daeva Gate was painted pale blue and held open by two brass statues of winged lions. A single Geziri guard stood there, clutching his coppery scythe as he tried to shepherd the nervous crowd through.

An angry voice caught her attention as they approached the fountain. "And what do you get for standing up for the faithful? For helping the needy and oppressed? Death! A gruesome death while our king hides behind the trousers of his fire-worshipping grand wazir!"

A djinn man dressed in a dirty brown robe and sweat-stained white turban had climbed on top of the fountain and was shouting to a growing group of men gathered below. He gestured angrily at the Daeva Gate. "Look, my brothers!" the man shouted again. "Even now, they are favored, guarded by the king's own soldiers! And this, after they've stolen an innocent new bride from the bed of her believing husband . . . a woman whose only crime was leaving her family's superstitious cult. Is this just?"

The crowd waiting to enter the Daeva Quarter grew, edging out toward the fountain. The two groups were mostly staying apart and giving each other wary glances, but Nahri saw a young Daeva man turn, looking annoyed.

"It is just!" the young Daeva argued back loudly. "This is our city. Why don't you leave our women alone and crawl back to whatever human hovel your dirt blood came from?"

"Dirt blood?" the man on the fountain repeated. He climbed to a higher block so that he was more visible to the crowd. "Is that what you think I am?" Not waiting for an answer, he produced a long knife from his belt and dragged it down his wrist. Several people in the crowd gasped as the man's dark blood dripped and sizzled. "Does this look like dirt to you? I passed the veil. I am as djinn as you!"

The Daeva man was not deterred. Instead, he stepped closer to the fountain, anger brewing in his black eyes. "That foul human word has no meaning for me," he snapped. "This is *Daeva*bad. Those who would call themselves djinn have no place here. Nor do their shafit spawn."

Nahri pressed closer to Dara. "Sounds like you have a friend," she muttered darkly. He scowled but said nothing.

"Your people are a disease!" the shafit man yelled. "A degenerate bunch of slavers still worshipping a family of inbred murderers!"

Dara hissed, and his fingers grew hot on her wrist. "Don't," Nahri whispered. "Just keep going."

But the insult clearly angered the Daeva crowd that remained, and more of them turned toward the fountain. A gray-haired old man defiantly raised an iron cudgel. "The Nahids were Suleiman's chosen! The Qahtanis are nothing but Geziri sand flies, filthy barbarians speaking the language of snakes!"

The shafit man opened his mouth to respond and then stopped, raising a hand to his ear. "Do you hear that?" He grinned, and the crowd went quiet. In the distance, she could hear chanting coming from the direction of the bazaar. The ground started to tremble, echoing with the pounding feet of a growing throng of marchers.

The man laughed as the Daevas started to nervously back away, the threat of a mob apparently enough to convince them to flee. "Run! Go huddle at your fire altars and beg your dead Nahids to save you!" More men poured into the plaza, anger in their faces. Nahri didn't see many swords, but enough were armed with kitchen knives and broken furniture to alarm her.

"This will be your day of reckoning!" the man shouted. "We

will tear through your homes until we find the girl! Until we find and free every believing slave you infidels hold!"

She and Dara were the last through the gate. Dara made sure she was past the brass lions and then turned to argue with the Geziri guard. "Did you not hear them?" He gestured at the growing mob. "Close the gate!"

"I cannot," the soldier replied. He looked young, his beard little more than black fuzz. "These gates never close. It's against the law. Besides, reinforcements are coming." He swallowed nervously, clutching his scythe. "There's nothing to worry about."

Nahri didn't buy his false optimism, and as the chanting grew louder, the soldier's gray eyes widened. Though she couldn't hear the djinn instigator over the shouts of the crowd, she saw him gesticulate to the mob of men below. He pointed defiantly at the Daeva Gate, and a roar went through them.

Nahri's heart raced. Daeva men and women, young and old, were rushing down the manicured streets and vanishing into the pretty stone buildings surrounding them. About a dozen men worked to quickly seal doors and windows, their bare hands the bright crimson of a blacksmith's tools. But they'd only completed about half the buildings, and the mob was close. Farther down the street, a toddler wailed as its mother pounded desperately on a locked door.

Something hardened in Dara's face. Before Nahri could do anything, he snatched the scythe away from the Geziri soldier and shoved him to the ground.

"Useless dog." Dara gave the doors a halfhearted tug, and when they didn't budge, he sighed, sounding more irritated than worried. He turned toward the crowd.

Nahri panicked. "Dara, I don't think . . ."

He ignored her and crossed the plaza toward the mob, twisting the scythe in his hands as if to test the weapon's weight. With the rest of the Daevas behind the gate, he was alone—a single man facing hundreds. The sight must have struck the crowd as amusing; Nahri caught sight of a few puzzled faces and heard laughter.

The shafit man hopped down from the fountain with a grin. "Can it be . . . is there at least one fire worshipper with some courage?"

Dara shaded his eyes with one hand and pointed the scythe at the crowd with the other. "Tell that rabble to go home. No one is tearing through any Daeva homes today."

"We have cause," the man insisted. "Your people stole back a convert woman."

"Go home," Dara repeated. Without waiting for a response, he turned back toward the gate. At Nahri's side, one of the winged lions seemed to shudder. She startled, but when she glanced over, the statue was still.

"Or what?" The shafit man started after Dara.

Still standing with his back to the crowd, Dara caught Nahri's eye as he pulled off the turban that partially covered his face.

"Get back, Nahri," he said, wiping off the mud that concealed his tattoo. "Let me handle this."

"*Handle* it?" Nahri kept her voice low, but anxiety swelled inside her. "Did you not hear the guard? There are soldiers coming!"

He shook his head. "They're not here now, and I've seen enough Daevas killed in my lifetime." He turned back toward the mob.

Nahri heard a few gasps of disbelief from the men nearest them, and then whispers began to race through the crowd.

The shafit man burst into laughter. "Oh, you poor soul, what in God's name have you done to your face? You think you're an Afshin?"

A stout man twice Dara's size in a blacksmith's apron stepped forward. "He has slave eyes," he said dismissively. "He's obviously deranged—who but a madman would wish to be one of those demons?" He raised an iron hammer. "Step aside, fool, or be struck down first. Slave or not, you're still only one man."

"I *am* only one man, aren't I? How kind of you to share your concerns—perhaps we should even the odds." Dara waved his hands toward the gate.

Nahri's first thought was that he motioned for her—which, while flattering, was a deeply flawed estimation of her abilities. But then the brass lion at her side shivered.

She backed away as it stretched, the metal groaning as the statue arched its back like a house cat. The one on the other side of the gate shook out its wings, opened its mouth, and roared.

Nahri wouldn't have thought any sound could rival the terror-inducing howl of the marid's river serpent, but these came close. The first lion cried back to its fellow just as loudly, a horrible growl mixed with the grating of rocks that shook her to her core. It belched a fiery plume of smoke, like coughing up a hair ball, and then strolled toward Dara with a sinewy grace completely at odds with its metal form.

Judging from the screams of the mob, Nahri suspected animating winged lions that breathed flames was not a regular occurrence in the djinn world. About half ran for the exits, but the rest hoisted their weapons, looking more determined than ever.

Not the shafit man—he looked entirely bewildered. He gave Dara a searching look. "I-I don't understand," he stammered as the ground started to rumble. "Are you working with—"

The shafit blacksmith was not similarly deterred. He raised an iron hammer and rushed forward.

Dara had barely raised his scythe when an arrow slammed into the blacksmith's chest, followed swiftly by another tearing through his throat. Dara glanced back in surprise as trumpeting filled the air around them.

A massive beast emerged from the gate leading to the bazaar. Twice the size of a horse, with gray legs as thick as tree trunks, the creature flapped a pair of fanlike ears and raised its long trunk to let out another angry bellow. An elephant, Nahri realized. She had seen one once, on a private estate she had robbed.

The elephant's rider ducked under the gate, a long silver bow in his hands. He coolly surveyed the chaos in the plaza. The archer appeared about her age—not that that meant anything among the djinn; Dara could pass as a man in his thirties, and he was older than her civilization. The rider also looked Daeva; his eyes and wavy hair were as black as hers, but he wore the same uniform as the Geziri soldiers.

He sat easily on the elephant, his legs propped up on a cloth saddle, his body swaying with the animal's movements. She saw him startle at the sight of the animated statues and raise his bow again before hesitating, likely realizing arrows were no match for the brass beasts.

More soldiers poured out from the other gates, pushing back the fleeing mob and fanning out to prevent any men from escaping. A coppery sword flashed, and someone screamed.

A trio of Geziri soldiers advanced on Dara. The closest drew his weapon, and one of the lions bounded over, growling as it whipped a metal tail through the air.

"Stop!" It was the archer. He quickly slid off the elephant, landing gracefully on the ground. "He's a slave, you fools. Leave him alone." He handed his bow to another man, and then raised his hands as he approached them. "Please," he said, switching to Divasti. "I mean you no—"

His gaze locked on the mark on Dara's temple. He made a small, choked sound of surprise.

Dara did not look similarly impressed. His bright eyes scanned the archer from his gray turban to his leather slippers, and then he made a face as if he'd downed an entire carafe of sour wine. "Who are you?"

"I . . . my name's Jamshid." The archer's voice came out in a whisper of disbelief. "Jamshid e-Pramukh. Captain," he added in a stammer. His gaze darted between Dara's face and the cavorting lions. "Are you . . . I mean . . . it's not—" He shook his head, abruptly cutting himself off. "I think I should take you to meet my king." He glanced at Nahri for the first time. "Your . . . ah . . . companion," he decided, "may join you as well if you desire."

Dara twisted his scythe. "And should I desire to—"

Nahri stomped hard on his foot before he could say something stupid. The rest of the soldiers were busy picking through the crowd, separating the men from the women and children, though Nahri saw some awfully young boys pushed up against the same wall as the men. Several were weeping and a few were praying, dropped in such familiar prostration that she had to tear her eyes away from the sight. She wasn't sure what passed for justice in Daevabad, nor how the king punished people who insulted him and threatened another tribe, but from the doomed looks in the eyes of the men as they were rounded up, she could make plenty of guesses.

And she didn't want to join them. She gave Jamshid a gracious smile through her veil. "Thank you for your invitation, Captain Pramukh. We would be honored to meet your king."

"THE FABRIC IS TOO THICK," NAHRI COMPLAINED. She sat back, letting the curtain go with a frustrated sigh. "I can't see anything." As she spoke, the palanquin that had been brought for them lurched forward and back, settling at an awkward angle that nearly spilled her into Dara's lap.

"We are ascending the hill that leads to the palace," Dara said, his voice low. He rolled his dagger in his hands and stared at the iron blade, his eyes flashing.

"Will you put that thing away? There are dozens of armed soldiers about—what are you going to do with that?"

"I'm being delivered to my enemy in a floral box," Dara replied and flicked the chintzy curtains with the dagger. "I might as well be armed."

"Did you not say dealing with the djinn was preferable to being drowned by river demons?"

He threw her a dark look and continued to twirl the knife. "To see a Daeva man dressed like them . . . serving that usurper—"

"He's not a *usurper*, Dara. And Jamshid saved your life."

"He did not *save* me," Dara replied, looking offended at the suggestion. "He prevented me from permanently silencing that wretched man."

Nahri let out an exasperated noise. "And murdering one of the king's subjects on our first day in Daevabad would help us how?" she asked. "We're here to make peace with these people, and find safe haven from the ifrit, remember?"

Dara rolled his eyes. "Fine," he sighed, toying with the dagger again. "But truthfully, I did not mean to do that with the shedu."

"The what?"

"The shedu—the winged lions. I wanted them to simply block the gate, but . . ." He frowned, looking troubled. "Nahri, I've felt . . . *strange* since we entered the city. Almost like—" The carriage lurched to a stop, and Dara shut his mouth. The curtains were yanked open to reveal a still nervous-looking Jamshid e-Pramukh.

Nahri ducked out of the litter, awed by the sight before her. "Is that the palace?"

It had to be; she could scarcely imagine what other building could be so enormous. Sitting heavy on a stony hill above the city, Daevabad's palace was a massive edifice of marble so big it blocked part of the sky. It wasn't particularly pretty, its main building a simple six-level ziggurat that stretched into the sky. But she could see the outline of two delicate minarets and a gleaming golden dome tucked behind the marble wall, hinting at more grandeur beyond.

A pair of golden doors were set in the palace walls, lit up by blazing torches. No . . . not torches, two more of the winged lions—shedu, Dara called them—their brass mouths filled with fire. Their wings were poised stiffly over their shoulders, and Nahri suddenly recognized them. The tattooed wing on Dara's cheek, crossed with the arrow. His Afshin symbol, the mark of service to the once royal Nahid family.

My family. Nahri shivered though the breeze was gentle.

As they passed the torches, Dara suddenly leaned close to whisper in her ear. "Nahri, it may be best if you remain . . . vague about your background."

"You mean I shouldn't tell my ancestral enemy that I'm a liar and a thief?"

Dara inclined his head against hers, keeping his gaze forward. His smoky smell surrounded her, and her stomach gave an involuntary flutter. "Say that the girl Baseema's family found you in the river as a child," he suggested. "That they kept you as a servant. Say you tried to keep your abilities hidden, and that you were just playing and singing with Baseema when you accidentally called me."

She gave him a pointed look. "And the rest of it?"

One of his hands found hers and gave it a gentle squeeze. "The truth," he said softly. "As much as possible. I know not what else to say."

Her heart sped as they entered a vast garden. Marble paths stretched out across the sunny grasses, shaded by manicured trees. A cool breeze brought the smell of roses and orange blossoms. Delicate fountains gurgled nearby, dappled by leaves and flower petals. The sweet trill of songbirds filled the air, along with the melody from a distant lute.

As they approached, Nahri could see that the first level of the massive ziggurat was open on one side with four rows of thick columns holding up the ceiling. There were flower-filled fountains set into the ground, and the marble floor was almost soft, perhaps worn down by millennia of feet. It was a white-veined green that resembled grass, bringing the garden indoors.

Although the space looked big enough for thousands, Nahri guessed that there were fewer than two hundred men there now, gathered around a stepped platform made of the same marble as the floor. It began to rise near the middle of the room with its highest level meeting the wall opposite the garden.

Nahri's gaze was immediately drawn to the figure at its front. The djinn king lounged on a brilliant throne set with dazzling jewels and intricate stonework, power radiating off his bronze-brown skin. His ebony robes smoked and twirled at his feet, and a beautifully colored turban of twisting blue, purple, and gold silk crowned his head. But from the way everyone in the room lowered their heads in deference, he needed neither rich clothes nor throne to indicate who ruled here.

The king looked like he'd once been handsome, but his graying beard and the paunch beneath his black robes attested to some age. His face was still sharp as a hawk's, however, his steel-colored eyes bright and alert.

Intimidating. Nahri gulped and looked away to study the rest. Aside from a retinue of guards, there were three other men on the marble platform's upper levels. The first was older, with hunched shoulders. He looked Daeva; a dark line of charcoal marked his golden brown forehead.

Two more djinn were on the next platform. One sat on a plump cushion and was dressed similarly to the king, his curly black hair mussed and his cheeks slightly flushed. He rubbed his beard, absentmindedly running his fingers around a bronze goblet. He was handsome, with an air of ease Nahri noticed was common in the rich and lazy, and bore a strong resemblance to the king. His son, she guessed; her gaze paused at a heavy sapphire ring on his pinkie. A prince.

A younger man stood directly behind the prince, dressed in similar fashion to the soldiers, though his turban was a dark crimson instead of gray. He was tall, with a scruffy beard and a severe expression on his narrow face. Though he shared the same luminous skin and peaked ears as purebloods, she had trouble identifying his tribe. He was nearly as dark as the Ayaanle salt traders, but his eyes were the steely gray of the Geziri.

No one appeared to notice them. The king's attention was focused on a pair of bickering men below. He sighed and snapped his fingers; a barefoot servant greeted his outstretched hand with a goblet of wine.

"—it's a monopoly. I know more than one Tukharistani family weaves jade thread. They shouldn't be allowed to band together whenever they sell to an Agnivanshi merchant." A well-dressed man with long black hair crossed his arms. A line of pearls draped his neck and two more encircled his right wrist. A heavy gold ring sparkled on one hand.

"And how do you know that?" the other man accused him. He was taller and looked a bit like the Chinese scholars she'd seen in Cairo. Nahri edged past Dara, curious to get a better look at the men. "Admit it: you're sending spies to Tukharistan!"

The king raised a hand, interrupting them. "Didn't I *just* deal with the two of you? By the Most High, why are you still doing business with each other? Surely there are other . . ." He trailed off.

The goblet fell from his hand as he stood, shattering on the marble floor, spatters of wine staining his robe. The hall fell silent, but he didn't seem to notice.

His eyes had locked on hers. Then a single word rushed from his mouth like a whispered prayer.

"*Manizheh?*"

16

NAHRI

Every head in the massive audience hall turned to stare at her. In the metal-toned eyes of the djinn—dark steel and copper, gold and tin—she saw a mix of confusion and amusement, as if she were the target of a joke yet to be revealed to her. A few tittering laughs rose from among the crowd. The king took a step away from his throne, and the noise abruptly stopped.

"You're alive," he whispered. The chamber was now so still she could hear him take a deep breath. The few remaining courtiers between her and the throne quickly backed away.

The man she assumed was a prince gave the king a bewildered look and then glanced back at Nahri, squinting to study her like she was some strange sort of insect. "That girl's not Manizheh, Abba. She looks so human she shouldn't have even passed the veil."

"*Human?*" The king stepped to the lower platform, and as he drew closer, a beam of sunlight from the screened windows caught his face. Like Dara, he was marked on one temple with a black tattoo; in his case, an eight-pointed star. The tattoo's edge had a smoky glow that seemed to wink at her.

Something in his face crumpled. "No . . . she is not Manizheh." He stared at her another moment and frowned. "But why would you think she's human? Her appearance is that of a Daeva pureblood."

It is? Nahri clearly wasn't the only one confused by the king's conviction. The whispers started back up, and the young soldier with the crimson turban crossed the platform to join the king.

He laid a hand on the king's shoulder, visibly concerned. "Abba . . ." The rest of his words followed in a hiss of incomprehensible Geziriyya, taking Nahri aback.

Abba? Could the soldier be another son?

"I see her ears!" The king shot back in annoyed Djinnistani. "How can you possibly think she's shafit?"

Nahri hesitated, uncertain of how to proceed. Were you allowed to just start talking to the king? Maybe she had to bow or . . .

The king suddenly made an impatient noise. He raised his hand, and the sigil on his temple flared to life.

It was as if someone had sucked the air from the room. The torches on the wall went out, the fountains ceased their gentle gurgle, and the black flags hanging behind the king stopped fluttering. A wave of weakness and nausea passed over Nahri, and pain flared in the various parts of her body she'd battered in the past day.

Beside her, Dara let out a strangled cry. He fell to his knees, ash beading off his skin.

Nahri dropped to his side. "Dara!" She laid a hand on his shivering arm, but he didn't respond. His skin was nearly as cold and pale as it had been after the rukh attack. She turned on the king. "Stop it! You're hurting him!"

The men on the platform looked as shocked as the king had when she first arrived. The prince gasped, and the older Daeva man stepped forward, one hand going to his mouth.

"The Creator be praised," he said in Divasti. He stared at Nahri with wide black eyes, a mixture of something like fear, hope, and ecstasy crossing his face all at once. "You . . . you're—"

"Not a shafit," the king interrupted. "As I told you." He dropped his hand, and the torches flared back to life. Beside her, Dara shuddered.

The Qahtani king hadn't taken his eyes off her once. "An enchantment," he finally concluded. "An enchantment to make you appear human. I have never heard of such a thing." His eyes were bright with wonder. "Who are you?"

Nahri helped Dara back to his feet. The Afshin was still pale and seemed to have trouble catching his breath. "My name is Nahri," she said, struggling under his weight. "That Manizheh you mentioned, I . . . I think I'm her daughter."

The king abruptly drew himself up. "Excuse me?"

"She's a Nahid." Dara hadn't recovered entirely, and his voice came out in a low growl that sent a few courtiers skittering farther away.

"A Nahid?" the seated prince repeated over the growing sounds of the shocked crowd. His voice was thick with disbelief. "Are you insane?"

The king raised his hand to dismiss the room. "Out, all of you."

He did not have to issue the order twice—Nahri didn't realize so many men could move that fast. She watched in silent fear as the courtiers were replaced by more soldiers. A line of guards—armed with those same strange copper swords—formed behind Dara and Nahri, blocking their escape.

The king's steely gaze finally left her face to fall upon Dara.

"If she's the daughter of Banu Manizheh, who exactly would that make you?"

Dara tapped the mark on his face. "Her Afshin."

The king lifted his dark brows. "This should be an interesting story."

"NONE OF THIS MAKES ANY SENSE," THE PRINCE declared when Dara and Nahri finally fell silent. "Ifrit conspiracies, rukh assassins, the Gozan rising from its banks to howl at the moon? A captivating tale, to be sure . . . perhaps it will earn you entrance to the actors' guild."

The king shrugged. "Oh, I don't know. The best tales always have at least a kernel of truth."

Dara bristled. "Should you not have your own witnesses to the events at the Gozan? Surely you have scouts there. Otherwise an army could be assembling at your threshold with you none the wiser."

"I'll consider that professional advice," the king replied, his tone light. He'd remained impassive as they spoke. "It *is* a remarkable story, however. There's no denying the girl is under some sort of curse—that she should be plainly pureblooded to me while appearing shafit to the rest of you." He studied her again. "And she does resemble Banu Manizheh," he admitted, a hint of emotion stealing into his voice. "Strikingly so."

"And what of it?" the prince countered. "Abba, you can't really believe Manizheh had a secret daughter? *Manizheh?* The woman used to give plague sores to men who looked too long upon her face!"

Nahri would not have minded such an ability right now. She'd spent the last day being attacked by various creatures and had little patience for the Qahtani's doubt. "Do you want proof that I'm a Nahid?" she demanded. She pointed at the curved dagger sheathed at the prince's waist. "Toss that over, and I'll heal before your eyes."

Dara stepped in front of her, and the air smoked. "That would be extremely unwise."

The young soldier, or prince, or whoever he was—the one with the scruffy beard and hostile expression—immediately edged closer to the prince. He dropped his hand to the hilt of his copper sword.

"Alizayd," the king warned. "Enough. And calm yourself, Afshin. Believe it or not, Geziri hospitality does not involve stabbing our guests. At least, not before we've been properly introduced." He gave Nahri a sardonic smile and touched his chest. "I am King Ghassan al Qahtani, as surely you know. These are my sons, Emir Muntadhir and Prince Alizayd." He pointed to the seated prince and the scowling young swordsman before gesturing to the older Daeva man. "And this is my grand wazir, Kaveh e-Pramukh. It was his son Jamshid who escorted you to the palace."

The familiarity of their Arabic names took her aback, as did the fact that two Daeva men served the royal family so prominently. *Good signs, I suppose.* "Peace be upon you," she said cautiously.

"And upon you as well." Ghassan spread his hands. "You'll forgive our doubts, my lady. It's only that my son Muntadhir speaks correctly. Banu Manizheh had no children and has been dead twenty years."

Nahri frowned. She wasn't one to share information easily, but she wanted answers more than anything else. "The ifrit said they were working with her."

"Working with her?" For the first time, she saw a hint of anger in Ghassan's face. "The ifrit were the ones who murdered her. A thing they apparently did with much glee."

Nahri's skin crawled. "What do you mean?"

It was the grand wazir who spoke up now. "Banu Manizheh

and her brother Rustam were ambushed by the ifrit on their way to my estate in Zariaspa. I . . . I was among the ones who found what was left of their traveling party." He cleared his throat. "Most of the bodies were impossible to identify, but the Nahids . . ." He trailed off, looking close to tears.

"The ifrit put their heads on spikes," Ghassan finished grimly. "And stuffed their mouths with the relics of all the djinn they enslaved in the traveling party, as an added bit of mockery." Smoke curled around his collar. "Working with her, indeed."

Nahri recoiled. She saw no hint of deception from the men on the platform—not on this matter at least. The grand wazir looked ill, and barely checked grief and rage swirled in the king's gray eyes.

And I came so close to falling into the hands of the demons who did that. Nahri was shaken, truly shaken. She considered herself skilled at detecting lies, but the ifrit had her almost convinced. She guessed Dara was right about them being talented liars.

Dara, of course, did not bother concealing his rage at the Nahid siblings' grisly demise. An angry heat radiated from his skin. "Why were Banu Manizheh and her brother even allowed outside the city walls? Did you not see the danger in allowing the last two Nahids *in the world* to go traipsing about outer Daevastana?"

Emir Muntadhir's eyes flashed. "They weren't our prisoners," he said heatedly. "And the ifrit hadn't been heard from in over a century. We scarcely—"

"No . . . he is right to question me." Ghassan's voice, quiet and devastated, silenced his elder son. "God knows I've done so myself, every day since they died." He leaned back against his throne, suddenly looking older. "It should have been Rustam alone. There was a blight in Zariaspa affecting their healing herbs, and he was the more skilled at botany. But Manizheh insisted on accompanying him. She was very dear to me—and very, very stubborn. A poor combination, I admit." He shook his head. "At the time, she was so adamant that I . . . ah."

Nahri narrowed her eyes. "What?"

Ghassan met her gaze, his expression simmering with an emotion she couldn't quite decipher. He studied her for a long moment and then finally asked, "How old are you, Banu Nahri?"

"I can't be sure. I think about twenty."

He pressed his mouth in a thin line. "An interesting coincidence." He did not sound pleased.

The grand wazir blushed, furious red spots blooming in his cheeks. "My king, surely you do not mean to suggest that Banu Manizheh—one of Suleiman's blessed and a woman of unimpeachable morals—"

"Had sudden cause twenty years ago to flee Daevabad for a distant mountain estate where she'd be surrounded by discreet and utterly loyal fellow Daevas?" He arched an eyebrow. "Stranger things have happened."

The meaning of their conversation suddenly became clear. A flicker of hope—stupid, naive hope—rose in Nahri's chest before she could squash it down. "Then . . . my father . . . is he still alive? Does he live in Daevabad?" She couldn't hide the desperation in her voice.

"Manizheh refused to marry," Ghassan said flatly. "And she had no . . . attachments. None that I was aware of, at least."

It was a curt answer that brooked no room for further discussion. But Nahri frowned, trying to puzzle things out. "But that doesn't make sense. The ifrit knew of me. If she fled before anyone learned of her pregnancy, if she was murdered on her journey, then . . ."

I shouldn't be alive. Nahri left the last part unspoken, but Ghassan looked equally stymied.

"I don't know," he admitted. "Perhaps you were born while they were still traveling, but I cannot imagine how you survived,

let alone wound up in a human city on the other side of the world."
He raised his hands. "We might never have those answers. I only
pray that your mother's final moments may have been lightened
by the knowledge that her daughter lived."

"Someone must have saved her," Dara pointed out.

The king raised his hands. "Your guess is as good as mine.
The curse affecting her appearance is a strong one . . . it might
not have been cast by a djinn."

Dara glanced down at her, something briefly unreadable in his
bright eyes before he turned back to the king. "She truly doesn't
appear a shafit to you?" Nahri could hear a hint of relief in his
voice. And it hurt, there was no denying it. Clearly, for all their
growing "closeness," blood purity was still important to him.

Ghassan shook his head. "She looks as Daeva as you do. And
if she's truly the daughter of Banu Manizheh . . ." He hesitated,
and something flickered in his face; it was replaced by his calm
mask in a moment, but she was good at reading people, and she
noticed.

It was fear.

Dara prodded him. "If she is . . . then what?"

Kaveh answered first, his black eyes meeting hers. Nahri
suspected the grand wazir—a fellow Daeva—didn't want the king
massaging this answer. "Banu Manizheh was the most talented
healer born to the Nahids in the last millennium. If you are her
daughter . . ." His voice turned reverent—and a little defiant.
"The Creator has smiled upon us."

The king shot the other man an annoyed look. "My grand
wazir is easily excited, but yes, your arrival in Daevabad might
prove quite the blessing." His eyes slid to Dara. "Yours, on the
other hand . . . you said you were an Afshin, but you've not yet
offered your name."

"It must have slipped my mind," Dara replied, his voice cool.
"Why don't you share it now?"

Dara lifted his chin slightly and then spoke. "Darayavahoush e-Afshin."

He might as well have drawn a blade. Muntadhir's eyes went wide, and Kaveh paled. The younger prince dropped his hand to his sword again, stepping closer to his family.

Even the implacable king now looked tense. "Just to be clear: are you the Darayavahoush who led the Daeva rebellion against Zaydi al Qahtani?"

The *what*? Nahri whirled on Dara, but he wasn't looking at her. His attention was locked on Ghassan al Qahtani. A small smile—the same dangerous smile he'd flashed at the shafit in the plaza—played around his mouth.

"Ah . . . so your people remember that?"

"Quite well," Ghassan said coolly. "Our history has a lot to say about you, Darayavahoush e-Afshin." He crossed his arms over his black robe. "Though I could have sworn one of my ancestors beheaded you at Isbanir."

It was a trick, Nahri knew, a slight to his honor meant to pull a better answer from the Afshin.

Dara, of course, rushed right into it. "Your ancestor did no such thing," he said acidly. "I never made it to Isbanir—you would not be sitting on that throne if I had." He held up his hand, and the emerald winked. "I was captured by the ifrit while battling Zaydi's forces in the Dasht-e Loot. Surely you can work out the rest."

"That doesn't explain how you stand before us now," Ghassan said pointedly. "You would have needed a Nahid to break the ifrit's slave curse, no?"

Though Nahri's head was swimming with new information, she noticed Dara hesitate before answering.

"I don't know," he finally confessed. "I thought the same . . . but it was the peri, Khayzur—the one who saved us at the river—who freed me. He said he found my ring on the body of a human traveler in his lands. His people don't typically intervene in our matters, but . . ." She heard Dara's throat catch. "He took mercy on me."

Something twisted in Nahri's heart. Khayzur had freed him from slavery *and* saved their lives at the Gozan? The sudden image of the peri alone and in pain, awaiting death from his fellows in the sky, played through her mind.

But Ghassan certainly didn't seem worried over the fate of a peri he'd never met. "When was this?"

"About a decade ago," Dara replied easily.

Ghassan looked taken aback again. "A decade? Surely you don't mean to say you spent the past fourteen centuries as an ifrit slave?"

"That's exactly what I mean to say."

The king pressed his fingers together, looking down his long nose. "Forgive me for speaking plainly, but I've known hardened warriors driven to gibbering madness by less than three centuries of slavery. What you're suggesting . . . no man could survive it."

What? Ghassan's dark words sent ice flooding into her veins. Dara's life as a slave was the one thing she hadn't pressed him on; he didn't want to talk about it, and she didn't want to think about the bloody memories she'd been forced to relive alongside him.

"I didn't say I survived it," Dara corrected, his voice curt. "I remember almost nothing of my time as a slave. It's difficult to be driven insane by memories you don't have."

"Convenient," Muntadhir muttered.

"Quite," Dara shot back. "For surely a—what did you say, a gibbering madman?—would have little patience for all this."

"And your life before you were a slave?"

Nahri startled at the sound of a new voice. The younger prince, she realized; Alizayd, the one she'd mistaken for a guard.

"Do you remember the war, Afshin?" he asked, in one of the coldest voices Nahri had ever heard. "The villages in Manzadar and Bayt Qadr?" Alizayd stared at Dara with open hostility, with a hatred that rivaled how Dara himself had looked upon the ifrit. "Do you remember Qui-zi?"

At her side, Dara tensed. "I remember what your namesake did to *my* city when he took it."

"And we'll leave it at that," Ghassan cut in, throwing his youngest son a warning look. "The war is over, and our peoples are at peace. A thing you must have known, Afshin, to willingly bring a Nahid here."

"I assumed it was the safest place for her," Dara said coolly. "Until I arrived to find an armed mob of shafit preparing to sack the Daeva Quarter."

"An internal matter," Ghassan assured him. "Believe me, your people were never in any danger. Those arrested today will be thrown in the lake by week's end."

Dara snorted, but the king remained impassive. Impressively so—Nahri sensed it took a lot to rattle Ghassan al Qahtani. She was not sure whether or not to be pleased by such a thing but decided to match his frankness. "What do you want?"

He smiled—a true smile. "Loyalty. Pledge yourselves to me and swear to preserve the peace between our tribes."

"And in return?" Nahri asked, before Dara could speak.

"I will declare you Banu Manizheh's pureblooded daughter. Shafit appearance or not, none in Daevabad will dare question your origin once I speak on such a thing. You'll have a home in the palace—your every material desire granted—and take your rightful place as Banu Nahida." The king inclined his head toward Dara. "I will formally pardon your Afshin and grant him a pension and position commensurate with his rank. He may even continue to serve you should you wish."

Nahri checked her surprise. She could not imagine a better offer. Which of course made her distrust it. He was essentially asking for nothing, in return for giving her everything she could imagine wanting.

Dara dropped his voice. "It's a trick," he warned in Divasti. "You will no sooner bend the knee to that sand fly than he will ask some—"

"The sand fly speaks perfect Divasti," Ghassan interrupted. "And does not require the bending of any knees. I am Geziri. My people don't share your tribe's love for overinflated ceremony. For me, your word is sufficient."

Nahri hesitated. She glanced again at the soldiers behind them. She and Dara were thoroughly outnumbered by the Royal Guard—not to mention the young prince clearly itching for a fight. However abhorrent the thought was to Dara, this was Ghassan's city.

And Nahri hadn't survived this long without learning to recognize when she was outmatched. "You have my word," she said.

"Excellent. May God strike us both down if we break it." Nahri flinched, but Ghassan only smiled. "And now that we have that unpleasantness behind us, may I be honest? You both look terrible. Banu Nahida, there appears to be a journey's worth of blood on your clothes alone."

"I'm fine," she insisted. "It's not all mine."

Kaveh blanched, but the king laughed. "I do believe I am going to like you, Banu Nahri." He studied her for another moment. "You said you were from the country of the Nile?"

"Yes."

"Tatakallam arabi?"

The king's Arabic was rough but comprehensible. Surprised, she nonetheless replied, "Of course."

"I thought so. It is one of our liturgical languages." Ghassan paused, looking thoughtful. "My Alizayd is a rather devoted student of it." He nodded at the scowling young prince. "Ali, why don't you escort Banu Nahri to the gardens?" He turned back to her. "You may relax, get cleaned up, have something to eat. Whatever you desire. I will have my daughter, Zaynab, keep you company. Your Afshin can stay behind to discuss our strategy with the ifrit. I suspect this isn't the last we've heard from those demons."

"That isn't necessary," she protested. She wasn't the only one. Alizayd pointed in Dara's direction, a flurry of Geziriyya coming from his mouth.

The king hissed a reply and raised his hand, and Alizayd shut up, but Nahri wasn't convinced. She didn't want to go anywhere with the rude prince, and she certainly didn't want to leave Dara's side.

Dara, however, reluctantly nodded. "You should rest, Nahri. You'll need your strength for the coming days."

"And you won't?"

"Oddly enough, I am perfectly well." He squeezed her hand, sending a rush of warmth straight to her heart. "Go," he urged. "I promise not to go to war without your permission," he added with a sharp smile at the Qahtanis.

As Dara released her hand, she caught sight of the king's careful gaze on the two of them. Ghassan nodded at her, and she followed the prince through an enormous set of doors.

ALIZAYD WAS HALFWAY DOWN THE WIDE, ARCADED corridor by the time she reached him. She jogged, trying to keep up with his long strides while casting curious glances at the rest of the palace. What she saw was well maintained, but she could sense the age of the ancient stone and crumbling facades.

A pair of servants bowed low as they passed, but the prince didn't seem to notice. He kept his head down as they walked. He clearly hadn't inherited his father's diplomatic warmth, and the openly hostile way he had spoken to Dara made her nervous.

Nahri sneaked a look at him from the corner of her eye. *Young* was her first impression. His hands clasped behind his back and his shoulders hunched, Alizayd carried his lanky body as if he'd recently sprouted into his alarming height and was still getting used to it. He had a long, elegant face, one that might have even been handsome had it not been furrowed in a scowl. His chin was scruffy, more the hope of a beard than anything substantial. Besides the copper scimitar, a hooked dagger was tucked in his belt, and Nahri thought she caught sight of another small knife bound to his ankle.

He glanced over, probably in the hope of studying her in a similar fashion, but their eyes caught, and he quickly looked away. Nahri cringed as the silence between them grew more strained.

But he was the king's son, and she was not easily deterred. "So," she started in Arabic, remembering what Ghassan said about him studying the language. "Think your father's going to kill us?"

She'd meant it as a poor joke to lighten the mood, but Alizayd's face twisted in open displeasure. "No."

The fact that he answered so easily—like he'd been mulling over the question himself—shocked her out of her feigned casualness. "You sound *disappointed*."

Alizayd gave her a dark look. "Your Afshin is a monster. He deserves to lose his head a hundred times over for the crimes he's committed." Nahri startled, but before she could respond, the prince pulled open a door and beckoned her through. "Come."

The sudden appearance of the late-afternoon light dazzled her eyes. The lilt of birdsong and monkey calls broke the quiet, occasionally cresting into the croak of a frog and the rustle of crickets. The air was warm and moist, so fragrant with the aroma of rose blossoms, rich soil, and wet wood that her nose stung.

As her eyes adjusted to the light, her amazement only grew. What stretched before them could hardly be called a garden. It was as vast and wild as the feral woods she and Dara had journeyed through, more like a jungle intent on devouring its garden roots. Dark vines sprawled from its depths like lapping tongues, swallowing the crumbling remains of fountains and ensnaring defenseless fruit trees. Flowers in near violent hues—a crimson that shone like blood, a speckled indigo like a starry night—bloomed across the ground. A pair of spiky date palms glittered in the sun before her, made entirely of glass, she realized, their plump fruit a golden jewel.

Something swooped overhead, and Nahri ducked as a four-winged bird—its feathers the variants of colors one would see in a setting sun—flew past. It vanished into the trees with a low growl that could have come from a lion ten times its size, and Nahri jumped.

"*This* is your garden?" she asked in disbelief. A tiled path stretched before them, broken by gnarled, thorned roots and shrouded by moss. Tiny glass globes filled with dancing flames floated over it, illuminating its twisting route into the garden's dark heart.

Alizayd looked insulted. "I suppose my people don't keep the gardens as immaculate as your ancestors did. We find ruling the city to be a more appropriate use of time than horticulture."

Nahri was losing patience with this royal brat. "So Geziri hospitality doesn't involve stabbing your guests, but does allow for threats and insults?" she asked with mock sweetness. "How fascinating."

"I . . ." Alizayd looked taken aback. "I apologize," he finally muttered. "That was rude." He stared at his feet and motioned toward the path. "If you please . . ."

Nahri smiled, feeling vindicated, and they continued. The path turned into a stony bridge hanging low over a glimmering canal. She glanced down as they crossed. The water was the clearest she'd ever seen, gurgling over smooth rocks and shining pebbles.

Before long they came upon a squat stone building rising from the vines and crowded trees. It was painted a cheerful blue with columns the color of cherries. Steam seeped from the windows, and a small herb garden hugged its exterior. Two young girls knelt among the bushes, weeding and filling a thatched basket with delicate purple petals.

An older woman with lined skin and warm brown eyes emerged from the building as they approached. Shafit, Nahri guessed, noticing her round ears and sensing the familiarity of a fast heartbeat. The woman wore her graying hair in a simple bun and was dressed in some complicated garment wound about her torso.

"Peace be upon you, sister," Alizayd greeted her when she bowed, in a far kinder tone than he had used with Nahri. "My father's guest has had a long journey. Do you mind caring for her?"

The woman gazed at Nahri with undisguised curiosity. "It would be an honor, my prince."

Alizayd briefly met her eyes. "My sister will join you soon, God willing." She could not tell if he was joking when he added, "She is better company." He didn't give her a chance to respond, turning abruptly on his heel.

An ifrit would be better company than you. At least Aeshma had briefly attempted to be charming. Nahri watched as Alizayd quickly returned the way they'd come, feeling more than a little uneasy, until the shafit woman gently took her arm and guided her into the steamy bathhouse.

In minutes, a dozen girls were attending to her; the servants were shafit of a dizzying array of ethnicities, speaking Djinnistani with snatches of Arabic and Circassian, Gujarati and Swahili, along with more languages she couldn't identify. Some offered tea and sherbet while others carefully assessed her wild hair and dusty skin. She had no idea who they thought she was, and they were careful not to ask but treated her as if she were a princess.

I could get used to this, Nahri thought what felt like hours later as she lolled in a warm bath, the water thick with luxurious oils, and the steamy air smelling of rose petals. One girl massaged her scalp, working a lather into her hair while another massaged her hands. She let her head fall back and closed her eyes.

She was far too drowsy to realize the room had gone silent before a clear voice jolted her out of her reverie.

"I see you have made yourself comfortable."

Nahri's eyes shot open. A girl sat on the bench opposite her bath, her legs delicately crossed underneath the most expensive-looking dress Nahri had ever seen.

She was stunning, with a beauty so unnaturally perfect Nahri knew in a moment not a drop of human blood ran through her veins. Her skin was dark and smooth, her lips full, and her hair carefully hidden under a simple ivory turban embellished with a single sapphire. Her gray-gold eyes and elongated features resembled the younger prince so sharply there could be no doubt who she was. Alizayd's sister, the princess Zaynab.

Nahri crossed her arms and sank back under the bubbles, feeling exposed and plain. The other woman smiled, clearly enjoying her discomfort, and dipped a toe into the bath. Diamonds winked from a gold anklet.

"You've got the whole palace in quite an excitement," she continued. "They're preparing a massive feast even now. If you listen, you can hear the drums from the Grand Temple. Your entire tribe is celebrating in the streets."

"I . . . I'm sorry . . . ," Nahri stammered, uncertain what to say.

The princess stood with a grace that made Nahri want to weep with envy. Her gown fell in perfect waves to the floor; Nahri had never seen anything like it: a rose pink net as fine as a spider's web, spun into a delicate floral pattern interlaced with seed pearls, and laid over a deep purple sheath. It didn't look like something made by human hands, that was for certain.

"Nonsense," Zaynab replied. "There's no need to apologize. You are my father's guest. It pleases me to see you content." She beckoned toward a servant bearing a silver tray, plucking a powdery white confection from it and slipping it into her mouth without getting a speck of sugar on her painted lips. She glanced at the servant. "Have you offered any to the Banu Nahida?"

The girl gasped and dropped the tray. It clattered to the ground, and a pastry rolled into the scented water. The servant's eyes were as wide as saucers. "The *Banu Nahida*?"

"Apparently so." Zaynab gave Nahri a conspiratorial smile, a wicked gleam in her eyes. "Manizheh's own daughter, bewitched to look human. Exciting, isn't it?" She gestured at the tray. "Better clean that quickly, girl. You've gossip to spread." She turned back to Nahri with a shrug. "Nothing interesting ever happens around here."

The studied casualness with which the princess revealed her identity left Nahri momentarily speechless with anger.

She's testing me. Nahri checked her temper and reminded herself of Dara's story about her origins. *I was raised a simple human servant, saved by the Afshin and brought to a magical world I barely understand. React like that girl would.*

Nahri forced an embarrassed smile, realizing this was only the first of many games she'd be playing in the palace. "Oh, I don't know how interesting *I* am." She gazed at Zaynab in open admiration. "I've never met a princess before. You're so beautiful, my lady."

Zaynab's eyes lightened with pleasure. "Thank you, but please . . . call me Zaynab. We're to be companions here, aren't we?"

God protect me from such a fate. "Of course," she agreed. "If you will call me Nahri."

"Nahri it is." Zaynab smiled and gestured her forth. "Come! You must be famished. I will have food brought to the gardens."

She was more thirsty than famished; the heat of the bath

had sucked every last bit of moisture from her skin. She glanced around, but her destroyed clothes were nowhere to be seen, and she had little desire to reveal more of herself before the frighteningly striking princess.

"Oh, come, there's no reason to be shy." Zaynab laughed, accurately guessing her thoughts. Mercifully, one of the servants reappeared at the same time, bearing a silken, sky blue robe. Nahri slipped into it and then followed Zaynab out of the bathhouse and along a stone path through the wild garden. The collar of Zaynab's dress dropped low enough to expose the back of her elegant neck, and Nahri could not help but study the golden clasps of the two necklaces she wore. They looked delicate. Fragile.

Stop, she chided herself.

"Alizayd fears he has already offended you," Zaynab said as she led Nahri to a wooden pavilion that seemed to appear from out of nowhere, perched over a clear pool. "I apologize. He has the unfortunate tendency to say exactly what's on his mind."

The pavilion was lined with a thick embroidered carpet and plush cushions. Nahri sank into them without instruction. "I thought honesty a virtue."

"Not always." Zaynab sat down across from her, elegantly folding herself onto a cushion. "He did tell me about your journey, however. What a grand adventure that must have been!" The princess smiled. "I could not resist the urge to peek in my father's court to see the Afshin before I came here. God forgive me, but that's a beautiful man. Even more handsome than the legends say." She shrugged. "Although I guess that's to be expected from a slave."

"Why would you say that?" Nahri asked, the question coming out sharper than she intended.

Zaynab frowned. "Do you not know?" When Nahri said nothing, she continued. "Well, that's part of the curse, is it not? To make them more alluring to their human masters?"

Dara hadn't told her that, and the thought of the handsome

daeva forced to obey the whims of a slew of enthralled masters was not something Nahri wished to dwell upon. She bit her lip, wordlessly watching as a handful of servants joined them on the pavilion, each bearing a silver platter loaded with food. The one closest to her, a stout woman with biceps as thick as Nahri's legs, staggered from the weight of her platter and nearly dropped it in Nahri's lap when she set it down.

"God be praised," Nahri whispered. There was enough food in front of her to break the fasts of an entire Cairo neighborhood. Piles of saffron-hued rice glistening with buttery fat and studded with dried fruit, mounds of creamy vegetables, stacks of fried almond-colored patties. There were sheets of flatbread as long as her arms and small clay bowls filled with more varieties of nuts, herbed cheeses, and fruit than she could identify. But it all paled compared to the platter in front of her, the one which nearly toppled the servant carrying it: a whole pink fish resting in a bed of bright herbs, two stuffed pigeons, and a copper pot of meatballs in a thick yoghurt sauce.

Her gaze fell upon an oval dish piled with spiced rice, dried limes, and glistening chicken pieces. "Is that . . . kabsa?" She was pulling the dish toward her, helping herself before Zaynab could answer. Starving, exhausted, and having subsisted on stale manna and lentil soup for weeks, Nahri didn't particularly care if she came off as uncouth. She closed her eyes, savoring the taste of the roasted chicken.

She caught sight of the princess's amused expression as she eagerly scooped up more of the spiced rice. "Are you such a fan of Geziri cuisine, then?" Zaynab smiled, the expression not quite meeting her eyes. "I've never known a Daeva to eat meat."

Nahri remembered Dara saying that, but shrugged it off. "I ate meat in Cairo." She coughed, a lump in her throat from swallowing so quickly. "Do you have any water?" she choked out to one of the servants.

Across from her, Zaynab delicately pecked at a bowl of glistening black cherries. She nodded toward a glass carafe. "There is wine."

Nahri hesitated, still a little leery of alcohol. But as she started to cough again, she decided a few sips wouldn't hurt. "Please . . . thank you," she added as a servant poured a generous goblet and handed it over. She took a long sip. It was far drier than the date wine Dara conjured up, crisp and cool. And rather refreshing; sweet without being overly so, with a delicate hint of some sort of berry.

"That's delicious," Nahri marveled.

Zaynab smiled again. "I'm glad you like it."

Nahri kept eating, taking a few sips of wine every now and then to clear her throat. She was vaguely aware of Zaynab droning on about the history of the gardens; the sun had grown hot, but a gentle breeze blew over the cool water. Somewhere in the distance, she could hear the faint sound of glass wind chimes. She blinked and leaned heavily into the soft cushions, a strange heaviness creeping over her limbs.

"Are you all right, Nahri?"

"Mmm?" She looked up.

Zaynab gestured toward Nahri's goblet. "You may wish to ease up on that. I hear it's rather potent."

Nahri blinked, struggling to keep her eyes open. "Potent?"

"Supposedly. I wouldn't know myself." She shook her head. "The lectures I would get from my little brother if he caught me drinking wine . . ."

Nahri looked at her goblet. It was full—she realized now just how careful the servants had been to keep it full—and she had no idea how much she'd consumed.

Her head swam. "I . . ." Her voice came out in an embarrassing slur.

Zaynab gave her a mortified look, pressing a hand to her heart.

"I'm sorry!" she apologized, her voice sugar sweet. "I should have guessed your . . . upbringing would not have exposed you to such things. Oh, Banu Nahida, do be careful," she warned as Nahri fell forward on her palms. "Why don't you rest?"

Nahri felt herself being helped into an impossibly soft mound of cushions. A servant started to fan her with a large paddle of palm fronds while another spread a thin canopy to block the sun.

"I . . . I can't," she tried to protest. She yawned, her vision going fuzzy. "I should find Dara . . ."

Zaynab laughed lightly. "I'm sure my father can handle him."

Somewhere in a back corner of her mind, Zaynab's confident laugh nagged at Nahri. A warning tried to break through the fog of her thoughts, raise her from the creeping exhaustion.

It failed. Her head fell back, and her eyes fluttered shut.

NAHRI SHIVERED AWAKE, SOMETHING COLD AND wet pressed against her forehead. She opened her eyes, blinking in the dim light. She was in a dark room, lying on an unfamiliar couch, a light quilt drawn up to her chest.

The palace, she remembered, *the feast*. The goblets Zaynab kept pressing on her . . . the odd heaviness that overtook her body . . .

She immediately drew up. Her head was not pleased at the swiftness of the movement and promptly protested with a pounding ache at the base of her skull. Nahri winced.

"Shhh, it's all right." A shadow separated itself from a murky corner. A woman, Nahri realized. A Daeva woman, her eyes as dark as Nahri's and an ash mark upon her brow. Her black hair was pulled into a severe bun, and her face was lined with what looked like equal measures of hard work and age. She approached with a steaming metal cup. "Drink this. It will help."

"I don't understand," Nahri muttered, rubbing her aching head. "I was eating and then . . ."

"I believe the hope was that you would pass out drunk among

a pile of meat dishes and embarrass yourself," the woman said lightly. "But you needn't worry. I arrived before any real damage was done."

What? Nahri pushed the cup away, suddenly less inclined to accept unknown drinks from strangers. "Why would she . . . who are *you*?" she demanded, bewildered.

A gentle smile lit the woman's face. "Nisreen e-Kinshur. I was the senior aide to your mother and uncle. I came as soon as I received word—though it took me some time to make my way through the crowds celebrating in the streets." She pressed her fingers together, inclining her brow. "It is an honor to meet you, my lady."

Her head still spinning, Nahri wasn't quite sure what to say to that. "Okay," she finally managed.

Nisreen motioned to the steaming cup. Whatever it was smelled bitter and a bit like pickled ginger. "That will help, I promise. Your uncle Rustam's recipe, one that won him many fans among Daevabad's merrymakers. And as for the first part of your question . . ." Nisreen lowered her voice. "You would be wise not to trust the princess; her mother Hatset never had much love for your family."

And what does that have to do with me? Nahri wanted to protest. She'd been in Daevabad barely a day; could she really have already earned herself an adversary at the palace?

A knock at the door interrupted her thoughts. Nahri looked up as a very familiar—and *very* welcome—face peeked in.

"You're awake." Dara smiled, looking relieved. "Finally. Feeling any better?"

"Not really," Nahri grumbled. She took a sip of the tea and then made a face, setting it down on a low mirrored table beside her. She swiped at a few of the wild strands of hair sticking to her face as Dara approached. She could only imagine what she looked like. "How long have I been asleep?"

"Since yesterday." He sat down beside her. Dara certainly

looked well rested. He'd bathed and shaved and was dressed in a long pine green coat that set off his bright eyes. He wore new boots, and as he moved she caught sight of the saddlebag he placed on the ground.

The coat and shoes took on a new meaning. Nahri narrowed her eyes. "Are you going somewhere?"

His smile faded. "Lady Nisreen," he asked, turning to the older woman. "Forgive me . . . but would you mind perhaps giving us a moment alone?"

Nisreen arched one black eyebrow. "Were things so different in your time, Afshin, that you'd be left alone with an unmarried Daeva girl?"

He pressed a hand against his heart. "I promise I mean nothing scandalous." He smiled again, a slightly rakish grin that made Nahri's heart skip a beat. "Please."

Nisreen apparently wasn't immune to the handsome warrior's charms either. Something in her face collapsed even as her cheeks grew a bit pink. She sighed. "*One* moment, Afshin." She rose to her feet. "I should probably go check on the workers restoring the infirmary. We'll want to begin training as soon as possible."

Training? Nahri's head pounded harder. She'd hoped to have at least a brief respite in Daevabad after their exhausting journey. Overwhelmed, she merely nodded.

"But, Banu Nahida . . ." Nisreen paused at the door and glanced back, concern in her black eyes. "Please take better care around the Qahtanis," she warned gently. "Around anyone not of our tribe." She left, closing the door behind her.

Dara turned back to Nahri. "I like her."

"You would," Nahri replied. She gestured again to his boots and bag. "Tell me why you're dressed like you're going somewhere."

He took a deep breath. "I'm going after the ifrit."

Nahri blinked at him. "You've lost your mind. Being back in this city has actually driven you insane."

Dara shook his head. "The Qahtanis' story about your origins and the ifrit doesn't make sense, Nahri. The timeline, this supposed curse affecting your appearance . . . the pieces don't fit."

"Who *cares*? Dara, we're alive. That's all that matters!"

"It's not all that matters," he argued. "Nahri, what if . . . what if there was some truth in what Aeshma said about your mother?"

Nahri gaped. "Did you *not* hear what the king said happened to her?"

"What if he was lying?"

She threw up her hands. "Dara, for the love of God. You're looking for any reason to distrust these people, and for what? To go on some half-baked quest?"

"It's not half-baked," Dara said quietly. "I didn't tell the Qahtanis the truth about Khayzur."

Nahri went cold. "What do you mean?"

"Khayzur didn't free me. He *found* me." Dara's bright eyes met her shocked ones. "He found me twenty years ago, covered in blood, barely aware, and wandering the same part of Daevastana in which your relatives supposedly met their end . . . an end you must have just escaped." He reached his hand out, grasping hers. "And then twenty years later—using a magic I still don't understand—you called me to your side."

He squeezed her hand, and she was acutely aware of his touch, his palm hard and calloused against her own. "Maybe the Qahtanis aren't lying, maybe that's the truth as far as they are aware. But the ifrit knew something—and right now that's all we have." There was a hint of pleading in his voice. "Someone brought me back, Nahri. Someone saved you. I have to know."

"Dara, do you not remember how easily they defeated us at the Gozan?" Her voice broke in fear.

"I'm not going to get myself killed," he assured her. "Ghassan's giving me two dozen of his best men. And as much as it pains me to say this, the Geziris are good soldiers. Fighting seems to be the only thing they do well. Trust me when I say I wish I did not have the experience to know this."

She threw him a dark look. "Yes, you might have mentioned your past in a bit greater detail before we got here, Dara. A *rebellion*?"

He flushed. "It's a long story."

"It always seems to be, with you." Her voice grew bitter. "So that's it, then? You're just going to leave me here with these people?"

"It won't be long, Nahri, I swear. And you'll be perfectly safe. I'm taking their emir." His face twisted. "I made it quite clear to the king that if something happened to you, his son would suffer the same."

She could only imagine how well that conversation had gone over. And she knew part of what Dara was saying made logical sense, but God, did the thought of being alone in this foreign city, surrounded by scheming djinn with unknown grievances, terrify her. She couldn't conceive of doing this alone, of waking without Dara beside her, of passing her days without his gruff advice and obnoxious comments.

And surely he was underestimating the danger. This was the man who'd jumped down the gullet of a rukh with the vague notion of killing it from the inside. She shook her head. "What of the marid, Dara, and the peris? Khayzur said they were after you."

"I'm hoping they're already gone." Nahri raised her brow, incredulous, but he continued. "They're not going to come after a large party of djinn. They can't. There are laws between our races."

"That didn't stop them before." Her eyes stung. This was all too much, too fast.

His face fell. "Nahri, I have to do this . . . oh, please don't cry," he begged as she lost the fight against the tears she was trying to hold in check. He brushed them from her cheek, his fingers hot against her skin. "You won't even know I'm gone. There's so much to steal here that your attention will be thoroughly occupied."

The joke did little to improve her mood. She averted her gaze, suddenly embarrassed. "Fine," she remarked flatly. "After all, you brought me to the king. That's all you promised—"

"Stop." Nahri startled as his hands suddenly cupped her face. He leveled his gaze on hers, and her heart skipped a beat.

But Dara went no further—though there was no denying the flash of regret in his eyes as his thumb lightly brushed her lower lip. "I'm coming back, Nahri," he promised. "You're my Banu Nahida. This is *my* city." His expression was defiant. "Nothing will keep me from either of you."

17

ALI

The boat before Ali was made of pure bronze and large enough to hold a dozen men. Beams of sunlight undulated across its gleaming surface, reflected off the distant lake below. The hinges holding the boat to the wall creaked hoarsely as it swayed in the breeze. They were ancient; the bronze boat had been hanging here for nearly two thousand years.

It was one of the execution methods of which the Nahid Council had been most fond.

The shafit prisoners in front of Ali must have known they were doomed, had likely realized it as soon as they were arrested. There was little begging as his men forced them into the bronze boat. They knew better than to expect mercy from purebloods.

They confessed. These are no innocent men. Whatever rumor incited them, they had taken up weapons with the intent of sacking the Daeva Quarter.

Prove your loyalty, Zaydi, Ali heard his brother say. He hardened his heart.

One of the prisoners—the smallest—suddenly broke away. Before the guards could grab him, he threw himself at Ali's feet.

"Please, my lord! I didn't do anything, I swear! I sell flowers in the midan. That's all!" The man looked up, pressing his palms together in respect.

Except that he wasn't a man at all. Ali startled; the prisoner was a boy, one who looked even younger than himself. His brown eyes were swollen from crying.

Perhaps sensing Ali's uncertainty, the boy continued, his voice desperate. "My neighbor just wanted the ransom! He gave my name, but I swear I did nothing! I have Daeva customers . . . I would never hurt them! Zavan e-Kaosh! He would vouch for me!"

Abu Nuwas yanked the boy to his feet. "Get away from him," he growled as he shoved the sobbing shafit into the boat with the rest. Most were praying, their heads lowered in prostration.

Shaken, Ali turned over the scroll in his hands, the paper worn thin. He stared at the words he was supposed to recite, the words he'd said too many times this week.

One more time. Just do this one more time.

He opened his mouth. "You have all been found guilty and sentenced to death by the noble and illuminated Ghassan al Qahtani, king of the realm and . . . Defender of the Faith." The title felt like poison in his mouth. "May you find mercy in the Most High."

One of his father's metallurgists stepped forward and cracked his charcoal-colored hands. He gave Ali an expectant look.

Ali stared at the boy. *What if he's telling the truth?*

"Prince Alizayd," Abu Nuwas prompted. Flames twisted around the metallurgist's fingers.

He barely heard Abu Nuwas. Instead he saw Anas in his mind.

It should be me up there. Ali dropped the scroll. *I'm probably the closest thing to the Tanzeem here.*

"Qaid, we are waiting." When Ali said nothing, Abu Nuwas turned to the metallurgist. "Do it," he snapped.

The man nodded and stepped forward, his smoldering black hands turning the hot crimson of worked iron. He grabbed the edge of the boat.

The effect was instantaneous. The bronze began to glow, and the barefoot shafit started to shriek. Most immediately jumped in the lake; it was certain to be a quicker death. A few lasted another moment or two, but it didn't take long. It rarely took long.

Except this time. The boy his age, the one who had begged for mercy, didn't move fast enough and by the time he tried to jump overboard, the liquid metal had licked up his legs and trapped him in the boat. In desperation, he grabbed for the side, likely meaning to heave himself over.

It was a mistake. The boat's sides were no less molten than its deck. The bewitched metal snatched his hands tight, and he shrieked as he tried to pull free.

"Ahhh! No, God, no . . . please!" He screamed again, an animal-like howl of pain and terror that tore at Ali's soul. This was why men immediately jumped in the lake, why this particular punishment struck such terror in the hearts of the shafit. If you did not find the courage to face the merciless water, you would slowly be burned to death by the molten bronze.

Ali snapped. No one deserved to die like this. He yanked his boots off and freed his zulfiqar, pushing the metallurgist out of the way.

"Alizayd!" Abu Nuwas shouted, but Ali was already climbing into the boat. He hissed; it burned far worse than he expected. But he was a pureblood. It would take a lot more than liquid bronze to harm him.

The shafit boy was pinned on all fours, his gaze forcibly directed on the hot metal. He wouldn't have to see the blow. Ali raised his zulfiqar high, meaning to bring it down through the doomed boy's heart.

But he was too late. The boy's knees gave way, and a wave of liquid metal washed onto his back, instantly hardening. Ali's blade thudded uselessly against it. The boy screamed louder as he jerked and twisted in a desperate attempt to see what was happening behind him. Ali reeled in horror as he raised his zulfiqar.

The boy's neck was still bare.

He didn't hesitate. The zulfiqar flared to life as he brought it down again, and the fiery blade sliced through the boy's neck with an ease that twisted his stomach. His head dropped, and there was merciful silence, the only sound the thudding of Ali's heart.

He took a ragged breath, fighting a swoon. The bloody scene before him was unbearable. *God forgive me.*

Ali staggered out of the boat. Not a single man met his eyes. Shafit blood drenched his uniform, the crimson stark against his white waist-wrap. The hilt of his zulfiqar was sticky in his hand.

Ignoring his men, he silently headed back toward the stairs that led to the street. He didn't make it halfway down before his nausea got the better of him. Ali fell to his knees and vomited, the boy's screams echoing in his head.

When he was done, he sat back against the cool stone, alone and shaking on the dark staircase. He knew he'd be shamed if someone came across him, the city's Qaid sick and trembling simply because he'd executed a prisoner. But he didn't care. What honor did he have left? He was a murderer.

Ali wiped his wet eyes and rubbed an itchy spot on his cheek, horrified to realize it was the boy's blood drying on his hot skin. He rubbed his hands and wrists furiously on the rough cloth of his waist-wrap and then wiped the blood from his face with the tail of his red Qaid's turban.

And then he stopped, staring at the cloth in his hands. He had dreamed of wearing this for years, had trained for this position his entire life.

He unwound the turban and let it drop in the dust.

Let Abba take my titles. Let him banish me to Am Gezira. It matters not.

Ali was done.

COURT WAS LONG ADJOURNED BY THE TIME ALI reached the palace, and though his father's office was empty, he could hear music from the gardens below. He made his way down and spotted his father reclining on a cushion next to a shaded pool. A glass of wine was at hand, as was his water pipe. Two women were playing lutes, but a scribe was there as well, reading from an unfurled scroll. A scaled bird with smoking feathers—the magical cousin of the homing pigeons humans used to send messages—was perched on his shoulder.

Ghassan glanced up as Ali approached. His gray eyes swept from Ali's uncovered head to his blood-spattered clothes and bare feet. He raised a dark eyebrow.

The scribe looked up and then jumped at the sight of the bloody prince, sending the startled pigeon into a nearby tree.

"I-I need to talk to you," Ali stammered, his confidence vanishing in his father's presence.

"I imagine so." Ghassan waved off the scribe and musicians. "Leave us."

The musicians quickly packed away their lutes, edging carefully past Alizayd. The scribe wordlessly placed the scroll back in his father's hand. The broken wax seal was black: a royal seal.

"Is that from Muntadhir's expedition?" Ali asked, worry for his brother outweighing anything else.

Ghassan beckoned him closer and handed him the scroll. "You're the scholar, aren't you?"

Ali scanned the message, both relieved and disappointed. "There's no sign of these supposed ifrits."

"None."

He read further and let out a sigh of relief. "But Wajed has finally met up with them. Thank the Most High." The grizzled old warrior was more than Darayavahoush's match. He frowned when he reached the end. "They're headed to Babili?" he asked in surprise. Babili was near the border with Am Gezira, and the idea of the Afshin Scourge so close to their homeland was unsettling.

Ghassan nodded. "Ifrit have been spotted there in the past. It's worth exploring."

Ali scoffed and tossed the scroll on a small side table. Ghassan leaned back on his cushion. "You disagree?"

"*Yes*," Ali said vehemently, too upset to keep his temper in check. "The only ifrit they're going to find are figments of the Afshin's imagination. You should never have sent Muntadhir off with him on this useless campaign."

The king patted the seat next to him. "Sit, Alizayd. You look ready to collapse." He poured a small ceramic cup of water from a nearby pitcher. "Drink."

"I'm fine."

"Your appearance would beg to differ." He pushed the cup into Ali's hand.

Ali took a sip but remained stubbornly on his feet.

"Muntadhir is perfectly safe," Ghassan assured him. "I sent two dozen of my best soldiers with them. Wajed's there now. Besides, Darayavahoush would not dare harm him while the Banu Nahida is under my protection. He wouldn't risk her."

Ali shook his head. "Muntadhir is no warrior. You should have sent me instead."

His father laughed. "Absolutely not. The Afshin would have

strangled you by day's end, and I'd be obliged to go to war, no matter what you said to deserve it. Muntadhir is charming. And he's going to be king. He needs to spend more time leading men and less time leading drinking songs." He shrugged. "Truthfully, what I wanted most was Darayavahoush away from the girl, and if he was willing to run off on his own accord?" He shrugged. "All the better."

"Ah, yes. Manizheh's long-lost daughter," Ali said acidly. "Who has yet to heal a single person—"

"On the contrary, Alizayd," Ghassan interrupted. "You should stay more ahead of palace gossip. Banu Nahri had a nasty fall when exiting the bath this morning. A careless servant must have left some soap on the floor. She cracked her head open in full view of at least a half-dozen women. An injury like that would have proven fatal to a normal girl." Ghassan paused, letting his words sink in. "She healed in moments."

The intent in the king's voice was chilling. "I see." Ali swallowed, but the idea of his father planning accidents for young women in the bathhouse was enough to remind him of his original purpose. "When do you think Wajed and Muntadhir will return?"

"A few months, God willing."

Ali took another sip of water and then set the glass down, working up his nerve. "You're going to need someone else to take over as Qaid then."

His father gave him a look that was almost amused. "I am?"

Ali gestured at the blood on his uniform. "A boy begged me for his life. Said he sold flowers in the midan." His voice broke as he continued. "He could not make it out of the boat. I had to cut off his head."

"He was guilty," his father said coldly. "They all were."

"Of what, being in the midan when your rumor started a riot? This is *wrong*, Abba. What you're doing to the shafit is wrong."

The king stared at him for a few long moments, the expression in his eyes unreadable. Then he stood. "Walk with me, Alizayd."

Ali hesitated; between the surprise Tanzeem orphanage and the secret Nahid crypt, he was beginning to hate being led places. But he followed his father as he headed toward the wide marble steps to the upper platforms of the ziggurat.

Ghassan nodded at a pair of guards on the second level. "Have you been to see the Banu Nahida?"

The Banu Nahida? What did the girl have to do with his being Qaid? Ali shook his head. "No. Why would I?"

"I hoped you would strike up a friendship. You are the one fascinated by the human world."

Ali paused. He hadn't spoken to Nahri since escorting her to the garden, and he doubted his father would be pleased to learn of his rudeness during that encounter. He settled for another truth. "I am not given to pursuing friendships with unmarried women."

The king scoffed. "Of course. My son the sheikh . . . always so dutiful to the holy books." There was uncharacteristic hostility in his voice, and Ali was startled when he saw how icy his father's eyes were. "Tell me, Alizayd, what does our religion say about obeying your parents?"

A chill went through him. "That we should do so in all matters . . . unless it goes against God."

"Unless it goes against God." Ghassan held his gaze for another long moment while Ali inwardly panicked. But then his father nodded at the door leading out to the next platform. "Go. There is something you should see."

They stepped out onto one of the upper tiers of the ziggurat. One could see the entire island from this height. Ali drifted toward the crenellated wall. It was a beautiful view: the ancient city hugged by its glowing brass walls, the neatly terraced and irrigated fields on its southern hills, the calm lake ringed by the emerald green mountains. Three thousand years of human architecture was spread before him, meticulously copied by the invisible djinn who'd passed through human cities, watching the rise and fall of their empires. Djinn-designed buildings stood apart, impossibly tall towers of twisting sandblasted glass, delicate mansions of molten silver, and floating tents of painted silk. Something stirred in his heart at the sight. Despite its wickedness, Ali loved his city.

A plume of white smoke caught his eye, and he turned his attention to the Grand Temple. The Grand Temple was the oldest building in Daevabad after the palace, an enormous yet simple complex at the heart of the Daeva Quarter.

The complex was so enshrouded by smoke that he could barely make out the buildings. That wasn't unusual; on Daeva feast days the temple tended to see an uptick in the number of people servicing the fire altars. But today wasn't a feast day.

Ali frowned. "The fire worshippers look busy."

"I've told you not to call them that," Ghassan chided as he joined him at the wall. "But, yes, it's been like this all week. And their drums haven't stopped yet."

"The streets are filled with their celebrations as well," Ali said darkly. "You'd think the Nahid Council had returned to throw us all in the lake."

"I cannot blame them," the king admitted. "If I were Daeva, and I witnessed an Afshin and Banu Nahida miraculously appear to stop a mob of shafit from breaking into my neighborhood, I'd take to wearing an ash mark on my head as well."

The words were out of Ali's mouth before he could stop himself. "Did the riot not go according to your plan, Abba?"

"Watch your tone, boy." Ghassan glared at him. "By the Most High, do you *ever* stop to consider the things in your head before you spout them? If you were not my son, you would be arrested for such disrespect." He shook his head and looked down upon the city. "You self-righteous young fool . . . sometimes I think you have no appreciation for the precariousness of your position. I had to send Wajed himself to deal with your scheming relatives in Ta Ntry and still you talk this way?"

Ali flinched. "Sorry," he muttered. His father stayed silent as Ali nervously crossed and uncrossed his arms, tapping his fingers on the wall. "But I don't see what this has to do with me resigning as Qaid."

"Tell me what you know of the Banu Nahida's land," his father said, ignoring his statement.

"Egypt?" Ali warmed to the discussion, glad to be on ground that was familiar to him. "It's been settled even longer than Daevabad," he started. "There have always been advanced human societies along the Nile. It's a fertile land, lots of agriculture, good farming. Her city, Cairo, is very large. It's a center of trade, and scholarship. They have several acclaimed institutes of—"

"That's enough." Ghassan nodded, a decision settling on his face. "Good. I'm glad to know your obsession with the human world isn't entirely useless."

Ali frowned. "I'm not sure I understand."

"I'm going to marry the Banu Nahida to Muntadhir."

Ali actually gasped. "You're going to do *what*?"

Ghassan laughed. "Don't act so shocked. Surely, you must see the potential in their marriage? We could put all this nonsense with the Daevas behind us, become a united people moving forward." Something uncharacteristically wistful flickered across his face. "It's a thing that should have been done generations ago, had our respective families not been so prudish about crossing tribal lines." His mouth thinned. "A thing I should have done myself."

Ali couldn't hide his flustered reaction. "Abba, we have no idea who this girl is! You're ready to take her identity as Manizheh's daughter on the secondhand word of some supposed ifrit and the fact that a bathroom fall didn't kill her?"

"Yes." Ghassan's next words were deliberate. "It pleases me for her to be Manizheh's daughter. It is useful. And if we say it is true—if we act on that assumption—others will as well. She clearly has some Nahid blood. And I like her; she seems to have an instinct for self-preservation sorely lacking in the rest of her kin."

"And that's enough to make her queen? To make her mother to the next generation of Qahtani kings? We know nothing else of her heritage!" Ali shook his head. He'd heard how his father had felt about Manizheh, but this was lunacy.

"And here I thought you would approve, Alizayd," the king said. "Are you not constantly railing about how blood purity does not matter?"

His father had him there. "I take it Muntadhir does not yet know of his impending nuptials?" Ali rubbed his head.

"He'll do as he's told," his father said firmly. "And we have time aplenty. The girl cannot legally marry until her quarter century. And I would like her to do so willingly. The Daevas will not be pleased to see her warm toward us. It must be done sincerely." He spread his hands on the wall. "You will have to take care in befriending her."

Ali whirled on him. "What?"

Ghassan waved him off. "You just said you didn't want to be Qaid. It will look better if you keep the title and uniform until Wajed returns, but I will have Abu Nuwas take over your responsibilities so you have time to spend with her."

"Doing what exactly?" Ali was stunned by how quickly his father had turned his resignation around in his own favor. "I know nothing of women and their . . ." He fought an embarrassed heat. ". . . *whatever* it is they do."

"By the Most High, Alizayd." His father rolled his eyes. "I'm not asking you to lure her into your bed—as thoroughly entertaining a spectacle as that would be. I'm asking you to *make a friend*. Surely that is not beyond your skill set?" He waved a dismissive hand. "Talk to her of that human nonsense you read. Astrology, your currency obsession . . ."

"Astronomy," Ali corrected under his breath. But he doubted some human-raised girl was going to be interested in the value of varying coin weights. "Why would you not ask Zaynab?"

Ghassan hesitated. "Zaynab shares your mother's distaste for Manizheh. She went too far in her first encounter with Nahri, and I doubt the girl will trust her again."

"Then Muntadhir," Ali offered, growing desperate. "You trust him to charm the Afshin but not seduce this girl? That's all he does!"

"They are going to be married," Ghassan declared. "Truthfully, regardless of what either of them thinks about it. But I'd rather things not go to that extreme. Who knows what kind of propaganda Darayavahoush filled her head with? We need to undo some of that damage first. And if she reacts badly to you, it's a lesson in how to proceed with Muntadhir without poisoning the well of their marriage."

Ali stared at the smoking temple. He had literally never had a conversation with a Daeva lasting longer than ten minutes that ended well, and his father wanted him to befriend a Nahid? A *girl*? That last thought alone was enough to send a shiver of nerves down his spine.

"There's no way, Abba," he finally said. "She'll see right through me. You're asking the wrong person. I don't have experience with that kind of deception."

"Don't you?" Ghassan stepped closer and rested his arms on the wall. His brown hands were thick and roughly calloused, the heavy gold ring on his thumb looking like a child's bangle. "After all, you successfully hid your involvement with the Tanzeem."

Ali went cold; he had to have heard wrong. Yet as he cast an alarmed glance down at his father, something else caught his eye.

The guards had followed them. And they were blocking the door.

A wordless terror gripped Ali's heart. He clutched at the parapet, feeling like someone had torn a carpet out from under his feet. His throat tightened, and he glanced at the distant ground, briefly tempted to jump.

Ghassan didn't even look at him; his expression was completely serene as he stared at his city. "Your tutors always praised your prowess with numbers. '*A keen mind your son has for figures,*' they told me. '*An excellent addition he'd make to the Treasury.*' I assumed they were exaggerating; I dismissed your harping on currency issues as another of your eccentricities." Something twitched in his face. "And then the Tanzeem started bedeviling my cleverest accountants. They declared their funds impossible to trace, their financial system a cunningly convoluted mess designed by someone with a detailed understanding of human banking . . . and far too much time on his hands.

"I hated to even suspect such a thing. Surely my son—my own blood—would never betray me. But I knew I had to at least audit your accounts. And the amount you withdraw regularly, Alizayd? I'd like to say you're either supporting a particularly cunning concubine or a strong addiction to human intoxicants . . . but you've always been obnoxiously vocal about your abhorrence of both."

Ali said nothing. He was caught.

A small, humorless smile played on his father's face. "Praise be to God, have I actually silenced you for once? I should have accused you of treason earlier in our conversation and saved myself your insufferable comments."

Ali swallowed and pressed his palms harder against the wall to hide their trembling. *Apologize.* Not that it would make a difference. Had his father really known for all these months that he'd funded the Tanzeem? What about the murder of the Daeva men?

The money, God, please let it just be the money. Ali couldn't imagine he'd still be alive if his father knew the rest. "But-but you made me Qaid," he stammered.

"A test," Ghassan answered. "Which you were failing miserably until the Afshin's arrival apparently reset your loyalties." He crossed his arms. "You owe a sincere debt to your brother. Muntadhir has been your most adamant defender. Says you tend to throw money at every sad-eyed shafit who comes crying your way. As he knows you best, I was persuaded to give you a second chance."

That's why he took me to the tomb, Ali realized, remembering how Muntadhir begged him to stay away from the shafit. His brother hadn't directly interfered with their father's test—that would have been his own treason—but he'd come close. Ali was struck by his devotion. All this time he'd been judging his brother's drinking, his shallow behavior . . . yet Muntadhir was probably the only reason Ali was still alive.

"Abba," he started again. "I . . ."

"Save your apology," Ghassan snapped. "The blood on your clothes, and the fact that you came to me with your grief this time instead of turning to some filthy shafit street preacher is enough to allay my doubts." He finally met Ali's terrified gaze, and his expression was so fierce that Ali flinched. "But you *will* win me this girl."

Ali swallowed and nodded. He said nothing. It was all he could do to remain upright.

"I would like to think that I don't need to waste my time detailing the various punishments that will befall you if you deceive me again," Ghassan continued. "But knowing how your type feels about martyrdom, let me make this clear. It will not be you alone who suffers. If you even think of betraying me again, I will make you lead a hundred such innocent shafit boys to that damned boat, understand?"

Ali nodded again, but his father didn't look convinced. "Say it, Alizayd. Tell me you understand."

His voice was hollow. "I understand, Abba."

"Good." His father clapped his shoulder so hard that Ali jumped and then motioned to his ruined uniform. "Now you should go wash up, my son." He let go of Ali's arm. "There's a lot of blood on your hands."

18

NAHRI

Nahri woke with the sun.

The dawn call to prayer whispered in her ear, drifting from the mouths of a dozen different muezzins high atop Daevabad's minarets. Oddly enough, the call never woke her in Cairo, but here, the cadence—so close but not quite the same—did every day. She stirred in her sleep, momentarily confused by the feel of the silken sheets, and then opened her eyes.

It usually took a few minutes for her to remember where she was, to recognize that the luxurious apartment surrounding her was not a dream and that the big bed, crowded with soft brocaded cushions and held off the richly carpeted floor with bowed mahogany legs, was hers alone. It was no different this morning. Nahri studied the enormous bedchamber, taking in the beautifully woven rugs and delicately painted silk wall coverings. A massive landscape of the Daevastana countryside, painted by Rustam—her uncle, she reminded herself, the idea of having

relatives still surreal—dominated one wall, and a carved wooden
door led to her own private bath.

Another door opened onto a chamber for her wardrobe. For
a girl who'd spent years sleeping on the streets of Cairo, a girl
who once counted herself fortunate to have two plain abayas in
decent shape, the contents of that small room were like things
out of a dream—a dream that would have ended with her selling
them all and raking in the profits, but a dream nonetheless. Silk
gowns, lighter than air and embroidered with thread of spun
gold; fitted felt coats in a rainbow of colors embellished with a
riot of jeweled flowers; beaded slippers so lovely and intricate it
seemed a shame to walk in them.

There were more practical clothes, as well, including a dozen
sets of the calf-length tunics and richly embroidered fitted pants
Nisreen said Daeva women typically wore. An equal number of
chadors, the floor-length cloak also endemic to the women of
their tribe, hung from glass globes with far more grace than they
usually hung from Nahri's head. She'd yet to get used to the ornate gold headpieces that held the chador in place, and had a tendency to step on the hem and send the whole ensemble crashing
to the ground.

Nahri yawned, rubbing the sleep from her eyes before leaning back on her palms to stretch her neck. Her hand landed on a
lump: She'd stashed several jewels and a gold armband in the lining of the mattress. She had similar caches throughout the apartment, gifts she'd been given by an unrelenting stream of rich
well-wishers. The djinn were clearly obsessed with gems, and she
didn't trust the number of servants passing through her rooms.

Speaking of which . . . Nahri slid her hand away and lifted
her eyes, gazing at the small unmoving figure kneeling in the
shadows across the room. "By the Most High, do you ever sleep?"

The girl bowed and then stood, Nahri's voice propelling her
into motion like one of those children's box toys that sprang up

when released. "I wish to be of service to you at all times, Banu Nahida. I pray you slept well."

"As well as I can while being watched all night," Nahri grumbled in Divasti, knowing the shafit servant couldn't understand the Daeva tongue. This was the third girl she'd had since arriving, having frightened off the previous two. Although Nahri had always found the idea of servants appealing in theory, the slavish devotions of these timid girls—children really—unnerved her. Their human-hued eyes were an all too familiar reminder of the strict hierarchy that governed the djinn world.

The girl crept forward, keeping her gaze carefully on the floor while bearing a large tin tray. "Breakfast, my lady."

Nahri wasn't hungry but couldn't resist a peek at the tray. What came out of the palace kitchens amazed her just as much as the contents of her wardrobe. Any food she wanted, in any quantity, at any time. Upon this morning's tray was a steaming stack of fluffy flatbreads sprinkled with sesame seeds, a bowl of blushing apricots, and several of the ground pistachio pastries with cardamom cream she liked. The scent of minty green tea rose from the copper kettle.

"Thank you," Nahri said and motioned toward the sheer curtains leading to the garden. "You can leave it out there."

She slid out of bed and wrapped a soft shawl around her bare shoulders. Her fingers brushed the small weight at her hip, as they did at least a dozen times a day. Dara's dagger. He'd given it to her before he'd gone off on his stupid, suicidal mission to hunt the ifrit.

She closed her eyes, fighting the ache in her chest. The thought of her easily provoked Afshin, surrounded by djinn soldiers, seeking out the same ifrit who'd nearly killed them was enough to catch her breath.

No, she told herself. *Don't even start.* Fretting over Dara would help neither of them; the Afshin was more than capable of taking care of himself, and Nahri didn't need any distractions. Especially not today.

"Shall I comb your hair, my lady?" her servant piped up, pulling her from her thoughts.

"What? No . . . it's fine like this," Nahri said distractedly as she brushed her messy curls off her shoulders and crossed the room for a glass of water.

The girl raced her to the jug. "Your robes, then?" she asked as she poured a glass. "I've had the ceremonial Nahid garments cleaned and pressed—"

"No," Nahri cut in, more sharply than she'd intended. The girl shrank back as if she'd been slapped, and Nahri winced at the fear in her face. She hadn't meant to scare her. "I'm sorry. Look . . ." Nahri wracked her mind for the girl's name, but she had been so bombarded by new information each day, it eluded her. "Could I have a few minutes to myself?"

The girl blinked like a frightened kitten. "No. I-I mean . . . I cannot leave, Banu Nahida," she pleaded in a tiny whisper. "I am to be available—"

"I can take care of Banu Nahri this morning, Dunoor." A calm, measured voice spoke up from the garden.

The shafit girl bowed and was gone, fleeing before the speaker parted the curtains. Nahri raised her eyes to the ceiling. "You'd think I ran around lighting people on fire and poisoning their tea," she complained. "I don't understand why people here are so afraid of me."

Nisreen entered the chamber without a sound. The older woman moved like a ghost. "Your mother enjoyed a rather . . . *fearsome* reputation."

"Yes, but she was a true Nahid," Nahri countered. "Not some lost shafit who can't conjure up a flame." She joined Nisreen on the pavilion overlooking the gardens. The white marble flushed pink in the rosy dawn light, and a pair of tiny birds twittered and splashed in the fountain.

"It's only been a couple of weeks, Nahri. Give yourself time." Nisreen gave her a sardonic smile. "Soon you'll be capable of conjuring up enough flames to burn down the infirmary. And you're *not* a shafit, no matter your appearance. The king said so himself."

"Well, I'm glad he's so certain," Nahri muttered. Ghassan had done his part in their deal, publicly declaring Nahri to be Manizheh's long-lost, *pureblooded* daughter, claiming her human appearance was the result of a marid curse.

Yet Nahri herself was still not convinced. With every passing day in Daevabad, she became more attuned to the differences between purebloods and shafit. The air grew warm around the elegant purebloods; they breathed deeper, their hearts beat more slowly, and their luminous skin gave off a smoky odor that stung her nose. She could not help but compare the iron scent of her red blood; the salty taste of her sweat; the slower, more awkward way her body moved. She certainly *felt* shafit.

"You should eat something," Nisreen said lightly. "You have an important day ahead of you."

Nahri picked up a pastry and turned it over in her hands before putting it back down, feeling nauseated. "Important" was an understatement. Today was the first day Nahri was going to treat a patient. "I'm sure I can just as easily kill someone on an empty stomach."

Nisreen gave her a look. Her mother's former aide was one hundred and fifty years old—a number she offered with the air of someone discussing the weather—but her sharp black eyes seemed ageless.

"You're not going to kill anyone," Nisreen said evenly. She said everything with such confidence. Nisreen struck Nahri as one of the most steadily capable people she'd ever met, a woman who'd not only easily thwarted Zaynab's attempt to embarrass Nahri, but had also handled over a century's worth of God only knew what sort of magical maladies. "It's a simple procedure," she added.

"Extracting a fire salamander from someone's body is simple?" Nahri shuddered. "I still don't understand why you chose this as my first assignment. I don't see why I even *have* a first assignment. Physicians train for years in the human world, and I'm expected to just go out and start cutting magical reptiles out of people after listening to you lecture for a few—"

"We do things differently here," Nisreen interrupted. She pushed a cup of hot tea in Nahri's hands and motioned her back inside the room. "Take some tea. And sit," she added, pointing to a chair. "You cannot see the public looking like that."

Nahri obeyed, and Nisreen retrieved a comb from a nearby chest and started on Nahri's hair, raking it down her scalp to separate the braids. Nahri closed her eyes, enjoying the feel of the comb's sharp teeth and the expert tugging of Nisreen's fingers.

I wonder if my mother ever braided my hair.

The tiny thought bubbled up, a crack in the armor Nahri had settled over that part of herself. It was a foolish notion; from the sound of things, Nahri had no sooner been born than her mother had been killed. Manizheh never had the chance to braid Nahri's hair, nor witness her first steps; she hadn't lived long enough to teach her daughter Nahid magic, nor listen to her complain about arrogant, handsome men eager to rush after danger.

Nahri's throat tightened. In many ways it had been easier to assume her parents neglectful bastards who'd abandoned her. She might not remember her mother, but the thought of the woman who birthed her being viciously murdered was not something easily ignored.

Nor was the fact that her unknown father might still be in

Daevabad. Nahri could only imagine the gossip swirling about *that*, but Nisreen had warned her that her father was a subject best avoided. The king was apparently not pleased to have learned of Manizheh's indiscretion.

Nisreen finished her fourth braid, weaving a sprig of sweet basil into the ends. "What's that for?" Nahri asked, eager for a distraction from her dark thoughts.

"Luck." Nisreen smiled, looking slightly self-conscious. "It's something my people used to do for girls back home."

"Back home?"

Nisreen nodded. "I'm from Anshunur originally. A village on the southern coast of Daevastana. My parents were priests; our ancestors ran the temple there for centuries."

"Really?" Nahri sat up, intrigued. After Dara, it was strange to be around someone who spoke so openly about their background. "So what brought you to Daevabad?"

The older woman seemed to hesitate, her fingers trembling upon Nahri's braid. "The Nahids, actually," she said softly. When Nahri frowned in confusion, Nisreen explained. "My parents were killed by djinn raiders when I was young. I was badly injured, so the survivors brought me to Daevabad. Your mother healed me, and then she and her brother took me in."

Nahri was horrified. "I'm sorry," she blurted out. "I had no idea."

Nisreen shrugged though Nahri spotted a flicker of grief in her dark eyes. "It's all right. It's not uncommon. People bring offerings to their temples; they're wealthy targets." She stood. "And I had a good life with the Nahids. I found a lot of satisfaction working in the infirmary. Though on the topic of our faith . . ." Nisreen crossed the room, heading for the neglected fire altar across the room. "I see you've let your altar go out again."

Nahri winced. "It's been a few days since I refilled the oil."

"Nahri, we've discussed this."

"I know. I'm sorry." Upon her arrival, the Daevas had gifted Nahri with Manizheh's personal fire altar, a guilt-inducing piece of metal and water, restored and polished to perfection. The altar was about half her height, a silver basin filled with water kept at a constant simmer by the tiny glass oil lamps bobbing upon its surface. A pile of cedar sticks smoldered on the small cupola that rose from the basin's center.

Nisreen refilled the lamps from a silver pitcher nearby and plucked a cedar stick from the consecrated tools meant to maintain the altar. She used it to relight the flames and then beckoned Nahri closer.

"You should try to take better care of this," Nisreen admonished, though her voice stayed gentle. "Our faith is an important part of our culture. You're worried about treating a patient? Then why not touch the same tools your grandparents once did? Kneel and pray as your mother would have before attempting a new procedure." She motioned for Nahri to bow her head. "Take strength from the one connection to your family you still have."

Nahri sighed but allowed Nisreen to mark her forehead with ash. She probably could use all the luck she could get today.

ABOUT HALF THE SIZE OF THE ENORMOUS AUDI-ence chamber, the infirmary was a spartan room of plain white-washed walls, a blue stone floor, and a lofty domed ceiling made entirely of tempered glass that let in sunlight. One wall was given over to apothecary ingredients, hundreds of glass and copper shelves of varying sizes. Another section of the room was her workplace: a scattering of low tables crowded with tools and failed pharmaceutical attempts, and a heavy sandblasted glass desk in one corner surrounded by bookshelves and a large fire pit.

The other side of the room was meant for patients and typically curtained off. But today the curtain was drawn back to reveal an empty couch and a small table. Nisreen swooped past with a tray of supplies. "They should be here any moment. I've already prepared the elixir."

"And you still think this is a smart idea?" Nahri swallowed, anxious. "I've not had the best luck with my abilities so far."

That was an understatement. Nahri had assumed being a healer to the djinn would be similar to being a healer among humans, her time spent correcting broken bones, birthing babies, and stitching up wounds. As it turned out, the djinn didn't need much help with those sorts of ailments—purebloods anyway. Instead, they needed a Nahid when it got . . . *complicated*. And what was complicated?

Stripes were common in infants born during the darkest hour of the night. The bite of a simurgh—firebirds the djinn enjoyed racing—would cause one to slowly burn up from the inside. Sweating silver droplets was a constant irritation in the spring. It was possible to accidentally create an evil duplicate, to transform one's hands into flowers, to be hexed with hallucinations, or to be turned into an apple—an incredibly grave insult to one's honor.

The cures were little better. The leaves from the very tops of cypress trees—and only the very tops—could be boiled into a solution that when blown upon by a Nahid opened up the lungs. A ground pearl mixed with just the right amount of turmeric could help an infertile woman conceive, but the resulting infant would smell a bit salty and be terribly sensitive to shellfish. And it wasn't just the illnesses and their associated cures that sounded unbelievable, but the endless list of situations that seemed entirely unrelated to health.

"It's a long shot, but sometimes a two-week dose of hemlock, dove's tail, and garlic—taken every sunrise outdoors—can cure a nasty case of chronic unluckiness," Nisreen told her last week.

Nahri remembered her stunned disbelief. "Hemlock is *poisonous*. And how is being unlucky an illness?"

The science behind it all made little sense. Nisreen went on and on about the four humors that made up the djinn body and the importance of keeping them balanced. Fire and air were to exactly even each other out at twice the amount of blood and four times the amount of bile. To become unbalanced could cause a wasting disease, insanity, feathers . . .

"Feathers?" Nahri had repeated incredulously.

"Too much air," Nisreen had explained. "Obviously."

And though Nahri was trying, it was all too much to take in, day after day, hour after hour. Since arriving at the palace, she had yet to leave the wing that housed her quarters and the infirmary; she wasn't sure she was even *permitted* to leave, and when Nahri asked if she could learn to read—as she'd dreamed of doing for years—the older woman had gotten strangely cagey, muttering something about the Nahid texts being forbidden before promptly changing the subject. Besides her terrified servants and Nisreen, Nahri had no other company. Zaynab had politely invited her for tea twice, but Nahri turned her down—she didn't intend to consume liquids near that girl again. But she was an extrovert, used to chatting with clients and roaming all over Cairo. The isolation and single-minded focus of her training had her ready to burst.

And she sensed her frustration was curbing her abilities. Nisreen repeated what Dara had already told her: blood and intent were vital in magic. Many of the medicines Nahri studied simply wouldn't work without a believing Nahid to produce them. You couldn't stir a potion, grind a powder, or even lay your hands upon a patient without a firm trust in what you were doing. And Nahri didn't have that.

And then yesterday Nisreen had announced—rather abruptly— that they were changing tactics. The king wanted to see her heal someone, and Nisreen agreed, believing that if Nahri was given the chance to treat a few carefully selected patients, the theories would make more sense to her. Nahri thought that sounded like a great way to slowly reduce Daevabad's population, but it didn't seem as if she had much say in the matter.

There was a knock at the door. Nisreen eyed her. "You'll be fine. Have faith."

Her patient was an older woman, accompanied by a man who looked like her son. When Nisreen greeted them in Divasti, Nahri sighed with relief, hoping her own people would be more sympathetic to her inexperience. Nisreen led the woman to the bed and helped her remove a long midnight-colored chador. Underneath, the woman's steel gray hair was arranged in an elaborately braided nest. Gold embroidery winked from her dark crimson gown, and large clusters of rubies hung from each ear. She pursed her painted lips and gave Nisreen a distinctly unimpressed look while her son—dressed in similar finery—hovered nervously over her.

Nahri took a deep breath and then walked over, pressing her palms together like she'd seen others of her tribe do. "Peace be upon you."

The man pressed his own hands together and fell into a low bow. "It is the greatest honor, Banu Nahida," he said in a hushed voice. "May the fires burn brightly for you. I pray the Creator blesses you with the longest of lives and the merriest of children and—"

"Oh, calm yourself, Firouz," the old woman interrupted. She considered Nahri with skeptical black eyes. "You're Banu Manizheh's daughter?" she sniffed. "Awfully human looking."

"Madar!" Firouz hissed, clearly embarrassed. "Be polite. I told you about the curse, remember?"

He's the gullible one, Nahri decided, and then she cringed, a little ashamed to have thought it. These people were patients, not marks.

"Hmm." The woman must have picked up on Nahri's attitude. Her eyes glittered like a crow's. "So you can fix me?"

Nahri plucked a wicked-looking silver scalpel off the tray and twirled it in her fingers. "Insha'Allah."

"She certainly can." Nisreen slid smoothly between them. "It's a simple task." She pulled Nahri off to where she'd already prepared the elixir. "Watch your tone," she warned. "And don't speak that Geziriyya-sounding human tongue in here. Her family is a powerful one."

"Ah, then by all means, let's experiment on her."

"It's a simple procedure," Nisreen assured for the hundredth time. "We've gone over this. Have her drink the elixir, look for the salamander, and extract it. You are the Banu Nahida; it should be as obvious to you as a black spot on the eye."

Simple. Nahri's hands were trembling, but she sighed and took the elixir from Nisreen. The silver cup warmed in her hands, and the amber liquid started to steam. She crossed back to the old woman and handed it to her, watching as she took a sip.

Her patient made a face. "This is really quite awful. Do you have anything to cut the bitterness? A sweet, perhaps?"

Nahri raised her eyebrows. "Was the salamander coated in honey when you swallowed it?"

The woman looked insulted. "I did not *swallow* it. I was hexed. Probably by my neighbor Rika. You know the one, Firouz? Rika with her pathetic rosebushes and that loud daughter with the Sahrayn husband?" She scowled. "Their whole family should have been tossed out of the Daeva Quarter when she married that turban-wearing pirate."

"I can't *imagine* why she would want to hex you," Nahri said lightly.

"Intention," Nisreen whispered as she came around with a tray of instruments.

Nahri rolled her eyes. "Lie back," she told the woman.

Nisreen handed her a silver bulb that tapered into a glistening sharp point. "Remember, just a light touch with this. It will immediately paralyze the salamander so you can extract it."

"That's assuming I can even . . . whoa!" Nahri gasped as a

lump the size of her fist suddenly rose up under the woman's left forearm, ballooning out her thin skin until it looked ready to burst. It wiggled and then raced up the woman's arm to vanish under her shoulder.

"Did you see it?" Nisreen asked.

"Didn't any of you?" Nahri asked in shock. The old woman gave her a disgruntled look.

Nisreen smiled. "I told you that you could do it." She touched Nahri's shoulder. "Take a deep breath and keep the needle ready. You should spot it again any—"

"There!" Nahri saw the salamander again, near the woman's abdomen. Quickly, she plunged the needle into the woman's stomach, but the bulge seemed to melt away.

"Ay!" The old lady cried as a drop of black blood blossomed against her gown. "That hurt!"

"Then stay still!"

The woman whimpered as she clutched one of her son's hands. "Don't yell at me!"

The bump reemerged near the old woman's collar, and Nahri attempted to jab it again, drawing more blood and provoking another shriek. The salamander squirmed away—she could see a clear outline of its body now—and raced around the woman's neck. "Eep!" the woman shrieked as Nahri finally just grabbed for the creature, her fingers closing on the woman's throat. "Eep! You're killing me! You're *killing* me!"

"I'm not . . . be quiet!" Nahri shouted, trying to focus on holding the salamander in place while raising the needle. She had no sooner uttered the words than the creature beneath her hand tripled in size, its tail wrapping around the woman's throat.

The old woman's face instantly darkened, and her eyes turned red. She gasped and clawed at her throat as she struggled to breathe.

"No!" Nahri desperately tried to will the parasite smaller, but nothing happened.

"Madar!" the man cried. "Madar!"

Nisreen dashed across the room and yanked free a small glass bottle from one of the drawers. "Move," she said quickly. She edged Nahri aside and tipped the woman's head back, prying open her jaws and pouring the contents of the bottle down her throat. The bulge vanished, and the woman started coughing. Her son pounded her back.

Nisreen held up the bottle. "Liquefied charcoal," she said calmly. "Shrinks most internal parasites." She nodded at the old woman. "I'll get her some water. Let her catch her breath, and we'll try again." She lowered her voice so only Nahri could hear. "Your intention needs to be more . . . *positive*."

"What?" Nahri was confused for a moment, and then Nisreen's warning became clear. The salamander hadn't started strangling the woman when the needle touched it.

It had done so when Nahri commanded her to be quiet.

I nearly killed her. Nahri took a step back and knocked one of the trays off the table. It clattered to the floor, and the glass vials smashed against the marble.

"I-I need some air." She turned toward the doors leading to the gardens.

Nisreen stepped in front of her. "Banu Nahida . . ." Her voice was calm, but didn't mask the alarm in her eyes. "You can't just leave. The lady is under your care."

Nahri pushed past Nisreen. "Not anymore. Send her away."

She took the stone steps leading down to the garden two at a time. She hurried through the manicured plots of healing plants, startling two gardeners, and then beyond, following a narrow path into the royal garden's wild interior.

She gave little thought to where she was going, her mind

spinning. *I had no business touching that woman*. Who was she kidding? Nahri was no healer. She was a thief, a con artist who occasionally got lucky. She'd taken her healing abilities for granted in Cairo where they were as effortless as breathing.

She stopped at the edge of the canal and leaned against the crumbling remains of a stone bridge. A pair of dragonflies glistened above the rushing water. She watched them dart and dip under a fallen tree trunk whose dark branches pushed out of the water like a man trying not to drown. She envied their freedom.

I was free in Cairo. A wave of homesickness swept over her. She longed for Cairo's bustling streets and familiar aromas, her clients with their love problems, and her afternoons of pounding poultices with Yaqub. She'd often felt like a foreigner there, but now knew it wasn't true. It took leaving Egypt to realize it was home.

And I'll never see it again. Nahri wasn't naive; behind Ghassan's polite words, she suspected that she was more prisoner than guest in Daevabad. With Dara gone, there was no one she could turn to for help. And it was clear she was expected to start producing results as a healer.

She chewed the inside of her cheek as she studied the water. That a patient had appeared in her infirmary barely two weeks after her arrival in Daevabad was not an encouraging sign, and she couldn't help but wonder how Ghassan might punish her incompetence should it continue. Would her privileges—the private apartment, the fine clothes and jewels, the servants and the fancy foods—start disappearing with each failure?

The king might be pleased to see me fail. Nahri hadn't forgotten the way the Qahtanis had received her: Alizayd's open hostility, Zaynab's attempt to humiliate her . . . not to mention that flicker of fear in Ghassan's face.

Movement caught her eye, and she glanced up, welcoming any

distraction from her grim thoughts. Through a screen of purple dappled leaves, she could see a clearing up ahead where the canal widened. A pair of dark arms splashed through the water's surface.

Nahri frowned. Was someone . . . *swimming*? She assumed all djinn were as wary of water as Dara.

A little concerned, Nahri picked her way over the bridge. Her eyes went wide when she entered the clearing.

The canal rose up straight in the air.

It was like a waterfall in reverse, the canal rushing from the jungle to pool against the palace wall before cascading up and over the palace. It was a beautiful, if not entirely bizarre sight that utterly captivated her before another splash from the misty pool drew her eye. She raced over, spotting someone struggling in the water.

"Hold on!" After the tumultuous Gozan, this little pool was nothing. She charged right in and grabbed the closest flailing arm, pulling hard to bring whoever it was to the surface.

"*You?*" Nahri made a disgusted sound as she recognized a very bewildered Alizayd al Qahtani. She immediately let go of his arm, and the prince fell back with a splash, the water briefly closing over his head again before he straightened up, coughing and spitting water.

He wiped his eyes and squinted as if not quite believing who he saw. "*Banu Nahri?* What are you doing here?"

"I thought you were drowning!"

He drew up, every bit the arrogant royal even when wet and confused. "I was not *drowning*," he huffed. "I was swimming."

"Swimming?" she asked, incredulous. "What kind of djinn swim?"

A flicker of embarrassment crossed his face. "It's an Ayaanle custom," he mumbled, snatching a neatly folded shawl from the canal's tiled edge. "Do you *mind*?"

Nahri rolled her eyes but turned around. On a sunny patch of grass ahead, a woven rug was laid out, crowded with books, a sheaf of notes, and a charcoal pencil.

She'd no sooner heard him splash out than he marched past her toward the rug. The shawl was wrapped around his upper body with the same fastidiousness Nahri had seen shy new brides cover their hair. Water dripped from his soaked waist-wrap.

Alizayd retrieved a skullcap from the rug and pulled it over his wet head. "What are you doing here?" he demanded over his shoulder. "Did my father send you?"

Why would the king send me to you? But Nahri didn't ask; she had little desire to continue talking to the obnoxious Qahtani prince. "It doesn't matter. I'm leaving . . ."

She trailed off as her eyes alighted on one of the open books on the rug. An illustration covered half the page, a stylized shedu wing crossed with a scythe-ended arrow.

An Afshin mark.

Nahri immediately went for the book. Alizayd got there first. He snatched it up, but she seized another, twisting away when he tried to grab it.

"Give that back!"

She ducked under his arm and quickly flipped through the book, searching for any more illustrations. She came upon a series of figures drawn on one of the pages. A half-dozen djinn, their arms exposed to show black tattoos spiraling up their wrists, and on some, spreading across their bare shoulders. Tiny lines, like rungs in an unsupported ladder.

Like Dara's.

Nahri had not given his tattoos much thought, assuming they had to do with his lineage. But as she stared at the illustration, a finger of cold traced her spine. The figures appeared to be from various tribes, and all had expressions of pure anguish drawn on their faces. One woman had her eyes lifted to some invisible sky, her arms outstretched and her mouth open in a wordless scream.

Alizayd grabbed the book back, taking advantage of her distraction.

"Interesting subject you're studying," she said, her voice biting. "What is that? Those figures . . . that mark on their arms?"

"You don't know?" When she shook her head, a dark look crossed his face, but he offered no further explanation. He tucked the books under his arm. "It doesn't matter. Come on. I'll take you back to the infirmary."

Nahri didn't move. "What are the marks?" she asked again.

Alizayd paused, his gray eyes seemingly sizing her up. "It's a record," he finally said. "Part of the ifrit curse."

"A record of *what*?"

Dara would have lied. Nisreen would have deflected and changed the subject. But Alizayd just pressed his mouth in a thin line and answered, "Lives."

"What lives?"

"The human masters they've killed." His face twisted. "It supposedly amuses the ifrit to see them add up."

The human masters they've killed. Nahri's mind went back to the countless times she'd observed that tattoo wrapped around Dara's arm, the tiny black lines dull in the light of his constant fires. There had to be hundreds of them.

Aware of the prince watching her, Nahri fought to keep her face composed. After all, she'd seen that vision in Hierapolis; she knew how thoroughly controlled Dara had been by his master. Surely he couldn't be blamed for their deaths.

Besides, however ghastly the meaning of Dara's slave mark, Nahri suddenly realized a much nearer threat lurked. She glanced again at the books in Alizayd's hand, and a surge of protectiveness flooded through her, accompanied by a prickle of fear. "You're studying him."

The prince didn't even bother lying. "It's an interesting tale the two of you have concocted."

Her heart dropped. *Nahri, the pieces don't fit . . .* Dara's hurried words came back to her, the mystery about their origins that had led him to lie to the king and race after the ifrit. He'd suggested the Qahtanis might not even realize something wasn't right.

But it was clear that at least one of them had some suspicions. Nahri cleared her throat. "I see," she finally managed, not entirely masking the alarm in her voice.

Alizayd dropped his gaze. "You should go," he said. "Your minders are likely getting worried."

Her *minders*? "I remember the way," Nahri retorted, turning back toward the garden's wild interior.

"Wait!" Alizayd stepped between her and the trees. There was a hint of panic in his voice. "Please . . . I'm sorry," he rushed on. "I shouldn't have said that." He shifted on his feet. "It was rude . . . and it's hardly the first time I've been rude to you."

She narrowed her eyes. "I'm getting accustomed to it."

A wry expression crossed his face, nearly a smile. "I would beg that you not." He touched his heart. "Please. I'll take you back through the palace." He nodded to the wet leaves sticking to her chador. "You needn't go traipsing back through the jungle because I have no manners."

Nahri considered the offer; it seemed sincere enough, and there was the slight chance she could accidentally knock his books into one of the fiery braziers of which the djinn seemed so fond. "Fine."

He nodded in the direction of the wall. "This way. Let me just change."

She followed him across the clearing to a stone pavilion fronting the wall and then through an open balustrade into a plain room about half the size of her bedroom. One wall was taken up by bookshelves, the rest of the room sparsely decorated with a prayer niche, a single rug, and a large ceramic tile inscribed with what looked like Arabic religious verses.

The prince went straight to the main door, an enormous antique of carved teak. He stuck his head out and made a beckoning motion. In seconds, a member of the Royal Guard appeared, silently installing himself at the open door.

Nahri gave the prince an incredulous look. "Are you *afraid* of me?"

He bristled. "No. But it is said that when a man and woman are alone in a closed room, their third companion is the devil."

She raised an eyebrow, struggling to contain her mirth. "Well then, I suppose we should take precaution." She eyed the water dripping from his waist-wrap. "Didn't you need to . . . ?"

Ali followed her gaze, made a small, embarrassed noise, and then promptly vanished through a curtained archway—the books still in hand.

What an odd person. The room was extraordinarily plain for a prince, nothing like her lavish apartment. A thin sleeping pallet had been neatly folded and placed upon a single wooden chest. A low floor desk looked out upon the garden, its surface covered with papers and scrolls all set at disturbingly perfect right angles to one another. A stylus rested alongside an immaculate inkpot.

"Your quarters don't look very . . . *lived* in," she commented.

"I haven't lived in the palace long," he called from the other room.

She drifted toward the bookshelves. "Where are you from originally?"

"Here." Nahri jumped at the close sound of his voice. Alizayd had returned without making a sound, now dressed in a long gray waist-wrap and striped linen tunic. "Daevabad, I mean. I grew up in the Citadel."

"The Citadel?"

He nodded. "I'm training to be my brother's Qaid."

Nahri tucked that bit of information in her head for later, captivated by the crowded bookshelves. There were hundreds of books and scrolls there, including some half her height and a good number thicker than her head. She ran a hand along the multihued spines, overtaken by a sense of longing.

"Do you like to read?" Alizayd asked.

Nahri hesitated, embarrassed to admit her illiteracy to a man with such a large personal library. "I suppose you could say I like the idea of reading." When his only response was a confused frown, she clarified. "I don't know how."

"Truly?" He seemed surprised, but at least not disgusted. "I thought all humans could read."

"Not at all." She was amused by the misconception—maybe humans were as much of a mystery to the djinn as the djinn were to humans. "I've always wanted to learn. I hoped I'd have the opportunity here, but it seems it's not to be." She sighed. "Nisreen says it's a waste of time."

"I imagine many in Daevabad feel the same way." Even as she touched the gilded spine of one of the volumes, Nahri could tell he was studying her.

"And if you could . . . what would you read about?"

My family. The answer was immediate, but there was no way she was revealing that to Alizayd. She turned to face him. "The books you were reading outside looked interesting."

He didn't bat an eye. "I fear those particular volumes are unavailable right now."

"When do you think they'll be available?"

She saw something soften in his face. "I don't think you'd want to read these, Banu Nahri. I don't think you'd like what they say."

"Why not?"

He hesitated. "War isn't a pleasant topic," he finally said.

That was a more diplomatic response than Nahri would have expected considering the tenor of their earlier conversation. Hoping to keep him talking, she decided to answer his initial question a different way. "Business." At Alizayd's visible confusion, she explained. "You asked what I would read about if I could. I would like to know how people run businesses in Daevabad, how they make money, negotiate with each other, that sort of thing." The more she thought about it, the better idea it seemed. After all, it was her own brand of business savvy that had kept her alive in Cairo, hustling travelers and knowing the best way to swindle a mark.

He went entirely still. "Like . . . economics?"

"I suppose."

His eyes narrowed. "Are you *sure* my father didn't send you?"

"Quite."

Something seemed to perk up in his face. "Economics, then . . ." He sounded strangely excited. "Well, I certainly have enough material on that."

He stepped closer to the shelves, and Nahri moved away. He really was tall, towering over her like one of the ancient statues that still dotted the deserts outside Egypt. He even had the same stern, slightly disapproving face.

He plucked a fat blue-and-gold volume from the top shelf. "A history of Daevabad's markets." He handed her the book. "It is written in Arabic, so it might prove more familiar."

She cracked open the spine and flicked through a few pages. "Very familiar. Still completely incomprehensible."

"I can teach you to read it." There was an uncertainty in his voice.

Nahri gave him a sharp look. "What?"

Alizayd spread his hands. "I can teach you . . . I mean, if you want me to. After all, Nisreen doesn't command my time. And

I can convince my father that it would be good for relations between our tribes." His smile faded. "He is very . . . supportive of such endeavors."

Nahri crossed her arms. "And what do you get out of it?" She didn't trust the offer at all. The Qahtanis were too clever to take at face value.

"You are my father's guest." Nahri snorted, and Alizayd almost smiled again. "Fine. I must admit an obsession with the human world. You can ask anyone," he added, perhaps picking up on her doubt. "Particularly your corner of it. I've never met anyone from Egypt. I'd love to learn more about it, hear your stories, and perhaps even improve my own Arabic."

Oh, I have no doubt you'd like to know lots of things. As Nahri considered his offer, she mentally sized up the prince. He was young, younger even than she was, she was fairly certain. Privileged, a bit ill-tempered. His smile was eager, a little too hopeful for the offer to have been a casual aside. Whatever his motivation, Alizayd wanted this.

And Nahri wanted to know what was in his books, especially if the information was damaging to Dara. If making this awkward boy her tutor was the best way to protect herself and her Afshin, then by all means.

Besides . . . she *did* want to learn how to read.

Nahri dropped onto one of the floor cushions. "Why wait, then?" she asked in her best Cairene Arabic. She tapped her fingers on the book. "Let's get started."

19

ALI

"You're going easy on me."

Ali glanced across the training-room floor. "What?"

Jamshid e-Pramukh gave him a wry smile. "I've seen you spar with a zulfiqar before—you're going easy on me."

Ali's gaze ran down the other man's attire. Jamshid was dressed in the same sparring uniform as Ali, bleached white to highlight every strike of the fiery sword, but while Ali's clothes were untouched, the Daeva guard's uniform was scorched and covered in charcoal smudges. His lip was bleeding and his right cheek swollen from one of the times Ali had sent him crashing to the floor.

Ali raised an eyebrow. "You have an interesting idea of easy."

"Nah," Jamshid said in Divasti. Like his father, he retained a slight accent when speaking Djinnistani, a hint of the years they'd spent in outer Daevastana. "I should be in far worse shape. Little burning pieces of Jamshid e-Pramukh all over the floor."

Ali sighed. "I don't like fighting a foreigner with a zulfiqar," he confessed. "Even if we're just using training blades. It doesn't feel fair. And Muntadhir won't be happy if he returns to Daevabad to find his closest friend in little burning pieces."

Jamshid shrugged. "He'll know to blame me. I've been asking him for years to find a zulfiqari willing to train me."

Ali frowned. "But why? You're excellent with a broadsword, even better with a bow. Why learn to use a weapon you can never properly wield?"

"A blade is a blade. I might not be able to summon its poisoned flames like a Geziri man, but if I fight alongside your tribesmen, it stands to reason I should have some familiarity with their weapons." Jamshid shrugged. "At least enough not to jump away every time they burst into flames."

"I'm not sure that's an instinct you should suppress."

Jamshid laughed. "Fair enough." He raised his blade. "Shall we continue?"

Ali shrugged. "If you insist." He swept his zulfiqar through the air. Flames burst between his fingers and licked up the copper blade as he willed them, scorching the forked tip and activating the deadly poisons that coated its sharp edge. Or would have, if the weapon were real. The blade he held had been stripped of its poisons for training purposes, and Ali could smell the difference in the air. Most men couldn't, but then again most men hadn't obsessively practiced with the weapon since they were seven.

Jamshid charged forward, and Ali easily ducked, landing a blow on the Daeva's collar before spinning off his own momentum.

Jamshid whirled to face Ali, trying to block his next parry. "It doesn't help that you move like a damn hummingbird," he complained good-naturedly. "Are you sure you aren't half peri?"

Ali couldn't help but smile. Strangely enough, he'd been enjoying his time with Jamshid. There was something easy about his demeanor; he behaved as though they were equals—showing neither the subservience most djinn did around a Qahtani prince nor the Daeva tribe's typical snobbery. It was refreshing—no wonder Muntadhir kept him so close. It was hard to even believe he was Kaveh's son. He was nothing like the prickly grand wazir.

"Keep your weapon higher," Ali advised. "The zulfiqar isn't like most swords; it's less a thrusting and jabbing motion, more quick slashes and side strikes. Remember the blade is typically poisoned; you only need to inflict a minor injury." He swung his zulfiqar around his head, the flames soared, and Jamshid veered back as expected. Ali took advantage of the distraction to duck, aiming another blow at his hips.

Jamshid leaped back with a frustrated snort, and Ali easily cornered him against the opposing wall. "How many times would you have killed me by now?" Jamshid asked. "Twenty? Thirty?"

More. A real zulfiqar was one of the deadliest weapons in the world. "Not more than a dozen," Ali lied.

They continued sparring. Jamshid wasn't improving much, but Ali was impressed by his grit. The visibly exhausted Daeva man was covered in ash and blood but refused a break.

Ali had his blade at Jamshid's throat for the third time and was about to insist they stop when the sound of voices drew his attention. He glanced up as Kaveh e-Pramukh, clearly in friendly conversation with someone behind him, stepped into the training room.

The grand wazir froze. His eyes locked on the zulfiqar at his son's throat, and Ali heard him make a small, strangled noise. "*Jamshid?*"

Ali immediately lowered his weapon, and Jamshid spun around. "Baba?" He sounded surprised. "What are you doing here?"

"Nothing," Kaveh said quickly. He stepped back, oddly enough looking more anxious than before as he tried to pull the door shut. "Forgive me. I didn't—"

The door pushed past his hand, and Darayavahoush e-Afshin strolled into the room.

He entered like it was his own tent, his hands clasped behind his back, and stopped when he noticed them. "Sahzadeh Alizayd," he greeted Ali calmly in Divasti.

Ali was not calm, he was speechless. He blinked, half expecting to see another man in the Afshin's place. What in God's name was Darayavahoush doing here? He was supposed to be in Babili with Muntadhir, far away on the other side of Daevastana!

The Afshin studied the room like a general surveying a battlefield; his green eyes scanned the wall of weapons and swept over the various dummies, targets, and other miscellany cluttering the floor. He glanced back at Ali. "Naeda pouru mejnoas."

What? "I . . . I don't speak Divasti," Ali stammered out.

Darayavahoush tilted his head, his eyes brightening with surprise. "You don't speak the language of the city you rule?" he asked in heavily accented Djinnistani. He turned to Kaveh and jerked a thumb in Ali's direction, looking amused. "Spa snasatiy nu hyat vaken gezr?"

Jamshid went pale, and Kaveh hurried between Ali and Darayavahoush, open fear on his face. "Forgive our intrusion, Prince Alizayd. I didn't realize you were the one training Jamshid." He placed his hand on Darayavahoush's wrist. "Come, Afshin, we should be leaving."

Darayavahoush shook free. "Nonsense. That would be rude." The Afshin wore a sleeveless tunic that revealed the black tattoo swirling around his arm. That he didn't cover it said a great deal, but perhaps Ali shouldn't be surprised—the Afshin had been an accomplished murderer long before he had been enslaved by the ifrit.

Ali watched as he ran a hand along the cracked marble lattice lining the windows and gazed at the multicolored paint chips clinging to the ancient stone walls. "Your people have not maintained our palace very well," he remarked.

Our palace? Ali's mouth dropped open, and he gave Kaveh an incredulous glance, but the grand wazir just lifted his shoulders, looking helpless.

"What are you doing here, Afshin?" Ali snapped. "Your expedition was not due back for weeks."

"I left." Darayavahoush said simply. "I was eager to return to my lady's service, and your brother seemed perfectly capable of managing without me."

"And Emir Muntadhir agreed?"

"I did not ask." Darayavahoush grinned at Kaveh. "And now here I am, getting a rather *informative* tour of my old home."

"The Afshin wished to see the Banu Nahida," Kaveh said, carefully meeting Ali's gaze. "I told him that unfortunately her time is occupied with training. And indeed, on that note, Afshin, I fear we must leave. I am due to meet—"

"You should go," Darayavahoush interrupted. "I can find my way out. I defended the palace for years—I know it like the back of my hand." He let the words lie for a moment and then turned his attention to Jamshid. His gaze lingered on the young Daeva's wounds. "You were the one who stopped the riot, yes?"

Jamshid looked positively awed that the Afshin was speaking to him. "I . . . uh . . . yes. But I was just—"

"You are an excellent shot." The Afshin looked the younger man over and clapped him on the back. "You should train with me. I can make you even better."

"Really?" Jamshid burst out. "That would be wonderful!"

Darayavahoush smiled and then deftly snatched the zulfiqar away from Kaveh's son. "Certainly. Leave this to the Geziri." He raised the blade and twisted it, watching as it sparkled in the sunlight. "So this is the famous zulfiqar." He tested the weight, looking it over with a practiced eye and then glanced at Ali. "Do you mind? I would not wish for the hands of a—what is it you call us? Fire worshipper?—to contaminate something so sacred to your people."

"Afshin—" Kaveh started, his voice thick with warning.

"You may go, Kaveh," Darayavahoush said, dismissing him. "Jamshid, why don't you join him? Let me take your place and spar a bit with Prince Alizayd. I have heard such *great* talk of his skills."

Jamshid glanced at Ali, looking apologetic and lost for words. Ali didn't blame him; if Zaydi al Qahtani came back to life and complimented his skill with a zulfiqar, Ali would also be speechless. Besides, the arrogant gleam in Darayavahoush's green eyes was fraying his last nerve. If the man wanted to challenge him with a weapon he'd never so much as held, so be it.

"It's fine, Jamshid. Go with your father."

"Prince Alizayd, that's not a—"

"Good day, Grand Wazir," Ali said sharply. He didn't take his eyes off Darayavahoush. He heard Kaveh sigh, but there was no disobeying a direct order from one of the Qahtanis. Jamshid reluctantly followed his father out.

The Afshin shot him a much cooler look once the Pramukhs were gone. "You did quite a bit of damage to the grand wazir's son."

Ali flushed. "Have you never injured a man while training?"

"Not with a weapon I knew my opponent could never properly use." Darayavahoush raised the zulfiqar to examine it as he circled Ali. "This is much lighter than I imagined. By the Creator, you would not believe the rumors about these things during the war. My people were terrified of them, said Zaydi stole them from the very angels guarding Paradise."

"That's the way of things, isn't it?" Ali asked. "The legend outweighing the flesh-and-blood figure?"

His meaning was clearly not lost on the Afshin, who looked amused. "You are probably right."

He charged then at Ali with a hard right strike that, if it had been a broadsword, would have knocked his head off from the force alone. But the zulfiqar was not that, and Ali easily ducked, taking advantage of Darayavahoush's stumble to sweep the broad side of his blade on his back.

"I've wanted to meet you for some time, Prince Alizayd," Darayavahoush continued, sidestepping Ali's next thrust. "Your brother's men were always talking about you; I've heard you're the best zulfiqari in your generation, as talented and as fast as Zaydi himself. Even Muntadhir agreed; he says you move like a dancer and strike like a viper." He laughed. "He's so proud. It's sweet. You rarely hear a man speak of his rival with such affection."

"I'm not his rival," Ali snapped.

"No? Then who becomes king after your father if something should happen to Muntadhir?"

Ali drew up. "What? *Why?*" A briefly irrational fear seized his heart. "Did *you*—"

"Yes," Darayavahoush said, his voice thick with sarcasm. "I murdered the emir and then decided to return to Daevabad and crow about it because I always wondered what it would be like to have my head on a spike."

Ali felt his face grow warm. "Aye, don't fret, little prince," the Afshin continued. "I enjoyed your brother's company. Muntadhir has a taste for life's pleasures and talks too much when he's in his cups . . . what's not to like about that?"

The comment threw him—as it was presumably meant to— and Ali was unprepared when the Afshin raised his zulfiqar and rushed him again. The Afshin feinted left and then spun—faster than Ali had ever seen a man move—before bringing the blade down hard. Ali blocked him but just barely, his own zulfiqar ringing with the force of the hit. He tried to push back, but the Afshin didn't budge. He held the zulfiqar with only one hand, not showing a hint of weariness.

Ali held tight, but his hands trembled on the hilt as the Afshin's blade neared his face. Darayavahoush leaned close, putting his weight into the sword.

Brighten. Ali's zulfiqar burst into flames, and Darayavahoush instinctively jerked back. But the Afshin recovered quickly, swinging his zulfiqar toward Ali's neck. Ali ducked, feeling the whiz of the blade as it passed just over his head. He stayed low to aim a fiery blow at the backs of the Afshin's knees. Darayavahoush stumbled, and Ali darted up and away.

He could kill me, Ali realized. One misstep was all it would take; Darayavahoush could claim it was an accident, and who would be able to dispute it? The Pramukhs were the only witnesses, and Kaveh would probably be overjoyed to cover up Ali's murder.

You're being paranoid. But when Darayavahoush struck out again, Ali met his advance with a bit more gusto, finally forcing him back across the room.

The Afshin lowered his zulfiqar with a wide grin. "Not bad, Zaydi. You fight very well for a boy your age."

Ali was getting sick of that smug smile. "My name isn't Zaydi."

"Muntadhir calls you that."

He narrowed his eyes. "You're not my brother."

"No," Darayavahoush agreed. "I am certainly not. But you do remind me of your namesake."

Considering that the original Zaydi and Darayavahoush had been mortal enemies in a century-long war that wiped out whole swaths of their race, Ali knew that wasn't a compliment, but took it as such anyway. "Thank you."

The Afshin studied the zulfiqar again, holding it so that the copper blade gleamed in the sunlight streaming through the windows. "Don't thank me. The Zaydi al Qahtani I knew was a bloodthirsty rebel fanatic, not the saint your people have turned him into."

Ali bristled at the insult. "*He* was bloodthirsty? Your Nahid Council was burning shafit alive in the midan when he rebelled."

Darayavahoush lifted one of his dark eyebrows. "Do you know

so much about the way things were a millennium before your birth?"

"Our records tell us—"

"Your *records*?" The Afshin laughed, a mirthless sound. "Oh, how I would love to know what those say. Can the Geziri even write? I thought all you did out there in your sandpits was feud and beg for human table scraps."

Ali's temper flashed. He opened his mouth to argue and then stopped, realizing just how carefully Darayavahoush was watching him. How intentionally he'd chosen his insults. The Afshin was trying to provoke him, and Ali would be damned if he was going to go along with it. He took a deep breath. "I can go sit in a Daeva tavern if I want to hear my tribe insulted," he said dismissively. "I thought you wanted to spar."

Something twinkled in the Afshin's bright eyes. "Right you are, boy." He raised his blade.

Ali met his next thrust with a clash of their blades, but the Afshin was good, improving at a frighteningly fast rate, as if he could literally absorb each of Ali's actions. He moved quicker and struck harder than anyone Ali had ever fought, had ever even imagined possible. The room grew hot. Ali's brow felt oddly damp—but of course that wasn't possible. Pureblooded djinn didn't sweat.

The power behind the Afshin's blows made it feel like sparring with a statue. Ali's wrists ached; it was getting difficult to maintain his grip.

Darayavahoush was backing him into a tight corner when he abruptly broke away and lowered his zulfiqar. He sighed as he admired the blade. "Ah, I have missed this . . . Peacetime may have its virtues, but there's nothing like the rush and clash of your weapon against the enemy's."

Ali took the moment to catch his breath. "I'm not your enemy," he said through gritted teeth, though he very much disagreed with the sentiment right now. "The war is over."

"So people keep telling me." The Afshin turned away, strolling slowly across the room and deliberately leaving his back unprotected. Ali's fingers twitched on his zulfiqar. He forced himself to push away the strong temptation to attack the other man. Darayavahoush wouldn't have put himself in such a position if he were not entirely confident he could defend it.

"Was it your father's idea to keep us separated?" the Afshin asked. "I was surprised by how eager he was to see me gone from Daevabad, even offering up his firstborn as collateral. And yet I'm still blocked from seeing my Banu Nahida. I was told there's a waiting list for appointments the length of my arm."

Ali hesitated, thrown by the abrupt change in subject. "Your arrival was unexpected, and she's busy. Perhaps—"

"That order did not come from Nahri," Darayavahoush snapped, and in an instant Ali felt the room grow hotter. The torch opposite him flared, but the Afshin didn't seem to notice, his gaze fixed on the wall. It was where most of the weapons were stored, a hundred varieties of death hanging from hooks and chains.

Ali couldn't help himself. "Looking for a scourge?"

Darayavahoush turned back around. His green eyes were bright with anger. Too bright. Ali had never seen anything like it, and the Afshin was not the first freed slave he'd met. He glanced again at the blazing torches, watching as they flickered wildly, almost as though they were reaching for the former slave.

The light faded from the Afshin's eyes, leaving a calculating expression on his face. "I hear your father intends to marry Banu Nahri to your brother."

Ali's mouth fell open. Where had Darayavahoush learned *that*? He pressed his lips together, trying to hide the surprise in his face. Kaveh, it had to have been. Considering the way those fire worshippers were whispering together when they entered the training room, Kaveh was probably spilling every secret he knew. "Did the grand wazir tell you that?"

"No. You just did." Darayavahoush paused long enough to enjoy the shock on Ali's face. "Your father strikes me as a pragmatic man, and marrying them would be a most astute political move. Besides, you are rumored to be some sort of religious fanatic, but according to Kaveh, you're spending a great deal of time with her. That would hardly be appropriate unless she was meant to join your family." His eyes lingered on Ali's body. "And Ghassan clearly doesn't mind crossing tribal lines himself."

Ali was speechless, his face warm with embarrassment. His father was going to murder him when he found out that Ali had let slip such information.

He thought fast, trying to come up with a way to undo the damage. "Banu Nahri is a guest in my father's home, Afshin," he started. "I'm simply trying to be kind. She wished to learn to read—I would scarcely say there's anything inappropriate about that."

The Afshin drew closer, but he wasn't smiling now. "And what are you teaching her to read? Those same Geziri records that demonize her ancestors?"

"No," Ali shot back. "She wanted to learn about economics. Though I'm sure you filled her ears with plenty of lies about us."

"I told the truth. She had a right to know how your people stole her birthright and nearly destroyed our world."

"And what of your part in such things?" Ali challenged. "Did you tell her that, Darayavahoush? Does she know why you're called the Scourge?"

There was silence. And then—for the first time since the Afshin entered the room with his smug smile and laughing eyes—Ali saw a trace of uncertainty in his face.

She doesn't know. Ali had suspected as much, though Nahri was always careful not to speak of the Afshin in his presence. Oddly enough, he was relieved. They'd been meeting for a few weeks now, and Ali was enjoying her company. He didn't like thinking that his future sister-in-law would be loyal to such a monster had she known the truth.

Darayavahoush shrugged, but there was a flash of warning in his bright eyes. "I was just following orders."

"That is *not* true."

The Afshin lifted one of his dark eyebrows. "No? Then tell me what your sand-fly histories say of me."

Ali could hear his father's warning in his mind, but he didn't hold back. "They speak of Qui-zi for one." The Afshin's face twitched. "And you were taking no orders once Daevabad fell and the Nahid Council was overthrown. *You* led the uprising in Daevastana. If you can call such indiscriminate butchery an uprising."

"*Indiscriminate butchery?*" Darayavahoush drew himself up, his expression scornful. "Your ancestors slaughtered my family, sacked my city, and tried to exterminate my tribe—you have great nerve to judge my actions."

"You exaggerate," Ali said dismissively. "No one tried to exterminate your tribe. The Daevas survived just fine without you around to destroy mixed villages and bury innocent djinn alive."

The Afshin snorted. "Yes, we survived to become second-class citizens in our own city, forced to bow and scrape to the rest of you."

"An opinion formed after spending, what, two days in Daevabad?" Ali rolled his eyes. "Your tribe is wealthy and well-connected, and their quarter is the cleanest and most finely run in the city. You know who are second-class citizens? The shafit who—"

Darayavahoush rolled his eyes. "Ah, there it is. It's not a discussion with a djinn until they start bemoaning the poor, sad shafit they can't stop creating. Suleiman's eye, find a *goat* if you can't control yourselves. They're comparable enough to humans."

Ali's hands tightened on the zulfiqar. He wanted to hurt this man. "Do you know what else the histories say about you?"

"Enlighten me, djinn."

"That you could have done it." Darayavahoush frowned, and Ali continued. "Most scholars believe you could have defended an independent Daevastana for a long time. Long enough to free a few of the surviving Nahids. Perhaps even long enough to retake Daevabad."

The Afshin went still, and Ali could tell he had struck a nerve. He stared at the prince, and when he spoke his voice was soft, his words intent. "It sounds like your family was very lucky the ifrit killed me when they did, then."

Ali didn't break away from the other man's cold gaze. "God provides." It was cruel, but he didn't care. Darayavahoush was a monster.

Darayavahoush lifted his chin and then smiled, a sharp smile that reminded Ali more of a snarling dog than a man. "And here we are discussing ancient history again when I promised you a challenge." He raised the zulfiqar.

It burst into flames, and Ali's eyes went wide.

No non-Geziri man should have *ever* been able to do that.

The Afshin looked more intrigued than surprised. He gazed at the flames, the fire reflected in his bright eyes. "Ah . . . now isn't that fascinating?"

It was the only warning Ali got.

Darayavahoush charged him, and Ali whirled away, flames licking down his own zulfiqar. Their weapons met with a crash, and Darayavahoush shoved his blade up and along Ali's until the hilt caught his hands. Then he kicked him hard in the stomach.

Ali fell back, rolling quickly away when Darayavahoush slashed down in a motion that would have sliced his chest open if he hadn't moved fast enough. *Well, I suppose Abba was right*, he thought, jumping up as the Afshin swept his zulfiqar at his feet. *Darayava-housh and I probably wouldn't have made very good travel companions.*

The Afshin's calm was gone and with it, much of the reserve Ali now realized the other man had been showing. He was actually an even *better* fighter than he'd let on.

But the zulfiqar was a Geziri weapon, and Ali would be damned if some Daeva butcher was going to beat him with it. He let the Afshin pursue him across the training room, their fiery blades clashing and sizzling. Though he was taller than Daraya-vahoush, the other man was probably twice his bulk, and he was hoping his youth and agility would eventually turn the duel in his favor.

And yet that didn't appear to be happening. Ali dodged blow after blow, becoming increasingly exhausted—and a little afraid.

As he blocked another charge, he caught sight of a khanjar glinting on a sunny window shelf across the room. The dagger peeked out among a pile of random supplies—the training room was notoriously messy, overseen by a kindly yet absentminded old Geziri warrior no one had the heart to replace.

An idea sparked in Ali's head. As they fought, he started letting his fatigue show—along with his fear. He wasn't acting, and he could see a glimmer of triumph in the Afshin's eyes. He was clearly enjoying the opportunity to put the stupid young son of a hated enemy in his place.

Darayavahoush's forceful blows shook his entire body, but Ali kept his zulfiqar up as the Afshin followed his lead toward the windows. Their fiery blades hissed against each other as Ali was pushed hard against the glass. The Afshin smiled. Behind his head, the torches flared and danced against the wall like they'd been doused in oil.

Ali abruptly let go of his zulfiqar.

He snatched the khanjar and dropped to the ground as Darayavahoush stumbled. Ali rolled to his feet and was on the Afshin before the other man recovered. He pressed the dagger to his throat, breathing hard, but went no further. "Are we done?"

The Afshin spat. "Go to hell, sand fly."

And then every weapon in the room flew at him.

Ali threw himself to the floor as the weapons wall purged itself. A spinning mace whooshed over his head, and a Tukharistani pole arm speared his sleeve to the ground. It was over in a matter of seconds, but before Ali could process what had happened, the Afshin stomped hard on his right wrist.

It took every bit of self-control not to scream as Darayavahoush ground the heel of his boot into the bones of Ali's wrist. He heard something crack and a searing pain rushed through him. His fingers went numb, and Darayavahoush kicked the khanjar away.

The zulfiqar was at his throat. "Get up," the Afshin hissed.

Ali did so, cradling his injured wrist through the ripped sleeve. Weapons littered the floor, the chains and hooks that had held them dangling broken on the opposite wall. A chill went down Ali's back. It was the rare djinn who could summon a single object—and that was with far more focus over a shorter distance. But this? And so soon after drawing flames from the zulfiqar?

He shouldn't be able to do any *of this.*

Darayavahoush didn't seem bothered. Instead, he gave Ali a coolly appraising look. "I wouldn't have thought such a trick your style."

Ali gritted his teeth, trying to ignore the pain in his wrist. "I suppose I'm full of surprises."

Darayavahoush looked at him for a long moment. "No," he finally said. "You're not. You're exactly what I would expect." He picked up Ali's zulfiqar and tossed it over; surprised, Ali caught it with his good hand. "Thank you for the lesson, but sadly, the weapon did not live up to its fearsome reputation."

Ali sheathed his zulfiqar, offended on its behalf. "Sorry to disappoint you," he said sarcastically.

"I didn't say I was disappointed." Darayavahoush ran his hand over a war ax protruding from one of the stone columns. "Your charming and cultured brother, your pragmatic father . . . I was starting to wonder what happened to the Qahtanis I knew . . . starting to fear my memories of the zulfiqar-wielding fanatics who destroyed my world were wrong." He eyed Ali. "Thank you for this reminder."

"I . . ." Ali was lost for words, suddenly fearing he'd done far worse than reveal his father's plans regarding Nahri. "You misunderstand me."

"Not at all." The Afshin gave him another sharp smile. "I was also once a young warrior from the ruling tribe. It's a privileged position. Such utter confidence in the rightness of your people, such unwavering belief in your faith." His smile faded; he sounded wistful. Regretful. "Enjoy it."

"I am nothing like you," Ali shot back. "I would never do the things you did."

The Afshin pulled open the door. "Pray you're never asked to, Zaydi."

20

NAHRI

"It's a lock."

"A *lock*? No, it cannot be. Look at it. It's obviously some advanced mechanism. A scientific tool . . . or, considering the fish, perhaps a navigational aid for the sea."

"It's a lock." Nahri took the metal object from Alizayd's hands. It was made of iron and shaped like an ornate fish with fluttering fins and a curved tail, and it had a series of boxy pictograms carved into one side. She pulled free a pin from her headscarf and turned the lock over to find the keyhole. Holding it close to her ear, she expertly picked it, and the bar swung open. "See? A lock. It's just missing its key."

Nahri triumphantly handed the ornamental lock back to Ali and leaned into her cushion, propping her feet up on a plump silk ottoman. She and her overqualified tutor were in one of the upper balconies of the royal library, the same place they'd been meeting every afternoon for the past few weeks. She took a sip of tea, admiring the intricate glasswork of the nearby window.

The impressive library had quickly become her favorite place in the palace. Even bigger than Ghassan's throne room, the huge roofed-over courtyard was filled with bustling scholars and arguing students. On the balcony across from them, a Sahrayn instructor had conjured up smoke into an even larger map than the one Dara had made for her during their desert crossing. A miniature boat of spun glass floated in its sea. The instructor raised his hands and a gust of wind filled its silken sails, sending it racing along a chart marked by tiny burning embers as several students watched. In the alcove above him, an Agnivanshi scholar was teaching mathematics. With each snap of her fingers, a new number appeared scorched on the whitewashed wall before her, a veritable map of equations her pupils were diligently copying.

And then there were the books themselves. The shelves soared out of sight to meet the dizzyingly high ceiling; Ali—who seemed utterly delighted by her interest in the library—had told her that its vast inventory contained copies of just about every work ever written, both human and djinn. Apparently there was an entire class of djinn who spent their lives traveling from human library to human library, meticulously copying its works and sending them back to be archived in Daevabad.

The shelves were also crowded with glittering tools and instruments, murky preservation jars, and dusty artifacts. Ali warned her away from the majority; apparently small explosions were not uncommon. The djinn had a propensity for exploring the properties of fire in *every* form.

"A lock." Ali's words pulled her attention back. The prince sounded disappointed. Two library attendants flew through the air behind him on carpets the size of prayer rugs, retrieving books for the scholars below.

"Efl," she corrected his Arabic. "Not qefl."

He frowned, pulling over a piece of parchment from the stack they'd been using to practice letters. "But it is written like this." He wrote out the word and pointed to its first letter. "Qaf, no?"

Nahri shrugged. "My people say efl."

"Efl," he repeated carefully. "Efl."

"There. Now you sound like a proper Egyptian." She smiled at Ali's serious expression as he turned the lock over in his hands. "The djinn don't use locks?"

"Not really. We find curses to be a better deterrent."

Nahri made a face. "That sounds unpleasant."

"But effective. After all . . ." He met her gaze, a slight challenge in his gray eyes. "A former maidservant just picked one rather easily."

Nahri cursed herself for the slip. "I had a lot of cupboards to open. Cleaning supplies and such."

Ali laughed, a warm sound she rarely heard that always took her a bit by surprise. "Are brooms so valuable among humans?"

She shrugged. "My mistress was stingy."

He smiled, peering into the lock's exposed keyhole. "I think I should like to learn to do this."

"Pick a lock?" She laughed. "Are you planning a future as a criminal in the human world?"

"I like to keep my options open."

Nahri snorted. "Then you'll need to work on your accent. Your Arabic sounds like something spoken by scholars in the ancient courts of Baghdad."

He took the jab in stride, returning it with a compliment. "I suppose I'm not making as much progress as you in our respective studies," he confessed. "Your writing has truly come a long way. You should start thinking about what language you'd like to tackle next."

"Divasti." There was no question. "Then I can read the Nahid texts myself instead of listening to Nisreen drone on."

Ali's face fell. "I fear you'll need another tutor for that. I barely speak it."

"Truly?" When he nodded, she narrowed her eyes. "You told me once that you know five different languages . . . and yet you couldn't find time to learn that of Daevabad's original people?"

The prince winced. "When you put it that way . . ."

"What about your father?"

"He's fluent." Ali replied. "My father is very . . . taken with Daeva culture. Muntadhir, as well."

Interesting. Nahri filed that information away. "Well, that settles it. You'll join me when I start. There's no reason for you not to learn."

"I look forward to being outmatched," Ali said. Just then, a servant approached bearing a large covered platter, and the prince's face lit up. "Salaams, brother, thank you." He smiled at Nahri. "I have a surprise for you."

She raised her eyebrows. "More human artifacts to identify?"

"Not exactly."

The servant pulled away the top of the platter, and the rich smell of sizzling sugar and buttery dough wafted past her. Several triangles of flaky sweet bread sprinkled with raisins, coconut, and sugar were stacked on a plate, the aroma and sight immediately familiar.

"Is that . . . feteer?" she asked, her stomach immediately grumbling at the delicious scent. "How did you get this?"

Ali looked delighted. "I heard there was a shafit man from Cairo working in the kitchen and requested that he prepare a treat from your home. He made this as well." He nodded at a chilled carafe of bloodred liquid.

Karkade. The servant poured her a cup of the cold hibiscus tea, and she took a long sip, savoring its sweetened tang before tearing off a strip of the buttery pastry and popping it in her mouth. It tasted exactly like she remembered. Like home.

This is my home now, she reminded herself. Nahri took another bite of feteer. "Try some," she urged. "It's delicious."

He helped himself while she sipped her karkade. Though she was enjoying the snack, there was something about the combination that was troubling her . . . and then it hit her. This was the same meal she'd eaten in the coffeehouse before she entered the cemetery in Cairo. Before her life was abruptly upended.

Before she met Dara.

Her appetite vanished, and her heart gave its usual lurch, whether from worry or longing she didn't know and had given up trying to sort out. Dara had been gone for two months—longer than their original journey together—and yet she woke every morning still half-expecting to see him. She missed him: his sly grin, his unexpected sweetness, even his constant grumbling—not to mention the occasional, accidental press of his body against hers.

Nahri pushed away the food, but the call to sunset prayer sounded out before Alizayd noticed. "Is it maghrib already?" she asked as she wiped the sugar off her fingers; the time always seemed to fly when she was with the prince. "Nisreen is going to kill me. I told her I'd be back hours ago." Her assistant—although she occasionally felt more like a disapproving schoolmistress or scolding aunt to Nahri—had made her distaste for both Prince Alizayd and these tutoring sessions quite clear.

Ali waited until the call to prayer was complete to respond. "Do you have a patient?"

"No one new, but Nisreen wanted—" She paused as Ali reached for one of his books, the sleeve of his pale robe falling back to reveal a badly swollen wrist. "What happened to you?"

"It's nothing." He pulled his sleeve down. "Just a training accident from the other day."

Nahri frowned. The djinn recovered quickly from non-magical injuries; it must have been a hard blow to still look like that. "Would you like me to heal you? It looks painful."

He shook his head as he stood, although she noticed now that he was carrying his supplies with his left arm. "It's not that bad," he said, averting his eyes as she readjusted her chador. "And it was well earned. I made a stupid mistake." He scowled. "Several, actually."

She shrugged, accustomed by now to the prince's stubbornness. "If you insist."

Ali placed the lock in a velvet box and handed it back to the attendant. "A lock," he mused again. "Daevabad's most esteemed scholars have themselves convinced this thing can calculate the number of stars in the sky."

"Couldn't they simply have asked another shafit from the human world?"

He hesitated. "That is not quite how things are done here."

"It should be," she replied as they left the library. "It seems a waste of time otherwise."

"I could not agree more."

There was an oddly fierce edge to his voice, and Nahri wondered whether or not to press him further. He'd answer, she knew; he answered all her questions. By God, sometimes he talked so much it could be difficult to get him to stop. Nahri normally didn't mind; the taciturn young prince she'd first met had become her most enthusiastic source of information about the djinn world, and strangely enough, she was beginning to enjoy their afternoons together, the one bright spot in her monotonous, frustrating days.

But she also knew the issue of the shafit was one which divided their tribes—the one which had led to the bloody overthrow of her ancestors at the hands of his.

She held her tongue, and they kept walking. The white marble corridor shone with the saffron-hued light of sunset, and she could hear a few latecomers still singing the call to prayer from the city's distant minarets. She tried to slow her steps, enjoying another few moments of peace. Returning to the infirmary each day—to inevitably fail at something new—was like donning weighted sackcloth.

Ali spoke again. "I don't know if you would be interested, but the traders who recovered that lock also found some sort of lens for observing the stars. Our scholars are attempting to restore it before the arrival of a comet in a few weeks."

"You're sure it's not just a pair of spectacles?" she teased.

He laughed. "God forbid. They'd die of disappointment. But if you like, I can arrange a viewing." Ali hesitated as a servant reached for the infirmary doors. "Perhaps my brother, Muntadhir, can join us. His expedition is due back by then and . . ."

Nahri had stopped listening. A familiar voice caught her attention as the infirmary door opened, and she rushed in, praying her ears weren't deceiving her.

They weren't. Sitting at one of her worktables, looking as harassed and handsome as always, was Dara.

Her breath caught in her throat. Dara was bent low in conversation with Nisreen, but he abruptly straightened up when he caught sight of Nahri. His bright eyes met hers, filled with the same swirl of emotions she suspected was on her face. Her heart felt ready to leap out of her chest.

By the Most High, get hold of yourself. Nahri shut her mouth, realizing it was hanging open as Ali entered the room behind her.

Nisreen shot to her feet, pressing her palms together. She bowed. "My prince."

Dara stayed seated. "Little Zaydi . . . salaam alaykum!" he greeted in atrociously accented Arabic. He grinned. "How is your wrist?"

Ali drew up, looking indignant. "You should not be here,

Afshin. The Banu Nahida's time is precious. Only those who are ill or injured—"

Dara abruptly raised a fist and then smashed it through the heavy, sandblasted glass table. The top shattered, sparkling shards of hazy glass cascading over the Afshin and the floor. He didn't even flinch; instead, he raised his hand and looked at the jagged pieces of glass embedded in his skin with mock surprise. "There," he deadpanned. "I'm injured."

Ali stepped forward with an angry expression, and Nahri sprang into action, Dara's lunatic act snapping her into focus. Likely breaking at least a dozen rules of protocol, she grabbed the prince by the shoulders and spun him around toward the door. "I think Nisreen and I can handle this," she said with forced cheer as she pushed him out. "You wouldn't want to miss prayer!" The astonished djinn was opening his mouth to protest when she smiled and shut the door in his face.

She took a deep breath to steady herself before turning back. "Leave us, Nisreen."

"Banu Nahida, that is not appropriate . . ."

Nahri didn't even look at the other woman, her gaze directed at Dara alone. "Go!"

Nisreen sighed, but before she could leave, Dara reached out to touch her wrist. "Thank you," he said with such sincerity that Nisreen blushed. "My heart is greatly lightened by knowing someone like you serves my Banu Nahida."

"It is my honor," Nisreen replied, sounding uncharacteristically flustered. Nahri couldn't blame her; she'd felt that way often enough in Dara's presence.

But she definitely was not feeling that way right now. She knew Dara could sense it; the moment Nisreen left, some of the bravado vanished from his face.

He gave her a weak smile. "You've taken very quickly to ordering people around."

Nahri picked her way through the remains of her destroyed table. "Have you completely lost your mind?" she demanded as she reached for his hand.

He stepped back. "I might ask you the same. Alizayd al Qahtani? Really, Nahri? Could you not find an ifrit to befriend?"

"He's not my friend, you fool," she said, grabbing again for his hand. "He's a mark. One I was having luck with until you sauntered into the palace and broke his wrist . . . stop wiggling away!"

Dara held his arm above her head. "Did I really break it?" he asked with an impish grin. "I thought so. His bones made the most pleasant sound . . ." He broke away from his reverie to glance down at her. "Does *he* know he's a mark?"

Nahri thought back to Ali's comment on her lock picking. "Probably," she admitted. "He's not as much of a fool as I hoped." She didn't dare mention the fact that their "friendship" had started when she learned Ali was reading up on Dara. That was not news she expected to be well received.

"You do know he's doing the same, yes?" There was a flicker of apprehension in Dara's face. "You can't trust him. I bet every other word out of his mouth is a lie meant to turn you toward their side."

"Are you suggesting my *ancestral enemy* has an ulterior motive? But I've spilled all my deepest secrets . . . what will I do?" Nahri touched her heart in mock horror and then narrowed her eyes. "Have you forgotten who I am, Dara? I can handle Ali just fine."

"*Ali?*" He scowled. "You've nicknamed the sand fly?"

"I call you by a nickname."

She could not have replicated Dara's reaction if she tried; his face twisted into a stormy mix of indignant hurt and pure outrage. "Wait." Nahri felt herself starting to grin. "Are you *jealous*?" When his cheeks flushed, she laughed and clapped her hands together in delight. "By the Most High, you are!" She took in his beautiful eyes and muscular frame, awed as usual by his presence. "How does that even *work* for you? Have you looked in a mirror this century?"

"I'm not jealous of the brat," Dara snapped. He rubbed his brow, and Nahri winced at the sight of the glass sticking out of his hand. "*He's* not the one they want you to marry," Dara added.

"Excuse me?" Her humor vanished.

"Did your new best friend not tell you? They want you to marry Emir Muntadhir." Dara's eyes flashed. "A thing which will not be happening."

"*Muntadhir?*" Nahri remembered very little about Ali's older brother except thinking that he looked like the type of man she'd easily fleece. "Where did you hear such an absurd rumor?"

"From *Ali's* own mouth," he replied, exaggerating the nickname. "Why do you think I broke his wrist?" Dara let out an annoyed huff and crossed his arms over his chest. He was dressed like a proper Daeva nobleman now, in a fitted dark gray coat that ended at his knees, wide embroidered belt, and baggy black pants. He cut a dashing figure, and as he shifted again, she caught a waft of the smoky cedar smell that always seemed to cling to his skin.

A low heat sparked in her chest even as he pressed his mouth in an irritated line. She remembered all too well the sensation of that mouth against hers and it was making her mind spin in reckless directions.

"What, nothing to say?" he challenged. "No thoughts on your impending nuptials?"

She had plenty of thoughts. Just not about Muntadhir. "You seem to object," she said mildly.

"Of course I object! They have no right to interfere in your bloodline. Your heritage is already suspect. You should be marrying the most high-caste Daeva nobleman they can find."

She gave him an even look. "Like you?"

"No," he said, flustered. "I didn't say that. I . . . it has nothing to do with me."

She crossed her arms. "Perhaps if you felt so concerned about my future in Daevabad, you might have *stayed* in Daevabad instead of running after ifrit." She threw up her hands. "So? What happened? You didn't ride in triumphantly with their heads in a bloody bag, so I'm guessing you didn't have much luck."

Dara's shoulders dropped—whether due to disappointing her or losing out on the chance to participate in the above scenario, she wasn't sure. "I'm sorry, Nahri." The anger had vanished from his voice. "They were long gone."

A tiny hope Nahri hadn't quite known she had been nursing snuffed out in her chest. But considering how dejected Dara sounded, she masked her own reaction. "It's all right, Dara." She reached for his good hand. "Come here." She plucked a long pair of tweezers from the worktable that was still standing and then pulled him toward a pile of floor cushions. "Sit. We can talk while I remove the pieces of furniture stuck in your hand."

They sank into the cushions, and he obediently held out his palm. It didn't look as bad as she feared: there were only about a half-dozen fragments in his skin and all were fairly large. There was no blood, a fact she didn't want to dwell on. Dara's hot skin was real enough for her.

She pulled free one of the shards and dropped it into a tin pan at her side. "So we know nothing more?"

"Nothing," he replied, his voice bitter. "And I have no idea where to turn next."

Her mind went to Ali's books—and to the millions crowding the library. There might be answers there, but Nahri couldn't even imagine where to start without help. And it seemed too risky to involve anyone else, even someone like Nisreen, who would probably be willing to help.

He looked crushed, far more than she would have expected.

"It's all right, Dara, really," she insisted. "Whatever happened in the past is just that: past."

A dark look crossed his face. "It's not," he muttered. "Not at all."

An aggrieved squawk suddenly sounded from behind the drawn curtain on the opposite side of the room. Dara jumped.

"Don't worry." Nahri sighed. "It's a patient."

Dara looked incredulous. "Are you treating birds?"

"By next week I might be. Some Agnivanshi scholar opened the wrong scroll, and now he has a beak. Every time I try to help, he sprouts more feathers." Dara drew up in alarm, casting a glance behind him, and she quickly held up a hand. "He can't hear us. He blew out his eardrums—and briefly mine—with all his carrying on." Nahri dropped another shard in the pan. "As you see, I have enough to occupy my mind here without fretting over my origins."

He shook his head but settled back down. "And how is that?" he asked, his voice gentler. "How are you doing here?"

Nahri started to toss off a flippant answer and then stopped. This was Dara, after all.

"I don't know," she confessed. "You know the life I lived before . . . in many ways this place is like a dream. The clothes, the jewels, the *food*. It's like Paradise."

He smiled. "I had a feeling you'd take a liking to royal luxury."

"But I feel as though it's an illusion, like I'm one mistake from having it all stripped away. And, Dara . . . I'm making so many of them," she confessed. "I'm a terrible healer, I'm outmatched when it comes to all these political games, and I'm just so . . ." She took a deep breath, aware she was rambling. "I'm tired, Dara. My mind is being pulled in a thousand directions. And my training, by God—Nisreen is trying to condense what seems like twenty years of study into two months."

"You're not a terrible healer." He gave her a reassuring smile. "You're not. You healed me after the rukh attack, didn't you? You just need to focus. Scattered minds are the enemy of magic. And give yourself time. You're in Daevabad now. Start thinking in terms of decades and centuries instead of months and years. Don't worry yourself over these political games. Playing them is not your place. There are those of our tribe far more qualified to do so on your behalf. Focus on your training."

"I suppose." The answer was typical of Dara: practical advice with a side of condescension. She changed the subject. "I didn't even know you were back; I take it you're not staying at the palace?"

Dara snorted. "I would sleep on the street before sharing a roof with these people. I'm staying with the grand wazir. He was a companion of your mother's; she and her brother spent much of their childhood on his family's estates in Zariaspa."

Nahri wasn't sure what to make of that. There was an eagerness about Kaveh e-Pramukh that unsettled her. When she first arrived, he was constantly dropping by the infirmary, bringing gifts and staying for hours to watch her work. She finally asked Nisreen to discreetly intervene, and she hadn't seen much of him since. "I'm not sure that's a good idea, Dara. I don't trust him."

"Is that because your sand-fly prince told you not to?" Dara eyed her. "Because let me tell you, Kaveh has a great deal to say on the subject of Alizayd al Qahtani."

"None of it good, I suppose."

"Not in the slightest." Dara lowered his voice. "You need to be careful, little thief," he warned. "Palaces are dangerous places for second sons, and that one strikes me as a hothead. I don't want you caught up in any political feuds if Alizayd al Qahtani ends up with a silk cord around his neck."

That image bothered her more than she cared to admit. *He's not my friend*, she reminded herself. *He's a mark.* "I can take care of myself."

"But you don't *need* to," Dara replied, sounding annoyed. "Nahri, did you not hear what I just said? Let others play politics. Stay away from these princes. They are beneath you anyway."

Says the one whose political knowledge is a millennium outdated. "Fine," she lied; she had no intention of turning away her best source of information, but she didn't feel like fighting. She dropped a final shard in the pan. "That's the last of the glass."

He offered a wry smile. "I'll find a less destructive way to see you next time." He tried to pull his hand away.

She held firm. It was his left hand, the same hand marked by what she now knew was a record of his time as a slave. The tiny black rungs spiraled out from his palm like a snail, twisting around his wrist and vanishing underneath his sleeve. She rubbed her thumb against the one at the base of his hand.

Dara's face darkened. "I take it your new friend told you what they mean?"

Nahri nodded, keeping her expression neutral. "How many . . . how far do they go?"

For once he gave up an answer without fighting. "Up my arm and all over my back. I stopped counting after about eight hundred."

She squeezed his hand and then let go. "There's so much you didn't tell me, Dara," she said softly. "About slavery, about the war . . ." She met his gaze. "About leading a *rebellion* against Zaydi al Qahtani."

"I know." He dropped his gaze, twisting his ring. "But I spoke truthfully to the king . . . well, about slavery, anyway. Save what you and I saw together, I remember nothing of my time as a slave." Dara cleared his throat. "What we saw was enough for me."

She had to agree. To her, it seemed a mercy that Dara couldn't remember his time in captivity—but it didn't answer the rest. "And the war, Dara? The rebellion?"

He looked up, apprehension in his bright eyes. "Did the brat tell you anything?"

"No." Nahri had been avoiding the darker rumors of Dara's past. "I'd like to hear it from you."

He nodded. "All right," he said, soft resignation in his voice. "Kaveh is trying to arrange a reception for you at the Grand Temple. Ghassan is being *resistant* . . ." His tone made it clear he didn't think much of the king's opinion. "But it would be a good place to talk without interruption. The rebellion . . . what happened before the war, it . . . it's a long story." Dara swallowed, visibly nervous. "You'll have questions, and I want to have time to explain, to make you understand why I did the things I did."

The birdman let out another screech, and Dara made a face. "But not today. You should check on him before he flies away. And I need to go. Nisreen is right about us being alone together. The sand fly knows you are here with me, and I would not wish to harm your reputation."

"Don't worry about my reputation," she said lightly. "I do enough damage on my own."

A wry smile played at the corner of his lips, but he said nothing, simply staring at her as if he was drinking her in. In the infirmary's soft light, Nahri found it difficult not to do the same, to not memorize the way the sunlight played in his wavy black hair, the jewel-like gleam in his emerald eyes.

"You look beautiful in our clothes," he said softly, running a finger lightly along the embroidered hem of her sleeve. "It's hard to believe you're the same ragged girl I pulled from a ghoul's jaws, the one who left a trail of stolen belongings from Cairo to Constantinople." He shook his head. "And to learn you're actually the daughter of one of our greatest healers." A note of reverence crept into his voice. "I should be burning cedar oil in your honor."

"I'm sure enough has already been wasted over me."

He smiled, but the expression didn't meet his eyes. He dropped his hand from hers, something like regret seeming to pass across his face. "Nahri, there is something we should . . ." He suddenly frowned, his head snapping up as if he'd heard a suspicious noise. He glanced at the door, appearing to listen for another second. Anger swept the confusion off his face. He abruptly rose to his feet, marching to the door and all but ripping it off its hinges.

Alizayd al Qahtani stood on the other side.

The prince didn't look even the slightest bit ashamed to have been caught. Indeed, as Nahri watched, he tapped his foot against the floor and crossed his arms, his steely eyes focused on Dara alone. "I thought you might need help finding your way out."

Smoke curled around Dara's collar. He cracked his knuckles, and Nahri tensed. But he went no further. Instead—still glaring at Ali—Dara directed his words to her, continuing to speak in the Divasti that Nahri was immediately relieved the prince couldn't understand. "I can't talk to you with this half-tribe brat lurking around." He all but spat the words in Ali's face. "Stay safe." He poked Ali hard in the chest to move him out of the doorway and left.

Nahri's heart sank at the sight of his retreating back. She threw Ali an annoyed look. "Are we spying on each other so openly now?"

For a moment, she expected the mask of friendship to drop. To see Ghassan reflected in Ali's face, to get a hint of whatever was really driving him to meet with her every day.

Instead she saw what looked like a war of loyalties play across his face before he dropped his gaze. He opened his mouth, then paused as if considering his words. "Please be careful," he said softly. "He . . . Nahri, you don't . . ." He abruptly shut his mouth, and stepped back. "I-I'm sorry," he stammered. "Have a good night."

21

ALI

Ali crept along the dusty shelf, crawling on his belly as he made his way toward the scroll. He stretched out his arm, straining to reach it, but his fingers didn't even graze the papyrus.

"I would be remiss if I didn't point out—again—that you have people who could do this for you." Nahri's voice drifted from outside the cryptlike shelves Ali was currently lodged between. "At least three library assistants offered to retrieve that scroll."

Ali grunted. He and Nahri were in the deepest part of the Royal Library's ancient archives, in a cavelike room hacked out of the city's bedrock. Only the oldest and most obscure texts were stored here, packed away in narrow stone shelves that Ali was swiftly learning were not intended for people to crawl through. The scroll they were after had rolled to the very back of its shelf, the bone-colored papyrus glowing in the light of their torch.

"I don't like having people do things of which I'm perfectly capable," Ali replied as he tried to inch a bit farther back. The rocky ceiling scraped his head and shoulders.

"They said there were scorpions down here, Ali. Big ones."

"There are far worse things than scorpions in this palace," he muttered. Ali would know—he suspected one of them was watching him right now. The scroll he was after was cuddled close to another twice its size, made from what looked like the hide of some sort of massive lizard. It had been shivering violently since he entered the shelf.

He'd yet to mention it to Nahri, but as Ali saw a flash of something that might have been teeth, his heart started to race. "Nahri, would . . . would you mind raising the torch a bit?"

The shelf immediately brightened, the dancing flames shadowing his profile. "What's wrong?" she asked, clearly picking up on the anxiety in his voice.

"Nothing," Ali lied as the lizard-hide scroll wiggled and flashed its scales. Heedless of scraping his head, Ali shoved himself deeper and snatched for the papyrus.

His fingers had just closed around it when the lizard-hide scroll gave a great bellow. Ali scrambled back, though not in time to avoid the sudden gust of wind that shot him out of the shelf like a cannonball, with enough force to throw him across the room. He landed hard on his back, the wind knocked from his lungs.

Nahri's worried face hovered over his. "Are you *all right*?"

Ali touched the back of his head and winced. "I'm fine," he insisted. "I meant to do that."

"Sure you did." She glanced nervously at the shelf. "Should we . . ."

From the direction of the shelf, there came the sound of a distinctly papery snore. "We're fine." He raised the papyrus scroll. "I don't think this one's companion wanted to be disturbed."

Nahri shook her head. Her hand flew to her mouth, and Ali realized she was trying to stifle a laugh.

"What?" he asked, suddenly self-conscious. "What is it?"

"I'm sorry." Her black eyes were bright with amusement. "It's just . . ." She made a sweeping motion over Ali's body.

He glanced down and then flushed. A thick layer of ancient dust covered his dishdasha and coated his hands and face. He coughed, sending up a bloom of fine powder.

Nahri held her hand out for the scroll. "Why don't I take that?"

Embarrassed, Ali handed it over and climbed to his feet, brushing the dust from his clothes.

Too late, he saw the snake stamped in the ancient wax seal. "Wait, Nahri, don't!"

But she'd already slipped a finger under the seal. She cried out, dropping the torch as the scroll flew from her other hand. It unfurled in the air, a glittering snake dashing from its depths. The torch hit the sandy ground and sputtered out, leaving them in darkness.

Ali acted on instinct, pulling Nahri behind him and drawing his zulfiqar. Flames danced up the copper blade, illuminating the archive with green-tinged light. In the opposite corner, the snake hissed. It was growing larger as they watched, gold and green bands striping a body the color of midnight. Already twice his height and thicker than a muskmelon, it loomed overhead, baring curved fangs that dripped with crimson blood.

Nahri's blood. Ali charged as it reared back to strike again. The snake was fast, but it had been created to deal with human thieves, and Ali was certainly not that. He lopped off the snake's head with a single strike of his zulfiqar, and then stepped back, breathing hard as it hit the dust.

"What . . ." Nahri exhaled. ". . . *in the name of God* was that thing?"

"An apep." Ali extinguished his zulfiqar, wiping the blade on his dishdasha before shoving it back in its sheath. The sword was far too dangerous to keep out in such close quarters. "I'd forgotten the ancient Egyptians were rumored to be rather . . . creative in protecting their texts."

"Perhaps we let someone who has a little more familiarity with the library retrieve the next scroll?"

"No argument here." Ali crossed back to her side. "Are you all right?" he asked, raising a fistful of flames. "Did it bite you?"

Nahri made a face. "I'm okay." She held out her hand. Her thumb was bloody, but as Ali watched, the two swollen wounds where the snake's fangs had penetrated shrank and then vanished under the smooth skin.

"Wow," he whispered in awe. "That really is extraordinary."

"Maybe." She shot the dancing flames in his palm a jealous look. "But I wouldn't mind being able to do that."

Ali laughed. "You heal from the bite of a cursed snake in moments, and you're jealous of a few flames? Anyone with a bit of magic can do this."

"*I* can't."

He didn't believe that for a moment. "Have you tried?"

Nahri shook her head. "I can barely wrap my mind around the healing magic, even with all of Nisreen's help. I wouldn't know where to begin with anything else."

"Then try with me," Ali offered. "It's easy. Just let the heat of your skin sort of . . . *ignite*, and move your hand like you might snap your fingers. But with fire."

"Not the most helpful explanation." But she raised her hand, squinting her eyes as she concentrated. "Nothing."

"Say the word. In Divasti," he clarified. "Later, you'll be able to simply think it, but for beginners, it's often easier to perform incantations out loud in your native tongue."

"All right." Nahri stared at her hand again with a frown. "Azar," she repeated, sounding annoyed. "See? Nothing."

But Ali didn't give up easily. He motioned toward the stony shelves. "Touch them."

"*Touch* them?"

He nodded. "You are in the palace of your ancestors, a place molded by Nahid magic. Draw from the stone like you would water from a well."

Nahri looked thoroughly unconvinced but followed him, placing her hand in the spot he indicated. She took a deep breath and then raised her other palm.

"Azar. Azar!" She snapped, loud enough to dislodge some dust from the nearest shelf. When her hand remained empty, she shook her head. "Forget it. It's not as if I'm having any success with anything else. I don't see why this would be any different." She started to drop her hand.

Ali stopped her.

Her eyes flashed at the same time his mind caught up with his actions. Fighting a wave of embarrassment, he nevertheless kept her hand pressed against the wall.

"You tried twice," he chided. "That's nothing. Do you know how long it took for me to call up flames on my zulfiqar?" He stepped back. "Try again."

She let out an annoyed huff but didn't drop her hand. "Fine. *Azar.*"

There wasn't even a spark; her face twisted with disappointment. Ali hid his own frown, knowing this should have been easy for someone like Nahri. He chewed the inside of his lip, trying to think.

And then it came to him. "Try it in Arabic."

She looked surprised. "In Arabic? You really think a human language is going to call up magic?"

"It's one that has meaning to you." Ali shrugged. "It doesn't hurt to try."

"I suppose not." She wiggled her fingers, staring at her hand. "Naar."

The dusty air above her open palm smoked. Her eyes widened. "Did you see that?"

He grinned. "Again."

She needed no convincing now. "Naar. *Naar.* Naar!" Her face fell. "I just had it!"

"Keep going," he urged. He had an idea. As Nahri opened her mouth, Ali spoke again, suspecting that what he said next would likely end either with her conjuring up a flame or punching him in the face. "What do you think Darayavahoush is up to today?"

Nahri's eyes flashed with outrage—and the air above her palm burst into fire.

"Don't let it go out!" Ali grabbed her wrist again before she could smother it, holding her fingers out to let the little flame breathe. "It won't hurt you."

"By the Most High . . . ," she gasped. Firelight danced across her face, reflecting in her black eyes, and setting the gold ornaments holding her chador in place aglow.

Ali let go of her wrist and then stepped back to retrieve their extinguished torch. He held it out. "Light it."

Nahri tipped her hand to let the flame dance from her palm to the torch, setting it ablaze. She looked mesmerized . . . and far more emotional than he'd ever seen her. Her typically cool mask had vanished; her face was shining with delight, with relief.

And then it was gone. She lifted an eyebrow. "Would you like to explain the purpose of that last question?"

He dropped his gaze, shifting on his feet. "Sometimes magic works best when there's a little . . ." He cleared his throat, searching for the least inappropriate word he could think of. "Ah, *emotion* behind it."

"Emotion?" She abruptly swept her fingers through the air. "Naar," she whispered, and a slash of fire danced in front of her. She grinned when Ali jumped back. "I suppose anger works just as well then." But she was still smiling when the tiny embers fell to the ground, winking out in the sand. "Well, whatever your intent, I appreciate it. Truly." She glanced up at him. "Thank you, Ali. It's nice to learn *some* new magic here."

He tried to offer a casual shrug, as if teaching potentially deadly skills to his ancestral enemy was something he did all the time—and not, as it suddenly dawned upon him, a thing that should have been considered more carefully. "You needn't thank me," he insisted, his voice slightly hoarse. He swallowed and then abruptly crossed to retrieve the scroll from where she'd dropped it. "I . . . I guess we should look at what we came down here for in the first place."

Nahri followed. "You really didn't have to go to all this trouble," she said again. "It was just a passing curiosity."

"You wanted to know about Egyptian marid." He tapped the scroll. "This is the last surviving account of a djinn meeting one." He unfurled it. "Oh."

"What?" Nahri asked, peeking over his arm. She blinked. "Suleiman's eye . . . what is *that* supposed to be?"

"I have no idea," Ali confessed. Whatever language the scroll was in was unlike any he'd ever seen, a confusing spiral of miniature pictograms and wedge-shaped marks. The letters—if they were letters—were crammed in so tight, it was difficult to see where one ended and the next began. From opposing corners, an inky path—a river perhaps, maybe the Nile—had been painted, its cataracts marked by more bizarre pictograms.

"I don't suppose we'll be getting any information from that," Nahri sighed.

Ali hushed her. "You shouldn't give up on things so quickly." An idea unfurled in his head. "I know someone who might be able to translate this. An Ayaanle scholar. He's retired now, but he might be willing to help us."

Nahri looked reluctant. "I'd rather not have my interest in this made public."

"He'll keep your secret. He's a freed slave—he'd do anything for a Nahid. And he spent two centuries traveling the lands of the Nile, copying texts before he was captured by the ifrit. I can think of no one better suited for the task." Ali rolled up the scroll.

He caught the confusion on her face, the connection not quite clear. But she said nothing. "You can just ask me," he finally said, when it was clear she wasn't going to speak.

"Ask you what?"

Ali gave her a knowing look. They'd been dancing around this topic for weeks—well, actually, they'd been dancing around lots of topics, but this one especially. "What you've wanted to ask since that day in the garden. Since I told you the significance of the mark on your Afshin's arm."

Nahri bristled, the warmth vanishing from her face. "I'm not discussing Dara with you."

"I didn't say *him* specifically," he pointed out. "But you want to know about slaves, don't you? You get all tense every time the slightest mention of them comes up."

Nahri looked even more annoyed to have been caught out, her eyes flashing. How wonderfully he'd timed this fight, to occur after he'd taught her to conjure up flames.

"And what if I do?" she challenged. "Is that a thing you'll race back to your father to report?"

Ali flinched. He couldn't say anything to that—he *had* been spying on her and the Afshin in the infirmary a few days ago, though neither of them had mentioned the incident until now.

He met her gaze. Ali wasn't used to Daeva eyes; he'd always found their ebony depths slightly off-putting, though admittedly

Nahri's were rather nice, her human features softening the harshness. But there was so much suspicion in her eyes—rightly so, of course—that Ali wanted to squirm. But he also suspected enough people in Daevabad, particularly the Afshin of whom she was so defensive, had lied to Nahri. So he decided to tell her the truth. "And what if I report it?" he asked. "Do you imagine your interest is surprising to anyone? You were raised in the human world on legends of djinn slaves. That you would want to know more is to be expected." He touched his heart, the corners of his mouth tugging up. "Come on, Nahid. A Qahtani fool is offering up free information. Surely your instincts are telling you to take advantage of it."

That drew a slight smile, tinged with exasperation. "Fine." She threw up her hands. "My curiosity is winning over my common sense. Tell me about slaves."

Ali raised the torch, nodding toward the corridor leading back to the main library. "Let's walk and talk. It'll look inappropriate if we're down here too long."

"The devil again?" He flushed, and she laughed. "You'd fit in well back in Cairo, you know," she added as she turned on her heel.

I do know. That was exactly the reason his father had chosen Ali for this assignment, after all.

"Is it like the stories, then?" Nahri continued, her Egyptian-laced Arabic rapid with excitement. "Djinn trapped in rings and lamps, forced to grant whatever wishes their human master desires?"

He nodded. "The slave curse returns djinn to their natural state, the way we were before the Prophet Suleiman—peace be upon him—blessed us. But the catch is that you can use your abilities only in the service of a human master. You're entirely bound to them, to their every whim."

"To their *every* whim?" Nahri shuddered. "In the stories, it's usually in good fun, people wishing for vast fortunes and luxurious palaces, but . . ." She bit her lip. "Humans are capable of some pretty terrible things."

"They have that in common with our race," Ali noted darkly. "With the marid and peri too, I'd imagine."

Nahri looked thoughtful for a moment, but then she frowned. "But the ifrit hate humans, don't they? Why give them such powerful slaves?"

"Because it's not a gift. It's raw, unchecked power," Ali explained. "Few ifrit have dared to directly harm humans since Suleiman cursed us. But they don't need to; a djinn slave in the hands of an ambitious human causes an immense amount of destruction." He shook his head. "It's revenge. That it eventually drives the djinn slave mad is merely an added benefit."

Nahri blanched. "But they can be freed, right? The slaves?"

Ali hesitated, thinking about the Afshin's relic hidden in the tomb far below his feet—the relic that had no business being there. How Darayavahoush had been freed without it was something not even his father knew. But there seemed little harm in answering her question; it wasn't as if Nahri would ever see the tomb.

"If they're fortunate enough to have their slave vessel—their ring or lamp or whatnot—reunited with their relic by a Nahid, then yes," Ali said.

He could practically see the wheels turning in Nahri's mind. "Their relic?"

He tapped the copper bolt in his right ear. "We get them when we're children. Each tribe has its own tradition, but it's basically taking . . . well, a *relic* of ourselves: some blood, some hair, a baby tooth. We seal it all up with metal and keep them on our person."

She looked a little disgusted. "Why?"

Ali hesitated, not certain how to put what he had to say delicately. "A djinn has to be killed to be made into a slave, Nahri.

The curse binds the soul, not the body. And the ifrit . . ." He swallowed. "We're the descendants of people they consider traitors. They take slaves to terrorize us. To terrorize the survivors who'll come upon the empty body. It can be . . . messy."

She stopped in her tracks, her eyes lighting with horror.

Ali spoke quickly, trying to allay the alarm in her face. "Either way, the relic is considered the best way to preserve a part of us. Especially since it can take centuries to track down a slave vessel."

Nahri looked sick. "So how did the Nahids free them, then? Did they just conjure up a new body or something?"

He could tell from her tone that she thought the idea was ridiculous, which is likely why she paled when he nodded. "That's exactly what they did. I don't know *how*—your ancestors were not ones to share their secrets—but something like that, yes."

"And I can barely conjure up a flame," she whispered.

"Give yourself time," Ali assured her, reaching for the door. "That's one thing we've got a lot more of compared to humans." He held the door for her, and then stepped out into the main rotunda of the library. "Are you hungry? I could have that Egyptian cook prepare some—"

Ali's mouth went dry. Across the crowded library floor, leaning against an ancient stone column, was Rashid.

He was clearly waiting for Ali—he straightened up as soon as Ali spotted him and headed in their direction. He was in uniform, his face perfectly composed, the picture of loyalty. One would never think the last time he and Ali had laid eyes on each other was when Rashid tricked him into visiting a Tanzeem safe house, threatening Ali with damnation for pulling his support of the shafit militants.

"Peace be upon you, Qaid," Rashid said, greeting him politely. He inclined his head. "Banu Nahida, an honor."

Ali edged in front of Nahri. Whether to protect his secret from her or to protect her from the vaguely hostile way Rashid's mouth curled when he said her title, Ali wasn't certain. He cleared his throat. "Banu Nahida, why don't you go ahead? This is Citadel business and won't take but a moment."

Rashid raised a skeptical eyebrow at that, but Nahri stepped away—though not before giving them both an openly curious look.

Ali eyed the rest of the library. Its main floor was a bustling place, filled at all hours with ongoing lectures and harassed scholars, but he was a Qahtani prince and tended to attract attention no matter his surroundings.

Rashid spoke up, his voice colder. "I'd say you're not pleased to see me, brother."

"Of course not," Ali hissed. "I ordered you back to Am Gezira weeks ago."

"Ah, you mean my sudden retirement?" Rashid drew a scroll from his robe and shoved it at Ali. "You might as well add it to your torch. Thank you for the *generous* pension, but it's not necessary." He lowered his voice, but his eyes flashed with anger. "I risked my life to help the shafit, Alizayd. I'm not a man to be bought off."

Ali flinched, his fingers curling around the scroll. "It wasn't meant in that manner."

"No?" Rashid stepped closer. "Brother, what are you *doing*?" he demanded in an angry whisper. "I take you to a home filled with shafit orphans, children who are sick and starving because we can't afford to care for them, and in response you abandon us? You retreat to the palace to play companion to a *Nahid*? A Nahid who brought the *Scourge of Qui-zi* back to Daevabad?" He threw up his hands. "Have you lost all sense of decency?"

Ali grabbed his wrist, holding it down. "Quiet," he warned, jerking his head toward the darkened archive from which he and Nahri had just emerged. "We're not doing this here."

Still glowering, Rashid followed him, but Ali had no sooner shut the door than the other man whirled on him again.

"Tell me there's something I'm missing, brother," he demanded. "Please. Because I cannot reconcile the young man Anas sacrificed himself to save with one who would force shafit into the bronze boat."

"I'm the city's Qaid," Ali said, hating the defensiveness in his voice. "Those men attacked the Daeva Quarter. They were tried and sentenced under our law. It was my duty."

"Your duty," Rashid scoffed, pacing away. "Being Qaid is not the only duty put upon you in this life." He glanced back. "I suppose you're not so different from your brother, after all. A pretty fire worshipper flutters her lashes and you—"

"That's enough," Ali snapped. "I made clear my intention to stop funding the Tanzeem when I learned you were buying weapons with my money. I offered you the retirement to save your life. And as for the Banu Nahida . . ." Ali's voice grew heated. "My God, Rashid, she's a human-raised girl from Egypt—not some fiery preacher from the Grand Temple. My father's guest. Surely you're not so biased against the Daevas that you oppose my befriending—"

"Befriending?" Rashid interrupted, looking incredulous. "You don't take *friends* from among the fire worshippers, Alizayd. That's how they trick you. Getting close to the Daevas, integrating them into the court and the Royal Guard—that's what's led your family astray!"

Ali's voice was cold. "Surely you see the hypocrisy in accusing another of tricking me into friendship." Rashid flushed. Ali pressed on. "I'm finished with the Tanzeem, Rashid. I couldn't help you even if I wanted to. Not anymore. My father found out about the money."

That finally shut down the other man's tirade. "Does he suspect you of anything else?"

Ali shook his head. "I doubt I'd be standing here if he knew about Turan. But the money was enough. I'm sure he has people watching my every move, not to mention my Treasury accounts."

Rashid paused, a bit of the anger gone. "Then we'll lie low. Wait a year or so for the scrutiny to die down. In the meantime—"

"No," Ali cut in, his voice firm. "My father made it clear that it was innocent shafit who would pay if he caught so much as a whiff of betrayal from me. I won't risk that. Nor do I need to."

Rashid frowned. "What do you mean you don't *need* to?"

"I made a deal with my brother," Ali explained. "For now, I fall in line with my father's plans. When Muntadhir's king, he'll let me take a stronger hand in managing issues with the shafit." His voice rose with excitement; his mind had been spinning with ideas since that day. "Rashid, think what we could do for the shafit if we had a king who openly supported our goals. We could organize work programs, expand the orphanage with money from the Treasury . . ."

"Your *brother*?" Rashid repeated in disbelief. "You think Muntadhir is going to let you help the shafit—with money from the palace, at that?" He narrowed his eyes. "You can't possibly be that naive, Ali. The only thing your brother's going to do to the Treasury is drain it to pay for wine and dancing girls."

"He won't," Ali protested. "He's not like that."

"He's *exactly* like that," Rashid replied. "Besides which, you haven't fallen in line, not really. If you were loyal, you would have had us arrested." He nodded rudely at the retirement papers. "I'd be dead, not pensioned off."

Ali hesitated. "We have different views on how to help the shafit. That doesn't mean I want you hurt."

"Or you know we're right. At least part of you does." Rashid let the words hang in the air and then sighed, suddenly looking a decade older. "You won't be able to continue like this, Alizayd," he warned. "To keep walking a path between loyalty to your family and loyalty to what you know is right. One of these days, you're going to have to make a choice."

I've made my choice. Because as much as Ali had initially disagreed with his father's plans regarding Nahri, he was starting to see where they could lead. A marriage between the emir and the Banu Nahida could bring true peace between the Daevas and the Geziris. And a Banu Nahida raised in the human world—who still looked human—might she not be able to nudge her tribe into being more accepting of the shafit? Ali sensed an opportunity, a true opportunity, to shake matters up in Daevabad and to make sure they landed right.

But he couldn't do it from a jail cell. Ali handed the retirement papers back. "You should take these. Go home, Rashid."

"I'm not going back to Am Gezira," the other man said cuttingly. "I'm not leaving Daevabad, Sister Fatumai isn't leaving the orphanage, and Hanno isn't going to stop freeing shafit slaves. Our work is larger than any of us. I would have thought Sheikh Anas's death taught you that."

Ali said nothing. In truth, Anas's death—what had led to it, what had come after—had taught Ali plenty. But they weren't lessons he suspected Rashid would appreciate.

Something cracked in the other man's face. "You were my idea, you know. My hope. Anas was reluctant to recruit you. He believed you were too young. I convinced him." Regret filled his voice. "Maybe he was right."

He turned away, heading for the door. "We won't bother you again, Prince. If you change your mind, you know where to find me. And I hope you do. Because on the day of your judgment, Alizayd . . . when you're asked why you didn't stand up for what you knew was just . . ." He paused, his next words finding Ali's heart like an arrow. "Loyalty to your family won't excuse you."

22

NAHRI

The palanquin that carried Nahri from the palace was a far cry from the one in which she had arrived, the cozy "floral box" she'd shared with an irritated Afshin. A symbol of her elevated station, it could have fit a half-dozen people, and was supported by twice that number. The inside was embarrassingly sumptuous, stuffed with brocaded pillows, an untouched cask of wine, and hanging silk tassels fragrant with frankincense.

And thoroughly covered windows. Nahri tried tearing at the silk panel again, but it was sewn tight. She glanced at her hand, struck by another possibility. She opened her mouth.

"Don't," Nisreen said sharply. "Don't even think of burning the curtains down. Especially not in that human language of yours." She clucked her tongue. "I knew that Qahtani boy was going to be a bad influence."

"He's proving a most useful influence." But Nahri sat back, throwing the covered windows an annoyed look. "This is the first time I've been able to leave the palace in months. You'd think I could actually *look* upon the city my ancestors built."

"You can see the Grand Temple when we arrive. Nahids are not expected to mix with the general populace; such a thing would disgrace you."

"I doubt that very much," Nahri muttered, crossing her legs and tapping a foot against one of the palanquin's support poles. "And if I'm in charge of the Daevas, can't I change the rules? Meat is now permitted," she intoned. "The Banu Nahida is allowed to interact with whomever she wants in whatever manner she wants."

Nisreen went a little pale. "That's not how we do things here." She sounded even more nervous than Nahri. The invitation to the Grand Temple had come yesterday without warning, and Nisreen had spent every minute of the past day trying to prepare Nahri with rushed lectures on Daeva etiquette and religious rituals that had mostly gone in one ear and out the other.

"My lady . . ." Nisreen took a deep breath. "I would beg—again—that you reflect on what this moment means to our people. The Nahids are our most cherished figures. We spent years mourning them, years believing their loss meant the end of everything until your—"

"Yes, until my miraculous return, I know." But Nahri didn't feel like much of a miracle. She felt like an imposter. She fidgeted, uncomfortable in the ceremonial clothes she'd been forced to don: a pale blue gown finely worked in silver thread and pants of spun gold, the hems heavy with seed pearls and lapis lazuli beads. White silk veiled her face, and a white chador—as light and fine as a puff of smoke—covered her hair, drifting to her feet. She didn't mind the chador, but the headpiece that held it in place—a heavy diadem of gold, glittering with sapphires and topaz and a band of tiny gold disks hanging over her brow—made her head ache.

"Stop fiddling with that," Nisreen advised. "You're liable to send the whole thing crashing down." The palanquin shuddered to a stop. "Good, we're here . . . oh, child, don't roll your eyes. That is hardly inspiring." Nisreen opened the door. "Come, my lady."

Nahri peeked out, stealing her first look at Daevabad's Grand Temple. Nisreen said it was one of the oldest buildings in Daevabad and it looked it, as imposing and massive as the Great Pyramids back in Egypt. It was a ziggurat like the palace, but smaller and steeper, a flat-topped step pyramid of three levels, brickwork covered by marble faience in a dazzling rainbow of colors and trimmed in brass. Behind the temple was a tower about twice its height. Smoke rose from its crenellated top.

A large courtyard stretched between the two buildings. A garden—far more orderly than the feral jungle of the palace—had been designed by a clearly discerning eye, with two long rectangular pools meeting to form a cross, outlined by lush flower beds in a riot of color. On either side of the pools, wide pathways stretched, inviting the visitor to linger, to amble slowly through the fragrant shade, past ancient trees with broad fan-shaped leaves. The entire complex was walled, the massive stones hidden by trellises dripping with roses.

It seemed a peaceful place, designed to encourage reflection and prayer—had a crowd of at least two hundred people not been excitedly swarming a single figure.

Dara.

Her Afshin stood at the heart of the garden, surrounded by a mob of admirers. Daeva children, many with imitations of his marks drawn on their cheeks, had dragged him to his knees and were pushing past each other to show the legendary warrior their skinny muscles and miniature fighting stances. Dara grinned as he replied to whatever it was they were saying. Though Nahri couldn't hear his words over the buzz of the crowd, she watched as he tugged affectionately on a small girl's braid, placing his cap on the head of the little boy standing next to her.

The adults looked just as mesmerized, awe on their faces as they pressed closer to the Afshin whose long-ago demise and defeated rebellion, Nahri realized, probably made him a rather romantic figure. And not just awe; as Dara smiled his all-too-charming grin, Nahri heard an audible—and distinctly female—sigh from the assembled crowd.

Dara glanced up, noticing Nahri before his admirers did. His smile grew more dazzling, which in turn sent her heart into an idiotic dance. A few of the other Daevas looked over, then more, their faces brightening at the sight of the palanquin.

Nahri cringed. "You said it would be only a few dozen people," she whispered to Nisreen, fighting the urge to duck back inside.

Even Nisreen looked taken aback by the size of the crowd headed in their direction. "I suppose some of the priests had friends and family begging to tag along, and then *they* had friends and family . . ." She made a sweeping gesture at the Grand Temple complex. "You *are* somewhat important to all this, you know."

Nahri muttered a curse in Arabic under her breath. Noticing the rest of the women had pulled their veils from their lower faces, she reached for hers.

Nisreen stopped her. "No, you keep yours on. Nahids—both men and women—always veil in the Grand Temple. The rest of us remove them." She dropped her hand. "That's the last I'll touch you, as well. No one is to touch you here, so don't reach out to your Afshin. In his day, a man would have gotten his hand lopped off for touching a Nahid in the Grand Temple."

"I'd wish them luck trying to do that to Dara."

Nisreen gave her a dark look. "He would have been the one doing the lopping, Nahri. He's an Afshin; his family has served yours in such a manner since Suleiman's curse."

Nahri felt the blood leave her face at that. But she stepped out, Nisreen behind her.

Dara greeted her. He appeared to be in some sort of ceremonial dress, a finely stitched felt coat dyed in the shimmering colors of a smoldering fire, loose charcoal pants tucked into tall boots. His uncovered hair fell in glossy black curls to his shoulders, his hat still being passed among his small fans.

"Banu Nahida." Dara's tone was solemn and reverent, but he winked before abruptly falling to his knees and pressing his face to the ground as she approached. The rest of the Daevas bowed, bringing their hands together in a gesture of respect.

Nahri stopped before a still-prostrate Dara, a little bewildered.

"Tell him to rise," Nisreen whispered. "He can't do so without your permission."

He can't? Nahri arched an eyebrow. Had she and Dara been alone, she might have been tempted to take advantage of such information. But for now, she simply beckoned him up. "You know you don't have to do that."

He climbed back to his feet. "It's my pleasure." He brought his hands together. "Welcome, my lady."

Two men had separated from the crowd to join them: the grand wazir, Kaveh e-Pramukh, and his son Jamshid. Kaveh looked like he was fighting back tears—Nisreen had told Nahri that he'd been very close to both Manizheh and Rustam.

Kaveh's fingers trembled as he brought them together. "May the fires burn brightly for you, Banu Nahida."

Jamshid gave her a warm smile. The captain was out of his Royal Guard uniform and dressed in Daeva fashion today, a dark jade coat trimmed in velvet and striped pants. He bowed. "An honor to see you again, my lady."

"Thank you." Avoiding the curious eyes of the crowd, Nahri glanced up as a small flock of sparrows flew past the smoking tower, their wings dark against the bright noon sky. "So this is the Grand Temple?"

"Still standing." Dara shook his head. "I have to admit, I wasn't sure it would be."

"Our people don't give up that easily," Nisreen replied, a note of pride in her voice. "We've always fought back."

"But only when necessary," Jamshid reminded her. "We have a good king in Ghassan."

An amused look crossed Dara's face. "Ever the loyal one, aren't you, Captain?" He nodded in Nahri's direction. "Why don't you escort the Banu Nahida inside? I need to speak with your father and Lady Nisreen a moment."

Jamshid looked a little surprised—no, he looked a little *concerned*, his eyes darting between his father and Dara with a trace of worry—but he acquiesced with a small bow. "Of course." He glanced at her, motioning toward the wide pathway that led to the Grand Temple. "Banu Nahida?"

Nahri threw Dara an irked look. She'd been looking forward to seeing him all morning. But she held her tongue, not intending to embarrass herself before the large Daeva crowd. Instead, she followed Jamshid down the path.

The Daeva captain waited and then matched his pace to hers. He walked with an unhurried air, his hands clasped behind his back. He was a little on the pale side, but he had a handsome face with an elegant, aquiline nose and winged black brows.

"So how are you finding life in Daevabad?" he asked politely.

Nahri considered the question. As she'd barely seen any of the city, she wasn't sure what sort of answer she could give. "Busy," she finally said. "Very beautiful, very bizarre, and very, very busy."

He laughed. "I can't begin to imagine what a shock this must be. Though from all sources, you are handling it with grace."

I suspect your sources are being diplomatic. But Nahri said nothing, and they kept walking. There was a deep, almost solemn, stillness to the garden air. Something strange, like an absence of . . .

"Magic," she said, realizing it aloud. When Jamshid gave her a confused frown, she explained, "There's no magic here." She made a sweeping gesture over the rather unassuming plant life surrounding her. There were no fiery floating globes, no jeweled flowers or fairy-tale creatures peering through the leaves. "Not that I can see anyway," Nahri clarified.

Jamshid nodded. "No magic, no weapons, no jewelry; the Grand Temple's meant to be a place of contemplation and prayer—no distractions allowed." He gestured to the serene surroundings. "We design our gardens as a reflection of Paradise."

"You mean Paradise isn't filled with treasure and forbidden delights?"

He laughed. "I suppose everyone would have their own definition of such a place."

Nahri kicked at the gravel path. It wasn't quite gravel, but rather flat, perfectly polished stones the size of marbles, in a vast array of colors. Some were speckled with flecks of what looked like precious metals while others were streaked with quartz and topaz.

"From the lake," Jamshid explained, following the direction of her gaze. "Brought up by the marids themselves as tribute."

"Tribute?"

"If you believe the legends. Daevabad was once theirs."

"Really?" Nahri asked, surprised. Though she supposed she shouldn't be. Misty Daevabad—ringed by fog-shrouded mountains and a fathomless magical lake—certainly seemed a place more suited for water beings than those created from fire. "So where did the marids go?"

"No one really knows," Jamshid replied. "They were said to be allied with your earliest ancestors; they helped Anahid build the city." He shrugged. "But considering the curse they placed on the lake before they disappeared, they must have had some sort of falling-out."

Jamshid fell silent as they approached the Grand Temple. Impossibly delicate columns held up a carved stone awning, shading a large pavilion fronting the entrance.

He pointed to the enormous shedu painted on the awning's surface, its wings outstretched over a setting sun. "Your family's crest, of course."

Nahri laughed. "This isn't the first time you've given this tour, is it?"

Jamshid grinned. "It is, believe it or not. But I was a novitiate here. I spent much of my youth training to enter the priesthood."

"Do priests in our religion typically ride around on elephants, shooting arrows to break up riots?"

"I wasn't a very good priest," he acknowledged. "I wanted to be like *him*, actually." He nodded toward Dara. "I suspect most Daeva boys do, but I went further, asking the king if I could join the Royal Guard when I was a teenager." He shook his head. "I'm lucky my father didn't throw me in the lake."

That shed some light on his earlier defense of the Qahtanis. "Do you like being part of the Royal Guard?" she asked, trying to remember the little she knew of the Daeva captain. "You're the prince's bodyguard, right?"

"The emir's," he corrected. "I can't imagine Prince Alizayd would ever *need* a bodyguard. Anyone raising a hand to him while he's wearing his zulfiqar is asking for a quick death."

Nahri had little argument there—she still remembered the swiftness with which Ali had dispatched the snake in the library. "And what's the emir like?"

Jamshid's face brightened. "Muntadhir's a good man. Very generous, very open—the type of man who invites strangers into his home and gets them drunk on his best wine." He shook his head, affection in his voice. "He's one I'd love to give this tour to.

He's always appreciated Daeva culture and patronizes a lot of our artists. I think he'd enjoy seeing the Grand Temple."

Nahri frowned. "*Can't* he? He's the emir; I'd think he could do whatever he likes."

Jamshid shook his head. "Only Daevas are allowed to enter the Grand Temple grounds. It's been that way for centuries."

Nahri glanced back. Dara was still next to the palanquin with Nisreen and Kaveh, but his gaze was on Nahri and Jamshid. There was something odd, almost subdued, in his face.

She turned back to Jamshid. He'd slipped off his shoes, and she moved to do the same.

"Oh, no," he said quickly. "You keep yours on. The Nahids are exempt from most restrictions here." He plunged his hands into a smoldering open brazier as they stepped into the shadow of the temple, sweeping ash up his forearms. He removed his hat, passing an ash-coated hand over his dark hair. "From this, as well. I think it's assumed you're always ritually pure."

Nahri wanted to laugh at that. She certainly didn't feel "ritually pure." Even so, she followed him into the temple, gazing about in appreciation. The interior was enormous and rather stark, simple white marble covering the floor and walls. A massive fire altar of finely polished silver dominated the room. The flames in its cupola danced merrily, filling the temple with the warm aroma of burning cedar.

About a dozen people, men and women both, waited below the altar. They were dressed in long crimson robes belted with azure cords. Like Jamshid, all were bareheaded except one, an elderly man whose peaked azure cap stood nearly half his height.

Nahri gave them an apprehensive look, her stomach fluttering with nerves. She'd felt like failure enough in the infirmary with only Nisreen to witness her mistakes. That she was now here, in the temple of her ancestors, greeted as some sort of leader, was terribly intimidating.

Jamshid pointed to the alcoves lining the temple's inner perimeter. There were dozens, crafted of intricately carved marble, their entrances framed by richly woven curtains. "We keep those shrines for the most lionized figures of our history. Mostly Nahids and Afshins, though every once in a while one of us with less prestigious blood sneaks in."

Nahri nodded to the first shrine they passed. Inside was an impressive stone statue depicting a thickly muscled man riding a roaring shedu. "Who's that supposed to be?"

"Zal e-Nahid, Anahid's youngest grandson." He pointed to the roaring shedu. "It was he who tamed the shedu. Zal climbed to the highest peaks of the Bami Dunya, the mountainous lands of the peri. There, he found the pack leaders of the shedu and wrestled them into submission. They flew him back to Daevabad and stayed for generations."

Nahri's eyes widened. "He wrestled a magical flying lion into submission?"

"Several."

Nahri glanced at the next shrine. This one featured a woman dressed in plated armor, one hand clutching a spear. Her stone face was fierce—but it was the fact that it was tucked under her own arm that really drew Nahri's attention.

"Irtemiz e-Nahid," Jamshid remarked. "One of the bravest of your ancestors. She held off a Qahtani assault on the temple about six hundred years ago." He pointed to a line of scorch marks Nahri hadn't noticed high up on the wall. "They tried to burn it down with as many Daevas stuffed inside as possible. Irtemiz used her abilities to quell the flames. Then she put a spear through the eye of the Qahtani prince leading the charge."

Nahri reeled. "Through his eye?"

Jamshid shrugged, not looking particularly fazed by this bloody bit of information. "We have a complicated history with the djinn. It cost her in the end. They cut off her head and threw her body in the lake." He shook his head sadly, pressing his fingers together. "May she find peace in the Creator's shade."

Nahri gulped. That was enough family history for the day. She moved away from the shrines, but despite her best effort to ignore them, one more caught her eye. Draped in rose garlands and smelling of fresh incense, the shrine was crowned by the figure of an archer on horseback. He stood up tall and proud in his stirrups, facing backward with his bow drawn to aim an arrow at his pursuers.

Nahri frowned. "Is that supposed to be—"

"Me?" Nahri jumped at the sound of Dara's voice, the Afshin appearing behind them like a ghost. "Apparently so." He leaned past her shoulder to better examine the shrine, the smoky scent of his hair tickling her nostrils. "Are those *sand flies* my horse is stomping?" He cackled, his eyes bright with amusement as he studied the cloud of insects around the horse's hooves. "Oh, that's clever. I would have liked to meet whoever had the nerve to slip that in."

Jamshid studied the statue with an air of wistfulness. "I wish I could ride and shoot like that. There's no place in the city to practice."

"You should have said something sooner," Dara replied. "I'll take you out to the plains just past the Gozan. We used to train there all the time when I was young."

Jamshid shook his head. "My father doesn't want me passing the veil."

"Nonsense." Dara clapped him on the back. "I'll convince Kaveh." He glanced at the priests. "Come, we've made them wait long enough."

The priests were bent in low bows by the time Nahri approached—or truthfully, they might have just been standing that way. All were elderly, not a black hair left in sight.

Dara brought his fingers together. "I present Banu Nahri

e-Nahid." He beamed back at her. "The grand priests of Dae-vabad, my lady."

The one in the tall peaked cap stepped forward. He had kind eyes crowned by the longest, wildest gray eyebrows Nahri had ever seen, a charcoal mark splitting his forehead. "May the fires burn brightly for you, Banu Nahri," he greeted her warmly. "My name is Kartir e-Mennushur. Welcome to the temple. I pray this is only the first of many visits."

Nahri cleared her throat. "I pray for that as well," she replied awkwardly, growing more uncomfortable by the second. Nahri had never gotten on well with clerics. Being a con artist tended to put her at odds with most of them.

At a loss for anything else to say, she nodded to the massive fire altar. "Is that Anahid's altar?"

"Indeed." Kartir stepped back. "Would you like to see it?"

"I . . . all right," she agreed, desperately hoping she wouldn't be expected to perform any of the rituals associated with it; everything Nisreen had attempted to teach Nahri about their faith seemed to have flown from her head.

Dara followed at her heels, and Nahri fought the temptation to reach for his hand. She could have used a little reassurance.

Anahid's altar was even more impressive up close. The base alone was big enough for a half-dozen people to bathe in comfortably. Glass oil lamps shaped like boats floated within, bobbing across the simmering water. The silver cupola towered overhead, a veritable bonfire of incense burning behind the gleaming metal. Its heat scalded her face.

"I took my vows in this very spot," Dara said softly. He touched the tattoo on his temple. "Received my mark and my bow and swore to protect your family no matter the cost." A mix of astonishment and nostalgia crossed his face. "I didn't think I'd ever see it again. I certainly didn't imagine by the time I did, I'd have my own shrine."

"Banu Manizheh and Baga Rustam have one as well," Kartir offered, pointing to the other side of the temple. "Should you wish to pay your respects later, I'd be glad to show you."

Dara gave her a hopeful smile. "Maybe in time you will as well, Nahri."

Her stomach turned. "Yes. Perhaps even one where my head is still attached to my body." The words came out far more sarcastic—and loud—than Nahri intended, and she saw several of the priests below stiffen. Dara's face fell.

Kartir swept between them. "Banu Nahida, would you mind coming with me a moment? There's something in the sanctuary I'd like to show you . . . alone," he clarified, when Dara turned to follow.

Nahri raised her shoulders, feeling that she didn't have much choice. "Lead the way."

He did, heading for a pair of hammered brass doors set in the wall behind the altar. Nahri followed, jumping when the door clanged shut behind them.

Kartir glanced back. "My apologies. I suspect there aren't enough working ears among my fellows and me to be bothered by the noise."

"It's all right," she said softly.

The priest led her through a twisting maze of dark corridors and narrow staircases, proving far spryer than she'd initially thought, until they came to a sudden dead end outside another pair of simple brass doors. He pulled one open, motioning her inside.

A little apprehensive, Nahri crossed the threshold, entering a small, circular room barely the size of her wardrobe. She stilled, taken aback by an air of solemnity so thick she could almost feel it upon her shoulders. Open-faced glass shelves lined the rounded walls, small velvet cushions nestled in their depths.

Nahri drew closer, her eyes widening. Each cushion was home

to a single small object, mostly rings, but also lamps, bangles, and a few jeweled collars.

And all shared the same feature: a single emerald.

"Slave vessels," she whispered in shock.

Kartir nodded, joining her at the nearest shelf. "Indeed. All those recovered since Manizheh and Rustam's deaths."

He fell silent. In the room's somber stillness, Nahri could swear she heard the gentle sounds of breath. Her gaze fell on the vessel closest to her, a ring so similar to Dara's she had to tear her eyes away.

He was just like this once, she realized, *his soul trapped for centuries. Sleeping until another brutal master woke him to do their bidding.* Nahri took a deep breath, struggling to compose herself. "Why are they here?" she asked. "I mean, without a Nahid to break the curse . . ."

Kartir shrugged. "We didn't know what to do with them so we settled for bringing them here, where they could rest near the flames of Anahid's original fire altar." He pointed to a beaten brass bowl standing upon a plain stool in the center of the room. The metal was dull and scorched, but a fire burned bright among the cedarwood scattered in its center.

Nahri frowned. "But I thought the altar in the temple . . ."

"The altar out there is what came after," Kartir explained. "When her city was complete, the ifrit subdued, and the other tribes brought to heel. After three centuries of hardship, war, and work."

He lifted the ancient brass bowl. It was a humble thing, rough and undecorated, small enough to fit in his hands. "This here . . . this is what Anahid and her followers would have used when they were first freed by Suleiman. When they were transformed and dropped in this foreign land of marids with barely any understanding of their powers, of how to provide for and protect themselves." He gently placed the bowl in her hands and met her gaze, his eyes intent. "Greatness takes time, Banu

Nahida. Often the mightiest things have the humblest beginnings."

Nahri blinked, her eyes suddenly wet. She looked away, embarrassed, and Kartir took the bowl, wordlessly replacing it and leading her back out.

He motioned to a narrow, sunlit archway at the other end of the corridor. "There is a rather lovely view of the garden from there. Why don't you rest a bit? I'll see if I can't get rid of that crowd."

Gratitude welled up inside her. "Thank you," Nahri finally managed.

"You needn't thank me." Kartir pressed his hands together. "I sincerely hope you won't be a stranger here, Banu Nahida. Please know that whatever you need, we are at your disposal." He bowed again and left.

Nahri emerged from the archway into a small pavilion. High on the third level of the ziggurat, it was little more than a nook hidden behind a stone wall and a screen of potted date palms. Kartir was probably right about the view, but Nahri had no desire to peek at the crowd again. She collapsed into one of the low cane chairs, trying to collect herself.

She let her right hand fall to her lap. "Naar," she whispered, watching as a single flame swirled to life in her palm. She'd taken to conjuring it up more frequently, clinging to the reminder that she was capable of learning *something* in Daevabad.

"May I join you?" a soft voice asked.

Nahri closed her palm, extinguishing the flame. She turned around. Dara stood at the archway, looking uncharacteristically abashed.

She waved at the other chair. "All yours."

He took the seat across from her, leaning forward on his knees. "I'm sorry," he started. "I truly thought this was a good idea."

"I'm sure you did." Nahri sighed and then removed her veil, pulling off the heavy diadem holding her chador in place. She didn't miss the way Dara's gaze drifted to her face, nor did she care. He could deal with some distress—he certainly gave her enough.

He dropped his gaze. "You've an admirer in Kartir . . . aye, the tongue-lashing I just received."

"Thoroughly deserved."

"Undoubtedly."

Nahri glanced at him. He seemed nervous, rubbing his palms on his knees.

She frowned. "Are you all right?"

He stilled. "I'm fine." She saw him swallow. "So, what do you think of Jamshid?"

The question took her aback. "I . . . he's very nice." It was the truth, after all. "If his father's anything like him, it's hardly surprising he's risen so high in Ghassan's court. He seems very diplomatic."

"They are both that." Dara hesitated. "The Pramukhs are a respectable family, one with a long record of devotion to your own. I was a bit surprised to see them serving the Qahtanis, and Jamshid seems to have a regrettably sincere affection for Muntadhir, but . . . he's a good man. Bright, kindhearted. A talented warrior."

Nahri narrowed her eyes; Dara had never been subtle and he was speaking of Jamshid with far too much feigned indifference. "What are you trying *not* to say, Dara?"

He blushed. "Only that you seem well matched."

"*Well matched?*"

"Yes." She heard something catch in his throat. "He . . . he would be a good Daeva alternative if Ghassan presses on with his idiotic scheme to marry you to his son. You're near in age, his family has loyalty to both yours and the Qahtanis—"

Nahri straightened up, indignant with rage. "And *Jamshid e-Pramukh* is the first name that comes to mind when you think of Daeva husbands for me?"

He had the decency to look ashamed. "Nahri—"

"No," she cut in, her voice rising in anger. "How dare you? You think to introduce me as some wise Banu Nahida one moment and attempt to trick me into marriage with another man in the next? After what happened that night in the cave?"

He shook his head, a faint flush stealing over his face. "That should never have happened. You were a woman under my protection. I had no right to touch you that way."

"I remember it as being mutual." But as the words left her lips, Nahri recalled that she had kissed him first—twice—and the realization twisted her stomach into a knot of insecurity. "I . . . was I wrong?" she asked, mortification rising in her voice. "Did you not feel the same way?"

"No!" Dara fell to his knees before her, closing the space between them. "Please don't think that." He reached for one of her hands, holding fast when she tried to jerk away. "Just because I *shouldn't* have done it doesn't mean . . ." He swallowed. "It doesn't mean I didn't want to, Nahri."

"Then what's the problem? You're unmarried, I'm unmarried. We're both Daeva . . ."

"*I'm not alive*," Dara cut in. He dropped her hand with a sigh, rising to his feet. "Nahri, I don't know who freed my soul from slavery. I don't know how. But I know that I died: I drowned, just like you saw. By now, my body is likely nothing but ash on the bottom of some ancient well."

A fierce denial rose in Nahri's chest, foolish and impractical. "I don't care," she insisted. "It doesn't matter to me."

He shook his head. "It matters to me." His tone turned imploring. "Nahri, you know what people are saying here. They think you're a pureblood, the daughter of one of the greatest healers in history."

"*So?*"

She could see the apology in his face before he answered. "So you'll need children. You deserve children. A whole brood of little Nahids as likely to pick your pocket as heal an injury. And I . . ." His voice broke. "Nahri . . . I don't bleed. I don't *breathe* . . . I can't imagine that I could ever give you children. It would be reckless and selfish of me to even try. The survival of your family is too important."

She blinked, thoroughly taken aback by his reasoning. The survival of her family? *That's* what this was about?

Of course. That's what everything *here is about.* The abilities that had once kept a roof over her head had become a curse, this connection with long-dead relatives she'd never known a plague on her life. Nahri had been kidnapped and chased halfway across the world for being a Nahid. She was all but imprisoned in the palace because of it, Nisreen controlling her days, the king shaping her future, and now the man that she—

That you what? That you love*? Are you such a fool?*

Nahri abruptly stood, as angry with herself as she was with Dara. She was done showing weakness before this man. "Well, if that's all that matters, surely Muntadhir will do," she declared, a savage edge creeping into her voice. "The Qahtanis seem fertile enough, and the dowry will probably make me the richest woman in Daevabad."

She might as well have struck him. Dara recoiled, and she turned on her heel. "I'm going back to the palace."

"Nahri . . . Nahri, *wait*." He was between her and the exit in a heartbeat; she'd forgotten how fast he could move. "Please. Don't leave like this. Just let me explain . . ."

"To *hell* with your explanations," she snapped. "That's what you always say. That's what today was supposed to be, remember? You promising to tell me about your past, not parading me in front of a bunch of priests and trying to convince me to marry another man." Nahri pushed past him. "Just leave me alone."

He grabbed her wrist. "You want to know about my *past*?" he hissed, his voice dangerously low. His fingers scalded her skin and he jerked back, letting her go. "Fine, Nahri, here's my story: I was banished from Daevabad when I was barely older than your Ali, exiled from my home for following orders *your* family gave me. That's why I survived the war. That's why I wasn't in Daevabad to save *my* family from being slaughtered when the djinn broke through the gates."

His eyes blazed. "I spent the rest of my life—my *short* life, I assure you—fighting the very family you're so eager to join, the people who would have seen our entire tribe wiped out. And then the ifrit found me." He held up his hand, the slave ring sparkling in the sunlight. "I never had anything like this . . . anything like *you*." His voice cracked. "Do you think this is easy for me? Do you think I *enjoy* imagining your life with another?"

His rushed confession—the horror behind his words—dulled her anger, the utter misery in his face moving her despite her own hurt. But . . . it still didn't excuse his actions.

"You . . . you could have told me all this, Dara." Her voice shook slightly as she said his name. "We could have tried to fix things together, instead of you plotting out my life with strangers!"

Dara shook his head. Grief still shadowed his eyes, but he spoke firmly. "There's nothing to fix, Nahri. This is what I am. It's a conclusion I suspect you'd have come to soon enough anyway. I wanted you to have another choice in hand when you did." Something bitter stole into his expression. "Don't worry. I'm sure the Pramukhs will provide you with dowry enough."

The words were her own, but they cut deep when turned back on her. "And that's what you think of me, isn't it? Regardless of your feelings, I'm still the dirt-blood-raised thief. The con artist after the biggest score." She gathered the edges of her chador, her hands shaking with anger and something else, something deeper than anger that she didn't want to admit to. She'd be damned if she was going to cry in front of him. "Never mind that I might have done those things to survive . . . and that I might have fought for you just as hard." She drew herself up, and he dropped his gaze under her glare. "I don't need you to plan my future here, Dara. I don't need *anyone* to."

This time when she left, he didn't try to stop her.

23

ALI

"This is extraordinary," Nahri said as she raised the telescope higher, aiming it at the swollen moon. "I can actually see where the shadow overtakes it. And its surface is all pocked . . . I wonder what could cause such a thing."

Ali shrugged. He, Nahri, Muntadhir, and Zaynab were stargazing from an observation post high atop the palace wall overlooking the lake. Well, Ali and Nahri were stargazing. Neither of his siblings had yet to touch the telescope; they were lounging on cushioned sofas, enjoying the attentions of their servants and the platters of food sent up from the kitchens.

He glanced back, watching as Muntadhir pressed a glass of wine on a giggling handmaid, and Zaynab examined her newly hennaed hands. "Maybe we should ask my sister," he said drily. "I'm sure she paid attention to the scholar while he was explaining."

Nahri laughed. It was the first time he'd heard her laugh in days, and the sound warmed his heart. "I take it your siblings don't share your enthusiasm for human science?"

"They would, if human science involved lying around like pampered . . ." Ali stopped, remembering his objective in be-friending Nahri. He quickly backtracked. "Though Muntadhir is certainly entitled to some rest; he did just return from hunting ifrit."

"Perhaps." She sounded unimpressed, and Ali shot Munta-dhir's back an annoyed look before following Nahri to the parapet. He watched as she lifted the telescope to her eye again. "What's it like to have siblings?" she asked.

He was surprised by the question. "I'm the youngest, so I don't actually know what it's like *not* to have them."

"But you all seem very different. It must be challenging at times."

"I suppose." His brother had only just returned to Daevabad this morning, and Ali couldn't deny the relief he felt upon seeing him. "I'd die for either of them," he said softly. "In a heartbeat." Nahri glanced at him, and he smiled. "Makes the squabbles more interesting."

She didn't return his smile; her dark eyes looked troubled.

He frowned. "Have I said something wrong?"

"No." She sighed. "It's been a long week . . . several long weeks, actually." Her gaze remained fixed on the distant stars. "It must be nice to have a family."

The quiet sadness in her voice struck him deep, and he didn't know whether it was her sorrow or his father's order that moved him to say what he did next. "You . . . you could, you know," he stammered. "Have a family, I mean. Here. With us."

Nahri stilled. When she glanced at him, her expression was carefully blank.

"Forgive me, my lords . . ." A wide-eyed shafit girl peeked up from the edge of the stairs. "But I was sent to retrieve the Banu Nahida."

"What is it, Dunoor?" Nahri spoke to the girl, but her gaze remained on Ali, something unreadable in her dark eyes.

The servant brought her palms together and bowed. "I'm sorry, mistress, I do not know. But Nisreen said it's most urgent."

"Of course it is," Nahri muttered, an edge of fear creeping into her voice. She handed the telescope back to him. "Thank you for the evening, Prince Alizayd."

"Nahri . . ."

She gave him a forced smile. "Sometimes I speak without thinking." She touched her heart. "Peace be upon you." She offered a brusque salaam to his siblings and then followed Dunoor down the stairs.

Zaynab threw her head back with a dramatic sigh as soon as Nahri was out of earshot. "Does the end of our intellectual family farce mean that I can leave as well?"

Ali was offended. "What is *wrong* with the two of you?" he demanded. "Not only were you rude to our guest, but you're turning away an opportunity to gaze upon God's finest works, an opportunity only a fraction of those in existence will ever be blessed to—"

"Oh, calm down, Sheikh." Zaynab shivered. "It's cold up here."

"Cold? We're djinn! You are *literally* created from fire."

"It's fine, Zaynab," Muntadhir cut in. "Go. I'll keep him company."

"Your sacrifice is appreciated," Zaynab replied. She gave Muntadhir's cheek an affectionate pat. "Don't get into too much trouble celebrating your return tonight. If you're late to court in the morning, Abba is going to have you drowned in wine."

Muntadhir touched his heart with an exaggerated motion. "Thoroughly warned."

Zaynab left. His brother stood, shaking his head as he joined Ali at the parapet's edge. "You two fight like children."

"She is spoiled and vain."

"Yes, and you're self-righteous and insufferable." His brother shrugged. "I've heard it enough times from both of you." He leaned against the wall. "But forget that. What's going on with this?" he asked, sweeping his hand over the telescope.

"I told you before . . ." Ali toyed with the telescope's dial, trying to sharpen the image. "You fix the location of a star and then—"

"Oh, for God's sake, Zaydi, I'm not talking about the telescope. I'm talking about this new Banu Nahida. Why are the two of you whispering like girlhood friends?"

Ali glanced up, surprised by the question. "Did Abba not tell you?"

"He told me you were spying on her and trying to turn her to our side." Ali frowned, disliking the baldness of the statement, and Muntadhir gave him a shrewd look. "But I know you, Zaydi. You like this girl."

"So what if I do?" He *was* enjoying his time with Nahri, he couldn't help it. She was as intellectually curious as he was, and her life in the human world made for fascinating conversation. "My earlier suspicions about her were wrong."

His brother let out an exaggerated gasp. "Were you replaced with a shapeshifter while I was gone?"

"What do you mean?"

Muntadhir pushed up to sit on the wide edge of the stone parapet separating them from the distant lake. "You've befriended a Daeva *and* admitted to being wrong about something?" Muntadhir tapped his foot against the telescope. "Give me that, I want to make sure the world has not turned upside down."

"Don't do that," Ali said, quickly stepping back with the delicate instrument. "And I'm not that bad."

"No, but you trust far too easily, Zaydi. You always have." His brother gave him a meaningful look. "Especially the people who look human."

Ali put the telescope back on its stand and turned his full attention to Muntadhir. "I take it Abba told you the entirety of our conversation?"

"He said he thought you were going to throw yourself off the wall."

"I'd be lying if I said I didn't consider it." Ali shuddered, recalling the confrontation with his father. "Abba told me what you did," he said softly. "That you defended me. That you were the one who convinced him to give me another chance." He glanced at his brother. "If you hadn't talked to me in the tomb . . ." Ali trailed off. He knew he'd have done something reckless if Muntadhir hadn't stopped him. "Thank you, akhi. Truly. If there's any way I can ever repay you . . ."

Muntadhir waved him off. "You don't have to thank me, Zaydi." He scoffed. "I knew you weren't Tanzeem. You've just got more money than sense when it comes to shafit. Let me guess, that fanatic gave you some wretched story about hungry orphans?"

Ali grimaced, a thread of old loyalty to Anas pulling at him. "Something like that."

Muntadhir laughed. "Do you remember when you gave your grandfather's ring to the old crone who used to pace the palace gates? By the Most High, you had shafit beggars trailing you for months." He shook his head, giving Ali an affectionate smile. "You barely came up to my shoulder back then. I was convinced your mother would throw you in the lake."

"I think I still have scars from the beating she gave me."

Muntadhir's face turned serious, his gray eyes briefly unreadable. "You're lucky you're the favorite, you know."

"Whose favorite? My mother's?" Ali shook his head. "Hardly.

The last thing she said to me was that I spoke her language like a savage, and even that was years ago."

"Not your mother's," Muntadhir pressed. "Abba's."

"*Abba's?*" Ali laughed. "You've had too much wine if you think that. You're his emir, his firstborn. I'm just the idiot second son he doesn't trust."

Muntadhir shook his head. "Not at all . . . well, all right, you *are* that, but you're also the devout zulfiqari a Geziri son is supposed to be, uncorrupted by Daevabad's delicious delights." His brother smiled, but this time the expression didn't reach his eyes. "By the Most High, if I'd given money to the Tanzeem, they'd still be picking smoldering bits of me out of the carpets."

There was an edge to Muntadhir's voice that made Ali uncomfortable. And even though he knew his brother was wrong, he decided to change the subject. "I was starting to fear that's how the Afshin would send you back to Daevabad."

Muntadhir's face soured. "I *will* need more wine if we're going to talk about Darayavahoush." He dropped off the wall's edge and crossed back toward the pavilion.

"That bad?"

His brother returned, setting down one of the food platters and a full goblet of dark wine before pushing back up on the wall. "God, yes. He barely eats, he barely drinks, he just *watches*, like he's waiting for the best time to strike. It was like sharing a tent with a viper. By the Most High, he spent so much time staring at me, he probably knows the number of hairs in my beard. And the *constant* comparisons to how things were better in his time." He rolled his eyes and affected a heavy Divasti accent. "If the Nahids still ruled, the ifrit would never dare come to the border; if the Nahids still ruled, the Grand Bazaar would be cleaner; if the Nahids still ruled, wine would be sweeter and dancing girls more daring and the world would just about explode in happiness." He dropped the accent. "Between that and the fire-cult nonsense, I was nearly driven mad."

Ali frowned. "What fire-cult nonsense?"

"I took a few Daeva soldiers along, thinking Darayavahoush would be more comfortable around his own people." Muntadhir took a sip of his wine. "He kept goading them into tending those damn altars. By the time we returned, they were all wearing ash marks and barely speaking to the rest of us."

That sent a chill down Ali's spine. Religious revivals among the fire worshippers rarely ended well in Daevabad. He joined his brother on the wall.

"I couldn't even blame them," Muntadhir continued. "You should have seen him with a bow, Zaydi. He was *terrifying*. I have no doubt that if his little Banu Nahida wasn't in Daevabad, he would have murdered us all in our sleep with the barest of efforts."

"You let him have a weapon?" Ali asked, his voice sharp.

Muntadhir shrugged. "My men wanted to know if the Afshin lived up to the legend. They kept asking."

Ali was incredulous. "So you tell them *no*. You were in charge, Muntadhir. You would have been responsible if anything—"

"I was trying to gain their friendship," his brother cut in. "You wouldn't understand; you trained with them in the Citadel, and judging from how they spoke of you and your damn zulfiqar, you already have it."

There was a bitterness to his brother's voice, but Ali persisted. "You're not supposed to be friends. You're supposed to lead."

"And where was all this common sense when you decided to spar alone with the Scourge of Qui-zi? You think Jamshid didn't tell me about that bit of idiocy?"

Ali had little defense for that. "It was stupid," he admitted. He bit his lip, remembering his violent interaction with the Afshin. "Dhiru . . . while you were gone . . . did Darayavahoush seem strange to you in any way?"

"Did you not hear *anything* I just said?"

"That's not what I mean. It's just that when we sparred . . . well, I've never seen anyone wield magic like that."

Muntadhir shrugged. "He's a freed slave. Don't they retain some of the power they had when they were working for the ifrit?"

Ali frowned. "But *how* is he free? We still have his relic. And I've been reading up on slaves . . . I can't find anything about peris being able to break an ifrit curse. They don't get involved with our people."

Muntadhir cracked a walnut in his hand, pulling the meat free. "I'm sure Abba has people looking into it."

"I suppose." Ali pulled the platter over and grabbed a handful of pistachios, prying one open and flicking the pale shell into the black water below. "Did Abba tell you the other happy news?"

Muntadhir took another sip of wine, and Ali could see an angry tremor in his hands. "I'm not marrying that human-faced girl."

"You act like you have a choice."

"It's not happening."

Ali pried open another pistachio. "You should give her a chance, Dhiru. She's astonishingly smart. You should see how fast she learned to read and write; it's incredible. She's worlds brighter than you for sure," he added, ducking when Muntadhir threw a walnut at his head. "She can help you with your economic policies when you're king."

"Yes, that's just what every man dreams of in a wife," Muntadhir said drily.

Ali gave him an even gaze. "There are more important qualities for a queen to have than pureblood looks. She's charming. She has a good sense of humor . . ."

"Maybe you should marry her."

That was a low blow. "You know I can't marry," Ali said quietly. Second Qahtani sons—especially ones with Ayaanle blood—

weren't allowed legal heirs. No king wanted that many eager young men in line for the throne. "Besides, who else could you want? You can't possibly think Abba would let you marry that Agnivanshi dancer?"

Muntadhir scoffed, "Don't be absurd."

"Then who?"

Muntadhir drew up his knees and set down his empty goblet. "Quite literally anyone else, Zaydi. Manizheh's the most terrifying person I've ever met—and I say that having just spent two months with the Scourge of Qui-zi." He shuddered. "Forgive my reluctance to jump in bed with the girl Abba says is her daughter."

Ali rolled his eyes. "That's ridiculous. Nahri's nothing like Manizheh."

Muntadhir didn't look convinced. "Not yet. But even if she's not, there's still the more pressing issue."

"Which is?"

"Darayavahoush turning me into a pincushion for arrows on my wedding night."

Ali had no response to that. There was no denying the raw emotion in Nahri's face when she first saw the Afshin in the infirmary, nor the fiercely protective way he spoke of her.

Muntadhir raised his eyebrows. "Ah, no answer now, I see?" Ali opened his mouth to protest, and Muntadhir hushed him. "It's fine, Zaydi. You just got back into Abba's good graces. Follow his orders, enjoy your extremely bizarre friendship. I'll clash with him alone." He hopped off the parapet. "But now, if you don't mind me turning my attention to more pleasurable matters . . . I am due a reunion at Khanzada's." He adjusted the collar on his robe and gave Ali a wicked smile. "Want to come?"

"To Khanzada's?" Ali made a disgusted face. "No."

Muntadhir laughed. "Something will tempt you one day," he called over his shoulder as he headed for the stairs. "Someone."

His brother left, and Ali's gaze fell again on the telescope.

They will be a poor match, he thought for the first time, remembering the curiosity with which Nahri had studied the stars. Muntadhir was right: Ali did like the clever Banu Nahida, finding her constant questions and sharp responses an oddly delightful challenge. But he suspected Muntadhir would not. True, his brother liked women; he liked them smiling and bejeweled, soft and sweet and accommodating. Muntadhir would never spend hours in the library with Nahri, arguing the ethics of haggling and crawling through shelves crowded with cursed scrolls. Nor could Ali imagine Nahri content to loll on a couch for hours, listening to poets pine for their lost loves and discussing the quality of wine.

And he won't be loyal to her. That went without saying. Truthfully, few kings were; most had multiple wives and concubines, though his own father was something of an exception, only marrying Hatset after his first wife—Muntadhir's mother—had died. Either way, it was a thing Ali never really questioned, a way to secure alliances and the reality of his world.

But he didn't like to imagine Nahri subjected to it.

It isn't your place to question any of this, he chided as he raised the telescope to his eyes. Not now and certainly not once they were married. Ali didn't buy Muntadhir's defiance; no one stood against their father's wishes for long.

Ali wasn't sure how long he stayed on the roof, lost in his thoughts as he watched the stars. Such solitude was a rare commodity in the palace, and the black velvet of the sky, the distant twinkling of faraway suns seemed to invite him to linger. Eventually he dropped the telescope to his lap, leaning against the stone parapet and idly contemplating the dark lake.

Half asleep and lost in thought, it took Ali a few minutes to realize a shafit servant had arrived and was gathering up the abandoned goblets and half-eaten platters of food.

"You are done with those, my prince?"

Ali glanced up. The shafit man motioned to the platter of

nuts and Muntadhir's goblet. "Yes, thank you." Ali bent to remove the lens from the telescope, cursing under his breath as
he pricked himself on the sharp glass edge. He had promised the
scholars that he would pack up the valuable instrument himself.

Something smashed into the back of his head.

Ali reeled. The platter of nuts crashed to the ground. His
head felt fuzzy as he tried to turn; he saw the shafit servant, the
gleam of a dark blade . . .

And then the terrible, tearing wrongness of a sharp thrust
in his stomach.

There was a moment of coldness, of foreignness, something
hard and new where there had been nothing at all. A hiss, as if
the blade were cauterizing a wound.

Ali opened his mouth to scream as the pain hit him in a
blinding wave. The servant shoved a rag between his teeth, muffling the sound, and then pushed him hard against the stone wall.

But it wasn't a servant. The man's eyes turned copper, red
stealing into his black hair. *Hanno.*

"Didn't recognize me, crocodile?" the shapeshifter spat.

Ali's left arm was bent behind his back. He tried to shove
Hanno off with his free hand, and in response, the shafit man
twisted the blade. Ali screamed into the rag, and his arm fell
back. Hot blood spread across his tunic, turning the fabric black.

"Hurts, doesn't it?" Hanno mocked. "Iron blade. Very expensive. Ironically enough, bought with the last of your money." He
shoved the knife deeper, stopping only when it hit the stone behind Ali.

Black spots blossomed in front of Ali's eyes. It felt like his
stomach was filled with ice, ice that was steadily extinguishing
the fire that dwelled inside him. Desperate to get the blade out,
he tried to knee the other man in the stomach, but Hanno easily
evaded him.

"'*Give him time,*' Rashid tells me. Like we're all purebloods with centuries to muse on what's right and wrong." Hanno pressed his weight on the knife, and Ali let out another muffled scream. "Anas *died* for you."

Ali scrambled for purchase on Hanno's shirt. The Tanzeem man yanked the knife out and plunged it higher, dangerously close to his lungs.

Hanno seemed to read his thoughts. "I know how to kill purebloods, Alizayd. I wouldn't leave you half dead and take the chance of you being rushed to that fire-worshipping Nahid people say you're fucking in the library." He leaned in close, his eyes filled with hate. "I know how . . . but we're going to do this slowly."

Hanno made good on the threat, pushing the knife higher with such an exaggerated, agonizing unhurriedness that Ali would swear he felt each individual nerve tear. "I had a daughter, you know," Hanno started, grief stealing into his eyes. "About your age. Well, no . . . she never got to be your age. Would you like to know why, Alizayd?" He wiggled the blade, and Ali gasped. "Would you like to know what purebloods like you did to her when she was just a child?"

Ali couldn't find the words to apologize. To plead. The rag fell from his mouth, but it didn't matter. All he could manage was a low cry when Hanno twisted the knife yet again.

"No?" the shapeshifter asked. "That's fine. It's a story better told to the king. I intend to wait for him, you know. I want to see his face when he finds these walls covered in your blood. I want him to wonder how many times you screamed for him to come save you." His voice broke. "I want *your* father to know what it feels like."

Blood puddled at Ali's feet. Hanno held him tight, crushing his left hand. Something stung from inside his palm.

The glass lens from the telescope.

"Emir-joon?" He heard a familiar voice from the stairs. "Muntadhir, are you still here? I've been looking—"

Jamshid e-Pramukh emerged from the staircase, a blue glass bottle of wine dangling from one hand. He froze at the bloody scene.

Hanno wrenched the knife free with a snarl.

Ali slammed his forehead into the other man's.

It took every bit of strength he could muster, enough to send his own head spinning and to draw a dull crack from Hanno's skull. The shapeshifter reeled. Ali didn't hesitate. He struck out hard with the glass lens and slashed his throat open.

Hanno staggered back, dark red blood pouring from his throat. The shafit man looked confused and a little frightened. He certainly didn't look like a would-be assassin now; he looked like a broken, grieving father covered in blood. Blood that had never been black enough for Daevabad.

But he was still holding the knife. He lurched toward Ali.

Jamshid was faster. He brought the wine bottle up and smashed it over Hanno's head.

Hanno dropped, and Jamshid caught Ali as he fell. "Alizayd, my God! Are you . . ." He glanced in horror at his bloody hands and then lowered Ali into a sitting position. "I'll get help!"

"No," Ali said, croaking the word, tasting blood in his mouth. He grabbed Jamshid's collar before he could rise. "Get rid of him."

The command came out in a growl, and Jamshid stiffened. "What?"

Ali fought for breath. The pain in his stomach was fading. He was fairly certain he was about to pass out—or die, a possibility which probably should have bothered him more than it did. But he was focused on only one thing—the shafit assassin lying at his feet, his hand clutching a blade wet with Qahtani blood. His father would murder every mixed-blood in Daevabad if he saw this.

"Get . . . *rid of him*," Ali breathed. "That's an order."

He saw Jamshid swallow, his black eyes darting between Hanno and the wall. "Yes, my prince."

Ali leaned against the stone, the wall icy cold in comparison to the blood soaking his clothes. Jamshid dragged Hanno to the parapet; there was a distant splash. The edges of his vision darkened, but something glittered on the ground, catching his attention. The telescope.

"N-Nahri . . . ," Ali slurred as Jamshid returned. "Just . . . Nahri—" And then the ground rushed up to meet him.

24

NAHRI

Urgent.

The word rang through Nahri's mind, tying her stomach into knots as she hurried back to the infirmary. She wasn't ready for anything urgent; indeed, she was tempted to slow her pace. Better for someone to die waiting rather than be murdered directly by her incompetence.

Nahri pushed open the infirmary door. "All right, Nisreen, what—" She abruptly shut her mouth.

Ghassan al Qahtani sat at the bedside of one of her patients, a Geziri cleric far into his third century who was slowly turning to charcoal. Nisreen said it was a fairly common condition among the elderly, fatal if untreated. Nahri had pointed out that *being* three hundred was a condition that should soon prove fatal, but treated the man anyway, putting him near a steamy vaporizer and giving him a dose of watery mud charmed by an enchantment Nisreen had coached her through. He had been in the infirmary for a few days, and had seemed fine when she left: fast asleep, with the burning contained to his feet.

A chill crept down her spine as she watched the fondness with which the king squeezed the sheikh's hand. Nisreen was standing behind them. There was a warning in her black eyes.

"Your Majesty," Nahri stammered. She quickly brought her palms together and then, deciding it couldn't hurt, bowed. "Forgive me . . . I didn't realize you were here."

The king smiled and stood. "No apology necessary, Banu Nahida. I heard my sheikh wasn't doing well and came by to offer my prayers." He turned back to the old man and touched his shoulder, adding something in Geziriyya. Her patient offered a wheezy response, and Ghassan laughed.

He approached, and she forced herself to hold his gaze. "Did you enjoy your evening with my children?" he asked.

"Very much." Her skin prickled; she could swear she felt the power literally radiating off him. She couldn't resist adding, "I'm sure Alizayd will report everything later."

The king's gray eyes twinkled, amused by her gall. "Indeed, Banu Nahida." He gestured at the old man. "Please, do what you can for him. I'll rest easier knowing that my teacher is in the hands of Banu Manizheh's daughter."

Nahri bowed again, waiting until she heard the door close to hurry to the sheikh's side. She prayed she hadn't already said or done something rude in front of him, but knew that was unlikely—the infirmary put her in a foul mood.

She forced a smile. "How are you feeling?"

"Much better," he rasped. "God be praised, my feet finally stopped hurting."

"There is something you should see," Nisreen said softly. She lifted the sheikh's blanket, blocking his view so Nahri could examine his feet.

They were gone.

Not only were they gone—reduced to ash—but the infection had swept up his legs to take root in his skinny thighs. A smoldering black line licked toward his left hip, and Nahri swallowed, trying to conceal her horror.

"I-I'm glad to hear you're feeling better," she said with as much cheer as she could muster. "If you'll just . . . ah, let me confer with my assistant."

She dragged Nisreen out of earshot. "What happened?" she hissed. "You said we fixed him!"

"I said no such thing," Nisreen corrected her, looking indignant. "There's no cure for his condition, especially at his age. It can only be managed."

"How is *that* managing it? The enchantment seems to have made him worse!" Nahri shuddered. "Did you not just hear the king crowing about what good hands he's in?"

Nisreen beckoned her toward the apothecary shelves. "Trust me, Banu Nahri, King Ghassan knows how serious the situation is. Sheikh Auda's condition is familiar to our people." She sighed. "The burn is advancing quickly. I sent a messenger to retrieve his wife. We'll just try to keep him as comfortable as possible until then."

Nahri stared at Nisreen. "What do you mean? There must be something else we can try."

"He's dying, Banu Nahida. He will not last the night."

"But—"

"You cannot help them all." Nisreen laid a gentle hand on her elbow. "And he's elderly. He's lived a good, long life."

That may have been so, but Nahri could not help thinking about how affectionately Ghassan had spoken of the other man. "It figures my next failure would be a friend of the king."

"Is *that* what's worrying you?" The sympathy vanished from her assistant's face "Could you not put your patient's needs above your own for once? And you've not yet failed. We haven't even started."

"You *just* said there was nothing we could do!"

"We'll try to keep him alive until his wife arrives." Nisreen headed toward the apothecary shelves. "He'll suffocate when the infection reaches his lungs. There's a procedure that will give him a little more time, but it's very precise and you'll have to be the one to do it."

Nahri didn't like the sound of that. She hadn't tried another advanced procedure since nearly strangling the Daeva woman with the salamander.

She reluctantly followed Nisreen. In the light of the flickering torches and blazing fire pit, her apothecary looked alive. Various ingredients twitched and shuddered behind the hazy, sand-blasted glass shelves, and Nahri did the same at the sight. She missed Yaqub's apothecary, full of recognizable—and reliably dead—supplies. Ginger for indigestion, sage for night sweats, things she knew how to use. Not poisonous gases, live cobras, and an entire phoenix dissolved in honey.

Nisreen pulled free a pair of slender silver tweezers from her apron and opened a small cabinet. She carefully plucked out a glimmering copper tube about the length of a hand and skinny as a smoking cheroot. She held it at arm's length, jerking away when Nahri reached for it.

"Don't touch it with your bare skin," she warned. "It's Geziri made, from the same material as their zulfiqar blades. There's no healing from the injury."

Nahri pulled back her hand. "Not even for a Nahid?"

Nisreen gave her a dark look. "How do you think your prince's people took Daevabad from your ancestors?"

"Then what am I supposed to do with it?"

"You will insert it into his lungs and then his throat to relieve some of the pressure as his ability to breathe burns away."

"You want me to stab him with some magical Geziri weapon that destroys Nahid flesh?" Had Nisreen suddenly developed a sense of humor?

"No," her assistant said flatly. "I want you to insert it into his lungs and then his throat to relieve some of the pressure as his ability to breathe burns away. His wife lives on the other side of the city. I fear it will take time to reach her."

"Well, God willing, she moves faster than him. Because I am not doing anything with that murderous little tube."

"Yes, you are," Nisreen said, rebuking her. "You're not going to deny a man a final good-bye with his beloved because you're afraid. You are the Banu Nahida; this is your responsibility." She pushed past her. "Prepare yourself. I'll get him ready for the procedure."

"Nisreen . . ."

But her assistant was already returning to the ailing man's side. Nahri quickly washed up, her hands shaking as she watched Nisreen help the sheikh sip a cup of steaming tea. When he groaned, she pressed a cool cloth to his brow.

She should be the Banu Nahida. It was not the first time the thought had occurred to Nahri. Nisreen cared for their patients like they were family members. She was welcoming and warm, confident in her abilities. And despite her frequent grumblings about the Geziri, there was no hint of prejudice as she tended to the old man. Nahri watched, trying to squash the jealousy flaring up in her chest. What she would give to feel competent again.

Nisreen looked up. "We're ready for you, Banu Nahri." She glanced down at the cleric. "It will hurt. You're sure you don't want some wine?"

He shook his head. "N-no," he managed, his voice trembling. He glanced at the door, the movement obviously causing him pain. "Do you think my wife—" He let out a hacking, smoky cough.

Nisreen squeezed his hand. "We'll give you as much time as we can."

Nahri chewed the inside of her cheek, unnerved by the man's

emotional state. She was used to looking for weakness in fear, for gullibility in grief. She had no idea how to make small talk with someone about to die. But still she stepped closer, forcing what she hoped was a confident smile.

The sheikh's eyes flickered to her. His mouth twitched, as if he might be trying to return her smile, and then he gasped, dropping Nisreen's hand.

Her assistant was on her feet in a flash. She pulled apart the man's robe to reveal a blackened chest, the skin smoldering. A sharp, septic odor filled the air as Nisreen's precise fingers ran up his sternum and then slightly to the left.

She seemed unbothered by the sight. "Bring the tray over here and hand me a scalpel."

Nahri did so, and Nisreen sank the scalpel into the man's chest, ignoring his gasp as she cut away a section of burning skin. She clamped the flesh open and beckoned Nahri closer. "Come here."

Nahri leaned over the bed. Just below the rush of foamy black blood was a billowing mass of glimmering gold tissue. It fluttered softly, slowing as it took on an ashen hue. "My God," she marveled. "Are those his lungs?"

Nisreen nodded. "Beautiful, aren't they?" She picked up the tweezers holding the copper tube and held it out to Nahri. "Aim for the center and gently insert. Don't go deeper than a hair or two."

Her brief sense of wonderment vanished. Nahri looked between the tube and the man's fading lungs. She swallowed, suddenly finding it difficult to breathe herself.

"Banu Nahida," Nisreen prompted, her voice urgent.

Nahri took the tweezers and held the tube over the delicate tissue. "I-I can't," she whispered. "I'm going to hurt him."

His skin suddenly flared, the lungs crumpling into powdery ash as the burning embers swept toward his neck. Nisreen quickly pushed aside his long beard, exposing his neck.

"The throat then, it's his only chance." When she hesitated, Nisreen glared. "Nahri!"

Nahri moved, bringing the tube swiftly down to where Nisreen pointed. It went in as easily as a hot knife through butter. She felt a moment of relief.

And then it sank deep.

"No, don't!" Nisreen grabbed for the tweezers as Nahri tried to pull the tube back up. A terrible sucking sound came from the sheikh's throat. Blood bubbled and simmered over her hands, and his entire body seized.

Nahri panicked. She held her hands against his throat, desperately willing the blood to stop. His terrified eyes locked on hers. "Nisreen, what do I do?" she cried. The man seized again, more violently.

And then he was gone.

She knew it immediately; the weak beat of his heart shuddered to a stop, and the intelligent spark flickered out of his gray gaze. His chest sank, and the tube whistled, the air finally escaping.

Nahri didn't move, unable to look away from the man's tortured face. A tear trailed from his sparse lashes.

Nisreen closed his eyes. "He's gone, Banu Nahida," she said softly. "You tried."

I tried. Nahri had made this man's last moments a living hell. His body was a wreck, his lower half burned away, his bloody throat torn open.

She took a shaky step away, catching sight of her own singed clothes. Her hands and wrists were coated in blood and ash. Without another word, she crossed to the washbasin and started fiercely scrubbing her hands. She could feel Nisreen's eyes on her back.

"We should clean him up before his wife gets here," her assistant said. "Try to—"

"Make it look like I didn't kill him?" Nahri cut in. She didn't turn around; the skin on her hands smarted as she scoured them.

"You didn't kill him, Banu Nahri." Nisreen joined her at the sink. "He was going to die. It was only a matter of time." She went to lay a hand on Nahri's shoulder, and Nahri jerked away.

"Don't touch me." She could feel herself losing control. "This is your fault. I told you I couldn't use that instrument. I've been telling you since I arrived that I wasn't ready to treat patients. And you didn't care. You just keep pushing me!"

Nahri saw something crack in the older woman's face. "Do you think I *want* to?" she asked, her voice oddly desperate. "Do you think I would be pushing you if I had any other choice?"

Nahri was taken aback. "What do you mean?"

Nisreen collapsed in a nearby chair, letting her head fall into her hands. "The king wasn't just here to see an old friend, Nahri. He was here to count the empty beds and ask why you're not treating more patients. There's a waiting list—twenty pages deep and growing—for appointments with you. And those are just the nobles—the Creator only knows how many others in the city need your skills. If the Qahtanis had their way, every bed in here would be filled."

"Then people need to be more patient!" Nahri countered. "Daevabad lasted twenty years without a healer—surely she can wait a bit longer." She leaned against the washbasin. "My God, even human physicians study for years, and they're dealing with colds, not curses. I need more time to be properly trained."

Nisreen let out a dry, humorless laugh. "You'll never be properly trained. Ghassan might want the infirmary filled, but he'd be pleased if your skills never went beyond the basic. He'd probably be happiest if half your patients died." When Nahri frowned, her assistant straightened up, looking at her in surprise. "Do you not understand what's going on here?"

"Apparently not in the least."

"They want you *weak*, Nahri. You're the daughter of Banu Manizheh. You marched into Daevabad with Darayavahoush e-Afshin at your side the day a mob of shafit tried to break into the Daeva Quarter. You nearly killed a woman out of irritation . . . did you not notice that your guards were doubled after that day? You think the Qahtanis want to let you *train*?" Nisreen gave her a disbelieving look. "You should be happy you're not forced to wear an iron cuff when you visit their prince."

"I . . . But they let me have the infirmary. They pardoned Dara."

"The king had no choice but to pardon Darayavahoush—he is beloved among our people. Were the Qahtanis to harm a hair on his head, half the city would rise up. And as for the infirmary? It is symbolic, as are you. The king wants a Nahid healer as a herder wants a dog, occasionally useful but entirely dependent."

Nahri stiffened in anger. "I'm no one's dog."

"No?" Nisreen crossed her arms, her wrists still covered in ash and blood. "Then why are you playing into their hands?"

"What are you talking about?"

Nisreen drew closer. "There is no hiding your lack of progress in the infirmary, child," she warned. "You entirely ignored the Daevas who came to see you at the Grand Temple—and then you stormed out without a word. You neglect your fire altar, you eat meat in public, you spend all your free time with that Qahtani zealot . . ." Her face darkened. "Nahri, our tribe doesn't think lightly of disloyalty; we've suffered too much at the hands of our enemies. Daevas who are suspected of collaboration . . . life is not easy for them."

"Collaboration?" Nahri was incredulous. "Staying on good terms with the people in power isn't collaboration, Nisreen. It's common sense. And if my eating kebab bothers a bunch of gossipy fire worshippers—"

Nisreen gasped. "What did you say?"

Too late Nahri remembered the Daevas hated the term. "Oh, come on, Nisreen, it's just a word. You know I didn't—"

"It's not just a word!" Furious red spots blossomed in Nisreen's pale cheeks. "That *slur* has been used to demonize our tribe for centuries. It's what people spit when they rip off our women's veils and beat our men. It's what the authorities charge us with whenever they want to raid our homes or seize our property. That *you*—of all people—would use it . . ."

Her assistant stood, pacing farther into the infirmary with her hands laced behind her head. She glared back at Nahri. "Do you even want to improve? How many times have I told you how important intention is in healing? How critical belief is when wielding magic?" She spread her hands, gesturing to the infirmary surrounding them. "Do you believe in *any* of this, Banu Nahri? Care anything for our people? Our culture?"

Nahri dropped her gaze, a guilty flush filling her cheeks. *No.* She hated how quickly the answer leaped to her mind, but it was the truth.

Nisreen must have sensed her discomfort. "I thought not." She took the crumpled blanket lying abandoned at the foot of the sheikh's bed and silently spread it over his body, her fingers lingering on his brow. When she glanced up, there was open despair in her face. "How can you be the Banu Nahida when you care nothing for the way of life your ancestors created?"

"And rubbing my head in ash and wasting half the day tending a fire altar will make me a better healer?" Nahri pushed off the washbasin with a scowl. Did Nisreen think she didn't feel badly enough about the sheikh? "*My hand slipped*, Nisreen. It slipped because I should have practiced that procedure a hundred times before being let anywhere near that man!"

Nahri knew she should stop, but shaken and frustrated, fed up with the impossible expectations dropped on her shoulders the moment she'd entered Daevabad, she pressed on. "You want to know what I think of the Daeva faith? I think it's a *scam*. A bunch of overly complicated rituals designed to worship the very people who created it." She bunched her apron into an angry ball. "No wonder the djinn won the war. The Daevas were probably so busy refilling oil lamps and bowing to a horde of laughing Nahids that they didn't even realize the Qahtanis invaded until—"

"Enough!" Nisreen snapped. She looked angrier than Nahri had ever seen her. "The Nahids pulled our entire race out of human servitude. They were the only ones brave enough to fight the ifrit. They built this city, this magical city with no rival in the world, to rule an empire that spanned continents." She drew closer, her eyes blazing. "And when your beloved Qahtanis arrived, when the streets ran black with Daeva blood and the air thick with the screams of dying children and violated women . . . this tribe of *fire worshippers* survived. We survived it all." Her mouth twisted in disgust. "And we deserve better than you."

Nahri gritted her teeth. Nisreen's words had found their mark, but she refused to concede such a thing.

Instead, she threw her apron at the older woman's feet. "Good luck finding a replacement." And then—avoiding the sight of the man she'd just killed—she turned and stormed out.

Nisreen followed. "His wife is coming. You can't just leave. Nahri!" she shouted as Nahri flung open the door to her bedchamber. "Come back and—"

Nahri slammed the door in Nisreen's face.

The room was dark—as usual, she'd let the fire altar go out—but Nahri didn't care. She staggered to her bed, fell face-first on the lush quilt, and for the first time since she arrived in Daevabad, probably for the first time in a decade, she let herself sob.

SHE COULDN'T HAVE SAID HOW MUCH TIME PASSED. She didn't sleep. Nisreen knocked on her door at least a half-dozen times, begging softly for her to come back out. Nahri ignored her. She curled into a ball on the bed, staring vacantly at the enormous landscape painted on the wall.

Zariaspa, someone once told her, the mural painted by her uncle, although the familial word felt as false as ever. These people weren't hers. This city, this faith, her supposed tribe . . . they were alien and strange. She was suddenly tempted to destroy the painting, to knock over the fire altar, to get rid of every reminder of this duty she'd never asked for. The only Daeva she cared for had rejected her; she wanted nothing to do with the rest.

As if on cue, the knocking started again, a lighter tap on the rarely used servants' door. Nahri ignored it for a few seconds, growing silently more enraged as it continued, steady as a dripping pipe. Finally she flung her blanket away and flew to her feet, stomping over to the door and yanking it open.

"What is it now, Nisreen?" she snapped.

But it wasn't Nisreen at her door. It was Jamshid e-Pramukh, and he looked terrified.

He staggered in without invitation, bowed under the weight of an enormous sack over his shoulder.

"I'm so sorry, Banu Nahida, but I had no choice. He insisted I bring him straight to you." He dropped the sack on her bed and snapped his fingers, flames bursting between them to illuminate the room.

It wasn't a sack he'd dropped on her bed.

It was Alizayd al Qahtani.

NAHRI WAS AT ALI'S SIDE IN SECONDS. THE PRINCE was unconscious and covered in blood, pale ash coating his skin.

"What happened?" she gasped.

"He was stabbed." Jamshid held out a long knife, the blade dark with blood. "I found this. Do you think you can heal him?"

A rush of fear swept through her. "Take him to the infirmary. I'll get Nisreen."

Jamshid moved to block her. "He said just you."

Nahri was incredulous. "I don't care what he said! I'm barely trained; I'm not going to heal the king's son alone in my bed-room!"

"I think you should try. He was most adamant, and Banu Nahida . . ." Jamshid glanced at the unconscious prince and then lowered his voice. "When a Qahtani gives an order in Daevabad . . . you obey." They'd switched to Divasti without her noticing, and the dark words in her native tongue sent a chill through her veins.

Nahri took the bloody knife and brought it close to her face. Iron, though she smelled nothing that would indicate poison. She touched the blade. It didn't spark, burst into flames, or evidence any sort of godforsaken magical malice. "Do you know if this is cursed?"

Jamshid shook his head. "I doubt it. The man who attacked him was shafit."

Shafit? Nahri stayed her curiosity, her attention focused on Ali. *If it's a normal injury, it shouldn't matter that he's a djinn. You've healed wounds like this in the past.*

She knelt at Ali's side. "Help me get his shirt off. I need to examine him."

Ali's tunic was so badly destroyed that it was small effort to finish ripping it open. She could see three jagged wounds, in-cluding one that seemed to go all the way through to his back. She pressed her palms against the largest one and closed her eyes. She thought back to how she'd saved Dara and tried to do the same, willing Ali to heal and imagining the skin healthy and whole.

She braced herself for visions, but none came. Instead, she caught the scent of salt water, and a briny taste filled her mouth. But her intentions must have been clear; the wound twitched under her fingers, and Ali shivered, letting out a low groan.

"By the Creator . . . ," Jamshid whispered. "That's extraor-dinary."

"Hold him still," she warned. "I'm not done." She lifted her hands. The wound had started to close, but his flesh was still discolored and looked almost porous. She lightly touched his skin, and foamy black blood rose to the surface, like pressing on a soaked sponge. She closed her eyes and tried again, but it stayed the same.

Though the room was cool, sweat poured from her skin, so much so that her fingers grew slick. Wiping them on her shirt, she moved on to the other wounds, the salty taste intensifying. Ali hadn't opened his eyes, but the rhythm of his heart stabilized under her fingertips. He took a shaky breath, and Nahri sat back on her heels to examine her half-completed work.

Something seemed wrong. *Maybe it's the iron?* Dara had told her on their journey that iron could impair purebloods.

I could stitch it. She'd done some stitching with Nisreen, using silver thread treated with some sort of charm. It was supposed to have restorative qualities and seemed worth a try. Ali didn't look like he was going to keel over and die if she took a few minutes to retrieve some supplies from the infirmary. But it was still a guess. For all she knew, his organs were destroyed and leaking into his body.

Ali murmured something in Geziriyya, and his gray eyes slowly blinked open, growing wide and confused as he took in the unfamiliar room. He tried to sit up, letting out a low gasp of pain.

"Don't move," she warned. "You've been injured."

"I . . ." His voice came out in a croak, and then she saw his gaze fall on the knife. His face crumpled, a devastated shadow overtaking his eyes. "Oh."

"Ali." She touched his cheek. "I'm going to get some supplies from the infirmary, okay? Stay here with Jamshid." The Daeva guard didn't look particularly pleased by that but nodded, and she slipped out.

The infirmary was quiet; the patients she hadn't killed asleep and Nisreen gone for now. Nahri set a pot of water to boil on the glowing embers in her fire pit and then retrieved the silver thread and a few needles, all the while studiously ignoring the sheikh's now-empty bed.

When the water came to a boil, she added a sludgy spoonful of bitumen, some honey, and salt, following one of the pharmaceutical recipes Nisreen had shown her. After a moment of hesitation, she crumbled in a prepared opium pod. It would be easier to stitch Ali up if he was calm.

Her mind ran rampant with speculation. Why would Ali possibly want to hide an attempt on his life? She was surprised the king himself wasn't in the infirmary to ensure that his son got the best treatment, while the Royal Guard swept the city, breaking down doors and rounding up shafit in search of conspirators.

Maybe that's why he wants it kept quiet. It was obvious Ali had a soft spot for the shafit. But she wasn't about to complain. Just a few hours earlier, she feared Ghassan would punish her for accidentally killing the sheikh. Now his youngest—his favorite, according to some gossip she'd overheard—was hiding in her bedroom, his life in her hands.

Balancing her supplies and the tea, Nahri tucked a copper ewer of water under one arm and headed back to her room. She edged the door open. Ali was in the same position he'd been in when she left. Jamshid paced the bedchamber, looking like he sorely regretted whatever chain of events had led him to this moment.

He glanced up when she approached and quickly crossed to take the tray of supplies. She nodded at a low table in front of the fireplace.

He set it down. "I'm going to go get his brother," he whispered in Divasti.

She glanced at Ali. The blood-covered prince looked to be in shock, his shaking hands wandering over the ruined sheets. "Are you sure that's a good idea?"

"Better than two Daevas getting caught trying to cover up an attempt on his life."

Excellent point. "Be fast."

Jamshid left, and Nahri returned to the bed. "Ali? *Ali*," she repeated when he didn't respond. He startled, and she reached for him. "Come closer to the fire. I need the light."

He nodded but didn't move. "Come on," she said gently, pulling him to his feet. He let out a low hiss of pain, one arm clutched against his stomach.

She helped him onto the couch and pressed the steaming cup into his hands. "Drink." She pulled over the table and laid out her thread and needles, then went to her hammam to retrieve a stack of towels. When she returned, Ali had abandoned the cup of tea and was draining the entire ewer of water. He let it fall back to the table with an empty thud.

She raised an eyebrow. "Thirsty?"

He nodded. "Sorry. I saw it, and I . . ." He looked dazed, whether from the opium or the injury she didn't know. "I couldn't stop."

"There's probably barely any liquid left in your body," she replied. She sat and threaded her needle. Ali was still holding his side. "Move your hand," she said, reaching for it when he didn't comply. "I need to . . ." She trailed off. The blood covering Ali's right hand wasn't black.

It was the dark crimson of a shafit—and there was a *lot* of it.

Her breath caught. "I guess your assassin didn't get away."

Ali stared at his hand. "No," he said softly. "He didn't." He glanced up. "I had Jamshid throw him in the lake . . ." His voice was oddly distant, as if marveling over a curiosity not connected to him, but grief clouded his gray eyes. "I . . . I'm not even sure he was dead."

Nahri's fingers trembled on the needle. *When a Qahtani gives an order in Daevabad, you obey.* "You should finish your tea, Ali. You'll feel better, and it'll make this easier."

He had no reaction when she started stitching. She made sure her movements were precise; there was no room for error here.

She worked in silence for a few minutes, waiting for the opium to take full effect, before finally asking, "Why?"

Ali set his cup down—or tried to. It fell from his hands. "Why what?"

"Why are you trying to hide the fact that someone wanted to kill you?"

He shook his head. "I can't tell you."

"Oh, come on. You can't expect me to fix the results without knowing what happened. The curiosity will kill me. I'll have to invent some salacious story to amuse myself." Nahri kept her tone light, occasionally glancing up from her work to gauge his reaction. He looked exhausted. "Please tell me it was because of a woman. I would hold that over you for—"

"It wasn't a woman."

"Then what?"

Ali swallowed. "Jamshid went to get Muntadhir, didn't he?" When Nahri nodded, he started to shake. "He's going to kill me. He's . . ." He suddenly pressed a hand to his head, looking like he was fighting a swoon. "Sorry . . . do you have some more water?" he asked. "I-I feel terribly strange."

Nahri refilled the ewer from a narrow cistern set in the wall. She started to pour him a cup, but he shook his head.

"The whole thing," he said, taking it and draining it as quickly as he had the first. He sighed with pleasure. She looked at him askance before returning to her stitches.

"Be careful," she advised him. "I don't think I've ever seen someone drink so much water so quickly."

He didn't respond, but his increasingly glazed eyes took in

her bedchamber again. "The infirmary is much smaller than I remember," he said, sounding confused. Nahri hid a smile. "How can you fit patients in here?"

"I've heard your father wants me treating more."

Ali waved dismissively. "He just wants their money. But we don't need it. We have *so* much. Too much. The Treasury is sure to collapse from its weight one day." He stared at his hands as he waved again. "I can't feel my fingers," he said, sounding surprisingly untroubled by this revelation.

"They're still there." *The king's earning money off my patients?* It shouldn't have surprised her, but she felt her anger quicken anyway. Collapsing Treasury, indeed.

Before she could question him further, a surge of wetness under her fingers caught her attention, and she glanced down in alarm, expecting blood. But the liquid was clear and as she rubbed it between her fingers, she realized what it was.

Water. It trickled through the fissures of Ali's half-healed wounds, washing free the blood and seeping past her stitches, smoothing out his skin as it passed. Healing him.

What in God's name . . . Nahri gave the ewer a puzzled glance, wondering if there'd been something in it she wasn't aware of.

Strange. But she kept at her work, listening to Ali's increasingly nonsensical ramblings and occasionally assuring him that it was okay that the room looked blue and the air tasted of vinegar. The opium had improved his mood, and oddly enough she started to relax as she noticed improvement with each stitch.

If only I could find such success with magical illnesses. She thought of the way the old man's frightened eyes locked on hers as he breathed his last. It was not something she would ever forget.

"I killed my first patient today," she confessed softly. She wasn't sure why, but it felt better to say it out loud, and God knew Ali was in no state to remember. "An old man from your tribe. I made a mistake, and it killed him."

The prince dropped his head to stare at her but said nothing, his eyes bright. Nahri continued. "I always wanted this . . . well, something like this. I used to dream of becoming a physician in the human world. I saved every coin I could, hoping one day to have enough to bribe some academy to take me." Her face fell. "And now I'm terrible at it. Every time I feel like I master something, a dozen new things are thrown upon me with no warning."

Ali squinted and looked down his long nose to study her. "You're not terrible," he declared. "You're my friend."

The sincerity in his voice only worsened her guilt. *He's not my friend*, she'd told Dara. *He's a mark*. Right . . . a mark who'd become the closest thing she had to an ally after Dara.

The realization unsettled her. *I don't want you caught up in any political feuds if Alizayd al Qahtani ends up with a silk cord around his neck*, Dara had warned. Nahri shuddered; she could only imagine what her Afshin would think of this midnight liaison.

She briskly finished her last stitch. "You look awful. Let me clean off the blood."

In the time it took her to dampen a cloth, Ali was asleep on the couch. She pulled off what remained of his bloody tunic and tossed it into the fire, adding her ruined bedding as well. The knife she kept, after wiping it down. One never knew when these things would come in handy. She cleaned Ali up as best she could and then—after briefly admiring her stitches—covered him with a thin blanket.

She sat across from him. She almost wished Nisreen was here. Not only would the sight of the "Qahtani zealot" sleeping in her bedroom likely give the other woman a heart attack, but Nahri would happily throw her hateful comments back in her face by pointing out how successfully she'd healed him.

The door to the servants' entrance smashed open. Nahri jumped and reached for the knife.

But it was only Muntadhir. "My brother," he burst out, his gray eyes bright with worry. "Where . . ." His gaze fell upon Ali, and he rushed to his side, dropping to the ground. He touched his cheek. "Is he all right?"

"I think so," Nahri replied. "I gave him something to help him sleep. It's best if he doesn't jostle those stitches."

Muntadhir lifted the blanket and gasped. "My God . . ." He stared at his brother's wounds another moment before letting the blanket fall back. "I'm going to kill him," he said in a shaky whisper, his voice thick with emotion. "I'm going to—"

"Emir-joon." Jamshid had joined them. He touched Muntadhir's shoulder. "Talk to him first. Maybe he had a good reason."

"A reason? *Look* at him. Why would he cover something like this up?" Muntadhir let out an aggravated sigh before glancing back at her. "Can we move him?"

She nodded. "Just be careful. I'll come check on him later. I want him to rest for a few days, at least until those wounds heal."

"Oh, he'll be resting, that's for sure." Muntadhir rubbed his temples. "A sparring accident." She raised her eyebrows, and he explained. "That's how this happened, do you understand?" he asked, looking between her and Jamshid.

Jamshid was skeptical. "No one's going to believe I did this to your brother. The reverse, maybe."

"No one else is going to see his wounds," Muntadhir replied. "He was embarrassed by the defeat, and he came to the Banu Nahida alone, assuming their friendship would buy him some discretion . . . which is correct, yes?"

Nahri sensed this wasn't the best moment to bargain. She ducked her head. "Of course."

"Good." He kept his gaze on her a moment longer, something conflicted in its depths. "Thank you, Banu Nahri," he said softly. "You saved his life tonight—that's a thing I won't forget."

Nahri held the door as the two men made their way out, the

unconscious Ali between them. She could still detect the steady beat of his heart, recalling the moment he'd gasped, the wound closing beneath her fingers.

It wasn't a thing she would forget either.

She closed the door, picked up her supplies, and then headed back to the infirmary to put them away—she couldn't risk making Nisreen suspicious. It was quiet, a stillness in the misty air. Dawn was approaching, she realized, early morning sunlight filtering through the infirmary's glass ceiling, falling in dusty rays on the apothecary wall and her tables. Upon the sheikh's empty bed.

Nahri stopped, taking it all in. The hazy shelves of twitching ingredients that her mother must have known like the back of her hand. The wide, nearly empty half of the room that would have been filled with patients griping about their maladies, assistants twining among them, preparing tools and potions.

She thought again of Ali, of the satisfaction she'd felt watching him sleep, the *peace* she'd felt after finally doing something right after months of failing. The favorite son of the djinn king, and she'd snatched him back from death. There was power in that.

And it was time for Nahri to take it.

SHE DID IT ON THE THIRD DAY.

Her infirmary looked like it had been ransacked by some sort of lunatic monkey. Peeled and abandoned bananas lay everywhere—she'd thrown several in frustration—along with the tattered remains of damp animal bladders. The air was thick with the stench of overripe fruit, and Nahri was fairly certain she'd never eat a banana again in her life. Thankfully, she was alone. Nisreen had yet to come back, and Dunoor—after retrieving the requested bladders and bananas—had fled, probably convinced Nahri had gone entirely mad.

Nahri had dragged a table outside the infirmary, into the

sunniest part of the pavilion facing the garden. The midday heat was oppressive; right now the rest of Daevabad would be resting, sheltering in darkened bedrooms and under shady trees.

Not Nahri. She held a bladder carefully against the table with one hand. Like the scores before it, she'd filled the bladder with water and carefully laid a banana peel on top.

In the other hand, she held the tweezers and the deadly copper tube.

Nahri narrowed her eyes, furrowing her brow as she brought the tube closer to the banana peel. Her hand was steady—she'd learned the hard way that tea would keep her awake but also make her fingers tremble. She touched the tube to the peel and pressed it down just a hair. She held her breath, but the bladder didn't burst. She removed the tube.

A perfect hole pierced the banana skin. The bladder beneath was untouched.

Nahri let out her breath. Tears pricked her eyes. *Don't get excited*, she chided. *It might have been luck.*

Only when she repeated the experiment a dozen more times—successful in each instance—did she let herself relax. Then she glanced down at the table. There was one banana peel left.

She hesitated. And then she placed it over her left hand.

Her heart was beating so loudly she could hear it in her ears. But Nahri knew if she wasn't confident enough to do this, she'd never be able to do what she planned next. She touched the tube to the peel and pressed down.

She pulled it away. Through a narrow, neat hole she could see unblemished flesh.

I can do this. She just needed to focus, to train without a hundred other worries and responsibilities dragging her down, patients she was ill-prepared to handle, intrigue that could destroy her reputation.

Greatness takes time, Kartir had told her. He was right.

Nahri needed time. She knew where to get it. And she suspected she knew the price.

She took a ragged breath, her fingers falling to brush the weight of the dagger on her hip. Dara's dagger. She'd yet to return it—in fact, she'd yet to see him again after their disastrous encounter at the Grand Temple.

She drew it from its sheath now, tracing the hilt and pressing her palm over the place he would have gripped. For a long moment, she stared at it, willing another way to present itself.

And then she put it down.

"I'm sorry," Nahri whispered. She rose from the table, leaving the dagger behind. Her throat tightened, but she did not allow herself to cry.

It would not do to appear vulnerable before Ghassan al Qahtani.

2 5

ALI

Ali dove under the canal's choppy surface and turned in a neat somersault to kick in the opposite direction. His stitches smarted in protest, but he pushed past the pain. Just a few more laps.

He slid through the murky water with practiced ease. Ali's mother had taught him to swim; it was the only Ayaanle tradition she insisted he learn. She'd defied the king to do it, showing up unexpectedly at the Citadel one day when he was seven, intimidating and unfamiliar in a royal veil. She'd dragged him back to the palace while he kicked and screamed, begging her not to drown him. Once in the harem, she'd pushed him in the deepest part of the canal without a word. Only when he surfaced—limbs flailing, gasping for air through his tears—had she finally spoken his name. And then she taught him to kick and dive, to put his face in the water and breathe from the side of his mouth.

Years later, Ali still remembered every minute of her careful instruction—and the price she'd paid for such defiance: they

were never allowed to be alone again. But Ali kept swimming. He
liked it, even if most djinn—especially his father's people—looked
upon swimming with utter revulsion. There were even clerics
who preached that the Ayaanle's enjoyment of water was a perversion, a relic of an ancient river cult in which they'd supposedly cavorted with marid in all sorts of sinful ways. Ali dismissed
the sordid tales as gossip; the Ayaanle were a wealthy tribe from
a secure and largely isolated homeland—they'd always provoked
jealousy.

He finished another lap and then drifted in the current. The
air was still and thick, the buzz of insects and the twitter of birdsong the only sounds breaking the garden's silence. It was almost
peaceful.

An ideal time to suddenly be set upon by another Tanzeem assassin. Ali tried
to put the dark thought out of his mind, but it wasn't easy. It had
been four days since Hanno tried to kill him, and he'd been confined to his quarters ever since. The morning after the attack,
Ali had awoken to the worst headache of his life and a furious
brother demanding answers. Wracked with pain, with guilt, and
his mind still in a fog, Ali had given them, bits of truth about his
relationship with the Tanzeem slipping out like water through
his fingers. It turned out his earlier hopes were correct: his father
and brother had only known about the money.

Muntadhir was decidedly *not* pleased to learn the rest.

In the face of his brother's growing rage, Ali had been trying
to explain why he'd covered up Hanno's death when Nahri had
arrived to check on him. Muntadhir had bluntly declared him a
traitor in Geziriyya and stormed out. He hadn't been back.

Maybe I should go talk to him. Ali climbed out of the canal, dripping on the decorative tiles bordering it. He reached for his shirt.
Try to explain . . .

He stopped, catching a glimpse of his stomach. The wound
was gone.

Stunned, Ali ran his hand over what had been a half-healed gash studded with stitches an hour earlier. It was now nothing more than a bumpy scar. The wound on his chest was still stitched, but that too looked remarkably improved. He reached for the third under his ribs and flinched. Hanno had driven the knife straight through him at that point, and it still hurt.

Maybe the canal water had some sort of healing properties? If so, it was the first Ali had heard of it. He'd have to ask Nahri. She'd been coming by most days to check on him, seemingly unfazed that he'd been dumped in her bedroom covered in blood only a few days ago. The only allusion she'd made to saving his life had been in her gleeful sack of his small library. She'd claimed several books, an ivory inkwell, and a gold armband as "payment."

He shook his head. She was odd, to be sure. Not that Ali could complain. Nahri might be the only friend he had left.

"Peace be upon you, Ali."

Ali startled at the sound of his sister's voice and pulled on his shirt. "And upon you peace, Zaynab."

She came around the path to join him on the wet stones. "Did I catch you *swimming*?" She feigned shock. "And here I thought you had no interest in the Ayaanle, and our—what do you like to call it—culture of scheming indulgence?"

"It was just a few laps," he muttered. He wasn't in the mood to fight with Zaynab. He sat, dropping his bare feet back into the canal. "What do you want?"

She sat beside him, trailing her fingers through the water. "To make sure you're still alive, for one. No one's seen you at court in nearly a week. And to warn you. I don't know what you think you're doing with that Nahid girl, Ali. You've no skill at politics, let alone—"

"What are you talking about?"

Zaynab rolled her gray-gold eyes. "The marriage negotiations, you idiot."

Ali suddenly felt light-headed. "*What* marriage negotiations?"

She drew back, looking surprised. "Between Muntadhir and Nahri." She narrowed her eyes. "Are you telling me that you didn't help her? By the Most High, she gave Abba a list of percentages and figures that looked like some report from the Treasury. He's furious with you—he thinks you wrote it."

God preserve me . . . Ali knew Nahri was clever enough to come up with such a thing on her own, but suspected he was the only Qahtani who had an accurate measure of the Banu Nahida's capabilities. He rubbed his brow. "When did all this happen?"

"Yesterday afternoon. She showed up at Abba's office, uninvited and unaccompanied, to say the rumors were tiring her, and she wanted to know where they stood." Zaynab crossed her arms. "She demanded an equal cut in patient payments, a pensioned position for her Afshin, a paid training sabbatical in Zariaspa . . . and by God, the *dowry* . . ."

Ali's mouth went dry. "Did she really ask for all that? Yesterday, you are sure?"

Zaynab nodded. "She also refuses to let Muntadhir take a second wife. Wants it written in the contract itself in recognition of the fact that the Daevas don't permit it. More time to train, no patients for at least a year, unfettered access to Manizheh's old notes . . ." Zaynab ticked off her fingers. "I'm sure I'm missing something. People said they were haggling past midnight." She shook her head, seeming both impressed and indignant. "I don't know who that girl thinks she is."

The last Nahid in the world. And one with some very compromising information on the youngest Qahtani. He tried to keep his voice smooth. "What did Abba think?"

"He felt the need to check his pockets after she left but was otherwise elated." Zaynab rolled her eyes. "He says her ambition reminds him of Manizheh."

Of course it would. "And Muntadhir?"

"What do you think? He doesn't want to marry some conniving, thin-blooded Nahid. He came straight to me to ask what it was like to be of mixed tribes, to not be able to speak Geziriyya—"

That surprised him. Ali hadn't realized such concerns had been among Muntadhir's reasons for not wanting to marry Nahri. "What did you tell him?"

She gave him an even stare. "The truth, Ali. You can pretend it doesn't bother you, but there's a reason so few djinn marry outside their tribe. I've never been able to master Geziriyya like you, and it's completely severed me from Abba's people. Amma's are little better. Even when Ayaanle pay me compliments, I can hear the shock in their voice that a sand fly accomplished such sophistication."

That took him aback. "I didn't know that."

"Why would you?" She dropped her gaze. "It's not like you've ever asked. I'm sure you find harem politics frivolous and contemptible anyway."

"Zaynab . . ." The hurt in her voice cut him deeply. Despite the antagonism that frequently characterized their relationship, his sister had come here to warn him. His brother had covered for him time and time again. And what had Ali done? He'd dismissed Zaynab as a spoiled brat and helped his father trap Muntadhir in an engagement with a woman he didn't want.

Ali stood as the sun sank behind the tall palace walls, throwing the garden into shadow. "I need to find him."

"Good luck." Zaynab pulled her feet from the water. "He was drinking by noon and made some comment about consoling himself with half the city's noblewomen."

"I know where he'll be." Ali helped her to her feet. She turned to leave, and he touched her wrist. "Have tea with me tomorrow."

She blinked in surprise. "Surely you have more important things to do than have tea with your spoiled sister."

He smiled. "Not at all."

IT WAS DARK BY THE TIME ALI REACHED KHANZA-da's salon. Music spilled into the street, and a few soldiers milled about outside. He nodded to them and steeled himself as he climbed the stairs leading to the rooftop garden. He could hear a man grunting; a woman's low cry of pleasure echoed from one of the dark corridors.

A servant moved to block the door when Ali arrived. "Peace be upon you, Sheikh . . . Prince!" the man corrected with an embarrassed flush. "Forgive me, but the lady of the house—"

Ali pushed past him and through the door, wrinkling his nose at the overly perfumed air. The roof was packed with at least two dozen noblemen and their retainers. Quick-footed servants twined among them, bringing wine and tending to water pipes. Musicians played and two girls danced, conjuring up illuminated flowers with their hands. Muntadhir lounged on a plush couch with Khanzada next to him.

Muntadhir didn't seem to notice his arrival, but Khanzada jumped to her feet. Ali raised his hands, readying an apology that died on his lips when he noticed a new addition to Muntadhir's drinking companions. He dropped his hand to his zulfiqar.

Darayavahoush grinned. "Peace be upon you, little Zaydi." The Afshin sat with Jamshid and a Daeva man Ali didn't recognize. They looked like they were having a good time, their goblets full, a pretty wine bearer perched beside them on the large cushioned bench.

Ali's gaze slid from the Afshin to Jamshid. Now there was a situation he had little idea how to handle. He owed the Daeva man his life several times over, for interrupting Hanno and getting rid of his body, for getting him to Nahri. There was no denying it—but God, did he wish it had been someone other than Kaveh's son. A word, an insinuation, and the grand wazir would be after Ali in a heartbeat.

Khanzada was suddenly in front of him, waving a finger in his face. "Did my servant let you in? I told him—"

Muntadhir finally spoke. "Let him pass, Khanzada," he called in a weary voice.

She scowled. "Fine. But no weapons." She snatched his zulfiqar away. "You make my girls nervous enough."

Ali watched helplessly as his zulfiqar was handed off to a passing servant. Darayavahoush laughed, and Ali whirled on him, but Khanzada seized his arm and dragged him forward with a surprising amount of force for such a delicate-looking woman.

She pushed him into a chair beside Muntadhir. "Don't make trouble," she warned before stalking off. Ali suspected the doorman was about to get quite the tongue-lashing.

Muntadhir didn't greet him, his vacant gaze focused on the dancers.

Ali cleared his throat. "Peace be upon you, akhi."

"Alizayd." His brother's voice was cool. He took a sip from his copper goblet. "What brings a holy man to such a bastion of sin?"

A promising start. Ali sighed. "I want to apologize, Dhiru. To talk to you about—"

There was a burst of laughter from the Daeva men across the way. The Afshin appeared to be telling some sort of joke in Divasti, his face animated, his hands waving for emphasis. Jamshid laughed as the third man topped off his goblet. Ali frowned.

"What?" Muntadhir demanded. "What are you staring at?"

"I . . . nothing," Ali stammered, surprised by the hostility in his brother's voice. "I just didn't realize Jamshid and Darayavahoush were so close."

"They're not close," Muntadhir snapped. "He's being polite to his father's guest." His eyes flashed, something dark and uncertain in their depths. "Don't be getting any ideas, Alizayd. I don't like that look on your face."

"What *look*? What are you talking about?"

"You know what I'm talking about. You had your supposed assassin thrown in the lake and risked your life to cover up whatever the hell you were doing on the wall. It ends there. Jamshid isn't talking. I asked him not to . . . and unlike some people here, he doesn't lie to me."

Ali was aghast. "You think I'm planning to hurt him?" He lowered his voice, noticing the curious gaze of a nearby servant—they might have been speaking Geziriyya, but an argument looked the same in any language. "My God, Dhiru, do you really think I'd kill the man who saved my life? Do you think me capable of that?"

"I don't know what you're capable of, Zaydi." Muntadhir drained his goblet. "I've been telling myself for months that this is all a mistake. That you're just some softhearted fool who threw his money around without asking questions."

Ali's heart skipped a beat, and Muntadhir beckoned for the wine bearer, falling silent only long enough for the man to finish pouring him more wine. He took a sip before continuing. "But you're not a fool, Zaydi—you're one of the brightest people I know. You didn't just give them money, you taught them to hide it from the Treasury. And you're far better at covering your tracks than I would have imagined. Your sheikh was crushed to death in front of you, and my God . . . you didn't *flinch*. You had the damn presence of mind to *dispose of a body* while you were dying yourself." Muntadhir shuddered. "That's cold, Zaydi. That's a coldness I didn't know you had in you." He shook his head, a hint of regret stealing into his voice. "I try to dismiss them, you know, the things people say. I always have."

Nausea welled in Ali. In the depths of his heart, he suddenly suspected—and feared—where this conversation was going. He swallowed back the lump rising in his throat. "What things?"

"You know what things." His brother's gray eyes—the gray eyes they shared—swam with emotion, a mix of guilt and fear and suspicion. "The things people always say about princes in our situation."

The fear in Ali's heart unspooled. And then—with a swiftness that took him aback—it turned to anger. To a resentment that Ali hadn't even realized, until this moment, he held tightly clamped, in a place he didn't dare go. "Muntadhir, I'm *cold* because I've spent my entire life at the Citadel training to serve you, sleeping on floors while you slept with courtesans on silken beds. Because I was ripped from my mother's arms *when I was five* so that I might learn to kill people at your command and fight the battles you'd never have to see." Ali took a deep breath, checking the emotions swirling in his chest. "I made a mistake, Dhiru. That's it. I was trying to help the shafit, not start some—"

Muntadhir cut in. "You and your mother's cousin are the only known financiers of the Tanzeem. They were amassing weapons for an unknown purpose, and an unknown Geziri soldier with access to the Citadel stole them zulfiqar training blades. You've yet to arrest anyone, though by the sound of things, you know their leaders." Muntadhir drained his goblet again and turned to Ali. "You tell me, akhi," he implored. "What would you think if you were in my position?"

There was a hint of fear—true fear—in his brother's voice, and it made Ali sick. Had they been alone, he would have thrown himself at Muntadhir's feet. He was tempted to do so anyway, witnesses be damned.

Instead, he grabbed his hand. "Never, Dhiru. *Never.* I would stick a blade in my heart before I raised it to you—I swear to God . . . Akhi . . . ," he begged as Muntadhir scoffed. "*Please.* Just tell me how to fix this. I'll do anything. I'll go to Abba. I'll tell him everything—"

"You're dead if you tell Abba," Muntadhir interrupted. "Forget the assassin. If Abba learns you were at that tavern when two Daevas were murdered, that you've gone all these months without arresting the traitor in the Royal Guard . . . he'll throw you to the karkadann."

"So?" Ali didn't bother to hide the bitterness in his voice. "If you think I'm plotting to betray you all, why not tell him yourself?"

Muntadhir gave him a sharp look. "Do you think I want your death on my conscience? You're still my little brother."

Ali immediately backed down. "Let me talk to Nahri," he offered, remembering the reason he'd originally come here. "Maybe I can convince her to lessen some of her demands."

Muntadhir laughed, a drunken, derisive sound. "I think you and my conniving fiancée have done enough talking—that's one thing I do intend to stop."

The music ended. The Daeva men started to clap, and Darayavahoush said something that made the dancers giggle.

Muntadhir's gaze locked on the Afshin like a cat after a mouse. He cleared his throat, and Ali saw something very dangerous—and very stupid—settle in his face. "You know, I think I'll deal with one of her demands right now." He raised his voice. "Jamshid! Darayavahoush!" he called. "Come. Take some wine with me."

"Dhiru, I don't think this is a good—" Ali abruptly shut up as the Daeva men came within earshot.

"Emir Muntadhir. Prince Alizayd." Darayavahoush inclined his head, bringing his fingers together in the Daeva salute. "May the fires burn brightly for you both on this beautiful evening."

Jamshid looked nervous, and Ali guessed that he'd been around a drunken Muntadhir enough to know when things were about to go very badly. "Greetings, my lords," he said hesitantly.

Muntadhir must have noticed his distress. He snapped his fingers and nodded to the floor cushion at his left. "Be at peace, my friend."

Jamshid sat. Darayavahoush grinned and snapped his fingers. "Just like that?" he asked, adding something in Divasti. Jamshid blushed.

Unlike Ali, however, Muntadhir was fluent in the Daeva language. "I assure you he is no trained dog," Muntadhir said coolly in Djinnistani, ". . . but my dearest friend. Please, Afshin," he said, indicating the spot next to Jamshid. "If you would sit." He beckoned for the wine bearer again. "Wine for my guests. And Prince Alizayd will take whatever you serve children who cannot yet handle drink."

Ali forced a smile, recalling how Darayavahoush had goaded him about his rivalry with Muntadhir while they sparred. There could hardly be a worse time for the Afshin to pick up on any hostility between the Qahtani brothers.

Darayavahoush turned to him. "So what happened to you?"

Ali bristled. "What are you talking about?"

The Afshin nodded at his stomach. "Injury? Illness? You're carrying yourself differently."

Ali blinked, too astonished to reply.

Muntadhir's eyes flashed. Despite their argument, there was a fiercely protective edge in his voice when he spoke. "Watching my brother so closely, Afshin?"

Darayavahoush shrugged. "You are not a warrior, Emir, so I don't expect you to understand. But your brother is. A very good one." He winked at Ali. "Straighten up, boy, and keep your hand away from the wound. You wouldn't want your enemies to observe such weakness."

Muntadhir again beat him to a response. "He is quite recovered, I assure you. Banu Nahri has been at his bedside daily. She is very attached to him."

The Afshin glowered, and Ali—being quite attached to his head as well as to Nahri—quickly spoke up. "I'm sure she's equally devoted to all her patients."

Muntadhir ignored him. "The Banu Nahida is actually the reason I wished to speak to you." He glanced at Jamshid. "There's a governorship available in Zariaspa, yes? I believe I overheard your father saying something about it."

Jamshid looked confused but replied, "I think so."

Muntadhir nodded. "A coveted position. Enviable pension in a beautiful part of Daevastana. Few responsibilities." He took a sip of his wine. "I think it would be a good fit for you, Daraya-vahoush. When we were discussing the wedding yesterday, Banu Nahri seemed worried about your future and—"

"What?" The Afshin's dangerous smile vanished.

"Your future, Afshin. Nahri wants to make sure you're well rewarded for your loyalty."

"Zariaspa is not Daevabad," Darayavahoush snapped. "And what wedding? She's not even past her quarter century. She's not legally permitted to—"

Muntadhir waved one hand, cutting him off. "She came to us yesterday with her own offer." He smiled, an uncharacteristically malicious gleam in his eyes. "I suppose she's eager."

He lingered on the word, imbuing it with more than a hint of vulgarity, and Darayavahoush cracked his knuckles. Ali instinctively reached for his zulfiqar, but his weapon was gone, taken by Khanzada's servants.

Fortunately, the Afshin stayed seated. But the motion of his hand drew Ali's attention, and he startled. Was the Afshin's slave ring . . . glowing? He narrowed his eyes. It appeared so. The emerald shone with the barest of lights, like a flame contained by a grimy glass lamp.

The Afshin didn't seem to notice. "I follow the Banu Nahida in all things," he said, his voice icier than Ali ever thought a man's could be. "No matter how abominable. So I suppose congratulations are in order."

Muntadhir started to open his mouth but thankfully, Khanzada chose that moment to approach.

She perched on the edge of Muntadhir's sofa and draped an elegant arm around his shoulders. "My beloved, with what serious business do you gentlemen mar this beautiful evening?" She stroked his cheek. "Such grumpy faces on all of you. Your inattention insults my girls."

"Forgive us, my lady," the Afshin interjected. "We were discussing the emir's wedding. Surely you will be in attendance?"

Heat rose in his brother's expression, but if Darayavahoush hoped to spark some sort of jealousy-fueled lover's spat, he had underestimated the courtesan's loyalty.

She smiled sweetly. "But of course. I shall dance with his wife." She slid into Muntadhir's lap, her sharp eyes staying on Darayavahoush's face. "Perhaps I can give her some guidance in how to best please him."

The air grew warm. Ali tensed, but the Afshin didn't respond. Instead, he drew in a sharp breath and reached for his head as if overcome by an unexpected migraine.

Khanzada feigned concern. "Are you well, Afshin? If the evening has overtired you, I have rooms where you may rest. Surely I can find you companionship," she added with a cold smile. "Your type is rather apparent."

She'd gone too far—she and Muntadhir both. Darayavahoush snapped back to attention. His green eyes flashed, and he bared his teeth in an almost feral grin.

"Forgive the distraction, my lady," he said. "But that truly is a beautiful image. You must fantasize about it often. And how lovingly detailed . . . right down to the little house in Agnivansha. Red sandstone, yes?" he asked, and Khanzada went pale. "On the banks of the Chambal . . . a swing for two overlooking the river."

The courtesan straightened up with a gasp. "How . . . you can't possibly know that!"

Darayavahoush didn't take his eyes off her. "By the Creator, how *very* much you want it . . . so much so that you'd be willing to run away, to abandon this pretty place and all its riches. You don't think he'd be a good king anyway . . . would it not be better for him to go off with you, to grow old together, reading poetry and drinking wine?"

"What in God's name are you going on about?" Muntadhir snapped as Khanzada jumped up from his lap, embarrassed tears in her eyes.

The Afshin fixed his bright eyes on the emir. "Her wishes, Emir Muntadhir," he said calmly. "Not that you share them. Oh, no . . ." He paused, edging closer, his eyes locked on Muntadhir's face. A delighted grin spread across his face. "Not at *all*, apparently." He looked between Jamshid and Muntadhir and then laughed. "Now *that's* an interesting—"

Muntadhir jumped to his feet.

Ali was between them in an instant.

His brother might not have been Citadel trained, but at some point in his life, someone had clearly taught him how to throw a punch. His fist caught Ali on the chin and knocked him clean off his feet.

Ali landed hard, shattering the table that held their drinks with a crash. The musicians clanged to a noisy stop, and one of the dancers screamed. Several people jumped to their feet. The crowd looked shocked.

Two soldiers had been loitering near the roof's edge, and Ali saw one reach for his zulfiqar before his fellow grabbed his arm. *Of course*, Ali realized. To the rest of the roof, it must have looked like the Emir of Daevabad had just purposefully punched his younger brother in the face. But Ali was also the future Qaid, an officer in the Royal Guard—and it was clear the soldiers weren't sure who to protect. Had Ali been any other man, they'd be dragging him away from their emir before he could respond. That's what they *should* have been doing—and Ali could only pray Muntadhir didn't realize the breach in protocol. Not after the fears his brother had just confessed to having where Ali was concerned.

Jamshid held his hand out. "Are you all right, my prince?"

Ali stifled a gasp as a stab of pain tore through his half-healed dagger wound. "I'm fine," he lied as Jamshid helped him to his feet.

Muntadhir gave him a shocked look. "What the hell were you thinking?"

He took a shaky breath. "That if you struck the Scourge of Qui-zi across the face after publicly insulting his Banu Nahida, he'd rip you into confetti." Ali touched his already swelling jaw. "Not a bad punch," he admitted.

Jamshid scanned the crowd and then touched his brother's wrist. "He's gone, Emir," he warned in a low voice.

Good riddance. Ali shook his head. "What was he talking about anyway? About Khanzada . . . I've never heard of an ex-slave being able to read the wishes of another djinn." He glanced at the courtesan. "What he said—was any of that true?"

She blinked furiously, glaring daggers. But not at him, Ali realized.

At Muntadhir.

"I don't know," she spat. "Why don't you ask your brother?" Without another word, she burst into tears and fled.

Muntadhir swore. "Khanzada, wait!" He rushed after his lover, vanishing into the depths of the house.

Thoroughly confused, Ali looked to Jamshid for some explanation, but the Daeva captain was staring determinedly at the ground, his cheeks strangely flushed.

Putting aside his brother's romantic entanglements, Ali considered his options. He was sorely tempted to rally the soldiers downstairs and have the Afshin found and arrested. But for what?

A drunken argument over a woman? He might as well throw half of Daevabad into prison. The Afshin hadn't struck Muntadhir, hadn't even truly insulted him.

Don't be a fool. Ali's decision settled, he snapped his fingers, trying to get Jamshid's attention. He had no idea why the Daeva captain looked so nervous. "Jamshid? Darayavahoush is staying with your family, yes?"

Jamshid nodded, still avoiding Ali's eyes. "Yes, my prince."

"All right." He clapped Jamshid's shoulder, and the other man jumped. "Go home. If he doesn't return by dawn, alert the Citadel. And if he *does* return, tell him he'll be expected at court tomorrow to discuss what happened here tonight." He paused for a moment, then added reluctantly, "Tell your father. I know Kaveh likes to be kept abreast of all Daeva matters."

"At once, my prince." He sounded eager to be gone.

"And, Jamshid . . ." The other man finally met his eyes. "Thank you."

Jamshid simply nodded and then hurried away. Ali took a deep breath, trying to ignore the pain lancing through him. His dishdasha clung wetly to his abdomen, and when he touched it, his fingers came away bloody. He must have reopened the wound.

He readjusted his outer black robe to cover the blood. Were it still day, he would have discreetly sought out Nahri, but it would be near midnight by the time he got to the infirmary, the Banu Nahida asleep in her bed.

I can't go to her. Ali was lucky he hadn't been caught in Nahri's bedroom the first time. A second was far too risky—especially considering the gossip likely to start circulating around the Qahtanis after tonight. *I'll bind it myself,* he decided, *and wait in the infirmary.* At least that way, if the bleeding got worse, she'd only be a room away. It seemed a reasonable plan.

Then again, most things had lately—right before they blew up in his face.

26

NAHRI

"Nahri. Nahri, *wake up*."

"Mmm?" Nahri lifted her head from the open book upon which she'd fallen asleep. She rubbed away a crease the crumpled page had left on her cheek and blinked sleepily in the dark.

A man stood over her bed, his body outlined in the moonlight.

A hot hand clamped over her mouth before she could scream. He opened his other palm; dancing flames lit his face.

"Dara?" Nahri managed, her voice muffled against his fingers. He dropped his hand, and she drew up in surprise, her blanket falling to her lap. It had to be past midnight; her bedroom was otherwise dark and deserted. "What are you doing here?"

He dropped onto her bed. "What part of 'stay away from the Qahtanis' did you not understand?" Anger simmered in his voice. "Tell me you didn't agree to marry that lecherous sand fly."

Ah. She was wondering when he'd hear about that. "I haven't agreed to anything yet," she countered. "An opportunity presented itself, and I wanted to—"

"An *opportunity*?" Dara's eyes flashed with hurt. "Suleiman's eye, Nahri, for once could you speak like someone with a heart instead of someone peddling stolen goods at the bazaar?"

Her temper sparked. "*I'm* the one without a heart? I asked you to marry me, and you told me to go produce a stable of Nahid children with the richest Daeva man I could find as soon as . . .'" She trailed off, getting a better look at Dara as her eyes adjusted to the darkness. He was dressed in a dark traveling robe, silver bow and arrow-filled quiver slung over his shoulder. A long knife was tucked in his belt.

She cleared her throat, suspecting she was not going to like the answer to her next question. "Why are you dressed like that?"

He stood up, the linen curtains blowing gently in the cool night air behind him. "Because I'm getting you out of here. Out of Daevabad and away from this family of sand flies, away from our corrupted home and its mobs of shafit clamoring for Daeva blood."

Nahri exhaled. "You want to *leave* Daevabad? Are you mad? We risked our lives to get here! This is the safest place from the ifrit, from the marid—"

"It's not the *only* safe place."

She drew back as a vaguely guilty expression crossed his face. She knew that expression. "What?" she demanded. "What are you keeping from me now?"

"I can't—"

"If you say 'I can't tell you,' I swear on my mother's name to stab you with your own knife."

He made an annoyed noise and paced around the edge of her bed like an irritated lion, his hands clasped behind his back, smoke swirling about his feet. "We have allies, Nahri. Both here and outside the city. I said nothing in the temple because I didn't want to raise your hopes—"

"Or let me have a say in my own fate," Nahri cut in. "As usual." Thoroughly annoyed, she flung a pillow at his head, but he easily ducked it. "And *allies*? What is that supposed to mean? Are you plotting with some secret Daeva cabal to steal me away?" She said it sarcastically, but when he flushed and looked away, she gasped. "Wait . . . *are* you plotting with some secret Daeva cabal—"

"We don't have time to get into the details," Dara interrupted. "But I'll tell you everything on the way."

"There's no 'on the way'—I'm not going anywhere with you! I gave my word to the king . . . and my God, Dara, have you heard how these people punish traitors? They let some great horned beast stomp you to death in the arena!"

"That's not going to happen," Dara assured her. He sat beside her again and took her hand. "You don't have to do this, Nahri. I'm not going to let them—"

"*I don't need you to save me!*" Nahri jerked her hand away. "Dara, do you listen to anything I say? *I* started marriage negotiations. *I* went to the king." She threw up her hands. "What are you even saving me from? Becoming the future queen of Daevabad?"

He looked incredulous. "And the price, Nahri?"

Nahri swallowed back the lump that rose in her throat. "You said it yourself: I'm the last Nahid. I'm going to need children." She forced a shrug, but couldn't keep the bitterness entirely out of her voice. "I might as well make the best strategic match."

"'*The best strategic match*,'" Dara repeated. "With a man who doesn't respect you? A family that will always view you with suspicion? *That's* what you want?"

No. But Nahri had made clear her feelings for Dara. He'd rejected them.

And in her heart she knew she was starting to want more in Daevabad than just him.

She took a deep breath, forcing some calm into her voice. "Dara . . . this doesn't have to be a bad thing. I'll be *safe*. I'll have all the time and resources to properly train." Her throat caught. "In another century, there might very well be a Nahid on the throne again." She glanced up at him, her eyes wet despite her best effort to check her tears. "Isn't that what you want?"

Dara stared at her. Nahri could see the emotions warring in his expression, but before he could speak, there was a knock at the door.

"Nahri?" a muffled voice called out.

A familiar voice.

Smoke curled around Dara's collar. "Forgive me," he started in a deadly hush. "Exactly which brother did you agree to marry?"

He was across the room in three strides. Nahri raced after him, throwing herself in front of the door before he could rip it off the hinges. "It's not what you think," she whispered. "I'll get rid of him."

He glowered but stepped back into the shadows. She took a deep breath to calm her racing heart and then opened the door.

Alizayd al Qahtani's smiling face greeted her.

"Peace be upon you," he said in Arabic. "I'm so sorry to . . ." He blinked, taking in the sight of her bedclothes and uncovered hair. He immediately averted his eyes. "I . . . er—"

"It's fine," she said quickly. "What's wrong?"

He'd been holding his left side but opened his black robe now, revealing the bloodstained dishdasha beneath. "I tore some of my stitches," he said apologetically. "I wanted to wait in the infirmary overnight, but I can't get the bleeding to stop and . . ." He frowned. "Is something wrong?" He studied her face, casting aside propriety for a moment. "You—you're shaking."

"I'm fine," she insisted, aware of Dara watching from the other side of the door. Her mind raced. She wanted to tell Ali to run, to yell at him for daring to come to her door unaccompanied— anything to get him safely away—but he did look like he needed help.

"Are you sure?" He took a step closer.

She forced a smile. "I'm sure." She considered the distance between the two of them and the infirmary. Dara would not dare follow her, would he? He could have no idea how many patients rested inside, how many guards waited in the outer corridor.

She nodded at Ali's bloody dishdasha. "That looks awful." She stepped through the door. "Let me—"

Dara called her bluff.

The door was ripped from her hand. Dara reached for her wrist, but a wide-eyed Ali grabbed her first. He pulled her into the infirmary, shoving her behind him, and she landed hard on the stone floor. His zulfiqar burst into flames.

In seconds, the infirmary was in chaos. A spray of arrows fired into the wooden balustrade, following Ali's path as his zulfiqar lit the curtain sectioning off the patient beds on fire. Her birdman shrieked, flapping his feathered arms from atop his bed of sticks. Nahri climbed to her feet, still a little dizzy from the fall.

Ali and Dara were fighting.

No, not fighting. *Fighting* was two drunks brawling in the street. Ali and Dara were *dancing*, the two warriors spinning around each other in a wild blur of fire and metal blades.

Ali leaped onto her desk, as graceful as a cat, using its height to strike Dara from above, but the Afshin ducked away in the nick of time. He smashed his hands together, and the desk burst into flames, collapsing under Ali's weight and tossing the prince to the burning ground. Dara aimed a kick at his head, but Ali rolled away, slashing the backs of Dara's legs as he went.

"Stop!" she cried as Dara hurled one of the desk's burning legs at Ali's head. "Stop it, both of you!"

Ali ducked the chunk of flying debris and then charged the Afshin, bringing the zulfiqar down at his throat.

Nahri gasped, her fears for the men abruptly reversing. "No! Dara, watch—" The warning wasn't out of her mouth before

Dara's ring blazed with emerald light. Ali's zulfiqar shuddered and dimmed, the copper blade twisting and then *wriggling*. It let out an angry hiss, melting into the shape of a fiery viper. Ali startled, dropping the snake as it reeled back to snap at him.

Dara didn't hesitate. He grabbed the djinn prince by the throat and slammed him into one of the marble columns. The entire room shook. Ali kicked him, and Dara smashed him into the column again. Black blood dripped down his face. Dara tightened his grip, and Ali gasped, clawing at Dara's wrists as the Afshin strangled him.

Nahri raced across the room. "Let him go!" She grabbed Dara's arm and tried to wrest him off, but it was like fighting a statue. "Please, Dara!" she screamed as Ali's eyes darkened. "I beg you!"

He dropped the prince.

Ali crumpled to the ground. He was a wreck, his eyes dazed, blood dripping down his face, more blossoming through his dishdasha. For once, Nahri didn't hesitate. She dropped to her knees, knocked his turban away, and ripped the neckline of his dishdasha to the waist. She pressed a hand against each wound and closed her eyes.

Heal, she commanded. The blood instantly clotted beneath her fingers, the skin smoothing into place. She hadn't even realized how immediate, how extraordinary it was until Ali groaned and started coughing for air.

"Are you okay?" she asked urgently. From across the room, she was aware of Dara staring at them.

Ali managed a nod, spitting a stream of blood. "Did . . . did he hurt you?" he wheezed.

By the Most High, is that what he thought he was interrupting? She pressed one of his hands. "No," she assured him. "Of course not. I'm fine."

"Nahri, we need to go," Dara warned in a low voice. "Now."

Ali looked between them, and shock bloomed in his face. "You're *running away with him*? But you . . . you told my father—"

There was a loud knock on the door leading to the outer corridor. "Banu Nahida?" a muffled male voice called. "Is everything all right?"

Ali straightened up. "No!" he boomed. "It's the Af—"

Nahri clapped her hand over his mouth. Ali jerked back, looking betrayed.

But it was too late. The banging on the door grew louder. "Prince Alizayd!" the voice shouted. "Is that you?"

Dara swore and rushed to the door to lay his hands on the door pulls. The silver instantly melted, winding across the doors in a lacelike pattern to lock them together.

But Nahri doubted it would keep anyone out for long. *He has to go*, she realized, something breaking in her heart.

And though she knew he had no one to blame but himself, Nahri still choked on the words. "Dara, you need to go. Run. Please. If you stay in Daevabad, the king will kill you."

"I know." He snatched Ali's zulfiqar as the coppery snake tried to slither past, and it instantly re-formed in his hands. He crossed to her desk and emptied a glass cylinder containing some of her instruments. He rifled through the random tools and plucked out a bolt of iron. It melted in his hands.

Nahri stilled. Even she knew he shouldn't have been able to do that.

But Dara barely winced as he reshaped the soft iron into a skinny length of rope. "What are you doing?" she demanded as he bent and yanked Ali's hands away from hers. He wrapped the soft metal around the prince's wrists, and it instantly hardened. The banging outside grew louder, smoke seeping under the door.

Dara beckoned to her. "Come."

"I already told you: I'm not leaving Daevabad—"

Dara pressed the zulfiqar to Ali's throat. "You are," he said, his voice quietly firm.

Nahri went cold. She met Dara's eyes, praying she was wrong, praying that the man she trusted above all others was not really forcing this choice upon her.

But in his face—his beautiful face—she saw intent. A little regret, but intent.

Ali chose that particularly ill-advised moment to open his mouth. "Go to hell, you child-murdering, warmongering—"

Dara's eyes flashed. He pressed the zulfiqar harder against Ali's throat.

"Stop," Nahri said. "I . . ." She swallowed. "I'll go. Don't hurt him."

Dara moved the zulfiqar away from the prince, looking relieved. "Thank you." He jerked his head at Ali. "Watch him a moment." He quickly crossed the room, heading toward the wall behind her desk.

Nahri felt numb. She sat beside Ali, not trusting her legs.

He stared at her with open bewilderment. "I'm not sure whether to thank you for just saving my life or accuse you of betrayal."

Nahri sucked in her breath. "I'll let you know when I figure it out."

Ali dared a glance at Dara and then lowered his voice. "We're not going to get away," he warned, his worried eyes meeting hers. "And if my father thinks you're responsible . . . Nahri, you gave him your word."

A heavy grinding sound interrupted them. Nahri looked up to see Dara painstakingly pulling apart the stone wall along its decorative edges, smoke and bright white flames licking at his hands. He stopped once the gap was large enough to squeeze through.

"Let's go." Dara grabbed Ali by the back of his robe and dragged him along, pushing him through first. The prince fell hard, to his knees.

Nahri flinched. She couldn't tell herself that Ali was just a mark anymore; he'd become a friend, there was no denying it. And he was a kid in comparison to Dara, decent-hearted and kind, whatever his faults.

"Give me your robe," she said curtly as Dara turned back to her. Nahri hadn't had time to dress, and she would be damned if she was going to be dragged through Daevabad in her bedclothes.

He handed it over. "Nahri, I . . . I'm sorry," he said in Divasti. She knew his words were sincere, but they didn't help. "I'm just trying to—"

"I know what you're trying to do," she rebuked him, her tone sharp. "And I'm telling *you*: I'll never forgive you if something happens to him—and I'll never forget what you did here tonight."

She didn't wait for a response; she didn't expect one. Instead, she stepped through the gap. She got one last glimpse of her infirmary, and then the wall sealed behind her.

THEY WALKED FOR WHAT FELT LIKE HOURS.

The narrow passageway Dara led them through was so tight that they had to literally squeeze through at points, scraping their shoulders on the rough stone walls. Its ceiling soared and dipped, rising to towering heights before plunging so low they were forced to crawl.

Dara had conjured up small fireballs that danced overhead as they journeyed through the otherwise pitch-black tunnel. No one spoke. Dara seemed intensely focused on sustaining whatever magic held the passage open while Ali drew increasingly ragged breaths. Despite being healed, the prince didn't look well. Nahri could hear his heart racing, and he kept bumping into the close walls like a dizzy drunk.

He finally stumbled to the ground, crashing hard into the backs of Dara's legs. The Afshin swore and turned around.

Nahri swiftly stepped between them. "Leave him alone." She helped Ali to his feet. He was sweating ash and seemed to have trouble focusing on her face. "Are you okay?"

He blinked and swayed slightly. "Just having some issues with the air."

"The air?" She frowned. The tunnel smelled a bit stale for sure, but she could breathe just fine.

"It's because you do not belong here," Dara said darkly. "This is not your city, not your palace. The walls know that even if you Geziri dogs do not."

Nahri glared at him. "Then let's hurry."

As they walked, the tunnel widened and grew steep, eventually shifting into a long set of crumbling steps. She braced herself against the wall, flinching when it turned damp beneath her hands. In front of her, she heard Ali take a deep breath of the humid air. As the stairs grew slippery with moisture, she would swear his steps looked surer.

Dara stopped. "It's flooded ahead."

The flames above their heads brightened. The steps ended in a pool of still black water that smelled as vile as it looked. She drew to a stop at the edge, watching the flickering lights reflect on the water's oily surface.

"Afraid of a little water?" Ali pushed past Dara and strode confidently into the dark pool, stopping when it reached his waist. He turned back. His ebony robe melted so easily into the black water that it looked like the liquid itself was draped over his shoulders. "Worried the marid will get you?"

"At home in there, aren't you, little crocodile?" Dara mocked. "Does it remind you of Ta Ntry's fetid swamps?"

Ali shrugged. "Sand fly, dog, crocodile . . . Are you just

working your way through the animals you can name? How many can be left? Five? Six?"

Dara's eyes flashed, and then he did something Nahri had never seen him do.

He stepped into the water.

Dara raised his hands, and the water *fled*, rushing over rocks and dashing through crevices. The drops that didn't make it sizzled underfoot as he passed through.

Nahri's mouth fell open. His ring was glowing, a bright green light, like the sun shining upon a wet leaf. She thought back to what he'd done to the shedu, to Ali's zulfiqar, to the iron bindings.

And suddenly she wondered just how many secrets Dara was holding back from her. Their kiss in the cave seemed very long ago.

The Afshin shoved a visibly shocked Ali forward. "Keep walking, djinn, and watch your mouth. It would greatly upset the Banu Nahida if I cut out your tongue."

Nahri quickly caught up to Ali.

"So his very presence boils water now?" Ali whispered, giving Dara's back a nervous look. "What manner of horrors is that?"

I have no idea. "Maybe it's just part of being a slave," she said weakly.

"I've known freed slaves. They don't have that kind of power. He probably went the way of the ifrit and gave himself over to demons long ago." He grimaced and looked down at her, lowering his voice even further. "Please, in the name of the Most High, tell me you don't truly intend to go off with him."

"You do remember the zulfiqar at your throat?"

"I will throw myself in the lake before I let that monster use my life to steal yours." He shook his head. "I should have just given you that book in the garden. I should have told you about the cities he destroyed, the innocents he murdered . . . you'd have stuck a knife in his back yourself."

Nahri recoiled. "I would never." She knew Dara had a bloody past, but surely Ali exaggerated. "It was a war—a war *your* people started. Dara was only defending our tribe."

"Is that what he told you?" Ali drew in his breath. "*Defending* . . . Nahri, do you know why people call him the Scourge?"

Something very cold crept down her spine, but she pushed it away. "I don't. But might I remind you that you were the one who came to me the other night covered in another man's blood," she pointed out. "Dara's hardly the only one keeping secrets."

Ali abruptly stopped. "You're right." He turned to her, his expression resolved. "It was the blood of a shafit assassin. I killed him. He was a member of a political group called the Tanzeem. They advocate—sometimes violently—for the rights of the shafit and are considered criminals and traitors. I was their primary benefactor. My father found out and ordered me to befriend you and convince you to marry my brother as penance." He raised his dark eyebrows, blood crusted at his hairline. "There. Now you know."

Nahri blinked, taking it all in. She had known Ali had his own agenda, the same as she did—but it stung to hear it laid out so plainly. "The interest in my country, in improving your Arabic . . . I take it that was all pretense?"

"No, it wasn't. I swear. However our friendship started, however I felt about your family . . ." Ali looked embarrassed. "It's been a dark few months. My time with you . . . it was a light."

Nahri looked away; she had to, she could not bear the sincerity in his face. She caught sight of his bloody wrists still bound in iron. *He survives this*, she swore to herself. *No matter what.*

Even if it meant running off with Dara.

They kept walking, Ali throwing the occasional hostile glance at Dara's back. "Perhaps now it's your turn."

"What do you mean?"

"Rather adept at picking locks and negotiating contracts for a maidservant, aren't you?"

She kicked at the ground, sending a few pebbles flying. "I'm not sure you'd still think of me as a light if I told you about my background."

"Nahri," Dara called out, interrupting their quiet conversation.

The cavern had ended. They joined Dara at a rocky ledge overlooking a low drop to a narrow sandy beach that surrounded a still lagoon. In the distance, she could see stars through a slice of sky. The lagoon was strangely luminous, the water a coppery blue that shimmered as if under a tropical sun.

Dara helped her onto the beach and handed her his knife as he dragged Ali down to join them. "I'll need your blood," he said, sounding apologetic. "Just a bit on the blade."

Nahri ran the knife over her palm, getting only a few drops before her skin stitched together. Dara took the knife back and whispered a prayer under his breath. The crimson blood burst into flames as it dripped off the blade.

The lagoon began to churn, a great sucking sound coming from its pit as the water rushed away, and something metallic rose in its center. As Nahri watched, an elegant copper boat burst from the pool's surface, beads of water skittering off its glimmering hull. It was fairly small, probably built to hold no more than a dozen passengers. There was no sail to be seen, but it looked fast, its stern tapering to a sharp point.

Nahri stepped forward, transfixed by the beautiful boat. "Has this been here all this time?"

Dara nodded. "Since before the city fell. The Qahtani siege was so brutal that no one had a chance to escape." He shoved Ali into the shallows. "Climb aboard, sand fly."

Nahri went to follow, but Dara caught her wrist. "I'll let him go," he said quietly in Divasti. "I promise. There are supplies waiting for us on the other side of the lake, a carpet, provisions, weapons. I'll leave him on the beach unharmed, and we'll fly away."

His words only worsened her feeling of betrayal. "I'm glad to know we'll be well-provisioned when the ifrit murder us."

She tried to pull away, but Dara held her tight. "The ifrit aren't going to murder us, Nahri," he assured her. "Things are different now. You'll be safe."

Nahri frowned. "What do you mean?"

In the distance, there came the sound of a shout, followed by an inaudible command. The voices were far, belonging to men still unseen, but Nahri knew how quickly the djinn could move.

Dara released her wrist. "I'll tell you when we're out of the city. I'll tell you everything you want to know. I should have before." He touched her cheek. "We'll get past this."

I don't know about that. But she let him help her onto the boat. Dara retrieved a copper pole that ran down the center of the deck. He jabbed it into the sandy bank, and they were off.

The boat slipped past the cavern's edge with a sizzle. When she glanced back, the rocky face appeared smooth and unblemished. She spotted the docks in the distance, swarmed by tiny figures with flickering torches and gleaming blades.

Ali gazed at the soldiers as the boat raced through the still water toward the dark mountains.

Nahri edged closer to him. "What you told me about your agreement with your father—do you think he'll punish you if I leave?"

Ali dropped his gaze. "It doesn't matter." She watched him tick off his knuckles—praying, counting, maybe just a nervous gesture. He looked miserable.

The words were out of her mouth before she could think better of them. "Come with us."

Ali stilled.

Stupidly, Nahri pressed on, keeping her voice low. "You might as well escape what comes next. Cross the Gozan with us and then go see that human world you're so fascinated with. Go pray in Mecca, study with the scholars of Timbuktu . . ." She swallowed, emotion stealing into her voice. "I have an old friend in Cairo. He could probably use a new business partner."

Ali kept his gaze on his hands. "You really mean that, don't you?" he asked, his voice oddly hollow.

"I do."

He briefly squeezed his eyes shut. "Oh, Nahri . . . I'm so sorry." He turned to look at her, guilt radiating from every line in his face.

Nahri backed away. "No," she whispered. "What have you—" The air flashed around her, and the words caught in her throat. She clutched the ship's railing and held her breath through the smothering embrace of the lake's veil. As with her first crossing, it lasted only a moment, and then the world readjusted. The dark mountains, the star-dappled sky . . .

The dozen or so warships loaded with soldiers.

They nearly crashed right into the closest one, a hulking wooden trireme that sat heavy in the water. The small copper boat slid by and smashed a few oars, but the men onboard were ready. The deck was loaded with archers, their bows drawn, while other soldiers threw down chains of spiked anchors to snag their vessel. One of the archers let loose a single flaming arrow high in the sky. A signal.

Ali climbed awkwardly to his feet. "My ancestors found the copper boat shortly after the revolution," he explained. "No one could raise it, so it stayed. And we learned how to conceal things on the other side of the veil centuries ago." He lowered his voice. "I'm sorry, Nahri, I really am."

She heard Dara snarl. He was on the other end of the boat

but drew his bow in the blink of an eye, aiming an arrow at Ali's throat. Nahri couldn't imagine what he was thinking. They were completely outnumbered.

"Afshin!" Jamshid appeared at the warship's edge. "Don't be a fool. Lower your weapon."

Dara didn't move, and the soldiers fanned out as if preparing to board. Nahri raised her hands.

"Zaydi!" There was a shout from the ship as Muntadhir pushed through the line of soldiers. He took in the sight of his bloodied brother in irons, an arrow aimed at his throat. Hatred twisted his handsome face, and he lunged forward. "You bastard!"

Jamshid grabbed him. "Muntadhir, don't!"

Dara gave Muntadhir an incredulous look. "What are *you* doing aboard a warship? Are the ballasts filled with wine?"

Muntadhir let out an angry hiss. "Wait until my father arrives. We'll see how bravely you talk then."

Dara laughed. *"Wait for my baba.* The anthem of every Geziri hero."

Muntadhir's eyes flashed. He glanced back, seeming to judge how far the other ships were and then gestured angrily at the archers. "Why are your arrows pointed at him? Target the girl and see how fast the great Scourge surrenders."

The smile vanished from Dara's face. "Do that, and I will kill every last one of you."

Ali immediately stepped in front of her. "She's as innocent as I am, Dhiru." She saw him glance at the other ships as well, seeming to make the same calculation as his brother.

And then it hit her. Of course they wanted to wait for Ghassan; Dara was completely defenseless in the face of Suleiman's seal. If they delayed until the king arrived, he was doomed.

He did this to himself. Nahri knew that. But her mind flashed back to their journey, to the sorrow that constantly haunted him, his anguish when he talked about his family's fate, the bloody memories of his time as a slave. He'd spent his life fighting for the Daevas against the Qahtanis. It was no small wonder he was desperate to save her from what must seem the worst possible fate.

And God, the thought of him in irons, dragged before the king, executed in front of a jeering crowd of djinn . . .

No. *Never*. She turned, a sudden heat in her chest. "Let him go," she begged. "Please. Let him leave, and I'll stay here. I'll marry your brother. I'll do whatever your family wants."

Ali hesitated. "Nahri . . ."

"Please." She grabbed his hand, willing the reluctance in his eyes to vanish. She couldn't let Dara die. The thought alone broke her heart. "I beg you. That's all I want," she added, and at the moment, it was true, her only desire in the world. "I only wish for him to live."

There was a moment of strange stillness on the ship. The air grew uncomfortably hot, the way it might at an approaching monsoon.

Dara let out a choked gasp. Nahri whirled around in time to see him stumble. His bow dipped in his hands as he frantically tried to catch his breath.

Horrified, she lurched toward him. Ali grabbed her arm as Dara's ring suddenly blazed.

When he looked up, Nahri stifled a cry. Though Dara's gaze was focused on her, there was no recognition in his bright eyes. There was *nothing* familiar in his face: his expression was wilder than it had been at Hierapolis, the look of something hunted and hurt.

He whirled on the soldiers. He snarled, and his bow doubled in size. The quiver transformed as well, growing flush with a variety of arrows that vied to outdo each other in savagery. The one he held notched ended in an iron crescent, its shaft studded with barbs.

Nahri went cold. She remembered her last words. The intent

behind them. She couldn't have truly—could she? "Dara, *wait!* Don't!"

"Shoot him!" Muntadhir screamed.

Ali shoved her down. They hit the deck hard, but nothing whizzed over their heads. She looked up.

The soldiers' arrows had frozen in midair.

Nahri strongly suspected King Ghassan was going to be too late.

Dara snapped his fingers, and the arrows abruptly reversed direction to flit through the air and cut through their owners. His own swiftly joined them, his hands moving so fast between the quiver and bow that she couldn't follow the motion with her eyes. When the archers fell back under the onslaught, Dara snatched up Ali's zulfiqar.

His bright gaze locked on Muntadhir, and his mad eyes flashed with recognition. "*Zaydi al Qahtani,*" he declared. He spat. "*Traitor.* I've waited a long time to make you pay for what you did to my people."

Dara had no sooner made his lunatic assertion than he charged the ship. The wooden railing burst into flames at his touch, and he vanished into the black smoke. She could hear men screaming.

, "Free me," Ali begged, thrusting his wrists into her lap. "Please!"

"I don't know how!"

The body—sans head—of an Agnivanshi officer landed beside them with a thud, and Nahri shrieked. Ali pushed awkwardly to his feet.

She grabbed his arm. "Are you mad? What are you possibly going to do like that?" she asked, gesturing to his bound wrists.

He shook her off. "My brother's over there!"

"Ali!" But the prince was already gone, disappearing into the same black smoke as Dara.

She recoiled. What in God's name had just happened to Dara? Nahri had spent weeks at his side—surely she had wished for things out loud without . . . well, whatever it was she had just done.

He's going to kill everyone on that boat. Ghassan would arrive to find his sons murdered, and then he'd hunt them to the ends of the earth, hang them in the midan, and their tribes would go to war for a century.

She couldn't let that happen. "God preserve me," she whispered, and then she did the most un-Nahri-like thing she could imagine.

She ran into danger.

Nahri boarded the ship, climbing up the broken oars and anchor chains, while trying very hard not to look at the cursed water gleaming below. She'd never forgotten what Dara told her about it shredding djinn flesh.

But the carnage on the trireme put the deadly lake out of mind. Fire licked down the wooden deck and crept up the rigging for the black sail. The line of archers lay where they'd fallen, pierced with dozens of arrows. One screamed for his mother as he clutched his ruined stomach. Nahri hesitated but knew she had no time to waste. She picked over the bodies, coughing and waving smoke away from her face as she stumbled over a stack of bloody oilcloth.

She heard screams from across the ship and spied Ali racing ahead. The smoke briefly dissipated, and then she saw him.

It was suddenly clear why—over a thousand years later—Dara's name still provoked terror among the djinn. His bow slung on his back, he had Ali's zulfiqar in one hand and a stolen khanjar in the other and was using them to make quick work of the soldiers remaining around Muntadhir. He moved less like a man and more like some raging war god of the long-ago era in which he'd been born. Even his body was illuminated, seemingly on fire just below the skin.

Like the ifrit, Nahri recognized in horror, suddenly unsure of just who or what Dara truly was. He shoved the zulfiqar into the throat of the last guard between him and Muntadhir and yanked it out bloody.

Not that the emir noticed. Muntadhir sat on the bloody deck with the arrow-riddled body of a soldier cradled in his arms. "Jamshid!" he screamed. "No! God, no—look at me, please!"

Dara raised the zulfiqar. Nahri drew to a stop, opening her mouth to shout.

Ali threw himself on the Afshin.

She'd barely noticed the prince, awestruck by the horrible sight of Dara doing death's work. But he was suddenly there, taking advantage of his height to jump on Dara's back and loop his bound wrists around the Afshin's neck like a noose. He drew up his legs, and Dara staggered under the sudden weight. Ali kicked the zulfiqar out of his hands.

"Muntadhir!" he screamed, adding something in Geziriyya that she couldn't understand. The zulfiqar had landed barely a body's length away from the emir's feet. Muntadhir didn't look up; he didn't even seem to have heard his brother's cry. Nahri ran, picking over bodies as quickly as she could.

Dara let out an aggravated sound as he tried to shake the prince loose. Ali pulled up his hands, pressing the iron bindings tight against the Afshin's throat. Dara gasped but managed to elbow the prince in the stomach and slam his back hard into the ship's mast.

Ali didn't let go. "Akhi!"

Muntadhir startled and looked up. In a second he had dived for the zulfiqar, at the same time Dara finally succeeded in throwing Ali over his head. He grabbed his bow.

The young prince hit the wet deck hard and slid to the boat's edge. He scrambled to his feet. "Munta—"

Dara shot him through the throat.

27

NAHRI

Nahri screamed and rushed forward as a second arrow went through Ali's chest. The prince staggered back, and his heel caught against the edge of the boat, throwing him off balance.

"Ali!" Muntadhir lunged for his brother but wasn't fast enough. Ali toppled into the lake with barely a splash. There was a large gulp, like the sound of a heavy rock landing in a still pool, and then silence.

Nahri ran to the railing, but Ali was gone, the only sign of his presence a ripple in the dark water. Muntadhir dropped to his knees with a wail.

Her eyes welled with tears. She spun on Dara. "Save him!" she cried. "I wish for you to bring him back!"

Dara swooned, staggering at her command, but Ali didn't reappear. Instead Dara blinked, and the brightness left his eyes. His confused gaze wandered the bloody deck. He dropped the bow, looking unsteady. "Nahri, I—"

Muntadhir jumped to his feet and snatched up the zulfiqar. "I'll kill you!" Flames swirled up the blade as he charged the Afshin.

Dara parried the other man away with his khanjar as easily as he might have swatted a gnat. He blocked another of Muntadhir's attempts and then casually ducked the third, elbowing the emir hard in the face. Muntadhir cried out; a spray of black blood spouted from his nose. Nahri didn't need to be a swordsman to see how clumsily he moved in comparison with the deadly swift Afshin. Their blades clashed again, and Dara shoved him away.

But then Dara stepped back. "Enough, al Qahtani. Your father doesn't need to lose a second son tonight."

Muntadhir didn't look particularly desirous of Dara's mercy— nor capable of being reasoned with. "Fuck you!" he sobbed, slashing wildly with the zulfiqar as blood ran down his face. Dara moved to defend himself. "Fuck you and your sister-fucking Nahids. I hope you all burn in hell!"

Nahri couldn't judge his grief. She stood frozen at the edge of the boat, her heart breaking as she stared at the still water. Was Ali already dead? Or was he being torn apart right now, his screams silenced by the black water?

More soldiers poured from the ship's hold, some holding broken oars like batons. The sight stirred her from her grief, and she climbed to her feet, her legs shaking. "Dara . . ."

He glanced up and abruptly raised his left hand. The ship cracked, a wall of splintered wood rising twice her height to separate them from the soldiers.

Muntadhir swung the zulfiqar at Dara again, but the Afshin was ready. He hooked his khanjar in the forked sword's tip and twisted it from Muntadhir's hands. The zulfiqar went skittering across the deck, and Dara kicked the emir in the chest, sending him sprawling.

"I'm sparing your life," he snapped. "Take it, you fool." He turned around and walked away, heading in her direction.

"That's right . . . run, you coward!" Muntadhir shot back. "That's what you do best, isn't it? Run away and let the rest of your tribe pay for your actions!"

Dara slowed.

Nahri watched Muntadhir's grief-stricken eyes trail the deck, taking in Jamshid's arrow-riddled body and the spot where his brother had been shot. A look of pure anguish, of *spite*—ragged and unthinking—filled his face.

He stood up. "Ali told me, you know, what happened to your kin when Daevabad fell. What happened when the Tukharistanis broke into the Daeva Quarter looking for *you*, looking for vengeance, and found only your family." Muntadhir's face twisted in hate. "Where were you, Afshin, when they screamed for you? Where were you when they carved the names of the Qui-zi dead into your sister's body? She was only a child, wasn't she? Long names, those Tukharistanis," he added savagely. "I bet they were only able to fit a few before—"

Dara screamed. He was on Muntadhir in less than a second, striking the emir so hard across the face that a bloody tooth flew from his mouth. The khanjar smoked in his other hand, and as he raised it, it transformed, the blade turning dull and splitting into a dozen or so leather strands studded with iron.

A whip.

"You want me to be the Scourge?" Dara shrieked as he lashed Muntadhir. The emir cried out and raised his arms to protect his face. "Will that please your filthy people? To make me into a monster yet again?"

Nahri's mouth fell open in horror. *Do you know why people call him the Scourge?* she heard the dead prince ask.

Dara brought the whip down again, ripping a strip of flesh

from Muntadhir's forearms. Nahri wanted to flee. This was not the Dara she knew, the one who taught her to ride a horse and slept by her side.

But she didn't flee. Instead, acting on a crazy impulse, she jumped to her feet and grabbed his wrist as he raised the whip again. He whirled around, his face wild with grief.

Her heart thudded. "*Stop*, Dara. Enough."

He swallowed, his hand trembling under her own. "It's not enough. It won't ever be. They destroy everything. They murdered my family, my leaders. They eviscerated my tribe." His voice broke. "And after everything, after they take Daevabad, after they turn me into a monster, they want *you*." His voice choked on the last word, and he raised the whip. "I will flay him until he's bloody dust."

She tightened her grip on his arm and stepped between him and Muntadhir. "They haven't taken me. I'm right here."

His shoulders dropped, and he bowed his head. "They have. You won't forgive me the boy."

"I . . ." Nahri hesitated, glancing at the spot where Ali had gone over. Her stomach turned, but she pressed her mouth in a firm line. "It doesn't matter right now," she said, hating the words as she spoke them. She nodded at the approaching ships. "Can you make it to shore before they get here?"

"I won't leave you."

She pressed the hand holding the whip. "I'm not asking you to." Dara glanced down, his bright eyes meeting her own. She took the whip from him. "But you need to let this go. Let it be enough."

He took a deep breath, and Muntadhir let out a groan as he curled in on himself. The hate returned to Dara's face.

"No." Nahri took his face in her hands and forced him to look in her eyes. "Come with me. We'll leave, travel the world." It was obvious there was no going back to what they'd had before. But she'd have said anything to get him to stop.

Dara nodded, his bright eyes wet. She tossed the whip in the lake and took his hand. She had just started to lead him away when Muntadhir stammered behind them, a strange mix of hope and alarm in his voice.

"Z-Zaydi?"

Nahri spun around. She gasped, and Dara threw a protective arm in front of her as the flicker of relief died in her chest.

Because the thing that was climbing up onto the boat was definitely not Alizayd al Qahtani.

THE YOUNG PRINCE STEPPED INTO THE FIRELIGHT and swayed like one not accustomed to land. He blinked, a slow reptilian movement, and she saw that his eyes had gone completely black, even the whites vanished under an oily dark cover. His face was gray, and his blue lips moved in a silent whisper.

Ali stepped forward and mechanically scanned the ship. His clothes were shredded, and water streamed from his body like a sieve, pouring from his eyes, ears, and mouth. It bubbled up from under his skin and dripped from his fingertips. He took another jerky step toward them, and in the improved light, Nahri could see his body, encrusted with all manner of lake debris. The arrows and iron shackles were gone; instead, waterweeds and disembodied tentacles tightly wrapped his limbs. Shells, shimmering scales, and razor-sharp teeth were embedded in his skin.

Muntadhir slowly stood up. The blood drained from his face. "Oh, my God. Alizayd . . ." He took a step closer.

"I wouldn't do that, sand fly." Dara was pale as well. He pushed Nahri behind him and reached for his bow.

Ali jerked to attention at the sound of Dara's voice. He sniffed the air and then turned on them. Water puddled at his feet. He'd been whispering since he climbed aboard, but as he drew nearer, she suddenly understood the words, muttered in a language unlike anything she'd ever heard. A flowing language that rushed and slithered and swam over his lips.

Kill the daeva.

Except of course it wasn't "daeva" he used, but rather a sound Nahri knew she could never reproduce, the syllables full of hate and pure . . . *opposition.* As if this other thing, this *daeva*, had no right to exist, no right to sully the waters of the world with smoke and flames and fiery death.

From behind his wet robe, Ali drew an enormous scimitar. The blade was green and mottled with rust, looking like something the lake had swallowed centuries ago. In the firelight, she saw a bloody symbol roughly carved high upon his left cheek.

"Run!" Dara cried. He shot Ali, and the arrow dissolved upon contact. He grabbed the zulfiqar and rushed the prince.

The symbol blazed bright on Ali's cheek. A wave of pressure burst through the air, and the entire ship shook. Nahri flew back into a stack of wooden crates. A jagged piece of wood sliced deep into her shoulder. It burned as she sat up, a wave of weakness and nausea sweeping over her.

Her powers were gone. And then she realized what must have been carved into Ali's cheek.

Suleiman's seal.

Dara.

"No!" Nahri climbed to her feet. In the center of the ship, Dara had fallen to his knees just like he had when Ghassan used the seal to reveal her identity. He looked up to see the thing that was Ali towering over him, raising the rusted blade over his head. He attempted to defend himself with the zulfiqar, but even Nahri could see that his movements were slowed.

Ali knocked it away with enough force to send the blade flying into the lake and then raised the rusty scimitar again. He started to bring it down toward Dara's neck, and Nahri screamed. Ali hesitated. She took a breath.

He changed direction, slashing down, cutting clean through Dara's left wrist and severing his hand.

Separating the ring.

Dara didn't make a sound as he fell. She could swear he seemed to look past Ali, to gaze upon her one final time, but she wasn't certain. It was hard to see his face; he'd grown as dim as smoke, and there was some woman screaming in her ear.

But then Dara grew still—too still—and crumbled to ash before her eyes.

28

ALI

Ali knew he was dying when he crashed through the lake's placid surface.

The icy water sucked him down and attacked him like a rabid animal, shredding his clothes and tearing at his skin. It scrabbled at his mouth and surged up his nose. A white-hot heat burst inside his head.

He screamed into the water. There was something *there*, an alien presence rooting through his mind, sifting through his memories like a bored student flipping through a book. His mother singing a Ntaran lullaby, the hilt of a zulfiqar in his hands for the first time, Nahri's laughter in the library, Darayavahoush raising his bow . . .

Everything stopped.

There was a hiss in his ear. *HE IS HERE?* the lake itself seemed to demand. The turbulent water stilled, and there was a warm press at his throat and chest as the arrows dissolved.

The relief was temporary. Before Ali could even think about kicking for the surface, something snaked around his left ankle and yanked him down.

He squirmed as waterweeds wrapped his body, the roots digging into his flesh. The images in his mind flashed faster as the lake devoured his memories of Darayavahoush: their duel, the way he'd looked upon Nahri in the infirmary, the fiery light that filled his ring as he charged the ship.

Words burst into his mind again. *TELL ME YOUR NAME.*

Ali's lungs burned. Two clams were trying to burrow into his stomach and a pair of toothy jaws clamped down on his shoulder. *Please*, he begged. *Just let me die.*

Your name, Alu-baba. The lake crooned the words in his mother's voice this time, a baby name he'd not heard in years. *Give your name or see what shall pass.*

The image of the hated Afshin was swept away to be replaced by Daevabad. Or what was once Daevabad and was now little more than a burning ruin, surrounded by an evaporated lake and filled with the ash of its people. His father lay slaughtered on the marble steps of the wrecked royal court, and Muntadhir hung from a smashed window screen. The Citadel collapsed, burying alive Wajed and all the soldiers with whom he'd grown up. The city burned; houses burst into flames and children screamed.

No! Ali writhed in the lake's grip, but there was no way to stop the awful visions.

Skeletally thin gray beings with vibrant wings bowed down in obedience. Rivers and lakes dried up, their towns overtaken by fire and dust while a land he recognized as Am Gezira was swept away by a poisonous sea. A lonely palace grew from Daevabad's ashes, spun from fired glass and molten metals. He saw Nahri. Her face was veiled in Nahid white, but her dark eyes were visible and filled with despair. A shadow fell over her, the shape of a man.

Darayavahoush. But with black eyes and a scar across his young face, lacking the handsome grace of a slave. Then his eyes were green again and older, his familiar smug smile briefly returning. His skin flared with fiery light, and his hands turned to coal. His eyes were golden now and utterly alien.

Look. The visions started to repeat, lingering on the images of his murdered family. Muntadhir's dead eyes snapped open. *Say your name, akhi,* his brother begged. *Please!*

Ali's mind spun. His lungs were empty, the water thick with his blood. His body was shutting down, a fuzzy blackness encroaching on the bloody visions.

NO, the lake hissed, desperate. *NOT YET.* It shook him hard, and the images grew more vicious. His mother brutalized, given over to hungry crocodiles with the rest of the Ayaanle while a crowd of Daevas cheered. The shafit, rounded up and set on fire in the midan. Their screams filled the air, the scent of crackling flesh making him gag. Muntadhir pushed to his knees and beheaded before the yellow eyes of a jeering group of ifrit. A mass of unknown soldiers pulling Zaynab from her bed and ripping her clothes . . .

No! Oh God, no. Stop this!

Save her, his father's voice demanded. *Save us all.* The iron bindings grew weak with rust and then burst apart. Something metallic was pressed into his hand. A hilt.

A pair of bloody hands wrapped around his sister's throat. Zaynab's terrified gaze locked on his. *Brother, please!* she screamed.

Ali broke.

Had he been less certain of his imminent death or had he been raised in the outer provinces where one was taught never to speak their true name, to guard it as they did their very soul, he might have hesitated, the request immediately understood for what it was. But assaulted by the images of his brutalized family and city, he didn't care why the lake wanted what it must have already learned from his memories.

"Alizayd!" he screamed, the water muffling his words. "Alizayd al Qahtani!"

The pain vanished. His fingers closed around the hilt without him willing them to do so. His body suddenly felt distant. He was barely aware of being released, of being pushed through the water.

Kill the daeva.

Ali broke through the lake's surface but did not gasp for breath; he did not need it. He climbed up the ship's hull like a crab and then stood, water streaming from his clothes, his mouth, his eyes.

Kill the daeva. He heard the daeva speak. The air was wrong, empty and dry. He blinked, and something burned on his cheek. The world grew quieter, gray.

The daeva was before him. Part of his mind registered shock in the other man's green eyes as he raised a blade to defend himself. But his movements were clumsy. Ali knocked his weapon away, and it flew into the dark lake. The djinn soldier in Ali saw his chance, the other man's neck exposed . . .

The ring! The ring! Ali changed the direction of his blow, bringing it down toward the glowing green gem.

Ali swooned. The ring clattered away, and the sword fell from his hand, now more a rusty artifact than a weapon. Nahri's screams filled the air.

"Kill the daeva," he mumbled and collapsed, the blackness finally welcoming him.

ALI WAS DREAMING.

He was back in the harem—in the pleasure gardens of his mother's people—a small boy with his small sister, hiding in their usual spot under the willow tree. Its bowed branches and thick fronds made a cozy nook next to the canal, hidden from the sight of any interfering grown-ups.

"Do it again!" he begged. "Please, Zaynab!"

His sister sat up with a wicked smile. The water-filled bowl rested in the dust between her skinny crossed legs. She raised her palms over the water. "What will you give me?"

Ali thought fast, considering which of his few treasures he'd be willing to part with. Unlike Zaynab, he had no toys; no trinkets and amusements were given to boys groomed to be warriors. "I can get you a kitten," he offered. "There's lots near the Citadel."

Zaynab's eyes lit up. "Done." She wiggled her fingers, a look of intense concentration brewing in her small face. The water shuddered, following the motion of her hands and then slowly rose as she spun her right hand, whirling like a liquid ribbon.

Ali's mouth fell open in wonder, and Zaynab giggled before smashing the watery funnel down. "Show me how," he said, reaching for the bowl.

"You can't do it," Zaynab said self-importantly. "You're a boy. *And* a baby. You can't do anything."

"I'm not a baby!" Wajed uncle had even given him a spear shaft to carry around and scare off snakes. Babies couldn't do that.

The screen of leaves was suddenly swept away and replaced with his mother's angry face. She took one look at the bowl, and her eyes flashed with fear. "Zaynab!" She yanked his sister away by her ear. "How many times have I told you? You are never to—"

Ali scurried back, but his mother wasn't interested in him. She never was. He waited until they had crossed the garden, Zaynab's sobs growing distant, before he crept back toward the bowl. He stared at the still water, at the dark profile of his face surrounded by the pale sunlit leaves.

Ali raised his fingers and beckoned the water closer. He smiled when it began to dance.

He knew he wasn't a baby.

THE DREAM RECEDED, SWEPT BACK IN THE REALM of childhood memories to be forgotten as a sharp bite of pain tugged at his elbow. Something growled in the very recesses of his mind, clawing and snapping to stay put. The tug came again, followed by a burst of heat, and the thing released.

"That's the last of it, my king," a female voice said. A light sheet fluttered over his body.

"Cover him well," a man commanded. "I would spare him the sight as long as possible."

Abba, he recognized as his memory came back to him in a shambles. The sound of his father's voice was enough to drag him free of the fog of pain and confusion miring his body.

And then another voice. "Abba, I'm begging you." *Muntadhir.* His brother was sobbing, pleading. "I'll do anything you want, marry anyone you want. Just let the Nahid treat him, let Nisreen help him . . . by God, I'll bind his wounds myself! Jamshid saved my life. He shouldn't have to suffer because—"

"Kaveh's son will be seen when mine opens his eyes." Rough fingers tightened on Ali's wrist. "He will be healed when I have the name of the Daeva who left those supplies on the beach." Ghassan's voice turned colder. "Tell him that. And pull yourself together, Muntadhir. Stop *weeping* over another man. You shame yourself."

Ali heard the sound of a chair kicked away and a door slammed shut. Their words were meaningless to Ali, but their voices . . . oh, God, their *voices.*

Abba. He tried again. "Abba . . . ," he finally choked out, trying to open his eyes.

A woman's face swam into view before his father could re-spond. *Nisreen*, Ali remembered, recognizing Nahri's assistant. "Open your eyes, Prince Alizayd. As wide as you can."

He obeyed. She leaned in to examine his gaze. "I see no trace of the blackness remaining, my king." She stepped back.

"I-I don't understand . . . ," Ali started. He was flat on his back, exhausted. His body burned; his skin stung, and his mind felt . . . raw. He looked up, recognizing the tempered glass ceiling of the infirmary. The sky was gray, and rain swirled on the trans-parent plates. "The palace was destroyed. You were all dead . . ."

"I'm not dead, Alizayd," Ghassan assured him. "Try to relax; you've been injured."

But Ali couldn't relax. "What about Zaynab?" he asked, his ears ringing with his sister's screams. "Is she . . . did those monsters . . ." He tried to sit up, suddenly realizing his wrists were bound to the bed. He panicked. "What is this? Why am I restrained?"

"You were fighting us; do you not remember?" Ali shook his head, and his father nodded to Nisreen. "Cut him loose."

"My king, I'm not certain . . ."

"I was *not* asking."

Nisreen obeyed, and his father helped him sit up, swatting his hands away when Ali tried to pull off the white sheet that had been tucked around him like swaddling cloth. "Leave that be. And your sister is fine. We are all fine."

Ali glanced again at the rain beating against the glass ceil-ing; the sight of the water was oddly alluring. He blinked, forcing himself to look away. "But I don't understand. I saw you—all of you—dead. I saw Daevabad destroyed," Ali insisted, and yet even as he said the words, the details were already starting to escape him, the memories pulled away like the tide while newer, firmer ones replaced them.

His fight with the Afshin.

He shot me. He shot me, and I fell in the lake. Ali touched his throat but felt no injury. He started to shake. *I shouldn't be alive.* No one survived the lake, not since the marids cursed it thousands of years ago.

"The Afshin . . . ," Ali stammered. "He-he was trying to flee with Nahri. Did you catch him?"

He saw his father hesitate. "In a manner of speaking." He glanced at Nisreen. "Take that away to be burned, and tell the emir to come back in here."

Nisreen rose, her black eyes unreadable. In her arms was a wooden bowl filled with what looked like bloody lake debris: shells and rocks, mangled hooks, a tiny decayed fish, and a few teeth. The sight stirred him, and he watched as she left, passing by two larger reed baskets on the floor. A dead gray tentacle the size of a viper shared one with roughly torn waterweeds. The toothy jaw of a crocodile skull peeked out from the second.

Ali drew up straight. *Teeth sinking into my shoulder, weeds and tentacles seizing my limbs.* He glanced down, suddenly realizing just how carefully the sheet had been tucked around his body. He grabbed for one end.

His father tried to stop him. "Don't, Alizayd."

He tore it away and gasped.

He'd been scourged.

No, not scourged, he realized as his horrified gaze ran over his bloody limbs. The marks were too varied to have been made by a whip. There were gashes that cut down to muscle and scratches that barely drew blood. A pattern of scales was etched into his left wrist, and spiky ridges marred his right thigh. Strips and whirls of flesh had been carved from his arms like one might have wound bandages. There were bite marks on his stomach.

"What happened to me?" He started to tremble, and when no one responded, his voice broke in fright. "What *happened*?"

Nisreen froze at the door. "Should I call for guards, my king?"

"No," his father snapped. "Just my son." He grabbed Ali's hands. "Alizayd, calm down. Calm down!" Nisreen vanished.

Water streamed down his cheeks, pooling in his palms and growing clammy on his brow. Ali stared in horror at his dripping hands. "What is this? Am I . . . *sweating*?" Such a thing wasn't possible: pureblooded djinn did not sweat.

The door burst open, and Muntadhir rushed in. "Zaydi . . . thank God," he breathed as he hurried to his bedside. His face paled. "Oh . . . *oh*."

He wasn't the only one shocked. Ali gaped at his brother; Muntadhir looked like he'd been on the wrong side of a street brawl. His jaw was bruised, stitches held together gashes on his cheek and brow, and bloody bandages wrapped his arms. His robe hung in shreds. He appeared to have aged thirty years; his face was drawn, his eyes swollen and darkly rimmed from crying.

Ali gasped. "What happened to you?"

"The Scourge was offering a demonstration of his title," Muntadhir said bitterly. "Until you turned him into a pile of ash."

"Until I did *what*?"

The king glared at Muntadhir. "I had not yet reached that part." He glanced at Ali again, his face unusually gentle. "Do you remember climbing back onto the boat? Killing Darayavahoush?"

"No!"

His father and brother exchanged a dark look. "What do you remember of the lake?" Ghassan asked.

Pain. Indescribable pain. But he didn't need to tell his worried father that. "I . . . something was talking to me," he remembered. "Showing me things. Awful things. You were dead, Abba. Dhiru . . . they cut your head off in front of a crowd of ifrit." He blinked back tears as his brother blanched. "There were men defiling Zaynab . . . the streets were burning . . . I thought it all real." He swallowed, trying to regain control. More sweat poured from his skin, soaking the sheets. "The voice . . . it-it was asking for something. My name."

"Your name?" Ghassan asked sharply. "It asked for your name? Did you give it?"

"I-I think so," Ali replied, trying to recall his scattered memories. "I don't remember anything after that." His father went still, and Ali panicked. "Why?"

"You don't give your name, Alizayd." Ghassan was clearly trying—and failing—to check the alarm rising in his voice. "Not freely, not to a creature who's not of our race. Giving your name means giving up control. That's how the ifrit enslave us."

"What are you saying?" Ali touched his wounds. "You think the ifrit did this to me?" He gasped. "Does that mean—"

"Not the ifrit, Zaydi," Muntadhir cut in quietly. Ali watched his brother's gaze dart to their father, but Ghassan didn't interrupt. "That's not what lives in the lake."

Ali's eyes went wide. "The *marid*? That's insane. They haven't been seen in thousands of years!"

His father hushed him. "Keep your voice down." He glanced at his eldest. "Muntadhir, get him some water." Muntadhir poured him a cup from the ceramic water pitcher on the table behind them, pressing it into his hand before stepping carefully away. Ali clutched it, taking a nervous sip.

Ghassan's face stayed grave. "The marid have been seen, Alizayd. By Zaydi al Qahtani himself when he took Daevabad . . . in the company of the Ayaanle man who commanded them."

Ali went cold. "*What?*"

"The marid were seen by Zaydi," Ghassan repeated. "He warned his son about them when he became emir, a warning passed down to each generation of Qahtani kings."

"*We don't cross the Ayaanle,*" Muntadhir intoned softly.

Ghassan nodded. "Zaydi said the Ayaanle alliance with the

marid earned us our victory . . . but that the Ayaanle had paid a terrible price for doing so. We were never to betray them."

Ali was shocked. "The marid helped us take Daevabad from the Nahids? But that-that's absurd. That's . . . *abhorrent*," he realized. "That would be . . ."

"A betrayal of our race itself," Ghassan finished. "Which is why it doesn't leave this room." He shook his head. "My own father never believed it, said it was just a story passed down over the centuries to frighten us." Ghassan's face fell. "Until today, I thought he might be right."

Ali narrowed his eyes. "What are you saying?"

Ghassan took his hand. "You fell in the lake, my son. You gave your name to a creature in its depths. I think it *took* it . . . I think it took *you*."

Ali drew up with as much indignation as he could from his soaking sheets. "You think I let a marid . . . what, *possess* me? That's impossible!"

"Zaydi . . ." Muntadhir stepped closer, his face apologetic. "I saw you climb back on the boat. You had all those things clinging to you, your eyes were black, you were whispering in some bizarre language. And when you used the seal, my God, you completely overpowered Darayavahoush. I've never seen anything like it."

The seal? He had used Suleiman's seal? *No, this is madness. Utter madness.* Ali was an educated man. He'd never read anything indicating that marid could possess pureblooded djinn. That *anything* could possess djinn. How would something like that have been kept a secret? And did that mean all the gossip—all the cruel rumors about his mother's people—was rooted in truth?

Ali shook his head. "No. We have scholars; they know the truth about the war. Besides, djinn can't be possessed by a marid. If they could, surely—surely someone would have studied it. It would be in a book—"

"Oh, my child . . ." His father's eyes were filled with sorrow. "Not everything is in a book."

Ali dropped his gaze, fighting back tears, unable to bear the pity in Ghassan's face. *They're wrong*, he tried to insist to himself. *They're wrong.*

But how else to explain the gaps in his memory? The horrific visions? The very fact that he was alive? He'd been shot in the throat and lungs, had fallen into water cursed to shred any djinn who touched it. And here he was.

A marid. He stared at his dripping hands as nausea swept over him. *I gave my name and let some water demon use my body like a shiny new blade to murder the Afshin.* His stomach churned.

From the corner of his eye, he saw the ceramic pitcher start to shake on the table behind his brother. God, he could *sense* it; he could feel the water aching to burst free. The realization shook him to the core.

His father squeezed his hand. "Look at me, Alizayd. The Afshin is dead. It is over. No one need ever know."

But it wasn't over. It never would be: sweat was pouring from Ali's brow even now. He was changed.

"Ali, child." He could hear the worry in his father's voice. "Talk to me, please . . ."

Ali sucked in his breath, and the water pitcher behind Muntadhir exploded, sending clay fragments skittering across the floor. The water gushed out, and Muntadhir jumped, his hand going for the khanjar at his waist.

Ali met his eyes. Muntadhir dropped his hand, looking slightly ashamed.

"Abba . . . he can't be seen like this," he said quietly. "We need to get him out of Daevabad. Ta Ntry. Surely the Ayaanle will know better . . ."

"I'm not giving him to Hatset's people," Ghassan said stubbornly. "He belongs with us."

"He's making water pitchers explode and drowning in his own sweat!" Muntadhir threw up his hands. "He's second in line for the throne. Two heartbeats away from controlling Suleiman's seal and ruling the realm. For all we know, the marid is still in there, waiting to seize him again." Muntadhir met Ali's frightened eyes. "Zaydi, I'm sorry, I truly am . . . but it is the height of irresponsibility to let you remain in Daevabad. The questions your condition will provoke . . ." He shook his head and looked back to their father. "You were the one who gave me the lecture when you made me emir. Who told me what would happen if the Daevas ever suspected how we won the war."

"No one is going to find out anything," the king snapped. "No one on the ship was close enough to see what happened."

Muntadhir crossed his arms. "No one? Then I take it you've already taken care of our supposed Banu Nahida."

Ali reeled. "What do you mean? Where's Nahri?"

"She's fine," the king assured him. "I haven't decided her fate yet. I'll need your testimony if I decide to execute her."

"Execute her?" Ali gasped. "Why in God's name would you execute her? That lunatic gave her no choice."

His father looked baffled. "Muntadhir said she ordered the Afshin to attack. That they were trying to escape when you killed him."

They were? Ali flinched. That hurt, he couldn't lie. But he shook his head. "That's not how it started. I came upon him trying to kidnap her in the infirmary. He told her that he'd kill me if she didn't go along with him."

Muntadhir snorted. "Convenient. Tell me, Zaydi . . . did they at least hide their laughter when they acted all this out, or did they just assume you too stupid to pick up on it?"

"It's the truth!"

"The truth." His brother scowled, his expression darkening. "How would you even recognize such a thing?"

Ghassan frowned. "What were you doing in the infirmary in the middle of the night, Alizayd?"

"It doesn't matter why he was there, Abba," Muntadhir said dismissively. "I told you he'd protect her; he's so lovestruck he doesn't even realize it. He probably *does* think she's innocent."

"I'm not *lovestruck*," Ali snapped, offended at the prospect. The rain beat harder against the roof, echoing the pounding in his heart. "I know what I saw. What I heard. And she's innocent. I will shout it in the streets myself if you try her."

"Go ahead!" Muntadhir shot back. "It would hardly be the first time you shamed us in the streets!"

Ghassan rose to his feet. "What in God's name are you two going on about?"

Ali couldn't answer. He could feel his control slipping. The rain drummed against the glass above him, the water achingly close.

Muntadhir glared at him, a warning in his gray eyes so clear he might as well have spoken it. "Twenty-one men are dead, Zaydi. Several because they fought to save my life, more because they came to rescue yours." He blinked, tears gathering in his dark lashes. "My best friend is probably going to join them. And I will be damned if that lying Nahid whore gets away with it because your word is unreliable when it comes to the shafit."

He let the challenge lay in the air. Ali took a deep breath, trying to quell the emotions churning inside him.

Something metallic groaned above their heads. A small leak sprang.

Ghassan glanced up, and for the first time in his life, Ali saw true fear on his father's face.

The roof gave out.

The water smashed through the ceiling, sending twisted copper piping and shards of glass flying through the infirmary. The rain poured in, streaming down Ali's skin and soothing his burning wounds. From the corner of his eye, he saw Muntadhir and his father duck under a remnant of ceiling. The king looked unhurt. Shocked but unhurt.

Not so his brother. Fresh black blood dripped down Muntadhir's face—a piece of glass must have gouged his cheek.

"Akhi, I'm sorry!" Ali felt guilt twist through him, mixing with his confusion. "I didn't mean to do that, to hurt you, I swear!"

But his brother wasn't looking at him. Muntadhir's blank gaze traveled the ruined infirmary, taking in the pouring rain and destroyed ceiling. He touched his bloody cheek.

"No . . . I'm sorry, Zaydi." Muntadhir wiped the blood from his face with the tail of his turban. "Tell Abba whatever truth you want. Make it good." He pressed his mouth in a grim line. "I'm done protecting you."

29

ALI

"As-salaamu alaykum wa rahmatullah." Ali turned his head and whispered the prayer into his left shoulder. "As-salaamu alaykum wa rahmatullah."

He relaxed his shoulders and turned his palms upward to offer his supplications, but his mind went blank at the sight of his hands. Though his wounds were healing remarkably fast, the scars remained stubborn, fading to thin dark lines that resembled the dead Afshin's tattoos so much it turned his stomach.

Ali heard the door open behind him but ignored it, refocusing on his prayers. He finished and turned around.

"Abba?"

The king slouched on the rug behind him. There were shadows under his eyes, and his head was bare. At first glance, he could have been a commoner, a tired old man in a plain cotton dishdasha taking a rest. Even his beard looked more silver than it had just a few days ago.

"P-peace be upon you," Ali stammered. "I'm sorry. I did not realize . . ."

"I didn't wish to disturb you." Ghassan patted the spot on the rug next to him, and Ali sank back to the floor. His father stared at the mihrab, the small carved niche in the corner indicating the direction to which Ali, and every other believing djinn, bowed in prayer.

Ghassan's eyes dimmed. He rubbed his beard. "I'm not much of a believer," he finally said. "Never have been. Honestly, I always assumed our religion to be a political move on the part of our ancestors. What better way to unify the tribes and preserve the ideas of the revolution than to adopt the new human faith of our homeland?" Ghassan paused. "Of course, I know that's utter heresy in the eyes of your kind, but think about it . . . did it not largely end the veneration of the Nahids? Give our rule the veneer of divine approval? A clever move. At least that's what I've always thought."

Ghassan continued to gaze at the mihrab, but his mind seemed a world away. "Then I saw that ship go up in flames with my children onboard, at the mercy of a madman I let into our city. I listened to the screams, terrified that one would sound familiar, that it would be calling my name . . ." Ali heard his throat catch. "I would be lying if I said my brow didn't press a prayer mat faster than that of the most zealous sheikh."

Ali stayed silent. Through the open balustrade, he could hear birds singing in the bright sunshine. The light filtered through the window screens, throwing elaborate designs on the patterned rug. He stared at the floor, sweat beading on his brow. He was becoming accustomed to the sensation.

"Have I ever told you why I named you Alizayd?" Ali shook his head, and his father continued. "You were born shortly after Manizheh and Rustam's murders. Dark times for our people, probably the worst since the war. Daevabad was crowded with migrants fleeing from the ifrit in the outer provinces, there was a secession movement brewing among the Daevas, the Sahrayn were already in open revolt. Many believed we were living in the end times for our race.

"People said it was a miracle when your mother became pregnant again after Zaynab's birth. Pureblooded women are lucky to have even one child, but two? And so close together?" Ghassan shook his head, a ghost of a smile on his face. "They said it was a blessing from the Most High, a sign of His favor over my reign." The smile faded. "And then you were a boy. A second son with a powerful mother from a wealthy tribe. When I went to Hatset, she begged me not to kill you." He shook his head. "That she could think such a thing of me as I counted your fingers and whispered the adhan into your ear . . . I knew then that surely we were strangers to each other.

"Within a day of your birth, I had two assassins from Am Gezira present themselves at court. Skilled men, the best at what they did, offering discreet ways to end my dilemma. Merciful, quick solutions that would leave no suspicion for the Ayaanle." His father clenched his fists. "I invited them into my office. I listened to their calm and reasoned words. And then I murdered them with my own hands."

Ali startled, but his father didn't seem to notice.

Ghassan stared out the window, lost in his memories. "I sent their heads back to Am Gezira, and when your name day came, I called you 'Alizayd' as I bolted your relic to your ear. The name of our greatest hero, the progenitor of our rule, so that all would know you were my own. I gave you to Wajed to raise as Qaid and throughout the years, when I saw you grow up in the footsteps of your namesake—noble, yet kind, a zulfiqari to be reckoned with . . . My decision pleased me. At times, I even found myself wondering . . ." He paused, shaking his head slightly, and then for the first time since entering the room, turned to meet Ali's gaze. "But I fear now that giving a second son the name of our world's most famous rebel was not my wisest decision."

Ali's gaze dropped. He could not bear to look his father in the eyes. He had imagined being filled with righteous anger when they finally had this confrontation, but now he just felt sick. "Muntadhir told you."

Ghassan nodded. "What he knew. You were careful not to give him names, but they were easy enough to ferret out. I executed Rashid ben Salkh this morning. It may be of small comfort that he took no part in the attempt on your life. Seems the shafit man acted alone in trying to avenge the riot. We're still looking for the old woman."

Hanno acted alone. Ali went numb as the guilt settled upon his shoulders. *So Rashid was exactly what he seemed.* A fellow believer, a man so dedicated to helping the shafit that he'd betrayed his tribe and risked his privileged life as a full-blooded Geziri officer. And Ali had gotten him killed.

He knew he should be apologizing—groveling at his father's feet—but the enormity of what he'd done erased any impulse to save his own life. He thought of the little girl they'd saved. Would she be out on the streets after Sister Fatumai was caught? Would all of them?

"She's an old woman, Abba. An old shafit woman who cares for orphans. How can you possibly think of someone like that as a threat?" Ali could hear the frustration in his voice. "How can you think of *any* of them as a threat? They just want a decent life."

"Yes. A decent life with you as their king."

Ali's heart skipped a beat. He glanced at his father to see if he was joking, but Ghassan's stony face indicated no jest.

"No, I don't imagine you wanted to put it together, though your brother certainly did. Rashid ben Salkh was removed from a posting in Ta Ntry years ago under suspicion of incitement. He was burning letters from the Ayaanle when he was arrested.

He confessed under torture but maintained your innocence." The king sat back. "He did not know the identities of his Ayaanle backers, but I have no doubt his death will bring consternation to more than a few members of your mother's household."

Ali's mouth went dry. "Abba . . . punish me for aiding the Tanzeem. I freely admit it. But . . . *that*?" He couldn't even bring himself to say the word. "Never. How can you possibly think I would take up arms against you? Against Muntadhir?" He cleared his throat, growing emotional. "You really think me capable of—"

"Yes," Ghassan said curtly. "I think you capable. I think you *reluctant*, but quite capable." He paused to regard him. "Even now I see the anger in your eyes. You might not find the courage to defy me. But Muntadhir—"

"Is my *brother*," Ali cut in. "I would never—"

Ghassan raised a hand to silence him. "And thus you know his weaknesses. As do I. His first decades as king will be tumultuous. He will mismanage the Treasury and indulge his court. He will crack down on your beloved shafit in an effort to seem tough and push aside his queen—a woman I suspect you care for a bit too much—for a bevy of concubines. And as Qaid, you will be forced to watch. With the Ayaanle whispering in your ear, with the loyalty of your fellow soldiers in hand . . . you will watch. And you will break."

Ali drew up. That cold place, the knot of resentment Muntadhir had briefly touched at Khanzada's, unspooled again. He wasn't accustomed to challenging his father so directly, but this wasn't a charge he would let lie. "*I would never*," he repeated. "I all but gave my life to save Muntadhir's on that boat. I would never hurt him. I want to *help* him." He threw up his hands. "That's what all this was about, Abba. I don't want to be king! I don't want Ayaanle gold. I wanted to help my city, to help the people we've left behind!"

Ghassan shook his head. He looked even more resolute. "I

believe you, Alizayd. That's the problem. Like your namesake, I think you want to help the shafit so much that you'd be willing to bring the city down just to see them rise. And I can't risk that."

His father said nothing else. He didn't need to. For Ghassan had always been clear when it came to his views on kingship. Daevabad came first. Before his tribe. Before his family.

Before the life of his youngest son.

Ali felt oddly light. He cleared his throat, finding it difficult to breathe. But he wasn't going to beg for his life. Instead, he hardened his heart, looking his father in the eye. "When do I meet the karkadann?"

Ghassan didn't drop his gaze. "You don't. I'm stripping you of your titles and Treasury accounts and sending you to Am Gezira. The other tribes will assume you went to lead a garrison."

Exile? Ali frowned. *That can't be it.* But as his father stayed silent, Ali realized there had been a warning in the story of his birth.

Foreigners might think it just a military assignment, but the Geziri would know better. When Alizayd al Qahtani—Alizayd the Ayaanle—showed up in Am Gezira impoverished and alone, the Geziri would know he'd lost his father's protection. That this second son, this foreign son, had been abandoned, and his blood could be spilled without retribution. Geziri assassins were the best and readily available. Anyone hoping to curry favor with his brother, with his father, with Kaveh, with any of the enemies Ali had made over the years—it didn't even have to be someone he'd personally angered. The Qahtanis had a thousand adversaries, even among their own tribe.

Ali *was* being executed. It might take a few months, but he'd end up dead. Not on a battlefield, fighting bravely in his family's name; nor as a martyr, clear-eyed in his choice to defend the shafit. No, instead he was going to be hunted down in an unfamiliar land, murdered before his first quarter century. His last days would be spent alone and in terror, and when he inevitably fell, it would be to people who would carve him up, taking whatever bloody evidence they needed for payment.

His father climbed to his feet, his slow movements betraying his age. "There is a merchant caravan headed to Am Gezira tomorrow. You'll leave with them."

Ali didn't move. He couldn't. "Why don't you just have me killed?" The question came out in a rush, half plea. "Throw me to the karkadann, poison my food, have someone cut my throat while I sleep." He blinked, fighting back tears. "Would that not be easier?"

Ali could see his heartbreak mirrored in his father's face. For all the jokes about how strongly he resembled his mother's people, his eyes were Ghassan's. They always had been.

"I can't," the king admitted. "I cannot give that order. And for that weakness, my son, I apologize." He turned to leave.

"And Nahri?" Ali called out before his father reached the door, desperate for any bit of consolation. "You know I spoke the truth of her."

"I don't know that at all," Ghassan countered. "I think Muntadhir is right; your word on that girl is unreliable. And it doesn't change what happened."

Ali had destroyed his future to tell the truth. It had better mean something. "Why not?"

"You slew Darayavahoush before her eyes, Alizayd. It took three men to drag her kicking and screaming from his ashes. She bit one of them so badly he needed stitches." His father shook his head. "Whatever was between the two of you is gone. If she did not consider us enemies before, she most certainly does now."

30

NAHRI

"Oh, warrior of the djinn, I beseech thee . . ." Nahri closed her swollen eyes as she sang, drumming her fingers on an overturned bowl sticky with crusty bits of rice. She'd taken it from the pile of moldering dishes at the door, remnants of the meals she'd barely touched.

She picked up a wooden shard from a smashed chair and cut deeply into her wrist. The sight of her blood was disappointing. It would work better if she had a chicken. If she had her musicians. Zars were to be precise.

The blood dripped down her arm and onto the floor before the wound closed up. "Great guardian, I call to you. Darayavahoush e-Afshin," she whispered, her voice breaking, "come to me."

Nothing. Her bedchamber stayed as quiet as it had been a week ago when she was locked away still covered in his ashes. But Nahri didn't let that dissuade her. She'd just try again, varying the song slightly. She couldn't remember the exact words she'd sung in Cairo so long ago, but once she got them right, it had to work.

She shifted on the floor, getting a whiff of unwashed hair as she pulled the filthy bowl over. She was slashing her wrist for the umpteenth time when the door to her room opened. A woman's dark silhouette was visible against the infirmary's blinding light.

"Nisreen," Nahri called, relieved. "Come. If you keep the beat on the drum, then I can use this plate as a tambourine, and—"

Nisreen rushed across the room and snatched the bloody shard away. "Oh, child . . . what is this?"

"I'm calling Dara back," Nahri answered. Wasn't it obvious? "I did it once. There's no reason I can't do it again. I just have to get everything right."

"Banu Nahri." Nisreen knelt on the floor and pushed the bowl away. "He's gone, child. He's not coming back."

Nahri pulled her hands away. "You don't know that," she said fiercely. "You're no Nahid. You know noth—"

"I know slaves," Nisreen cut in. "I helped your mother and uncle free dozens. And, child . . . they cannot be separated from their vessels. Not for a moment. It's all that binds their soul to this world." Nisreen took Nahri's face between her hands. "He's gone, my lady. But you are not. And if you'd like to keep it that way, you need to pull yourself together." Her eyes were dark with warning. "The king wants to speak to you."

Nahri stilled. In her mind, she saw the arrow tearing through Ali's throat and heard Muntadhir screaming as Dara scourged him. A cold sweat broke across her skin. She couldn't face their father. "No." She shook her head. "I can't. He's going to kill me. He's going to give me over to that karkadann beast and—"

"He's not going to kill you." Nisreen pulled Nahri to her feet. "Because you're going to say exactly what he wants to hear and do exactly as he orders, understand? That is how you survive this." She pulled Nahri toward the hammam. "But we're going to get you cleaned up first."

The small bathhouse was steamy and warm when they entered, the wet tiles redolent of roses. Nisreen nodded at a small wooden stool in the misty shadows. "Sit."

Nahri obeyed. Nisreen dragged over a bowl of hot water and then helped her out of her filthy tunic. She poured the bowl over her head, and the water streamed down her arms, turning gray as it rinsed the ashes from her skin.

Dara's ashes. The sight nearly undid her. She choked back a sob. "I can't do this. Not without him."

Nisreen clucked her tongue. "Now where is the girl who killed ifrit with her blood and offered up fiery, blasphemous lectures on her ancestors?" She knelt and wiped Nahri's dirty face with a damp cloth. "You're going to survive this, Banu Nahri. You must. You are all we have left."

Nahri swallowed back the lump in her throat, a thought occurring to her. "But his ring . . . maybe if we found it . . ."

"It's gone." A bitter edge crept into Nisreen's voice as she rubbed a nub of soap into a lather. "There's nothing left; the king had the boat burned and sunk." She massaged the soap into Nahri's long hair. "I've never seen Ghassan like this."

Nahri tensed. "What do you mean?"

Nisreen lowered her voice. "Darayavahoush had help, Nahri. The king's men found supplies on the beach. Not much—it might have been only one man, but . . ." She sighed. "Between that and the demonstrations . . . it's chaos." She poured a bucket of clean water over Nahri's head.

"The *demonstrations*? What demonstrations?"

"There have been Daevas gathering at the wall every day, demanding justice for Darayavahoush's death." Nisreen handed her a towel. "To kill a slave is a great crime in our world, and the

Afshin . . . well, I suspect you saw for yourself in the temple how people felt about him."

Nahri flinched, remembering the sight of Dara playing with the Daeva children in the garden, the awed faces of the adults clustering around him.

But Nahri also remembered all too well who was to blame for the carnage on that boat—and the one death she didn't imagine the king would ever forgive. "Nisreen . . . ," she started as the other woman began to comb her hair. "Dara killed Ali. The only justice Ghassan's going to—"

Nisreen drew back in surprise. "Dara didn't kill Alizayd." Her face darkened. "I should know; I was forced to treat him."

"Treat him . . . Ali's *alive*?" Nahri asked, incredulous. The prince had been shot, drowned, and then seemingly possessed by the marid; she hadn't even considered the possibility that he still lived. "Is he okay?"

"'*Is he okay?*'" Nisreen repeated, looking aghast at the question. "He murdered your Afshin!"

Nahri shook her head. "It wasn't him." There had been nothing of Ali in the oil-eyed wraith who climbed aboard the boat chanting in a language like the rush of the sea. "It was the marid. They probably forced him—"

"He probably volunteered," Nisreen cut in coldly. "Not that we'll ever know. Ghassan's already had him smuggled back to Am Gezira—and warned me that if I spoke of what happened, he'd cut your throat."

Nahri recoiled. But not just at the threat. At her own sudden memory of Ali's rushed apology on the boat. He *had* said nothing, letting them rush into the trap he knew awaited.

Nisreen seemed to read her mind. "My lady, forget the Qahtanis. Worry about *your* people for once. Daevas are being killed—hung from the palace walls—simply for demanding justice, for a mere *inquiry*, into the death of one of our own. Daeva men are being dragged from their homes, interrogated and tortured. We've been stripped of royal protection, our quarter left undefended—half our shops in the Grand Bazaar have already been looted." Her voice broke. "Just this morning, I heard word a Daeva girl was snatched from her palanquin and raped by a mob of shafit men while the Royal Guard stood by."

The blood left Nahri's face. "I . . . I'm sorry. I had no idea."

Nisreen sat on the bench opposite her. "Then *listen* to me. Nahri, the Qahtanis are not your friends. This is how it always happens with them. One of us steps out of line—one of us *thinks* about stepping out of line—and hundreds pay the price."

The door to the hammam swung open. A Geziri soldier barged in.

Nisreen jumped to her feet, blocking Nahri from sight. "Have you no decency?"

He rested his hand on his zulfiqar. "Not for the Scourge's whore."

The Scourge's whore? His words sent a rush of fear through Nahri. Her hands were shaking so badly that Nisreen had to help her dress, pulling a loose linen gown over Nahri's head and tying her shalvar pants.

Nisreen draped her own black chador over Nahri's wet hair. "Please," she begged in Divasti. "You're the only one left. Forget your grief. Forget our words here. Tell the king whatever he needs to hear to grant you mercy."

The impatient soldier seized her wrist and pulled her toward the door. Nisreen followed. "Please, Banu Nahri! You must know he loved you; he wouldn't want you to throw away—"

The soldier shut the door in Nisreen's face.

He dragged Nahri along the garden path. It was an ugly day; gray clouds bruised the sky, and an icy wind brought a smattering of rain against her face. She pulled the chador tight around her and shivered, wishing she could disappear into it.

They crossed the rain-slick pavilion toward a small wooden gazebo nestled between a wild herb garden and an ancient, sprawling neem tree. The king was alone and looked as composed as ever, his black robes and brilliant turban not the slightest bit damp.

Despite Nisreen's warning, Nahri didn't bow. She squared her shoulders, looking him dead in the eye.

He dismissed the soldier. "Banu Nahida," he greeted her. His expression was calm. He motioned to the opposite bench. "Why don't you sit?"

She sat, ignoring the urge to slide to the side of the bench farthest from him. His eyes hadn't left her face.

"You look better than when I saw you last," he commented lightly.

Nahri flinched. She only vaguely recalled the king's arrival on the boat. The way Suleiman's seal had crashed down a second time while soldiers dragged her, thrashing and screaming, from Dara's ashes.

She wanted to get this conversation over with as quickly as possible—to get *away* from him as quickly as possible. "I know nothing," she said, rushing. "I don't know who helped him, I don't know what—"

"I believe you," Ghassan interrupted. Nahri gave him a surprised look, and he continued. "I mean, I don't particularly care, but for what it's worth, I do believe you."

Nahri fidgeted with the hem of her chador. "Then what do you want?"

"To know where you stand now." Ghassan spread his hands. "Twenty-one men are dead and my streets aflame. All because that damnable Afshin decided—in what I imagine was a hotheaded moment of the deepest stupidity—to kidnap you and my son and flee Daevabad. I've heard strikingly different accounts of how this happened," he continued. "And I've decided on one."

She arched an eyebrow. "You've *decided* on one?"

"I have," he replied. "I think two drunk men got in an idiotic brawl over a woman. I think one of those men—still bitter about losing a war, driven half mad by slavery—snapped. I think he decided to take what belonged to him by force." He gave her an intent look. "And I think you're very fortunate that my younger son, injured in the brawl earlier, was in the infirmary to hear your screams."

"That's not what happened," Nahri said heatedly. "Dara would never—"

The king waved her off. "He was a volatile man from an ancient and savage world. Who can really understand why he chose to lash out the way he did? To steal you from your bed like some uncivilized brute from the wilds of Daevastana. Of course you went along; you were terrified, a young girl under his sway for months."

Nahri was normally good at checking her emotions, but if Ghassan thought she was going to publicly paint Dara as some barbarian rapist and herself as a helpless victim, he was mad.

And he wasn't the only one with leverage. "Does this charming story of yours include the part where your son was possessed by the marid and used Suleiman's seal?"

"Alizayd was never possessed by the marid," Ghassan said, sounding completely self-assured. "What a ridiculous thing to suggest. The marid have not been seen for millennia. Alizayd never fell in the lake. He was caught in the ship's rigging and climbed back aboard to slay the Afshin. He's a hero." The king paused and pressed his lips into a bitter smile, his voice wavering for the first time. "He always was a talented swordsman."

Nahri shook her head. "That's not what happened. There were other witnesses. No one is going to believe—"

"It is far more believable than Manizheh having a secret daughter hidden away in a distant human city. A girl whose very bearing would suggest an almost entirely human pedigree . . .

forgive me, what did we say it was? Ah, yes, a curse to affect your appearance." The king pressed his long fingers together. "Yes, I sold that story quite well."

His frankness took her aback; she had thought it odd how easily the king accepted her identity when even she herself doubted it. "Because it's the truth," she argued. "You were the one to mistake me for Manizheh when I first arrived."

Ghassan nodded. "A mistake. I cared greatly for your mother. I saw a Daeva woman walk in with an Afshin warrior at her side, and my emotions briefly overtook me. And who knows? You may very well be Manizheh's daughter—you clearly have some Nahid blood . . ." He tapped the seal on his cheek. "But I see human in you as well. Not much; if your parents were clever, they could have hidden it—there are plenty in our world who do. But it's there."

His confidence shook her. "You would have let Muntadhir marry someone with human blood?"

"To secure peace between our tribes? Without hesitation." He chuckled. "Do you think Alizayd the only radical? I have lived long enough—and seen enough—to know that blood does not account for everything. There are plenty of shafit who can wield magic with as much skill as a pureblood. Unlike my son, I recognize that the rest of our world is not ready to accept such a thing. But as long as no one else learned what you were . . ." He shrugged. "The exact composition of my grandchildren's blood would not have bothered me one whit."

Nahri was speechless. She could take little heart in Ghassan's assertion that shafit were equals—not when he could so easily disregard such a truth for political reality. Doing so bespoke a cruelty she had not seen in Dara's far more ignorant brand of prejudice.

"So expose me," she challenged. "I don't care. I'm not going to help you slander his memory."

"'Slander his memory'?" Ghassan laughed. "He's the Scourge of Qui-zi. This lie pales in comparison with his actual atrocities."

"Says a man committed to using lies to further his reign."

The king lifted one of his dark eyebrows. "Do you want to hear how he earned that title?"

Nahri stayed silent, and the king regarded her. "But of course. For all the interest in our world, all the things you asked my son . . . you've shown curiously little appetite for your Afshin's bloody history."

"Because it doesn't matter to me."

"So it will not bother you to hear it." Ghassan sat back, pressing his hands together. "Let us talk of Qui-zi. The Tukharistanis were once your ancestors' most loyal subjects, you know. Steadfast and peaceful, devoted to the fire cult . . . With just one flaw—they intentionally broke the law regarding humans."

He tapped his turban. "Silk. A specialty of the humans in their land and an immediate hit when it was introduced to Daevabad. But its creation is a delicate task—too delicate for hot-blooded djinn hands. And so the Tukharistanis invited a select few human families into their tribe. They were embraced and given their own protected city. Qui-zi. None could leave, yet it was considered a paradise. As one would expect, the daeva and human populations mixed throughout the years. The Tukharistanis were careful not to let anyone with human blood leave Qui-zi, and silk was so prized that your ancestors turned a blind eye to the city's existence for centuries.

"Until Zaydi al Qahtani rebelled. Until the Ayaanle swore their allegiance and suddenly any daeva—forgive me, any *djinn*— with a trace of sympathy for the shafit fell under suspicion." The king shook his head. "Qui-zi could not stand. The Nahids needed to teach us all a lesson, a reminder of what happened when we broke Suleiman's law and got too close to humans. So they devised such a lesson and selected an Afshin to carry it out, one too young and too stupidly devoted to question its cruelty." Ghassan eyed her. "I'm sure you know his name.

"Qui-zi fell almost immediately; it was a merchant city in the wilds of Tukharistan with few defenses. His men sacked the houses and burned a fortune in silk. They weren't there for riches, they were there for the people.

"He had every man, woman, and child scourged until they bled. If their blood wasn't black enough, they were immediately killed, their bodies tossed in an open pit. And they were the lucky ones; the purebloods faced a worse fate. The throats of their men were packed with mud and then they were buried alive, enclosed in the same pit as their dead shafit fellows and any pureblooded woman unfortunate enough to be carrying a suspect pregnancy. The boys were castrated so that they would not carry on their fathers' wickedness, and the women given over to rape. Then they burned the city to the ground and brought the survivors back to Daevabad in chains."

Nahri was numb. She balled her hands into fists, her nails digging into the skin of her palms. "I don't believe you," she whispered.

"Yes, you do," Ghassan said flatly. "And truthfully had that put an end to the rebellion, prevented the far greater number of deaths and atrocities in the war to come . . . I'd have put a whip in his hand too. But it didn't. Your ancestors were ill-tempered fools. Forget the slain innocents, they destroyed half of Tukharistan's economy. A commercial grievance wrapped in moral outrage?" The king tutted. "By year's end, every remaining Tukharistani clan had sworn loyalty to Zaydi al Qahtani." He touched his turban again. "Fourteen hundred years later, their finest spinners send me a new one every year to mark the anniversary."

He's lying, she tried to tell herself. But she could not help but recall the perpetually haunted Afshin. How many times had she heard the dark references to his past, seen the regret in his eyes? Dara admitted to once believing that the shafit were little more than soulless deceptions, that blood-mixing would lead to another of Suleiman's curses. He said he'd been banished from Daevabad when he was Ali's age . . . punished for carrying out the orders of her Nahid ancestors.

He did it, she realized, and something shattered inside her, a piece of her heart that would never repair. She forced herself to look at Ghassan, struggling to stay expressionless. She would not show him how deep a wound he'd just struck.

She cleared her throat. "And the point of this tale?"

The king crossed his arms. "Your people have a history of making foolish decisions based on absolutes instead of reality. They're still doing it today, rioting in the streets and rushing to their deaths for a demand no sensible person would expect me to grant." Ghassan leaned forward, his face intent. "But in you, I see a pragmatist. A shrewd-eyed woman who would negotiate her own bride price. Who manipulated the son I sent to spy on her to the point where he sacrificed himself to protect her." He spread his hands. "What happened was an accident. There is no need to derail the plans we had *both* set in place, no reason we cannot repair what was broken between us." He eyed her. "So tell me your price."

A price. She would have laughed. There it was. That's all anything really came down to: a price. Looking out for herself and no one else. Love, tribal pride . . . they were worthless in her world. No, not just worthless, they were *dangerous*. They'd destroyed Dara.

But there was something else in what Ghassan had just said. *The son who sacrificed himself* . . . "Where's Ali?" she demanded. "I want to know what the mar—"

"If the word 'marid' comes out of your mouth again, I will have every Daeva child in the city thrown into the lake before your eyes," Ghassan warned, his voice cold. "And as for my son, he is gone. He will not be here to defend you again."

Nahri drew back in horror, and he let out an irritated sigh.

"I'm growing impatient, Banu Nahri. If my slandering one of the most murderous men in history bothers your conscience, let's devise another tale."

She didn't like the sound of that. "What do you mean?"

"Let's talk about you." He tilted his face, studying her like she was a chessboard. "I can easily reveal you as shafit; there are a number of ways—none particularly pleasant—in which to do so. That alone would turn most of your tribesmen against you, but we might as well go further, give the masses something to gossip about."

He tapped his chin. "Your disregard for your people's fire cult is almost too easy, as are your failures in the infirmary. We'd need a scandal . . ." He paused, a calculating expression crossing his hawkish face. "Perhaps I spoke wrongly about what happened in the infirmary. Maybe it was Darayavahoush who found you in the arms of another man. A young man whose name makes Daeva blood boil . . ."

Nahri recoiled. "You would never." It was obvious they were speaking plainly, so she didn't pretend not to know of whom he spoke. "You think people are howling for Ali's blood now? If they thought he—"

"Thought he what?" Ghassan gave her a condescending smile. "In what world do men and women pay the same price for passion? You'll be the one blamed. Indeed, people will assume you particularly . . . *talented* to have seduced such a religious man."

Nahri shot to her feet. Ghassan seized her wrist.

The seal flashed on his cheek, and her powers vanished. He tightened his grip, and she gasped, unaccustomed to how sharp the feeling of pain was without her healing abilities.

"I welcomed you," he said coldly, all jest gone. "I invited you into my family, and now my city is aflame and I will never look upon my youngest again. I am in no mood to suffer a foolish little girl. You will work with me to fix this, or I will make sure every

Daeva man, woman, and child holds you responsible for Darayavahoush's death. I will paint you as a whore and a traitor to your
tribe." He released her wrist. "And then I will give you over to
that mob at my walls."

She clutched her wrist. She had no doubt Ghassan spoke truthfully. Dara was dead, and Ali gone. There was no Afshin to fight
for her, no prince to speak for her. Nahri was alone.

She dropped her gaze, for the first time finding it difficult to
meet his eyes. "What do you want?"

THEY DRESSED HER IN THE CEREMONIAL GARMENTS
of her family: a sky blue gown heavy with gold embroidery, white
silk veiling her face. She was glad for the veil—she hoped it hid the
shame burning in her cheeks.

Nahri barely looked at the contract as she signed it, the paper
that bound her to the emir as soon as she reached her first quarter century. In another life, she might have eagerly devoured the
detailed inventory, the dowry that made her one of the wealthiest
women in the city, but today she didn't care. Muntadhir's signa-
ture below hers was an indecipherable scrawl—the king had literally forced his hand just before her future husband spat at her feet
and stormed off.

They went to the massive audience hall next, the place in
which she'd first laid eyes on the Qahtanis. Nahri could sense
the size of the crowd before she entered, the anxious breathing
and quickened heartbeats of thousands of pureblood djinn. She
stared at her feet as she followed the king onto the green marble
platform, stopping at the level just below him. Then she swallowed and lifted her gaze to a sea of stony faces.

Daeva faces. Ghassan had ordered a representative of every
noble family, every trading company and craft guild, every priest
and scholar—anyone of elite standing in the Daeva tribe—to come
hear Nahri's testimony. Despite dozens of arrests and public ex-

ecutions, her tribesmen continued to protest at the palace walls, demanding justice for Dara's murder.

She was here to end that.

Nahri unfurled the scroll she'd been given. Her hands shook as she read out the charges she'd been ordered to say. She did not deviate from the script once nor did she allow herself to dwell on the words condemning the man she loved in the most vulgar of terms, the words destroying the reputation of the Afshin who'd sacrificed everything for his people. Her voice stayed flat. Nahri suspected her audience was savvy enough to realize what was going on, but she didn't care. If Ghassan wanted a performance, he should have thought to ask for one.

Even so, there were tears in her eyes when she finished, and her voice was thick with emotion. Filled with shame, she dropped the scroll and forced herself to look at the crowd.

Nothing. There was no horror, no disbelief among the black-eyed Daevas before her. Indeed, the vast majority looked just as impassive as they had when she first walked in.

No, not impassive.

Defiant.

An old man stepped out from the crowd. Wearing the bright crimson robes of the Grand Temple, he made for a striking sight; an ash mark split his lined face and a tall, azure cap crowned his soot-covered head.

Kartir, Nahri recognized him, remembering the kindness he'd shown her back in the temple. She cringed now as he took another step toward her. Her stomach clenched; she expected some sort of denouncement.

But Kartir did nothing of the sort. Instead, he brought his fingertips together in the traditional Daeva show of respect, dropped his gaze, and bowed.

The priests behind him immediately followed suit, and the motion rippled out across the crowd as the entire audience of

Daevas bowed in her direction. No one said a word. Nahri drew in her breath, and then from just behind her, she heard a heart begin to beat faster.

She stilled, certain she was imagining things and then glanced back. Ghassan al Qahtani met her gaze, an unreadable expression in his eyes. The sun brightened in the window behind him, reflecting off the dazzling gems in his throne, and she realized what he sat upon.

A shedu. The throne was carved in the shape of the winged lion that was her family's symbol.

Ghassan sat upon a Nahid throne.

And he didn't look pleased. She suspected the impromptu display of Daeva unity was not what he intended. She felt for him—truly. It was frustrating when someone upended your well-laid plans.

It's why you never stopped plotting alternatives.

His face turned colder, and so Nahri smiled, the first time she'd done so since Dara's death. It was the smile she'd given the basha, the smile she'd given to hundreds of arrogant men throughout the years just before she swindled them for all they were worth.

Nahri always smiled at her marks.

EPILOGUE

Kaveh e-Pramukh ran the last ten steps to the infirmary. He shoved open the heavy doors, his entire body shaking.

His son lay inside on a fiery bed of smoking cedar.

The sight stole the air from his lungs. Forbidden care until Kaveh—in the words of the king, "sorted out what was going on with your traitorous tribe of fire-worshipping fanatics"—Jamshid was still in the uniform he'd been wearing when he rushed out of their house that terrible night, his white waist-wrap now entirely black with blood. He lay twisted on his side, his body contorted and held up by pillows to avoid pressure on the arrow wounds in his back. A thin layer of ash covered his skin, dotting his black hair. Though his chest rose and fell in the flickering light of the infirmary's wall torches, the rest of his body was still. Too still.

But not alone. Slumped in a chair at his bedside was Emir Muntadhir, his black robe rumpled and streaked with ash, his gray eyes heavy with grief. One of Jamshid's unmoving hands was between his own.

Kaveh approached, and the emir startled. "Grand Wazir . . ." He dropped Jamshid's hand, though not before Kaveh noticed how closely he'd laced their fingers together. "Forgive me, I—"

"Bizhan e-Oshrusan," Kaveh breathed.

Muntadhir frowned. "I don't understand."

"That's the name your father wants. Bizhan e-Oshrusan. He was one of the Daeva soldiers on your expedition; it was he who left the supplies on the beach. I have evidence and a witness who will testify to such a thing." Kaveh's voice broke. "Now please . . . let me see my son."

Muntadhir immediately stepped away, relief and guilt lighting his face. "Of course."

Kaveh was at Jamshid's side in a second. And then he was numb. Because it was impossible that he should be standing here while his child lay broken before him.

Muntadhir was still there. "He . . ." Kaveh heard Muntadhir's voice catch. "He didn't even hesitate. He jumped in front of me the moment the arrows started flying."

Is that supposed to bring me comfort? Kaveh brushed the ash from his son's closed eyes, his fingers trembling from rage as much as grief. *It should be you in a bloody uniform, and Jamshid weeping in royal finery.* He suddenly felt capable of strangling the young man beside him, the man he'd watched break his son's heart time and time again, whenever the rumors surrounding them grew a bit too pitched—or whenever something new and pretty caught his eye.

But Kaveh couldn't say that. The charges he wanted to fling at Muntadhir would likely end with Kaveh being declared the Afshin's accomplice and one of the arrows in Jamshid's back shoved into his heart. Ghassan al Qahtani's eldest son was untouchable—Kaveh and his tribe had just learned all too well how coldly the king dealt with people who threatened his family.

It was a lesson Kaveh would never forget.

But right now, he needed Muntadhir gone—every second he lingered was another Jamshid suffered. He cleared his throat. "My emir, would you please give that name to your father? I would not wish to delay my son's treatment any further."

"But of course," Muntadhir said, flustered. "I . . . I'm sorry, Kaveh. Please let me know if anything changes with his condition."

Oh, I suspect you'll know. Kaveh waited until he heard the door shut.

In the firelight, piles of fresh timber and crates of glass ceiling tiles threw wild shadows across the ruined room. Nahri's patients had been moved while the infirmary was under repair, and she was safely away—in a meeting with the priests at the Grand Temple that Kaveh knew would go long. He'd chosen the time deliberately; he didn't want to implicate her in what he was about to do.

From his belt, he pulled free a small iron blade. It was more scalpel than knife, its handle wrapped in layers of protective linen. Kaveh cut a careful slit in Jamshid's bloody tunic, ripping a gash large enough to reveal the small black tattoo that marked the inside of his son's left shoulder blade.

At first appearance, the tattoo was unremarkable: three swirling glyphs, their lines stark and unadorned. Plenty of Daeva men—especially in Zariaspa, the Pramukhs' wild corner of Daevastana—still partook in the old tradition of marking their skin with the proud symbols of their lineage and caste. A way to honor their heritage, it was one part superstition, one part fashion, the pictograms themselves so ancient that no one could really decipher them. Beloved but useless.

Jamshid's tattoo was not useless. It had been burned into his skin by his mother just hours after his birth and for years had been the surest safeguard of his life. Of his anonymity.

Now it was killing him.

Please, Creator, I beg you: let this work. Kaveh lay the scalpel at the tip of the first swirling glyph. The ebony-marked flesh hissed at the touch of the iron, the magic protesting. His heart racing, Kaveh cut away a sliver of skin.

Jamshid drew in a sharp breath. Kaveh stilled as a few drops of black blood blossomed at the cut. They dripped away.

And then the skin below stitched itself back together.

"What do you think you're doing?" a woman's voice behind him demanded. Nisreen. She was at Kaveh's side in seconds, pushing him away from Jamshid, and pulling the torn flaps of his uniform back over the tattoo. "Have you lost your mind?"

Kaveh shook his head, his eyes welling with tears. "I can't let him suffer like this."

"And revealing him will end that suffering?" Nisreen's eyes scanned the dark room. "Kaveh . . . ," she warned in a low whisper. "We have no idea what will happen if you remove that mark. His body has never healed itself. There's been an arrow lodged in his spine for a week; there's no telling how the magic might respond to such an injury. You could kill him."

"He could die if I don't!" Kaveh wiped his eyes with his other hand. "He's not your child, you don't understand. I have to do something."

"He's not going to die," Nisreen assured him. "He's endured this long." She pressed down on Kaveh's wrist, lowering the knife. "They're not like us, Kaveh," she said softly. "He has his mother's blood—he'll survive this. But if you remove that mark, if he heals on his own . . ." She shook her head. "Ghassan will have him tortured for information—he'll never believe his innocence. The Qahtanis will rip through our tribe for answers; there will be soldiers tearing through every grassy knoll, every home in Daevastana." Her eyes flashed. "You will destroy everything that we've worked for."

"It's already gone," Kaveh argued, his voice bitter. "The Afshin is dead, Banu Nahri will have a Qahtani baby in her belly in a year, and we've not even heard from—"

Nisreen took the knife from his hand and replaced it with something hard and small. It stung his palm. Iron, he realized, as he held it up in the light to examine it. A ring.

A battered iron ring with an emerald that shone as if it were on fire.

Kaveh immediately closed his fingers over the ring. It scorched his skin. "By the Creator," he breathed. "How did you—"

She shook her head. "Don't ask. But don't despair. We need you, Kaveh." She nodded at Jamshid. "He needs you. You need to get back into Ghassan's good graces, to make him trust you enough that you can return to Zariaspa."

He gripped the Afshin's ring as it grew hotter. "Dara tried to kill my *son*, Nisreen." His voice cracked.

"Your son was on the wrong side." Kaveh flinched, and Nisreen continued. "He won't be again. We'll make sure of it." She sighed. "Did you find someone to take the blame for the supplies?"

He offered a mute nod. "Bizhan e-Oshrusan. He asked only that we make arrangements for his parents. He . . ." Kaveh cleared his throat. "He understood that he was not to be taken alive."

Nisreen's face was somber. "May the Creator reward his sacrifice."

There was silence between them. Jamshid stirred in his sleep, the motion threatening to upend Kaveh all over again.

But it was also the reminder he needed. For there was still a way to save his son. And for that Kaveh would do anything; he'd grovel before the king, cross the world, face the ifrit.

He'd burn down Daevabad itself.

The ring seemed to pulse in Kaveh's hand, a thing alive with a beating heart. "Does Nahri know?" he asked softly, raising his hand. "About this, I mean?"

Nisreen shook her head. "No." A protective edge entered her voice. "She has enough to worry about right now. She needs no distractions, no false hope. And truthfully . . . she's safest not knowing. If we're caught, her innocence might be her only defense."

Kaveh nodded again, but he was tired of being on the defensive. He thought of the Daevas that Ghassan had already executed, the merchants beaten up in the Grand Bazaar, the girl raped in front of the Royal Guard. Of his son—nearly killed defending a Qahtani and then denied treatment. Of the martyrs in the Grand Temple. Of all the other ways his people had suffered.

Kaveh was tired of bowing to the Qahtanis.

A small flicker of defiance bloomed in his chest, the first he'd felt in a long time. His next question came out in a desperate whisper. "If I can get the ring to her . . . do you really think she can bring him back?"

Nisreen gazed at Jamshid. Her eyes were filled with the type of quiet awe most Daevas felt in the presence of one of their Nahids. "Yes," she said firmly. Reverently. "I think Manizheh can do anything."

GLOSSARY

Beings of Fire

DAEVA: The ancient term for all fire elementals before the djinn rebellion, as well as the name of the tribe residing in Daevastana, of which Dara and Nahri are both part. Once shapeshifters who lived for millennia, the Daeva had their magical abilities sharply curbed by the Prophet Suleiman as a punishment for harming humanity.

DJINN: A human word for "daeva." After Zaydi al Qahtani's rebellion, all his followers, and eventually all daevas, began using this term for their race.

IFRIT: The original daevas who defied Suleiman and were stripped of their abilities. Sworn enemies of the Nahid family, the ifrit revenge themselves by enslaving other djinn to cause chaos among humanity.

SIMURGH: Scaled firebirds that the djinn are fond of racing.

ZAHHAK: A large, flying, fire-breathing lizard-like beast.

Beings of Water

MARID: Extremely powerful water elementals. Near mythical to the djinn, the marid haven't been seen in centuries, though it's rumored the lake surrounding Daevabad was once theirs.

Beings of Air

PERI: Air elementals. More powerful than the djinn—and far more secretive—the peri keep resolutely to themselves.

RUKH: Enormous predatory firebirds that the peri can use for hunting.

SHEDU: Mythical winged lions, an emblem of the Nahid family.

Beings of Earth

GHOULS: The reanimated, cannibalistic corpses of humans who have made deals with the ifrit.

ISHTAS: A small, scaled creature obsessed with organization and footwear.

KARKADANN: A magical beast similar to an enormous rhinoceros with a horn as long as a man.

Languages

DIVASTI: The language of the Daeva tribe.

DJINNISTANI: Daevabad's common tongue, a merchant creole the djinn and shafit use to speak to those outside their tribe.

GEZIRIYYA: The language of the Geziri tribe, which only members of their tribe can speak and understand.

General Terminology

ABAYA: A loose, floor-length, full-sleeved dress worn by women.

ADHAN: The Islamic call to prayer.

AFSHIN: The name of the Daeva warrior family who once served the Nahid Council. Also used as a title.

AKHI: Geziri for "my brother," an endearment.

BAGA NAHID: The proper title for male healers of the Nahid family.

BANU NAHIDA: The proper title for female healers of the Nahid family.

CHADOR: An open cloak made from a semicircular cut of fabric, draped over the head and worn by Daeva women.

DIRHAM/DINAR: A type of currency used in Egypt.

DISHDASHA: A floor-length man's tunic, popular among the Geziri.

EMIR: The crown prince and designated heir to the Qahtani throne.

FAJR: The dawn hour/dawn prayer.

GALABIYYA: A traditional Egyptian garment, essentially a floor-length tunic.

HAMMAM: A bathhouse.

ISHA: The late evening hour/evening prayer.

MAGHRIB: The sunset hour/sunset prayer.

MIDAN: A plaza/city square.

MIHRAB: A wall niche indicating the direction of prayer.

MUHTASIB: A market inspector.

QAID: The head of the Royal Guard, essentially the top military official in the djinn army.

RAKAT: A unit of prayer.

SHAFIT: People with mixed djinn and human blood.

SHEIKH: A religious educator/leader.

SULEIMAN'S SEAL: The seal ring Suleiman once used to control the djinn, given to the Nahids and later stolen by the Qahtanis. The bearer of Suleiman's ring can nullify any magic.

TALWAR: An Agnivanshi sword.

TANZEEM: A grassroots fundamentalist group in Daevabad dedicated to fighting for shafit rights and religious reform.

ULEMA: A legal body of religious scholars.

WAZIR: A government minister.

ZAR: A traditional ceremony meant to deal with djinn possession.

ZUHR: The noon hour/noon prayer.

ZULFIQAR: The forked copper blades of the Geziri tribe; when inflamed, their poisonous edges destroy even Nahid flesh, making them among the deadliest weapons in this world.

ACKNOWLEDGMENTS

This book began as a private project that would never have seen the light of day were it not for the support and encouragement—sometimes rather forceful!—of the wonderful people below.

First, to my friends and faculty at the American University of Cairo: thank you for sharing your country's awe-inspiring history, for guiding me through the sites that would have made up Nahri's world, and for renewing my faith in a way I didn't realize until much later. Any mistakes or misrepresentations are mine alone.

To my husband, Shamik, whose curiosity about what I was always typing on my computer started this entire journey, thank you. You're the best friend and beta reader a fellow nerd could ask for, and you've been my rock.

The fantastically talented people of the Brooklyn Speculative Fiction Writers' group—particularly Rob Cameron, Marcy Arlin, Steven R. Fairchild, Sondra Fink, Jonathan Hernandez, Alex Kirtland, Cynthia Lovett, Ian Montgomerie, Brad Park, Mark Salzwedel, Essowe Tchalim, and Ana Vohryzek—who whipped this manuscript into shape and became friends in the process.

Jennifer Azantian, my wonderful agent and Nahri's and Ali's

greatest cheerleader, thank you for taking a chance on some random writer from Twitter; for making what seemed a dream become reality; and for being a steadying presence the many times I needed one.

Priyanka Krishnan, my amazing editor, who helped guide me through the rough patches, and whose warmth and diplomatically worded comments always make me smile—I'll try not to kill too many of the characters you love.

To the rest of the Voyager team, including Angela Craft, Andrew DiCecco, Jessie Edwards, Pam Jaffee, Mumtaz Mustafa, Shawn Nicholls, Shelby Peak, Caro Perny, David Pomerico, Mary Ann Petyak, Liate Stehlik, and Paula Szafranski: I will always appreciate the hard work that went into making this book, and the enthusiasm everyone had for it. And to everyone else at Harper who loved and supported this book, I thank you. You have been a great group to work with. A very sincere thanks to Will Staehle, as well, for designing a cover that literally took my breath away the first time I saw it.

I'd never have gotten this far without my extraordinary parents—my mother, Colleen, who shared her love of reading with me, and my father, Robert, who then drove me to the library and bookstore what must have seemed every weekend of my childhood—your love and hard work made me the person I am today. Thanks go to my brother, Michael, as well, for teaching me the meaning of sibling love *without* having to battle for a throne. To Sankar and Anamika, who stepped up to help the moment this all became real; you will always have my deepest gratitude.

To my daughter, my greatest source of happiness: you're too young to read this now, but thank you for letting me work on this at home, albeit with a level of toddler negotiation that is frighteningly reminiscent of a certain con artist. I love you.

And last, but certainly not least, a sincere thank-you to my ummah: to the past that inspired me, the present that embraced me, and the future we'll build together . . . jazakum Allahu khayran.

About the author

About the book

Read on

Insights,
Interviews
& More . . .

Meet S. A. Chakraborty

Author photograph by Melissa C. Beckman

S. A. CHAKRABORTY is a speculative fiction writer from New York City. Her debut, *The City of Brass*, is the first book in the Daevabad Trilogy. When not buried in books about Mughal miniatures and Abbasid princes, she enjoys hiking, knitting, and re-creating unnecessarily complicated meals for her family. You can find her online at www.sachakraborty.com or on Twitter at @SChakrabs, where she likes to ramble about history, politics, and Islamic art. ∾

A Prologue to
The City of Brass

Muntadhir

"DHIRU." A HAND SHOOK HIS SHOULDER. "DHIRU."

Muntadhir al Qahtani groaned, burying his face in his pillow. "Go away, Zaynab."

His sister's small body landed next to his, jolting the bed and sending a fresh throb of pain into his pounding skull. "You look awful," she said cheerfully. He felt her pluck away the hair plastered to his cheek. "Why are you all sweaty? Were you . . ." She let out a scandalized—and rather thrilled—gasp. "Were you drinking?"

Muntadhir pressed the silk pillow over his ears. "Uhkti, it's too early for this. Why are you in my room?"

"It's not that early." Zaynab's hands scrabbled around, tickling him, and she laughed as he tried to wriggle away. Abruptly, her fingers stilled, closing over something lying near his head.

"Is this an earring? Dhiru, why do you have a woman's earring in your bed?" Excitement lit her voice. "*Oh*, does it belong to that new singing girl from Babili?"

In a moment of utter panic, Muntadhir shot out his hand to sweep the other side of the mattress. Relief swept through him when he found it empty; the earring's owner must have already left, thank God. That was *not* something he needed his gossipy, thirteen-year-old sister to see.

He rolled over, squinting in the dark; Muntadhir's servants all knew to pull the shades before the Emir woke from one of his "evenings," so Zaynab came to him in blurry pieces: her gray-gold eyes, her mischievous smile . . . the intricate gold and emerald jhumka dangling from her fingers. . . .

"Give me that." Muntadhir snatched the earring back as Zaynab giggled. "Could you at least make yourself useful and pour me a glass of water?"

Still grinning, Zaynab bounced off the bed and carefully poured the contents of his blue glass pitcher into a goblet, making a face as she examined it. "Why does this smell funny?"

"It has medicine for my head in it."

She came back and offered the cup to him gracefully. "You shouldn't drink wine, akhi. It's forbidden."

"So many things are forbidden, little bird." Muntadhir drained the glass. He wasn't setting the best example for his sister, but at least last night's drinking had—technically—been in the service of his kingdom.

Zaynab rolled her eyes. "You know I hate when you call me that. I'm not a child anymore."

"Yes, but you still flit around everywhere, listening and seeing things that are not your business." Muntadhir tapped the top of her head. "A tall bird," he teased. "You and Ali are going to leave me behind with all this growing."

She fell back onto the bed. "I tried to see him," she complained, sounding glum. "Wajed brought the cadets over from the Royal Guard to spar. I went to the arena, and Abba made me leave. He said it was 'inappropriate,'" she added, flicking a hand dismissively.

Muntadhir was sympathetic. "You are getting older, Zaynab, as you said," he pointed out gently. "You shouldn't be around all those men."

Zaynab glared at him. "You smell like wine and have some lady's earring in your bed. Why do you get to do whatever you want, and I can't even leave the harem anymore? If we were back in Am Gezira, I'd be able to go out. Our cousins do all the time!"

"But we're not in Am Gezira, and our cousins aren't princesses," Muntadhir said. He didn't entirely disagree with Zaynab, but he didn't feel up to debating Daevabad's archaic traditions with his sister right now either. "Life is different here. People will talk."

"So, let them talk!" Zaynab balled her hands, her fists punching the silk blanket beneath her. "It's not fair! I'm *bored*. I can't even go to the market park in the Ayaanle Quarter anymore. That was my favorite place. Amma used to take me there every Friday to see the animals."

Her lower lip trembled, making her look much younger than her thirteen years. "Ali too."

Muntadhir sighed. "I know, ukhti. I'm sorry . . ." Zaynab looked away and Muntadhir's chest tightened. "I'll take you, alright?" he suggested. "No one is going to stop me. We'll go by the Citadel on the way and drag Ali out, too."

Zaynab's face instantly brightened. "Really?"

He nodded, giving one of her braids a little tug. "I'll insist I need a particularly small zulfiqari to keep us safe. As long as *you* promise to deal with his chattering. He'll probably subject us to an entire afternoon's lecture on the history of the market park."

"It's a deal!" She smiled again, the grin lighting up her whole face. "You're a good brother, Dhiru."

"I try." He nodded toward the door. "Now will you let me go back to sleep?"

"You can't. Abba wants to see you."

Muntadhir's mood soured at once. "About what?"

Zaynab shrugged. "I didn't ask. He seemed annoyed." She inclined her head. "You should probably hurry."

"I see. Thanks for letting me know so quickly." His sister merely laughed at his sarcasm, and he shooed her away with a sigh. "Go on, you troublemaker. Let me get dressed."

Zaynab skipped off, and Muntadhir rolled out of bed, swearing under his breath. He hadn't expected to see his father until this evening; had he known he'd be summoned so early, he would never have had so much to drink last night.

He splashed rosewater over his face, then rinsed his mouth and ran his hands through his hair and over his beard, attempting to smooth their disarray. He exchanged his rumpled waist-cloth for a crisp dishdasha patterned with blue diamonds, then grabbed his cap and turban cloth and hurried out, winding his turban rapidly as he half-jogged toward the arena. His limbs felt heavy; his abused body did not appreciate the speed at which it was being compelled to move.

When he finally reached the arena, Muntadhir ▶

took the stairs leading to the viewing platform with great care, easing one foot ahead of the other, but trying not to appear impaired. Ghassan would not be pleased to see him lurching around like a newborn karkadan.

The pavilion that overlooked the palace arena was well-shaded, with drapes of brightly patterned gold and black silk and thickly planted potted ferns rising overhead to protect Daevabad's royals and their privileged retainers from the city's merciless midday heat. A half-dozen servants waved wetly gleaming palm fans, dipping the branches into a fountain of enchanted ice before churning air in the darkened space.

Muntadhir breathed deeply outside the curtained archway, inhaling the smoky scent of frankincense and trying to calm his pulse. His mouth tasted sour and thick, last night's wine not entirely gone. Not that it mattered. He could be impeccably turned out, and Ghassan would see through the façade—he always did. His father had a stare that opened a man up and dissected him out as he squirmed. And he was most accomplished at turning that stare on his eldest son.

At least today he'd be able to counter it with some useful information. Steeling himself, he stepped through the curtain.

He winced. Light came in dappled rays through the drapes. The chatter of the men on the pavilion, the clash and sizzle of the zulfiqars below, and the delicate music coming from a pair of lutes all competed to make his head pound in a dizzying manner. Ahead, he caught sight of his father sitting on a thick brocaded cushion, his attention focused on the arena.

Muntadhir began to move toward him, but he didn't get halfway there before a young Daeva man abruptly stepped in front of him. Muntadhir jerked back in surprise, barely keeping his balance.

"Emir Muntadhir! Peace be upon you! I hope you are having a most excellent of mornings!"

The man was dressed in the garb of a priest . . . or maybe some sort of priest-in-training—

Muntadhir was not up to deciphering the intricacies of the Daeva faith right now. A short crimson jacket went to the fellow's knees, underneath which he wore striped azure and fire-yellow trousers. A cap of the same color sat upon his curly hair.

The effect was bright. Very bright. Far too bright for this particular morning, though there was something about the man's long-lashed black eyes, overly enthusiastic manner and rural Divasti accent that tugged at Muntadhir's memory.

The pieces slowly came together in his foggy head. "Upon you, peace," he answered warily. "Pramukh, yes? Kaveh's son?"

The other man nodded, grinning. He was actually rocking back and forth on his heels with excitement, and Muntadhir suddenly wondered if he wasn't the only one who'd had too much to drink.

"Jamshid! That is . . . I am meaning, that is my name," the other man replied, bumbling the Djinnistani words. He blushed, and even in his preoccupied state, Muntadhir could not help but note that it was rather fetching. "I cannot tell you how thrilled I am to join your service, Emir." He brought his fingers together in the Daeva blessing, then added a smart Geziri salute for good measure. "You will find none more loyal than me!"

Joining my service? Muntadhir stared at Jamshid in complete confusion for a few heartbeats before his gaze slid to his father. Ghassan wasn't looking at him, confirmation in Muntadhir's mind that he'd just become the pawn in some new scheme.

He returned his attention to the bouncing, starry-eyed priest. His eyelashes really were suspiciously long, the effect captivating.

Muntadhir cleared his throat, shutting down the thought. There was no damn way this man was joining his service. He feigned a smile, inclining his head to motion Jamshid out of his way. "Would you mind . . ."

"But of course!" Jamshid sprang back. "Should I wait for you outside?"▶

"You do that." Muntadhir neatly stepped past him without a backward glance.

Ghassan didn't look up as Muntadhir approached. His admiring gaze was still locked on the ground below.

"Look at him fight," his father said by way of greeting. Appreciation and proud awe—two sentiments he rarely directed toward Muntadhir—were clear in his voice. "I have never seen someone so young handle a zulfiqar with such skill."

There was only one person who'd earn such praise from Ghassan al Qahtani, and as Muntadhir glanced down upon the sand, apprehension rising in his chest, he spotted Alizayd. His little brother was sparring against a soldier who looked to be twice his height and three times his bulk. Both fighters had their blades aflame, and a group of young cadets were ringed out in a wide circle around them, cheering their royal fellow.

Muntadhir frowned, stepping forward as he caught sight of the greenish haze at the heart of the whipping fire. "That's not a training blade."

Ghassan shrugged. "He's ready to move on."

Muntadhir whirled on his father. "He's *eleven*. Citadel cadets don't start using live blades until they're fifteen, if not older." He tensed, cringing as the weapons met with a clash. "He could be killed!"

Ghassan waved him off. "He would not have advanced if Wajed and his instructors did not think him prepared. I spoke to him, as well. He desires the challenge."

Muntadhir bit his lip. He knew his little brother well enough to know it wasn't the challenge Ali desired. It was the chance to prove himself. To prove to his fellow cadets—boys taken from hard-scrabble villages in Am Gezira, the ones now shouting him on—that the half-Ayaanle prince was just as good as they were. Better. And child or not, there was no denying the deadly focus in Ali's eyes when he returned his opponent's strike, taking advantage of his small size to duck under the man's arm.

My future Qaid. The young man who, but for a quirk of timing and politics, could be in his older brother's thoroughly privileged position.

Troubled, Muntadhir forced himself to look away. "May I sit, Abba?" Ghassan nodded at a cushion, and Muntadhir sank into it. "Forgive my tardiness," he continued. "I didn't realize you wished to speak to me so early."

"It's noon, Muntadhir. If you didn't drink until dawn, this wouldn't seem early." Ghassan threw him an exasperated look. "You are too young to be so reliant on wine. If it doesn't put you in an early grave, it will make you a weak king."

Muntadhir had no doubt which of those possibilities bothered his father more. "I'll try to temper my intake," he said diplomatically. "Though last night was not without its uses."

He fell silent as a servant approached to pour him a cup of coffee from a steaming copper carafe. Muntadhir thanked him and took a long sip, willing the drink to dispel the pounding in his head.

"What uses?" Ghassan prodded.

"I think your suspicions about al Danaf are correct," he replied, naming one of the northern Geziri governors. "I was out with his cousin last night, and he was making some rather interesting promises to one of my female companions. I'd say they've either learned to conjure gold from rocks or they're skimming from the caravan taxes due to the Treasury."

"Proof?"

Muntadhir shook his head. "But his wife is from a powerful clan. I suspect they would be none too pleased to learn of the offers he was making to another woman." He took another sip of the fragrant coffee. "I thought I'd pass him over to you." It was their usual way: Muntadhir learning what he could by using his charm, and his father stepping in when it was time to turn to different—darker—methods.

Ghassan shook his head, his mouth pressed in a grim line. "That bastard. To think I was considering him for your sister's hand."▶

Muntadhir froze, the cup halfway to his lips. "What?"

"It would be smart to strengthen our relationship with the north. Alleviate some of the tension that has built over the past few decades."

"You'd give your daughter to a snake a half-century older than her just to alleviate some tension?" Muntadhir's voice was sharp. "She doesn't even speak Geziriyya. Do you have any idea how lonely she'd be out there? How miserable?"

Ghassan waved him off the same way he'd waved off Muntadhir's concerns about Ali's safety. It was a profoundly irritating gesture. "It was only a thought. I would not do anything without talking to her."

As though her opinion would matter. Muntadhir knew his father meant no true unkindness . . . but Zaynab was a princess, a powerful piece in the deadly game that was Daevabad's politics. Her future would be determined based on whatever course Ghassan deemed best for their reign.

"And the reason you had me summoned— does it have to do with Kaveh's rather loud son thinking that he's joining my service?"

Ghassan glanced at his son. "He *is* joining your service. He's offered himself for the Daeva Brigade. He'll train at the Citadel with the aim of becoming your personal guard, and in the meantime, he can join your circle. He's apparently quite the talented archer."

An *archer*? Muntadhir groaned. "No. Do not make me take some country noble with aspirations of being an Afshin under my wing. I beg you."

"Don't be such a snob." Ghassan's gaze returned to the arena as Ali landed another blow. "Jamshid is a temple-educated Daeva noble. I'm sure he'll fit in with your little retinue of poets and singers well enough. Indeed, I want you to make sure of it."

Muntadhir frowned at the intent in his father's voice. "Is something going on?"

"No." Ghassan's mouth tightened. "But I think it would be valuable if Jamshid was in your orbit and if he was loyal—truly loyal. It cannot hurt us to have a reliable Daeva so highly placed." He shrugged. "And were that reliable Daeva to be in the Grand Wazir's household . . . all the better."

Even though they were speaking quietly in Geziriyya, Muntadhir darted a peek past his father's shoulder at the surrounding nobles to make sure no one was listening. "Do you suspect Kaveh of something?"

"You sound hopeful."

Muntadhir hesitated. He had been uneasy with his father's choice to name Kaveh e-Pramukh as Grand Wazir a few years back, but he'd been too young—and too fearful of disagreeing with his father—to protest.

Ghassan must have sensed his thoughts. "Speak your mind, Emir."

"I don't trust him, Abba."

"Because he is Daeva?"

"No," Muntadhir replied, his voice firm. "You know I'm not like that. I trust many Daevas. But there are some we will never win over. I can feel it. You can *see* it. Behind the polite smiles, there's resentment in their eyes."

Ghassan's expression didn't waver. "And you think Kaveh is one of them? He has done very well as Grand Wazir."

Muntadhir twisted the silver ring on his thumb. "I think a man as close as he reportedly was to Manizheh and Rustam is a man we should be careful of," he said delicately. "Abba, there are times Kaveh looks at me . . . it's like he sees an insect. He never lets it color his actions, but I'd bet coin that behind his walls, he's calling us sandflies in need of swatting."

"All the more reason to put someone behind those walls."

"And his son is the best option?" Muntadhir asked. "You could easily place a proper spy in his household."

Ghassan shook his head. "I don't want a spy. I want his son. I want someone I can use, someone Kaveh *knows* I can use, and a person he wouldn't dare risk."▸

Muntadhir knew what his father was truly saying. It was a dynamic he'd seen play out before: The sons of political opponents taken into the Citadel, ostensibly for honorable careers, but also so there would be a ready blade at their throat should their parents step out of line. Wives "invited" to serve as companions for the queen, then detained in the harem when suspicion fell upon their husbands.

The memory of Jamshid's eager smile sent prickles of guilt across his skin. "Do you intend to harm him?" he finally asked.

"I hope not. You have a talent for dazzling people. There are courtiers who would spill blood to be one of your companions." Ghassan's eyes narrowed. "So, take that bright-eyed, aspiring Afshin, and make him your closest friend. Show Kaveh's son the charm, the riches, the women . . . the paradise his life could be. And make damn sure he knows his fortunes are tied to ours. It should not be difficult, Muntadhir."

Muntadhir considered this. Knowing his father, he supposed he should be pleased Ghassan was asking him only to befriend Jamshid, not poison him or frame him in some sort of scandal. "That's it? Make him one of my companions?"

There was a flicker in his father's eyes he couldn't decipher. "I would not be averse to you encouraging his tongue to spill about his life back in Zariaspa. About what he knows of his father's relationship with the Nahid siblings."

Muntadhir ran a finger around the edge of his coffee cup. Whether it was the wine still churning in his belly or his father's words, he'd lost his taste for it.

"Understood. If that is all . . ."

Ali's cry drew his attention. Muntadhir turned just in time to see his brother's zulfiqar go spinning out of his hand.

Relief flooded through him. He doubted Ali wanted to lose, but the sooner his little brother was done playing with that fiery, poisoned death blade, the better.

Except Ali's opponent didn't stop. He charged after him, kicking his brother square in the chest. Ali fell hard, sprawling in the sand.

Muntadhir shot to his feet in outrage.

"Sit," Ghassan said flatly.

"But, Abba—"

"*Now.*"

Muntadhir sat, his skin burning as Ali's opponent stalked after him. The other cadets were frozen. His brother seemed suddenly, horrifically, young and small; a scared little kid scrambling backward, his terrified gray eyes darting between the looming bulk of his opponent and the spot where his zulfiqar had landed.

Men died trying to master the zulfiqar. The training was ruthless, meant to separate out those who could properly wield and control such a destructive weapon from those who couldn't. But surely not here. Not the king's *son*, not before his own eyes.

"Abba," Muntadhir tried again, tensing as Ali barely ducked the next strike. Flames whipped around the warrior's copper sword as he lunged. "Abba, stop this. Tell him to stand down!" His voice broke in fear.

His father said nothing.

Ali's expression abruptly changed; determination sweeping over his features. He grabbed a handful of sand and hurled it in his opponent's face.

The man jerked back, his free hand going to his eyes. It was enough time for Ali to hook his foot around the other man's ankles, knocking him off balance and sending him tumbling to the ground. Ali drew his khanjar in the next moment, ramming it into the hand holding the zulfiqar. He did it again and again, and then again, the brutal movement drawing blood from the other warrior.

His opponent dropped the zulfiqar.

Muntadhir let out a shaky breath. Despite his father's order, he'd risen back to his feet, drawing close to the platform's edge. He must have been visible for Ali glanced up, meeting his eyes.

In the space of time it took for his little brother to give Muntadhir a trembling smile, his opponent had drawn his own khanjar.

He smashed the dagger's handle across Ali's face.

Ali yelped in pain, blood pouring from his ▸

nose. Muntadhir's angry shout was drowned by the sound of the whistle marking the end of the match.

His hand dropped to his own khanjar, which he intended to put through the throat of the man below immediately.

Ghassan grabbed his wrist, jerking him close. "Stop."

"I'm not going to stop! Did you see what he did?"

"Yes." His father's voice was firm, but Muntadhir didn't miss the dart of his eyes back to Ali before they settled on his eldest's face. "The match had yet to be called. Alizayd shouldn't have lost focus."

Muntadhir wrenched his arm free. "*Shouldn't have lost focus*? They were both disarmed! A man does that to your son and you say nothing?"

Anger flashed across Ghassan's face, but it was a weary sort of anger. "I would rather see his nose broken than hear of his death on some faraway battlefield. He is learning, Muntadhir. He's going to be Qaid. It is a violent, dangerous life, and neither you nor I do him any favors by softening his training."

Muntadhir looked at his little brother. His white sparring uniform was now filthy, stained by scorch marks, blood, and the arena's dirty sand. Ali pressed a grimy sleeve to his nose to stem the bleeding as he limped over to retrieve his zulfiqar.

The sight broke Muntadhir's heart. "Then I don't want him to be Qaid," he burst out. "Dismiss him from the Citadel. Let him enjoy whatever is left of his childhood and then let him have a normal life."

"He's never going to have a normal life," Ghassan said softly. "He is a prince from two powerful families. Such people do not have normal lives in our world."

Muntadhir said nothing, feeling sick as Ali re-sheathed his zulfiqar, the blade looking too big against his small body.

Ghassan joined him at the pavilion's edge. "It is not for Alizayd alone that I do these things," he chided, not ungently. "You have good political instincts, Muntadhir. You are charming, you are an excellent diplomat . . ." He put a hand on Muntadhir's shoulder. "But you are neither an ambassador, nor a wazir. You are my successor. You need to harden your heart, or Daevabad will crush you. And you cannot risk that, my son, not for a moment. The city rises and falls with its king."

Daevabad comes first. Muntadhir's lip curled. It was his father's mantra. The thing he said when brutally putting down those who dared to dissent. When ruining the lives of his young children.

Things Muntadhir would one day be expected to do.

Nausea welled inside him. "I . . . I should take Jamshid to the Citadel." It was the first excuse he could think of.

Ghassan lifted his hand. "Go in peace."

"Upon you blessings." Muntadhir touched his heart and brow, backing away.

Jamshid was still there, and he was no less exuberant the second time, leaping to his feet as though someone had touched him with a hot coal when he saw Muntadhir approaching. "Emir!"

"Please stop that." Muntadhir rubbed his head. He had no desire to go to the Citadel. Despite his promise to his father, the only thing he felt like doing was drinking away their conversation, and the memory of Ali's pained cry and Zaynab's sad eyes. But his usual cup companions were likely still hungover in their beds, and Muntadhir knew his own weaknesses enough to know he was in no state to drink alone.

He narrowed his eyes at Jamshid. "Does your priesthood forbid wine?"

Jamshid lifted a thick eyebrow, looking baffled. "No?"

"Then you're coming with me."

JAMSHID STROLLED THE length of the carved wooden balcony. "This is an extraordinary view," he admired. "One can see all of Daevabad from here."

Muntadhir made a grunt of assent from his ▶

cushion but didn't move. He didn't feel like looking down at the city he'd be expected to one day tyrannize, even if it was beautiful.

Jamshid turned around, leaning against the railing. "Is something the matter, Emir?"

"Why would you ask that?" Muntadhir said.

"You look a bit sad." Jamshid shrugged. "And I'd heard you were more talkative."

Muntadhir stared at the man in disbelief. People did not ask if the Emir of Daevabad was *sad*. Not even his closest companions spoke so freely. Ah, they would have noticed his reticence surely, but they wouldn't dare question it. Instead, they'd compose poems to praise him or offer up diverting tales, all while discretely beginning to water down his wine.

But Muntadhir couldn't find it in himself to be annoyed. After all, palace etiquette probably wasn't taught at the Daeva's Grand Temple. "Tell me of yourself," he said instead. "Why did you wish to leave the priesthood? Are you no longer a believer?"

Jamshid shook his head. "I'm still a believer. But I didn't think shutting myself up with dusty texts the best way to serve my people."

Now that was intriguing. "And your father agreed? Kaveh seems so orthodox."

"My father is in Zariaspa on family business." Jamshid's knuckles paled as he tightened his grip on the wine cup. "He doesn't know."

"You left the Grand Temple and joined the Royal Guard without your father's permission?" Muntadhir was astonished . . . and a bit impressed. That was *not* the way things were typically done among Daevabad's powerful noble families, and the man before him didn't seem the rebellious type. At all.

Jamshid looked amused by his reaction. "Does your father know everything about you?"

There was a spark in the other man's dark eyes that, combined, with the question, sent a sharp buzz down Muntadhir's spine. He drew up, his gaze flickering over the other man. Under different circumstances, he might have wondered if there had been an undercurrent of intent lingering in those words. He might have been tempted to find out; with a flash of the smile he knew had broken a fair number of hearts in Daevabad, and an invitation to sit.

But very few people in Daevabad looked at Muntadhir al Qahtani with such directness . . . and even fewer spoke to him with the kind of genuine warmth that emanated from Jamshid. He cleared his throat, trying to ignore the blood rushing under his skin. "My father knows everything," he found himself saying.

Jamshid laughed, a rich sound that sent Muntadhir's stomach fluttering. "I suppose that's true." He left the balcony, coming closer. "That must be difficult."

"It's terrible," Muntadhir agreed, suddenly having a hard time looking away from the other man. He wasn't a great beauty but there was something pleasing about his winged brows and slightly old-fashioned mustache. Still in his temple attire, Jamshid looked as though he might have stepped out of one of the chipped paintings of the Nahid Council that clung to the palace's ancient walls.

Jamshid sat without invitation and then quickly stood back up, looking embarrassed. "Forgive me . . . am I allowed? I know there's all sorts of protocol."

"Sit," Muntadhir urged. "Please. It's nice to take a break from protocol."

Jamshid smiled again. It seemed to be a thing he did easily—Muntadhir supposed people who grew up without having to worry about ridiculous court etiquette and its related political intrigue all did so. "My father would disagree. He's always worried we're showing our 'terrible' country ways." Jamshid made a face. "You'd think after a decade in Daevabad, I would have lost my accent."

"I like your accent," Muntadhir assured. He took a sip of his wine. "Why did you leave Zariaspa?"

"My father wanted me educated at the Grand ▸

Temple. Or so he says." He drank from his cup, his dark eyes fixing on the sky. "I suspect it was easier to start fresh here."

"What do you mean?" Muntadhir asked, his curiosity getting the better of his urge not to follow his father's orders so immediately.

Jamshid glanced at him, surprise in his dark eyes. "My mother . . . I assumed you knew."

Muntadhir winced. He did know, and his words had been clumsy. "Forgive me. Your mother died when you were young, correct? I didn't mean to bring it up."

"I don't mind," Jamshid said quickly. "Truly. I don't get to speak about her with anyone. My father refuses." His expression clouded. "She died when I was born, and they weren't married. I think she might have been a servant, but no one will tell me anything more about her. They're too ashamed."

Muntadhir frowned. "Why? You have your father's name. Is it that much of an issue?"

"For Daevas, yes. My people are obsessed with tracing their roots back on every which side." He drank back the rest of his cup. "It determines what we do, who we marry . . . everything." He spoke lightly, but Muntadhir didn't miss the flash of pain in his face. "And half of my roots are missing."

"Maybe that just means you're free to write your own destiny. Maybe it's a gift." Muntadhir said softly, thinking of his Ali and Zaynab.

Jamshid stilled, his eyes locked on Muntadhir's, his expression serious. When he finally spoke, his voice was solemn. "I had heard . . ." He paused. "That you tend to become overly poetic when drunk."

Muntadhir's eyes went wide as heat rushed to his face. Had Jamshid just . . . *insulted* him? Outside his family, no one dared speak to Daevabad's emir with such disrespect. They probably feared the king would execute them.

But as Jamshid's eyes suddenly danced with mirth and a laugh escaped his lips, it was not anger Muntadhir felt. He didn't know *what* he felt; there was a strange lightness dancing in his chest that was entirely unfamiliar.

Even so, he tried to muster an indignant glare. "Your father is right to worry over your manners," Muntadhir shot back. "I was trying to be nice, you ass!"

"Then I am blessed indeed to join your service." Jamshid smirked, and Muntadhir realized his father's cold assignment was going to be much more difficult than he had anticipated. "You'll have plenty of time to teach me." ❧

Reading Group Guide

1. *The City of Brass* is told from two perspectives: Nahri's and Ali's. Whose did you find more compelling, and why?

2. Nahri struggles with her magic, her heritage, and with finding her path once she is brought to Daevabad. Did you sympathize with her struggles? How does her view of her gifts—and herself— change as the story progresses?

3. Ali also struggles, primarily with the question of whether he owes his loyalty to his family, or to the people he believes they should be protecting (the shafit). Do you feel he made the right choices? What might you have done differently, in his place?

4. Dara is a character who contains many layers, and whose past is filled with question marks. Were you surprised when you learned of his dark history as a warrior? Do you feel his relationship with Nahri could have survived those revelations?

5. Were you familiar with any of the folklore S. A. Chakraborty drew upon in creating the world of the djinn? If so, which elements? What was your favorite aspect of the world she created?

6. Did you come away feeling any of the characters were true villains or true heroes? Why or why not?

7. Take a look at the map and the description of the six djinn tribal regions in the front of the book. If you were to visit one of the tribes, which would it be?

8. The political feuding of the djinn is complex, tangled, and dates back centuries. Did you see any parallels to real world events, either historical or contemporary, in your reading?

9. Chakraborty draws upon a specific storytelling tradition—the type of which is used in classic Middle Eastern folk tales such as *One Thousand and One Nights*. It is exciting and action-packed, and yet meant to draw you deeper and deeper into a world in a slow and powerful way. Did you feel she succeeded?

10. *The City of Brass* is the first book in a trilogy. What do you hope will happen next?

An Excerpt from
The Kingdom of Copper

Coming January 2019 from Harper Voyager

Alizayd al Qahtani didn't make it a month with his caravan.

"Run, my prince, run!" The sole Ayaanle member of his traveling party cried as he staggered into Ali's tent one night while they were camped along a southern bend of the Euphrates. Before the man could expand on his warning, a blood-dark blade burst from his chest.

His weapons already at hand, Ali flew to his feet. He slashed the back of the tent open with a strike of his zulfiqar and fled into the night.

They pursued him on horseback, but the Euphrates glistened close ahead, black as the star-drenched night reflected in the river's coursing surface. Praying his weapons were secure, Ali plunged straight into the water as the first arrows shot past, one narrowly missing his face.

Ali swam fast, the motion as instinctual as walking, faster than he ever had, with a grace that would have taken him aback had he not been preoccupied with saving his life. Arrows struck the water around him, following his course, and so he dived deep, the water growing colder and more opaque. The Euphrates was wide here, and sluggish. It took him time to cross, to navigate his way past submerged rocks and water weeds to the shallows on the opposite side.

It was only when he was climbing out that the sick realization swept over him: he had not needed to emerge for air the entire time.

But there was little time to contemplate that—not when he could see mounted archers pacing the opposite bank. The first assassins to come for him after his father's cold decree.

Ali was not waiting around to see if they could find out a way to cross the river. Instead, he ran, racing headlong toward the horizon until his legs gave out and he collapsed in exhaustion.

He awoke in a sea of golden sand.

The dawn sun was gentle on his scarred skin. Ali climbed cautiously to his feet, but a single glance revealed he was alone. In every direction was desert; the sky a bright, hot bowl turned upside-down. He took a shaky breath, glancing down at his filthy and still damp dishdasha. He had nothing else save his zulfiqar and khanjar. He'd lost his sandals in the river and left his turban in his tent. He had no food, no water, and a desert to cross.

Despair lapped at the edges of his mind. Ali hadn't expected to survive long; that his exile was a death sentence was obvious to anyone with knowledge of the politics of his tribe. But he'd hoped to put up a decent fight, to at least *arrive* in Am Gezira, even if it was only for the slight comfort of dying in his ancestral land. Angry tears pricked his eyes.

He wiped them away. No, this would not be how things ended for him, weeping tears of self-pity as he wasted away in some unknown patch of sand. Ali was Geziri. When the time came, he would die dry-eyed and with the declaration of faith on his lips, a blade in his hand.

He fixed his eyes southwest, in the direction of his homeland, the direction he'd prayed his entire life. He went through the motions to cleanse himself for prayer, the motions he'd made multiple times a day since his mother had first shown him.

He raised his palms, closing his eyes. *Guide me*, he begged. *Protect those I was forced to leave behind and when my time comes . . .* he caught his breath *. . . when my time comes, please have more mercy on me than my father did.*

Ali touched his fingers to his brow. Then he rose to his feet.

Having nothing but the sun to guide him through the unbroken expanse of sand, Ali followed its relentless path across the sky, ignoring—and then growing accustomed to—its merciless heat upon his shoulders. The hot sand scorched his bare feet—and then it didn't. He was a djinn, and though he couldn't drift and dance as smoke among the dunes as his ancestors might have done before Suleiman's blessing, the desert would not kill him. He walked each day until exhaustion overtook him, only breaking to pray and sleep. He let his mind—his despair at how completely he'd ruined his life—drift away, replaced by the simple motion of placing one foot in front of the other.

Hunger gnawed at him. Water was no problem—Ali had not thirsted since the marid took him. He tried hard not to think about the implication of that, to ignore the newly restless part of his mind that delighted in the sweat beading on his skin and dripping down his limbs.

Finally, the landscape began to change. Rocky cliffs emerged from the sandy dunes like massive, grasping fingers, and he scoured the craggy bluffs for any sign of food. He'd heard rural Geziri were able to conjure entire feasts from human scraps, but Ali had never been taught the magic. He was a prince raised to be a Qaid, surrounded by servants his entire privileged life. He had no idea how to survive on his own.

Desperate and starving, he ate any bit of greenery he could find down to the roots. It was a mistake. One morning, several weeks after fleeing his caravan, he awoke violently ill. Ash crumbled from his skin, and he vomited until all that came up was a fiery black substance that burned the ground.

Hoping to find a bit of shade in which to recover, Ali tried to climb down from the cliffs, but he was so dizzy that he couldn't even see straight. He lost his footing on the loose gravel almost immediately and slipped, tumbling down a sharp incline.

He landed hard in a stony crevasse, smashing his left shoulder into a protruding rock. There was a wet pop, and a searing heat burst down his arm. His fingers went numb.

Every breath sent a surge of pain through his throbbing shoulder. *Get up. You will die here if you do not get up.* But Ali's limbs refused to obey. Blood trickled from his nose, filling his mouth.

He blinked back tears as he stared at the stark

cliffs outlined against the bright sky. A glance at the crevasse revealed nothing but sand and stones. It was—rather fittingly—a dead place. He supposed it could be worse—he could be tortured by his family's enemies, beheaded by an assassin's crude blow.

But God forgive him, Ali did not want to die.

He closed his eyes, trying to find some peace in the holy passages he'd memorized so long ago, but it was difficult. The faces of those he'd left behind in Daevabad kept breaking through the encroaching darkness, their voices taunting him as he slowly slipped into unconsciousness.

And then, sometime later—Ali was never sure how long—he woke to an impossibly foul substance being forced down his throat.

His eyes shot open and he gagged, his mouth full of something crunchy and metallic and *wrong*. His vision swam, slowly focusing on the silhouette of a broad-shouldered man squatting beside him. The man's face came to him in patches: a nose that had been broken more than once, a matted black beard, hooded gray eyes.

Geziri eyes.

The man laid a heavy hand on Ali's brow and spooned another thick helping of the disgusting gruel into his mouth. "Eat up, little prince."

Ali choked. "W-what is that?"

The other djinn beamed. "Oryx blood and ground locusts."

Ali's stomach immediately rebelled. He turned his head to vomit, but the man clamped his hand over Ali's mouth and massaged his throat, forcing the revolting mixture back down.

"Ay, do not be doing that. What kind of man turns down food that his host has so thoughtfully prepared?"

"Daevabadis." A second voice spoke up, and Ali glanced down at his feet, catching sight of a woman with black braids and a face that might have been carved from stone. "No manners." She held up Ali's zulfiqar and khanjar. "Lovely blades."

A breeze swept through the crevasse, and Ali shivered, soaked in sweat as usual. ►

25

The man held up a gnarled black root. "Did you eat something like this?" When Ali nodded, he snorted. "Fool. You're lucky not to be a pile of ash right now." He shoved another spoonful of the bloody gristle at Ali. "Eat. You'll need your strength for the journey home."

Ali pushed it away weakly. "Home?"

"Ain Luhayr," the man said, as if it was the most obvious thing in the world. "Home. It is but a week's travel west."

Ali shook his head. "No. I . . . I'm going south. To Um Jubal," he clarified, naming the forbidding mountain chain along Am Gezira's humid southern coast his ancestors had once called home. It was the only place he could think to find allies.

"Um Jubal?" The man laughed. "You are mostly dead and you think to cross Am Gezira?" He quickly shoved another spoonful of gruel in Ali's mouth. "There are assassins looking for you in every shadow of this land. Word is the fire-worshippers will make rich the man who kills Alizayd al Qahtani."

"Which is what *we* should be doing, Lubayd," the other raider cut in. "Not wasting our provisions on a southern brat."

"You'd kill a fellow Geziri for foreign coins?" The question came out with more scorn than Ali had intended.

"I'd kill an al Qahtani for free."

Ali startled at the hostility in her voice. The first man—Lubayd—sighed and shot her an annoyed look before turning back to Ali. "You'll forgive Aqisa here, prince, but it's not a good time to be visiting our land. We haven't seen a drop of rain in years." He put down the clay cup. "Our spring is drying up, we're running out of food, our children are starting to die . . . we send messages to Daevabad pleading for help. And do you know what our king says, our fellow Geziri king?"

"*Nothing*," Aqisa spat. "Your father doesn't even respond. So, do not speak of tribal ties to me, al Qahtani."

The hatred in her face sent a chill down his

spine. Ali eyed the zulfiqar in her hands. At least
he kept his blade sharp—hopefully, they'd be in
no mood to make him suffer as they executed
him. He swallowed back another wave of bile,
the oryx blood thick in his throat. "Well . . ." he
started weakly. "Then in that case, I agree." He
nodded at Lubayd's gruel. "You needn't waste that
on me."

There was a long moment of silence. Then
Lubayd burst into laughter, the sound ringing out
across the crevasse.

He was still laughing when he grabbed Ali's
injured arm without warning and yanked it
straight.

Ali cried out, black spots blossoming across
his vision. But as his shoulder slid back into place,
the searing pain immediately lessened. His fingers
tingled, sensation returning to his numb hand in
excruciating waves.

Lubayd grinned. He pulled free his ghutrah,
the cloth headdress worn by northern Geziri
djinn, and quickly fashioned it into a sling. Then
he hauled Ali to his feet by his good arm. "Keep
your sense of humor, boy. I think you're going to
need it."

A massive white oryx waited patiently at
the mouth of the crevasse; a line of dried blood
crossed one flank. Ignoring Ali's protests, Lubayd
shoved him onto the animal's back. Ali clutched
its long horns watching as Lubayd wrestled his
zulfiqar away from the other raider.

He dropped it in Ali's lap. "Let that shoulder
heal and perhaps you'll swing this again."

Ali gave the blade an incredulous look. "But I
thought . . ."

"We'd be killing you?" Lubayd shook his head.
"No. Not yet anyway. Not while you are doing
that." He motioned back to the crevasse.

Ali followed his gaze. His mouth fell open.

It wasn't sweat that had soaked his robe. A
miniature oasis had sprung up around him
while he lay dying. A spring gurgled through the
rocks where his head had been, trickling down
a path shrouded with new moss. A second ▶

spring bubbled up through the sand, filling the depression his body had left. Bright green shoots covered a bloody patch of gravel; their unfurling leaves were wet with dew.

Ali took a sharp breath, scenting the fresh moisture on the desert air. The potential.

Lubayd gestured to the greenery. "I have no idea how you did that, Alizayd al Qahtani," he said flatly. "But if you can draw water into a barren patch of sand in Am Gezira, well . . ." He winked. "You're worth far more than a few foreign coins."

⌐